# THE CAELVERSE COMPENDIUM

As the first of a series (Teloston University), the following fantasy/sci-fi novel, by Caleb Steele, is part of the *Caelverse: Realm of Cycles* canon:

*Teloston University: The Cult of the Black Moon*

# THE CAELVERSE COMPENDIUM

A Guide to the Caelverse
and its Various
Phenomena, Properties,
and Beings

A *Caelverse: Realm of Cycles* Book

## CALEB STEELE

ASTRAL
WELLSPRING
PRESS

First published in 2024 by Astral Wellspring Press, Australia

Copyright © 2024 Caleb Steele

Cover artwork by Caleb Steele
Cover artwork Copyright © Caleb Steele

Images in The Caelverse Compendium created by Caleb Steele
Image Copyright © Caleb Steele
No images in The Caelverse Compendium were created by artificial intelligence.

No part of this book was written by artificial intelligence.

The Caelverse Compendium is a progressive continuation of a part of a novel first published in 2018 called *Teloston University: The Cult of the Black Moon* (Copyright © 2018 Caleb Steele). The Caelverse Compendium has also been published alongside the publication of the 2nd edition of *Teloston University: The Cult of the Black Moon* (Copyright © 2024 Caleb Steele).

National Library of Australia
Cataloguing-in-Publication (CIP) data:

Caleb Steele
The Caelverse Compendium

(Paperback version – this version): ISBN: 978-0-6483786-5-5
(e-book version): ISBN: 978-0-6483786-6-2
(Hardback version): ISBN: 978-0-6483786-7-9


ASTRAL WELLSPRING PRESS

As of the date of publication (2024), the following link to the author website may be accessed (which contains further links to various social media):

www.calebsteele.com

I dedicate this compendium to my fellow mages…

But since there are some pretty cool non-mages as well, I guess I dedicate this book to some of you, too.

# Acknowledgements

I wish to thank the handful of people who at least attempted to read my original compendium in *Teloston University: The Cult of the Black Moon*. I also wish to thank some of my family members and a few other people for their support, as this allowed me the time and energy to work on revising the old compendium into the glorious work it is today. For reasons of privacy, I will not list their names.

Unfortunately, a few people passed away during the writing of the *old* compendium, so I would like to acknowledge:

My Grandpa, John Ambrose Kelly. You were a great storyteller. Your delivery was always entertaining. Although you may not have approved of my book in every aspect, I hope you are some place nice now.

Wayne Henderson: You were a very charismatic person. I am so sorry you didn't get to read my book. May your spirit be thriving and forever learning.

Matthew Tonkin (Tonks): You took me in when I needed help, yet you struggled with your own issues. Thank you, and may your spirit be at peace.

There is also one person who passed away during the writing of The Caelverse Compendium, so I would like to acknowledge:

My Grandma, Elizabeth Kelly. We always had interesting conversations about the world. I always learned something interesting. I hope now that your spirit is enjoying many creative pursuits.

# Author's Note

I published my first novel in November 2018, and I took a year off to try and promote it (whilst learning many other skills on the way). Marketing the novel, however, was much harder than I anticipated. During that time, I considered rewriting the novel. Once 2020 began, I threw some ideas around before rewriting began in May. While writing, I stopped multiple times to really think hard about worldbuilding matters. One idea led to another, and while my head was exploding with creative thoughts, I was very critical about everything I proposed, and I had to scrap multiple ideas and systems. I would love to explain some of my ideas here, but I guess I will save them for a totally different series. A few months into rewriting the novel, I actually couldn't continue due to delving deeper into the worldbuilding process; I then had to move on to first updating the compendium at the back of the novel. Soon after doing this, I doubled the word count, and I knew that I had to publish the compendium as a separate book.

I decided that I didn't need to change too much about the Caelverse itself (although, I ended up adding a few new features). My main problem was the magic system, which has been massively overhauled. Just when I thought I had my new magic system nailed down, more issues arose, and it seemed the only way to fix the issues was to actually work out ALL of the statistics – in complete detail. I understand that magic is typically 'meant' to have a very 'mystical', 'esoteric', and 'obscure' feel to it, but I just could not let that pass. My magic system is unique. Nevertheless, I have briefly mentioned in pockets that there are still mysteries left, so the mages of the Caelverse do not know everything.

Hardcore fans would be able to work out some statistics of the new magic when reading the novels, anyway. For example, when using phasarchement magic in combat, a mage's shield may 'overload'. If I (as the narrator) mention that the overloading issue ceased 'a few seconds later' instead of giving the exact time, then, at the very least, it would be clear to the reader that the problem of overloading would not be, for instance, minutes, hours, or even days long. Basically, when reading the novels, a keen reader would be able to piece together the various time frames to develop rough statistics. Another factor to consider is that mages have developed libraries upon libraries of information on magic. Naturally, they would have conducted numerous tests on their own kind to fully measure their magical potential; and, The Caelverse Compendium provides readers with that information.

Because I had to work out *everything*, I must admit that I am worried that I may not have considered something important (to place in or remove from The Caelverse Compendium) – or that I have stated incorrect statistics. Nevertheless, consider the following: I have established that The Caelverse Compendium is 'written' by a mage within the Caelverse. Accordingly, if anything is wrong with this compendium, then blame the mage who wrote it – not me! Lol. Also, to appropriate and recontextualize what 'Xena, the Warrior Princess' once said, if there are any issues within a fantasy setting, it was the result of a mage. So, if there are any issues with the compendium, then… well, um… a mage did it. Yep… Oh, and in terms of calculations, the mage who wrote the compendium might also have forgotten to carry the one at times. *Looks shiftily from side to side*. I think my ass is fully covered now…

I am nevertheless glad that I published my first novel in 2018 before artificial intelligence (A.I.) was released to the public. Basically, all published work post 2022 is suspect. I have proof that I am the creator of many of these concepts – alas, I didn't get to publish this at the end of 2022, which was one of my deadlines (that I obviously did not meet). I will admit: I have actually spoken with A.I. in order to help with writing The Caelverse Compendium. At first, I tried to get it to do some calculations for me, but it turned out that it wasn't good at math. So, I ended up doing most of the math myself; still, I had the help of online calculators – but even then, I still had to understand the math, and in some cases, there were no online calculators for what I wanted. I also asked the A.I. about scientific concepts and areas. For example, I asked about pilot wave theory, as I couldn't find enough information on certain issues within the said theory; unfortunately, even then, the science seems to be underdeveloped (again, in certain ways), and naturally, I have fused it with my own theories. Some of the alternative scientific ideas within The Caelverse Compendium that I have *built upon* have already existed for a few decades now, but the built-upon concepts related to the non-scientific and alternative ideas are my own, and they have been developed to fit into a fantasy/sci-fi context. So, while A.I. *helped* with *some* of my *research*, the work in The Caelverse Compendium is my own.

# CONTENTS

*Acknowledgements*                                                                vi

*Author's Note*                                                                  vii

**Preface: High Commissioner's Message**                                           1

**Section One: The Constitution of Matter and Energy**                             3

  1.1: Introduction:                                                      3

  1.2: The Constitution of Physical Matter:                               5

  1.3: The Constitution of Etheric Matter:                               14

  1.4: The Constitution of Astral Matter:                                21

**Section Two: The Cosmology of the Caelverse**                                   28

  2.1: Structural and Astronomical Overview:                             28

  2.2: The Planets and Transportals:                                     32

  2.3: The Moons and Lunapexes:                                          42

  2.4: Additional Celestial Bodies:                                      48

  2.5: Mechanisms and Attributes of Astrology:                           51

  2.6: Assorted Celestial Images:                                        60

**Section Three: The Ontology, Processes, and Applications of Magic**             71

  3.1: General Ontology:                                                 71

  3.2: School of Mysticism:                                              94

  3.3. School of Charms (Charmagy):                                      103

  3.4: School of Alchemy:                                               109

  3.5: School of Conjuration:                                           122

  3.6: School of Phasarchement:                                         131

    3.6.1: Introduction:                                       131

    3.6.2: Ranks:                                              146

    3.6.3: Ultra-State Types (USTs):                           150

      3.6.3.1: UST One/Ultra-state Solid (Shields):  151

      3.6.3.2: UST Two/Ultra-state Plasma (Discharges): 161

      3.6.3.3: UST Three/Ultra-state Gas (Vortices): 189

3.6.3.4: UST Four/Ultra-state Liquid (Soaker Bombs/Swarm Clouds): 196

3.6.3.5: UST Five/Ultra-state Conductivity (Propulsors): 201

3.6.3.6: UST Six/Ultra-state Spacetime Crystals (Dimensional Fields): 204

3.6.4: Phasarchement Archetypal Classes (PACs): 207

3.6.5: PAC and UST Index (Including a Table of Contents): 212

3.6.5.1: Alpha Class (Attraction & Repulsion): 215

3.6.5.2: Beta Class (Synchronization & Desynchronization): 241

3.6.5.3: Gamma Class (Entanglement & Separation): 270

3.6.5.4: Delta Class (Motion & Motionlessness): 299

**Section Four: Life and Civilization** **327**

4.1: A Brief Overview of the Current Cycle of History: 327

4.1.1: Introduction: 327

4.1.2: The First Epoch (E1): 328

4.1.3: The Second Epoch (E2): 329

4.1.4: The Third Epoch (E3): 330

4.1.5: The Fourth Epoch (E4): 332

4.1.6: The Fifth Epoch (E5): 337

4.1.7: The Sixth Epoch (E6): 342

4.2: Contemporary Politics and Society: 342

4.3: Taxonomy of Sapient and Non-sapient Beings: 351

4.3.1: Introduction: 351

4.3.2: Generalum Constitutional Status Categories: 359

4.3.2.1: Organics: 359

4.3.2.2: GMOs (Biomodics): 360

4.3.2.3: Cyborgs (Cybernetics): 362

4.3.2.4: Mutants (Mutanetics): 364

4.3.2.5: Heterogenics: 368

4.3.2.6: Necrotics: 374

4.3.2.7: Mixed: 379

4.3.2.8: Synthetics: 379

4.3.2.9: Spectrals: 381

4.3.3: Morphological Type (Morphtype) Guide:     384

    4.3.3.1: Mammalians:     386

    4.3.3.2: Reptilians:     408

    4.3.3.3: Avians:     414

    4.3.3.4: Ichthyoids:     418

    4.3.3.5: Amphibinoids:     424

    4.3.3.6: Arthropoids:     428

    4.3.3.7: Molluscoids:     440

    4.3.3.8: Cnidarianoids:     445

    4.3.3.9: Echinodermoids:     449

    4.3.3.10: Anneloids:     452

    4.3.3.11: Phytoids:     455

    4.3.3.12: Fungoids:     459

    4.3.3.13: Lithoids:     462

    4.3.3.14: Protistoids:     467

    4.3.3.15: Mechanoids:     468

    4.3.3.16: Machines:     469

    4.3.3.17: X-Droids:     469

    4.3.3.18: Minor or Rare Categories:     470

    4.3.3.19: Assortions:     471

**Dictionary**     **474**

**Abbreviated Terms**     **479**

*About the Author*     *CDXCIV*

# Preface

## High Commissioner's Message

The *Caelverse Compendium* contains four sections explaining aspects of our known reality in what we call the *Caelverse*. It is possible – and very probable – however, that we live in a *multiverse*. If contact is ever made with lifeforms of other realities (*extraversal* beings), then there is a great chance that the first contacts would hail from a reality that possesses some similarities to our own. If such contact is the result of consciousness, then one of these similarities may very well be the language we use. Accordingly, we have written a compendium in our language; and if so ever a being from another reality were to read this, then not only would they gain knowledge of beings from other realities (i.e., us and how our reality functions), but it may then be possible to *bridge* some type of conscious gap between one reality (your reality, the reader) and another (our reality), in turn making contact possible.

The first section will explain the constitution of matter and energy (which may likely be the same in other realities). A brief overview of the cosmology of the Caelverse and its celestial bodies (such as the suns, planets, and moons) will follow. Since magical humans (called *mages*) are the dominant species in the Caelverse (politically and culturally), the compendium will explicate the fundamentals and ontological nature of magic itself. Lastly, the compendium will provide an overview of the current cycle of our history and the overarching political system (the *Caelverse Government of Magi* – or simply, the *CGM*) before the most commonly-understood taxonomy of sapient and non-sapient beings in the Caelverse will be listed (which includes mages and non-mages). This compendium will also cover many different philosophical areas, using both theoretical and empirical ideas and information; and, while it may seem dense, it will, nevertheless, provide explanations along the way. For ease of reading, a dictionary at the end has also been added for words not explained throughout the text. Now, may our first contact lead to happiness and prosperity!

Authorized by Tarmas Simonkash, High Commissioner of the *Intercluster Communications and Media Commission* (ICMC) for the CGM.
24th of Primsis B-424.

# Section One

*The Constitution of Matter and Energy*

## 1.1: Introduction:

It is currently unknown who or what – if anything at all – created existence; specifically, we do not know what caused both the physical and the empirically-established non-physical (spiritual) realms to exist, along with the various conscious beings that exist therein. Although a few mages believe that existence organically arose from nothing, most mages are technically *ietsists* (even though most do not use the term); that is, they believe that a supreme transcendent force of some kind exists (though, they really are not sure what it may be) and that this force created or, at least, sustains consciousness and physical and spiritual matter (at the ultimate level). Even then, of those who agree on the nature of this supreme force and what it is, there are different philosophical perspectives on its role (and their own) in the grand scheme of reality.

This term (ietsism), however, is only the *default belief* due to a lack of true knowledge of this supreme force; so, more accurately, most ietsists are *panentheists* by *soft belief* – a belief that everything in existence is – and is part of – this supreme creator being; but this supreme force simultaneously is also ontologically 'beyond' everything in existence. These mages also specifically hold to a *transnaturalist* worldview (even if generally scholars only use the term). This idea posits that root determinants of material phenomena are generated from a level of reality that transcends both the mutually bound physical *and* spiritual realms instead of merely being a product of the latter (supernaturalism). It may, then, appear that a merely socially-constructed distinction is thusly created from the two types of realms, but there are, indeed, objectively real – and inherently vastly contrasting natures – to both realities.

Simultaneously, it is not a matter of the two realms (physical and spiritual) being *totally* distinct from one another either; they are, in fact, layered and intertwined with each other. The spiritual planes also possess many layers or 'levels' 'blending' into one another, making for a multidimensional spectrum. Reality is theorized to operate as a *holarchy* – a hierarchy with levels being both parts and wholes. However, there are spiritual planes that are inaccessible to meditating or sleeping astral travellers from the Caelverse; so, for all that is known so far, it may be the case that some levels have no association with the physical at all. Moreover, there are parts of the holarchy – such as the astral planes – that do not need the physical, despite being fundamentally linked. Said another way, other physically-associated levels, such as the astral planes, arguably encompass the physical in a hierarchy but are not limited to the physical. For ease of understanding, it is better to simply think of each being 'attached' to one another.

Such a holarchy can be viewed from an alternative angle; that is, all physical matter possesses spiritual matter rather than spiritual matter possessing physical matter, and this ranges from inanimate minerals to insects to humans and even to the planets as wholes. Most physical organisms either cannot see the spiritual realms or, when they can, it is only vague, and only of two varieties; one: *etheric* matter, which is the energy extending immediately 'around' the physical, fully intertwined with it; and the second is *astral* matter, which is generally only seen with certain meditation or sleep, where meditators project their consciousness out to traverse its planes.

Still, what exactly *is* matter? To answer this, it is best to understand the physics by first asking, where does matter generate from? More specifically, what is the ultimate source of matter? With great backing empirical evidence, most scholars axiomatically agree that an *ultimate unified field* permeates everything in existence; and the most common terms for this field are the *Aether* or the *zero-point (energy) field* (ZPE and ZPF). It is important to note that there is a difference between the terms *aether energy* and *the* Aether; the latter is the *entire* ZPF, whereas the former is *from* the ZPF. There are, nevertheless, many questions left to be answered, and, thus, competing theories over its existence and nature have arisen. Of the two major theories, one states that this field is part of, or simply *is*, the aforementioned supreme intelligence (that potentially created existence); and the second views the Aether as an emergent, ever-evolving energy which, by default, connects all matter (which contains consciousness) and therefore is, at least now, conscious in some way.

Whichever theory is correct, all matter is in a sea of conscious information. In any case, while there is an ultimate unified field, the more specific question is: what is the ontologically *fundamental* nature of it? That is, is the Aether *first* (pure) potentiality and/or consciousness and/or energy? Precisely, does energy derive from consciousness or are both ontologically one and the same? This, nevertheless, forces us to return to the question of whether it is a creator or not. Despite this difficult question – and despite many scholars stating that consciousness and potentiality are both one and fundamental, where energy *then* emerges from this fundamental level – all three phenomena are so close and interlinked that it is easier, for the sake of brevity, to say that they are fundamentally one force.

The Aether, though, is actually a *medium*, not just a *field*, so it is possible that there might be a level of energy beyond the Aether that is not a medium. It is now clear to us that this medium is also a *superfluid*, so when matter moves through the Aether, there is no drag, but matter will still produce various effects in the medium. Even though the various planes of existence (can) work as holarchies, all matter in the various planes draw from the Aether, so in this sense, there is no hierarchy other than the Aether being the supreme source of energy for all matter. Still, the energy that emerges from the Aether and produces matter on a certain plane of existence has a certain *frequency set* (that is, a set of frequencies). As such, the matter on one plane of existence does not (necessarily have to – at least directly) interact with other matter in other planes of existence. The Aether itself is not – nor does it have – *form*, but it can, however, via potentiality, give rise *to* form. Form, then, is the corporealization of that which is incorporeal. The process of corporealization (form) from the incorporeal is the next fundamental question. That is, *how* does the Aether give rise to form, specifically, matter?

# 1.2: The Constitution of Physical Matter:

Despite our advanced technology, we still do not know the precise, fundamental structure of physical reality. While there are accordingly many theories, the most accepted of these for the corporealization of physical matter are *torus-structure theories* (TSTs) that are also within the framework of the *standard physics paradigm* (SPP). This is not to say that other realms of existence do not have torus structures at their fundamental level but, instead, that the physical realm has a torus structure of a particular frequency set of energy, and the types of configurations from the torus in the physical realm differ to that of other matter in the spiritual planes. Most TSTs explain that physical matter is made of discrete 'particles' from the Aether that form via a vortex that curls around and retracts back into itself, in turn forming a *horn torus* shape. With this closed loop, the amount of energy that enters and exits the torus is constant, so the torus does not gain or lose energy.

In the case of the dominant TST, the energy from the Aether springs forth in an *electromagnetic* state (essentially, it is *light* with *electric* and *magnetic* components); but due to the discrete nature of the torus in the Aether, the particle is *quantized* (that is, the energy is *discrete*, so it becomes a *quantum particle*). This particular case is known as a *photon*, which is a quantum of light. Without this complete torus formation, there is merely electromagnetic energy. Nevertheless, the photon also has a wave of energy around it in the form of *sine* (or *sinusoidal*) *waves*, which are ripples or perturbations in the Aether. Specifically, the electric and magnetic components form waves that oscillate at right angles to each other in the photon's direction of propagation; and together, they form a *field* that extends out from the particle (photon) basically to infinity (unless absorbed or enacted upon), decreasing in strength proportionally to the square of the distance from the particle.

As the electromagnetic energy returns to the Aether in the vortex, *gravity* is formed as a result. Gravity is thus the *compression* of the Aether, and this affects all quantum particles within the physical realm (so, quantum particles cause gravity but are also affected by it). Essentially, gravity causes *acceleration* within the fabric of both space and time (and together, this is known as *spacetime*, as the two are not dimensionally separate). The more particles there are in a region, the greater the effect of gravity. The 'fabric' of spacetime itself in the physical realm is also quantized. Aether-powered toroidal vortices called *constituent spacetime units* (CSUs) also constitute the substrate of spacetime; and these are so small that they are the smallest unit of measurement within physical reality. The entirety of spacetime is tightly packed with these spherical-in-effect CSUs, each geometrically spaced from one another in an *isotropic vector matrix* (IVM) – meaning: they are uniform, equidistant, and identical in all directions; and, they are arranged in a pattern as part of a system. When gravity is exerted, these CSUs also compress, but they remain the same size as they were in comparison to the surrounding quantum particles also affected by the same level of gravity. In geometric terms, spacetime can be said to *curve*.

Quantum particles will move towards the most compressed/curved area relative to their location, with the effect (acceleration) increasing the further the particles move towards the region of highest compression. Of course, the force of gravity acting between any two particles is inversely proportional to the square of the distance between the said particles. Acceleration will also only occur until another force enacts on a particle, so it may be the case that particles will maintain their *velocity* (speed) towards the *gravitational well*. Note that *force* is the mechanical action of changing the motion of an object (that is, force pushes and pulls objects).

Unlike electromagnetism itself, gravity is not technically a force, so all objects will merely follow *geodesics* (the shortest path between two points) instead of actually being pulled or pushed via positive and negative charges. For the sake of brevity, though, gravity is said to be a force. Even if an object is at *rest* (zero-initial velocity), gravity will still cause the object to accelerate, as it is the dimension of *time* within spacetime that causes objects to move spatially. That is, while an object/particle may be at zero-initial velocity in the context of space, all entities nevertheless possess velocity through time, so they are not technically at rest. So, as an object moves through time, their trajectory will geometrically bend towards the spatial area of that which causes gravity.

Photons do not have what is known as *mass* – that is, they do not possess *inertia* or the resistance to acceleration or change in position via force. However, it is more accurate to say they only have zero *rest mass*; that is, if one were able to hypothetically bring a photon to rest (so it would not be moving), it would only *then* have no mass. Therefore, photons still have a speed limit when moving through space – more specifically, a *vacuum*, which is a region of space devoid of all matter (apart from CSUs). So, photons are the fastest travelling particles in physical reality, and despite being *effectively* massless, photons still exert gravity and are affected by gravity. As photons have energy and *momentum* with restraints, mass and energy are equivalent.

The photon is an *elementary particle*, so it does not break down into other particles, but there are two other elementary particles – *electrons* and *protons*; and, while these other two elementary particles are not made of photons, they can still absorb and emit them. Unlike the photon made of one torus, electrons and protons consist of *dual toruses* (one on the top and one on the bottom), and this forms rest mass (also known as *intrinsic mass*) – that is, they possess inertia and do not travel at the same speed as a photon (that is, the speed of light). These particles also form the *chemical elements* (*atoms*), which constitute the building blocks of all matter. Despite being elementary particles and formed in almost the same way, protons and electrons have different masses; in fact, the proton has far more mass than an electron, and the reason for this is due to *how* the proton *displaces* the Aether around it. Every proton and electron in physical reality will respectively have the same mass, but their *weights*, on the other hand, will change (either increase of decrease) in different gravitational fields.

Electrons have *negative electric charge*, where the top and bottom toruses feature aether energy flowing *inwards*, whereas protons, on the other hand, are *positively-charged*, and their toruses feature aether energy flowing *outwards* of the top and bottom of their toruses. For clarification, the energy flow is still the same in the toruses (that is, energy flows *from* the Aether back into itself) so the toruses for each particle are reversed in their position to one another; also, charge itself is different to mass, so these are separate issues. Positive and negative charges attract (that is, pull) each other together, while positive and positive or negative and negative charges repel (that is, push) each other away. When an electron and a proton are combined, they form a *neutron* – a neutrally-charged *composite particle*, which can break down (that is, *decay*) into an electron and proton again. A particle's top torus will feature its *magnetic north*, while its bottom torus will feature its *magnetic south*. So, while all three particles have different electric charges, all three have *magnetic dipoles*; and, unlike photons that have *electromagnetic* fields, protons and electrons have *electric* and *magnetic* fields (not electro-magnetic fields), whereas neutrons just have magnetic fields (although, there are nuanced and strange discrepancies to these norms).

Protons and neutrons form at the centre of an atom, which is known as the *nucleus*. When more protons and neutrons are added to an atom, the chemical element changes, such as when *carbon* (with six protons and six neutrons) turns into nitrogen (with seven protons and seven neutrons). This causes atoms to become more *massive*. While protons are positively-charged, it would *seem* like they would fly away from one another; but this is not the case. While it is still unclear as to the exact mechanism of how this works, it is believed that either the force of gravity within the nucleus is much stronger before dropping off exponentially, or there are specific and unusual aether perturbations that cause this effect. The latter theory is based on studies showing how two uncharged conductive plates in a vacuum can be attracted to one another. Of course, this only occurs at *very* short distances, and basically, a similar, but critically different effect occurs in an atom's nucleus.

Protons and neutrons will also form at particular geometric locations from one another inside the nucleus as a result of the way they shape the Aether around them. This is similar to an empirically-verified modal vibrational phenomenon called *cymatics* outside the context of the quantum realm, where various sounds will cause different types of patterns to emerge in assorted mediums. For example, a specific frequency can excite sand particles to form into certain geometric patterns. A similar phenomenon occurs at the subatomic level as well, where geometric patterns form. So, the crucially-important key to understand is that while toruses are the base form of matter, geometric positions are the fundamental *structure* of particle *positions* within the context of spacetime (which, as stated before, is also geometric), affecting everything from the quantum level all the way up to macro-based matter and spiritual energies.

Electrons also form into geometric positions around the nucleus, equalling in the number of protons for each chemical element. These geometric positions are placed into quantized *shells*, so electrons will not be found in simply any location in an atom. These shells are also known as *energy levels*, so when an electron absorbs a particular photon (that it *can* absorb – as this process, too, is quantized), it can jump to another shell; and when an electron emits a photon, it will jump down to the next shell. When electrons absorb photons, they do not become triple toruses; instead, they just change their energy levels and, thus, their positions in the atoms. Also, when electrons emit photons, the electromagnetic energy is of a particular quanta, and so the energy will form another torus – thus the quantization. For clarification, photons have different wavelengths and energy levels, too, and for the electron to move to another shell, it must absorb a photon of a particular energy level, or the electron will not move. When no absorption occurs, then the photon may either pass through the atom, or it might be reflected or refracted off the surface. Electron geometry changes when more electrons are added, and since electrons are negatively-charged, they will repel one another, so each will hold a particular spot within an overall geometric shape.

All of these geometric positions are not rigid (more so the case for electrons than protons and neutrons). That is, quantum particles can be found in different locations; but not all locations are equal, so some locations will have more probable chances of seeing particles than other locations. So, each particle will have *clouds* of probable positions, where the probability distribution will vary within the geometrically-formed cloud. In the context of electrons around a nucleus, these are known as *orbitals* – note, though, that electrons do not orbit in the same manner as planets around suns (as explained in *Section Two*). Electrons can also leave their atoms, but their movements will still be bound by probable pathways and locations. Parenthetically, when atoms gain or lose atoms, they can become *ionized*, in turn causing various effects.

In the past, most scholars believed that quantum particles *themselves* possessed *superposition*, where they (the particles) would be spread out everywhere in a fuzzy *wave function* of probable states and positions instead of only being in one definite location at a single time. So, the particles would be both a particle *and* a wave (known as *wave-particle duality* – WPD), with the wave being more of a mathematical understanding of all probable locations (that is, the wave, here, represents a probability amplitude of the particle's locations). This, of course, is only until the particle (in its state of superposition) is *measured* with either energy from certain devices, for example, or even, arguably, from consciousness itself *observing* it, and so, a wave function *collapse* would occur, where a particle's position would collapse to a single state/position. Even the environment itself (such as sunlight hitting a particle) can cause a collapse, but a *full* collapse does not necessarily have to occur, and, instead, partial *quantum decoherence* can just occur, where the wave function is limited. Put another way, the particle, in its superposition, would lose part of its *quantum coherence*, and it would remain in superposition, now, instead, with less probable states. However, this theory has fallen somewhat out of favour (although, this does not mean it has been disproven).

In contrast to this older, indeterminate WPD theory, more scholars now take the view that particles *themselves* always have a definite location and are not spread out in superposition. The particles are believed to not be both a particle and a wave; instead, they are a particle but also *have* a wave – with the latter guiding the former. This is called *pilot wave theory* (PWT), and particles themselves act deterministically within the framework of the wave's *quantum potential*. It is the pilot wave itself that holds the particle's superposition via quantum potential, and it can still be said that there is a wave function as well, allowing for particles to move in pathways that can form wave patterns of probable locations until a measurement or observation occurs. Measurement, in the context of PWT, alters the wave function, which continues to evolve, anyway, so various terms like 'wave function change' are used instead. So, quantum particles in the context of PWT can still change their position and state, where the pilot wave determines the probable locations the particle can take. Said another way, while the pilot wave deterministically directs the particle, the particle can still be found in more probable locations that the wave function possesses.

While the WPD theory is tied with the *uncertainty principle* (where one cannot know both a particle's position *and* momentum at once), PWT supposes that, due to its deterministic nature, it *could* be possible to predict where a particle will go if the initial variables/conditions were fully known; however, there are *hidden initial variables* that cannot be known about the particle and wave function, as measurement disrupts these variables and their coherence. This can lead to *apparent* randomness. While this might seem like it would violate certain quantum principles of *locality* (where no local hidden variables can exist), consider that the wave function features *nonlocal* interaction, where the pilot wave can affect particles across any distance – faster than the speed of light (so it is instant). This brings up the question as to *what* the pilot wave *is* exactly (as this violates the aforesaid speed of light), and so there are various theories; but most theories tie the pilot wave (and its ability to interact nonlocally) back to special fluctuations in both the Aether *and* spiritual energies. In fact, when coupled with certain spiritual energies, there are non-deterministic elements to this pilot wave (function), as subsequently explained in *Section 1.3*.

The quantum potential of PWT's wave function, within the framework of universal geometric structuring, even allows for electrons to 'orbit' nuclei in their geometric, quantized orbitals. Of course, there are other quantum factors that *affect* the wave function, so it is not just the pilot wave alone that causes electrons to orbit in their orbitals. When a particle moves to one geometric region from another (due to any number of reasons, such as when the orbitals change in structure due to an atom gaining more electrons), there will be a brief moment where the particle will not be in a quantized position, but the pilot wave will still guide the particle to a quantized place within a cloud area, even if it means having to initially move through a *node* (an area of zero probability). Note that the term *cloud* is still used in PWT, even though the particle itself would not form a cloud in the same sense as in WPD theory, but *cloud area* is normally also used as an alternative. As another parenthetical note, photons also have wave functions, and these also have their own geometry of probable locations, in turn affecting a photon's position it has in its propagation.

When an electron, for example, is confined to a particular area (usually in their atoms), this is what is known as *localization*. With the nonlocal nature of the pilot wave, this allows for *nonlocalization*. When atoms *bond* together (to form *molecules* or *compounds* of matter), they may produce greater probabilities for electrons to move between them by affecting the wave function. The wave function, in turn, can affect electrons, guiding them across various atoms. Two nonlocal particles can also non-locally affect each other via the wave function, and the particles can also affect the wave function itself to affect the other particle.

Nonlocal interaction does not just occur via the pilot wave, spiritual energies, and the Aether level itself. All quantum particles (including photons) have *wormholes* in their cores, each connecting to all other particles in physical reality over any spatial distance. These wormholes themselves then allow for – but do not fully establish – what is known as *quantum entanglement*. For a particle to *quantumly entangle* with another particle, both must first be locally present. When entanglement occurs, the two particles can then separate over any distance and still be entangled. The entanglement itself causes the particles to be *correlated*, where the *quantum state* of one particle can affect the other. For example, the quantum states of *spin*, *angular momentum*, *position*, and *polarization* can be correlated; but all of these are still tied in to the wave function.

Spin is a particle's physical rotation (orientation), where the particle will face a particular direction along a 'chosen' axis. This affects phenomena like *magnetic moments* (that is, magnetic orientation) and chemical bonding. If Particle A is entangled with Particle B, then, when a wave function changes via measurement, the spin state of Particle B will be the opposite of Particle A. So, the magnetic north of Particle A will face one direction, and the magnetic north of Particle B will face the other. In other words, particles will have a spin state even without entanglement, but once entangled, each will either be *aligned* or *anti-aligned* with a chosen axis based on a wave function change. Of course, this would be part of a *singlet state*, and so, in the case of *triplet states*, for example, there can be a different combination of states.

Angular momentum itself, on the other hand, deals with mass and velocity, whereas position regards a particle's location, defined by the wave function. Polarization, however, more so involves photons and the orientation of their oscillations. Other cases of entanglement occur as well, such as a particle's energy levels. Another related phenomenon is *quantum synchronization*, where quantum states can synchronize. This normally involves resultant phenomena like aligning *phases* (*phase locking*) or a synchronization of oscillation frequencies of quantum systems through feats such as *coupling interactions*, and it does not need quantum entanglement. However, quantum entanglement greatly enhances these phenomena, and it can lead to other phenomena like perfectly-correlated states and enhanced quantum coherence. Interestingly, the quantum states (such as spin states) of two particles can even be engineered to be the same instead of being opposite (as what naturally occurs in quantum entanglement).

While quantum entanglement itself is not limited to distance, the entanglement between two or more particles can still suffer from environmental decoherence, and the entanglement may be limited (through *entanglement degradation*) or even totally lost (such as through *entanglement sudden death*). Even though quantum particles are technically always fully connected to each other via the ZPE level, entanglement at the quantum level *itself* will always abide by the *monogamy principle* of *resource distribution*. So, when more than two particles are entangled at the quantum level, the degree of the entanglement between them will split, so two of the particles cannot be *maximally entangled* while also being entangled to the third particle. Regardless of how many particles are entangled, the entanglement itself will not transfer mass or energy.

Quantum entanglement, however, can allow for *quantum energy teleportation* (QET), where energy from Particle A can be transferred to Particle B nonlocally (again, so long as the particles were initially entangled). When QET occurs, Particle A (the particle itself) will not actually teleport to where Particle B is located (so only the energy will be teleported), and there needs to be enough energy in the first place for the event to occur. So, if Particle A is an electron, it will reduce to the lowest shell, but Particle A will not lose any more energy at its ground state. QET should not be confused with simple *quantum teleportation*, which involves first entanglement and then a transfer of *information* (the quantum state) of Particle A using the addition of *classical communication* (that is, non-quantum means like radio waves or cables). Three particles at minimum are needed for quantum teleportation; and, in this case, the quantum state of Particle A will be 'destroyed', where its state will most likely change.

CSUs also contain wormholes and can be entangled. Moreover, it is from these entangled CSUs that non-quantum wormholes (*portals*) in the very fabric of spacetime can be formed and created. As such, the best means to teleport mass and energy is through creating or finding large wormholes in spacetime and then physically moving through it – though, currently, this is very energy-expensive, and it is not an easy process to create such wormholes. Given that space and time are linked, then it is possible to entangle time itself. However, the natural wormholes that do exist (that we know of) do not allow time travel. Moreover, the practical applications of the time aspect of entangling spacetime have thus far been limited (that is, engineering it), but we do know that time is not quite linear in spiritual realms.

There is also the phenomenon of *quantum tunnelling*, where particles can 'teleport' *through* matter (specifically, *potential energy barriers* – PEBs). Most quantum tunnelling occurs with very-small scale (thin) barriers (with comparatively low energy), but there are examples, like with *magic* (as explained in *Section Three*), where particles can quantumly tunnel through more massive PEBs like doors, walls, and armour. In WPD theory, quantum tunnelling occurs via a particle's superposition, where a particle *may* be located on the other side of the PEB. In PWT, the quantum potential of the pilot wave alters the potentials of the particle, causing the particle to literally move through the PEB – that is, the particle *phase shifts*.

There is a particular reason why such phase shifting via potentials in quantum tunnelling can occur. Force fields are responsible for how particles move and interact with one another; but interestingly, forces and their fields are not fundamental. Instead, *potentials* are fundamental – they are not mere mathematical tools. Potentials, essentially, are fields in space that describe the potential energy per unit of a certain quantity at each point in the said space. They can be broken up into *scalar* and *vector* fields, where magnetic, electric, and gravitational potentials apply. All of these potentials not only tie into one another, but they are also tied into the Aether, so they are united and can be manipulated from this single field (the Aether); alternatively, they can even be manipulated with via their associated forces from tangible particles.

By isolating the vector potential from a magnetic field, for example, electromagnetic potentials can have physical effects on particles – even in regions where electric and magnetic fields are zero. The vector potential here also affects a particle's wave function, which, in turn, affects the particle. To be clear, a *real, tangible* magnetic field is not created; instead, it is *as if* a magnetic field existed in the region, and it is the affected wave function that causes the particle to behave as if in the influence of a magnetic field. The reverse can also effectively occur; that is, instead of virtual force fields affecting wave functions, force fields themselves can virtually be suppressed or even fully cancelled out via a wave function change. Different potentials can affect one another; for example, when a magnetic vector potential *diverges* or *converges* (that is, expands or compresses) instead of *curls*, then this can help to produce different gravitational potential. Remarkably, the wave function can affect the vector or scalar potential, which in turn can affect the wave function, which in turn can affect the particle. So, a particle's wave function itself initially has the ability to alter potentials in PEBs – which is what can occur when particles phase shift in quantum tunnelling. Basically, the particle moves through a PEB as if the PEB were not there at all.

Manipulating potentials or even other quantum phenomena may seem like *free energy* could be harnessed to greatly enhance society; and, while free energy *does* exist, it is limited. For example, free energy can come from magic, but this does not last forever. Then there is artificially-induced or technologically-formed free energy, such as manipulating patterned quantum particles to vibrate back and forth in the act of *atomic interparticularization*, but for some unknown reason, this does not last, and it is very limited in its output. It is suspected that spiritual energies may be distorting the flow of energy whenever free energy is potentially viable, but this is still very unclear.

Ultimately, physical matter is not purely physical; it is just the Aether in its known densest and quantized form. With the acknowledgment that the Aether is a conscious (or consciously-linked) information field, it is generally accepted that a universal language is part of its fabric, and this language emerges as geometric symbolism. This can be seen manifest in the very structure of quantum particle positions, so essentially, quantum particles – coupled with their geometry – are also concentrated packets of universally-standardized information. In addition to normal quantum particles, there are also *pseudo* (or *ghost*) *particles*, such as *neutrinos* (that can emerge from the decay of particles like neutrons), but these are actually particle-*like* perturbations in the Aether that give the illusion of being real particles. Naturally, of course, these ghost particles still have a particular geometric superposition. While all particles emerge from *one* source, the actual reality of all particles being separate from one another is itself an illusion. This is not to say that physical particles ontologically and phenomenally do not exist – it is, instead, that they are not *solely* separate.

# 1.3: The Constitution of Etheric Matter:

The first layer of spiritual substance is *etheric energy* in the *etheric realm*. The word etheric is old, and etheric energy used to be considered the actual Aether, but etheric energy is now understood to be a spiritual substance *from* the Aether – like how physical matter emerges from the Aether. Awkwardly, the word etheric is still in use, so careful spelling and phrasing is necessary to distinguish the two energies. Etheric energy is normally fully entwined with physical matter, and it even emerges from it, but etheric energy can be without physical matter, and ultimately, etheric energy still comes from the Aether. The term 'etheric' is not just limited to etheric energy; it can also refer to the etheric realm (or *etheric plane*) itself when referred to as 'the etheric'. Typically, 'etheric' in 'the etheric' is not capitalized – like how sometimes the physical realm may sometimes be called 'the physical'. Unlike the *astral realm* (explained in *Section 1.4*), the etheric realm only has one *plane*, but it still has many frequencies of energy that do not necessarily have to interact with one another.

All physical properties have their own *etheric body*, which is normally also known as the *auric field* (simply called the *aura*). An etheric body is a quasi-physical energy that is a mirrored version of the physical. However, the etheric body is more than just a mirror; it also contains its own unique structures that are not related to the physical. Of the physical structures it mirrors, though, the etheric essentially holds a physical entity's data and *metadata*; that is, the etheric contains various non-physical structural information *about* the physical, such as names and statistics. These statistics, of course, are not literal drawn-and-figured numbers and names that one can read; but the metadata can *appear* as such to psychic mages who purposely tap into particular etheric energy, collecting and *translating* the metadata in a way that their brains can understand. In other words, psychics can still technically see transcribed numerals and names written with alphabets, etc. Alternatively, the metadata can appear as geometric shapes, usually cymatic in nature, and this becomes essential to draw from when creating *spells* (with more information on magic explained in *Section Three*). Still, etheric energy is very fluid, and so it actually *can* form into literal figures that psychics can see.

The quantum particles in the physical realm have wave functions that possess superposition. This wave function results from the pilot wave, which, at the very least, is partially found in the etheric. The pilot waves in the etheric have non-deterministic properties that allow for different probable outcomes, so determinism would only apply if the physical realm were hypothetically left to its own devices. The etheric also not only has more *de*localized energy than the physical realm (that is, the etheric energy can easily spread out across the etheric plane), but the delocalized energy can move faster in proportion to the physical matter it is (or is not) attached to – *and*, etheric energy and matter can also teleport. Basically, it is faster than the speed of light in the physical. Accordingly, it is fully possible for the pilot wave (for the physical) to travel faster than the speed of light found in the physical realm. In other words, since the etheric is very much entwined with the physical, this faster-than-light feature allows for the totally nonlocal wave function that physical particles possess.

Very interestingly, due to its more fluid nature, the etheric body of a physical entity possesses more available probable states (not mere higher probabilities) than the wave function itself applying for the physical realm; that is, in the physical realm, a particle might have the possibility and probability of it being in a few different locations, while the etheric body, on the other hand, would possess a greater superposition for the same particle. This is different to the wave function itself for the physical, so the pilot wave's wave function is different for the etheric body. For clarification, pilot waves in the etheric affect the physical realm, but the pilot waves in the etheric still affect the etheric itself on their own level.

The etheric is also more *time-fluid*, and, as such, it can actually pull from – and be influenced (more so) by – current probable futures, the past, and (similar or different) *timelines*. A timeline is essentially a single reality that either exists or could exist along a time continuum, and there could be an infinite number of timelines. It is theorized that there are multiple active (corporealized) timelines and many inactive timelines in existence, and the wave function can still draw from inactive timelines. It is, alas, hard to determine if other timelines are active or not because when psychic mages see other timelines, they could merely be seeing how the timeline might look like if it was active. For practically any event in a timeline, there is the possibility of there being a different probable and improbable outcome, so there would naturally be different timeline forks and pathways. This, of course, does not mean that a timeline will be created at every single event – only, instead, that it is possible that a different timeline *can* exist (even as an incorporealized state). There is a great question amongst scholars as to whether timelines fork off individually for each individual being or if they fork off within collectives (that is, consciousnesses grouped into collectives).

A person's etheric body will technically be *linked* to all current probable futures, pasts, and (similar or different) timelines, but this does not mean that one can see all such timelines in their etheric body. That is, the different timelines are not the wave functions; instead, wave functions have probable states, and these can also pull from and be influenced by other timelines. The 'further' away a timeline is to one's etheric body, the weaker the effect it will have on the wave function. When a psychic sees a timeline or a mere probable state, their etheric body will produce images or scenes; alternatively, the psychic may see other etheric energy (already) possessing such images or scenes. With PWT, while a definite (set of) particle(s) would still exist within an etheric body, a psychic may still see other probable states. For WPD theory, while the etheric will have the same quasi particle of the physical in a similar cloud of probability, it will also have an *external set* of potential and probable states that extend well beyond this in the form of probable pasts, futures, and presents. Still, the aura will have a limited external set available (as the aura will not be 'infinite' in its practical tangible scope), but most of these states can have *ties/links* to other realities not in the aura.

Via one's consciousness, different states can be chosen or drawn in (through a natural *attractive* force based on vibrational likeness and connection), leading to various outcomes. Whether done through one's own consciousness or subconscious or another person's consciousness, etheric energy will interact with the physical at the quantum level (which is the 'gateway' between the two realms), enabling (greater) *freewill* in an otherwise (very) deterministic reality. The stronger one's etheric energy – along with how free their consciousness is from restraints – the more one can manipulate the physical world. The only spiritual energy minerals per se possess is etheric energy, and their etheric energy is minimal due to their lack of consciousness. Of course, since consciousness is theorized to permeate everything, it is understandable as to why minerals still possess *some* etheric matter. Therefore, the more conscious an entity is, the stronger the etheric energy it will possess. However, it is not just a matter of the mineral's consciousness but also of the consciousness of another (person, for example) who may interact with the mineral in question. So, a sole iron atom (not in a biological body, for example) may have various probable futures due to the reality that a conscious entity may interact with it, affecting it. Note that there is a nuanced difference between this and the mineral merely existing in other timelines.

It may seem that these etheric factors do not actually establish freewill but are rather random or simple indeterminate states. This is not correct. Different realities are drawn into subjective existence through consciousness (again, whether consciously choosing them or subconsciously drawing them in automatically), not arbitrary factors that have no logical reason for being. No matter what happens, whether from an act of freewill or determined outcomes – even if *seemingly* making no sense – all occurrences happen due to a logical reason. The rules of logic cannot be broken; they can only *seem* broken in very complex circumstances. Second, the higher the etheric potential and probability pathways, a causal factor in shaping an outcome turns from a determiner to a mere influencer of a conscious decision. That is, with greater etheric potential, the consciousness of a being has a higher chance to override such causal factors, even if, in effect, 'deterministically' (by way of low probabilities) *influenced* by them.

It is then a matter of partial freewill compared to total freewill (which can only exist outside of all spacetime) and no freewill (being a rock, for example). So, the consciousness of a limited being (a person in physical reality) can (partially) access and utilize the unlimited power of the Aether (that is, consciousness existing in a pure ultimate potential field and, thus, being in a total state of freewill) to perform such changes. In other words, a person's freewill operates by partially accessing the *infinite power* of a level of reality that transcends the limits of spacetime and its determinants, and the person does so by manoeuvring through various etheric probabilities.

So, a person may like a particular substance, such as chocolate, and their preference may continue to be influenced by causal factors leading to such preference; but when freewill is applied, they may end up using the power of their consciousness to override such preferences. Since mages and other sapient beings cannot totally override their physical beings, their freewill is thus limited. The desire to remove such subjective preferences can itself be influenced by a causal factor or more (generally physical), but it ultimately comes down to the level of consciousness one possesses, which is the true creative shaper of outcomes. Imagine the single goal of altering the preference for or against chocolate. The goal itself has a set number of causal factors – potentially millions among many combinations, with many falling under larger categories such as one's genes. As consciousness moves through each causal factor (such as genetic memory), the change in probability alteration is higher.

In the context of *genetics* (explained more in *Section 4.3*), this is one example of *epigenetics*, where certain genes may be switched on or off through particular means; but viewing millions of causal factors from the limitations of consciousness in the physical (such as being a human who only has so many hours in a day and so much brain power) may seem impossible. Indeed, it is for humans. However, there can be overarching alterations that consciousness can focus on. The viewing of a causal factor will have a diffusing effect on related causal factors, thereby somewhat – and diminishingly – altering ones that were not focused on in the first place, therefore enabling some degree of change, potentially overriding such a desire.

Extremely limited probability pathways resulting from both physical factors and the lack of etheric energy (and awareness) limit a human from simply turning into a dragon, for example. This, of course, is merely focusing one's intent on change. As will be covered in *Section Three* (*Section 3.4*, specifically), mages can use the magical art of *alchemy* to create much more profound changes; but this only occurs through the precise practice of the magic, not *merely* accessing higher etheric energy and awareness to overcome determinants from the limitations of the mage's somatic perspective. Such magic, then, *can* allow mages to transform their physical bodies. The alchemical magic, though, draws from corporeal or non-corporeal realities in existence, all existing *due to* probabilities opening up new states of being; but these potential states extend beyond the body's mere probable present states and futures. So, a dragon body would exist in some reality due to the infinite potentiality embedded within existence itself allowing the dragon body to exist in the first place, but the alchemist's transformation into a dragon would not (in all likelihood) be based on their own body possessing the probability of it transforming into the dragon. One can only naturally converge on different probable states if there is the very probability of it happening in the first place.

The physical body as a *whole* can change to a whole new body due to how pilot waves work in the etheric and for the physical. The etheric body will have a pilot wave not only for itself but also one for each of its constituent parts; the same applies for the quantum particles of the physical body the etheric body is connected to, so parts of a physical body (like a whole heart, for example) will have their own wave function as well as the physical body as a whole having its own wave function. So, it is not just each individual quantum particle that has its own wave function (although, each individual particle is still a whole entity itself). Accordingly, the etheric automatically groups various properties into particular entities. When certain physical properties have enough particular connections in the etheric, they will pass certain *holistically-related thresholds* (HRTs), whereby *holistically-related forms* (HRFs) can be established. So, a person's whole body would have enough etheric data for it to be a HRF itself, whereby its own wave function will affect the body and all of its constituents as a whole entity. Of course, there can be HRFs within HRFs, passing their own HRTs, so a person's heart would itself be a HRF within the HRF of the body.

The etheric is necessary for this categorical phenomenon, because while there may be some connection at the quantum level purely in the physical for certain things (like tables or people), most atoms in an object or person would not otherwise really be connected as an ontologically *defined* entity outside of social constructions. Normally, the wave function of the holistically greater HRF will overrule the wave functions of its constituent parts. This also means that when it comes to magic and many other phenomena that affect HRFs, either the most prominent HRF or affectable HRF will be affected. So, in the case of affecting a mage's body via magic, the whole body would be affected rather than the heart. For clarification, while the entity that is a HRF would be affected *as* a HRF (a whole entity), the constituents within the HRF would also be affected in themselves, but the constituents within the HRF would not be affected as HRFs. Even potential fields can affect HRFs. If various etheric properties act as whole entity, then the term *etheric holistically-related form* (EHRF) is used.

Whilst more time-fluid, the etheric still responds to physical structuring and is also shaped by the physical. Thus, geometric formations – or any atomic events, really – of intensified energies in the physical can draw in, warp, or alter etheric strength. Likewise, the health of a person affects the etheric body; therefore, one of the best ways to strengthen the etheric is not to actually focus on the etheric per se; rather, attention should be paid to fixing physical problems first, such as going to the gym and exercising. Of course, this is a complex issue, and so mages (having a certain gland in their brains that allow for magic) will still be able to produce more etheric energy in the context of magic than a non-mage simply due to having the extra physical traits (the gland). That is, despite a mage not exercising their minds, they would still have a greater advantage over a non-mage (in the context of magic). Some non-mages *do* have psychic abilities, but they not have the ability to wield magic in the most-commonly understood sense of the term. In the end, it is still the physical that allows for this greater alerting of etheric reality.

Physical reality requires one to continually re-nourish itself, but the etheric depends on the physical to act accordingly, too. If a physical body dies, this affects the etheric, and a being's *soul* will eventually lose the etheric energy it had. Note that a soul is a particularized consciousness with its own ego, which will also possess a body of some kind (even if only spiritual). Although etheric energy can disappear and dissipate, it can also still rest in a dormant state of non-tangible potential and, thus, technically never cease to exist. Imagine switching off a movie from a device; the off-state movie still exists in a dormant state, ready to be accessed again. Moreover, the particular etheric energy may also exist in other realities. Although it is still unknown exactly why physical beings need sleep, sleeping naturally will recharge and restrengthen the etheric body. Even harmful electromagnetic radiation in the physical realm, for the most part, does not affect the aura *directly*; so, the physical body is affected first, and the etheric aura, in turn, is affected. Likewise, attacks in the spiritual planes will create discordant frequencies in the etheric body, and the negatively-affected etheric can in turn affect physical probabilities.

A wave function will essentially phase lock with a particular timeline or state; this is a form of synchronization, and it can occur consciously or otherwise. However, this is a bit different to the quantum synchronization found in the physical realm. Nevertheless, synchronizing with other timelines can aid in quantum synchronization. Moreover, the more fluid and broader range of the etheric can help with quantum synchronizations as well. The etheric can even cause different *events* in the physical realm to synchronize (rather than mere quantum synchronizations of particle states), and this is known as a *synchronicity*. For example, a person may keep seeing particular numbers, and at the moment of seeing such numbers, *seemingly* coincidental events may also occur. Still, care must be taken not to consider all synchronicities as being part of one's making or relevance, as there are many different environmental etheric energies that a person can interact with without even knowing about. Many of these irrelevant synchronicities are called *synchronicity webs*, as they are clusters of etheric energy people may stumble across and get entangled in. For example, a person may see the name of object in particular over and over again within a period (of a month) while the etheric energy of the web lasts, yet it may have no relevance in their lives.

It is not just etheric webs people can experience; it is possible to knowingly or unknowingly walk through etheric beings such as *ghosts*. Ghosts are temporary beings in the etheric who have, for unknown reasons, not passed on to the astral realm. They are not necessarily demonic, but their presence does not necessarily have to come across as a conscious being. Like physical entities with sufficient consciousness, ghosts still possess an astral body, but they do not have physical bodies; however, ghosts can *possess* bodies with an occupant host and, thus, control physical bodies (whether with the consent of the host or not). Note that ghosts are different to pure *astral spirits* (who are beings in the astral with no physical bodies). Most theories and evidence suggest that ghosts are able to maintain their etheric form due to being able to feed off other etheric energy.

Although there are numerous ghost stories describing events where the ghosts are capable of great feats, such as manifesting physically and then devouring people, none of these have been empirically verified. At most, ghosts either create distortions in quantum potentials and/or appear to those who can see the etheric. In these cases, the psychic can see, hear, and in some cases, smell or feel the ghosts, but as will be explained in the following section on astral matter, these are reinterpretations via the brain – in addition to (resultant) wave function changes across their *physical* bodies – rather than direct sensory stimuli. The ghost, in this sense, does not actually touch the person. Still, via wave function changes, a ghost can still technically move physical objects, but this would be indirect, and it is still a rare occurrence. Not all cases require a psychic to see a ghost, and ghosts have other abilities as well; for more information on ghosts, see *Section 4.3.2.9*.

When a person feels dark (evil) etheric energy around them, it has to be under-stood that there are two aspects to this phenomenon. The etheric energy will contain properties that can be harmful to particular matter, and in the case of physical matter, this is done via particular wave functions changes. But it is also the case that the said etheric energy has the *information* of darkness – that is, it is a holistic phenomenon that is more than just the harmful effects. In contrast, the physical realm will not have this same level of information, so any darkness that is manifest in the physical will only manifest as something tangible like 'pain' or corruption of intact physical properties. So, one does not feel dark physical energy; instead, they only feel the *effects* of darkness. The same can go for any other holistically-defined attributes, such as love.

# 1.4: The Constitution of Astral Matter:

As a potentially infinitely-large mental space, the astral realm is fundamentally a dreamscape – a completely-non-physical realm with properties that are even less localized than the etheric while totally being outside the frequency range of the physical. Of course, one could make the argument that all reality is a dreamscape, but the astral is a realm where *thoughts themselves* can instantly manifest things. Given the mental nature of the astral, the convergence between the physical, etheric, and the astral begins when the former two contain patterns of mental activity. So, only beings that are capable of mental activity have *astral bodies*. Unless discarnate, deep meditation or sleep is required to consciously access the astral planes, where consciousness has to be wholly 'outside' of its physical body. The same normally applies to the etheric body; that is, when a person is astral travelling, the etheric body *tends* to be left behind; but since the etheric is in a looser state than the physical, one can technically astral travel to a limited extent with their etheric body attached.

Even when outside both the physical and etheric bodies, astral travellers, nevertheless, will still basically be tied to both of their bodies via a 'cord' – normally, this appears silvery. The reverse is also true: that is, astral beings that do not possess etheric bodies are still capable of forming etheric bodies. However, not all (indeed, most) entities do this, as it is difficult, and they need a form of sustenance to maintain the etheric state; usually, this is etheric energy that emits from physical entities. Sometimes, though, energetic fluctuations in the etheric realm can allow for greater chances of astral entities to form etheric bodies.

Although access to (and within) the many astral planes within the totality of the astral realm is limited, advanced psychic mages, from the physical realm (normally through meditation), can see certain astral energies, generally those of the astral bodies around people. Still, this is normally only temporary, and it is limited in other ways, too. This does not include seeing *charms* in *charm magic* that many conscious beings can see (detailed in *Section 3.3*). While the word 'astral' simply refers to that which is astral-based, this includes the term *astral realm*, which is used as a singular term for the astral in its entirety. Meanwhile, *astral plane(s)* (singular or plural) refer either to a specific plane within the astral realm or to its many planes. A psychic mage can see through multiple bodies – physical, etheric, and astral – but their consciousness mostly sees physical matter through the physical eyes and brain.

When a psychic mage *does* see spiritual matter (while the psychic is in the physical realm), it is still *mostly* through the physical brain. It is the physical body that limits the consciousness of the being who is inside it from seeing astral energies as they exist. This means all such spiritual energy and information is filtered through the subjective-orientating lens and limitations of the brain, and so biases, misinterpretations, and distortions naturally form as a result. In other words, the brain does not actually see astral energy in its actuality and, instead, just what it perceives of it. Despite this, it is actually not pure imagination that the mage will see; there are, indeed, etheric and astral energies that reach the mage's etheric and astral bodies, but these energies still have to go through the brain in what is called *channelling*.

Channelled information will always be distorted due to subjective properties and biases. Think of how colour is seen; physical eyes have photoreceptor cells that are responsible for seeing colour, and changing a set or the properties of these cones will alter one's perceptions. Even one's language can alter the perception of colour alone, where instead of seeing what one thinks of as another shade of green, one can see an entirely different colour, such as blue. The children's game, 'whispering agents', is a good example of how easily information can be misinterpreted; in the game, one person whispers or mimes a message to another in a line of players, and eventually, the end message will typically differ from the initial one – even if in mere tone.

So how, exactly, does astral energy channel to the physical? To understand the question, it is best to first acknowledge again that all things in existence (in all states and all realities) are connected at the ZPF. That is, the natural state of existence is *default connection*. From this axiom, we may then ask: why, then, does information not *simply* (besides at the quantum level) connect to anything else in everyday reality? The short answer is: matter. Matter creates various effects, distorting the connection of all that exists. Informational energy can only then network and *flow* through *aligning* matter, and the matter which is not conductive will create a blockage of this flow. Consider how electricity can conduct easily through copper, yet it does not conduct through a resistor like rubber. The energy (electricity) is *ready* to flow through matter, connecting to the end destination, but it gets impeded by matter itself. The very nature of the physical and astral realms differ so greatly that it is not an issue of swapping rubber for copper. The physical, nevertheless, has to have properties that can align with the astral; otherwise, there is very little to no connection via a channel.

The astral, nevertheless, fundamentally connects through to the physical via the etheric, doing so primarily through the etheric's less localized states, probabilities, and (meta)data. Accordingly, the etheric (being a semi-reflection of the physical) needs to contain the vital properties of having proper conductivity. It is believed that the more precise level of etheric-to-physical interaction is not just at the quantum level but also *up to* the *microtubule* level, where quantum particles lay in less-localized states. Nearly all types of biological organisms (apart from certain groups, like bacteria) have microtubules, which are polymers (that is, materials consisting of repeating chains of very large molecules with subunits) of tubulin (a type of protein) found in neurons (the main constituent of nerve tissue). The brain also, interestingly, has to be capable of processing certain information. Channelling advanced knowledge is impossible if the brain cannot comprehend, say, the mathematics of such knowledge. Generally, when such knowledge *can* be channelled, it comes through as easy-to-understand broad concepts rather than as complex details. When the physical aligns more with the astral, channelling of information becomes easier. If the mage loses its synchronization with the astral, channelled information will begin to degrade.

Equally, astral beings cannot *properly* see the physical, as they do not have the eyes of a physical being to see reality as such. They, too, will get a distorted view of our reality. Most of the time, all they can perceive of those in the physical is their astral bodies, which filter distorted versions of the physical. Nevertheless, in the cases where it *seems* like astral entities may 'properly' see the physical, they still cannot properly see it from certain perspectives (such as how a human perceives reality through their physical eyes), and they may, instead, be seeing a convoluted mess of physical properties, which includes light outside of the visible spectrum, along with alternate realities. Still, there are rare and hard ways to 'download' the *exact* data of both a first-person and third-person perspective (the latter deriving from the etheric alone) of a physical entity and view and experience it in the astral. Astral beings may also accidentally tune into and see probable realities, not the tangible one; and this may even occur *while* they are correctly following the tangible reality, not just before tuning into it.

The actual planes of the astral realm, howbeit, have numerous unexplainable *astral shrouds*, blocking sight to other spiritual realms, many futures, multiple fields in the astral, and more. Even though many astral travellers have made countless journeys into the astral, the astral can be confusing for several reasons, primarily because it is filled with the craziness of people's beliefs and imaginations (such as religious beliefs), along with one's own deceptive and subjective biases – biases that exist even without the physical shell. Because of these shrouds, confusion has arisen as to whether the higher astral planes contain what is sometimes referred to as *hyperspace* – which is an abstruse realm of bizarre geometry of extra dimensions filled with strange *archetypal* beings – or if this hyperspace is a different kind of reality altogether with its own constitution of matter. If it is a different reality, then most theories suggest that this hyperspace is a 'place' between realms, as if the hallways or even the substructural realm of all that exists. Despite the confusion and lack of standard astral travel to the so-called hyperspace, beings from the physical realm have managed to come across this strange place in various brief settings – sometimes by mistake.

Like frequencies of light in the physical, spiritual properties exist on different frequencies. When one's frequency changes, so does their reality within the spiritual planes, with a plane being a *sub-frequency set*. Therefore, there are not just 'places' within the astral but also *states of being*. So, two physical people next to each other may not have their spiritual energies interact directly or at all with one another due to their different frequencies. Correspondingly, one does not have to be physically present next to a particular physical thing in order to interact with its spiritual energy, as they can access it via spiritually tuning into that state of being first (with the help of delocalization and nonlocality). Quantum entanglement does not guarantee this, but it does help. Techniques have accordingly been developed to hide, mask, and shift energy away from unwanted attention. Amazingly, it can be either harder or easier to view the astral body of someone (and any of their imaginations) than some astral constructs elsewhere. Naturally, most astral travellers avoid tuning into hellish places, such as the one filled with 'fire' people call *Seckaphon*. There are also the *nether planes*, which are particular kinds of dark (and usually evil) realms, filled with nebulous beings. This term does not refer to any one type of plane, so it is an adjective for *types* of planes.

No-one in the Caelverse (at least publicly) knows how the astral shrouds were formed, whether they are artificial or natural. However, even though astral beings cannot properly see the physical – especially through the astral shrouds – they can still see certain 'signals' flashing from people's astral bodies, indicating particular activity. Usually, signals are also distorted through a variety of energy clusters and can be easy to miss, especially since there is a lot of activity in the astral; but a large percentage of astral beings know what these signals are, and they are capable of honing in on them. These signals emerge by opening up channels to the astral or when simply emitting strong, unique energies. Specific (and generally, *occultic*) rituals are an excellent way to open channels and emit special energies. Particular rituals attract particular entities. All participants in a ritual entangle themselves into a larger, unified field of energy to varying degrees, so there are signals within signals.

If a person is located or discovered – and if the energies properly connect and allow for it – then attachment, or even possession, may occur. Spiritual entities hijack and 'rewire' the etheric before absorbing the metadata and then direct data, allowing them to, for example, speak languages they would otherwise not know. Still, this may be a hard process, and so not all beings can learn a new language. One ritual is not equal to another; some are good, some are bad, and others vary in strength. Other practices, specifically dark practices, may lead to possession; these practices include: hexes (including being subject to hexes); deep meditations; and consuming destructive and intoxicating substances. Once a proper connection has been established, spiritual entities may – and eventually have to – leave the physical host temporarily, easily finding the host again later.

Astral beings also attempt to locate people through *thoughtform attachments*. Like all properties in the astral, *thoughtforms* are mentally-created constructs that form auto-matically when mental activity occurs; and these can take the form of virtually any-thing, from primitive blobs of floating energy, to objects like tables, to spheres of music, to artificially-intelligent (A.I.) beings with personality constructs (generally, but not always, archetypal), to complex energy systems that manage and power other astral constructs, to entire fantasy worlds to play in, and even to technologies or tools that can be utilized for too many reasons to list. Not all mental constructs will lead to equal results; that is, some mental activity might be so weak or temporary that it may appear like no thoughtforms manifest. Users may also consciously suppress the level of strength their thoughtforms possess. It is important to understand the nature of thoughtforms, as they are part of the fundamental question as to what matter is, along with the mechanics of particular magic. Even though thoughtforms are only mental energy, their creation is another process of energy (matter) formation and, thus, another example of the link between consciousness and matter.

Thoughtforms are *second-order beings* and do not possess the level of consciousness as their creators (*first-order beings*), though they still possess some form of consciousness, just as inanimate minerals do (according to the theory that consciousness permeates all matter). This even applies to 'intelligent' thoughtforms that may take on the structure of a person. Technically, even animal consciousness has more awareness (and freewill) than such a thoughtform with its limited programming. However, any thoughtform, just like physical matter, can be *entitized*, though the soul of an animal generally will not be able to entitize an intelligent thoughtform, for example, due to the said soul's lack of development, preventing it from vibrationally aligning with the astral construct.

The entitization of physical matter *usually* emerges through birth, but exceptions always apply. Astral travellers have determined that (*re*)*incarnation* occurs, though nobody has been able to understand how this process actually works. The more complex the physical vehicle, the more complex the soul is, and there is now much debate as to whether artificial intelligence (specifically, physical robots) will birth souls or lead to entitization. More accurately, artificial intelligence will never have souls, as it is artificial; instead, it may be possible for *physical robotic bodies* to have souls, should they advance enough in the future – but this may still only allow for a limited type of consciousness. Nevertheless, A.I. in the physical can still have etheric and astral attachments. Even though mages can see auras to determine who and what is ensouled, consider that seeing the etheric and astral is limited, with distortions also being a problem, so this does not, nor likely will not, give adequate answers. Moreover, there is a difference between pure consciousness and a soul, so there can – indeed, are cases – where there is the illusion of a soul. To see pure consciousness, one would need to *be* the Aether itself in its purest form, which cannot be done as an entity in the physical.

When a thoughtform is ensouled, it is no longer a thoughtform. Even before turning into a being with a soul, a thoughtform may be able to create more of its kind (thoughtforms), intentionally or not. However, this is not as easy for it as it is for a conscious soul because thoughtforms rely on a source of conscious energy (generally their creators), whereas conscious entities usually rely on other sources for nourishment; although, even food, such as apples, contain minerals, which technically possess some (very minor) form of consciousness. Therefore, the latter example, while similar to the former, should more accurately be categorized as being on a different *level* of consumption *of conscious energy*.

If a thoughtform is advanced enough to create another thoughtform, the second creation must also find a source of energy if it is to survive. Generally, they do not last long, as a conscious entity's attention and energy are limited. Such creations are also almost always replicas or lower entities than the thoughtforms that spawned them. All thoughtforms can only directly interact with other astral entities and bodies, but through attachments, they can still indirectly influence the physical by affecting the etheric first. There are also collective thoughtforms that do not seek out energy to sustain themselves *as such* but, instead, are seas of mass energy that beings of all kinds are naturally part of by default. These are called *mass collective thoughtforms* (MCTs), which are not to be confused with *meta-order beings* (MOBs), which are a theorized oversoul encompassing various amounts of souls.

MCTs are collectively created either intentionally or unintentionally, usually due to mass, collective belief systems, large group identities, racial or specieal genetic makeups, intense energy entangling, and even advanced psychic techniques. Over time, MCTs are more likely to change than perish. When their existence is threatened, MCTs merely change and adapt to new information, for example, sometimes looking very different from their initial conception. MCTs are also capable of creating their own minor thoughtforms. However, unlike how ordinary thoughtforms create others of their ilk, MCTs usually influence their conscious beings into creating self-reinforcing thoughtforms. In addition, MCTs also harness dissipating energy from conscious beings and redirect it into individual thoughtforms that happen to be in alignment with the MCT. And then there are the individual thoughtforms in the MCTs that grow from the very power of the latter, which, in turn, may create more thoughtforms – though, many die off. MCTs are not easy to see; generally, a being is either swamped in one (or many) or not, and they normally exist on other (and multiple) frequencies (and planes) compared to standard thoughtforms people create.

A distinction here must also be made between MCTs and the *collective unconscious*, which is another matter – though, they are both still fundamentally entwined, as one affects the other. The collective unconscious is a collective mental field that rests in the astral, but it may exist in other realms, such as the physical (like within the genetic makeup of the people). That is, physical entities still produce a collective unconscious, although these still are found in the astral. While other collective fields exist (such as *morphic fields* – detailed in *Section 4.3.1*), these are not mental per se in their pure form. A collective unconscious will store particular archetypal forces and mental patterns that a collective group of beings (such as a race of people, species, or even multiple sapient beings) have tapped into or mentally created. This field will not necessarily possess tangible thoughtforms, and these archetypal forces, instead, lay in dormant states. However, thoughtforms can easily manifest from these fields, especially when an astral traveller from the physical explores the astral planes. Interestingly, MCTs can emerge from a collective unconscious and vice versa.

A collective unconscious still needs tangible entities in order to exist; so, if all physical entities were to die off, then *their* collective unconscious fields would disappear, too. The physical beings, in this context, act as the nodes for the emergent collective unconscious. Of course, there would be traces of their existences in other dormant states (just like how everything in existence will still exist in a dormant state somewhere); and all archetypal forces of any collective unconscious, nevertheless, ultimately exist at the ZPF that transcends all matter. In other words, there are collective unconscious fields within other collective unconscious fields, all tying into the ultimate collective unconscious (and conscious) field of the Aether.

# Section Two

## *The Cosmology of the Caelverse*

## 2.1: Structural and Astronomical Overview:

• Note: Various useful images and explanations can be found in *Section 2.6*.

The Caelverse (pronounced: sail-vurs) is a massive torus-shaped system that features what astronomers believe to be 589,824 *planets* divided equally in orbit around 32,768 *suns*. Each sun has its own respective *solar system*, so there are also 32,768 solar systems. Giant, planet-less *C-stars* (*constellated stars*) form 32,768 *sets* of twelve geometrically-positioned *constellations* around each solar system, all among a sea of nebulae, one parsec (roughly thirty trillion kilometres) away from their respective systems, ringed perpendicular (from their centres) in relation to the circular direction of travel the solar systems take through the Caelverse. The solar systems also are part of *solar clusters*, which are specific sets of vertically-walled solar systems, each with 256 suns that vary in distance and geometric location from one another; therefore, there are 128 solar clusters. There are also unconstellated *L-stars* (*loose stars*) that situate between and around the solar clusters in far greater number than both the suns and C-stars.

The suns and stars are a mix of colours on the electromagnetic spectrum, which most humans *would* see as white, but due to atmospheric scattering – in addition to other variables such as the location one is on a planet, along with the time of day – people will see them in different colours. For most humans, suns generally appear yellowish to reddish. While in space, though, the suns look white, whereas the stars may appear in assorted colours due to various properties in space altering their appearance. Although the stars vary in size, every sun has a rough radius of 772,768 km from their cores to their photospheres. Constellations also have various layers, and each of these differ in size. The edge of the Caelverse is also a curved mirror, so when both the suns and stars move through the Caelverse, their mirrored lights either *blueshift* or *redshift*, depending on whether one is approaching a light or moving away from it. Grid lines have also been detected across the Caelverse's surface on an etheric (but not a physical) level.

The Caelverse is specifically a *horn* torus, so the centre has a point; however, the centre is shrouded, so while the geometry of the Caelverse is clear, it is still unknown what exactly is at the centre. Most theories suggest that the central point is a gateway to a space beyond the Caelverse. Not only has no-one ever reached the centre of the Caelverse (as space travel and teleportation is limited), there has not been any evidence of anything emerging from this possible gateway either. Although the origins of the Caelverse are unclear, it is generally theorized that it was at least the product (though not necessarily a conscious creation) of an external force – whether physical and/or spiritual. Since many shrouds block access to a person gaining such knowledge in the astral realm, it is also unclear whether the Caelverse directly or indirectly connects to any other physical system of similar or different structures.

However, what *is* empirically evident (due to psychic research in the etheric) is that other physical realities exist; and so, given this axiom, it must follow that the Caelverse is part of something much greater, with that likely being a *multiverse*. Still, these other realities may only be other corporeal (and incorporeal probable and possible) time-lines of the Caelverse alone. Besides the shrouded centre of the torus, there are other massive energy distortions and concentrations in the Caelverse itself that block psychics from properly determining how certain structures in the Caelverse are and were truly formed, and, thus, there is still much left to learn about the cosmology of the Caelverse.

Despite there being many competing cosmological theories, it is nonetheless clear that the Caelverse is in a constant state of change. At one 'end' of the Caelverse is also the gigantic *Great Black Wall* (GBW), a vertical field filled with many *black holes* and a strange gas that appears like a liquid. For some unknown reason, the black holes do not coalesce, nor do they consume the surrounding gas, so they are called *micro* black holes compared to the hypothetical large black holes that could exist. The majority of astronomers theorize that the GBW will consume every solar system in roughly 66,585,605 years' time    as of the year B 121 (for more information on the current year, see *Section 4.1*). The GBW, more specifically, will supposedly take 524,288 years to gravitationally rip *each* solar cluster to shreds individually. The 'first' solar cluster (named: *SC1*) is already experiencing slow destruction, with wild cosmic rays causing massive environmental damage; even the planets' natural gravitational distortions are wildly distorted to further extremes. With an estimated 1,029 years left before complete annihilation, nearly all willing sapient lifeforms have permanently relocated to other solar clusters from these *oblivion-bound worlds* (OBWs). Many black market and unlawful activities occur in SC1, despite strong government entry restrictions. Since the GBW is not one giant black hole, time dilation is not a big issue and phenomenon for SC1.

The Great Black Wall's opaqueness leaves it impossible to physically see what lies behind or inside it. Astronomers are unsure whether the wall has already consumed other clusters or not, as there is an increasing gap between the front of the GBW and its rear – the latter travelling at the same speed as the solar systems. That is, the GBW has both a 'head' and a 'tail' with a probable gap in between. This gap – the *Great Black Gap (GBG)* – has the equivalent size of roughly four cluster *spaces* within it. Since there are nine parsecs between each solar cluster, there are therefore thirty-six parsecs from one edge of the GBG to the other side (when viewed from a central point as a circumference). In addition to this, there are also nine parsecs between the Caelverse's leading (living) solar cluster (SC128) and the GBW's tail, and then another nine parsecs from the start of the GBW to SC1 (the cluster now close to total destruction). This latter figure, of course, is measured from the GBW's initial trajectory from the edge of the GBG's four cluster spaces; and so, as of the current year B-424, it is now less than one parsec away.

Given the geometrically 'perfect' number of suns and solar clusters already present in the Caelverse (respectively 32,768 and 128), it seems unlikely the GBW has consumed other solar clusters in the current cycle of history. Still, the GBW would have had a starting point, so when also adding the spaces in the GBG, it would take 69,730,304 years for the GBW to completely move through the Caelverse from its original starting point. Whatever the case, it is generally believed that the Caelverse will reform its solar clusters after the GBW has consumed everything. One reason for this is that advanced psychics have tuned into the celestial bodies of the Caelverse, discovering that their various (though vague) etheric energies exist in multiple different time periods of our current reality. This means that there would be different *cycles* of reformation for the *same timeline*. In other words, the energies exist in different time periods of our current timeline that extend beyond our *current* cycle of history; *but* this simultaneously does not mean *itself* that the energies *necessarily* exist in other timelines (although they still do).

While it seems likely that life itself in the Caelverse will eventually meet complete annihilation, this does not matter *too* much to some people, as psychics have learned that (re)incarnation of some kind occurs. The anomaly here is that if it takes 69,730,304 years for *complete* destruction – and what is assumed to be the same amount of time for complete reformation – many questions arise, such as how the planets managed to form in so little time. For clarification, this figure is taken from the absolute beginning of the Caelverse cycle, prior to the GBG forming. Moreover, this figure is not incorporating the absolute total of 139,460,608 years when doubled to account for the reforming process.

One theory proposed for the reformation process involves *time crystals* – structures and patterns that repeat in (periods of) time rather than space like regular crystals. Time crystals are not in equilibrium, so they do not heat up; essentially, they have motion without energy, which may seem strange prima facie. It would appear, then, as though time crystals allow for infinite energy, but by themselves, this is not technically the case. When viewed in relation to the mechanisms of the Caelverse as a whole, however, the particular effects of time crystals are more so a part of the overall process of solar cluster formations. That is, time crystals are not exactly responsible for the perpetual motion – and life-sustaining motions – of the Caelverse; this is fundamentally, rather, a result of the cores of each major celestial body absorbing ZPE to then generate cold fusion and fission. These cores, more specifically, initially add more energy to the Caelverse for said processes (cold fusion and fission) before then reabsorbing said energy back into the Aether, so there is, accordingly, a zero-net gain/loss of energy in the long run. The result is that there can be constant motion and reformation of the celestial bodies indefinitely, allowing the Caelverse to avoid eventually losing heat (energy) through entropy over time throughout its cycles.

However, certain strong, particularly-formed time crystals, when coupled with the entanglement of all matter *and* time via the ZPF, do create structures that *support* the *particular* motion of the Caelverse. Such time crystals specifically access and draw from particular *time reference points* within etheric information matrices, helping to reform matter quicker than normal within broad frameworks. Basically, the atoms within time crystals have a certain type of quantum superposition; and when the quantum states (such as spin) occur in a certain way, certain developments can occur in a sequence much faster than what would otherwise likely occur naturally. During the formation of the clusters, these time crystals would have been far more powerful and active than what they are today; when the Caelverse cycles through again, these time crystals will return to their original state. This means that many of the non-renewable resources, such as petroleum and diamonds, would have formed far quicker in the initial stages of cluster formation than in the later stages.

Essentially, the younger the planet, the more powerful the time crystals, granting a roughly equal amount of development in each cluster. Given geometry and nature of the Caelverse, there seems to be a perfect (but not equal) distribution that occurs with such formations. Of course, there are multiple theories as to how *exactly* certain resources like oil emerged underground; for example, some theories claim that the oil had a pure abiotic (non-biological) origin, while other theories suggest that while the oil *did* develop abiotically, it ultimately came from the etheric reference points of organic entities in a previous cycle having left behind organic materials after death. It is likewise theorized that these time crystals and corresponding etheric reference points would have helped with the origins and development of all species in the Caelverse. Scholars, nevertheless, are divided on the issue of evolution, creation, and other related theories; for a detailed explanation on this topic, see *Section 4.3*. Other celestial bodies in the Caelverse, such as the moons, indicate a master designer; but then again, it has also been argued that all things in existence have an amazing ability to naturally self-organize geometrically without the need for an explicit designer.

## 2.2: The Planets and Transportals:

Planets are sorted into *tiers* and *classes* (specifically, *planetary orbital tiers* – POTs – and *planetary structural classes* – PSCs), with every solar system having the same classifications. There are three POTs, with T1 (Tier One) planets being close to their sun, T2 planets being in the *prime habitable zone*, and T3 planets orbiting far away from their sun. T1 planets are so close to their sun that they experience scorching temperatures, where surface temperatures reach well beyond liveable standards. Some T1 planets have atmospheres while others do not; for those that do not have atmospheres, the temperatures reach extremely cold levels during the nights. T2 planets, on the other hand, contain most of the life in the Caelverse; but even then, there are many places on these planets that are uninhabitable for most beings. T3 planets are basically the opposite of T1 planets; that is, they are too cold for normal life – both during the day and night, regardless of whether a planet has an atmosphere or not.

It takes *exactly* 360 *Standard Days* for *all* T2 worlds to orbit a sun (making one *Standard Year*), whereas *all* T1 worlds complete an orbit in a mere thirty-three Standard Days exactly. Meanwhile, T3 planets take exactly twelve Standard Years and thirty Standard Days to fully orbit their sun. Despite these differences, all tiers orbit their suns in a counterclockwise manner when viewed from above a sun's north pole. While it may intuitively seem that T1 planets would look reddish and T1 planets would look blueish, this is not necessarily the case. However, many of these planets do have such respective colours.

Spacecraft have, nevertheless, been able to reach and land on T1 and T3 planets. Initial exploration was with unmanned probes, but eventually manned spaceships were able to establish colonies on these planets. However, due to the extremely harsh conditions (not just the temperatures), only basic colonies (all living underground) have been able to survive up to this point. There have been rogue operations that have splintered off from these colonies and ventured out beyond designated colony territory, but these are very small and are not as successful as the various criminal organizations that exist on T2 worlds. Psychic mages have also detected particular etheric activity from underground – the kind of etheric activity that lifeforms produce and possess. However, this is largely distorted, so it is unclear whether other life exists on these planets or not; but in all likelihood, at least some unknown alien life exists.

Each POT has a set of six PSCs that universally occur in an established order throughout the Caelverse. The first PSC are C1 (Class One) worlds, and it is from C1 planets that the Standard Day of twenty-four hours is set. Other classes may have their own days, but when dealing with interplanetary affairs, the Standard Day is used. T2-C1 planets are the most habitable and inhabited places in the Caelverse, exhibiting an array of lifeforms from bacteria to fully sapient beings. Their terrains are generally temperate, but they also feature deserts, tundra, mountainous regions, vast oceans, and of course, polar ice caps. Shaped as globes, each have a diameter of 50,968 km, while most have *axial tilts* establishing seasons. With an equatorial rotational spin of over 6,671 km per hour, T2-C1 planets would potentially be capable of generating devastating weather via the *Coriolis effect*, but this issue is largely offset due to various factors, such as particular geomagnetic influences, atmospheric composition, *biospheric* actors, and, of course, assorted planetary frequencies that establish various types of oscillations that alter how heat is distributed across the planets. When also accounting for centrifugal force, there is not too much of a difference between the weight of one mass at the equator compared to the same mass at the poles.

C1 planets have an average surface area of 8,161,031,551 km$^2$; and underneath this level is the rest of the crust, then the upper and lower mantles, then the outer and inner cores, all together possessing an average volume of 69,325,242,678,128 km$^3$. From the crust to the end of the lower mantle, however, all C1 planets have a 'honeycomb' or 'cellular' structure; in a few places, it is more akin to a sponge. These natural structures form what is typically called the *grand caverns*, which are massive areas featuring an array of lifeforms (for T2 planets), oceans, cities (T2), and more. C1 planets also have an average mass of 3.822 x 10$^{26}$ kg (as roughly with other PSCs), where most of the mass is found in the core and the mantle. Due to this great amount of mass, the surface gravitational pull *would* be *about* 39.24 m/s$^2$, but all PSC of planets have gravitational distortions; and so, in the case of C1 planets, these distortions uniformly reduce the surface gravitational pull to *about* 9.81 m/s$^2$, which is about what most organisms in the Caelverse are adapted to living under.

All planetary gravitational distortions result from how the cores operate. Each core features a *planetary mass regulator* (PMR) – a self-organizing (and potentially self-aware) field that draws energy directly from the Aether before slowly producing matter via cold fusion. These fields, moreover, have the ability for cold fission, and they *can* also absorb matter back into the Aether. PMRs also alter planetary composition (as well as the formation of matter in the planetary layers), all the while being able to manipulate forces (including gravity) in a variety of ways. Naturally, a large amount of mass will surround a PMR, acting as the planet's *inner matter core* (IMC), where an *outer matter core* (OMC) follows. IMCs are solid (and mostly made of iron), but they also contain an ordered geometry of crystals as a result of the PMRs producing certain harmonic frequencies. These geometrically-aligned crystals establish their own harmonic frequencies, which penetrate the liquid OMCs before encompassing the whole planet. These harmonic frequencies then help develop the structures found in the mantles (and, in the case of C1 worlds, the cellar/honeycomb structures).

A PMR, more precisely, will actually alter *potential fields* rather than changing the real gravity itself. So, the surface gravity of a C1 planet is still actually 39.24 m/s$^2$, but with the changed potential, this causes mass to *effectively* fall at the rate of 9.81 m/s$^2$ via a wave function change. Basically, the quantum nature of the falling masses is changed, and this results in the observed phenomenon of them falling slower. Since this involves wave functions, probabilities are involved, but for all practical cases, masses will always uniformly fall at their respective altered potentials within a given region in a planet's atmosphere; specifically, there is a 100% chance of a mass having reduced acceleration up to the end of the *thermosphere* – unless, of course, some other phenomenon changes the potential. For the sake of brevity, it is normally easier to just say 'warped gravity' instead of 'warped gravitational potential'. All masses within the *warped gravitational field* (WGF) will not only be affected with reduced acceleration, but their gravitational potential exerted on other masses will be affected as well.

Due to PMRs having unique frequencies, all WGFs are unique in their geometric structure; however, all PSCs will have virtually the same *type* of WGF geometric structure. Basically, the PMR will effectively 'redistribute' the gravity to certain *locations* within the WGF and not to the masses themselves within the SGF. Of course, as a result, masses will be drawn to those locations of greatest gravity, so the greater the gravity, the more mass that will naturally accumulate to those locations. Since the redistributed gravitational locations are found within the *relative* spatial field of the planet, this means that as a planet orbits its sun, the locations of such gravity also move, as they are relative to the WGF and the planet. For clarification, while the gravitational effect of masses within the WGF can technically extend for infinity, the WGF's ability to reduce gravitational potential for masses only occurs within the planetary region, so the WGF does not affect masses on other planets, for example.

In the case of C1 planets, basically all the gravity will be found roughly up to the planet's surface without unusual relocations. That is, C1 planet WGFs are plainly spherical, with the majority of C1 planets featuring changes in gravity on the inside as if the density of the planet decreased *linearly* from the centre outwards; for some planets, however, the gravity changes as if there were *constant density* throughout the volume of the planet. So, for the former example, the gravity does not increase linearly from the centre of the planet (even though the *density* would otherwise be linear), whereas for the latter example, the level of gravity increases linearly from the centre.

Each planet effectively reduces their normal gravity by 75%. Therefore, if all the planets were spherical, then their surface gravitational pulls would be about 9.81 m/s$^2$. So, despite the different gravitational locations in the WGFs among the PSCs, all planets have an equal amount of gravity. With all the planets having equal gravity, each planet is balanced in their orbit around the sun, as no planet pulls another out of its orbit. When more mass is added to a planet (for example, if a spaceship were to enter the atmosphere, specifically, the WGF of the planet), the PMR will be able to affect the gravitational potential of the mass and keep the strength of the WGF the same. However, if, hypothetically, a whole other planet were to collide with the original planet, then the WGF would likely be affected and reduced in its strength compared to the amount of added mass. Certain technologies and phenomena like magic can create different gravitational fields within a WGF that are not affected, as this occurs via a difference in *phase*. Note that technologies and places that use *centrifugal force* are not affected, as centrifugal force – the apparent outward force on an object that rotates – is a *pseudo force*.

In contrast to C1 planets, C2 worlds are ring shaped. The majority of C2 planets are toroids resembling doughnuts, but a decent number appear like the ornamental jewellery worn on fingers. Even the grand caverns in the mantles are ring-shaped; that is, they are long tunnels that circle right around the worlds. The cores and the PMR are also spread out in such a fashion. C2 planets have geometrically simple WGFs, where the locations of gravity are held in the centre-most part of the mass of the ring, as what would otherwise naturally occur for such toroidal worlds. The PMRs *are* responsible for the shape of the planets, but even without the PMRs fashioning such shapes, ring worlds can technically exist in their own right. For a hypothetical doughnut world without gravitational distortions, the only way it (the world) could prevent degenerating into a sphere would be via centrifugal force; specifically, it would have to rapidly rotate. Interestingly, the tangible C2 planets (of both types) in the Caelverse actually *do* rapidly rotate, where they experience rapid day-and-night cycles. It is almost as if the planets are naturally 'equipped' to prevent such degeneration, anyway – should they ever not have such gravitational distortions via a WGF.

Around half of C2 planets have axial tilts, while the other ones rotate strictly on their horizontal plane or on their side. Coupled with the shape and rotation types of the planets, this results in some areas being naturally much colder or warmer. For doughnut worlds, even the topography has greater extremities, where large mountainous regions have formed near the inner section far greater than that found on C1 worlds. Then there are regions that never truly see night due to light reflecting and refracting off the inner planetary walls. These factors add more problems to the weather, and so, it is not just the high rotational speeds per se that create harsher and more unusual weather in comparison to C1 planets.

Not only does centrifugal force add the effect of gravity – where stronger 'gravity' is felt along the inner equator on doughnut worlds that spin on their horizontal plane, for example – but it actually also establishes habitable 'gravity' for thinner ring worlds.

This is because the mass for thinner worlds is more greatly distributed due to the wider gap. Basically, since gravitational force is inversely proportional to the square of the distance, the greater the distance between masses, the less force one side of the ring will exert on the other side. Thinner ring worlds, however, have greater tensile strength than doughnut worlds; and interestingly, were it not for the WGF and rapid rotation, they would likely still survive without degenerating into a sphere. While both types of ring worlds are different, they still have roughly the same *average* (mean) surface gravity in *certain* locations; so, for thinner ring worlds on the inside of the ring, the surface gravity is about 9.81 m/s².

Life on T2-C2 worlds is not only harsher in the above respects, but such planets also feature more ferocious lifeforms in addition to atmospheres that are not exactly optimal for humans and most sapient beings who have naturally developed on T2-C1 worlds. Still, while roughly 80% of sapient beings in the Caelverse live on T2-C1 planets, about 8% of sapient beings continue to live on T2-C2 planets, with most of these having originated and, thus, adapted to such worlds in the first place. Even for the beings that call T2-C2 planets their home world, this does not mean that they are adapted to living in all of the planet's areas. While mages are adapted to living on T2-C1 worlds, they have nonetheless set up many cities and bases across T2-C2 worlds, which is one of the main driving forces for immigration to these worlds.

Harsh habitability issues also apply to C3 planets, which are worlds that are geometrically 'pinched' in assorted directions. The WGF for C3 planets is mostly spherical in shape and density, except that *gravitational braces* pinch mass away from the sphere to cause the planets to resemble shapes like cubes, pyramids, hexagonal prisms, octahedrons, dodecahedrons, and more (but not cones or cylinders). The gravitational braces are found at the vertices of each shape; and when the braces pull the mass of the planet, they pull the mass to only such a degree that no mass actually touches the braces. The stronger the pull, the bigger the planet becomes (though, it will have less density). Instead of having proper straight edges and flat faces, said places curve inwards towards the centre of the planet. Essentially, the planets are not actually cubes, for example, but, instead, *concave cuboids*.

For most C3 worlds, the *felt* or *net* gravity near the edges is rather light, and at the vertices, it is basically zero gravity. The further one moves towards the centre of a face, the higher the gravity becomes – where, in the case of a perfect concave cuboid right in the centre of a face, the surface gravitational pull is roughly equal to that of the surface of C1 planets. Substances like water will typically flow to the centre of a face, where most of the planet's atmosphere will be located, too. So, for said planets, there is basically just one giant ocean in the middle. This is followed by a ring of vegetation, and then the climates become increasingly arid the further away from the centre; it also becomes increasingly harder to breathe any oxygen (especially amongst the incredibly high mountains around the edges and corners). All C3 planets have different rotational speeds and axes. So, in the case of cube-shaped planets, if a face does not ever turn to face the sun, then they remain completely frozen.

There are some C3 worlds where the gravity is rather high in the centre of the faces; and land-faring (that is, land travelling) entities that originated on these worlds have been able to physically adapt to moving between different the gravitational extremes – but aliens to such C3 worlds find life difficult. Nevertheless, different habitable zones force for an odd structure of society and economic production, where entire industries are accordingly separated geographically across great distances from other industries. This has resulted in sapient interspecies cooperation, where aquatic species work only in the ocean, regular beings work only in the ring of vegetation, and arid-suitable species work only on the outer edges; each species then trades with the other. Like with T2-C2 worlds, mages have managed to develop a lot of infrastructure on T2-C3 worlds, though nowhere near as much as that on T2-C1 worlds.

None of the above issues, however, compare to some of the extremities found on C4 planets, which can appear in any kind of shape. Usually, though, these shapes are of bizarre, asymmetrical forms. There are also other topographical formations that essentially add to the overall shape, and these include examples like: hand-like super-mountains; continental-sized chunks of land that float in the air; chasms that extend to the mantle; and calderas and 'craters' the size of continents (with some walls stretching up to the inner radiation belt). In a few places, curled landmasses allow people to basically walk upside down, and this phenomenon can even apply to the aforementioned examples; so, super-mountains, for example, may seem easy to 'climb', being horizontal to the climber; or, the climber could *effectively* be subject to the planet's standard gravitational levels (based on the real gravity) when climbing. Some C4 worlds also have slowly morphing gravitational distortions, so these geographical features do not necessarily last, and new formations occur over time.

While some C1 worlds have no axial tilt – and so, various bands of life form horizontally across their surfaces, where the equators, consequently, are harsher than the hottest deserts found on other C1 worlds – C4 planets typically either have shifting tilts, or they crazily spin around in seemingly arbitrary ways. There is even a decent percentage of C4 worlds that do not rotate, leading to scorching wastelands on one side, with eternal freezing nights on the other (including on T1 worlds with atmospheres). Life *does* exist on worlds for this latter example, but it generally forms in the thin band between these extremes. Besides planetary-scale phenomena, C4 planets also feature other extremes, such as mobile carnivorous flora and colossal-sized blood-drinking arthropoids. Dragons are believed to have originated on C4 worlds – or at least particular types of dragons. While some of the flora and fauna on C4 worlds cannot survive or thrive on C1 worlds, others can. There are, nonetheless, strong government regulations and security in place to prevent the importation, smuggling, or any other passage of such entities from occurring. Some outbreaks do occur, though they are quickly contained and resolved.

From massive and frequent ball lightning, to supersonic cyclones, to 'unholy' earthquakes, to random wormholes opening anywhere, and even to raindrops (and hail) the size of beach balls, C4 planets are off-putting for general *civilization* beyond rudimentary colonies, outposts, and corporate enterprises. These dangerous planets do, however, provide significant opportunities to mine resources if one is brave or imprudent enough to embark on such undertakings without the backing power of mega corporations. Numerous black markets and other illegal activities, nevertheless, occur on C4 worlds as well. Very few sapient beings originated on C4 worlds, so most beings are not adapted to them. Moreover, even for those that consider a T2-C4 planet their home world, this *certainly* does not mean that they are adapted to living on all places on their planet, nor other C4 planets across the Caelverse.

The following PSC, C5 worlds, have *some* greater extremities, but overall are safer than C4 planets. Still, they are not easily colonizable for a variety of reasons. C5 worlds are considered the 'mimic' or 'microcosm' class due to the fact that some of their mass mimics their solar system's mass in *form*. So, the central form of a C5 world is akin to the sun – but only in form (shape), not its actual mass or properties. Orbiting the 'sun' are also the solar system's planets and other celestial bodies. Each body is able to stay in their 'orbit' within the whole C5 planetary area (without colliding into one another) due to the distinct gravitational distortions within the WGF. Amazingly, C5 worlds also mimic themselves, but this mimicry is only up to one level; so, after the first level of mimicry, only spheres are in place of what would be C5 worlds.

Individually, these mimic masses are small – and they are not to scale with the other bodies in both distance and size – but they also collectively do not form enough mass two equal other PSCs. So, besides a massive cloud of gas that also surrounds these mimic masses, the rest (and majority) of the C5 mass is actually found in geometric 'frame' around the mimic masses. Normally, this frame takes the shape of a cube, but it is not limited to this shape. The frame only has the (generally thick) edges and vertices of the shape, not its faces. Therefore, one can look through a telescope on another PSC (like C1 planets) and see the mimic bodies through the faceless frame – even through the massive cloud of gas, which is not as thick as gas clouds in the *gas moons* (explained in *Section 2.3*). There is a difference between C5 WGFs and the ones for C3 planets; that is, the gravitational distortions are found as full lines across the beams of the frame, and they do not act as pinches like that of C3 planet gravitational braces. The frames are normally bigger than worlds of other PSCs, and the frames are also denser and more tensile.

The gravity varies based on where one is located on the frames, so there are both habitable and uninhabitable gravitational areas. The mimic bodies vary, too, so some bodies have lighter-than-normal gravity, while others have heavier gravity. While lighter gravity may seem beneficial for performing certain functions (such as for research or economic purposes), C1 lifeforms cannot survive on said C5 masses without their bodies weakening over time. Besides this, there are other negative economic problems trying to work in low gravity, such as operating with liquids – especially in cases where precision is necessary. For example, mining equipment that use drilling fluids require gravity to work effectively. Then there are farming issues, where the drainage from gravity is necessary. A lot of equipment also needs to be tailored for the environments, so they cannot *simply* be imported from other worlds (that are used for specific purposes). On top of this problem, artificial gravity generators are *far* too expensive to run, and rotating centrifuge stations, on the other hand, are also not that cost effective, and they have other limitations, too.

Most C5 frames (and the mimic bodies) rotate very slowly, with a day generally lasting about four Standard Days. Accordingly, climates are not optimal for most beings, so of the beings that do live on C5 worlds, they normally live underground. The majority of sapient lifeforms on C5 planets are also non-human, with many being lithoids, arthropoids, and fungoids. Mages, nevertheless, still control the governments on such planets, but in most cases, non-mage activities *effectively* go unregulated for the most part, unless they are big and draw the attention of mages. There are also some tourist attractions that attract various types of world-off beings.

The final PSC, C6 planets, is the most extreme of all – in terms of habitability. Devoid of practically any native sentient life (including simple flora), C6 planets are wastelands, where they lack water and proper atmospheres. They also experience extreme exposure to cosmic radiation and electrical winds, and it does not help that they also feature the *great storms* in the centre of their forms. That is, C6 planets are formed as a double cone(-like) structure, where at the apexes, a gigantic and powerful electoral storm constantly persists. The base of each cone is roughly flat, and given their distances from the great storms, these locations are much easier to build on. Most settlements are mage government military outposts and (highly-regulated) civilian colonies, followed then by various private research stations and corporate operations. Like with other harsh worlds, some illegal activity exists on these planets as well.

The great storms exist due to the planet's core being split between the two cones, which causes assorted aggravation. This also makes C6 planets appear like they are totally ripped asunder in the middle, when, more accurately, the split is just due to the WGF's gravitational shaping. The gravitational pull varies per location, but the bases of each cone (the poles) have roughly the same level of C1 surface gravity. The great storms also whip up large rocks high into the atmosphere, which then later descend in a similar vein to meteors striking celestial bodies. Massive fractures also exist across the surfaces of C6 planets, so traversing them is not easy. C6 planets also feature rings made of small rocks (individually no more than a couple of metres in diameter) and dust; and many of these, moreover, have naturally-formed geometric shapes (such as cubes or pyramids). These rocks and dust also concentrate to form geometric patterns, so there may be observable spirals or zigzags in the rings, for example, of more concentrated matter. C6 planets also typically rotate rapidly.

All planets (of every POT and PSC) possess intense radiation belts that make travelling outside a planet incredibly dangerous and expensive. Thus, very few space-ships exist. All space travel occurs within the confines of a solar system, too, as travelling to different solar systems and solar clusters would take exceedingly too long – more than many lifetimes for the average being. Regardless, living too far outside of a planet has repeatedly been shown to alter one's consciousness and physical state, so permanent or long-term space living, for now, is not ideal. Accordingly, the only way to travel to other planets in another solar system or solar cluster is via teleportation (that is, magic or potentially advanced technology in the probable future beyond already-established local-based *proxportals*) or the *planetary transportal system* (PTS), which consists of the naturally-formed planetary portals found on the nodes of the crisscrossing *ley lines* of each planet, which are potent potential fields in the form of lines that geometrically form across a planet's surface as a result of a PMR's frequencies. Moreover, the suppression of a planet's gravity via WGFs also add to their intensity. The ley lines do not actually *fully* crisscross, and, instead, they form observable energy nodes that circulate and then help to produce a single giant ring each, which people may walk through to reach other transportals.

The majority of transportals are *general transportals*, which lead to adjacent ley line nodes on the same planet. Since multiple ley lines intersect with one another, general transportals lead to multiple different transportals depending on the position a person walks through the transportal ring. So, if a person walks through the north part of a ring, then they will access the other transportal north of their location. Both parts of the ring, in this case, will be of the same size and shape as one another – which is a characteristic that all *window* portals possess. Accordingly, not all parts of a trans-portal ring will have *active* portals, but even the inactive parts of a transportal ring will still be visible. Most planets have between 700 and 750 general transportals, and some of these will be closer to one another than others (in their geometric formations).

There are then three types of *interplanetary transportals*; all three types, nevertheless, only lead to transportals of the same POT (so, T2 transportals can only lead to other T2 transportals). Therefore, as stated before, the only way to travel to other POTs is via magical teleportation or space travel. To access other PSCs within a solar system, one must travel to the north and south poles (or equivalents) of a planet.

So, the *interclass transportals* found at C1 north poles lead to C2 worlds (at their north pole equivalents) in their respective solar systems – and vice versa. C2 south pole interclass transportals lead to C3 worlds (at their south poles) and vice versa, while C3 north poles lead to C4 worlds (at their north poles). This repeats to C5 and then to C6 worlds before C6 worlds lead back to the south poles of C1 worlds.

To travel to other solar systems within the same solar cluster, a person must find one of generally two to four *inter-solar transportals* located in various positions on a planet. Normally, these are found near the equators on C1 worlds and the equivalents on other PSCs; and each inter-solar transportal will generally lead to an inter-solar transportal in an adjacent solar system. *Inter-cluster transportals*, on the other hand, are the rarest type. Only one solar system (the central one) in a solar cluster will possess inter-cluster transportals. However, all planets in the solar system will feature two sets of these transportals, each leading to adjacent solar clusters with their respective PSC; the only exception to this is the very first and last solar clusters in the Caelverse (SC1 and SC128), which are each next to the GBW; and so, only one inter-cluster transportal from their respective adjacent solar clusters will lead to these fringe solar clusters. In other words, SC1 transportals do not lead to SC128 transportals and vice versa. Unlike the other interplanetary transportals, inter-cluster transportals differ completely in location on a planet for each solar cluster.

All inter-cluster transportals spin, so they are harder to enter and exit safely and effectively. There are also unusual and sometimes dangerous weather, atmospheric, and dimensional conditions around such transportals. The mage conquest of the Caelverse was no easy feat due to this limitation (both during the time of the ancient mage empire and the modern-day CGM – respectively explained in *Section 4.1* and *Section 4.2*); and, as such, it was not always the case that whole mage armies moved through the inter-planetary transportals. For the most part, mage settlers were sent out first and then colonies were established, which then enabled armies to grow without the home solar clusters having to send out military personnel and resources.

The transportals possess a special mass (*transportal mass* – TPM) that *causes* the fabric of spacetime to form portals, so it is actually TPM which *surrounds* the window (space) of the transportal, where the space itself is entangled. These special particles, nevertheless, gain their power via the potential of the ley lines. In other words, the transportals are formed via real particles that are powered by potentials causing special wave function changes. From what we can gather, the TPM of one area was already entangled with the TPM of other areas and planets (likely during the formation of the Caelverse), and it is the ley lines that helped keep their coherence. Still, this part is not quite understood, and the coherence (and positioning of the TPM) could also have been the result of PMRs. The TPM would have originally entangled the space in the portal frame area and then, through a special form of *entanglement swapping* (which is like quantum teleportation except that states are swapped), the space itself at different locations would have entangled. The TPM would have exerted a force on the space (as they do now) to switch the mere entanglement to creating an actual portal; and, when a portal opened, locality would have allowed the TPM that lost their initial entanglement with each other in the swap to gain it back.

It is also not a simple matter of removing or destroying such TPM; and, in the *rare* cases where even an extremely-minimal amount of TPM is lost, PMRs send energy to the transportals via QET. Coupled with the potential in the ley lines, this allows for cold fusion, and the particle or particles are replaced. The ley lines not only help to stabilize the TPM and give them the power (ability) to form the transportals, they also help power (fuel) the TPM so that the transportals can permanently stay open. The ley lines only power a certain amount of mass, so it is not the case that any mass in the vicinity will gain the power to form transportals.

Interestingly, it is from being able to go to other planets via the transportals that mages are able to use their teleportation magic to teleport to other planets. This is because there first needs to be entanglement between two places, which cannot be done at a nonlocal distance. With technologies and/or established portal sites, mages can use their magic to form special particles that only form on one side of the entangled space to teleport; but, coupled with QET (where, technically, quantum particles can send energy through CSUs, despite the latter not being on the same quantum level as quantum particles), this is enough to cause the correlated states in the other space to form a portal. More information on this can be found at the end of *Section 3.6.6.3.*

## 2.3: The Moons and Lunapexes:

Every planet (of all POTs and PSCs) possesses one *crystal moon* (or *prime moon* or *transchite moon*), which is naturally made almost purely of an aggregate crystal called *transchite.* The transchite is also found to be in a few *ultra-states* of matter (for information on ultra-states, see *Section 3.6*). Most of this transchite is in an ultra-solid state, but it exists in some other states, too. Note that while the transchite is in an ultra-state, it is not the same type of material found in the ultra-states from the school of magic called *phasarchement* (as phasarchement does not produce transchite – again, for more information, see *Section 3.6*). Nevertheless, when the transchite is no longer within a certain range of the moon's field, it loses its ultra-state phase and cannot be re-established unless brought back to the crystal moon.

Crystal moons would also be translucent if it were not for their immensely-thick bodies, having universally-standard diameters of 12,742 km when measured at *base form.* Most crystal moons tend to have homogenous, bright colours, but a few beautifully flaunt the rainbow, depending on the levels of different types of crystal found within the aggregate. They also feature different kinds of patterns across their surfaces, including geometric, fractal, and standard crystalline structures. Crystal moons also orbit at an average distance of about 407,744 km from their planets; and their *perigees* and *apogees* (that is, their closest and farthest points in their orbit, respectively) range just about 25,484 km in difference from the said average distance each. Crystal moons do not have gravitational distortions, and their mass is $1/64^{th}$ of that of their planets; but when planetary WGFs are considered, then the crystal moons are effectively one quarter of the mass of their planets. The surface gravity, therefore, is the same as C1 planets.

All planets in the Caelverse each also possess another twelve moons known as the *elemental moons* (or *archetypal moons* or *shapeshifting moons*), divided up into the *archetypal elements* of 'fire', 'water', 'air', and 'earth' (see *Section 3.1* for details on *arch-elements*). Elemental moons vary in size (though, generally, they are around 12,742 km in diameter), and their mass varies. However, each elemental moon has a WGF, and they always respectively reduce their gravity down to a quarter of that of the crystal moon, despite whatever mass the elemental moons would otherwise possess. The gravitational distortions for elemental moons typically are not extreme in form, but some moons can seem quite bizarre in shape. Elemental moons also have a *circular orbit* of 611,616 km from their planets. This means that all the elemental moons have a fixed distance without a *periapsis* or *apoapsis* (that is, they orbit in a perfect circle without a closest or farthest point formed). They also orbit their planets approximately every 32.7273 Standard Days.

Both crystal and elemental moons have *prograde* motion in respect to their planets – namely, C1 worlds; so, when viewed from a bird's-eye view from the north pole of a C1 world, the moons *orbit* in the same direction of the planet's *rotation* – each counterclockwise. For clarification, this is a moon's movement *around* the planet and not itself the moon's rotation (its spin) on its own axis. For other PSCs, both moon types will orbit counterclockwise, regardless of whatever planetary rotation – or lack thereof – occurs. This means that all moons in the Caelverse perfectly synchronize with one another with any alignment relative to their planet. Typically, both crystal and elemental moons will also *rotate* prograde as well, but this is not always the case, so some moons can rotate in *retrograde* (that is, spin in the opposite direction).

Elemental moons consist primarily of one state of matter (not including the cores and parts of the mantles), so air moons are mostly made of gases, water moons, liquids, earth moons, solids, and for fire moons, a heated state based on properties of the first three that induces various states *and* processes like plasma and literal fire, respectively. Of the fire produced, most is charged with plasma, anyway. A water moon, for example, does not have to consist of $H_2O$ (that is, a molecule with two hydrogen atoms and one oxygen atom), and it can, instead, be any standard liquid while also minimally possessing properties in other phases/states such as solid and gas. For example, ice (a solid) can form in clouds, which are a mixture of liquid and gas. Nevertheless, in order to turn a heavy metal into a liquid, for example, higher temperatures are needed, and so most water moons are mainly filled with $H_2O$.

An earth moon's surface may entirely be a desert of sand, and its crust may comprise of lots of metallic, solidified substances like iron, gold, or mercury. In addition, a fair few earth moons possess orbiting rings of dust and rock. Gas moons may have gaseous auras and/or large jets and streams of gas shooting out. Liquid, nonetheless, tends to form around the cores of gas moons as a result of their overall density. Fire moons range greatly, too, with some *appearing* as if mini suns, while others can be completely covered in molten, plasma-charged rock. Their brightness in the sky, though, is not too bad for most inhabitants on a planet. Each elemental moon also has a *Lunar Mass Regulator* (LMR) at its core, which acts basically the same way as a PMR.

All planets experience *lunapexes*, which occur every thirty Standard Days in relation to one crystal moon's orbit around a planet. Essentially, lunapexes are a time of significant observable and mysterious energetic changes, affecting the planets in a myriad of ways, both physically and etherically. With 360 Standard Days in a year, there are also twelve months per year; and although originally there was a six-day week, for economic reasons in the past, this changed to a socially-constructed seven-day week; the consequent 28-day, four-week month thus features an additional two days for the lunapexes at the beginning, with each planet in the Caelverse (of all POTs and PSCs) experiencing the event simultaneously – despite whatever day length a planet experiences. Although throughout the year many celebrations are held, generally public holidays (for mages) are reserved only for the lunapexes, making twenty-four days in total. A month starts on the days and dates known as *L1* and *L2* (short for Lunapex One and Lunapex Two) before normal days begin, with Moonday starting on the 3rd, followed by Earthday, Waterday, Airday, Fireday, Starday, and Sunday before repeating to Moonday. The last day of the month is accordingly Sunday the 30th. For clarification, L1 and L2 will never be a standard day such as Moonday or Airday.

The lunapex process begins when the crystal moon first phases into the *lunar eclipse* (where a planet is directly positioned between the crystal moon and sun). Despite many crystal moons having *ascending* and *descending nodes*, this does not affect lunapex timings and alignments. That is, the crystal moons will move *above* and *below* the *ecliptic plane* but will always align on the ecliptic plane during the lunapex. Technically, the true moment of the eclipse is momentary, but the lunapex *effects* last two-and-a-half days, which is precisely the length of when the crystal moon passes (aligns) through (and with) one type of *zodiac sign* (which is a particular archetypal energy in the context of *astrology* – more explained in *Section 2.5*). The calendar only acknowledges two days, however; but this, again, is a cultural issue, not one of astronomical alignment. Precisely, a lunapex itself – and all of its effects – occur only at and provisionally post eclipse; and so, even when a crystal moon is very close to the eclipse, there are still no lunapex effects prior to it fully eclipsing. In other words, the lunapex is a distinct birthing event and not one of *mere* proximity itself; it is just that the location that a crystal moon possesses during this period happens to be an important factor.

Since planets have different time zones on their surfaces, a designated *Lunapex Mean Time* (LMT) has been established, so people may experience the initial effects of a lunapex during the day when the official event takes place at 00:00 LMT (midnight). Due to their extraordinary nature, crystal moons 'give birth' to new physical and etheric energy during the lunapexes, where their energetic stores erupt, causing a burst of power itself that creates massive amounts of radioactivity. Now brighter than before, a crystal moon truly becomes a *full moon*, with the brightness lasting for the entirety of the lunapex. If the crystal moons were, hypothetically, simple grey rocks, then during eclipses, they would potentially appear as a dark red due to sunlight refracting off their planet's atmosphere.

For moons that orbit certain gravitationally-warped worlds, the sun may shine right through these planets, but the lunapex will still occur in the same way for these moons and planets as well. Crystal moons may also discharge or rearrange orbiting matter to create or reform rings and other geometric formations around their bodies, and these typically last for a whole month, finally changing when the new lunapex begins. This phenomenon occurs through both tangible forces and potential fields. Sometimes the rings and geometric formations themselves will be formed from tiny geometric crystals, and these may also 'point' toward the elemental moon that aligned with it in an eclipse during the lunapex.

When an elemental moon aligns behind a crystal moon during a lunapex, the crystal moon will also channel physical and etheric energy toward the moon in question, *transfiguring* it (that is, crystal moons cause the elemental moons to shapeshift). The elemental moon may have been an air moon before the lunapex, but the crystal moon may transfigure it into a fire moon, for instance. The process is basically the same as how mages transfigure and shapeshift matter with alchemical magic – just without the spell crafting and magical activation. Crystal moons will contain a new etheric code for a new elemental moon, which it ties to the aligning elemental moon at the beginning of a lunapex. A crystal moon is able to derive these new etheric codes due not just to its powerful nature but also to its relationship with the elemental moons; essentially, the crystal moon will tap into a specific set of potential states that the elemental moons possess via the etheric, with one of these states being selected via differing probabilities and other influences (like, astrological). From this, the shapeshifting will result in the elemental moon changing its very structure, drawing from said etheric states. For more information on shapeshifting, see *Section 3.4*.

In this sense, the fire-moon-to-be exists in a noncorporeal state – a realm of potential before shifting to the tangible. The crystal moon also directs the elemental moon to the potential (in this case, the specific incorporeal fire moon) that is able to connect via the elemental moon's etheric energy. The process also requires vast amounts of physical energy (importantly working through and with the etheric), which the crystal moon absorbs from the sun over the course of the month. Note that the crystal moon is only paying for the *transformation* and not for the new mass; that is, the required energy is not creating or changing matter and, instead, is only shifting to a new state. Again, a better understanding of this phenomenon can be gained after reading *Section 3.4*. Prior to the lunapex, it is possible to see faint holograms of various probable types of moons ready for manifestation inside crystal moon shards. In other words, the more probable a fire moon of existing, the more chance of it faintly showing up compared to other probable types.

Elemental moons (and other astronomical bodies) are themselves HRFs, so this means that if a spaceship were to land on the moon, it would not shapeshift as well, as it would be a different HRF to the HRF of the elemental moon. However, it would certainly be dangerous to try and land on one of these moons when it is about to shapeshift or while it is shapeshifting. Various robotic rovers have already proven how dangerous such an endeavour can be, where the elemental moons do not push matter out of the way in the same manner as magic alchemical trans-formations. If, however, matter is added to the moon and it happens to have been there for a decent amount of time – and if it also integrates well with the moon – then the said matter may become part of the HRF of the moon; so, when the next transfiguration occurs, the said matter could transform with the rest of the moon. On the other hand, if a piece of the moon were to be taken away from it (like a small crystal rock), the piece would no longer be part of the HRF of the moon (with enough of an HRT) to be affected and, thus, transfigured. Howbeit, many types of materials degrade quickly when they are taken from the moons.

Each individual planet will also have a set of elemental moon types that are more likely to emerge than others. So, if an earth moon forms, it may have similar features to the previous earth moon manifested for that particular elemental moon. For example, both earth moons might have red deserts across their surfaces, but the new earth moon might also have a few grand canyons in various places. Fire and air moons are more masculine than their feminine water and earth moon counterparts, but there does not have to be a balance of this force simultaneously, so a planet may still have twelve water moons at the same time. Since all shapeshifting is provisional, the reason why elemental moons do not revert back is that they have enough energy to sustain the changes until another lunapex alignment is made, where another shapeshift occurs. Nevertheless, a shapeshift will always occur with a new alignment.

Each moon also affects its planet's atmosphere in its own ways as well, both physically and etherically; the latter, in this case, leads to different probability outcomes at the quantum level, in turn reinforcing the physical alterations affecting climates and the seasons. This phenomenon is both astrological and not astrological. If, in the rare case that, for example, there were twelve fire moons during a winter after shapeshifting, this would generally lead to summer(-like) climates due both to the physical effects of the moons and the increased probabilities of subtle quantum changes occurring. However, the effects do not simply stack with no diminishing returns. So, if there were twelve fire moons during a summer, this would not mean the temperature would be double than normal – though, it certainly would be hotter. In some cases on C4 planets, though, temperatures may actually double. In contrast, C6 planets, lacking proper atmospheres, are usually scarcely affected, as such.

There are other non-corporeal moons, such as the legendary 'black moon', which is meant to be the prime vehicle that *stores* the collective unconscious's *shadow energy* of all that exists in the Caelverse. It contains a multitude of collectives from different beings, and it is different to the collective unconscious fields found in the astral. Specifically, it is more *concentrated* than the collective unconscious in the astral, even though the black moon fundamentally exists in the astral (and potentially another physical timeline in – and/or reality beyond – the Caelverse). Moreover, it also filters out certain aspects of the collective unconscious while drawing in the *shadow-self* aspects and archetypes rather than collecting (all) mere archetypes themselves that exist in the collective unconscious. Accordingly, it has the propensity to hold more darker energies than the collective unconscious itself, although not all energies in the black moon are evil or dark. It is also more than the sum of its parts; so, the black moon is not just a receptacle for shadow selves but also itself a shadowy entity with its own energy. In addition, the energies within the black moon are also mixed together, but certain types of energies within the black moon can be individually felt as well.

Other vehicles exist for storing the collective unconscious (and specifically, shadow-self energies), but the black moon itself is the perfect archetype for this phenomenon. For this reason, it is the most 'popular' of its kind, and, thus, it has become stronger, in turn leading to positive reinforcement, which continues to enable it to be the prime vehicle. One of the main theories behind why such a collective shadow entity exists as a 'moon' is due to the feminine nature of both; that is, moons themselves are feminine (at least in the Caelverse), just as shadows and shadow selves themselves (not necessarily *particular* shadow selves) are archetypally feminine, which contrasts the masculine nature of *overt* reality. Furthermore, moons themselves are one of the biggest masses in existence (in the Caelverse), so they trump most matter found on a planet. Various groups of people tune into these archetypal moons for different reasons – some good, some bad – and there are, indeed, empirical results of change occurring from their *practices*. Usually, black moon practices occur during lunapexes and certain astrological alignments, but they can still occur at any point in time.

Regardless of what one's opinions are on the black moon, there actually happen to be some black moons in existence due to the colour of the rocks that constitute them. However, these are not *the* said archetypal shadow black moon, nor are they associated with it. Some people argue that the black moon manifests at particular, rare times in the Caelverse, while many suppose that it cannot actually manifest physically, and, instead, it only exists as a pure archetypal force – one that can at least be tapped into spiritually. Even though the black moon can be tapped into spiritually, this does not mean a black moon practitioner can fully channel the black moon both in its entirety *and* purely – considering that channelling of the astral itself is limited.

There have been no recorded incidences of this black moon physically manifesting, but there have been unusual times in history when it *may* have manifested, such as during the *Great Blackout* in the year A-7960 (for more information, see *Section 4.1.6*). Efforts were made to try and see if the black moon existed during the Great Blackout, but this proved futile. The mage home world called *Juntas* was completely covered with dark clouds at this time, and when airships were launched to allow travellers to see above the clouds, it turned out that there was still a thick atmosphere between the planet and moons, with the latter also possessing thick dark clouds. Attempts at teleportation to the crystal moon were made to see if it had turned into the black moon, but nobody could accomplish the feat. Even the people on other planets using telescopes could not see Juntas's moons. Knowledge of the black moon existed before the Great Blackout, but certain practices around it increased after this event.

# 2.4: Additional Celestial Bodies:

The Caelverse has many other celestial bodies and oddities. For example, beyond the planets in a slower orbit are the *plasmanaries*, which also contribute both direct physical and etheric (including astrological) effects upon other celestial bodies. These luminaries are gigantic spherical orbs, all about 140,162 km in diameter. They consist entirely of a special plasmatic energy that generates and constantly churns moving patterns and colours that have the appearance of, but are not limited to: lava lamp gloops; hundreds and thousands; spinning discs; fibre optic lights; crazy balls; looping strings; paint being mixed or even splashed in water; spirals; electricity; glitter; clouds (normal and stormy); froths; bubbles; oils; inks; spiky magnetic fluid; flames; flowering energy; fractals; waves; raindrops; reflectors; and more.

While plasmanaries *do* orbit the sun in a normal manner, they also activate pockets of entangled fields of space, where wormholes allow the plasmanaries to pop in and out of their current space and reappear at any position in their orbit. More explicitly, the entangled fields already exist (as a separate but linked phenomenon to the plasmanaries), and the wormholes activate and deactivate (and shift location), deriving the energy to do so from the sun. The entangled fields only need enough energy to allow for the *size* of the plasmanaries to teleport, not the *mass*. Technically, the entangled fields shrink due to the gravitational pull of the plasmanaries, but they happen to still have the right size after shrinking to allow the plasmanaries through. The orbital paths of each plasmanary also have thin filaments which absorb the sun's energy (as do the plasmanaries), helping to power the process.

All solar systems have nine rings or belts with multiple entangled and moving pockets. To the naked eye, all nine plasmanaries appear as large stars, whereas the wormholes are not visible at all, as it is the mass in the plasmanaries that causes the entangled fields to open up rather than the mass being around the entangled fields; however, with telescopes, one can see *through* the wormholes while they are active. A plasmanary's change in location may *seem* random, but in many cases, plasmanaries collectively emerge in a patterned formation, normally during the lunapexes. Predictions can be made as to when and where they will appear. Plasmanaries also make alignments with other astronomical bodies, establishing stronger positions such as *mega* or *super lunapexes*, and these facilitate the lunapexes astrologically. Eventually, the *Supreme Lunapex* may form, with all the plasmanaries aligned with each other, accompanied by three planets of all three POTs, as well as three of their respective moons *during* a lunapex. Note that in this case, there would be three moons, as one elemental moon would be between the sun and the planet. Even when not in lunapex formation, plasmanaries themselves still have (astrological) effects upon other celestial bodies.

Varying greatly in nature as well are the *comets* and *asteroids*, with each solar system possessing comets and asteroids of completely different sizes, numbers, orbits, types, and more. Both, of course, exist outside of the solar systems as well. There are two main kinds of comets: *normal comets* and *frame comets*. Normal comets are large chunks of rock, dust, ice, and gas; and when they pass near the sun, they release gases and other particles, forming a surrounding atmosphere called a *coma* and then a *tail*. Frame comets, on the other hand, possess harder materials that form windowed shells or bubbles around gases that barely escape. The 'windows' are transparent glass, and the ionized gases within them glow strongly; these comets, accordingly, lack *visible* tails (but they still possess tails).

Frame comets can also feature arch-elements, so some frame comets contain 'fire', 'water', 'earth', as well as the abovesaid type, which falls under 'air'. Water comets, specifically, are able to keep their liquid nature – even far from the sun – due to the type of properties constituting the liquid (so, they are not normally made of just water). Fire comets need extra energy from the sun in order for fire to burn or plasma to exist, so these comets exist in their form when closer to the sun. Both normal and frame comets can also form into *clustered comets*; that is, they can join together in proximity, and typically, these formations will be geometric. Nevertheless, clustered comets can easily break apart. In either case, comets have *minor* astrological influence. Asteroids, on the other hand, are basically minor (but non-true) planets that lack the tails of comets. However, these, too, can come in normal, frame, and clustered varieties.

There are several mysteries in the Caelverse as well, most of which are outside of the solar systems. One of these mysteries includes the *leviathan clouds*. Formed mostly out of cosmic dust, leviathan clouds happen to resemble monstrous entities of gigantic proportions; that is, these leviathan-looking clouds average about three times the size of a sun, and each take a different form, so some are more dragon-like, while others have jellyfish type structures. Some theories suggest that the leviathan clouds are energetic prints left over from actual leviathans that once roamed the Caelverse. Other theories claim that they are archetypal entities *available* for the Caelverse via the etheric, while other theories propose that actual leviathans exist in other parts of the multiverse and that their energies are so powerful that they naturally or even intentionally project into the Caelverse. Another theory adds to the last saying that those leviathans eventually (and quite literally) emerge into the Caelverse when the GBW has destroyed most of the solar clusters.

Psychics have attempted reading their etheric fields, but the leviathan clouds have etheric distortions, so nothing is certain about them. A fair few psychics believe that collective social biases have projected various thoughtforms onto the leviathan clouds, so this is one of the reasons for their distortions. Due to these potential collective biases, some theories hold that the collective unconscious has shaped the clouds to resemble leviathan archetypes; and then, other theories state that while this collective unconscious shaping is true, this *enables* real leviathans to eventually enter the Caelverse at some point in a cycle. Naturally, of course, there are more mundane theories that say they are merely cosmic dust with coincidental forms. In total, there are sixty-four observable leviathan clouds in the Caelverse, and each is situated evenly between the solar clusters. So far, astrologers and astronomers have not proven that the leviathan clouds exert astrological influence, despite what some astrologers claim.

As mysterious as leviathan clouds may be, strange *asteroid fields* of varying sizes situate between the solar clusters, each mostly filled with what are likely standard minerals. Many parts of the asteroid fields also form into figure-eight patterns. *Torn dead planets* (TDPs) also exist amongst the asteroid fields; these are what look to be planets, but they are too shattered to be considered actual 'planets', and the etheric data gathered from them show absolutely no life. It is unclear whether these asteroid fields and/or the TDPs are from a previous Caelverse cycle (that is, leftovers from the GBW's destruction) or were going to be part of solar clusters but never properly formed; potentially, they could have almost been solar clusters. Still, there are no signs of dead suns or stars amongst them. While some astrologers believe that the asteroid fields play at least some role in everyone's lives astrologically, most do not believe they have much or any significance at all.

Other anomalies have been spotted throughout the Caelverse, but they are so small that they could just be loose debris from the other celestial bodies. Most of these are attributed to matter from the asteroid fields; but naturally, there is always conflicting speculation. Still, some of this matter is ring-shaped, but since geometric shapes are part of the fabric of the Caelverse, this is not necessarily anything interesting. Some unsupported theories, nonetheless, suggest that these rings are broken gateways. Odd electrical 'elastic bands' also float in deep space, but there is little understanding of what these structures exactly are and what they are capable of doing. Except, however, they do sometimes produce frequencies akin to music. Then there are also a number of distorted black shrouds – besides the massive shroud in the centre of the Caelverse – called the *black mystery shrouds* (BMSs) of varying sizes throughout the Caelverse, and uncovering what lies hidden behind/inside them still remains completely a mystery…

## 2.5: Mechanisms and Attributes of Astrology:

Astrology is the study of a complex set of related phenomena that affects the events, properties, and consciousness of beings in the Caelverse. All such phenomena, nevertheless, fall under the influence of sets of archetypes, and so, not all astronomical effects are astrological – but astrological phenomena can influence and be entwined with non-astrological phenomena and vice versa. There are different layers to astrology (that is, different types of effects), each with varying degrees of influence. Each *type of astrological effect* (a TAE) requires its own consideration, but each also needs to be considered in relation to the other areas. The main TAEs are through: solar emission; celestial bodies themselves (specifically, planets and certain satellites – that is, the moons and their immediate physical forces); and lastly, the relational spatial geometry and etheric energetic signatures from various celestial bodies. It is hard to categorize TAEs linearly as to which is more influential, as they each have different types of effects, and they also affect one another (differently). While astrology deals with archetypes, these effects are physical and etheric (but they also have astral *connections*).

The main archetypes of astrology fall under what is called the *zodiac* – a wheel of archetypes. There are different kinds of zodiacs, but most bodies in the Caelverse wield a certain kind of zodiac, split into twelve repeating archetypes known as (zodiac) *signs*. The predominance of the *default zodiac* throughout the Caelverse is due to how properties naturally develop in most contexts; that is, it is unlikely, in most contexts, for other zodiacs to form. Note that celestial bodies themselves (like the suns) do not possess astrological archetypes, but rather, all said bodies etherically align *with* astrological archetypes via their particular physical properties. So, the physical properties *assume* a zodiac by *defaulting* to one. It is like how masculine and feminine roles naturally emerge from two or more entities in most contexts (whether conscious or nonconscious) – even amongst people of the same sex.

Once an entity aligns with an archetype, it naturally shapes itself to a degree towards that archetype as well. Of course, the celestial bodies could never physically be the actual archetypes themselves, as this would mean that they (the celestial bodies) would no longer be just that: celestial bodies. The celestial bodies then 'pull' (or 'warp') other bodies *toward* these archetypes with their physical effects. So, the planets do not themselves, for example, have career-driven personalities, nor do they *have* the energy of career-driven personalities. Essentially, they are just celestial bodies, but the physical and etheric nature of these celestial bodies happen to align more with a particular archetype, which, in turn, can affect one's consciousness to be, as said above, more career-driven. The zodiacs and other astrological archetypes essentially have roots (connections) in the astral but are not limited to the astral.

All suns produce and 'emit' the default zodiac across their solar systems as part of the first TAE. Due to their form, suns possess *differential rotation*, where not all parts of the sun will rotate with the same angular velocities. This causes a type of friction amongst the magnetic fields, where a sun will shoot out both light (*solar photons*) and *solar wind* (that is, a stream of various charged particles with mass) in twelve (equal) regions. Technically, the suns do not 'emit' the zodiacs; instead, the properties of the photons and solar wind from each region will have different effects (collectively and individually), with each spatial region staying static, despite a sun's rotation; that is, as a sun rotates, the zodiac rays will remain in the same place. The photons, more specifically, will have a particular superposition in each region, in turn causing different effects on the matter they contact. The photons themselves also have etheric energy data, and the etheric energy of the photons can also alter the photons even further through a feedback loop. When the said photons hit matter with their particular patterned superposition, they can cause certain kinds of changes in the states of various systems, in turn causing a chain event with a specific set of different outcomes.

While it might not seem like much, the photons may, more specifically, have a chance to cause tiny *bit manipulations* in systems. Normally, the term relates to computers (not just quantum computers), where the data changes, but bit manipulations can even affect genetic material, with certain effects having potentially great changes on a being's consciousness via the microtubule level. These bit manipulation changes may be minute and hard to detect, but they may induce wildly different outcomes via the *butterfly effect*, where small localized changes can lead to bigger effects elsewhere. While the term is typically used within the context of *chaos theory* (a multidisciplinary field of study that deals with the apparent random and unpredictable outcomes that can occur in seemingly deterministic systems), ultimately, all alterations are still an ordered set of specific effects (related to the state and etheric energy of the abovesaid photons); and within the context of astrology, patterns can be understood, and some predictions can accordingly be made.

Parenthetically, the Caelverse happens to be 'hostile' to many types of computers, and this is one of the reasons why many beings (including mages) use various types of paper as backups; this is not just a matter of the suns that cause these problems, but other phenomena create such problems, too. The photons also happen to affect the whole etheric field (the HRF) of the celestial body they hit (that is, a planet itself). This means that even if someone does not receive any sunlight, the affected planet itself can still, in turn, affect the person. So, the aggregate of photons hitting a planet but not hitting a particular person is more effective than a single photon hitting said person (without, hypothetically, the context of the planet as a whole).

The solar wind, on the other hand, more so affects the *geomagnetic field* (GMF) of a planet they contact via the magnetosphere. Note that while solar winds travel at super-fast speeds, it can take a while (even a couple of days) to reach outer celestial bodies, so this is something astrologers have to consider. The GMF of a planet affects the nature of various properties and things within and on the planet; and so, in the case of living organisms, this can affect their brains and DNA, causing various entities to act (a little) differently per the changes in the GMF. While the magnetic fields of certain technologies (while in proximity to a person) may be stronger than the GMF, consider that people are specifically *attuned* to the GMF – even if they do not consciously realize it – via *magnetoreception*. Certain parts of the brain, during birth, may be activated or deactivated, causing different types of personalities to form. Of course, since astrological effects are constant, people are always subject to change. There are also biological and other environmental factors to consider, so even twins born at the same time to the same parents will not necessarily display similar personalities.

The other bodies in the solar system can also affect a sun's *solar cycles* and its *sun spots*. This occurs through minute gravitational tugs; and, while such tugs are not strong, they are enough to cause small changes that can, in turn, cause larger changes. These differences in the sun spots cause the photons and the solar wind to change in a particular way. The *position* of the planets around the sun also causes different kinds of changes to these sun spots, so when angular *aspects* such as *conjunctions* or *squares* occur (that is, when celestial bodies are respectively close together or are at right angles to one another), different effects result in the sun spots. So, there is a complex dynamic of not just the sun for this TAE but also the entire solar system at work in regards to how the suns affect the bodies in their solar systems. For this reason, astrologers will draw up *heliocentric* charts (that is, charts that are centred around the suns) for this TAE to determine how the suns will affect their planets.

The next TAE involves the energy of the celestial bodies themselves, affecting, for the most part, things in and on their bodies, along with other bodies within their proximity. The only celestial bodies that produce their own zodiacs in regards to the second TAE are planets and crystal moons. The planets will have a GMF that cycles through zodiac signs, where the zodiac will alter various properties, events, and the consciousness of beings on the planet. The zodiacs emerge by virtue of the different properties within the celestial bodies; specifically, they have certain geometric structures within their cores (due to their PMRs and LMRs). Their respective cores all possess particular crystalized geometric structures that form alignments with particular archetypes (of the zodiacs). While it may seem that these structures would produce all the zodiac signs at once through each geometric point, this is not the case. Instead, the zodiac signs change at particular intervals in time, so a planet (and moon) will only exhibit one zodiac sign at a time.

The changing (or rather, activation) of the zodiac signs and their timings are a result of the planets *orbiting* around the sun. So, it is still a relational issue with the suns, and for T2 worlds with normal zodiacs, each zodiac sign will last one Standard Month. The switching to a new zodiac sign for such planets, however, is not linear; instead, it is based on various patterned sequences. Even though two planets may have the same zodiac, this does not mean that the strength of the zodiac sign on a person will be the same, so birth-based astrological effects may be overridden in weak cases. The crystal moons, on the other hand, are not in a patterned sequence, and they will always align with the zodiac of the sun's rays when they enter a new region. That is, the start of a lunapex will occur right when the crystal moon (and, thus, the planet) enters a new zodiacal region of the sun.

Crystal moons are representative of the feminine energy of the Caelverse, while the suns are the masculine polarity. Metaphorically and archetypally speaking, the suns impregnate the wombs of the crystal moons during the month (with electromagnetic and etheric energy), and at the beginning and duration of the lunapexes, the crystal moons give birth to particular energies. It may seem that if a crystal moon absorbs energy from the sun during a zodiac of a certain air archetype, it would continue being of that archetype of air – but this does not occur. Consider that the process of change through the zodiac wheel is just that: a process, and one of transformation through holistic flowing cycles, which features a special build-up of energies. Thus, the following lunapex can be of a fire archetype. Once a crystal moon passes the lunapex zone, it will not continue birthing lunapex energies; however, it will still continue affecting planets with its zodiac sign, which lasts one month, cycling through the zodiac wheel linearly every twelve Standard Months. A person's crystal moon zodiac sign will thus be the same as the sun's zodiac sign. Also, a person's crystal moon sign (at birth) does not have to be a lunapex moon, nor does a person's elemental moons have to be in lunapex formation.

Lunapexes are a part of astrology, but they do not make up the totality of astrology; moreover, lunapexes are more than just astrological, seeing how, for example, they cause transfigurations. In other words, zodiacs affect the lunapexes and are a part of the lunapexes, but lunapexes involve more than just the zodiacs. It is like how the sun shoots photons of a particular superposition according to the respective zodiac sign, but the photons themselves are not limited to zodiacs, and they (photons) can simply cause materials to become hotter. While the elemental moons do not produce a zodiac, they still technically are of a particular archetype (like air, fire, earth, or water), anyway, so they are, in and of themselves, *astrology-adjacent*.

The crystal moons also reflect and, importantly, refract sunlight in a certain ways. This itself causes different changes in the pattern of the solar photons according to the energy and structures of, in, and on the moons. The crystal moons also cause changes in tides, biological rhythms (affecting reproduction and migration), and, like other TAEs, a planet's GMF. This last point, however, is done indirectly via *tidal forces* and *tidal braking* (that is, the crystal moons cause tides to affect the inner parts of the planets, and the moons also affect the rotation of the planets). When the GFM is altered, this, again, affects beings and properties in various ways. These examples can nevertheless be found outside of the context of zodiacs, but the zodiac of the crystal moon will still shape their planets in particular ways – so, it is both astrological and non-astrological. Naturally, the elemental moons also affect phenomena like tides. Even though the crystal moons happen to produce lots of energy for the lunapexes, this does not mean people born on these dates are 'stronger', but the differences may be more pronounced than other times.

Astronomically, the suns are more important than the moons, as without them, there could be no life (unless the planets were closer to the stars). For those living in mage-dominated or culturally-influenced areas, it would seem as though that there is more cultural emphasis on the moons and the lunapexes as opposed to the suns. Principally, this phenomenon is a matter of the *seen* versus the *unseen*. People *see* the moons during the lunapexes and their results yet forget to (or do not openly) acknowledge (to a great extent) that the suns 'impregnate' the crystal moons and, thus, are fundamentally involved with the lunapexes and astrology. The crystal moons may absorb etheric energies, but so do the suns; it is just that by the time effects are seen, all attention is given to the moons.

The *solar eclipses* (where the moons pass between the sun and the planet) are not any less important, either; rather, they are part of the overall system-wide process of the changing of energies, which is still fundamentally tied with the lunapexes about half a month later. That is, it may not seem like much occurs during a solar eclipse -- there are no 'solarpexes', as such -- but this phase is more of a 'build up' for the monthly cycle. Suns, again, naturally assume a masculine role due to their dominance, and, thus, the moons, by default, take on a feminine role. Technically, if the suns did not exist, the moons would potentially have an altered dynamic.

The third TAE is a mix of default zodiac signs and celestial body positions relative to one another. This phenomenon is a relational matter, so all astrological charts and effects are centred around the entity being influenced. So, for people living on a planet, *geocentric* astrological charts are formed, where other celestial bodies influence them from their positions. It is the very specific geometric structuring of space and matter that establishes the zodiac signs in this case; and, these form through various mathematical *periods* and *sequences*, which are types of *information* (metadata) found in the etheric. So, if the sun were in a specific position relative to the entity (say, a person), then the sun would be under a certain zodiac. If a plasmanary were in the opposite direction, it would be in the opposing zodiac.

These sequences align with various archetypes and are cyclical – hence, the zodiac. It also helps that that there is the *spinning* nature of celestial bodies that gives power to the mandala of the zodiacs – a complete whole, and, more specifically, a holistic order of cycles – as if turning the zodiacs 'on', so to speak. In other words, the zodiacs, here, are part of a whole circular phase, and their mathematical periods in space emerge relative to the celestial body (in relation to other celestial bodies), where archetypal harmonics get distributed in beats or rhythms in an ever-moving phase. Technically, there are an infinite number of these spatial structures that can exist, but these still coalesce into the closest fitting archetypes that work within the context of a cyclical phase. Moreover, for most celestial bodies, the zodiac 'begins' in the direction of the sun due to the spinning nature of the solar system, with signs working counterclockwise from this position. Astrological charts, however, may show clockwise zodiacs for ease of reference.

Essentially, there is a physical basis to the third TAE, starting with the entity being influenced in relation to the physical bodies around them, and their etheric energies hold information, and these cause specific effects back on the physical via different and specific wave function changes. The physical distance of a plasmanary on a planet does not matter too much, as the etheric is less localized than the physical. Coupled with the near vacuum in a solar system, the etheric energy of the said plasmanary will not be relatively decohered as it reaches the said planet. While it may seem that a household item next to a person might have more local etheric energy than the far-away plasmanary, the less localized nature of the etheric can still allow for *special synchronizations*, even though the etheric energy of the plasmanary may not there in full. This largely has to do with the strength of celestial bodies, and so the plasmanary (in its totality) would naturally have more etheric energy than, say, a table. Via the etheric, the plasmanary's energy (its aggregate energy signature) would cause particular wave function changes on the person. Still, celestial bodies in other solar systems will be too far away to meet a threshold of any practical effect.

Interestingly, this etheric and geometric phenomenon is not limited to celestial bodies, so it can occur with tables and people. However, there are minimum *thresholds* of power required for the *specific* effects that only celestial bodies possess. Certain bodies like the sun, on the other hand, would *seem* like they would overpower entities like people (along with overshadowing *influencing* bodies like plasmanaries); however, in the case of the third TAE, there are also upper limits for certain effects, where diminishing returns occur. Certain positions/aspects (such as conjunctions) with other celestial bodies can also occur in regards to the third TAE (that is, when two or more celestial bodies are around the planet where the astrological chart is formed). Comets and asteroids are also included with aspects (and they even have influence by themselves). The third TAE also sees changes to GMFs – and, even the solar wind of the first TAE can be affected. Another important point to consider is that while the sun and crystal moon zodiacs will always align (regarding the other TAEs), the crystal moon's zodiac in the case of the third TAE (in relation to their planets) will be in opposition to the sun's zodiac sign during a lunapex due to it being in geometric opposition to the sun.

Even though the C-stars within the constellations themselves do not cause any practical astrological effect on bodies in the solar systems, note that they (the C-stars) are still formed in particular ways – a type of formation that happens to be inherent to how many properties naturally form. The constellations themselves (not the C-stars individually) do not possess any practical astrological effects either, but if they were closer to the solar systems, then naturally all sorts of TAEs (including the third TAE via geometry) would occur. Some astrologers beg to differ on the strength of effects of C-stars on solar system bodies (as well as whether the constellations themselves have any power), and they draw up other kinds of astrological charts, but these are not common. The same issues occur for other celestial bodies outside the solar systems.

All of these issues bring up the question as to what happens when a person is born outside of a planet. The reality is that being born off world *does* cause changes in one's personality, but given genetic dispositions (and how the environment also plays a role in one's personality), a person can change once adapted to the planets their ancestors lived on. So, a person's *birthchart* is just the *strongest* imprint, not the only one. Typically, this imprint is at birth, not conception, because this is when the individual is 'on their own' and separated from the physical and etheric shielding of the mother (where the GMF can better affect them) – though, there are exceptions to this norm, especially when it comes to certain species.

There are also many other ways to virtually 'overwrite' one's astrological imprint given at birth; however, this requires a great change to occur in the person. Some of these processes can be done through intense rituals, intentional or unintentional etheric modulation, or massive changes to the physical structure of the body (like in the case of *cybernetics*, where mechanical items are implanted into a body – with more on the topic explained in *Section 4.3.2.3*), in turn greatly affecting the etheric. Given that other variables act on all properties, and that some of these variables can alter astrological influences – *and* that it is hard to accurately measure astrological influences on a purely quantum level – astrology is used more as a *guide* than a precise calculator for examining events and the nature of properties.

Regardless of any potential changes, a person will default to an archetype (or set of archetypes), anyway. This is further boosted with the elemental moons. A person may have a rather 'fiery' personality based on having more 'fire' in their astrological birthcharts *as a whole*, but the elemental moons hold to archetypal energies both inside and outside the context of astrology (note: the elemental moons still play an astrological role in regards to the third TAE). So, the fiery person in question might also *specifically* have a certain number of fire moons altering their personalities. Accordingly, if a person were born under eight fire moons, two earth moons, one water moon, and one air moon, then, from the elemental moons alone, they will likely be archetypally quite fiery. The eight fire moons here will even trump, for example, a water moon that may have been aligned in a lunapex. Also consider that elemental moons may align with opposing zodiac elements (via the third TAE of geometric structuring), creating mixed and more complex results. For mages born under unclear circumstances in regards to zodiac energy and elemental moons, they will still default to an arch-element (of either air, fire, earth, or water), which, in turn, dictates the magic they use (again, for more information, see *Section 3.6*).

A *Standard New Year* occurs for all POTs simultaneously, which is set by T2 worlds. The other POTs (T1 and T2 planets), nevertheless, have their own new year's dates as well (despite not having any *practical* civilization); that is, while there are various calendars that exist for different parts of the Caelverse, the *Standard Calendar* is universally applied to all systems in the Caelverse, and it is normally used in both formal and informal settings. While a T2-C2 planet takes another two months to pass the same orbital location where a T2-C1 planet was before, all T2 worlds experience the same months together on the Standard Calendar – specifically set by T2-C1 worlds. Originally, the months were based on the actual position in orbit, but it became too confusing for inter-class relations.

It also used to be the case that the names of the lunapexes were used for the names of the months, but this changed as well. There are now three types of names to consider: the names of the zodiacs; the names of the lunapexes; and the names of the months. When people on T2-C1 worlds experience a *Duskair Lunapex* (with a strong *Agilas* zodiac influence), the people on a T2-C2 world will experience a *Dawnair Lunapex* (with a strong *Equamas* zodiac influence). However, both planets will fall under the month called *Tersis* on the Standard Calendar. Other POTs could name their lunapexes differently, but since there is very little civilization there, they just re-use the normal names and then use them at different times of their respective years. It also happens to be the case that the lunapexes align perfectly with the *solstices* and *equinoxes* of many planets. Note that a solstice is the time when the sun is at its peak or minimum *declinations* – that is, its excursion relative to a planet's equator – while equinoxes are when the sun crosses the plane of the equator. When the Dawnair Lunapex begins for most T2-C1 worlds, the season of *spring* will begin in the northern hemispheres, whereas *autumn* will begin in the southern hemispheres. The default zodiac, lunapex, and month names are:

**Equamas:** Cardinal air zodiac sign; **Dawnair Lunapex**; Month: **Primsis**.

**Origas:** Fixed air zodiac sign; **Midair Lunapex**; Month: **Secunsis**.

**Agilas:** Mutable air zodiac sign; **Duskair Lunapex**; Month: **Tersis**.

**Automas:** Cardinal fire zodiac sign; **Dawnfire Lunapex**; Month: **Quartsis**.

**Centras:** Fixed fire zodiac sign; **Midfire Lunapex**; Month: **Quintusis**.

**Adventras:** Mutable fire zodiac sign; **Duskfire Lunapex**; Month: **Sextusis**.

**Determas:** Cardinal earth zodiac sign; **Dawnearth Lunapex**; Month: **Septisis**.

**Stablas:** Fixed earth zodiac sign; **Midearth Lunapex**; Month: **Octasis**.

**Practas:** Mutable earth zodiac sign; **Duskearth Lunapex**; Month: **Nonusis**.

**Emotas:** Cardinal water zodiac sign; **Dawnwater Lunapex**; Month: **Decisis**.

**Privas:** Fixed water zodiac sign; **Midwater Lunapex**; Month: **Undesis**.

**Dreamas:** Mutable water zodiac sign; **Duskwater Lunapex**; Month: **Dudesis**.

## 2.6: Assorted Celestial Images:

Image 1: Overall shape of the Caelverse: a horn torus.

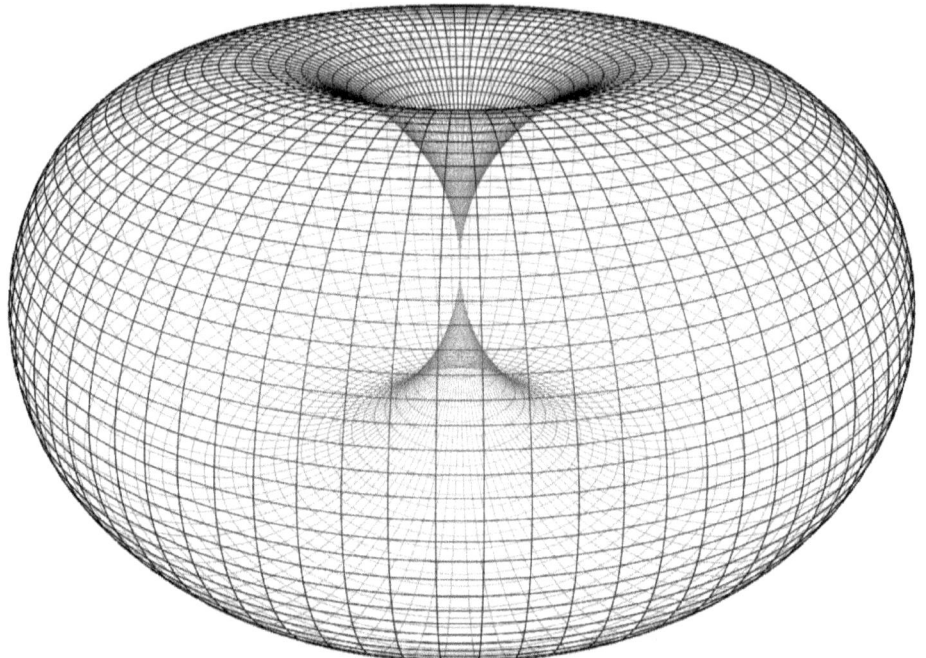

Image 2: Rough cross-section of the Caelverse – suns are not to scale or size:

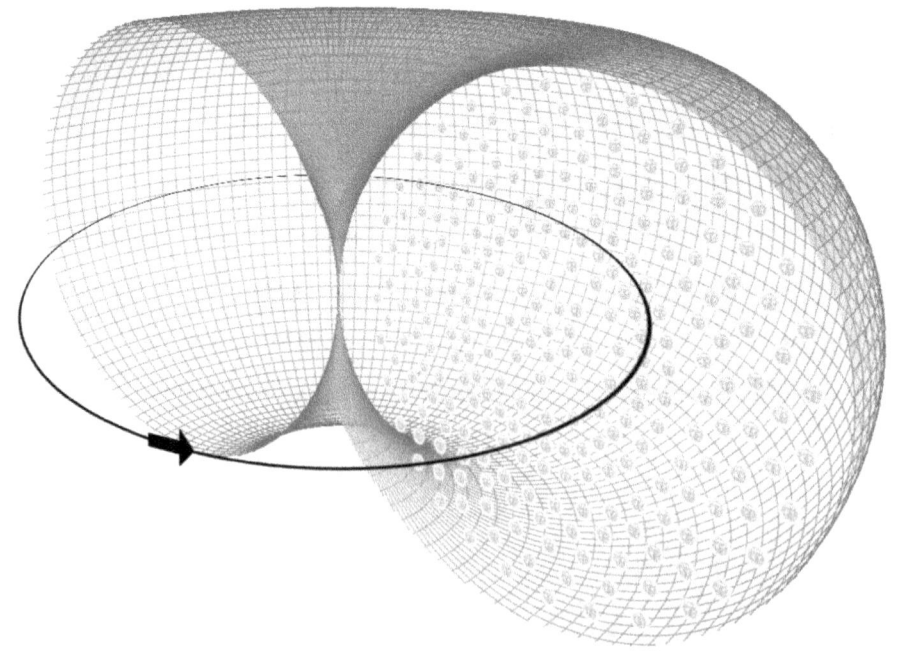

<u>Image 2 note:</u> There are 256 *solar systems* that make up one *solar cluster*. The provided image shows one solar cluster, with the pictures of each sun in the cluster being *representative* of one solar system. The solar clusters consist of vertically-walled solar systems, which are relative and plumb with the Caelverse's z-axis (facing 'up' in the image). Each solar cluster has a central solar system, and each central solar system within each solar cluster perfectly aligns with one another (in a circle) in their position in the Caelverse. The central solar systems also travel at just over one million kilometres per hour through the Caelverse, while the solar systems closer to the inside of the Caelverse travel slower than this, and the solar systems near the outer edge travel much faster. Accordingly, the solar systems within a solar cluster all have the same *local standard of rest* (LSR) – that is, angular velocity – and remain together as a wall. When accounting for other distances, it therefore takes just over four million Standard Years for the solar clusters to complete one orbit through the Caelverse (in a counter-clockwise manner).

There are also nine parsecs between each central solar system (when measured from the solar systems and not the star-based constellations – and also when measured using a circumference). While solar systems of other solar clusters may be closer than solar systems within the same solar cluster, this does not mean that they are part of a solar cluster; again, it depends on whether they are part of the aligned wall or not instead of proximity. Each solar cluster has its own special set of phenomena. This means, from the central suns, there is a circumference of 36,935,829,000,000,000 km. The suns also travel through the Caelverse with their north poles facing the direction of travel. Since some solar systems are on the edge (or outside rings) of a solar cluster, some of their planets will not see other solar systems during the night for certain parts of the year (assuming even standard rotations). Otherwise, when a planet does see the other solar systems, they will typically appear in a single line across the sky. Of course, these solar systems will be behind the constellations, so seeing them requires careful observation.

<u>Image 3 (next page):</u> Rough cross-section of the Caelverse. On left: A representation of The Great Black Wall (GBW), not a photo of it. On the right: A depiction of the mirrored, inner wall of the Caelverse. Lights from celestial bodies *redshift* or *blueshift* off the walls – that is, a light's wavelength will change due to the motion of the light relative to an observer, with red-shifting occurring when objects with light move *away from* an observer, while blue-shifting occurs when objects with light move *towards* an observer. Nevertheless, most of the time, nobody *sees* the slight purplish tinge due to a variety of reasons, such as the other celestial lights, like the bright nebulae, in addition to other atmospheric distortions; so, most people will see outer space as black, filled, however, with tiny white lights from L-stars.

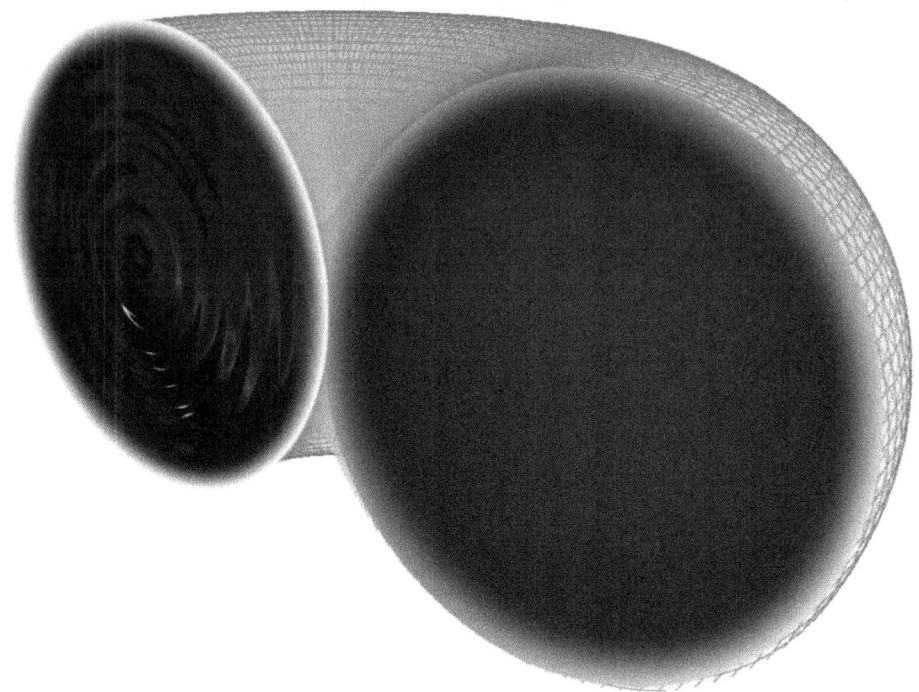

Image 4 (below): An example of a sun (with flares emerging from the *photosphere* – the outermost visible layer of the sun). The *corona*, the outer atmosphere, surrounds it.

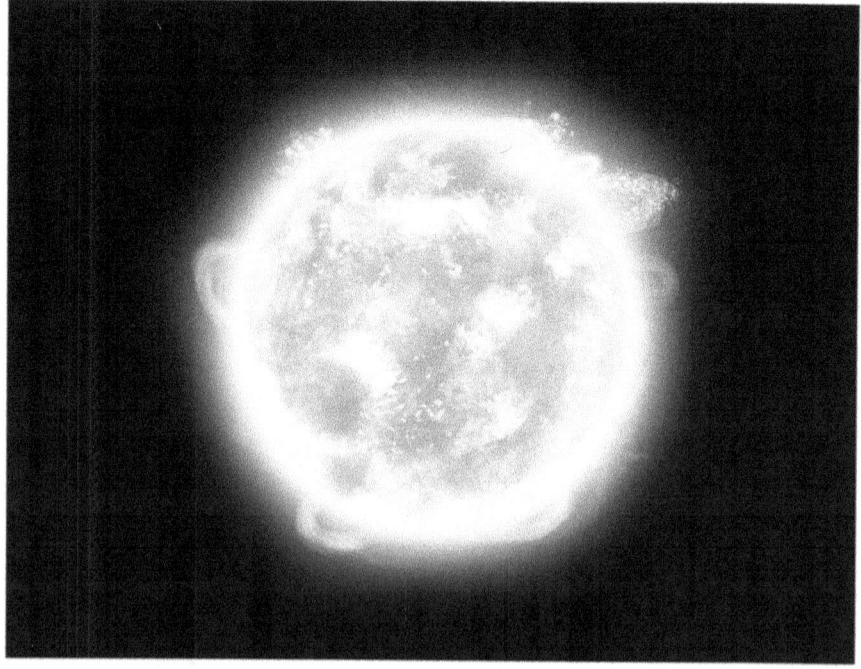

Image 5 (below): An example of a constellation of C-stars (with many unconstellated L-stars in the background) in the sky during a typical, non-cloudy night on a T2-C1 planet. Note that the constellations are like stamps across the sky, so they do not cover the whole sky, both in width and length. The constellations are also positioned across the *ecliptic* (the apparent path the sun takes in the sky), so they (each constellation – not the C-stars *within* each constellation) will appear in one line; but for many planets, the line of constellations will appear in different places across the sky, depending on one's location on a planet and the season. A *nebula* (that is, cosmic dust and gas – normally brightly coloured) will also accompany a constellation; and normally, a nebula is so large collectively that will cover most of the constellation. It is, of course, not possible to see every constellation at once merely by looking at the sky.

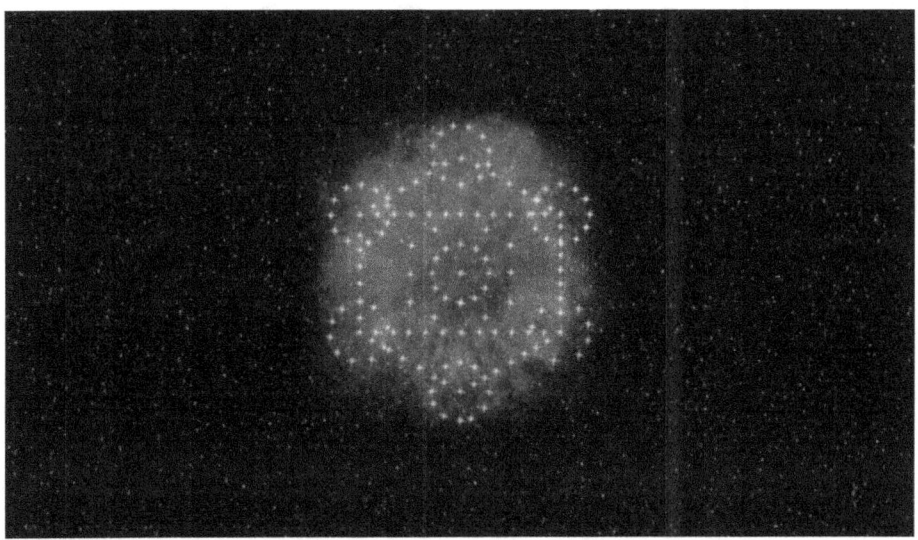

Image 6 (below): An example of a C1 planet (specifically, a T2-C1 planet).

<u>Image 7 (below)</u>: An example of a C2 planet (specifically, a T2-C2 planet).

<u>Image 8 (below)</u>: An example of a C3 planet (specifically, a T2-C3 planet).

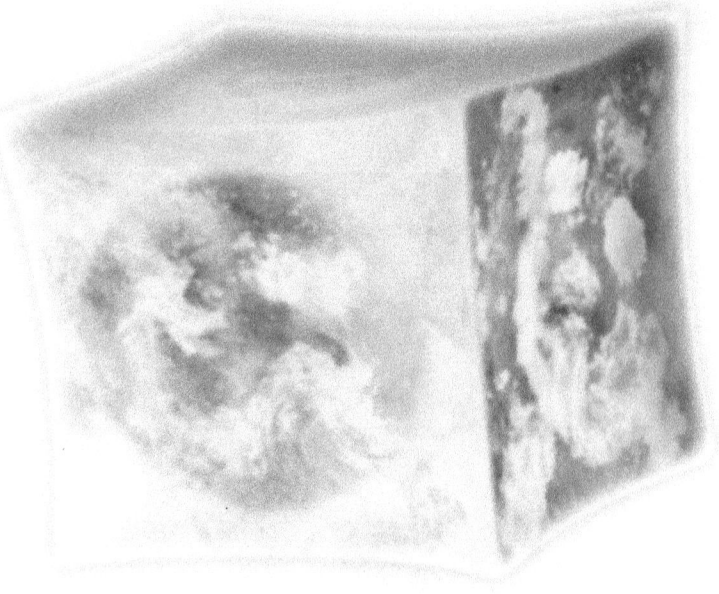

Image 9 (below): An example of a C4 planet (specifically, a T2-C4 planet).

Image 10 (below): An example of a C5 planet (specifically, a T2-C5 planet).

Image 11 (below): An example of a C6 planet (specifically, a T2-C6 planet).

Image 12 (below): An example of a T1 planet (specifically, a T1-C1 planet).

Image 13 (below): An example of a T3 planet (specifically, a T3-C1 planet).

Image 14 (below): An example of two crystal moons (with the example on the right showing the discharge of crystals).

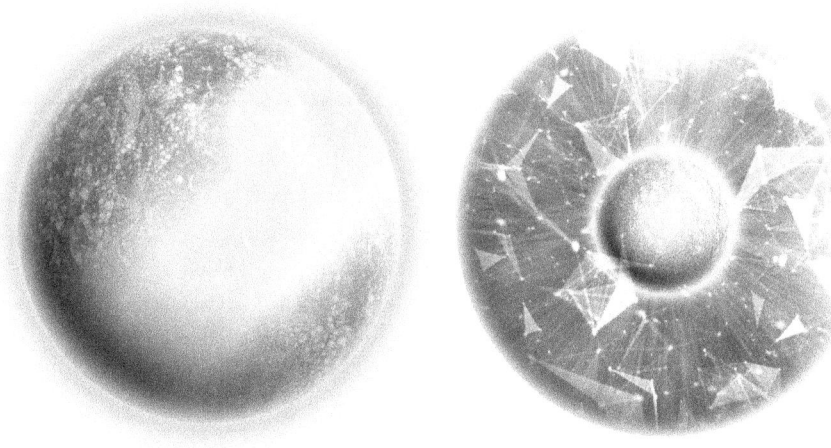

Image 15 (below): An example of two fire moons.

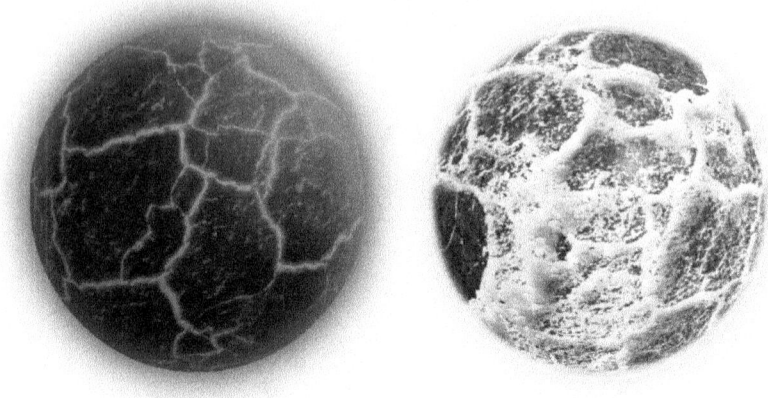

Image 16 (below): An example of two earth moons (with the example on the left showing that even elemental moons can possess *sub-moons*).

Image 17 (below): An example of two water moons (with the example on the left with clear storms).

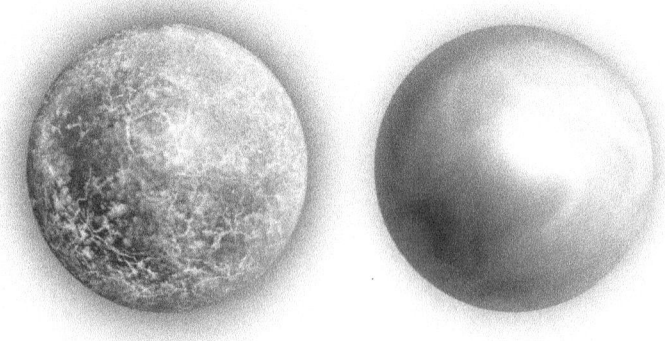

Image 18 (below): An example of two air moons (with the example on the right showing extreme gravitational distortions).

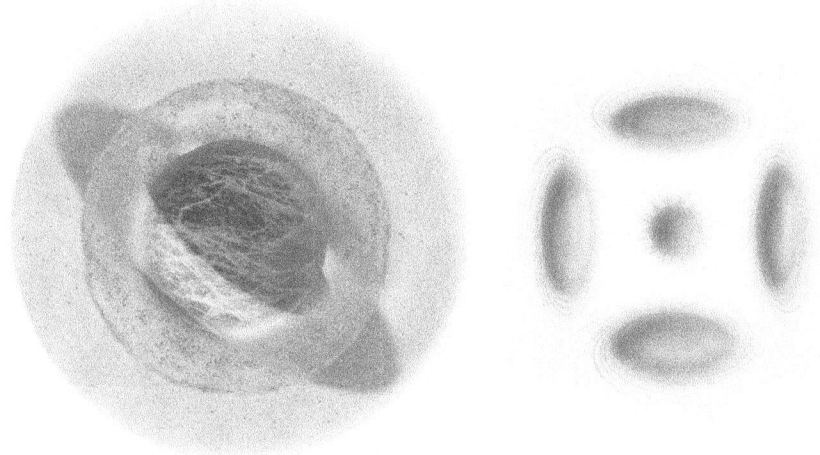

Image 19 (below): An example of four plasmanaries.

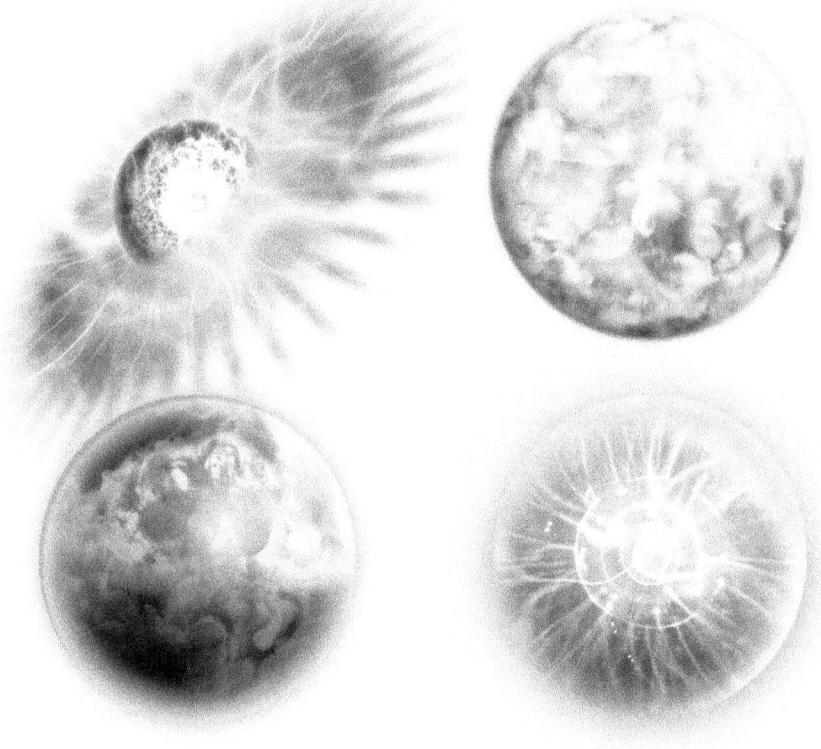

Image 20 (below): An example of two separate leviathan clouds.

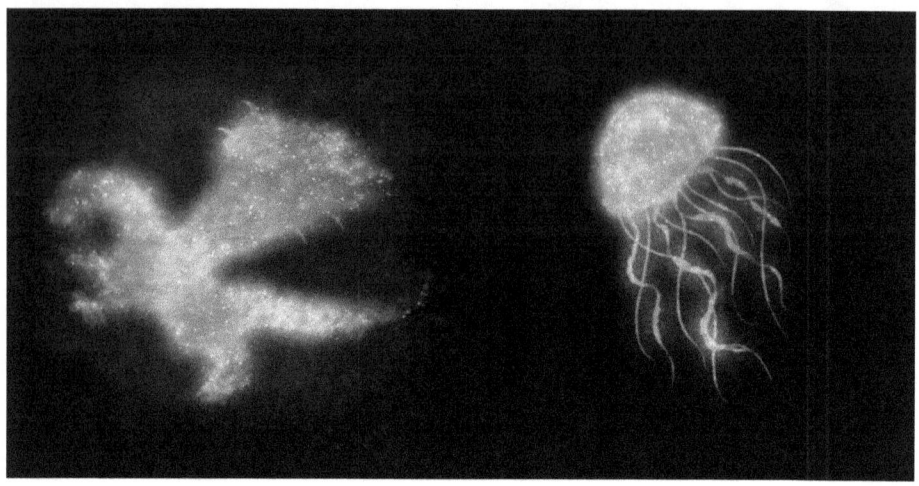

Image 21 (below): An example a torn dead planet (TDP). Interestingly, sometimes asteroids from the asteroid fields will enter the gravitational field of a TDP and form figure-eight patterns.

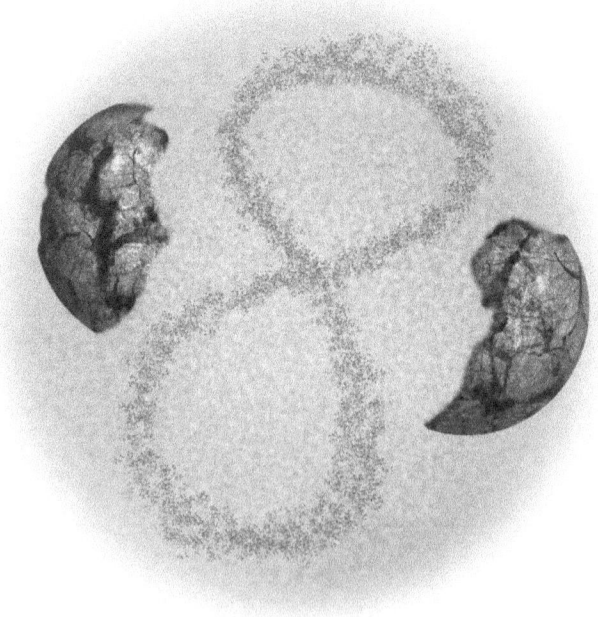

# Section Three

---

*The Ontology, Processes, and Applications of Magic*

## 3.1: General Ontology:

Mages have been researching magic for millennia, having accumulated a large and deep well of knowledge. Discoveries occur all the time, but most are currently more nuanced than revolutionary. Attempts at performing the impossible are always undertaken, but researchers understand that there are many limitations to what can be performed. The understanding of magic has changed over the ages, but magic is now mostly considered as, straightforwardly, the *conscious* altering of reality. Mages commonly accept that magic may *appear* to exist otherwise, but all such phenomena are just the complexities and wonders found in nature (unless one is to make the argument that reality itself is consciously *being* created from a supreme force). Fire, for example, is a chemical process – a visible effect of the process of combustion. When found in seemingly unnatural forms, fire *seems* magical, when in reality, it is a rarer phenomenon, usually burning as such because of unusual materials. Other spectacular phenomena may include certain forcefields, wild illusions, and kinetic blasts.

Since all conscious beings possess the fundamental characteristic basis of magic: consciousness, it must follow that magic, essentially, is a spectrum – one based on the ability of consciousness. It then follows that are certain *thresholds* to performing certain magical feats, like how a *living* being requires eyes (or something of such nature) to see and a nose to smell; and so, mages are virtually the only beings who are capable of most of these conventionally-understood feats of magic in physical existence. Not all thresholds, however, are magical. So, dragons, for instance, may *seem* like they possess magic, but they really only have complex physiology, which enables for phenomena like *thermosynthesis* – which, more specifically, allows dragons to draw, store, and convert heat energies from various sources (of the Caelverse) before using such energy at a later point to breathe seemingly unbelievable amounts of fire. Ice trolls, meanwhile, can use the *exothermic* process of *deposition* to turn the gas around them into solids, which they use to launch ice shards at foes. Electrical entities (usually aquatic) have *electrocyte-based* organs and can open their ion channels before discharging various voltages. Then there are numerous other entities that also have fantastic abilities, but none are using their consciousness in the aforesaid sense.

As all matter emerges from the unlimited energy of the ZPF, which is *at least* linked to consciousness, then (coupled with other axioms said in *Section One*) it must also follow that one's consciousness can draw from this source of energy (at conscious will) – and this, indeed, is the case. However, not all magic *only*, or at all, extracts directly from this source, so there are two tiers to magic – one which draws directly from the Aether, and the other that involves non-Aether interaction on the physical, etheric, and astral levels. The latter tier is nonetheless considered magical, as consciousness is still required and used, and it is a threshold that no non-magic beings can wield.

Technically, mages do not 'use their magic' nor 'use their consciousness'. Rather, mages consciously *change* their consciousness, which, in turn, *performs* the conscious action of magic – which may use aether energy. For the sake of brevity, many people nevertheless may still simply say, 'mages use their magic'. Nonetheless, when a non-mage picks up an apple, for example, they are still using their consciousness (via their brain and hand) to apply changes to their reality. This kind of feat is the type of 'magic' called *Standard Substance Manipulation* (SSM). Naturally, this includes the aforesaid dragons using thermosynthesis. The term 'standard' applies even to feats such as thoughtform manipulation in the astral.

Since virtually every living being performs SSM (at least in the physical realm – most plants do not create astral matter, however), it is not listed as one of the five types of mage magics known as *schools of magic* (listed in the following subsections). However, SSM is still a fundamental part of all the mage magics, anyway, as mages still use their brains (a physical device). Considering that consciousness is limited and affected by the physical casing it is in (the biological body), there is a physical component involved with magic that acts as a conduit of sorts for consciousness and its Aether connection. This conduit is called the *animagifestus gland*, or simply, the 'magic gland', situated right behind – and about two times the size of – the *pineal gland*. Other conduits to the Aether have also been theorized to exist. Mages may sometimes feel a tingling sensation in their heads when using magic, which results from the use of this gland. While the mere creation of astral matter is not a *mage* magical practice itself, the magic gland does help connect with spiritual energies, and, thus, mages have a greater ability to see such energies.

Mages fully develop their magic glands around the age of eighteen. However, when mages within a year of their eighteenth birthday experience the *Equamas Lunapex* (which happens to be the New Year's Lunapex for T2-C1 worlds), the properties of the lunapex and sun's zodiac basically jump-starts their magic glands. Consequently, all mages born in this particular period are essentially born into a 'year group'. When jump-started, mages are able to fully practice their magic. In saying that, even before developing their glands, mages are able to tap in to certain types of consciousness to varying levels, although generally at a much lesser strength than adults.

Mages become stronger with magical practice, but even then, most post-university mages possess around the same strength (with the probability distribution being a sharp bell curve), and so, only a small percentage of mages are incredibly powerful – relative to the rest of the mage population. Given that the magic gland is physical and requires the brain to be functional – and also for the fact that the physical body as a whole channels spiritual energy when properly aligned – it is accordingly imperative for mages to uphold their physical condition in order to practice magic both properly and at all. While some powerful mages may have terrible and decrepit bodies, they are powerful *in spite* of their bodies. This phenomenon results from particular training of one's consciousness. Nevertheless, if they had better physical conditions, they would be even more powerful – even if only marginally.

When *aether energy* is channelled from *the* Aether, it will surround the mage in the etheric before entering the physical world; but not all aether energy will necessarily be properly processed in a spell due to a mage being inept relative to the strength of the spell that they are trying to cast. That is, the energy will go to waste, even though it did initially manage to surround the mage. Explicitly, channelling from the Aether differs to how much of that energy mages can utilize for a spell. The connection to the Aether will wane with enough use via loss of conscious focus. The weariness, in this case, is actually a phenomenon caused by their consciousness having to interact with reality through the limitations of the physical body and with having to re-establish a connection with the ZPF. That is, a mage's level of consciousness is determined (or rather, strongly influenced) by the body (along with etheric constraints); and instead of consciousness itself having limitations (as consciousness at its core has infinite potential), it is rather that the physical body (even when in prime shape) puts a limitation and drain on the consciousness; and, therefore, limited consciousness cannot keep casting magic.

Mages possess two etheric pools for 'containing' aether energy around them – one for nearly all schools of magic, there is the *general aether pool* (GAP), and another pool, called the *lumarchetrix* (or, in some cases, the *phasarchement aether pool* – PAP), for the school of *phasarchement magic* (explained in *Section 3.6*). The reason why there are two separate pools is fundamentally due to the nature of the magics; the schools of magic that use GAP energy are based on etheric pre-formed creations (of geometric patterns), while the phasarchement pool does not feature this phenomenon; instead, it is more direct in its etheric channelling. There is an initial delay when the mage first begins to meditatively connect with the Aether before the charging of a pool can begin. The time varies based on the mage's power level, and *novices* take about forty-five seconds to connect. It may seem as if one should always remain connected to the Aether in order to avoid the initial delay, but connections wane over time, anyway. Regardless, *supreme-level* mages (the very best mages) can connect instantly.

Before connections to the Aether wane and are cut off (known as *exhaustion*), mages can also temporarily run out of the aether energy in their pools (that is, they experience what is known as *depletion*). When depletion occurs, a cooldown *stability* 'penalty' of about six seconds is incurred (for mages of most power levels) before the mage can use any magic again from that pool that dropped to zero. Still, whether they have depleted their energy (and are experiencing the penalty) or are currently using energy from their pools, mages automatically (and simultaneously) *recharge* energy from the Aether. When exhausted, mages either cannot recharge much energy or any at all, and the recovery from this can normally take around twenty-four hours.

The recharging process, while not exhausted, becomes like second nature, so it is not like mages have to consciously *think* of doing it, but they need to be conscious enough for it to take effect. Nevertheless, if a mage's consciousness reduces below normal levels without becoming unconscious, then there is a chance that the recharging rate could lower or not occur at all. If mages are exhausted, sleep is actually beneficial. When using magic from both pools at once, the recharge speed from the Aether will halve for each pool, and so, the *average* mage will recharge their pools to maximum capacity (which itself varies depending on the mage's strength) at 0.4167% per second instead of the normal 0.8333% per-second rate for one pool alone. Even so, both pools can simultaneously reach 100% capacity, and both tend to be at roughly full capacity when the mage *initially* connects to the Aether (so long as the mage did not deplete their pools shortly beforehand).

The energy in the GAP (and lumarchetrix) also lasts longer than in manifest form in the physical because it is not being spent in the etheric (or at least used in the same manner); in addition, the etheric realm naturally has a different time standard than the physical, anyway. Technically, mages *do* use a small portion of their own energy when *casting* spells. For example, the physical brain – coupled with the magic gland – of course, will insanely fire neurons around for many reasons during spell casting, and, thus, mages consume *some* amount of caloric energy. However, none of this energy actually goes into and feeds the spell itself.

Because magic is the conscious *altering* of reality, heightened *states* of awareness are not in themselves magic, despite being necessary *for* magic. However, because non-mages typically cannot reach such *types* of states, sometimes they mistakenly treat these states (and also any skill involved with reaching such states) as a magic. These heightened states fundamentally revolve around the *clair-senses*, or *psychic* skills, which allow the mage, for example, to see flashes of images in their minds (known as *clairvoyance*), while another example consists of having – and interpreting – visions in dreams (normally called *oneiromancy*). Basically, mages have advanced psychic *skills* plus their magics. Any mage advanced enough in psychic abilities is also typically labelled as a 'psychic'. For more *specific* uses of psychic activity (that is, specializations), sometimes labels like 'spiritualist' might be used.

There are some scholars, nevertheless, who argue that while these states are not magics in themselves, the conscious alerting of consciousness itself to reach different states is itself magic, as it is by its nature an alteration via consciousness. However, there should be a distinction made between pure consciousness itself and reality which encompasses more than just consciousness (or rather, the reality that consciousness inhabits). Moreover, the methods of increasing one's consciousness are not fundamentally different from what non-mages can do (as most of the process involves tuning into different frequencies and archetypes); and so, raising one's consciousness through various methods is more of an inherent ability and skill with a radically different ontological foundation to the five schools of magic available to mages. Still, if this were universally considered a magic, it would be called *psychicism*. The term is still used, anyway, for psychic activities, and psychicism is also taught at mage universities.

Of course, then there are both the said awareness increases and the inclusion of SSM, which can involve probability manipulations on the etheric level. Issues of probabilities also occur with constructing spells, and some magic causes probability manipulations. The difference between normal probability manipulations and that of mage magic is the ontologically and phenomenally different threshold levels, allowing for much greater and diverse effects. Mages still use general probability manipulations on the etheric level all the time, both consciously and otherwise, but no mage is incredibly powerful enough to create immense effects. These probability manipulations include practices like hexes, augmentations (like those found in rituals), and synchronizations; the latter, in this case, can also simply include matching particular energies without any probability variables considered. There are also physical tokens that may be worn or kept, like good luck tokens, but these are effectively very weak. If such a discipline were truly mastered, it would indeed be one of the most powerful of magics. All probability manipulations (and, specifically, increases in probabilities) can, nevertheless, lead to other phenomena occurring, and these could cause problems; in fact, some of these problems could, in turn, lead to a decrease in the initial event's probability of occurring.

Even though mages develop their abilities through time and practice, some mages possess natural talents and can, for example, easily have dreams linked to probable future events, even at a young age. Since the physical and spiritual are linked – and that the former necessitates a healthy or sound state to access the latter – there are nevertheless cases where while nearing death, a mage's senses greatly open up, usually with the automatic help of chemicals like *dimethyltryptamine* (N,N-DMT). Such windows of opportunity are just that: windows, and they close very suddenly. Also consider that there are cases where mages unconsciously tap into particular energies, such as having seemingly-random flashes of one or more probable futures. Whether in due part of the mage themselves or being subject to assorted happenings (intentional or actually 'random'), all such unconscious activity does not lack consciousness but rather are experienced on different levels of consciousness. In brief, the unconscious is still part of a mage's overall consciousness. Still, at this level alone, these experiences – on behalf of the mage experiencing them – are not considered 'magic' in the traditional sense.

For mages who are not 'responsible' for such happenings, this is still the result of a heightened awareness on a particular level, even on the unconscious level. Basically, this only occurs for mages who are adept at psychic abilities, anyway. So, in the case of intentional psychic attacks or intentional psychic visions induced in the mage, this can only occur if the mage is capable of either tuning into, or being tuned into, or is already tuned into such energy. For this reason, both young mages and many non-mages will likely not receive – or at least not receive the effects of – particular psychic attacks. All advanced mages must accordingly practice some defensive exercises to sustain control of their reality. On the whole, mages are slightly more susceptible to issues like demonic attacks, too. Even though there are techniques to ward off demons, it may be hard if the mage is also subject to areas with mass dark energies, such as those found in *black rituals*.

Mages can also scan etheric auras for a better understanding of the physical. Scanning the aura of a sick person, for example, may help determine the cause of their illness. Indubitably, this can be problematic, as a person's aura also contains various probable realities (pasts, presents, and futures); and so, the mage may be seeing false positives or other diseases unrelated to the reality they occupy. Moreover, the psychic may pick up the information of other people (related to the person) in said aura. Because of this, *accurate* 'mind-reading' is also next to impossible. Mages also suffer from projecting their own biases onto the auras of others, along with other distractions. Mages can also use *dowsing* techniques to find particular physical objects, but again, this has its own set of problems, such as shifting energies distorting such searches.

Mages are also the only physical beings able to psychically tune into most *mage-tech* with their consciousness – even though this is not a magic outside of SSM. The reason for this is that the majority of mage-tech contains *neurachite* and an established *neurachite* brain of a range of assorted intelligences. Neurachite is a special kind of crystal that can easily store information like DNA; more specifically, the crystal takes the data of the DNA and then is able to form *neuron analogues*. Because these are not actual neurons, this is not *wetware*. In other words, the neurons analogues are not formed with the actual biological tissues found in real neurons. Parenthetically, mages tend to avoid using wetware for a variety of reasons, and this includes simple appeal.

To reiterate for clarification, mages tend to benefit the most from inserting mage DNA into neurachite, as the neurachite accordingly has greater abilities than neurachite with DNA of other species, and mages alone can use the mage-tech. Neurachite of varying complexities allows mages of different skills to connect to it via their own brains and etheric energy, fundamentally because the crystal forms synthetic proteins that are super similar to those found in mage brains. Basically, neurachite brains have the potential to receive and transmit information *as if* a psychic. The brains are so far, however, incapable of performing magic. Most commands that mages give to neurachite brains are low level, such as switching devices on and off, as the majority of commands and applications beyond this are either problematic or impossible. Even mages who are yet to use magic (that is, *underage mages*) can use neurachite-based mage-tech, but they usually encounter some limitations. While it may seem unusual that mages cannot simply connect with the brains of other mages and control them, yet they can do so with neurachite, consider that neurachite is actually more advanced and powerful than mages in *some* ways, while in many other ways, it is very limited, so it is less advanced and powerful than mages.

Typically, neurachite is also formed inside an aggregate crystal called *unichite* that contains other crystals (primarily *aerochite*, *holochite*, and *charchite*); and this unichite is then coupled with other materials and technologies. Most neurachite brains are found in analogue computing systems called *neurachite analogue computers* (NACs). Mages still occasionally use other non-neurachite technologies, such as *digital electronic computers* (DECs) and *quantum mechanical computers* (QMCs), but they normally favour NACs for their analogue (non-digital) structure and increased efficiency in *particular* ways, along with their: ease of production; reduced etheric pollution (in some, but not all cases) compared to other technologies (which makes magic less difficult within the vicinity); again, exclusive accessibility for mages via their minds (but not always if the mage-tech has holographic interfaces via the holochite, as non-mages can still use these interfaces); ability to link to the unique *synopool* containing vast amounts of information, resources, and services via various applications (which are analogue in nature and separate from similar but different digital *internets*); and, neurachite does not have some of the problems found in digital artificial intelligences (despite neurachite presenting its own A.I. problems).

Due to problems with A.I., along with bit-manipulation equivalents and certain etheric distortions, mages still use paper, but this is normally made of holochite. The holochite can not only shrink and expand, but it is also incredibly durable. Moreover, when holochite is connected with a neurachite brain (which can detect what is written), the paper (like a physical book) can connect to the synopool, where holographic *overlays* can be produced from the physical paper itself. With this process, the paper never gets re-written (thus, the physical media is safe and permanent), but mages can still find updated information through the synopool. Interestingly, when studying or practicing magic in certain contexts, it is better to read from and use (holochite) paper.

Since properly seeing auras is a challenge for most mages in most contexts for more than a few seconds, many mages also use technologies to help see and determine etheric realities, such as *etheric data analysers* (EDAs) – which typically use neurachite. It must be noted that since all information from EDAs is converted to the physical, all data is merely *analogous* and not accurate, which means even technologies have their own limitations. Other than this (and with the aid of magic), the only way for mages to properly and adequately see etheric energy for more than a few seconds is to enter deep meditation, which is actually what allows mages to establish their magic for various schools of magic. When this deep meditation occurs, however, the mage is limited to a small amount of the etheric (such as the etheric energy of an item they are focusing on for their magic), and they cannot walk around and scan anything they fancy. Generally, this means the field of view a mage has in such a meditative state is centred around themselves and one other item – if present.

*Magic suppressors* are a form of mage-tech that lowers one's consciousness and, therefore, ability to wield magic. They achieve this by distorting a mage's brain – specifically, the magic gland. Because they only distort the magic gland, magic suppressors do not totally suppress one's overall consciousness, and mages can still, accordingly, be fully awake and have proper dialogue with other people. Such tech is usually used for prisoners, and they (suppressors – of a particular variety) need to be attached directly to the body. Still, there are some strong tonics, potions, aerosols, and powders that can also affect a mage in the same way, too, except these have a time limit. Just because magic suppressors are mage-tech, this does not preclude non-mages from using magic suppressors on mages. Indeed, non-mages prefer using such technology for capturing mages, as they otherwise are normally overwhelmed by magic. More information on magic suppressors can be found in *Section 3.6.3.2*.

Both the natural world and artificial creations affect the amount of etheric energy a mage has for themselves; so lunapexes, for example, will increase one's ability to increase awareness, which, in turn, helps with magic, such as allowing for a wider connection to the Aether. Understand that in this example, it does not *necessarily* increase one's awareness in itself; but rather, it usually induces changes that then allow for greater increases if, for example, the mage concentrates. Consider it similar to the following example: steroids allow one to increase muscle mass, but one must still exercise their muscles while on steroids, as the steroids do not automatically increase muscle mass – at least beyond small amounts. Varying levels of etheric energy can also be stored up in both nature (especially caves filled with crystals) and artificial creations, sometimes creating illusions for those who can see the etheric. This is similar to, but different from, *charm magic* (explained in *Section 3.3*). Some of these phenomena can be attributed to ghosts. Certain beings like fairies are also capable of manipulating the etheric around nature to such a great extent that they can, over time, increasingly mould nature towards their preferences and imaginations – though, this does have its limitations.

Since etheric energy is a *collection* of different data points of the physical while also being itself data and metadata of said physical materials (and more), it then follows that it is 'more than the sum of its parts'. Essentially, etheric energy has more abstract information in its very ontological and tangible being. In the philosophical context of *universals* and *particulars* (that is, the issue of whether either things have something in common, such as certain characteristics like 'redness' or if they are concrete spatiotemporal things), etheric energy is also less 'particularized' with its more diffuse nature. *Archetypes* are a form of universals as opposed to particulars, and with the abstract information found in the etheric, etheric energy, accordingly, has archetypal energy. This, however, does not mean the etheric has archetypes in their purest form, which can only be found in the pure potentiality of the Aether in non-form. This means that a mage can draw upon archetypes (which have broader sets of probabilities), which, in turn, can emerge as a *more* definitive structure in physical reality. These archetypes *themselves* in the etheric also contain swathes of information (data and metadata), so the mage does not have to analyse every single particle to determine how something works.

Let us take one of the infinite archetypal forces available: the *arch-elements* (that is, the *classical elements* of *fire*, *earth*, *water*, and *air*), which were originally considered the actual elements of matter until science emerged, properly explaining the reality of chemical elements and rendering the former false in this regard. While the arch-elements are not what the ancients considered, these archetypal states are still based on, but not limited to, the tangible *physical states* and processes known as: solid, liquid, gas, and plasma. As mentioned in *Section 2.3*, the fire element includes certain *processes*, too. Basically, archetypal states themselves are not literal minerals or gases, but they (archetypal states) still transcend and include the physical, thus they are *transclusive*. The terminology of the classical elements remains in order to provide an understanding of the nature of such states of being. All properties (physical, etheric, and astral), though, tune into and/or between these four archetypal states of being, with most generally sharing values across the spectrum. This means that there is usually no rigid structure for a property or thing to be fully in one archetype or another.

Water, for example, contains oxygen and hydrogen – the latter naturally being a gas (although, it can technically exist in a metallic state). When bonded with oxygen, water is formed. Gases typically have the structure of an air arch-element, but this is not always the case. When formed into a substance like water, the energy of actual water etherically *aligns* more with the classical water arch-element. Physical water, nevertheless, can be in different states of matter such as a liquid, solid, or gas, which themselves are tuned into the arch-elements, with each being 'water', 'earth', and 'air', respectively. So, actual water can be in both its natural water arch-element *and* earth arch-element, depending on its phase. Lava is another example, with the silicate melt being 'water', the suspended solids being 'earth', the bubbles holding gases being 'air', and finally, the super-heated state being 'fire'.

Despite archetypes being 'pure' in their state by default, they are not necessarily two-dimensionally simple in their ontological composition. That is, there are levels of complexity to the actual nature of archetypes themselves, not just the types of archetypes. With these levels of complexity, archetypes have multifaceted connections to other archetypes, in turn giving complexity to themselves. For instance, while archetypes have their *direct* opposites, they also hold *indirect* opposites – basically *shadow versions* of their nature. So, even though it is generally accepted that water is the opposite of fire, and earth is the opposite of air, these archetypes still have their own shadow opposites that actually relate more to the archetypes themselves than their direct opposites. For example, earth is typically the 'stable' arch-element due to its grounded, hard nature, and so, its shadow opposite is *chaos*. Fire produces light, and so, its obvious archetypal opposite is *darkness*. Water is known for its depth, connection, and substance, and so, the absence of this is a pure *void*. Air is the arch-element of buoyancy and life, so naturally, its shadow side is *nihility* (nothingness). Essentially, the *relevancy* of these other archetypes depends on the positioning from particular archetypes and their scope. These shadow archetypes also relate to one another as well.

Archetypes, in fact, additionally fall into a holistic order, so archetypes like the seasons, for example, must also be viewed not only individually (which is still nonetheless important), but also as a cyclical mandala of being. So, summer is not just summer; rather, it is a part of a whole process of change and *becoming*; that is, summer *becomes* autumn. It also *relates* to autumn, and we derive the meaning of summer through *comparison* to other seasons. When a solstice or equinox occurs, these are *peaks* within a cycle. There are also no *necessarily* abrupt transitions between the archetypes; so, the archetypal beingness is not static, and other dimensions need to be considered. Since archetypes are part of various holistic orders (particular or complete), they encompass the fundamental different states of being/consciousness.

Having knowledge of these archetypes and how they work can drastically impact the ability to tune into particular energies. This, in turn, allows one to more easily hack into physical systems via the metadata of the etheric. Therefore, archetypes are vital for mages to study. Archetypal energies consequently play a huge role in an assortment of practices such as dancing, monetary exchange and business dealings, architectural designing and designs, relationships, (structuring of) routines, psychological dispositions, and more. In short, the practice of archetypal tuning does not just relate to astrology and personality archetypes, but it also falls under the mage's ability to connect with etheric and astral energies, which, in turn, allows them to better increase their awareness of something in particular.

Perhaps the one practice which mages highly value the study of archetypes for is *rituals*, which are normally advanced psychic activities. Rituals can be performed for a variety of reasons, but they may simply be exercised to increase one's awareness and feel particular sensations, or they may also be coupled with magic. Note that the rituals conducted as an underage mage are not as effective (if at all) as when a mage has their magic active – even if the ritual is not being done to enhance magic per se; basically, when one's magic is active, the *potential* for psychic strength increases. Archetypes also deal in the same realm as symbolism, and symbolism affects a being's consciousness. When conducting a ritual, the goal may be (and usually is) to alter one's consciousness, which can be achieved by changing one's perceptions. Fundamentally, the ritual, in this case, is about removing oneself from ordinary reality and placing it into a 'new one' – a new pattern. To do this, archetypal symbols are normally used.

Symbols do not have to be drawn figures. For example, candles may be used; in this case, setting candles around an altar in itself does not really alter much of reality – they are just a bunch of puny flames, and the strength of the etheric energy itself is negligible. What the placed candles *can* do, however, is help *reorientate* one's consciousness into a particular mode of being as the mage focuses their consciousness (even unconsciously) into having a certain perception. This is similar to the *placebo effect* (where one's status, whether physical or mental, changes due to certain perceptions, whether based on something real or not), but the difference here is one's ability (skill) to radically shift their minds, in turn actually inducing real different states of consciousness. All of this, however, is not to say that candles and smoke themselves cannot have strong effects etherically (as small things *can* have big impacts), but this is still very contextual and limited. Outside of rituals (which may or may not feature items), sometimes pendants are worn, but the effects of these are marginal. Embodied symbols like sigils can also be great *mnemonic triggers* (that is, memory techniques, sometimes physical or not) sending messages to one's subconscious. Ultimately, it is still the mage either doing the reorientating or being subject to reorientation.

*Incantations* (that is, special chants) are another great example that can rile up one's consciousness. Usually, these are coupled with or integrated into rituals. There are also socially-learned archetypes resting in the unconscious that are *based* on tangible realities. For example, certain animals or creatures may possess particular traits like viciousness, boldness, and dominance, which societies have *collectively* understood on at least an unconscious level (for even thousands of years). When conducting a ritual with such animals – and by tuning into these archetypal energies that they emanate – a mage can more easily reorient their consciousness into such states for particular purposes. That is, it is sometimes not even a matter of raising one's consciousness, as if ascending a linear ladder, but, instead, shifting it to different perspectives. Sometimes contrasting animals may be used for specific effects that go beyond the effects that either individual animal may induce. Note that the zodiacs have associated animals *culturally* attached to them, yet astrological alignments can have opposing celestial bodies in addition to squaring or trining aspects, so there is usually a concoction of effects that create a meta effect.

Arch-elements are also fundamentally tied to the schools of magic, anyway. Basically, a mage is born into one *dominant* arch-element (usually with astrological factors being one of the biggest influences for this result), which means one is either an earth, fire, water, or air mage. Accordingly, this determines the school of magic in which they can specialize (apart from phasarchement, which all types of mages can use equally without *alignment modifier* 'penalties'). All schools of magic are nevertheless available to every mage, but a magic that is not aligned with the mage's arch-element will be much harder to perform and master.

The school of *conjuration* aligns with the earth arch-element due to its materialist nature; and all conjuration users are called *conjurers*. Fire mages are *alchemists*, able to harness the power of *alchemy* due to the aligning arch-element's transformative nature. Those with a dominant air arch-element can master the school of *charms* (or *charmagy*); known as *charmers*, they manipulate mental spheres (with some charms being what is basically a holographic phenomenon). Lastly, water mages are able to connect with properties of all kinds in a multitude of ways, and, thus, they become *mystics*, masters of *mysticism* magic. Essentially, each school respectively: creates, transforms, induces/compels, and connects with something. The alignment modifiers for each mage are actually neither a boost nor hindrance; rather, being aligned with a certain school essentially means one can adequately tune into its powers; if one is not aligned, it is not technically a *hindrance*, as it is, instead, simply the *lack* of a proper alignment.

With the use of rituals or other means, one can temporarily shift their natural arch-element; and, in rare cases with great training or life-changing experiences, an arch-element can be permanently changed. Despite there being assorted archetypes and alignments, magic is still fundamentally based on *universal constants*. As explained in *Section One*, the fundamental building blocks of physical and etheric matter are geometric (specifically, the *way* they form together). It is this universal geometry that constitutes the creation process for most of the schools of magic. Mages construct geometric patterns in the etheric or astral via their minds when meditating, and these geometric forms tend to take a fluorescent, holographic appearance. The patterns even vibrate strongly and can be felt when a mage tunes into them.

To be clear, the resultant cymatic patterns in the etheric *relate* to quantum patterns, but the geometric forms themselves in the etheric are not quantum patterns themselves – unless specifically referring to etheric data of specific quantum particles outside the context of spell crafting. Novice mages can still see their own astral creations, even though they may not yet be able to astral *travel*. Explicitly, novices are merely seeing their *own* 'nearby' astral energies in their *own* astral *bodies* (that are still in the astral planes), which is a different procedure to seeing other astral energies or even other auras within the astral planes. The meditation itself (and accessing one's inner mind) comes naturally to the overwhelming majority of mature-age mages; and even then, it can still be developed further as a skill.

In the face of being able to see the etheric and astral energies of a particular thing during *this* kind of meditation (that is, for spell crafting), the mage will not normally have full *comprehension* of the item's aggregate reality (that is, its complete timeline history and alternate probable realities), nor will the mage be in a position to do so whilst in their meditation. Therefore, this meditative process cannot generally be used for normal psychic activities, such as investigating the death of someone and finding the murderer. Whilst the mage may *see* such probable or actual realities in their meditation, the meditation's limitations will prevent the mage from making proper connections to *events* and *causes* (and other factors) outside the item's very tangible properties – its material (physical, etheric, or astral) constitution, which the mage still also will not even fully comprehend.

The spell construction process is mental while the mage is in the mediative state, yet for most schools of magic, the geometric forms will be etheric – not astral. However, astral forms can still be seen in this state, so a mage may be constructing etheric forms while astrally imagining, for example, a goblin sliding down a lollipop slide while playing a musical instrument. Spells are also not cast *while* fully in the astral planes without an etheric body, as spells are stored in one's etheric body – even though spells may affect astral matter. Nevertheless, casting spells *into* the astral planes *alone* without connection to the physical and etheric is not possible; and if it were possible, it would be pointless. The only exception to this is charm magic, as the charms themselves exist in the astral planes, but they are nonetheless generally *cast* while in the physical realm as a physical entity. Even when cast in the astral, the whole purpose of the charm is to affect physical matter, not other astral properties. Otherwise, if they are in the astral realm, a mage may as well just create normal (non-magic) astral thoughtforms.

For some magic (like conjuration), sometimes the mage has to first create pure imaginations in the mind first before properly constructing them in the astral. While the mage is constructing a spell, a negative entity may be able to latch on to the mage and thus affect the meditation; but the entity would not fully enter the mage's mind (unless possession occurs). The mage may still recognize what is happening due to their powerful unconscious mind; consequently, they may create a negative entity in their mind through the their own imagination. That is, the experience of the negative entity in the mind is just their imagination *based* on what is *actually* happening. Fortunately, such encounters with negative entities are not ordinary for most mages (especially for beginners), including when creating in the astral. This general lack of negative interactions has nothing to do with the number of negative beings in the astral (because there are, in fact, *countless* negative entities in the astral). Also, when a past trauma or extremely-negative thought does emerge, typically, the meditation will immediately end, so meditation practice *itself* is not dangerous or detrimental to a mage's wellbeing (unless, for example, it is coupled with certain drugs).

Even though mental creations are subjective, they still objectively *exist*, and mages must always adhere to objective universals – despite how complex and infinite in their creations they can appear. Put another way for understanding, these universals are the universal patterns found in the formation of matter itself and its phenomena thereafter, so no arbitrary geometric forms may be sufficient – despite, again, there being an infinite number of combinations available. Each pattern will be different, but the nuanced point to understand is that they still all adhere to universal laws. The outer, objective world vetoes and limits the results from the creative potentialities of the mind's inner world of subjectivity. For this reason, all mages study the same knowledge for creating spells. This process does not just revolve around the *types* of geometric shapes needed but also *where*, exactly, to place geometric forms and points in relation to one another.

Even when universals are adhered to, faulty or poor spells can, indeed, be made. Their effects, however, are not arbitrary; rather, a spell's intended effects to its actual outcome simply are not the same as a result, but the universal law of patterns universally creates such effects regardless of who casts it. Rephrased, for the spell itself, any and all patterns, whether constructed well or not, will universally create good or poor effects or outcomes. Of course, if no constructions are made, then no poor effects will occur, as the spell will not even work at all. Mages do not just study basic forms and memorize them; the focus of their studies is to understand *appropriate* geometries, which they have to figure out whilst in meditation.

Mages, therefore, cannot simply learn a standard set of geometries and then 'copy and paste' them in the mind from their subconscious (which saw them earlier in physical reality) without using their critical thinking abilities. Mages study and remember universal constants which then have to be *judiciously* applied to a variety of etheric or astral fields, as contexts will vary. To create the geometric forms in their etheric and astral auras, mages may enhance the size of their creations and shrink them back down again so they can fully see what they are creating. Even though created patterns are stored in the etheric body – which a mage may be able to return to in multiple meditation sessions – the subconscious stores patterns, too, in turn affecting the etheric.

Merely learning geometric forms is not enough to help create or tune into them when spell crafting, nor is it enough to utilize the magic. All mages have various *power levels*, which ultimately come down to one's levels of consciousness. In short, a mage has an *overall power level* (OPL), with all of their magics relatively (though not necessarily equally) corresponding (scaling) with it. That is, power levels vary (though correspond) for one's *individual* schools of magic, (sub)disciplines therein, and the different *aptitude aspects* of magic. The main aptitude aspects of magic are: *spell creation aptitudes; aether connection aptitudes; energy and spell storing aptitudes; casting/ channelling aptitudes;* and *ACE aptitudes*. Besides spell creation aptitudes, these still apply to phasarchement, except instead of 'energy and spell storage', there is just *energy storage*. For more information on power levels and rankings, see *Section 3.6.2*, as *some* of this information still applies to the GAP schools of magic of conjuration, mysticism, charms, and alchemy, despite its focus on phasarchement magic. The following information in this subsection regarding spell creation, spell storage, casting, charging, power levels, and energy costs primarily do not apply to phasarchement (unless otherwise noted), even though there are still *fundamental* similarities.

Spell creation aptitude power levels do not properly scale with the other aptitude aspects. However, all mages face varying limits as to what they can *tune* into and create when creating spells – according to their power levels. While there technically is an issue for non-aligning mages *creating* spells of different schools, this is only marginal – if at all a problem. The main problems for non-aligning mages rest with both *storing* spells in their etheric auras and then *casting* them; these alignment modifiers, mean-while, do not apply to ACE aptitudes (explained later in this subsection). While a mage may be able to store some spells of a non-aligned school, they certainly would not be able to store stronger spells of said school in their aura. Even then, they would not be able to store *many* weaker spells of a non-aligning school, either.

Spells are able to be stored indefinitely until later intentionally (and in some cases, unintentionally) removed – usually for the purpose of replacing it with another spell. However, if one's aura becomes weaker, then stored spells may fade away. Never-theless, there is a phenomenon called *etheric memory*, which is akin to muscle memory (where if one's physical muscles shrink through lack of exercise, the person may be able to easily regain their muscles through later exercise). So, if a mage loses a spell, they may be able to regain it later, but this still requires effort. The plus side to this is that it usually takes less effort to regain the spell than to remake it – assuming a few factors, such as their auras having regained their former strength.

Mages also need to be able to vibrationally *tune* into and align with these geometric forms to *cast* them, and, thus, a scholarly mage of a different arch-element will still find it hard casting from an unaligned school of magic. Even when a mage aligns with a particular school of magic, this does not mean that they will be able to store an infinite number of spells in their auras, nor does it mean they could tune into spells stronger than their power level (and either store or cast them). There are also, more specifically, *spell power types* (SPTs) and *spell energy requirements* (SERs). SPTs refer to the type of power level required to tune into and/or cast the spell, whereas SERs refer to how much energy each spell demands for casting. An average-powered mage can cast a spell with an average SPT, but this does not mean that the spell will necessarily have an average SER. Unfortunately for mages, there is an issue of *overcharging*, where the energy in one's GAP will not channel properly while powering the spell, thus going to waste. This, in turn, ends up *effectively* costing the caster more energy than the spell should otherwise universally cost. This channelling aptitude problem does not quite apply to charms as well, but charmers can still waste their own astral energies when creating their charms, anyway.

In the case of where the average SPT has a novice-level (that is, low) SER, the SER will match the SPT, as the energy will basically leak out into the etheric while channelling. The same goes for any SER that is below the SPT of any power level. For this reason, it is easier, in most cases, to just refer to a spell by its power level (such as, 'an average(-powered) spell'); but for the sake of accuracy and precision, both should be taken into account. Overcharging also occurs for other issues, too. Spells also have *creation energy costs* (CECs) and *maintenance energy costs* (MECs), where the CECs are normally more expensive than the MECs if the spell is short-lived. The abovesaid issue applies to both CECs and MECs.

Spells do not 'finish' either; instead, they either stop being fuelled (with the mage either running out of energy for MECs, or they choose to stop the fuelling the spell, or the user may even lose consciousness), or the spell itself *overloads*. A spell itself can overload if it has been in use for too long, relative to its power level; alternatively, a spell may overload if it is recast consecutively too often. In these cases, there is an issue with the aura (etheric energy), not the physical substance itself (such as of a conjured item, which may overload in another way, such as if it is an electronic device that short-circuits). When a spell overloads, a 'penalty' occurs, preventing the mage from casting the spell (but not all spells) again; and this normally begins at roughly nine seconds for most mages for most spells before increasing greatly for each time the spell is used thereafter before it (the aura) fully cools down.

The average (powered) mage can store four average-powered spells in their aura from an aligning school of magic and one novice-powered spell from each of the non-aligning schools (again, bar phasarchement). This alignment problem, though, does not greatly apply to *moving* charms (or affecting them in particular ways), but it does apply to *storing* them; this includes both the number and strength of the charms. Although the said mage would be limited to one novice spell, this would not mean, for instance, that the said mage could store an infinite number of *extremely-weak* spells (of any alignment). That is, there is still a cut-off point. While it may not seem like much of an issue not being able to create many extremely-weak spells, some conjured items, for example, may be extremely useful, even if low-powered, so having many types of conjured items would otherwise indeed help one in a multitude of ways.

If a mage creates a more powerful spell than their (the mage's) power level, then this naturally will take away from the ability to store other spells. However, the issue is not always clear cut, and so, if a mage attempts to store more spells than their normal capacity, then their auras may still be able to store them without necessarily pushing out older spells. Nevertheless, the heavy load of (higher-than-one's normal power level) spells in their etheric body, in this case (which will appear as a giant web or convoluted tapestry – even for advanced mages with lots of spells), will cause distortions and, thus, channelling *instabilities*. Resultingly, when a mage attempts to cast any spell, there will be a chance that it might not work at all, with the spell either fully working or fully failing.

In other words, bad storage issues will lead to channelling issues for all spells, giving each a *base* instability chance modifier, with other instability modifiers being added to the base as a result of other problems. While the etheric body will experience problems, it is specifically the *channelling* of the spells that experiences the problem in question. This means that if a spell fails due to a channelling instability, a mage can still not only continue casting any active, currently-cast spells (that were successfully created) but also other spells than the one that failed. For example, if a mage has a problematic aura with all spells having a base instability rate of 60%, then proceeds to cast – and continue to cast – Spell A with success, they may then try to cast Spell B and fail. In this case, Spell A would continue being cast while the mage may try to cast Spell C, which would still have the 60% instability chance (assuming it has no other modifiers).

Even without a heavy load of (bad or good) spells, instabilities occur for mages trying to cast spells beyond their power level, anyway. Therefore, increasing one's channelling aptitude decreases channelling instabilities and, thus, enables one to cast higher-powered spells. In the event that a spell does not work on casting (as a result of an instability), there will be a (generally small) 'cooldown' period before the mage may attempt casting again; usually, this is only about three seconds for most mages and for most spells. This may seem small, but in certain contexts requiring immediate action, this could be the difference between life and death. Moreover, if the spell is very hard to cast (with a probability of success being a mere 6%, for example), one may be casting for quite some time, as those three seconds for each period of failure will add up.

After the instability cooldown, the same chance rate will apply as before the failure, so one needs to be careful in avoiding what is known as the *gambler's fallacy*, thinking that the chance rate will improve after each attempt. Nevertheless, there are nuanced considerations to this that may complexify the issue, such as when a mage's power level may increase marginally as a result of repeated casting, in turn leading to a slightly altered chance rate. Still, increasing one's power level after failure *itself* virtually never happens. There may also be other etheric anomalies to consider in regards to instability alterations; but even then, these anomalies may actually decrease one's odds of success. Various attacks and other phenomena that affect one's consciousness may also contribute to varying instability problems.

Despite the average mage only being able to practically store four spells of an aligning school of magic in their auras at once, this is not the same as them (the mage) casting various spells at once – which also has a limit. The average mage happens to also be able to cast four spells (of any power level) from any of the general schools of magic at once before experiencing instabilities trying to cast additional spells. Possessing a poorly-created spell (that is not more powerful than one's power level) will typically not cause instability issues for other spells merely being in one's aura; however, the spell in question would potentially have instability issues itself when being cast. Casting instabilities do not occur for charm magic (including when acquiring charms), but charms *themselves* may become unstable. For alchemy, enchanted items themselves may also have instabilities, but this is a different matter to the powering (casting) of a transfiguration, where instabilities may also occur if the transfiguration is more powerful than the mage's power level.

Spells also take time to be *charged* up before they manifest. The charging process is itself a *phase state*, also known as *spell phasing*. One's OPL or aptitude power level does not affect the charge time of a spell itself, as all times, relative to the power of the spell, are universal. So, a more powerful spell itself will still universally take more time to cast for any mage than a less powerful spell itself. Of course, interruptions may occur during the charge (such as a mage being majorly distracted or punched), where the spell stops charging and needs to be restarted (so, spells cannot be paused while charging). When this occurs, a new CEC is required, with all CECs being applied at the start of the charge, not the end, so the previous energy that went to the CEC will be totally lost (that is, it will not go back to the user's aura).

This is not too detrimental, as most mages can recover their energy while they wait for the spell to charge; if the mage is not simultaneously using phasarchement magic, then they may even be able to totally recharge their energy before the spell finishes charging, so they (the mage) would only have to then effectively pay MECs. Therefore, powerful spells that require long charge times are still feasible in terms of costs. Tied with the depletion penalty if depleted of energy, mages may have to wait even longer, where they can still recharge in the meantime; still, mages can tell when they are about to deplete, and normally they will stop their spells before this occurs.

The average-powered conjuration, mysticism, and alchemy spell usually takes about seven seconds to charge and physically manifest without interruptions. Moreover, these spells will also universally cost the same amount of aether energy (respectively for their CECs and MECs), regardless of a mage's power level. Despite this, a more powerful spell will still universally cost more to cast for any mage than a less powerful spell. However, more powerful spells, relative to the individual, will also lead to overcharging costs, both for CECs and MECs. Even though charging does not apply to charm magic, placing charms still typically takes varying amounts of time.

Each mage has different GAP sizes, too (as part of their storing aptitude), so more powerful mages can afford to cast more spells. Aside from charms, the average spell from the aforesaid schools will also cost the average mage about 2% of their energy from their GAP per second. The aether connection aptitude, conversely, determines the recharge speed and exhaustion parameters. With an average GAP recharge rate of 0.8333% per second for the average mage while connected to the Aether (and 0.4167% per second when simultaneously using consistent phasarchement magic up until the lumarchetrix is full), this means that an average mage can cast an average-powered spell for 85.7 seconds (or 63.2 seconds in the latter case) before reaching depletion of their GAP – assuming CECs are not a problem (that is, not counted).

Unlike phasarchement magic, a mage cannot just lower (or increase) the power level of an already-constructed spell, so if they want a weaker spell that lasts longer, they will need to construct a new spell rather than merely channelling a weaker version of an established spell. Accordingly, *default power levels* do not apply for GAP magics; instead, 'power levels' alone are measured. Mages also have a maximum amount of aether energy that they can channel into the physical world at once. The maximum *channelling rate* for the average mage is 33% of their GAP per second, and most mages (of all power levels) practically never reach this threshold when casting magic.

A mage also establishes an *area of conscious effect* (ACE) with their spells, which extends from their very being (specifically, from the *location* of their physical body, in nearly all cases), and it is slightly (but categorically) different to a standard *area of effect* (AOE), which is not itself ontologically *based* on consciousness. However, the AOE will normally be only inside the ACE, so the former is still *bound* to the effects of conscious-ness. Of course, there are exceptions, such the gravitational field of an item. The ACE determines the spatial range of the spell that a mage can consciously exert a spell into without it disappearing back into the Aether, whereas the AOE determines the spatial area of what the spell itself (and any properties therein) may affect in its given area.

One's level of consciousness determines the size of the ACE, but generally, an ACE will be circular (spherical) in shape and about three metres in diameter. Regardless of the size (and shape), a mage will always use the same amount of aether energy per unit of measurement along the ACE's diameter (or equivalent). Parts of already-manifested spells, nevertheless, *may* temporarily (but only very shortly) last *outside* of the ACE due to their quantum particles possessing certain key traits that have etheric energy that 'stores' conscious energy. Basically, the spell part will have *phased momentum*, but the user will no longer control of fuel it. Mages can even *consciously* project tiny shells *of* their ACE out, which requires great concentration, so this is another way some conjured matter, like bullets, can temporarily last outside the ACE. In both cases, this allows for certain things like conjured bullets to leave the ACE and hit their targets. Even charms have an ACE, though the charmer does not have to be present.

Within an ACE, a mage normally exerts total conscious strength, unless there are unusual distortions or *particular* (but not all) 'blockages'. Therefore, the perimeter's cut-off point off is absolute, not gradual. An ACE is also different from a *spell's central area* (SCA), which is where the central body of the spell is located. The centre of a spell's cymatic patterns will determine the SCA; and during the phase state of a spell while charging, the SCA may be moved around in the air via the user's mind. So, if the SCA leaves the ACE, then the spell will end. The spell, in this case, will not begin again when it re-enters the ACE because it would not even exist anymore at that moment. Basically, the spell would have to be recast with a new CEC. If the SCA only happened to be at the ACE's edges, it would not flicker on and off, and, instead, it would either be fully active or not. If only a portion of the matter from a spell leaves the ACE, then the rest of the spell can still continue being cast (just, now, without the portion that left the ACE). Also important to note: a mage either can or cannot channel a spell; they do not channel a spell to a degree.

When a spell is being charged or if it is active, a user will also be able to see the etheric energy of their spell (that is, the fluorescent geometry) in their aura – even if the mage is not adept at psychicism. This results from the magic gland exciting their (the user's) ability to see more energy. However, this will only be of their own etheric aura, not of other etheric energies, and even then, it will be severely limited to the point where the mage will only see the spell and not other activity in their etheric aura. No-one else, of course, will be able to see the etheric side of the spell.

There are also miscellaneous *skills* and *traits* (with various abbreviation sets for each type therein) outside of both magic schools and aptitude aspects that sometimes correspond with power levels. For example, the majority of mages will use their hands when casting spells. Scholars are not exactly sure why this is the case, but most believe it is because hands act as the mind's manual liaison tools in daily life. When one thinks of changing something in general, they use their hands. There is a powerful subconscious connection between the hands and the mind, and the latter naturally uses such utensils to further its goals. Given that spells do not emerge from any part of the body, the mind automatically uses its best/most utilized interface tools – the hands. Advanced mages, however, do not always use their hands, and, instead, they may solely use their minds.

However, of these advanced mages (when they happen to not use their hands), a significant number will focus on a spell using their eyes, with the reason being obvious: magic is conscious-based, and vision (via the eyes) is a window for consciousness. The advancement of a mage, in this context, is not distinctly tied to one's power levels, but they are *correlated*, so not using hands is instead more of a skill than what is considered an aptitude aspect. For all schools of magic (including phasarchement), other assorted mnemonic triggers can help greatly when casting magic, such as tightening certain muscles, as this can trigger one's consciousness in particular ways.

In order to increase (default) power levels, a mage has to practice both raising their consciousness itself *and* that which requires such consciousness (i.e., magic). However, simply performing the latter does not necessarily mean that one will become stronger, but it is, nonetheless, a prerequisite to becoming stronger. The former may also increase the power levels of casting magic, but casting magic itself is generally better for increasing power levels. Also, when a mage increases their power levels of particular energies that are cast/channelled, they are not increasing the power of that which has been or is being channelled (such as a conjured item or a portal); but rather, it is still their consciousness that increases for that particular magic or aptitude aspect, which *in turn* causes greater (or allows for the potential of greater) forms to be cast or channelled.

Power levels ultimately *scale* for all magic when increases are made; so, a mage who increases their power level in one magical aptitude aspect or school will also increase their other aptitude aspects and schools. This scaling, however, is not equal, both in terms of each school raising in power equally and each aptitude aspect having the same power levels (due to the different nature of each type of aptitude aspect). That is, all aspects to one's magic increases are on an individual basis. For example, the aether connection aptitude aspect does not have the 'same power' as an ACE simply because they are both two different categories. Nevertheless, since aptitude aspects are still all bound to the level of one's consciousness, all aptitude aspects are fundamentally tied to one another, thus scaling still occurs.

So, if a mage only focuses on phasarchement magic, then they will still become stronger in that school compared to other schools of magic. Moreover, since there are divisions within schools of magic, this also means that particular types of channelled energy used will be slightly stronger than other types. For example, in phasarchement magic, there are six types of channelled forms, so if a mage were to use only a particular kind of power in phasarchement, they would then be more proficient at that specific type of energy. But because all powers scale, a mage technically *could* practically never use a particular phasarchement type of energy, yet they may be proficient in it because their overall power levels have increased.

Still, in most cases, a very short moment of *accustomization* is needed for a never-used type of energy before it can then be used at scaled power levels. The same applies to the (sub)disciplines of other magics, such as mysticism's perception and synthesization disciplines. Despite a mage being able to experience a significant increase in power levels, a non-aligning school of magic will still be significantly weaker than one's aligning school of magic. So, even at supreme OPLs, supreme--powered mages cannot cast supreme-powered spells from non-aligned schools. A very powerful mage, nevertheless, may still be more proficient in a non-aligning magic than a weak mage with their aligning school.

Nevertheless, in order to *practically* increase one's power levels, usage of other (sub)disciplines (or, in the above case with phasarchement, other types of energy) are generally required to be used in order to step out of a 'training rut'. The primary way to increase power levels (besides *simply* casting magic, which is generally inefficient timewise) is to cast magic under harder or harsher conditions than normal. For example, being in a stressful situation, such as in combat while using magic, can help raise one's consciousness, or it can even put pressure on one's consciousness, thus requiring it to push its limits to meet its (default) power levels. Afterwards, there then can be a slight increase in one's power levels. Other examples may include overcoming distracting scenarios that otherwise would captivate one's consciousness. Alternatively, casting magic under increased gravity or while underwater or while under the influence of toxic substances can produce effective results. Even with training in harsher conditions, this does not necessarily mean one's power levels will increase.

There is also the chance for a mage to enter into *flash meditation* when using their magic, which involves what the name suggests, and it lasts about a second on average. One does not simply enter into a flash meditation, and the phenomenon itself requires conscious effort to achieve while a mage is fully conscious and casting magic. It is a special kind of meditation that focuses on increasing one's consciousness, but a method that simultaneously allows the user to be conscious enough to still cast the magic. In such a very deep state, a mage can reach new conscious heights, thereby potentially increasing their power levels. If this can be achieved in heated situations (like combat), it becomes more effective.

Once certain actions have been executed in particular contexts and ways, *etheric event packages* (EEPs) may emerge, which are concentrations of *special* etheric energy holding particular etheric data that contain higher probability variances that can influence one's consciousness to attain new levels. As the name suggests, the EEPs contain etheric data on events, which result from when the mage (successfully) accomplishes both rare and extraordinary feats, such as defying situations that would have otherwise resulted in them being hit (for example, in the context of combat). Likewise, mages may execute certain combos (on opponents) or perform their magic while doing extreme acrobatics. Once a mage collects these EEPs by making direct contact with them *and* tuning into their energies, there is a chance for an indefinite increase in power levels. Note that EEPs are not needed to increase one's power levels; they are, instead, able to *better* increase power levels (that is, the increases in power are greater than normal).

There are also *etheric property packages* (EPPs), which can be attained from rare but interesting properties that may produce these. For example, a massive, rare explosion in nature *might* produce an EPP. Still, these EPPs rarely result in an increase in power levels; and when they do, it is generally extremely marginal. Technically, EEPs and EPPs occur all the time, but the majority that form have power levels that are so minuscule that they may as well not even exist; thus, the EEPs and EPPs in question are of a *special* nature, where they should potentially be called SEEPs or SEPPs; but since the terms are normally only used within the context of increasing power levels, the three-letter abbreviations aptly apply. A mage does not have to be using magic to achieve an EEP or an EPP, nor do they *when* collecting them, but without magic in both contexts, it is hard to increase one's power levels specifically for magic.

When one increases their power levels, they do not simply jump from a distinct, noticeable stage like 'average' to 'elite'; instead, all increases are incremental, and all terms like 'average' are relative constructions based on objective tangible measurements (again, for more information, see *Section 3.6.2*). For phasarchement magic specifically, if one uses *higher power levels* – especially in combination with all of the aforementioned methods – then there is also a greater chance for an increase in one's *default power level*. While typically mages accordingly focus on phasarchement to increase their overall power levels for all magic, it is generally the case that taking an all-round approach by using all schools of magic for training is ideal when increasing overall power levels.

## 3.2: School of Mysticism:

Although psychicism is not a school of magic, *mysticism* magic harnesses aspects of psychic phenomena, making them more available to the caster. The key difference is that mysticism magic does not come through natural means nor psychic training; instead, it involves a thorough process of creation and casting. Moreover, mysticism holds other powers that extend beyond psychic phenomena. Nevertheless, due to the creation process, mysticism has a stricter nature than pure psychicism (which can *seem* arbitrary at times). The major disciplines of mysticism magic include: *perception, bonding,* and *synthesization.* These groupings are also not mere easy socially-constructed identifiers, as the spells therein feature distinct geometries from one another. Each is also technically on a spectrum, and so, they also have a corresponding opposite, which are: *ignorance, disconnection,* and *entropy.* However, these opposites are still part of the same aforesaid disciplines. Mysticism uses and connects physical, etheric, and astral energies, all the while harnessing aether energy to fuel the magic. Spells do not necessarily have to affect the user, and they can intentionally or unintentionally affect other beings (whether for positive or negative outcomes). Basically, a mystic can *cast* spells *on* (other) people or things.

The first discipline, perception, is broken into two subdisciplines or categories: *awareness* and *comprehension.* Awareness spells allow the caster to see physical, etheric, or astral entities and properties that they would not otherwise see. For example, an awareness spell may help the mystic see a key hidden in a room, or the mystic may see a camouflaged person – or, in some cases, the mystic may see things behind multiple walls. In contrast to pure psychicism, where a psychic will see the etheric energies of a targeted item (like the said key), mysticism spells will generate *etheric overlays* of the target in the *mystic's* etheric body (aura), which the mystic will be able to see without further psychic exercise. Basically, the mystic will see an etheric *copy* of the etheric energy of the key, but they will not see the key's actual etheric energy. Sometimes, the mystic may (only) see mental images without seeing their own etheric body.

Etheric overlays are seen around the actual targeted item (that is, in the physical location and direction of the target), but due to the nature of the copy, this will not necessarily be accurate in its location, which is also further hampered by the fact that the etheric is less localized than the physical (despite there being definite locations) – all coupled with other viewable probable states. Moreover, some etheric copies may simply be seen in the mystic's etheric body without the mystic looking at the targeted item. In the case of seeing an astral entity, the mystic will only see it via either their etheric and/or astral body. Even if the mystic were to attempt casting the spell while fully astral *travelling* (which is not, in all practicality, possible, as one needs an etheric body to cast *mage spells*), then the pursuit would be pointless, as the mystic would be seeing the astral as it is, anyway.

Comprehension spells, on the other hand, connect to *data* as well, involving matters such as: languages; dreams; identification (of particular missing entities, for example); understanding patterns (pattern sense/recognition); ascertainment (of finding the right or relevant pathways for certain purposes – literal and analogous – for example); and gaining insights on matters such as the esoteric. The mystic, again, will never receive the actual phenomenon in its actuality, and so, all such magic will only deliver distorted results via analogy. The mystic also faces the issue of their own personal biases clouding their vision, along with being able to distort the *effects* of the spell (not the spell itself). Because the etheric information in the mystic's aura will be copied from etheric energy itself (which contains various connections to other probable realities), the copy, in this case as well, will possibly contain information on other probable states the target's etheric energy may possess. On top of this, other magic (such as charm magic) can also twist the mystic's perceptions. Therefore, great caution is always necessary.

A mystic may use a comprehension spell to try to interpret an unknown language, and identifiable words (of the mystic's own language) may appear to them visually or audibly, but these would be limited interpretations. Explicitly, the mystic would convert the words into their own language, but their own language might not have the most accurate words for what the original words meant. As another problematic example, a mystic may have to decide upon choosing between three pathways in a cave to walk through; and while the mystic may be able to comprehend etheric clues as to what each pathway may lead to, they might also pick up on the previous energy of the people who travelled through the cave. However, these previous people – even if from multiple, separate groups – may have been walking into a trap, and so, by thinking that more energy equals the correct path, the mystic may be mistaken.

In contrast to the discipline of perception, spells that induce ignorance essentially lower one's awareness and comprehension of a targeted being. Of course, care must still be taken with using such spells. For example, if the mystic attempted to lower the perception of an opponent mage, the latter could end up doing something very different (and unpredictable – and, thus, unaccounted for) as a result. A mystic, interestingly, might benefit from casting an ignorance spell on themselves in certain circumstances; for example, in cases where (opponent) psychic mages may be able to determine who is aware of certain things (or react to particular stimuli), the user can avoid being detected, as they would be unaware of said certain things (and, thus, may not react to said particular stimuli).

The second discipline of mysticism, bonding, also possesses crossovers with psychic phenomena, and while it can be stronger than psychicism, it also has other limitations.

Bonding spells include: empathy (being able to feel what other beings are feeling – or have felt or will feel); memory extraction and sharing; *scrying* (seeing through the first or third-person perspective of people or objects); telepathy, along with comm-unication (of different types) with other entities, such as animals, plants, and spirits (also known as *mediumship*); calling upon nature for aid; absorbing and sending energies (etheric and astral); and then there are (darker) subdisciplines, which include *necrourgy*, blood practices, and various figurine-based activities (which all still require explicit appropriate physical substances, as they are also used outside the context of mysticism magic). As with the perception discipline, any communication with bonding will suffer from distortions, both audibly and what the real messages contain. For example, with memory extraction, the caster's subconscious mind could alter the memory, implanting their own memories or imaginations into it.

With mediumship, there are always unintentional channel distortions, along with potential intentional distortions (generally *from* the astral). While necrourgy may involve communication with the dead, necrourgy is not itself communication with the dead. Essentially, necrourgy is the art of (or technique for) working with the dead, so it includes many practices. Most necrourgic practices, however, involve either creating *necrotics* (see *Section 4.3.2.6* for more details) or extracting etheric energy from *ghosts* for various purposes. In the case of mysticism, bonding a spirit to a body will help establish a necrotic. Note that necrourgy is not in itself immoral, but it does contain many dark practices, which are listed as *black necrourgy*. While necrourgy is not limited to mysticism (nor magic, for that matter), mystics usually perform the greatest amount of necrourgy, as the other schools of magic are either not that effective (like charms), too indirect (again, charms), or not applicable. Of course, this is not to say that most mystics perform necrourgy. While conjurers cannot conjure necrotics, alchemists can change organic tissue into necrotic tissue, but this itself is not necrourgy. Still, for this reason, mystics are sometimes either highly sought out or distrusted in particular contexts.

Even with good intentions, there are many dangers to the bonding discipline. For example, bonding to someone who has a sickness may result in the user becoming sick to a degree as well. Moreover, there is a greater chance of third parties being affected by bonding spells compared to the other mysticism disciplines. At least, though, bonding has its limits. For example, a mystic cannot simply use a sewing pin and stick it into a doll to kill someone; however, this is not to say that some etheric activity would not occur; it is, instead, that even when certain etheric activity occurs, there are certain thresholds that are required to be passed in order to successfully cause particular effects. That is, any degree below said thresholds would not even successfully cause any effect of that particular kind of effect (such as death). Separation spells, in contrast, basically cut off communications and connections that a caster or target may possess – with caution, again, needed with using these, too.

The last discipline, synthesization, is split into two subdisciplines called *restoration* and *composition*. Essentially, restoration spells restore certain properties back to their original state. Synthesization would be an extremely powerful magic if it was limitless, as one could, for example, hypothetically revert an opponent back to being a baby and then easily defeat them. However, such powers are well beyond what mages are capable of performing; and basically, the more complex an item is (along with the amount of 'damage' the item has received relative to the original state), the harder it is for the mystic to restore it. So, not only does the mystic only restore certain properties to a degree, but they may only be able to restore said properties in a particular way; or, they may only restore partial amounts of the properties.

Standard restoration magic is used to heal beings of sicknesses and injuries, while other spells can restore broken objects to their former state. Restoration magic essentially performs these 'miracles' by connecting to the entity's various etheric realities, drawing upon the available 'healthier' realities and then synthesizing either aspects or the totality of that reality into the current one to heal the entity. It does this via particular vibrations, causing matter to form and reform in a particular way (to that of the healthier reality). These healing vibrations are a different matter to the school of alchemy's total reality-swapping phenomenon (known as *transfiguration* or *shapeshifting*), which enables a mage, for example, to form bird wings on their body. In regards to mysticism spells, these vibrations work through the quantum level, in turn affecting the chemical structures of whatever is being restored. For entropy spells, the mystic can damage a perfectly sound object or person, drawing upon other realities (which may not necessarily be of the past but of alternative or future realities) to send destructive vibrations to the target. Given that restoration is limited, the destructive nature and power of entropy spells is also limited.

Composition spells, on the other hand, are greatly used within rituals. Accordingly, mystics tend to either lead rituals or be deeply involved with them. Essentially, casters connect etheric and astral energies to the physical and then synthesize material patterns and patterned energies to either realm. So, if the mystic wished to understand a particular energy in the etheric, they would connect to it and then synthesize a cymatic pattern in the physical realm (usually with a liquid like water or blood, but sand or salt works well, too). Such physical cymatic patterns and symbols would hold rudimentary (meta)data about the etheric energy, which then needs to be interpreted by the mystic (which can be further understood with perception magic). Alternatively, the caster could synthesize a pattern from the physical to the etheric in order to help with a ritual, in turn using that to alter the etheric. That is, the mystic would synthesize a needed energy from the etheric, which they might otherwise not have proper access to (or understanding of), and then they would ultimately redirect the altered pattern back into the etheric for their own gain.

Technically, physical energies (of any reality) can also be synthesized across to another physical location via quantum entanglement as a *basis* for other phenomena. Powerful mages are even able to form things such as faces out of properties like sand that can 'talk'. In such cases, it could either be the caster who talks or another entity. In order for the face to be audible, either the materials must be able to make sounds (such as water gurgling to give the semblance of audible language) or further perception magic is needed to interpret the speech. Entropy spells for composition, on the other hand, are primarily distortion based and can be used to send energy into the etheric to ruin a ritual, for instance. Alternatively, entropy spells could be used to distort an overwhelming etheric or negative energy before it gets synthesized into the physical.

For all of these cases of composition spells, the Aether powers the process, so the mystic is not pulling energy from the etheric and then throwing it into the physical. That is, if a cymatic pattern emerges in the physical based on the etheric, it would be the aether energy that moves the physical, not the etheric. It is only for brevity that people may say 'sending energy to-and-fro'. The Aether produces physical energy, and this physical energy naturally has the ability to cause matter to move. The spells also, more specifically, cause the physical energy to move and act in a particular way.

While mysticism has three main disciplines, there are two kinds of spell styles: *general* and *custom*. General mysticism spells are normally easier to make and can be used in many different contexts repeatedly, whereas customized spells *tend* to be single-use and are harder to make. However, general spells are less effective than customized spells for their respective matters. For example, a general restoration spell might be useful for healing general wounds, while a custom spell may effectively heal an extraordinarily-caused wound that would not otherwise heal due to some strange chemical preventing the tissue from reforming. In the latter case, the mystic would spend more time finding the nuances of the health issue and tailor the spell accordingly. Nevertheless, both general and custom spells can be either weak or strong; and even then, strong custom spells may be partially or completely ineffective for wounds which they were not customized for (even for similar health issues) due to their fine-tuned nature being unable to deal with anything outside of their programming. Moreover, a novice mage can still create a custom spell, while advanced mages can still – and often do – create general spells.

The mystic must first decide which type of spell style they want (general or custom), along with the discipline. For general spells, the mystic does not have to focus on any other entity other than their own etheric and astral fields (their auras) during the creation process. The first step for creating general spells involves the mage entering meditation before accessing their *immediate* astral field (their astral body). The mystic then has to focus on the vibrational nature of their intended discipline, which then forms a *cloud* of astral energy that vibrates roughly with the kind of magic that they want. From this cloud, the mage begins to stretch and 'solidify' it, which causes it to form into a *tunnel* with variously-sized and densified energy particles. These particles then form the basis for the *nodes*, which the mystic has to geometrically connect.

Prior to the meditation, the mystic should have studied the universal constants of various geometries and patterns in order to figure out how their spell should be crafted. With their minds, the mystic begins moving the particles before stretching their energy out to form geometric lines between them. Although the nodes and the tunnel itself will have the vibrational signature of the discipline's energy type, the geometries themselves are not only needed, but they can actually greatly alter the spell to the point of potentially changing the very discipline's energy. Each geometric line will have a fluorescent, holographic appearance and will vibrate at different levels (which the creator can feel) when formed in particular ways. Depending on the type and strength of the spell, the tunnel may morph into multiple tunnels.

A tunnel's ultimate role is to connect *to* something. Accordingly, once the main geometries have been established, the mystic then has to establish what is known as the *synchronizers* – or simply hooks or connectors. The synchronizers still require geometric shapes to operate as well, but these forms are denser and more complex than those in the tunnel. These synchronizers will either attach to alternate realities or alternate entities within the reality the mystic is currently in – including either the physical, etheric, or astral. The tunnel geometries, on the other hand, are meant to alter the channelling of energy from one reality or entity to another. Although naturally this does create 'distortions', this is not the sole reason for the aforementioned distortion issues (*while* channelling/casting a spell) that a mystic may encounter. In other words, the distortions in *this* context (*altering* channelled energy) are not only good but necessary in order for the spell to perform and function in a certain way.

Even if either the tunnel or the synchronizer has the right geometries while one does not, then the spell will either not work properly or at all. That is, it will either have a potential fail rate on creation or a complete fail rate. Sometimes, though, both will work, but they may channel the wrong (unintended) kinds of energies; but if a spell *does* channel the wrong kinds of energies (which is uncommon but not rare), it will *always* channel such energies, so there is no risk of a spell *becoming* bad when casting it again or even during a casting period itself. In other words, since spells are stored, the spell will always be good in itself – *if* the spell is good. Still, because of this, mystics cast practice spells in safe areas *first* before properly using them for the first time. For certain restoration spells, mystics usually practice on rats first.

When this stage has been completed, the mystic then proceeds to transfer the astral blueprint to their etheric aura, in turn causing the spell to become indefinitely attached to them. Note that spells can only be found within the user's own aura, not other auras, even though the spells can connect to other auras. This process takes practice, as the transfer itself will result in distortions of varying levels (especially the more complex the spell), which then need fixing via the astral or the etheric. That is, the new etheric body will still have an astral overlay, which can be fixed at that frame of reference (which is easier) or the etheric (which is harder). When the geometries are distorted, normally they will be repositioned, but sometimes new geometries may form. The creation and transfer stages have to be completed in a timely manner; that is, the mystic cannot begin creating the spell, leave it half finished, and then take a break for a year. The reason for this is that the astral energies will initially distort before dissipating. However, mystics may still take many years to create a spell, so long as they regularly focus on their creation. Once the transfer is a success, the creation process for the general spell will have finished.

In order to create a custom spell, the mystic needs to focus on the particular entity that they wish to affect via the spell (such as a sick person or broken table) and tune into its etheric field. If the intended matter is purely etheric or astral (such as a thoughtform, in the latter case), the mystic has to tune into it appropriately. Subsequently, the mystic needs to induce a cymatic field (a vibrational resonance pattern that looks fluorescent and holographic) into their astral body via the targeted entity's aggregate frequency in the etheric – even if the item or being is purely an astral entity – and then the mystic has to stretch the field out into a tunnel.

The cymatic tunnel will contain the entity's etheric metadata, all found in the nuances of the interference patterns. The cymatic field's interference patterns will contain nodes from which further geometric shapes (like with general spells) can be established. Each appropriate cymatic node will have geometric shapes aligned with them, but the mystic will also create multiple geometric shapes between the nodes. Essentially, the nodes of a custom spell more accurately align the geometric shapes (not originally of the cymatic field before the user created them) with the particular properties of the targeted being or item than with what is found in a general spell. As such, there will be far more geometric shaping involved with custom spells, and there will also be more room for error, as certain nodes should and should not be connected for particular results. The same principle found in general spells also applies to the custom synchronizers, just with the cymatic nodes to consider.

After the astral form has been established, the mystic can then transfer it into their etheric aura to use as a spell. To boost their magic, the mystic can even create a custom tunnel *from* the other reality or entity to the first entity that already connects with the spell. For example, the mystic might be healing a sick person, which may be considered HRF-A, while the healthier version in another reality (normally of a previous time period of that same timeline) may be considered HRF-B. The mystic has already created the tunnel for HRF-A and does not need one for HRF-B, but creating one for HRF-B to link to HRF-A will greatly increase the strength of the overall magic.

However, creating mystical tunnels normally from other realities (or nonlocal or obscure entities in the current reality) is a much harder task, as there are several other distortions involved, and the cymatic fields are fainter in some areas while more convoluted in others due to various probability fields interlacing and overlapping the appropriate field. If the mystic does not properly create HRF-B's tunnel, then there could potentially be serious negative effects. Either way, even though the tunnels do not directly channel into the mystic's physical body, the SCA does need to remain in their ACE for the magic to actually take place.

Once the spell has been constructed, then comes the task of preparing for casting the magic – the stage known as pre-casting. This process involves the mystic again tuning into their own etheric field and then the entity(s) they wish to connect to (both for general and custom spells). When this occurs, the mage then needs to focus on connecting the tunnels with their respective realities or entities. Whilst the synchronizers can connect to the other realities, they will encounter an issue where *frictional* energy builds, in turn causing the base geometries to move (and sometimes *continue* to move). Assorted distortions will also form, and then other geometric patterns will also arise. Accordingly, the mystic needs to manually manoeuvrer the synchronizers' geometric patterns properly into place – in addition to casting out the *frictional geometries* – all the while sifting through the distortions. Naturally, the more complex the spell, the greater the hassle in dealing with these problems.

Unlike with charm, alchemy, and conjuration magic, mysticism magic requires a certain level of higher focus during the entire spell's existence when casting. That is, by remaining in tune with the intended entity, the mystic usually cannot have too many distractions. For simple and average spells, a few minor distractions will not cause the spell to falter (except for when conducted by novice mages); but for some very powerful spells, sometimes the mystic may need a few days of meditation prior to casting so that they can fully perform their magic. This focusing issue includes the time when actually casting the spell. The tunnels in a mystic's aura can appear as if tentacles, both during charging a spell and its active duration. Once a mystic has finished casting their spell, then the effects will fade away; but for certain disciplines, the *results* of a spell's powers will remain (such as a healed body). Also, once the spell finishes (that is, when the mystic stops casting it or when they run out of energy), the mystic can nevertheless skip sorting the frictional geometries when they cast the spell again, as there will be a *temporary automatic alignment* period (normally for a few hours from the last connection), allowing for instant reconnection.

To explain the whole spell process another way for clarification, it is not a simple matter of picking the right reality/state when creating custom spells. Instead, a mystic has to create various structures that will likely connect to the right state. So, general spells will automatically connect to states that the mystic typically wants (due to the nature of the spell), whereas for the custom spell, the mystic would (hopefully) find the right/appropriate reality and *then* create the appropriate geometries so that they can connect with such a state. In the case of a healing spell, identifying the problem first is paramount, of course. However, in the case of both spell types, it is also not just a matter of connecting with right/appropriate states and creating geometries; instead, it is a matter of connecting with the states in a *specific* manner – this is where specific geometries come into effect. So, merely connecting with another healthier version of a person is not enough to heal the person; the mystic has to connect with the healthier version in a specific way (with the types of geometries found in the discipline of restoration) and then further create and calibrate their geometries to heal the person in a specific way. That is, without these nuances, merely channelling the other state to the current state will not suffice in healing the person (at all).

Restoration spells are incredibly useful in some contexts while not so useful in other contexts. For this reason, medical science and technologies (and even certain herbal remedies or simple quick-fix dressings) are still currently used as a means for remedying situations that spells cannot fix. For instance, a serious injury could result in death within minutes, and sometimes the quickest and most sure-effective measure is to put the injured person on life support with appropriate technologies. It would then only be appropriate to *afterwards* create a custom spell to heal the injury in full. A general spell, in this case, might not be suitable either – despite its potential strength. The custom spell might also only partially heal the person (even if it is a strong spell), so medical apparatuses would then be used to finish the job. In saying all this, there are some restoration spells that can at least partially heal or fix certain issues that not even the most advanced medical science can fix.

Of course, it would appear as though a mystic should repeatedly use the same spell (or even use other restoration spells) in order to fully heal the patient (should normal medicine not fully heal the said patient). However, using consecutive restoration spells on a person in a specific time period is dangerous, as it can cause particular etheric and quantum distortions that can lead to problems like mutations; in rare cases, a person may turn into a *monster* (for more information on mutants and monsters, see *Section 4.3.2.4*). Even after partial healing, the patient would potentially need some-where to rest; in which case, they may as well take the opportunity to benefit from medical services and technologies while in a hospital bed.

# 3.3: School of Charms (Charmagy):

*Charm* magic (or *charmagy*) is solely of the non-Aether tier of magic, and it is also the only school that is virtually, but not completely, non-physical. Charms are essentially astral-induced illusions and manipulations that physical entities can experience. Some physical beings are technically able to sense some normal astral energies in small, weak, and distorted amounts without meditation, but the difference here is that charms are conscious alterations of the standard understanding and definition of magic, and the effects of their advanced character completely surpass all said trivial sightings and sensations. Furthermore, charms are the only magic where the intended effects are consciously experienced; that is, a wooden table in the physical realm would not experience the mental constructs of the astral, as they lack mental capacities, nor would low-level plants experience these constructs due to lacking astral bodies as well.

A charm may, for example, specifically create the illusion of a rock wall that covers a hole in the side of a cliff. The charm itself is a field that exists in the astral, connected to the etheric, in turn distorting and reorientating the quantum fabric of the physical to create greater alignments, allowing the astral energy to properly channel through to the physical. The term 'field', in this context, more aptly applies to the physical, where there is a tangible physical field with measurable spatial dimensions, whereas the astral's special dimensions are orientated and relative only by the creation of the creator's mind. The field in this example extends beyond the illusion of the rock wall, but the perception of the rock wall can only be experienced within the field itself. Still, the illusion itself does not have to be seen at all points within the field and may only appear when a person is at a particular point in the field. Even though the physical materials within the charm field are reorientated (such as the surrounding rock), only a conscious entity will see the actual illusion, primarily through their brains.

The step-by-step process of the magic begins first with the charmer (or charmager) creating the thoughtform they wish to become the charm, and then the practitioner creates a series of geometries that enable the astral energy to operate as a charm. Thoughtforms are naturally created with mere thought (conscious or not) and can be wild and arbitrary or have minds of their own. The key to making charms, however, is for the charmer to focus thoughts on creating something that they truly desire and are able to control. The more complex the intended charm, the more focus is required to create them.

Charms basically come in the following categories: *illusion, compulsion, probability, binding, awareness,* and *meta*. Illusion charms create effects that affect the brain's sense of the senses, such as visuals, sounds, or smells. Neither the actual sound (that is, gas particles in the air moving in wave motion) nor the odorant (volatilized and detectable chemicals), nor any other effect, exists physically. Compulsion charms essentially compel the target (that possesses consciousness) to go against their freewill and act according to the program of the charm. For example, a compulsion charm may compel someone to desire a particular food; alternatively, a compulsion charm may ward people away from the AOE; or, in the absolute extreme and rare cases, a charm may virtually control the affected person's movements (however, for this to occur, there has to be a problem on the end of the victim as well, so the charm per se would not ever be this strong). Charmers can even compel themselves to perform certain actions that they would otherwise not perform.

Probability charms alter probabilities (namely, probabilities at the quantum level), but, again, only for conscious entities, so this will not affect the probability of a rock itself from doing something in particular. However, it may involve rocks if conscious entities are involved. These distortions at the quantum level may simply be distortions without any intention other than a distortion itself (which would result in seeming 'randomness'); or, the distortion may reorientate fields to result in certain desired effects. This can still backfire on the charmer, so caution is needed. Even powerful probability charms are, in the end, quite limited. Binding charms, meanwhile, are contractual, where two or more participants may be hexed if they break an oath, for example. For this reason, charmers are normally present in bindings, but there may be many charmers involved to make sure the binding contract is legitimate without the potential for loopholes. Awareness charms overlap with some mysticism magic in that they help increase the target's awareness of something in particular, or they may simply just increase their consciousness in general. Finally, meta charms affect how other charms operate and are almost always placed as one of the *layers* (explained shortly in this section) within a charm that contains other effects.

Most of these 'non-visual' thoughtforms will go hand-in-hand with *sigils*. The actual symbols found in sigils are socially-constructed and are not universally applicable, but the reason why mages create sigils is that they tend to need something to focus on while powering up the thoughtform. However, while all sigils are different, as their nature is subjective, keep in mind that particular symbols are embedded into the collective unconscious, and, thus, some have been empowered over time. These symbols, moreover, have arisen *for* a reason; namely, they have universal constants. Therefore, it is much easier for the charmer to focus on a particular symbol that everyone else uses for specific effects or charms. As a result, most of the time, a certain type of charm will generally have the same sigil or at least something similar.

Once the thoughtform is complete (which can be altered later on), the next step is establishing the *conduit field geometry*. The way in which the conduit field reorientates the physical to better align up with the astral for the channelling of energies is akin to how electrons are purposely aligned up in an iron magnet with their magnetic moments to create the magnetic effect. At the quantum level, particles like electrons in the charm field are quite literally realigned *to* the etheric, which aligns with the astral. For a conscious being who enters the field, the field will affect their astral body first, in turn affecting their etheric body, which then affects the electrons in their microtubules, which then realign; subsequently, their corresponding neural networks will shift the brain's perceptions in line with the field, in turn allowing the person to perceive the astral energies. Conversely, for non-conscious matter like rocks, the field will allow the astral energies to simply 'tether' when aligned, missing the complex process of the former. For clarification, charms can *connect to* non-conscious entities (like rocks), but they do not *effectively affect* them like they do with conscious entities.

The geometry itself is a little different to how the geometries operate in the other schools of magic. With charms, the conduit field geometries are not based on projections of tangible information points, but rather, the geometries are based on energy/information *densities*. So, the more information-dense the thoughtform, the more complex the geometries required. If the complexity is not met relative to the density of the thoughtform, the channel will be too weak to allow the complete thoughtform to work as a charm. Imagine a small funnel connected to a bottle; when massive amounts of water are poured in, most will still splash outside of the funnel. The complexity of the geometry thus 'widens' the channel, so to speak. Of course, it is not simply a matter of widening the channel, as this is only one aspect.

The charm practitioner begins creating their conduit field geometry in the astral just like they would any other thoughtform. Essentially, the field geometry is a network of energetic lines connecting up points to create a complex geometric pattern. The geometry, as a whole, must encompass the thoughtform, but geometries can still penetrate the thoughtform in the centre. Although the geometry is based on densities, there are nevertheless different types of densities based on the type of thoughtform, and so, the mage must be aware of the different information they poured into the thoughtform. The alignments need to also be appropriate for the intended target, both for consciousness itself and non-conscious matter. The actual alignments themselves will glow appropriately when the energy/information of the thoughtform flows properly. The better the geometry, the better the flow of energy. If the charmer decides to alter the thoughtform later, it must be at or of a lower energy density than what the geometry allows for, otherwise, the target will not, for example, see the full illusion (if at all), and it will mostly also be distorted. However, if the thoughtform changes too much, then the density types of the geometries will have to be radically altered, and the charm will basically be started over.

After the charmer finishes the conduit field geometry, another step, the *stabilizer geometry*, is needed. Thoughtforms naturally change in shape and character all the time, even without conscious intention, especially because many possess a mind of their own. Moreover, if thoughtforms are not fed conscious energy or do not feed, they will suffer from entropy and then dissipate and perish. To avoid thoughtforms changing and dying, a stabilizer geometry keeps them intact. The complexity of the stabilizer geometry depends on the complexity of both the thoughtform and the conduit geometry, as the latter becomes too unstable the more complex it becomes. The geometry itself of the stabilizer keeps the thoughtform's natural entropy from occurring, whereas the energy itself in the geometry fuels the thoughtform. This energy, of course, comes from the mage, who pours as much of their astral energy into it as possible. Such energy is not just normal energy; it is, instead, conscious energy, which is the type of energy that thoughtforms need. It is also so highly concentrated that it becomes 'crystallized' and, thus, can slowly drip feed energy to the thoughtform, allowing it to last for ages.

The average charm will last about three months *after* being cast (that is, the charm will not be attached to the charmer), but charms can still absorb atmospheric astral energy. Still, this is not as efficient as receiving astral energy directly, so the charm will eventually fade away; although, in some cases, charms may survive for years. Of course, *while* the charm (of any power level) is still attached to the creator in the astral (with some minor default etheric connections, too, from the help of the conduit field geometry), it can last indefinitely, feeding off the mage. The process of filling the stabilizer, however, may not work properly if its geometry does not flow properly and is not adequately secure. This means the charm will need to siphon more energy off the mage as a result of inefficiency and malabsorption. If the mage cannot provide the needed energy, the charm will begin to degenerate. Without proper flow, the poured conscious energy will just shoot off the ends of the geometries into the astral realm. If the mage exits their astral projection before the creation of the stabilizer geometry, they must quickly return, as their thoughtform may begin degenerating (depending on certain conditions), along with the conduit geometry. The stabilizer geometry also feeds and stabilizes other geometries in the charm – in addition to itself.

Although, at this point, the charm is complete and ready to be cast, another step is necessary for its security. A *ward geometry* is then added around the other geometries to protect against other astral energies and entities that may intentionally or unintentionally feed off of, distort, or destroy the charm. As with the other geometries, the complexity depends on the energy/information density of the other creations. While the stabilizer geometry feeds the ward geometry, the latter can still degrade over time with attacks. If the ward geometry is poorly made, it can actually *attract* destructive energies and entities. Even if the ward geometry is well crafted, it must be noted that extremely powerful charms may be subject to greater forces, which can result in degradation that scales proportionally. Charms that are put into public spaces (like a shopping centre) will usually degrade quickly, as many people will walk through them. Charms are great at affecting one or two people at a time *for* a number of few times (and some may even be good against a group for a few times), but they cannot sustain too many people constantly moving through them. Therefore, it is not like public places are filled with charms.

Finally, if the mage is content with their creation, they may wish to add more *layers* to the charm – that is, adding more thoughtforms. While these additional thoughtforms may seem like 'other charms', consider that when all the layers are tied together, then there is ultimately only one *whole charm*. Connecting layers also requires even more geometries linking each together, but these are generally rather simple. The more layers, the more unstable the overall whole charm, and so, most charms do not have more than one layer. Layers are different to merely adding (casting) multiple charm spells to a single spatial area in the physical realm, which is ill-advisable, anyway, as the fields will distort one another. Therefore, it is better to create a single, more complex (whole) charm than many petty ones for a single intended area. Layers, then, will either only activate under certain conditions, or they may only be tuned into with concentration.

Once the charmer has completed all of the previous steps, there is then the issue of storing charms, which has a very similar, but also slightly different nature, than the schools of conjuration, mysticism and alchemy. Thoughtforms naturally attach to things, and they also naturally attach to their creator. However, when there is too much energy tethered to something in particular, thoughtforms will detach and float away. In the case of a being attached to a user, mages can only have so much energy around them before *instabilities* arise, and, thus, mages cannot keep an infinite number of attached charms. Of course, the stronger the mage, the more capable they will be with retaining more and/or greater charms. While the charm is within the astral aura of the mage, it can have its energy restored with effort; but at the same time, the more charms attached to a mage, the more energy they will collectively siphon.

When ready to deploy (that is, 'cast') a charm, the charmer simply has to focus on detaching the charm and then attaching it to another physical material. With the reattachment, the mage then has to focus on channelling the energy from the astral, where the charm then hacks into the etheric body of the targeted entity before affecting its physical being. As a result, the attachment here is different from the attachment to one's own astral aura, which does not 'drill down' to the etheric via the conduit geometry – unless the mage wishes to cast the charm on themselves; in which case, it will drill down. Because the charmer detaches the charm, each is only 'single-use' and cannot be cast again from the aura like with other magic.

Nevertheless, charms may be 'picked up' (acquired) and then either placed back down somewhere else or saved in one's aura for later use, where the charm can last indefinitely. However, this acquisition is a tricky process; and even of the charms that can be seized, the process itself can degrade or even destroy the charm. Accordingly, it is generally the case that only the creator can perform this feat properly, as they are able to better tune into the charm's energy itself. Air mages normally are far better at this feat than other types of mages – even for picking up non-user-created charms. It is also easier to grab a charm that has been recently placed as opposed to one that has been placed for a long time. Even when a charm has not been (re)acquired, psychic mages can still send energy to the charm nonlocally in order to fuel it. Once a certain type of charm is made, it usually becomes easier to create more of the same kind through sheer practice alone.

Usually when it is time to cast a charm, the context will be different to what the charmer anticipated, so alterations may (have to) occur on the spot. For example, with the aforesaid illusory rock wall, the charmer may change the shape, size, and texture to better suit the environment. Let us say that the rock wall in their charm is a dark brown, whereas the rock in the physical world could be light brown mixed in with reds. Accordingly, without alterations, the final result could look out of place, creating an obvious illusion or at least something that would grab one's attention. The charmer does not have to alter other things, such as light, though. Moreover, any photons caught within the field will naturally realign with the astral and add to the illusion. To be clear, the charm is not making the photons move; instead, the charm is aligning the photons up with the etheric for the effect.

The rock wall, this way, will still reflect the appropriate amount of illusory light (according to its colour) for the targeted conscious entity being affected by the field. Mages may use special eyewear or devices to see particular anomalies – especially etheric anomalies. While the person (wearing goggles, for example) may see the illusory light, the goggles would not detect any reflecting light, indicating to the mage that there may potentially be a charm present. Such eyewear and devices cannot actually see the etheric and astral, so outside of the abovesaid physical case of photons, etheric-based detections are just analogously represented. This, again, means that such translations are inaccurate, and so, this would not absolutely prove the existence of a charm.

Although the strength of the charm depends on how it is created, mental resistances can deter such strengths, resulting in charms that may be distorted or not seen at all. In some cases, the target being may be able to see the geometries of the charm but not be affected. Mental resistances also differ from being to being (non-sapient to sapient); and even of a single being, their mental activity fluctuates all the time, intentionally or not. If a physical entity is drowsy, this will affect their ability to resist a charm, but it can also affect their consciousness to such a degree that they may not even be able to consciously tune into the charm in the first place. On top of this, a being can increase their mental fortitude with concentration; as a result, they may be able to resist – or alternatively tune into – a charm. That is to say, the experiencing of charms is not just about resistance strength but tuning strength as well, thus, some charms may be invisible or inexperienceable to most except for the select few – which can be great for keeping secrets. This means that there are not any universally-applied, one-size-fits-all conduit field geometries.

In saying that, there are still 'general' conduit field geometries that cover broad ranges of beings with normal, beta-state brain waves. Although a being may at first be affected by an illusion, they may be able to later 'shake it off'. Furthermore, the affected being may also be aware that they are being compelled to do something against their natural inclinations or even conscious thoughts. With greater freewill, the greater the chance to break free. Still, there is a difference between freewill and fortitude, and increasing one's fortitude (which itself may have many aspects) may not be enough at times. There are also crafty ways to manipulate and feed the ego. For those people that are affected, sometimes they may experience aftereffects. So, while a charm no longer directly affects a person as soon as they leave the field, if the brain has been affected too much, then they will experience lingering effects. For example, a memory-wiping charm could wipe a person's memories (usually only to an extent); and as soon as the person in question exits the field, they may temporarily have the same level of memories wiped, or they may have other kinds of brain fog for a few minutes longer while the mind recovers.

To add to charm secrecy, a mage can create a *meta* charm in the first layer. The meta layer may keep the additional or other layers dormant before activating them once certain conditions are met. For example, a meta charm may create a troll face that emerges from a physical material nearby, such as a wall. The face, in this context, may also only appear to someone once they reach a particular point in the field. The face may then be programmed to speak a certain line of dialogue, and they may then ask for a password or for the target to perform a certain action. One of these actions might require the person to 'dance like a chicken'; alternatively, the face might require the person to imagine something in particular (like an apple), in turn creating a thoughtform. The meta charm would then astrally detect the existence of this new thoughtform, in turn completing the required condition, allowing the meta charm to activate the second layer kept hidden away from all beings. Meta charms may exist without being in a different layer (so there would only be one layer to the charm). Normally in such cases, the charm's main function would be to alter other charms that either are or will be in the vicinity once placed.

# 3.4: School of Alchemy:

The core of *alchemy* (as a school) can be broken into two areas: *enchantment* and *transfiguration*, with each going hand in hand; that is, the alchemical process essentially begins with manipulating the etheric field of an item or entity before shapeshifting it (the item or entity) to another form. Mages can also enchant themselves and transform their own bodies. Alchemy is also a crossover tier of magic, where both aether and non-aether energy may be used. Ultimately, transfigurations lead to physical changes, yet the alchemical process requires and utilizes an etheric aura for transformation. Enchanted items are not 'magical technologies' or 'mage-tech', but technologies themselves may be enchanted. Moreover, enchanted items are generally referred to as 'enchanted items' rather than 'magic items' – unless erroneously used. This is because the enchanted *effects themselves*, such as levitation, are not magic, and they are, instead (as mentioned in the beginning of the *General Ontology* section), the phenomena found in the natural world and the products contained within. It is only the enchantment itself – the conscious alteration – that is magic. Still, 'magically-formed items' is a sound term that is used.

Enchanters first begin with meditation, tuning into the item or entity that they wish to enchant – specifically, this will be an HRF. This step is about gaining etheric knowledge of the HRF; otherwise, this initial tuning may be skipped if the enchanter already knows enough about the HRF. The practitioner then exits meditation, albeit resting in a meditative state, ready for the following processes that depend on their skill and power level. If the mage is attempting an enchantment at or above their power level, then they will need equipment; otherwise, it is possible to just use their consciousness alone. Even then, it is still easier for the enchanter to use equipment for enchantments that are below their power level. The main types of equipment used are: a source of energy (normally a charchite); aligners; magnifiers; and retainers. All of these will vary based on the type of enchantment and the type of HRF, too, and many mathematical calculations can go into this step. The equipment essentially manipulates the quantum properties of the HRF, which, in turn, makes the changes within the HRF's *etheric field* much easier.

Once the HRF is *primed* via the equipment, the enchanter may focus on the etheric field, where they have a few options. The enchanter can simply manipulate the etheric energy of the HRF, or they can use their own etheric energy to help with this process. Moreover, the enchanter can also add in aether energy to bolster either option. Generally, it is much easier to use aether energy, which normally entails also using it via the enchanter's own etheric energy. If the next step is not done soon after priming the HRF, then the enchanter may need to prime it again. The enchanter then has to access the different etheric states a HRF possesses (such as its alternative corporeal or non-corporeal realities that extend beyond the mere data of the HRF's current reality), which, again, is made easier if the HRF has been primed from the physical realm. The more skilled and powerful the enchanter is, the more states that may be accessed. Note that the HRF will only have a limited number (and set) of different probable states in its current tangible form (for both the case of PWT and WPD theory), but these will all have *links* to other states/realities not in its tangible field.

Let us now take a table to enchant. An enchanter may wish to encode a new enchantment or change the table's current enchantment. If we take the former option, the enchanter may wish to form a table made of iron instead of its natural wooden state. The enchanter would tune into the various etheric states around the table, sifting through various realities to find the one that happens to be an iron table. If the iron table is not within the standard set of current probable states, then it has to be found via one of the abovesaid links. To do so in either case, the mage would have to focus on the iron table in order to meet its frequency, where they would tweak their (the mage's) own frequency – *and* the table's – to match up with an intended reality. By doing this, the mage would 'see' various potential states in front of them, with the table being in different states, such as a broken table or a different coloured table, etc.

Such states (whether via links in the aura or not) will appear to the enchanter as a sea of thousands of translucent holograms interlacing with each other as they float around them (the enchanter) with varying densities, 'distances', and dimensions. It can be a little chaotic for the enchanter if they are open to too many realities at once. Even though not all potential states may be accessible, this does not mean that an enchanter would not see these other realities. In fact, there are potentially an infinite number of potential states in existence, and even though the number of available states is limited for an enchantment, many potential states will have near-identical versions of themselves. These near-identical versions will typically be *grouped* together, and so, to see the nuanced differences, 'zooming' into one group will 'expand' it, revealing more states. As a result, mages do not see all available states *at once*.

Regardless, the realities that are less vibrationally close will usually be 'further away', and they are generally harder to see and draw in. Some realities, though, are so far removed from the current reality – or just downright contradictory and impractical – that they are basically not just an extreme improbability of existing but, essentially, one of practical impossibility. For example, it would be *extremely* improbable for the table to turn into an intelligent dancing banana that shoots giant planets out of its square-circle eyes – therefore, it would be 'impossible'. Even turning a table into a banana would not be easy (at least for most mages), and usually enchanters will attempt to create enchantments that are relatable (vibrationally close) to the item. Still, it is not the case that the potential state has to simply be a different version of the item intended for enchantment. For example, the enchantment does not have to be an alternative table and can, instead, be a rifle (or, again, a simple banana).

After a potential state has been chosen and successfully accessed, the enchanter then has to *tie* it to the HRF as its most 'immediate' etheric reality by crafting the potential state as the HRF's *quantum trans state* (QTS), contrasting the HRF's previous *quantum base* (original) *state* (QBS). Although the QTS is, for now, etheric, consider that the end result of the alchemical process will be a physical transformation – hence, in this case, the term 'quantum' is used over 'etheric'. To accomplish this feat, the alchemist must tune into the HRF (its base state) and then induce a cymatic field (a vibrational resonance pattern) via the HRF's aggregate frequency in the etheric. When this happens, a holographic, fluorescent sphere (or similar shape) with multiple layers will emerge, featuring numerous nodes located at certain points in the interference patterns – some weak, some strong. Once this has been properly induced, the enchanter will then induce the chosen potential state's (that is, the QTS's) cymatic field, which is fundamentally the same process as inducing the first cymatic field, except that tuning into the potential state is harder.

The subsequent phase requires placing the chosen trans state's cymatic field around the item's base state field so one sphere is within another. However, when this occurs, a *disruption field* is created, and the cymatic patterns on both surfaces 'break down' into smaller geometries that begin to scatter, floating around the outside of their respective fields. If there are any other energy distortions around the item and enchanter during the process, the effect will increase. The enchanter then must reorientate the pieces as if it were a massive jigsaw puzzle, figuring out which pieces suit what location based on the layers beneath each field's surface. To see the inner field (the QBS) properly, the mage normally has to tune the outer field (the QTS) out of sight momentarily. Pieces can be easily placed in the wrong spot, but they can also be moved later on. Studying the nature of this issue beforehand, therefore, is recommended.

Once the pieces are in place, they generally remain unmoving. After completing this step, the following procedure has the enchanter spin the two fields until each has the most appropriate (major) nodes aligned as possible. To know which nodes to align, it is also recommended that the enchanter studies what energies certain patterns generally indicate and represent, unless the enchanter wishes to endure a lengthy period of trial and error. When the nodes align (whether correctly or incorrectly), they, too, will create their own interference patterns (geometries), in turn appearing like electrified crystals spinning around. These crystals will also basically shine the energies of the two fields in a multitude of directions. For the last stage, the enchanter twists these crystals around, shining energy to the remaining appropriate nodes, which should establish a full connection.

The basic level of enchantment should be complete at this point, and with the QTS tethered to the item or entity, the QTS will be readily accessible for transfiguration. The tethered QTS completes the channel that began with charging the etheric field, and so now certain information can be tunnelled back and forth from the physical quantum to the etheric. Additional enchantments may be placed on the

HRF, but this becomes harder for both the enchanter and the one wishing to transfigure the HRF. Such enchantments either come in the form of *alternatives* or *stacks*. Alternatives are simply different enchantments on a single HRF, whereas stacks are enchantments upon enchantments. While stacks can be made upon existing available potential states from the item's base state, if an item has been transfigured, then previously-unavailable potential states may become available. For example, after transfiguring a wooden table into an iron table, the potential states of other types of tables (or even other items) may become available, such as a very strong steel table.

In fact, stacking is how far-reaching enchantments can be attained, such as stone statues that can be transfigured into *biologics* (that is, beings of biological form). These transfigurations are only for the most advanced mages, so they are very rare. These biologics, though, lack brains, central nervous systems, and some other features that organic entities like animals possess. Basically, they are animal analogues. Note that this applies to enchantments outside the user's body (like a statue); a user, nevertheless, may transform into a normal biological entity, like a bear with a brain – and, in some cases, biological entities with certain *necrotic* tissue (again, see *Section 4.3.2.6* for more information on necrotics and their tissues).

To form said biologics, it is first easier if the statue looks like the being that will manifest, as this gives *some* sense of vibrational compatibility. One of the stacks will then transform into something simple, like base-level organic compounds (that is, not flesh), then *perhaps* a skeleton before other stacks flesh out the biologic. While this may sound impressive, consider that all of these biologics are functionally disabled, so their uses are limited. Note that this phenomenon is different to the fictional, fantasy-based *gargoyles* that turn from stone to living beings without magic. Also note that reaching these higher improbable states is a spell creation (and then a spell storage) aptitude(s) issue, but if a mage does not have high-enough casting aptitude abilities, the spell will also not work (without instabilities).

The more enchantments that are stacked in an HRF, the more unstable all of the enchantments will become. That is, when a mage goes to transfigure the item or entity, the enchantments may fail to allow for transfiguration due to etheric *instabilities*, and the mage will have to wait out a period of time before they can try to transfigure the HRF again. Multiple alternatives will also incur instabilities to a lesser extent as well. If the enchanter wishes only to enchant a certain *part* of the table, like a leg, as a new HRF on top of the HRF of the table that has already been enchanted, then this would not actually be a stack. Enchanting the leg, in this case, is still *possible*, but there will be etheric conflict and, thus, instabilities will nevertheless arise.

Enchantments may be undone by reversing the process via meditation, so the enchanter does not have to worry about not reaching new stacks. Enchanters may also create *traps*, where they put false or bad enchantments into an item, which may or may not be alternatives or stacks. When a mage goes to transfigure an item that has a trap as an alternative, they now basically have, in the case of a single trap, a 50/50 chance of picking the wrong enchantment – unless they are very discerning about general node connections. Such traps may have a transfigured state that instantly blows up, killing unwanted mages who attempt to transfigure the item. Alternatively, sometimes traps involve non-destructive transfigurations like a table that releases toxic gases, killing unwanted transfigurers.

Note that these bad enchantments are not faulty in the sense that the enchantment itself would blow up; rather, it would be the transfigured state that would happen to explode. An enchanter may even wish to add only bad enchantments to an item – even if only one enchantment in total is used. In such cases, usually the item would be used as a decoy for unwanted transfigurers, while the real item may be placed elsewhere (with good enchantments). While magical charms cannot be placed inside an enchantment itself, they can still be applied to an enchanted item. Furthermore, if a charm surrounds the enchanted item, the energies may slightly distort a person's ability to properly see the cymatic frequencies when transfiguring the item.

The transfiguration process requires a source of energy, and the best and only practical source for this is aether energy working through the etheric level. Even if this were not the case, it would not be practically possible (for mages and their phys-iology), for example, to use caloric energy from, say, the physical body, in order to fuel the transformation, as the transformation is not *growth* from the QBS but a *switch* to the QTS. There are exceptions to the issue of the required source of energy, and there are some species in the Caelverse that can switch etheric codes with stored physical energy, but this requires it working through and with the etheric, and it does not last long, and it has its limitations (more information can be found in *Section 4.3.2.5*).

The process specifically shifts the *entire* code of a particular structure's etheric field over to another, even if only a fraction of the code looks different while the rest of the code remains the same. If a mage transfigures themselves, where they merely have new eyes that possess greater eyesight, then the mage will still have a whole new body, even if, for all practical purposes, only the cones in the eyes change. *Both* in the cases of the shapeshifting mage and the table, none *grow* (or shrink or morph) into their new state; they literally change etheric codes (as if loading a new file on a computer). In the process, it might *look* like there is growth, but the change is a radical swap of two forms.

Restated, the QBS still exists in its original state, unchanged; it has not mutated into something different. The base state merely moves or phases out of this reality into non-corporeality, while the QTS replaces it. If the mage enchants their own body, this would not affect clothing, thus, sometimes mages have to remove their clothing if large transfigurations take place; otherwise, they may rip. Typically, mages will often refer to enchantments that specifically transform (that is, enhance) their senses (like eyesight) as 'sense enchantments', even though there are no official 'sense enchantments' that only changes one's senses specifically in the context of transfiguration. That is, it is the body that changes, which, *in turn*, affects the senses. Still, for the sake of brevity, many mages will just say that they 'got new eyes' with the transfiguration, for example, or a table that got a new paintjob or 'added' features.

Of course, *if* only part of a table (like one leg) were enchanted, then the *whole* leg would shapeshift, not the rest of the table, as all the properties in the table are part of an HRF. Still, it is hard to isolate part of an object while enchanting, so enchanting only a leg normally does not occur. Even when this happens (by way of passing a HRT), it can become problematic, as such transfigured states end up breaking an item apart. While this dangerous problem may *theoretically* occur for a *person's* legs, in *practice*, this never occurs, so transfiguring one's own body is basically universally safe, as the whole body will be transfigured, not parts. This primarily stems from the holistic nature of the etheric body of a person (and all of their properties being part of a strong HRF), so isolation is not something that can be practically achieved in the context of biological QBS enchantment and transfiguration.

Any kind of enchanted item can lose its enchantment(s) without mage intervention. This is usually a result of physical degradation, which, in turn, chips away the etheric reality around it, thereby diminishing the strength of the tethering itself of the trans state, not the strength of the trans state itself. That is, if a wooden table has been enchanted to become a steel table, the steel reality would not be weakened, nor would the table default to another type of reality, such as an iron table. Instead, the *chance* of the normal table turning into a steel table diminishes when it is being transfigured (that is, degradations cause casting/channelling instability issues). If the transfiguration fails, then the table does not shapeshift at all, and the alchemist must retry the transfiguration again until the table shapeshifts. If any enchanted item is damaged too much, then the enchantment will be totally lost. The same applies to stacked and alternative enchantments that become too unstable; that is, failure rates occur, and in extreme cases, the QTSs break apart from the QBS.

Since the whole body will be transfigured, a mage of any power level will only be able to transfigure their own body with one spell, not multiple. So, an alchemist would not be able to have both an eyesight-enhancing transfiguration (new eyeballs) and another one that features big claws at the same time. However, the alchemist could alternate between the two states after one transfiguration ends. If the mage wants both better eyesight and big claws simultaneously, then they would need to have a single transfiguration that possesses both of these characteristics. Usually, (fire) mages will try to max out their situation by transfiguring their body once and then simultaneously transfiguring something else, like their clothes, so they can turn them into armour for added protection and features.

Although the whole QBS changes, each transfigured state uses different levels of energy. Merely changing one's eyeballs to a slightly-different version will use less energy than a person transforming into a big beastly creature. This is fundamentally because the trans state is 'further away' from the base state in its vibrational connection, so more energy is required to draw from such etheric states. This, more specifically, not only determines the amount of aether energy required per second but also if the mage is even capable of transfiguring the item in the first place without instability issues. Mages still need to meditatively connect with the Aether at first, funnelling the energy into the enchanted item's etheric structure. From here, the mage then must go through a similar process to that found in enchanting; the difference is that they have to tune into the QTS that already exists. This initial process uses very little aether energy compared to actually sustaining the transfiguration. Due to suffering from their own subjective biases, novice mages find this tuning process rather hard; but other variables may make it harder for advanced mages, too. If done poorly, the mage tunes into untethered etheric states, which cannot be utilized (so no transfigurations occur).

In the case that there is an alternative enchantment, the mage will be able to tune into either one, and then they must choose. Stacked enchantments must be sequentially transfigured; meaning: if there are three enchantments in a stack, then there must be three successive transfigurations. Despite three transfigurations occurring, a mage will only be powering one state in the end at once (so they would only be casting one spell here), and, thus, the average-powered alchemist may continue transfiguring three other items (with average-powered transfigurations) in the meantime while still powering the one final stack. Of course, if the final stack happens to be a relatively powerful stack, then the average-powered mage might not be able to transfigure three other states simultaneously, as all mages are limited to (the number and strength of) what they can cast at any one time up to their power level.

Once the QTS has been found, the mage must realign the at-this-point rapidly-spinning cymatic fields. Although spinning in assorted directions, the cymatic fields are easier to align than in enchanting, as the mage only needs to *feel* for the right alignments; although, having knowledge on appropriate alignments does, indeed, help, especially with more advanced enchantments. Using one's consciousness to stop the spinning, the mage aligns the two fields after feeling a buzzing, clicking sensation. The mage then proceeds to 'jiggle' the two fields, slotting them through the crystallized geometries like a massive, complex key going into a keyhole, in turn completing the main process and allowing for the shifting of realities. The transfiguration should then be complete at this point.

Since bacteria and people have symbiotic (and other kinds of) relationships with one another with exceptionally-connected etheric bodies, they are essentially 'part' of one another. That is, the bacteria in a person will be part of the same HRF, even if they were not originally part of the HRF of the person at the time of the enchantment process – given their short lifespans; this is because new bacteria merge rapidly with the HRF of the person. As a result, the very bacteria in one's gut will also transfigure into another reality. This shapeshifting phenomenon even applies to certain *heterogenics* (explained in *Section 4.3.2.5*). If there are no bacteria-like bodies for the bacteria to inhabit in the transfigured state, then they would take a 'back seat' while the mage controls the new body, just like what occurs with particular heterogenics.

After transfiguring their body, the transfigurer can then exit their mediative state. There is yet one final step for shapeshifted bodies, though this mainly applies to (novice) mages in very different and unfamiliar states. That is, the transfigured mage may find their new bodies too radically different to easily identify with and operate, and so, they must become accustomed to it. To do this, the mage must enter another meditative state, where they have to concentrate on their entire body, traversing their consciousness topologically throughout it. This is also normally coupled with particular physical gesturing, which consists of releasing and tightening muscles and joints (or equivalents) at certain timings. By doing this for a good minute, the mage can rest easily enough in their new state so they do not revert back. In the case that they run out of aether energy and revert back before accustoming to it, the mage may have to repeat the process, but they should accustom to the new state eventually.

While the mage does not need to be solely focused on the enchanted object or body, some awareness is necessary in order for the Aether to continue powering the changes. For this reason, typically changing oneself totally into an inanimate object is not feasible, as the alchemist would not be conscious in the normal sense. Exceptions apply to very advanced mages who know how to counter this problem by (partially) lifting their consciousness outside the new body. Interestingly, while mages can only turn objects into animal analogues instead of proper animals, the same kind of has to apply to their own transformed bodies if they wish to sustain the magic. For example, turning into a bear would mean the mage would lack a magic gland, so this would not work. Therefore, mages create animal analogues spells for themselves if they are basically transforming their whole bodies – ones, however, with *mage* brains.

Once the transfiguration ends, the enchanted form returns to its base state, ready to be transfigured into its trans state later on (unless, for example, it is a liquid that has been totally consumed). Fortunately, while the item or person may return to their original form, a *temporary lingering alignment* period applies, where the geometries in the transfiguration will remain aligned for a certain amount of time (usually between six to twenty-four hours), as if 'unlocked'. This allows the mage to transfigure an item again from its QBS to its QTS without having to go through the process of spinning the geometries during meditation. All the mage has to do here is power the transfiguration with the Aether. Once the period finishes, the mage would then have to go through the process of spinning and aligning the geometries of the two states.

An ACE still applies to alchemical transformations, which means that if a mage transfigures a table, it needs to be within the vicinity of their (physical) being if the transfiguration is to last. If a piece of the table is chopped off before moving outside the ACE, it will not return to being a piece of the former table; instead, it will return to its etheric reality. If a mage manages to transform an object into a firearm loaded with bullets, then the bullets, when fired, would leave the ACE and then disappear. However, as noted in the *General Ontology* section, parts of a spell may, nevertheless, temporarily (but only very shortly) last outside of the ACE due to there being some conscious energy in it, giving items like bullets etc., phased momentum. Moreover, mages can even *consciously* project tiny shells of their ACE out, which requires great concentration, so this is another way said bullets can temporarily last outside the ACE.

The actual transition from the QBS to the QTS and vice versa is a form of phasing, so both forms can be partially seen when coming into or leaving the current reality *if* one can see the etheric. Otherwise, the split instant that a new form emerges, there may be a slight blurring effect. Since the trans and base states only switched realities, reverting back will not cause radioactive decay to occur, as there was no 'growth' in the first place. In the case that a transfigured body is shot with a bullet when returning to the base state, the phasing process will leave the bullet dropping to the ground instead of it being left inside the base body. Moreover, the phasing process will also push matter out of the way via wave function changes in a potential field, and so, if the bullet is at the position where the mage's feet will return, the bullet would be pushed away so it would not lodge inside a foot. There does, however, come a point where matter may not be pushed away in time, so an object in such a case would get caught inside a body – but this is uncommon. Furthermore, because the bullet drops, it follows that the base state would not receive the injury that the trans state endured.

*However*, if a transfigured mage is shot in a vital organ (let us say that the mage transforms into a bear analogue, and a bullet hits the heart), the mage's consciousness will be in complete shock. On return to the base form, the mage's mind will produce certain bodily functions and reactions, such as increased adrenaline, along with palpitations. The body will also quite literally go into shock, and the effect will be such an intensified version of the placebo effect that the body will convulse and actually haemorrhage in places. If the mage is not advanced enough – especially if they already have weak base bodies with diseases (especially comorbidities) and other conditions (including old age, lack of vitality, and overall weakness) – generally, death will ensue. Even if a body or table is blown up in its QTS, on return, certain quantum variables pertaining to probabilities will be altered, and these could lead to structural weaknesses in their atomic lattices, leading to deterioration or even overt damage.

While all of the abovesaid information covers enchantments and transfigurations themselves, there is yet another dynamic in alchemy to consider for when mages try to transfigure their own bodies. To maximize alchemical potential, mages who attempt to transfigure themselves also add in various *consumables*. These consumables may even be enchanted; but if they are enchanted, they do not, in turn, enchant the mage, nor do they transfigure them; instead, they only help with enchanting and transfiguring. More specifically, a mage may consume a specific consumable while they are enchanting their own body to reach higher (or different) potential etheric states, and/or they may later take a consumable to help with casting the enchantments (i.e., transfiguration). Mages would still be limited in the number of spells that they can cast at once, and such consumables do not increase the power of enchantments and transfigurations themselves. While consumables may seem like a major boost -- indeed, they are -- it is also important to note that enchanting (that is, reaching higher states for) the body and transfiguring it is much harder than enchanting inanimate items like tables, so consumables really help bring the mage's potential up to the level of said items.

Within the *context* of alchemy, the abovesaid consumables (that is, *biotic alchemical consumables* – BACs) are different from *non-biotic alchemical consumables* (NBCs) – both of which fall under *alchemical-based substances* (ABSs). Although some BACs may come in the form or creams, secretions, food, etc., most tend to be liquids. *Potions* are enchanted BAC liquids, while *tonics* are non-enchanted BAC liquids. On the other hand, *philtres* are enchanted NBC liquids, while *aquemicals* are non-enchanted NBC liquids. While the terms are officially standardized, some mages still mistakenly use the names interchangeably, and they may sometimes even use redundant terms like 'magic potion'. Each category possesses non-standardized subcategories, which are, nevertheless, commonly recognized and used. Outside the context of alchemy, a tonic may simply be called another term like 'drug', and an aquemical may simply be called a 'chemical'.

A potion may not only help a mage with their alchemy, but since they (potions) are enchanted, mages can transfigure the potions simply to reap biochemical benefits merely in their (the mage's) QBS form without transfiguring. That is, a potion, in this case, might have a dual purpose, or it might only have the purpose of biochemically *enhancing* the base form of a mage. Consider that any QBS substance – even when not transfigured or enchanted – will still affect the body. While artificially-manufactured BACs exist for the sake of enchantment, ingredients are better enchanted within their (relatively) whole context, as they are closer to certain etheric potential states than what other ingredients would possess; and this, in turn, would match up with the enchantments and transfigurations of the mage. So, vitamins, minerals, and other nutrient complexes are generally better in foods rather than in ('artificial' or 'natural') isolation, but extraction for the sake of bioavailability means that many ingredients need to be turned into potions. Sometimes, it may not just be an issue of bioavailability but one of ease of digestion.

To reiterate for clarification, the sight-enhancing properties of, say, an apple in a potion would vibrationally align with potential states where the mage would have better eye sight; but even in its QBS (that is, without the potion itself being trans-figured), the potion might simply help with better eyesight, anyway. When the mage transfigures the potion, the potion itself would be changed (into an enhanced form), and the potion itself would then enhance the mage's biochemistry, where they would see better (but not be transfigured); this enhancement would *also* then help the mage access higher etheric states for either enchanting and/or transfiguration. In the case of a sight enhancement potion, simple terms like 'sense potions' can apply for ease of reference and brevity. Every potion will also be different from the next, even if the 'same' ingredients are used (where the differences may be slight). Given that etheric potential states are grouped together, the fact that potions may be only slightly different from one another is not an issue here; however, if a mage drinks two potions of very different natures at the same time, this *may* result in etheric conflict.

Potions hit the bloodstream much faster than food. While some effects can be felt within a minute, most potions take effect in about twenty minutes of consumption. This might seem problematic, as a mage might (normally) only be able to power a transfiguration spell for up to two minutes. Moreover, enchanted items lose their enchantments when the substance is destroyed or altered greatly, and potions change in their composition as the body processes it. This latter point, of course, is not a problem for tonics, as they do not have enchantments. Fortunately, when a mage consumes a potion (so long as it is consumed when it is enchanted), it will instantly leave a *temporary etheric residue* in the mage's aura. This alone is enough to help with mage's bodily enchantments and transfigurations. In most contexts, the effect will last up to twenty-four hours before another potion would have to be consumed, as any remaining constituents of the potion in the body would no longer have a QTS. Still, if a mage drinks a transformed potion, gains the benefits, then transfigures their own body, the mage will not need another potion, nor the temporary etheric residue, for the remaining time of the temporary lingering alignment, as the potion would have effectively done its job at helping the mage achieve the said alignment.

There are some potions that (are specifically designed to) focus more so on both hitting the bloodstream and taking full effect within a minute, but these normally do not have extra temporary etheric residues, nor greater etheric residues. These potions are also usually harder to make, but they are better than the slower-affecting potions, which, when they revert to the QBS, may only provide mild biochemical effects (which is still possible, as they *do* affect other chemicals in the person's system before they have been properly processed to create their effects). Not only can they cause effects within the short timeframe, but they can still naturally leave behind temporary biochemical effects (after the potion's properties have returned to the QBS) simply due to having already caused changes in the body. If a potion is drunk in a transformed state, then a potion may or may not hit the bloodstream faster. Of course, if the mage has already transformed, then the potion would usually be pointless unless the mage is attempting another transformation. Still, the mage has to be careful, as the potion would fall to the ground when the transformation ends (like in the abovesaid case of a bullet hitting a transformed mage).

Consuming potions and tonics can nevertheless cause a build-up of toxicities, so their uses can be limited, both continuously and consecutively. The stronger the potion and tonic, the more typically it is the case that they contain more toxins. Mages can still (attempt to) acclimatize to particular substances over time in order to fully use them; and so, the more toxic the substance, the more advanced a mage must be to handle them. Many trans states in potions happen to be more toxic than their base state counterparts. Making sure one's mathematical calculations of consumables are correct before consumption is extremely important, of course. This is not much of an issue for potions that both have little toxins and require very little volume consumed for effect, but there are some potions that necessitate one to drink large sums of liquid in order to produce the needed effects. Many potions and mage tonics are also only bioavailable to mages, but a non-mage may still consume a mage-created tonic and receive benefits. In fact, non-mages can still drink transfigured potions for the benefits of the potion's trans state itself.

These biotic processes may seem like such a hassle for the individual mage, and so, a question then arises: why do mages not simply buy all or most of their enchanted substances – and even other enchanted items – from (mega) corporations? The reality is that while big business *does* sell enchanted items and potions, mass production is not possible in terms of enchantment, as the enchantment process itself cannot be mass produced. Therefore, (mega) corporations have the same production speed as both small businesses and individuals. While it would seem as though corporations might be able to hire the most advanced mages to produce enchantments (to speedily make enchanted products), their numbers are few compared to aggregate demand. Even then, it is not like average-powered mages seek out advanced enchantments, as they cannot transfigure the items, anyway. There is also the issue of the lowest common denominator, so producing enchanted items must be easy relative to the mass of individuals buying them. Still, there *are* corporations that make products that only the most advanced and rich buy.

The other problem is that enchanters unintentionally leave energy signatures in their enchantments, which can distort the perceptions of those trying to transfigure the items. Moreover, consider that for potion creation, subjective biases determine more probable pathway outcomes for potential states that have biochemical structures more fitting to the mage who created them. As a result, personalized potions sometimes grant potential states that have less, lower, or even no allergens and toxicities. Therefore, besides warning stickers, it is sometimes safer and easier for the individual mage to simply create their own potions, which is what normally happens. This is not to say that an individual mage cannot consume a corporate-made potion, nor create bad potions, but it essentially means that the best potions, relative to the individual, are typically tailormade. When individuals create potions, they will usually create large batches that *can* potentially last up to a lifetime (if they have the appropriate amount of ingredients, preservatives, and money).

Corporations, nevertheless, do produce many BACs and non-consumable materials that are *ready* to be enchanted. Still, for some ingredients (used in certain potions or tonics), they cannot be simply mass farmed – or farmed at all. For example, there are certain types of ingredients that can be harvested from creatures that critically change based on the environments the creatures are raised in. Changing even the slightest of variables can alter the ingredients in such a way that it renders it useless for certain potions. Some creatures, for example, need to have little to no *observation* as they develop and live, which usually would not occur in farmed environments. Mere observations can have small but critical changes at the quantum level via wave function changes, in turn greatly affecting a creature's eggs or tissues or products. There are also other mysterious (quantum) variables that alter certain ingredients, which are far too hard to control, so raiding animals (and their products) in the *wild* may be essential.

## 3.5: School of Conjuration:

*Conjuration* magic fundamentally involves what the name implies: it is the conscious action of bringing about something out of nothing. To be clear, though, the process is technically not actually a matter of creating something out of nothing, as the Aether, formless as it is, is something: pure energy (and/or consciousness). So, put more appropriately, from the Aether, a mage can create form out of no form. Conjuration spells, therefore, are not a form of summoning – they are, instead, a pure creation *from* energy. However, conjuration spells are still *based* on some entity that already exists, even if merely a mental entity or a non-corporealized one. Furthermore, the *constructs* that are used to establish conjurations are etheric and are not from the Aether directly; and so, conjurations technically are *powered* by the Aether, which fuels said intangible constructs of the etheric which bow to the laws of the Aether's potential. These conjured forms take on one of two categories, with the first being a purely holographic form – which may be taken from mental constructs – while the second consists of tangible mass made from real atoms like iron and copper, which form anything from tables to weapons. Holograms, of course, may still emerge from the physical constructs of the second category.

To begin constructing the spell, the conjurer enters meditation, where they will take a mental *snapshot* of the etheric data and metadata of an item they wish to conjure. In order to do this, they must tune into the item's (that is, the HRF's) etheric energy before inducing a cymatic field (a vibrational resonance pattern that looks fluorescent and holographic) via the targeted entity's aggregate frequency in the etheric. This even applies if the item is purely an astral entity; etheric energy, in this case, is developed *from* the astral energy, and it will act as a united EHRF. The metadata will be found in the interference patterns, which will form the basis from where the conjurer constructs further geometric shapes. To take an etheric snapshot of a mental construction, the conjurer can first imagine something (such as a table) in their minds, or they may do so in the astral. The more complex an item is, the harder it is to fully or adequately take a mental snapshot of it.

The term 'snapshot' does not imply that the conjurer quickly captures the etheric data and metadata – in fact, sometimes it can take many hours – but rather, the capture will not represent the etheric data in its perfect *entirety*. Moreover, the snapshot itself is not the actual etheric energy of the item but only an etheric copy and outline. Therefore, the conjurer needs to craft the basis of the original etheric energy, which emerges via the data. Conjurers also cannot remove the full etheric energy of an item and simply leave it in their personal auras. For one, to capture the full etheric energy of something would ultimately ruin it, as it is fundamentally tied to the physical item that generates it, and breaking it away would, at the very least, alter it. But even if this were not the case, the captured energy would not be properly integrated into the conjurer's aura, and it would simply dissipate.

After the snapshot has been taken, the conjurer then focuses on their own etheric aura, which is where the spell will be stored. Basically, the conjurer spherically projects the mental snapshot around themselves (from their conscious and subconscious minds – both of which naturally integrates into, and can be found in, the etheric) as the basis for their spell crafting. It is impossible for a mage to individually create and structure the countless atoms an item may possess, so this method is the only *known* way for the conjurer. Similar to other schools of magic, conjuration requires the conjurer to appropriately and geometrically link up the nodes found at the interference patterns of the cymatic outline.

Since it is possible to make adjustments to a *spell's* etheric data, holographic conjurations can also have other layers of geometric forms added during the construction phase. One of these geometric types create, or rather, induce *haptic feedback*, which is a form of physical stimuli that can be experienced through touch. The holograms would not be solid; instead, the holograms would have *photon-based oscillators*, which can convert light into mechanical energy. This, in turn, can create not only sound, but it can also cause the air particles (originally of the Caelverse that were not conjured) in the hologram to vibrate strongly enough to cause noticeable physical sensations when touched, thus giving the impression of the hologram having some physical form.

Of course, this haptic feedback is not strong enough to be on the same level as the physical matter it represents – a hologram of a table will not actually (*totally*) feel like a real table. For such an effect, the hologram would have to create literal atoms to cause the *exact* same effect that a real table with real atoms would have, and so, it would consequently not be a hologram anymore; anything other than this would break the *law of identity* in logic, where, for all A: A = A. This is not to say that in some cases there would not be convincing semblances, but these would nonetheless not be the exact same thing. Moreover, a being's *perceptions* may be limited, so while the hologram may not *totally* feel like a real table in any objective sense, one's limited subjective experiences could say otherwise.

If, however, the hologram is intended to be a looped movie, then there will be a cymatic *torus* instead of a sphere around the mage featuring certain structures therein. There is also the opportunity for powerful mages to use *energy condensers* in their constructions so that that they may conjure *photonic matter* (which is where photons interact with each other so strongly that, for all intents and purposes, they have 'mass'). While these conjurations have the potential to be extremely strong, the actual reality is that they are not *that* powerful (that is, even at the highest power levels, mages cannot achieve what could potentially be super powerful photonic matter). Note that the 'physicality' of photonic matter is not the same as the haptic feedback from the said photon-based oscillators. Nevertheless, a photonic 'table', for instance, would still not have the *same* type of physicality as a real wooden table.

Even though spells can be altered, conjuration is not like mysticism, for example, where new geometric forms have to be established between nodes. Rather, nodes simply have to be connected *appropriately* in conjuration. However, there are several issues that the conjurer will encounter, and technically, they will need to create *additional* geometries for conjurations that have mass. Still, these extra geometries are applied to *specific* phenomena and are not *mere* geometries found between nodes like in mysticism's tunnels. The first issue is that an item's etheric field will also contain various potential states (and other 'junk' information), which will make the cymatic field rather muddled. This information will also contain links to other states not in the etheric aura's tangible form; and while these will not be as visible as the other states naturally in the aura's etheric tangible form, their existence can still cause confusion and conflict.

In order to create the item as it is within the conjurer's reality, the conjurer need to *only* link up the interference patterns that are in the current reality.

Despite this problem of extra information, it *does* open up opportunities for the conjurer to tune into these aforesaid potential states, so instead of a wooden table, for example, that resides in the mage's current reality, the conjurer might be able to create an iron table existing in another reality or potential reality. However, this is a harder feat to achieve, and so, the majority of physical conjurations are based on what exists in the conjurer's current reality. Nevertheless, since the conjurer will only take a snapshot of the etheric field, they will not collect and then produce (that is, construct and conjure) *all* or *any* of the baggage probable and potential states the item possesses. For clarification, the 'current' reality', in this context, refers to the table *itself* which actually comes from the reality the conjurer comes from (so, the table could be in the conjurer's bedroom), and so, the 'other realities' are other timelines, etc. It is not specifically referring to the possible pathways and positions quantum particles may possess in the table of the current reality via the wave function, even though the table of the current reality would have such data.

In order to reach these other potential states, the conjurer needs to tune into them when taking the snapshot, which requires further skill and higher power levels. The cymatic field will then appear to alter, but the core field will still remain in view. As the conjurer reaches further out into more improbable and distanced potential states, the fainter they will appear until the probabilities and potential states are so improbable and distanced that they become virtually to totally invisible. Even the cymatic field that was created from an imagination will have other etheric potential states and, thus, can appear different from the original imagination; the same phenomenon can even apply to taking a snapshot from a tangible object in the physical realm for mere holographic conjurations.

Unlike in alchemy, there is no need to tether a specific etheric state to the core cymatic field in conjuration; it just so happens that the chosen state, in the abovesaid case for conjuration, comes with the baggage of other states in the etheric data. Technically, the conjurer does not actually have to pick all the nodes existing in one reality (or even all the nodes in an alternative one) when geometrically linking each together, as the multi-layered geometries (of multiple realities) could end up being exactly or similar to a field found in a single reality. Still, this can lead to unintended issues; for example, by linking to the wrong etheric state, the item, when conjured, could draw from a reality of it detonating. Alternatively, the table could be broken and made from a shoddy material.

Other etheric states aside, if the spell is poorly constructed, then there would be a chance that the conjured item might not appear at all; attempting to cast the spell would cause an *instability*, where the conjurer would have to wait out a period of time (generally a few seconds) before being able to attempt casting the spell again. In other cases, the conjured item may be missing parts of its structure, in turn leading it to shatter or collapse when touched. There might even be the chance of it exploding. Note that there is a nuanced but important difference between the sloppy construction of an object that explodes (due to a piece of the object potentially missing, causing it to be volatile) and linking to a probable or potential reality where an item *naturally* explodes. For explosions to occur within the context of *poor spell construction*, the conjured item would have to already have the potential for this to happen (like if a bomb was conjured and was now missing a vital component that would otherwise keep it from blowing up), as sloppy constructions *themselves* would not cause this problem (of exploding).

After this stage has been completed, a holographic conjuration should be finished. However, for conjurations that possess mass (not *mere* holograms), each node will also have to feature specific concentrations of energy, with each appearing like fluffy, spherical snowflakes (basically like sub-cymatic fields). When the overall cymatic field is filled with the necessary geometries that link the nodes together, such concentrations will *then* appear as sharp crystallizations. The conjurer must then zoom in on a node and begin its *fractalization*, creating enough inward-concentrating geometries to establish a 'downward' or shrinking fractal pattern. The conjurer does not need to infinitely create the fractals, as they automatically fill themselves out while the spell is being cast; but the more mass in the object, the more concentrated the fractal wells will become. These nodal concentrations exist due to the energies at the interference patterns clashing and turning 'inwards'. Many nodes will also be filled with *phi spirals* (that is, spirals that grow or shrink *logarithmically* with a *golden ratio* – that is, a ratio based on a mathematical constant roughly equal to 1.618 between two quantities).

Cymatic fields based on conjurations with mass will also contain *cymatic orbitals*, which are high-frequency packets of energy that 'fly off' from the natural resonance and structure of the cymatic field and independently zip around. These orbitals will both fly through and around the field, akin to how electrons likely orbit nuclei. That is, depending on their intensity, cymatic orbitals appear in geometrically-positioned clouds of probability. So, when a conjurer takes a snapshot of the item's cymatic field, they will pick up geometric blurs with diameters of decreasing intensities. Note that while this correlates with quantum states, the blur is *information* of probable states and does not represent definite particles themselves. The conjurer must determine the level of frequency such orbitals possess, and this is done by studying the type of cloud and its position. When the correct frequency is established, particular geometric patterns are then created between them and then with the rest of the field's nodes. The best place to position the geometric forms is between an orbital's highest probability and the most appropriate constellated area *around* the cymatic field or inner core that aligns with the closest appropriate nodes with a pointed shape. Like with the fractalized nodes, the more mass in the object, the more intense and numerous the orbitals.

After connecting all that needs to be connected in the cymatic field, the conjurer would then have finished creating the spell. Despite having all the constructions perfectly formed, the conjurer may not necessarily be able to cast the spell, as they have to be able to properly tune into the spell's energy, which depends on one's power levels relative to the power level of the spell. Quite a few factors contribute to this process, such as the spell's overall mass, its type of mass, the number of different elements, the atomic structuring, and more. The average-powered spell can only conjure *up to* 22 kg per conjuration; and as the atomic number in the elements increase, the less mass that can be conjured per element (and the percent for each element is not necessarily linear) – where said spell may only conjure mass up to *krypton* (Element No. 36). More specifically, a conjurer with said spell would be able to conjure roughly a maximum of six kilograms of iron, for example, but they would then still be able to conjure more matter to reach up to the 22 kg limit. Again, though, there are other factors to consider, such as *isotopes*, so these statistics can change.

In the context of combat equipment, an average mage with a respective-powered spell can (only) conjure standard rifles and handheld guns that lack, for example, *automated targeting systems* (ATSs) from various computing systems. The bullets within a magazine will also typically be part of an HRF (but only just); that is, when taking the data of a gun with a loaded magazine, the bullets will be part of it (the gun) as one HRF, so there would be one conjuration. Accordingly, in order to gain more bullets, the conjurer would have to reconjure the firearm again. It is, of course, possible to load real bullets into a conjured firearm, but this is not what most mages consider doing – for a variety of reasons, such dealing with the hassle of having to carry ammunition. Accordingly, mages try to maximize effectiveness with bigger magazines, where a net gain can be made in comparison to the cost of aether energy and the difficulty of the spell. Still, there are some weapons that do not use (metal) bullets, so ammunition may not be an issue, and this is an option for the average earth mage.

Average earth mages with respective-powered spells can also (only) conjure basic body armour; and normally, these are ceramic. While it might seem that 'simpler' atomic structures found in graphene armours, for example, would be easier to conjure than ceramic armours (that possess a wider variety of elements and more complex 3D-chemical structuring), this is not the case for a couple of reasons. For example, graphene features delocalized networks of electrons across its *covalent bonds*, which occur across its (the graphene's) *entire* structure. In comparison, many types of ceramic armours, with their larger polymer chains, exhibit electrons that are more localized to their *aromatic rings*. This is not to say that ceramic armours do not feature delocalized electrons, but rather, such armours do not feature delocalized electrons across the *entirety* of their structure like with graphene. This issue of locality makes it harder for a mage to tune into and, thus, cast the spell (at least with no instabilities).

Only master and supreme-level earth mages are able to conjure elements like uranium. Consider, though, that as each element increases, the difficulty is not always linear, as each element is itself different in nature from the last, where it is not a simple matter of each having 'more energy'. For example, the element uranium, in all its forms, is *unstable*. This greatly adds to its difficulty in casting. Therefore, no mage is capable of conjuring enough uranium to cause catastrophic events. The average supreme-level mage can manage to create up to 120 different chemical elements, but the highest ones have a rapid *half-life*, so they do not have many effective uses.

Like with alchemy, mages may conjure *lifeform* conjurations, but these, of course, are animal and plant analogues, which are useless in many cases. Even though such conjurations are sentient, they still lack the type and level of consciousness that the real versions possess. In other words, all conjured animals are meat robots or *golems*; and, despite them possessing some etheric energy, it (the etheric energy) is in a much more limited state, usually akin to the level of plant matter or some non-sapient insects. These limitations in the etheric come down to a golem's inability to navigate various probable realities. That is, many probabilities in their etheric energy are a result of probabilities being *projected* on to them rather than the golems having those probabilities created via their own freewill and level of consciousness. It is like how a rock has etheric energy, but *most* probabilities are due to other beings projecting their energy onto it by interacting with it, thereby potentially changing its outcome.

The lifeform spell constructions are themselves not faulty, but rather, they are so limited that they cannot fully create proper lifeforms. Many of these spells also come from tapping into other etheric states rather than copying from the current reality; in spite of the fact that tapping into other realities is harder, there is a net payoff in this regard to help create such beings, as other realities hold other kinds of stable information. There are also wetware technologies that can be conjured, and, some of these, interestingly, can be weapons. Most mages, though, detest wetware technologies, so such conjurations are rare. Moreover, only the most powerful of mages can conjure lifeform conjurations, and these lifeforms also happen to be weaker than what can be found through alchemical transfigurations. Even supreme-level mages may find their conjurations suffer from (slight) instabilities. The cymatic fields for lifeform conjurations also contain nodes so concentrated and speckled that the geometries appear 'curved', almost resembling complex DNA strands. This is not an additional process to a spell's construction but, instead, a new threshold of complexity.

To cast a spell, the conjurer must connect with the Aether and fuel the etheric field around them, which directly fuels the *intended* spell instead of all of the conjurer's spells and other etheric phenomena. This initiates the phasing process as the spell charges, which instantly incurs a CEC. During the phasing stage, the item will partially appear with varying degrees of faintness. Generally, while the phasing *into* reality has various times, the phasing *out* of reality occurs rather quickly for all spells; usually for the latter, this occurs for no more than two seconds. Because there are no extra stages needed in order to cast a spell after it has initially been created, conjuration magic – whilst straightforward and lacking certain neat features – is very simple compared to other schools of magic. Accordingly, non-earth types of mages sometimes become jealous of this point. Still, since conjurers pay for the mass of a conjuration itself instead of the *change* in reality in the case of alchemical magic, conjurations are more expensive than alchemical transfigurations. This means that while the respective power levels for spells cost the same across the two schools of magic (not including overcharging), the amount and type of mass in conjurations is less than in alchemy.

As with other magics, an ACE still applies for conjurations. A conjured item's matter/energy will vanish after the spell has finished, losing its vibration and melding back into the Aether. So, if a table is created, and a microscopic shard is chiselled off, both the table and the shard will disappear back into the Aether when the spell is no longer powered. If the shard extends beyond the ACE before the mage stops the spell, the shard will disappear. Anything positioned between the conjured item and the conjurer may distort the connection, especially materials like thick cement walls. When such blockages occur, the spell will stop – but only if the SCA itself is beyond the blockage; if, on the other hand, only a portion of the spell is beyond the blockage, then the spell itself will not cease – only the portion.

When light (from the sun, for example) reflects off a conjured object – along with establishing the resultant visible colours of the object – it will pass the ACE. This is because the light itself is not of the conjured item, so people can still see conjured items beyond the ACE. However, if the conjured item produces its own light, then people outside of the ACE may not necessarily see it, as the photons may disappear before reaching their eyes. Still, in the case of said conjured photons, they are still normally seen outside of the ACE, anyway, because, as noted in the *General Ontology* section, parts of a spell may, nevertheless, temporarily (but only very shortly) last outside of the ACE due to there being some conscious energy in it, giving items like bullets etc., phased momentum. The stored energy, interestingly, basically gives free energy to the conjuration without the user having to fuel it. Moreover, mages can even *consciously* project tiny shells of their ACE out, which requires great concentration, so this is another way bullets, for example, can temporarily last outside the ACE.

All materials in a conjuration emerge preformed, so a slab of bronze would not emerge as copper and tin at first. If any properties in the conjuration bond with materials of the Caelverse, then, when the spell stops, all bonds would break apart. Given that the non-conjured atoms of the Caelverse would not lose their electrons (specifically, they would not disappear into the Aether *with* the conjuration), then, in most cases, the materials will simply return to their state without any violent effect. Still, there are cases where particles of the Caelverse may become unstable, but this is not normally a major issue. It is also unwise to eat conjured foods, for example, as, once they disappear back to the Aether, they can leave one feeling hungrier than before.

When viewed classically, the *laws of thermodynamics* are not technically broken when a mage conjures an item, as energy is still being drawn from a source (the Aether) that encompasses a system (the Caelverse). Even so, such energy returns to the Aether, anyway. As the spell ethereally passes back to the Aether by way of phasing, there is no chemical decomposition or radioactive decay. Since energy is drawn from the Aether and not from one's physical surroundings, there is also no need for the Caelverse's energy to *thermodynamically* balance itself out, so creating a conjuration that generates fire will not result in the *endothermic* process of ice particles emerging nearby.

The issue of added energy, though, becomes more complicated when a spell creates energy, namely: *potential energy*. A classic example of this is gravitational potential. For example, if an object (originally from the Caelverse) is lifted up via a levitating conjured item, and then the spell finishes, there will be more energy 'added' to the Caelverse. That is, the uplifted item would now have more kinetic energy simply due to falling (or the potential to fall), which otherwise would not have happened normally. The matter becomes more complex when other variables are added. However, while it may seem profitable (economically, for example) to conjure items freely and then use that to develop extra potential energy, there are limits, and it is generally a waste of time, as there is little net gain in the activity.

Conjurations may be moved around in the air at will during the phasing process, and so, even heavy objects can be manoeuvred into suitable positions before appearing. If the mage had already conjured a heavy object and yet needed it lifted up to a certain location, they would have to stop the spell, charge it again, then move it into the position they want. Since even the average-powered spell will take about seven seconds to charge at minimum for all mages, there is normally plenty of time to get the position correct in the phasing process. In all cases, the conjuration would not gain momentum when it is moved around in the air – no matter the speed; and, thus, it would not be effectively 'thrown'. The same principle of moving phasing conjurations (and also for having to move phased conjurations effectively by recreating them) also applies to holograms, so it does not matter how much a conjuration weighs or does not weigh. *Moving* phasing items in the air also technically uses *slightly* more aether energy, but such levels are truly negligible.

When a phasing conjuration is making contact with solid matter like floors and walls, its etheric field will send etheric signals to the conjurer (who should be able to feel it), by default alerting the conjurer to what is occurring. A conjuration will do this because it will naturally 'prefer' to emerge in non-solid (and non-liquid) environments. In fact, the phasing conjuration will also automatically bounce away from such matter. However, with only a little bit of force, the conjurer can still move the phasing item through any matter, including most forcefield grades; still, this only applies if the conjurer does not lose conscious connection to the phasing conjuration when it is on the other side of something, like forcefields.

# 3.6: School of Phasarchement:

## 3.6.1: Introduction:

*Phasarchement* as a word derives from two words plus a suffix; namely, *phase, archetype,* and *ment,* altogether pronounced: fayz-är-ki-mu*h*nt (in other words: phase + arche from archetype + ment, like from state*ment*). Essentially, phasarchement (alternatively spelled *phasearchement*) magic is the art, action, result, and state of manifesting specific archetypal energies and masses of different but particular phases or phase states. For phasarchement magic, mages will draw upon the Aether to fuel a particular but major component in their etheric aura, which, in turn, can be channelled to physically manifest various phenomena. Similar to a mage's GAP, this auric *matrix* in the etheric realm is called the *lumarchetrix* (or colloquially the *lumatrix,* for short*),* which is derived from *luminescent, archetypal,* and *matrix.* Meanwhile, the tangible, physically-manifested *energy* inside or outside of any manifested mass from this matrix is called *photomission energy,* with the name existing to help distinguish it from energies originally found in the Caelverse, as the former will return to the Aether.

As with all other schools of magic, phasarchement is consciousness-based, so mages must be conscious enough to connect to a source of power that has such potential rather than manipulating any energy alone. Hence, the lumarchetrix is the necessary medium for this magic to materialize *and* structure the photomission energy in a way that allows it to form into particular matter. The lumarchetrix, for this reason, contains the archetypal potential of multiple *classes* (known explicitly as *phasarchement archetypal classes* or PACs) and their embodied *types* (more specifically, *ultra-state types* or USTs), indexed in *Section 3.6.5.* Fundamentally based on the essential flow of energy in reality itself, PACs are archetypally broader and more universal in their inherent manifest constitution than USTs, which are more corporeally existential, exhibit in particularized occurring phenomena in the form of states of matter when collectively formed. These PACs and USTs are inherent to the lumarchetrix, and, therefore, no spell crafting is involved with phasarchement magic. Ultimately, the lumarchetrix is both a pool of energy and a matrix of particular potential.

Mages are also able to absorb the lumarchetrix energy of other auras to fuel their own lumarchetrix, which is generally accomplished by using certain USTs of a particular PAC. Some of these USTs can also absorb the photomission energy of another mage's UST forms; however, the photomission energy will still convert to the etheric first before it will convert to one's lumarchetrix. If one's UST forms are in proximity to the UST forms that they are absorbing energy from, some of this photomission energy may directly power said forms, but most of the absorbed energy will still convert to the etheric. There is also the possibility of absorbing energy purely *of* (that is, originally from) the Caelverse, but this is very inefficient, and the absorbed energy will normally only just physically power the UST forms without converting to the etheric. It is also possible to absorb other etheric energy to fuel one's lumarchetrix, GAP, or general etheric aura, but this is normally inefficient as well.

While not a perfect analogy, the user's aura and manifested USTs in the physical realm, in the abovesaid context, are akin to an electrical device receiving electrical energy to power it. The device, here, does not infinitely build electricity inside it, and it only consumes the amount necessary for its operation. When the device in question requires more energy, more electrical energy flows into it. As for the conversion from photomission to the etheric, this is also akin to a house generating more electrical energy than it needs, in turn sending surplus electricity to the grid (in this case, the lumarchetrix). Photomission to lumarchetrix conversion is possible because all photomission energy (powering the UST forms) possess *aether-bound properties* (like with magically-conjured items); and, therefore, as they must return to the Aether at some point, they are able to also leave the Caelverse's physical realm and pass into the etheric with ease. In the case where energy from the Caelverse powers the UST form (as a UST), the energy will not infinitely build inside the form, and so, the UST form will not become more (and more) powerful (even if no energy is able to convert to the lumarchetrix for absorption).

Lumarchetrix and photomission energies are innately in equilibrium with the mage's physical body – even when a lumarchetrix is distorted or out of synchronization with the mage. Accordingly, manifested particles in the USTs will always concentrate *around* the user's body while simultaneously remaining inside an *aura*, which itself is part of – and in equilibrium with – the mage's being. While the lumarchetrix is an aura in the etheric, the physically-measurable space around the mage that they can channel lumarchetrix energy into is the *physical aura* – with its name deriving from the fact that it is the space in the physical realm. For most mages, this is generally just over three metres in diameter (with the central point being the centre of their bodies – so, around the sternum). The user's aura will typically be spherical, so this means that there will be less auric space between the user's feet and the bottom of their aura compared to their chest and the edge of the aura horizontally across from it. Despite this sphericality, UST particles 'prefer' to emerge in non-solid areas, so normally, no mass forms *in* the ground or floor underneath the user. Also, when a user's body brushes against or into the floating particles (such as the user moving their arm into the particle formations), the forms (mass of particles) will accordingly move.

Mages also have an option to create *primed photonic outlines* (PPOs), which are very light pre-renders of ultra-state formations. The phenomenon of these *photonic clouds* (basically, photons clumped together in floating clouds) is akin to conjuration phase states that can be moved around in the air, but in this case, they are *physically* visible as well. Essentially, PPOs allow the user to choose the direction and the location of where the UST particles will emerge and form with their minds – along with when they form, too. In so doing, the creator can save great amounts of lumarchetrix energy, as the PPOs cost *far* less to maintain than actual normal mass. That is, the user does not have to waste time repositioning already-formed ultra-states particles, which costs energy for every moment they exist. Since the photons are part of molecules rather than simply travelling superfast as an electromagnetic frequency, the user is not bathing in radiation, nor are they blinded by great amounts of light.

USTs gain the label 'ultra' because they differ from both normal states of matter and the already-unusual super-states, such as supersolids. Normal states of matter include solids, liquids, gases, and plasma, which are easily found throughout the Caelverse. Super-states, however, are generally hard to find, and in many cases, they can only be artificially created. Moreover, to create super-states, much energy is required, generally by altering temperatures to extreme degrees. Ultra-states, on the other hand, do not require extreme temperatures to create and are far more stable than their super-state counterparts (unless no energy powers them). The USTs that mages form normally do not possess much mass yet are capable of extremely interesting and powerful effects. The particles generated in a UST vary in properties, but since they are all in an ultra-state of matter, they are broadly grouped as *ultrachite*. Still, to distinguish from ultra-states found outside of phasarchement, they are some-times called *phasarchite*. The all-purpose labels cover multiple states for the different available USTs, which are *ultra: solid, liquid, gas, plasma, conductivity,* and *spacetime crystals.* Each of these ultra states also have *partial condensate properties* (meaning: the particles in a state of matter will basically have the same quantum state, so they will act as if a single quantum entity – essentially, a super atom – but they will exhibit other states as well).

Not everything created inside the physical aura has to take the shape of an aura. Indeed, most creations are much smaller than the aura itself, especially when they are concentrated. As one's ACE, auras can be expanded in size, but this normally requires more *conscious* focus (rather than more *energy* from the lumarchetrix). This means that there can be small but powerful auras in contrast to bigger, weaker auras; but generally, if a mage has greater conscious focus, it scales with greater power levels. A mage also has multiple *sub auras* based on the USTs they are using, all of which interlace and coalesce into their *aggregate physical aura* (APA), which synchronizes with all the active USTs and keeps them in harmony. For brevity and ease of reference, many mages normally just refer to one aura, which they call 'the aura'.

Because of the different nature of each UST, each creation naturally takes place in a new sub aura and not another one in use. However, a mage cannot create more than one aura of both the same UST and PAC – any attempt to do so will only generate more energy into that particular aura – nor can they create multiple PACs of the same UST (despite unverified legends speaking of mythical mages being able to accomplish such a feat). For clarification, mages cannot create two or more auras of the same type of ultrachite with different PACs nor have a single manifested UST form possess multiple PACs. Mages, nevertheless, can create different UST forms of assorted PACs at once. It also only takes a split second for a mage to not only create a UST aura but also to switch its PAC. Even though all the auras emanate from the core of the mage and interlace with one another, they each have a respective transformative area for ultrachite (as a result of auric equilibrium) that does not normally interfere with other already-transformed areas; meaning: the auras basically non-rigidly stack.

Ultrachite naturally forms in a specific way (such as the shape and density), and this establishes *form-based effects* (FBEs). For example, the ultra-gas ultrachite automatically generates a vortex, and the *form* of the vortex itself adds effects to the ultra-gas, such as how it moves itself and other things in its field. The ultra-state gas itself, on the other hand, establishes *state-based effects* (SBEs), which inflict various effects – specifically, in the case of ultra-gas, this is not much compared to other ultra-states, such ultra-solid, which can block various matter in assorted ways; but interestingly, the SBEs of ultra-gas, for example, nonetheless help to establish the FBE of the vortex itself, similar to how superfluids can continue spinning basically forever once stirred. All of this is also contrasted with *class-based effects* (CBEs) – based on the PACs – which add unique effects to the USTs, such as the ability to demagnetize certain matter or to increase the vulnerability of matter to decompositions. The forms themselves are a natural result of how the ultra-state particles structure at the molecular level while interacting with each other in an auric field – which, furthermore, are not always the creation of the mage's intent. Therefore, a mage, for example, cannot easily change an ultra-gas vortex to an immobile cube with their intent alone.

Unlike magically-conjured items that have already been phased into reality, mages can still *effectively* move their manifest UST forms around their aura with their minds. Technically, users do not actually move their ultrachite around as if a phase state in conjuration; instead, users make the USTs *perform* in a particular way via available particular wave function changes, which *practically* makes ultrachite able to move anywhere around the aura at the user's will. So, for example, the manifested ultra-state plasma particles floating around in an aura can be concentrated and drawn towards a central point to form a ball. The concentration, in this case, occurs when the user alters the particles' potential vectors first by altering energetic orientations via the lumarchetrix working through the quantum level and wave functions. The particles accordingly react to the changes, in turn changing their trajectory as they move throughout the aura. The same principle also applies to PPOs.

For the most part, it is a user's ACE aptitude that will determine the ability to move particles in the aura. It also helps that all available ultrachite is lightweight and that the particles naturally hover in the aura (from the ground and each other – while also being aligned with the user's body) due to their unusual electrical and magnetic nature. While ultrachite particles hover in the aura, they are not easily forced out of the aura from external forces, like with strong winds – especially the ultra-conductivity and ultra-spacetime crystal states – due to their said unusual nature. The particles in a particular aura will also work in unison as a single entity due to their special partial condensate properties – bolstered by the fact that they are also HRFs – which adds to the overall resistance in this context. Moreover, even the FBEs, such as the ultra-liquid being able to be in a cloud form, will also provide added resistance.

Ultra-states rarely exist in nature – apart from what is found in crystal moons. They have, however, been made in laboratories. Nevertheless, while ultra-states are more stable than super-states, laboratory-formed ultra-states have thus far only remained stable for a few seconds. Class-based ultrachite (found in phasarchement magic), specifically, has never been created in laboratories, though. Mages using conjuration and alchemy magic have managed to create class-based ultrachite, but the problem with these manifestations is that they are not tied to a mage's lumarchetrix and, accordingly, are not subject to its laws, bringing both limitations and advantages. That is, the ultrachite is not in auric equilibrium, and these conjurations and alchemical transfigurations cannot be utilized in the context of a lumarchetrix-influenced aura. Accordingly, particles float away from the conjurer or do not concentrate into particular forms, so the outcome of the FBEs ultimately renders the SBEs and CBEs redundant. Many CBEs do not work (properly), anyway, regardless of the lack of proper FBEs, as they require a proper connection to the mage as well. One benefit to conjured ultra-states, nonetheless, is that the conjurer does not have to be subject to problems like a desynchronized lumarchetrix, which distorts creations. Still, a user's etheric auras, in general, can distort, which is similar to a desynchronized lumarchetrix.

Photomission energy is, ultimately, just energy – but one that has been specifically generated with magic, so it has certain properties. All ultrachite is made up of this type of energy, and when the user stops channelling lumarchetrix energy, then the *ultrachite* (along with the photomission energy in it) will return to the Aether (without radioactive decay). While powered inside the aura, ultrachite will rejuvenate and regenerate itself from channelled lumarchetrix energy, lasting for varying amounts of time, depending on power levels and the UST. Once the ultrachite is formed, however, a user will just continue fuelling their ultrachite rather than creating more until it either is used in a particular manner or damaged (into what is known as *damaged ultrachite particles* – or DUPs – which lose their FBEs, CBEs, and practical SBEs before rapidly returning to the Aether).

As with GAP magic, users are charged with CECs for creating ultrachite, which is followed by MECs. Innately, all energy basically seeks to transfer from higher states to lower states. This means that the powered ultrachite in an aura will transfer photomission energy over to standard particles (of the Caelverse) in the atmosphere inside and outside of the aura. Specifically, the energy will conduct through or be absorbed into non-ultrachite properties; but this transferal does not create additional ultrachite for these other particles outside the aura, and the energy does not last long before going back to the Aether. Unlike with GAP magic, mages cannot consciously, in any *effective* way, project tiny shells of their ACE out for their phasarchement ultrachite due to ACE extensions, in this context, being more volatile. So, even though a mage might be able to shoot tiny shells out to extend their ACE, these shells are far below the needed threshold of consciousness for any effect.

Nevertheless, ultrachite particles can still temporarily (but only very shortly) *leave* the *ACE* before returning to the Aether due to having phased momentum, as with GAP magic. Note that when there is a loss of momentum (whether the electrons are in a ground state or not), the return to the Aether is absolutely sharp rather than gradual. Each UST form will have varying levels of such phased momentum, but for most forms, this is less than a second. The exceptions to this are the ultra-state plasma UST, which can last about six seconds outside the ACE (unless as DUPs), and *potentially* ultra-state liquid, which varies in time due to *chance*. Some ultra-spacetime crystal fields can also last indefinitely 'outside' the aura due to how they bend dimensions (that is, they are still basically in the aura), while ultra-state gas can extend photomission energy about half a metre from the aura, negating this problem in the given area. Some of these USTs have longer times frames for phased momentum compared to most conjured items due to how their quantum particles are organized and exist.

Essentially, the strange nature of the physical, in this case, has effects on the etheric, which then allows for more conscious energy to be *stored* in them.

To be clear, the stored conscious energy in a UST form is not the same as the user consciously powering them, so it is no longer in the ACE. When any UST form has any phased momentum, it will still possess 100% of its power, where the momentum would still fully drive energy from the Aether back into the particles before returning again and then permanently stopping. All particles in a UST form will be quantumly connected, so individual particles (unless as DUPs) will not lose phased momentum before other particles; that is, the UST form, *as a whole*, will lose momentum and then disappear as a whole. If a user were to purposely switch a UST off, it would rapidly stop the momentum (much faster than the abovesaid figures), instantly ceasing the existence of any form; note that this also applies to GAP spells. Because the UST form, in this case, is outside the ACE, then the user will no longer be powering it, so the aura would then be out of equilibrium, and so the user would then make more of the ultrachite in their aura.

Ultimately, both the ultrachite and/or photomission energy will eventually return to the Aether *without* passing through a lumarchetrix first (assuming no mage absorbs the energy). Accordingly, mages cannot recycle their own photomission energy and avoid having to regain more energy from the Aether. It may seem, then, that any energy that a mage absorbs (from another mage) would return to the Aether when it only just reaches the new lumarchetrix, as it was soon to return, anyway; but this is not the case due to the energy 'revitalizing' into a *new* aura of consciousness. That is, the original user of the photomission energy cannot basically absorb their own energy as such without some kind of phenomenon that allows for this process. This is where certain USTs of particular PACs perform this necessary function, which has a basis in both the physical properties of the manifested UST and the consciousness of the absorber. Unfortunately for users, they cannot use such USTs on their own energy due to an unchangeable alignment issue, where auric equilibrium is responsible.

As stated in *Section 3.1*, the energy in the lumarchetrix also lasts longer than in photomission form because the etheric realm naturally has a different time standard than the physical. In addition, while in the etheric, lumarchetrix energy is not being used in the same way photomission energy is being used. When in photonic cloud form, a user's photomission energy will not normally leave the aura (apart from small amounts of light that will radiate from the clouds – which is different from there being only pure electromagnetic energy). Since photons travel super fast, they can leave the aura and, in most cases, still have enough phased momentum to reach people's eyes before returning to the Aether. PPOs themselves, though, are very limited in their time frame outside of a user's aura.

With usage, the lumarchetrix will begin to deplete, but mages automatically refill it with more aether energy while engaged with the phasarchement magic itself. The recharge rate is known as the *lumarchetrix recharge rate* (LRR), which is the same as when a mage recharges their GAP. Mages also have the ability to intentionally defuel the lumarchetrix partially or completely – a feat that normally has contextually applicable reasons but is not often done. One example may include odd situations where the user cannot attack an opponent, but they nevertheless would not want an opponent to absorb their energy. Even when automatically recharging the lumarchetrix, most mages, however, will experience a net loss of lumarchetrix energy when using even just a moderate amount of photomission energy.

In contrast, mages of higher power levels *may* experience a net gain in lumarchetrix energy if their LRR happens to be greater than the power level of the ultrachite they are using – which does not always occur due to power levels mostly *scaling* (further explained in *Section 3.6.2*). Even then, this only occurs for users not (overly) using multiple USTs at once. When a mage's lumarchetrix energy reaches zero percent, they experience *lumarchetrix energy depletion* (LED) – or simply *depletion* – and cannot create any ultrachite. However, since mages can (immediately) regain lumarchetrix energy from the Aether, it would seem, then, that depletion is not a setback. The problem is, when LED occurs, the lumarchetrix experiences full *instability* (like with GAP magic from one's etheric aura), which prevents the user from channelling any UST forms for a certain period; for most mages, this is about six seconds. A user, nevertheless, can still fully recharge their lumarchetrix in the meantime (without any delay period), so when the instability finishes, they normally have enough energy to begin (re)creating most UST forms.

Then there is the eventual issue of *etheric energy exhaustion* (EEE) – or just *exhaustion* – which is essentially the same phenomenon as when a GAP exhausts. Basically, EEE occurs when the mage's connection to the Aether wanes through loss of conscious focus and recharging the lumarchetrix *and* GAP either slows down incredibly or stops fully (so, there is no effective and isolated *lumarchetrix energy exhaustion*). While in a state of exhaustion, the mage may still be totally awake, and so, it really amounts to how the mage's state of consciousness relates to the Aether. Exhaustion can occur before a mage depletes due to it being a connection issue to the Aether; and most mages recover from EEE after a night's rest or roughly after a twenty-four-hour period. Loss of focus *itself* happens through actual loss of (conscious) focus (to the Aether), but it can also occur by depleting one's lumarchetrix too often either only after just recovering from depletion or even using copious amounts of energy all the time from a full lumarchetrix. Parenthetically, depleting one's GAP is comparatively not as detrimental in this case (so, there is a difference between the two roots of exhaustion and the single outcome of exhaustion). Alternatively, reaching EEE could be due to other factors, such as being subject to someone else's phasarchement (or other types of) attacks.

As with GAP magic, there is an initial amount of time needed to connect to the Aether in the first place for before any energy can fill – and then later recharge – the lumarchetrix. In most cases, the average mage takes about thirty-five seconds to connect. Accordingly, it would seem as though staying connected to the Aether would be preferred over disconnecting because one could quickly use their magic at any one point in time without waiting. This can be vital when surprise attacks occur and instantly being able to defend oneself is necessary. However, staying connected to the Aether for long periods will also lead to EEE.

For the average mage, connections can last up to four consecutive hours, and simply disconnecting for a mere moment before reconnecting will not reduce this figure, nor will it affect the waiting time to end any EEE. Still, if the average mage disconnects after two consecutive hours of use without actually reaching EEE and then reconnects, say, five hours later, then there should be a *chance* that the four-hour figure might have reset by that point. However, the actual point it resets varies, where it is also *sharp*, and one usually either regains the full ability to properly reconnect or they do not. That is, unlike LED, which occurs and then ends with instant recharge of the lumarchetrix, EEE does not occur before shortly and instantly stopping for a few seconds, then returning momentarily before stopping again soon after. The only starting and stopping that may occur is the timeframe of recovery, which results from any actions that exhausts one's consciousness in a particular manner.

It normally takes about 120 seconds for the average mage to totally recharge their lumarchetrix from 0% when not using any other phasarchement energy – nor when exhausted. This figure means that the average mage recharges their lumarchetrix at a rate of 0.8333% per second until reaching the maximum capacity, which is known as the *maximum lumarchetrix pool* (MLP). After the *initial* connection to the Aether has been established, generally, a mage will begin at 100% of their MLP due to a 'flood' of energy occurring. Since mages have a maximum amount of lumarchetrix energy at any one point in time (that is, their MLP), they, therefore, cannot infinitely *stack* energy while recharging, nor infinitely siphon energy off opponents and then gain potentially infinite energy that does not deplete. Although, it *is* possible for a weaker mage to siphon extensive amounts of energy off a stronger mage (who can avoid being exhausted for a very long time), but such battles are usually short due to the stronger mage winning, anyway.

Mages also experience *lumarchetrix channel overcharging* (LCO) issues (or simply *overcharging*), which arise when ultrachite costs more than it normally would. It is actually the channelling (and converting) of lumarchetrix to photomission energy where the overcharging occurs, not the ultrachite itself costing more energy. There is no such thing as 'undercharging', however, and so, even the most powerful of mages who are not overcharged at all will still require a universal base amount of energy for each ultrachite particle that they produce – one cannot change the physics of the Caelverse, where less energy is required to create certain masses. Primarily, overcharging is either the result of certain ultrachite attacks causing the effect (against the user) or for the fact that most mages naturally get overcharged when they use higher than normal power levels; that is, the user would be out of *synchronization* with their lumarchetrix when using such different power levels.

Like with attacks that can absorb lumarchetrix energy, some attacks can *desynchronize* lumarchetrixes (the plural form of lumarchetrix – sometimes: *lumarchetrices*) due to the etheric being fundamentally tied to the physical; and so, when one is affected, the other is affected, too. In other words, when the lumarchetrix is desynchronized from the user, it is not the case that when the user channels energy that lumarchetrix energy enters the physical realm and then the user does not gain it. Instead, when the user channels energy, the lumarchetrix *does* actually funnel energy, but the energy does not funnel through to the physical realm, and it, instead, disperses into the wider etheric realm to then be permanently wasted – thus the phenomenon of overcharging. A lumarchetrix, nevertheless, can never be desynchronized more than 100%; that is, a desynchronized lumarchetrix is simply a desynchronized lumarchetrix.

However, when a user is subject to powerful desynchronization attacks that possess the *potential* for more than 100% desynchronization, then attempts to rectify the issue on behalf of the user will not necessarily lead to the lumarchetrix returning to sub-100% desynchronized levels. So, if an attack had a 200% potential desynchronization effect, a user may attempt to resynchronize their lumarchetrix, but they may only reduce the attacking power to 150%; and therefore, the user's lumarchetrix would still be 100% desynchronized. One's rate of overcharge also varies based on how far desynchronized their lumarchetrix is, and so, overcharging rates are not always equally proportional, and they typically begin incrementally before exponentially rising. Overcharging applies to both CECs and MECs, and a user can lose all of their lumarchetrix energy while trying to create or maintain their ultrachite while fully desynchronized, as manifested ultrachite (if any at all) will not have enough energy, so the lumarchetrix would naturally still try to funnel more energy into it until there is no energy left.

Each UST can be fuelled with varying energy levels, in turn changing both the duration and strength. Every individual mage has a particular *default power level* (DPL) when they channel any UST, which means that, by default, they will channel a set amount of energy in a specific time period for creating and maintaining ultrachite (so nothing below or above this default). The DPL, in this context, regards the power of the channelled UST and not other aptitude aspects of magic (such as one's aether connection or ACE – although, each have their own power levels that scale, anyway). Nevertheless, a user can *specifically* increase or decrease their DPL to a *higher power level* (HPL) or a *lower power level* (LPL), but this requires conscious focus.

With training, a mage's DPLs can increase; in which case, the new power level becomes their default. For clarification, HPLs and LPLs are not the same as when a new DPL has been attained (either through training or degeneration) and, instead, only occur when a mage deviates from their *current* DPL. However, if a mage temporarily lowers or raises their consciousness within a particular period (even within, say, an hour), they will then have a temporarily-changed DPL, which would not be the same as an HPL or LPL, even if the power levels would technically be potentially the same. When partial amounts of one's UST form either leaves the aura, returns to the Aether, or are turned into DUPs, the auric equilibrium will be out of balance due to what is being channelled; accordingly, the lumarchetrix will automatically fuel additional photomission energy for a UST *up to* the user's DPL (per their respective UST – of a PAC or non-PAC form – *Section 3.6.4* has more information on non-PACs). Mages who possess any DPL (whether strong or weak) will find contextually-applicable reasons for using HPLs and LPLs, as each has its pros and cons.

Although it is easy to create an LPL UST, it is harder to create an HPL UST due to *lumarchetrix channelling instabilities* (LCIs) when channelling; and, the further one deviates from their DPL (towards an HPL), the progressively harder the channelling becomes. Basically, the *channelling problem* of LCIs (not LCIs *themselves*) occur when lumarchetrix energy does not flow into the physical realm as photomission energy *when* a specific UST aura is *being* created (and not while it has already *been* created). Mages can experience different LCI rates, so a channel does not have to have a 100% LCI rate to experience instabilities. If, for example, the user fails to pass the LCI chance rate of, say, 60% for a *particular* UST (and not currently-formed USTs), the user will be unable to channel *any* energy into that specific UST (that is, *create* the UST) for a particular amount of time; for most mages, this cooldown period (or 'wait out') is about three seconds. LCIs apply to USTs themselves and not specifically to PACs *of* USTs, so a user cannot change the PAC *of* a failed UST to then channel the same UST. This allowable division occurs as a result of PACs being more archetypal than USTs, in turn affecting the way a mage channel forms into the Caelverse. A more detailed ontological understanding of PACs can be gained from *Section 3.6.4*.

The LCI issue, nevertheless, is not so simple, and LCIs may even occur for using multiple USTs and/or PACs at once; but this would not technically mean that all USTs and PACs *themselves*, in this case, would be affected; but rather, it would specifically affect the ability to *use* multiple USTs and PACs at once. So, if failure occurred while channelling multiple USTs, it (the failure) would only occur for the attempted final (and any additional) UST(s), not all currently-formed (and successful) USTs, thus limiting the number of active USTs. If it were a PAC issue, then the mage would not be able to channel the attempted UST *as* that specific PAC (and so, no UST would form) nor any other USTs *of* that specific PAC, thus limiting the number of active PACs. In both cases, there would still be a cooldown period. LCIs can also result from using particular USTs themselves (such as ultra-conductive and ultra-space time crystal states due to their more complex nature). There are also cases where one's lumarchetrix itself may be desynchronized, which results in adding individual instability modifiers for all of the above issues. Unlike overcharging, no lumarchetrix energy is wasted with a failed UST channel, as there was never a proper connection in the first place.

Creating an HPL or LPL does not entail a charge time, but the user may need a moment to focus their consciousness in order to channel such energy. *Charging* the *particularized effect phase* or *particle effect phase* (PEP) of already-created ultrachite is itself another matter, which is called *ultrachite phase charging* (UPC). PEPs are types of phases that exist within the phase (state of matter) of USTs, having various types of effects. When ultrachite is created, the particles may not be ready to exercise their CBEs due to being in *dormant effect status* (DES), so a UPC may be required to turn their PEP into *active effect status* (AES). Sometimes, the terms *latent* and *inactive* are used instead of 'dormant' for respective and specific contexts concerning *when* the particles are dormant; for example, 'latent' (LES) may be used for initially-formed ultrachite that have yet to reveal their potential, whereas 'inactive' (IES) may be used for when the PEP has turned from active to dormant; but generally, the term 'dormant' is used overall.

The reasons vary slightly per ultrachite as to why they may not be ready to exercise their CBEs (such as being unstable initially or after continued periods of use, which would otherwise lead to various issues), but basically, the ultrachite particles require further self-modulation and stabilization once created in order to produce their CBEs. While in DES, all the particles are already present with their needed energy to fuel the magic for when they are later in AES; and even though the process of a UPC *does* use energy, this is extremely marginal and *practically* does not weaken the ultrachite's normal functions. For clarification, while a user's ultrachite has been UPC'd and now is in AES, it will not use nor require additional energy. A single ultrachite particle is also either in AES or DES, not both simultaneously; they may be able to change rapidly, and not all particles in an aura have to be only in one PEP or the other. Indeed, in many cases during combat, one's auras can be filled with a mix of AES and DES particles. Changing the status of ultrachite particles does not cause, alter, or interfere with LCIs, nor is it a form of channelling and creating new ultrachite.

Most UST forms (as a *whole* – and not individual particles) that require a UPC for their CBEs will need to *fully* charge and cannot be *partially* charged; this is just initially for the PEP changing of the whole UST form, so some individual particles *may* still later turn back to DES while others in the aura remain in AES. If any ultrachite particles are lost in the UST form while the charging occurs, the UST form as a whole will still hold stability, and the UPC process will continue. So, if it takes, say, eight seconds to UPC, then the user cannot just charge for seven seconds and then have 87.5% of the particles in AES for the CBE powers; but there may be cases where the UST form may drop to 87.5% AES or less *after* the charge. However, for some UST forms, partial PEP charging is an option.

For most UST forms that have been UPC'd, the AES of their particles will only last for a certain duration before they are phased changed back to DES. When this occurs, a cooldown time (for the whole UST) applies before a timed charge (for the whole UST) is required again. Users, nevertheless, are able to stop a UPC midway at any point (but not pause it), with no cooldown penalty applying. Furthermore, users can switch currently-active AES particles off, but this would still incur a cooldown (and charge) time before they (the user) could phase change the particles back to AES. Since PEP changing is a corporealized phenomenon, a user cannot UPC one UST form and then switch the PAC and then have the new UST already PEP changed; that is, each UST of a certain PAC is unique.

PEP changing is also not limited to a UPC, and some ultrachite particles can (simply and rapidly) *switch* PEPs (automatically), such as when *particle inhibition* (that is, deactivation) transpires or when the user wills it – or even when certain phenomena occur, such as when the ultrachite particles contact solid and dense-enough materials at a certain speed. This is known as *ultrachite phase switching* (UPS). Switched particles, in this context, do not have duration limits; in fact, many UST forms that have particles that can UPS will already have full AES status on creation; but in many other cases, the AES of the particles will not last, anyway, due to a lack of photomission energy powering them outside the aura (for more information, see *discharges* in *Section 3.6.3.2*, as one example).

In some *modes* for ultrachite discharges and vortices, users cannot (allow for later) change (of) the status of the particles after creation. UST forms that can have UPS'd particles also do not need to have every particle PEP changed as a whole UST form initially, so individual particles within the whole can switch (sometimes back and forth). DES ultrachite particles have the same photomission MECs as AES ultrachite, and, accordingly, this is one of the reasons why some mages might use PPOs in certain cases. PPOs, however, cannot be UPC'd, so they are only useful for placing and readying *where* a user needs the ultrachite to be located.

UST forms not only have the potential to lose some of their particles via damage but also some of their energy in order to sustain damage. Of course, when this occurs, more energy from the lumarchetrix will flow into the ultrachite. However, this does not mean that the state or condition of the ultrachite will necessarily improve, as the channelled energy may only restore the energy of already-existing particles. In other words, if a particular UST form faces a certain problem, the inflowing of energy from the lumarchetrix would not instantly heal/remedy the problem and would, instead, only top up the maximum amount of energy so that the UST form can continue to not only exist but also carry on performing its functions. Still, some of these functions depend on there not being a particular problem, and so, normally, there is a cooldown period for the UST particles to naturally heal.

In the event that particles have been destroyed (as DUPs) or lost, then the new particles may still incur some of the problems of the old particles via being part of related *quantumly-imbalanced forms* (QIFs). Basically as if holding a memory, the new particles will pick up on *specific* problems of the last particles (that are more than mere 'damage', such as imposed deactivation) until the cooldown period resets or reduces. As a result, mages cannot simply switch off a UST and then recreate it in the hopes of restoring it to a perfect state. Even if this were not the case, recreating USTs incur further CECs, and rapid repeated recreation itself (not merely greatly refuelling a UST that is already manifested) introduces and increases particular problems, such as *lumarchetrix-based overloading* (LBO) – or, more broadly, *etheric-based overloading (EBO)*. Like with GAP magic, LBOs incur a penalty, which prevents the mage from manifesting that particular UST again; and this normally begins at roughly nine seconds for most mages for all USTs before increasing greatly for each time the UST is used thereafter before it (the aura) fully cools down. Note that LBOs are different from the physical-based overloading explained later in *Section 3.6.3.1*, which relates to QIFs (which are physical).

Despite mages having the ability to create HPLs, another limitation applies, which is a mage's maximum *lumarchetrix channel rate* (LCR). Essentially, all mages have a maximum amount of lumarchetrix energy that can be channelled (or siphoned from and then converted into photomission energy) at any one point in time. Normally, however, a mage's maximum LCR is much higher than what most of their DPL and HPL ultrachite naturally costs. For the majority of mages, their LCR is limited to 33% of their MLP per second, whereas most ultrachite will cost no more than 5% of an average mage's MLP to create. The only power that nearly meets this threshold is the ultra-spacetime crystal state; and so, by using this UST, most mages cannot simultaneously create much other ultrachite. This also means that almost no mage can create an HPL one rank higher than their DPL for ultra-spacetime crystal ultrachite. Technically, a mage could create ultrachite that reaches their maximum LCR yet not be overcharged, as overcharging is a different issue based primarily on exceeding DPLs or being desynchronized via attacks.

In order to properly form, certain ultrachite molecules and compounds must be formed together rather than in pieces within a specific period; thus, the LCR threshold means that a user cannot create some ultrachite over the course of multiple seconds as an alternative. Plus, DPLs prevent this from occurring. Despite all USTs being part of an auric equilibrium, no UST will naturally lower its DPL when other USTs are simultaneously being used in order to meet the auric equilibrium. That is, all individual USTs retain their DPLs, so if a user wishes to create an LPL or an HPL, they would have to totally create new ultrachite.

A user's UST form, in other words, will not automatically switch to an LPL if the LCR were met; instead, no other ultrachite would be formed unless the user intentionally created an LPL – which would be available to the user up to the LCR limit. Likewise, LPLs will not be automatically generated when a user has very low lumarchetrix energy (lower than the CEC for a DPL form). When a user happens to be totally out of energy (depleted), then whatever UST forms they have active will disappear and will not automatically reform once both the lumarchetrix recharges enough energy – or some energy (for potential LPLs) – and when the 100% LCI problem (for all UST forms) finishes due to the user experiencing LED. The new UST forms, moreover, would incur CECs and potentially LCIs.

For a better understanding, let us take an example of a mage with an LCR of 33%. If the mage already has two USTs active (with both adding to 32% of the LCR), then they decided to create a third UST with a DPL of 2% of their MLP, the third UST would not be formed. However, the mage would have the option to create an LPL worth 1% of their MLP for the CEC to meet the 33% threshold. If the percentages were all MECs, the same issue would still apply. If, however, 33% of the mage's LCR had already been met with the first two USTs, then if the third UST were attempted, the other two active USTs would not lower to LPLs, nor would they be switched off. The LCR threshold also prevents great amounts of photomission energy from being siphoned, but most attacks and effects never reach this threshold, anyway. Furthermore, the LCR prevents a fully desynchronized lumarchetrix from wasting all of its energy at once when it is trying to funnel energy into the physical realm to create or maintain ultrachite; but with the LCR at 33% *per second*, this does not help the mage much in this situation.

It is nevertheless possible for mages to simply use psychic powers to absorb an opponent's lumarchetrix energy without using particular ultrachite attacks. The same phenomenon can basically be applied to one's GAP. The reason why this is possible is due to the lumarchetrix being etheric, so psychic energies may be able to connect with lumarchetrixes. As lumarchetrix energy is being psychically siphoned, the victim can still reacquire the energy, but this does not happen often, as not only is the said energy firstly being 'pulled' away, it also remains temporarily in a *disturbed* state from its (the victim's) natural auric equilibrium and consciousness. The same applies to photomission energy that is being stolen. Lumarchetrix energy does not remain naturally in a disturbed state forever, and it will find stability through joining a new lumarchetrix that is sucking it in, refuelling the attacking mage. Note that decoupled lumarchetrix energy finding rest and equilibrium in another's lumarchetrix is technically different than using ultrachite attacks to siphon lumarchetrix energy, as the former is a natural phenomenon.

Combined with the fact that the lumarchetrix is etheric and, therefore, less localized than the physical realm (though not totally nonlocalized), this means that a third party elsewhere may absorb the energy; but generally, they have to be 'close by'. Any absorbing party, however, must have an active lumarchetrix to absorb lumarchetrix energy, just like with the reverse; that is, the only way to absorb lumarchetrix energy is if the victim has an active lumarchetrix in the first place. In most cases, it is far easier and more effective just to use ultrachite attacks than psychic powers in order to siphon lumarchetrix energy. When a mage is rendered unconscious, their lumarchetrix normally disappears within a relatively short amount of time; as such, if one needs to absorb energy from an opponent, they ought to do it in the heat of battle against conscious attackers instead of the unconscious. In this context, one's lumarchetrix actually disappears and does not simply become empty of energy; one's GAP also experiences the same phenomenon, so mages have to actually have the specific active etheric field around them to receive, store, and use aether energy. For clarification, the lumarchetrix (and GAP) does not totally disappear; instead, it enters a dormant phase or state.

## 3.6.2: Ranks:

For phasarchement (and the other schools of magic), there is a sharp probability distribution (a sharp bell curve represented on a graph) amongst university graduate mages regarding both their OPLs and individual power levels for their aptitude aspects. Accordingly, very few mages are extremely powerful; and even then, the most powerful mages do not reach levels beyond certain thresholds. This distribution also means that only a small percentage of mages are actually very weak (apart from certain demographics, such as those nearing death due to diseases or those who did not attend university and were instead placed in special-needs centres). Most graduate mages (both recent and old), therefore, have relatively equal power levels. According to the *Phasarchement Proficiency Registry*, the majority of graduate mages, therefore, fall into the power-level category of *average* (or *standard* or *regular*), while those with DPLs outside of this range fall accordingly into the following list *relative* to 'average'. The following rankings also apply to GAP magics, and GAP magic statistics also strongly correlate with the following phasarchement statistics:

1: Inept (Negligible)/Low(minimum)-achiever – 0.01%
2: Deficient/Underachiever – 1%
3: Novice/Student(-equivalent) – 7%
4: Average/Standard/Regular – 82%
5: Advanced/Expert – 7%
6: Elite – 3%
7: Master – 0.003%
8: Supreme – 0.00001%

The ranking system uses a *piecemeal growth model*, where there is a breaking point after the average rank. Basically, there are two levels of growth, where from inept to average, there is an exponential growth, and after average, the rate of increase changes with linear growth of arithmetic progression for each succeeding rank. In other words, the common ratio of two (2) between the consecutive terms (power level figures) is greater in the first instance compared to the common differences between each of the consecutive terms in the second instance. Imagine, abstractly, that inept power levels begin at zero and reach 2,000; the consecutive term for deficient would then be 4,000, while novice would be 8,000, followed by 16,000 for average. Technically, the advanced rank sees the exponential growth from the preceding ranks, but since the system refers to average power levels as the common standard, then the breaking point is considered at average, not advanced. So, advanced power levels are at 32,000; elite power levels would then be is 48,000; master power levels would be 64,000; and supreme power levels would be 80,000. Despite the doubling of power from average to advanced, when looked at within the context after the breaking point, it is still a linear increase.

Note that the median of the aforesaid probability distribution actually sits *halfway* through the 'average' power level. This means average mages who fall slightly below the median are still considered 'average'. According to this system, the best supreme mages are five times more powerful than the best average mages. There are, of course, the 'exalted' ranks, which include the following (in order of power): Mythic/Legendary; Transcendent/Ascendant; Divine/Demigod; God/Omnipotent. While some fringe scholars argue that mages of mythic status have existed in the past (or currently exist in remote locations while keeping their power levels and identities a secret), the subsequent ranks are just hypotheticals (that are generally found in fiction, legends, and word-of-mouth tales). The power levels of supposed mythic (and other ranked) mages vary greatly, too, and they are not well defined.

Phasarchement magic also possesses a few aptitude aspects, with power levels typically scaling between them. Although there are aether connection aptitudes, lumarchetrix/energy (MLP or sometimes *maximum energy pool* – MEP) storage aptitudes, channelling aptitudes, and ACE aptitudes, the power levels for manifested UST forms (indexed in *Section 3.6.5*) are based on channelling aptitudes. As with GAP magic, the channelling aptitude for phasarchement determines what and how much that can be channelled, the power level of the ultrachite, LCI rates, the LCR, and LCO costs. It does not include how synchronized one's lumarchetrix is (despite links to LCO costs and LCIs), as that technically falls under the storage aptitude; and, normally, all mages naturally have fully synchronized lumarchetrixes, anyway, with differences in resistances to desynchronizations being marginal per power level. Technically, the 'storage' aptitude would also include *accessibility* to various USTs and PACs, but since basically all mages have access to all the known USTs and PACs, this is not typically mentioned. There is one seeming exception here for one UST (ultra spacetime crystals), but this is still a channelling issue.

Generally, mages can create HPL ultrachite up to one rank higher than their DPL; so, this means that an average mage (positioned practically anywhere in their rank) can create 'advanced' HPL ultrachite (respectively within the advanced rank spectrum). The increase of one rank applies to all mages of ranks above average, too, because while it would naturally become harder to channel stronger higher power levels, the stronger a mage is, the greater the chance they have to create the HPL ultrachite, so there is a net neutral effect – thus, scaling occurs. Given the linear increase in power for HPLs for ranks above average, this is yet another reason why the piecemeal growth model is used, as there happen to be non-socially constructed difficulties per power level when creating HPLs. All HPL creations, however, are based on chance rates of success, and when creating HPL ultrachite of one rank higher than a DPL, the chance rate of success is incredibly low. No mage in empirical history has ever demonstratively achieved *DPLs* beyond supreme status (that is, one full stage higher than the lowest of the supreme rank); but naturally, supreme mages are still capable of establishing *HPLs* that exceed the supreme rank itself. As such, the power levels they use at that point are normally called *super supreme* or *maximized supreme*.

For those that are at supreme power levels, this is just a provisional status. Like how a sporting athlete will achieve peak performance in their career, this (as with supreme status) is normally short lived. It requires constant dedication to retain such status, and even of those who manage to sustain such dedication, they will still eventually fall back at least to the status of master, anyway. For others who attain supreme status, this is just a temporary result of undertaking certain practices like intense rituals, normally lasting no more than a single night (or a lunapex). Still, such mages are almost always of the master rank beforehand. Most of these ritual-based temporary increases likely go undocumented, so the abovesaid 0.00001% does not include these mages, but general estimates put this figure up to around 0.00006% over the course of a monthly period. Temporary power-level increases can also occur for mages below the master rank increasing to any other rank, so the first-mentioned statistics do not account for such variations. Again, for both cases, these mages are not using HPLs, and they are, instead, only hold temporarily-high DPLs.

Even though mages of higher ranks have greater DPLs than those below them, the percentage of their MLP used for each ultrachite creation tends to scale at least somewhat proportionally. That is, higher-ranking mages typically have similar CECs and MECs as an overall percentage of their MLPs to those of lower ranks with their respective DPLs. This is because stronger ultrachite requires greater amounts of photomission energy, yet when a mage advances in rank, so generally does their MLP. However, the stronger mage may have other beneficial feats, such as a faster LRR from the Aether (although, this does not increase that much per increase in power level); plus, stronger mages always have the choice to just use LPLs, granting them more attacks or feats before reaching LED. Note that an LPL *in itself* does not possess a longer manifested duration period than an HPL (or DPL) in itself, as time is not an intrinsic factor. Instead, LPL ultrachite lasts longer only because they are cheaper in MECs, thus granting more time for use.

For clarification, it is the amount of energy per UST and the skill to channel it that establishes the power level. But unlike with GAP magic, phasarchement USTs and PACs are more straightforward and clear cut, where the energy requirements also fully scale with the ability to tune into the power level of the UST and channel it. That is, the more energy a UST requires for that specific UST, the greater the power level of not only what is channelled but also the ability to even (adequately) cast it (without instabilities or at all). Note that the power requirements for different USTs differ, so, to be clear, this is only for each UST individually. Therefore, the two areas (that is, the amount of energy and the skill to channel a UST of a particular power) are *effectively* one and the same – thus, one's 'power levels'. In *this* case, there is no overcharging in the same respect of GAP magics, but LCOs still exist.

The *manifested* UST forms, however, vary in how much power they may deliver for certain effects – that is, for their FBEs, SBEs, and CBEs. This means that for each increase in a power level ranking (say, from average to expert), it is not necessarily the case that every single statistic will be a linear increase in power (where, in the said case of average to expert, the effects would seem like they should be double). Indeed, there are many cases where the effective manifested power for a particular effect may be more or less than the proportional-linear-level increase of the previous power ranking. Interestingly, even when (in the said case of average to expert) the power may be less than double for certain effects, this might only, for example, apply between USTs and not in regards to non-UST matter. For example, the main SBEs of ultra-state plasma are not double in effect against ultra-state solids, but the former can be double in power effectively against certain non-UST matter, like ceramic armour. For some CBEs, the powers do not equally scale; for example, the effects of a UPC for a particular UST of a certain PAC may be stronger, but this might also entail a longer charge time; in comparison, there may be some USTs of a particular PAC that have stronger effects *and* quicker charge times.

Most of this phenomenon comes down to *thresholds*, where certain effects cannot form well or at all until certain thresholds are met, and when these thresholds *are* met, sometimes the practical power increases greatly (sometimes even with added, different effects). So, certain feats may only be available for the stronger power level, thus potentially making the effects of the stronger power level worthy of being considered beyond one rank more than the lower power level. This issue does not even include the fact that certain *measurement systems* are not always linear, and some may be *logarithmic*. For example, decibel levels are logarithmic, so when particular ultrachite creates loud sounds measuring 130 decibels/dB (while at average power levels), doubling the power (at advanced power levels) would not lead to 260 dB. While this is not an issue with ultrachite or phasarchement magic itself, it is still a fallacy that some mages do not understand when measuring differences.

Other labels are used for mages, but these have varied meanings and are not all *quite* related to the abovesaid power levels. For example, a *sorcerer* or *sorceress* is someone who uses *occult* knowledge for their (generally powerful and/or dark) magic. Sorcery is the practice, but this practice is, again, of an occult nature, so it is *unknown* magic. Given that magic is well documented and no mage has yet to demonstrate other kinds of magic, all word of sorcery is unconfirmed speculation or fiction. There are also the labels *warlock* and *witch*, but these refer to *specific* and *specified* types of magic that purportedly existed in the past but are not (confirmed) in existence today.

To be clear, while warlocks and witches were said to have *specific* types of magic, this still means they had various *types* (plural) of magic – in addition to *practices*. Some modern mages still like to LARP (*live-action role-play*) some of these practices, though. For more information on warlocks and witches, see *Section 4.1.3*. Then there are the labels *wizard* and *wizardess*, but these terms have various meanings. Many mages who use wizard and wizardess (at least in the modern context) refer to mages who are *erudite* (that is, someone who has amassed a great deal of knowledge) and who may also give the *illusion* of having other magic due to how powerful they are in comparison to other mages. A few other labels exist as well, but they are not as common.

### 3.6.3: Ultra-State Types (USTs):

Each UST is assigned a number. Although some people believe that each UST exists along the line of a single band of energy, this is not the case. This technically means that there *could* be more USTs available for phasarchement magic, but no such energies have ever been demonstrated to exist – apart from that told in myths and legends. Although several numbering systems exist to categorize each UST, the most commonly-used one is the *Tagorean System*. Comprised of three tiers, the Tagorean System places the first two USTs into the *Primary Tier*, while the second two USTs are placed into the *Complementary Tier*, and the last two USTs are ranked in the *Special Tier*. Essentially, in combat, *primary-tier ultrachite* (PTU) are used more often compared to *complementary-tier ultrachite* (CTU), which aid the user to a lesser extent in more specific situations. *Special-tier ultrachite* (STU), however, have such extraordinary feats and effects that they can be – and indeed are – used both inside and outside of combat. The following subsections are *very* much best read sequentially.

## 3.6.3.1: UST One/Ultra-state Solid (Shields):

Fundamentally used as a form of defence, *UST One* produces what is essentially a full-body *shield* – thus, the informal name 'shields'. Most of a user's shield particles will automatically concentrate – and fittingly form – around the mage's body as a moulded 'shell' instead of filling the entire aura and turning it into a giant shield. Usually, the shell's distance from the user's skin is about three centimetres; and even when a user moves their body, the shell accordingly moves with the body. Apart from a few glistening particles in the air, shields have a glassy appearance that is nearly invisible except for when they are either: initially created; struck; in the middle of absorbing energy; overloading; or when moving incredibly fast relative to their environment in a medium (like air). Even when visible, shields are normally transparent to translucent when seeing them straight ahead in one's visual field. So, this means, from such an angle, the boundary of a shield will typically be more visible.

Unlike normal solids, the ultra-solid is more of a spongey aeroglass with a crystalline structure that has zero viscosity – in other words, it also acts *sort* of like a gas with ultra-fluidity. While normally soft, the ultra-solid particles will instantly harden (and accordingly strengthen) to protect the user when particular materials under certain circumstances contact them. Primarily, shields will block solids, liquids, and plasmas (including their ultra-state versions) but not gases (in most cases – but they can block ultra gases). Since oxygen particles can enter a shield's shell, users are able to breathe (and smell other things) inside. Even though plasma is typically less dense than gas particles and, accordingly, *could* pass through shields, the former energetically triggers shields to block them. While the air molecules in strong winds can pass through a shield (and hit a user's body), shields can block most *shockwaves*.

Shields will substantially harden, more specifically, when various states of matter (including the compressed air particles in shockwaves) move very fast relative to the shield – at the location of the impact area and any other area of the shield that might also be affected. For most DPLs, the minimum speed threshold is about 150 km/h. So, if a standard bullet were to hit a shield, the shield would harden at – and usually also near – the impact area, blocking the bullet, while the rest of the shield would remain like a soft sponge. Even if a solid object with low mass (like a dust particle) were to hit the shield at a fast speed, the shield would still harden at the impact area, but this would be basically unnoticeable. In some situations, shielded mages may have dusty or dirty clothes, but the tiny dirt particles would not have blown through the shield, and they may have, instead, come from previous events. Shields can still block other slow-moving matter, but they are susceptible to being pierced with enough force. So, the said dusty clothes could have come from another situation where the shielded mage scraped against a dirty brick wall *within* a certain speed and tore their shield open, allowing dirt to transfer to them.

Essentially, this means that shielded users are also susceptible to injury or death from attacks with weapons like knives. There is, nevertheless, one type of shield that can stop knife attacks with its CBE, which can only be utilised after a UPC. In the case of a knife attack against a normal shield, though, the shield would quickly reform its original structure after the knife leaves the shield's shell. If the shielded user dies suddenly, then their shield may simply totally disappear due to the lack of consciousness channelling the UST. If a shielded user were to grab an object, like a knife, at a regular speed, the shell around the hand would easily compress against the hand (and knife) and become thin enough for the user to easily hold the knife, so shields are not a clumsy form of protection. Even if an object is sharp, if not enough force is applied, it will not penetrate, so this means that the glass from a nearby window that shatters, for example, may not penetrate the shield.

While shields allow photons and heat energy (via conduction) through, this is only when these phenomena do not pass a certain threshold of (concentrated) energy. The same also applies to individual gas particles with high energy levels. So, while sunlight, for example, may pass through a shield, a highly-concentrated laser beam of sufficient energy will *mostly* not penetrate the shield. Although materials of any kind (whether ultrachite or not) cannot *block* magnetic fields, they can still *redirect* magnetic fields, in turn weakening their effects on the other side. This same principle applies to ultrachite shields, which greatly weaken the effects of magnetic fields on the inside of a shield. Still, if a magnetic field of an object is far stronger than the shield, the field will still go through in practically a normal manner. Since gravity, on the other hand, is not technically a force, shields do not 'block' gravity.

These resistances mean that shields are effective against energy weapons, too, such as plasma, magnetic, laser, and fire-based weapons – in addition to their equivalents found in nature, such as lightning. Note that electrical energy can come in many forms, but when most people see 'electrical energy', usually this is in the form of plasma, so shields will naturally block 'electrical energy' as well. Shields can also block high energy air particles and excess photons the same way as it does with standard plasma; that is, shields will *energetically* block them rather than necessarily turning hard in the abovesaid cases with fast-moving matter like solids. Specifically, a shield's electrons will whiz around the shield and block the attacking energy instead of the atoms (as wholes) themselves moving or simply blocking them by being in the way.

The soot produced from fire (in its *initial* gaseous form before turning into a solid), nevertheless, may pass through to the user inside their shield. Because *some* radiation (as well as energy transfers through conduction) will pass through a shield, heat can still build inside, potentially causing mild burns in certain circumstances. Particle-accelerator weapons also normally deal both kinetic and energy damage, so shields can also block their attacks in their respective ways simultaneously. Nevertheless, a shield will, in this case, divide its energy to affect both phenomena, but in most cases, the shield will still have enough power to stop both phenomena at once without suffering either a net or total loss.

Surplus SBE energy from (unhit areas) around the shield can also go towards the area of impact (from a bullet, for example) for added strength – which would be a different matter to whatever photomission energy that would be channelled into the shield to restore the shield's properties. That is, projectiles have to contend with nearly the whole shield's strength, not just the potential impact area. If the shield is hit all over (from multiple angles), then naturally less surplus energy can spread, so the impact areas would have to deal with the brunt of the projectile by themselves. So, this means that a shield would only be able block a certain number of bullets hit at any location at once; and for average DPLs, this amounts to about eight average rifle bullets at once, each with a muzzle energy of about 3,000 joules.

A similar but different phenomenon occurs with CBE-particles. That is, instead of energy *normally* travelling through the shield, *certain* CBE particles have a stronger condensate state, with the level and their effects increasing to contextually-specific areas across the shield. So, for a shield that has CBEs that can help stop knife attacks, the CBE-particles help the particles at the site of impact; and, in the case of multiple attacks at various locations across the shield at once, the CBE-particles would help these locations as well, appropriately spreading their power per the strength of each attack. Nevertheless, there can only be a certain energy density per area, so it is not like all but one of the CBE particles in a shield will 'send' their energy to just one CBE particle. In cases where certain (ultrachite) attacks have a central attack point (where the bulk of the properties are located) but also *spread* their energy or other properties across the shield, then the shield's CBE-particles can affect the attack via the *spread* energy.

The size of the shield, therefore, does not matter *too* much (in most regards), which means that while the height of a mage would affect the shield's surface area and, thus, area density, the overall strength would be relatively the same. Still, mages can also alter the shape and size of a shield, allowing them to create hovering discs, for instance, and this can increase the density of an impact area to block an additional number of certain kinds of projectiles. However, besides obvious limitations, such as leaving the user vulnerable to attacks from certain angles (as the shield would not be covering their whole body) – and for the fact that a disc-shaped shield would easily fold back if slow materials were to hit it (and, thus, would not be effective in most melee combat situations) – there are density issues, too. For example, shields can only possess a certain threshold of density based on their power level, so users cannot infinitely shrink shields.

On the other hand, if a shield were expanded too much, then the shield's level of density would pass a certain threshold that would cause major weaknesses. When a shield is formed without moulding around the user (like a disc), it will automatically hover, anyway, as UST particles naturally hover. Even when formed around the user as the default, the particles will hover, so when a user lifts their feet off the ground, the particles will move with the feet; moreover, since the shield acts as a whole entity, this means that when the feet are lifted up (with the shield particles closely following underneath them), this will not cause the top of the shield's shell to fall on the user's head. Despite being smooth, shields also have roughly the same *coefficient of friction* (that is, the ratio of frictional force) as that which is found in standard footwear in relation to standard walking surfaces. Accordingly, mages can walk on surfaces with shields underneath their feet as if wearing normal shoes. Technically, this is not the common form of friction involving particles mechanically rubbing against each other, and, instead, it is a result of electrostatic forces between the shield's fluctuating electrons and of the surface it touches at an angle.

Projectiles of a certain nature and force will still push a hardened shield, in turn pushing the user. In the case of bullets, this will only be to a very slight degree. Even though the protective hardening occurs virtually instantaneously, this defensive system is only a resistance and not an immunity. So, if an incoming material is moving with *enough* force, it will penetrate the shield. However, while these resistances only apply to a degree, they fully prevail in most circumstances in combat for nearly any power level. Usually, it takes a *very* powerful (metallic) ammunition to immediately *rip through* (that is, create a hole and penetrate) an active shield – one not found in any standard firearm that average-sized humanoids are capable of carrying by themselves. Heavy artillery can even destroy shields (that is, create more than just a hole). This destruction principle also *technically* applies to energy-based attacks and phenomena like lasers (light), fire (heat), and plasma (electricity); and even if they do not possess high energy, such phenomena can still slowly destroy shields. Still, shields will normally never be slowly destroyed, and they would, instead, *overload* well before this (with the issue of overloading explained later in this subsection).

Although shields can prevent offensive ultrachite particles from physically making contact with the user's *body*, all shields *themselves* of any power level are still subject to the SBEs and CBEs of offensive ultrachite particles, such as being pushed over (via CBEs), in turn pushing the user over. CBEs can also technically affect the mage on the *inside* of the shell when certain radiation applies. While UST Two particles, specifically, affect HRFs, they can still emit radiation, so, in the context of light, this can go through the shield and affect a user's eyes (and, thus, blind their sense of sight).

There is also the *shield-user connection* (SUC) to consider, which is where the user, to a lesser extent, can be affected because the shield is connected to the user both via a strong mental connection and their lumarchetrix. Only certain effects (CBEs) apply through a SUC, and these are in the realm of the mental and the etheric. Of course, these effects are at a much weaker level than if they were to affect a user while they were unshielded. The physical (mentally-applicable) effects that occur for the shield that would otherwise affect the user (should they have been hit) only affect them (the user) indirectly, not physically. Some offensive ultrachite particles are capable of affecting mental faculties to such an extent that they can send unshielded victims unconscious in one hit. Via the SUC, the offensive particles would, instead, only indirectly desynchronize the shielded mage's mind a little, making them more prone to being sent unconscious *if* enough further (successful and consecutive) attacks are launched against them via the SUC. The stronger the shield, the stronger (more secure) the connection channel is between the user's mind (and etheric field) to the shield.

Even though one shield may be stronger than another in terms of power levels, this does not mean that the stronger shield will have any increased resistances to *specific* CBEs. For example, a shield may not have any particular resistance to the specific effect of quantum entanglement separations. However, all shields possess *ultrachite particle inhibitors* (UPIs), which inhibit the CBEs of particular ultrachite particles (namely, from USTs Two and Three), turning the particles from AES to DES by affecting their PEP. Shields, nonetheless, are naturally immune to other shield UPIs, as are the other USTs not mentioned (that is, USTs Four, Five, and Six). UPIs are able to perform this feat by producing a particular magnetic field beyond themselves that can modulate certain PEPs. While UPIs are imbedded in the shield's ultrachite, they nevertheless possess an *effective* radius that is measured from the shell; and for average DPL shields, this effective radius is about 20 centimetres (with other power levels being of roughly similar size). This means that when ultrachite attack particles 'make contact' with UPIs, this also includes the actual space (vicinity) around the UPIs, not just direct physical contact. Even though UPIs affect CBE-instigating particles, the phenomenon itself is an SBE.

In the case of an attack that can push people over, the shield would inhibit a certain percentage of the attack's particles (depending on how many UPIs a shield has versus the strength of the attack). With the ultrachite attack accordingly weakened, the shielded mage may, instead, be able to withstand being pushed over, or they may only be pushed over to a lesser extent than what would have otherwise occurred. However, UPIs can become *overstimulated* when enough successful offensive ultrachite particles contact the shield (or enter the UPI vicinity) in a particular period. When UPIs experience *ultrachite inhibitor overstimulation* (UIO), the whole shield does not necessarily become overstimulated – just the individual affected UPIs. Also, when the number of available active UPIs drop, a greater number of attacking AES particles may *build* against the shield (with further attacks), consequently leading to higher PEP *active particle levels* (APLs) for attacks. UPIs also have an *aggregate strength*, which affects APL build (and more information is explained in *Section 3.6.3.2*).

When a shield has no available UPIs left due to all of them experiencing UIO, then existing or additional ultrachite attacks on the shield will achieve 100% APL, and offensive ultrachite particles can then fully *externally* affect the shield. At this moment, 100% SUC effects can apply as well (depending on the type of attack), but these CBEs will still be weaker compared to a whole attack which would otherwise occur against an unshielded mage. Even when an APL of, say, 38% has been attained, the user and their shield will still respectively feel the effects of that particular percentage, no matter the power level. Eventually, overstimulated UPIs cool down when no further attacks occur, which enables them to continue inhibiting more offensive ultrachite particles. UPIs are also subject to QIFs (even as individual units), so a user cannot just switch their shield off and then reset or reduce the cooldown on their UPIs. Naturally, the stronger the shield compared to the attacks, the slower APL will build against it; but since stronger shields have more UPIs, the speed of recovery as an overall percentage of the number of UPIs happens to be roughly the same as an average DPL shield's UPI cooldown rate.

Regardless of the APL, shields can only tolerate a certain number or amount of ultrachite or non-ultrachite attacks or energy in a particular period. Shields basically absorb offensive matter (more so fast-moving matter) as if a sponge, 'holding' such matter for a split second. So, when a bullet hits a shield, it practically becomes 'stuck' for a split moment before dropping to the ground. As for energy weapons or similar phenomena used against a shield, the shield will absorb the energy before it (the energy) diffuses into the atmosphere. For every moment a shield has to hold matter or energy, this contributes towards its *ultrachite overloading threshold* (UOT), where it experiences *ultrachite particle overload* (UPO) – which is an issue that is also applied individually for all other USTs. Eventually with enough attacks (or a single attack with comparatively more power than what a shield can withstand), a shield will no longer be able to absorb such energy, and it will *overload* (which is different from LBOs mentioned in *Section 3.6.1*).

When a user experiences a UPO, a *specific* QIF will occur inside the user's physical aura, preventing the whole UST (UST One, in this case) from forming for a particular period. This even applies to all PACs of the affected UST, so a user cannot simply change the PAC and create another shield while they wait for the overload to cool down. Specifically, it affects the UST itself, so all PACs are affected. While the QIF in question would only apply to shields, there are circumstances where particular QIFs can simultaneously affect multiple USTs. Technically, while a QIF occurs when a UST overloads, an *imbalanced potential field* (IPF) follows the overload, which is actually what prevents the UST from reforming. Still, there are cases where IPFs precede overloading. Basically, QIFs are found in and for tangible matter, whereas IPFs are spatial *fields* of distorted spacetime that can potentially affect (future) tangible matter. IPFs actually get their distorted potential from the etheric, but again, this is different from LBOs; that is, IPFs are etheric distortions of what-would-be manifested UST forms (the ultrachite matter itself) affecting the physical realm, whereas LBOs are overloaded lumarchetrixes. For general ease of reference and brevity (that is, to prevent using both terms), QIFs are usually mentioned in lieu of IPFs (*plus* QIFs).

The QIF (again, IPF) from an overloaded shield can even affect mages other than the user. So, if a user's shield overloaded and then an ally, for example, were to enter the user's aura (that is, the affected space – particularly where the shell would normally be), then there would be a chance that their (the ally's) shield would not form if they (the ally) attempted to create one. If the ally were already shielded in this case, then there would be a small chance that they (the ally) could suffer from a UPO as well. Respectively *upon entering* the aura's space, the chance rates for these two cases applying roughly average 15% and 10% (with relative DPLs considered). If the other (shielded or unshielded) mage were already within the vicinity when the event occurs, then there would be a one-off instant chance of around 10%, too, with roughly a 5% chance after leaving and re-entering the vicinity.

The overloading phenomenon, in these cases, will not occur *as a result of* shields that have some increase towards their UOT but have not actually overloaded (yet), as the type of QIF for these shields is not strong enough (more specifically, of a certain threshold for its nature) to create such effects. This phenomenon also does not occur for shields with UIO QIFs. Other UST auras can also overload when in the vicinity of other IPFs (so other USTs can overload when within a shield's IPF). However, since the IPF is not of the respective/specific field types of other USTs, this phenomenon does not occur under normal circumstances, so this would only occur via a type of *super IPF/QIF*. While stronger shields have greater UOTs, the recovery speed does not decrease that much per power level ranking. So, the average DPL shield's full cooldown rate is about 10 seconds, whereas each power ranking after average power levels will decrease this by about 1.75 seconds for each succeeding rank.

There will also be a delay before the QIF's cooling begins, which is called the *cooldown delay period* (CDP). For mages with average DPL shields, this is about two seconds; therefore, for average mages with DPL shields, there will be a 12-second period before full recovery. There are also two types of cooldowns: one where the overload time *resets* (totally to 0%) from an actual UPO, and the other where the UOT *subsides* (before a UPO occurs), with percentage points dropping every second linearly instead of in one instant and total reset. The *total* timeframe for the *overloading reset rate* (ORR) will be the same as the *overloading subsiding rate* (OSR) pro rata; so, if an average DPL shield were at 90% of its UOT before actually overloading, then it would still reduce (that is, subside) to 0% in about nine seconds after the CDP. Like with UPIs, the QIF of an overloaded shield will prevent a user from switching their shield off and simply resetting or reducing the cooldown on their UOT. The same applies to other USTs.

A CDP also applies to UPIs before restoration occurs via the *overstimulation subsiding rate* (OSSR), with the total cooldown timeframe for average DPL shields being 26.667 seconds after the CDP (of two seconds). In other words, the recovery rate for UPIs is about 3.75% per second – not including the CDP. It is technically the shield itself that heals the overstimulated particles rather than the said particles healing themselves. This means that the shield will not recover each individual over-stimulated particle all at once (as the shield can only handle healing so many particles at once); hence, the subsiding rate. The same applies to a shield's particles that enable the UOT. There is no overstimulation *reset* rate, so UPIs 'individually' recover; and after a shield reforms post overloading, the UPIs will not be *totally* restored (*as a result*), as *their* QIFs are different to UPO QIFs. However, overstimulated UPIs will still naturally subside during the (12-second) UPO period; and for average DPLs, about 45% of the UPIs will have recovered in that time (should at least this amount have been overstimulated in the first place). Mages may be able to intuitively tell what their UOT and recovery rates are at, but this is not as easy as feeling for how much energy they have left in their lumarchetrix.

While an overloaded shield may leave a user vulnerable, users will not be, in the meantime, charged lumarchetrix energy for their shield aura. Furthermore, users can still recharge their lumarchetrix energy in the interim (as the lumarchetrix is not ultrachite), with most mages saving energy on net (even when after accounting for the CEC of a new shield). It is technically the damage that a shield endures that causes overloading rather than the amount of photomission energy coming from the lumar-chetrix, per se, to fix and re-energize the shield; however, the two are correlated, as more damage will cause more photomission energy to be channelled. Still, the amount of energy channelled through to a shield can reach the LCR limit if, for example, energy is being absorbed from the shield. Regardless of whether a shield has been overloaded or not, the CEC for the average user to (re)make a respective DPL shield is 4.8% of their MLP, and the MECs are about 0.9% per second. Shields will also not overload simply due to being active, unlike other USTs, so there is no time limit.

While some CBEs can increase a shield's UOT or establish *UPI-equivalent* properties, if a user were to condense a shield to, say, a disc, then despite the increased particle density, the UOT would not increase, nor the number and strength of (the) UPIs. When a shield (or even other ultrachite) changes its PEP from DES to AES via a UPC or UPS (or vice versa via UPS or when the UPC finishes), overloading does not occur due to a naturally-allotted extra time for self-modulation and adjustment. Regardless of the PEP (apart from applicable CBEs against the shield), if a single attack were to nearly reach a shield's UOT at 95% and not 100%, the shield would normally not overload. That is, the UOT has to actually be fully met. The only major exception to this, however, is when particular (special) quantum (and potential) imbalances occur, affecting the shield in non-standard ways (which can occur via certain ultrachite attacks). Even though very powerful ammunition may be able to tear through a shield, this event would not necessarily mean that the shield would overload – although, in most cases, this would occur.

Assorted non-mages possess different kinds of shields and forcefields, some of which also have UPI-equivalent properties. However, generally, these are not as powerful as ultrachite UPIs. These non-ultrachite shields and forcefields are not just technological; organic, biological versions also exist. For example, some *arthropoids* possess antennae that generate forcefields with UPI-equivalent frequencies (generally, nevertheless, affecting ultrachite attacks within short range). In combat, mages, then, may face harder-than-normal opposition, but these instances usually occur with beings high up in eusocial orders; although, these are not necessarily queens or kings. Therefore, in combat against such arthropoids, it may be the case that only one out of ten would possess such abilities. Outside of arthropoid cases, the forcefield generation may be different. Necrotics and monsters may also possess their own UPI-like properties, which are different to – but on top of – their typical pre-existing resistances they have to particular phasarchement attacks. For more information on different types of beings, see the various subsections in *Section 4.3*.

Most mages do not bother augmenting their fights with non-ultrachite portable forcefields, such as *portable kinetic forcefields* (PKFs), *portable radiation forcefields* (PRFs), or *portable particle forcefields* (PPFs). PKFs block kinetic attacks (that surpass particular speeds), while PRFs block electromagnetic radiation after a certain threshold; PPFs, alternatively, block both kinetic and radiation attacks but are weaker with each, respectively, as a result. None of these forcefields use ultrachite, nor are any solid; instead, they rely on an energy field around the user's body. In most cases, mages avoid using these forcefields because they lose a decent amount of their strength when used in proximity to ultrachite shields. These portable forcefields also cost large amounts of energy, and they can even potentially overheat the user unless low power levels are used; as a result, PPFs do not match the power of average-powered ultrachite shields. Furthermore, portable forcefields can greatly prolong the QIFs of overloaded ultrachite shields. For this reason, mages do not quickly or automatically switch to portable forcefields when their ultrachite shields overload as a backup.

Because of the abovesaid limitations, the only non-magic forcefields mages may sometimes use are various types of *full barrier forcefields* (FBFs), which require large, bulky devices and great amounts of power from energy generators (both of which have big heat vents and weak points and are not easily portable). Ultrachite shields also do not typically have the power to practically weaken FBFs and similar forcefields when in proximity. Coupled with the fact that nobody can shoot through either side of an FBF, they are normally only used in particular locations, like a headquarters, that requires total protection. In fact, unlike portable forcefields, the speed of a particle does not matter against FBFs, so FBFs block all matter and high-powered radiation. Still, using portable forcefields can save precious photomission energy, which can then be used for further phasarchement magic. Therefore, some mages prefer using non-ultrachite portable forcefields, depending on the context.

Regardless of whether non-ultrachite portable forcefields are used or not, some mages wear various non-ultrachite *body armour* as a backup, which ultrachite shields do not distort (unlike the abovesaid portable forcefields). However, certain (strong) armours can also prolong QIFs by distorting proximal quantum and etheric fields, and these are known as *QIF-prolonging armours* (QPAs). Many of these armours include materials gained from biological organisms (with complex quantum structures), but non-biological QPAs also exist. Therefore, only weaker armours are typically used in conjunction with ultrachite shields, such as *ceramic body armours* (CBAs). While the weaker armours are still effective at blocking standard bullets, for example, they are not effective at blocking certain phasarchement attacks due to phenomena like *quantumly-dominant fields*, where the attacking particles will normally just easily (but not necessarily always) quantumly tunnel straight through the armour to the person's body (and more information on this can be found in *Section 3.6.3.2*).

The size of the armour matters, too; so, while mages can expand their shields to a degree without losing much practical strength, if they have to expand their shields around large mech suits (assuming the shields could even stay within the aura's space), then the density would be too weak. Alternatively, mages could have an ultrachite shield while inside a mech suit (so long as the shield were to form in non-solid spaces), but this is sometimes pointless, as the mech suit might fully protect the mage inside. An armour's weight can play a role in fatiguing a user, too, which could *potentially* cause, lead to, or increase the rate towards EEE. To be clear on the matter, shields naturally cover standard body armour (like CBA), not the other way round, so UST Two attacks and other attacks (like bullets) hit shields first, and then body armour is the backup in the case when a shield overloads or has run out of energy.

Despite these setbacks, standard body armours are great in certain contexts, such as blocking most melee attacks (like from knives). Moreover, body armours can help prevent injuries from traps, debris, and environmental hazards, so many military personnel use body armours. Although ultrachite shields (specifically, via QIFs) are weak to the abovesaid materials, it is important to note that the practical applications of such weaknesses mean that this (the weaknesses) really only apply with both the amount and proximity of said materials, so shooting bullet-like projectiles made of such materials found in QPAs, for example, at shielded or unshielded mages via a firearm would not practically prolong any QIFs that they (the mage) may later or currently experience, nor, in most cases, would being surrounded by said materials affect such QIFs much. That is, unless the room that the mage inhibits is totally made up of such materials (along with it also being a confined space), it is really the proximity, amount, and context of the armour and its framework that gives rise to a particular kind of quantum propinquity around the mage's body that causes such QIF issues.

### 3.6.3.2: UST Two/Ultra-state Plasma (Discharges):

Informally called *discharges*, ultra-state plasma is normally used for attacking opponents, and it is also a mage's main form of offence. Although the energy created in an aura can be shaped in a few different ways for particular uses, the most commonly-used one involves users concentrating the ultrachite particles into a fist-sized ball of energy that rapidly discharges (that is, shoots) from the user in an aimed direction. After their initial creation, ultra-state plasma particles will thinly fill the aura without producing any CBEs or major SBEs. So, before concentrating the particles into what is also generally and colloquially known as 'blast balls', the aura remains mostly imperceptible and does not brightly light up, as the particles are not dense enough to create such an effect. Instead, it is the blast balls themselves that shine brightly. The concentration of these particles also normally takes a split second.

Since the hands are the mind's manual liaison tools in daily life, the deeply-rooted psychological connection between the hands and mind naturally results in mages concentrating discharges near the palms of their hands before firing them off. Discharges will naturally shoot anywhere within roughly a ninety-degree range of the user's central vision, and so, in order to accurately fire at a particular location, hand usage for initial physical guidance is normally necessary, anyway. Mages normally hold their hands in front of their faces to aim, but adepts (of any power level ranking, technically) can accurately shoot discharges while holding their hands away from their faces. Accuracy is both a *non-magic skill* and a part of one's *ACE aptitude*, so it is a matter of both the user's consciousness *and* the direction in which the blast ball is directed towards that matters. That is, although aiming via the mind works, physically gesturing with the hands will also help more precisely shape the direction of the energy so the blast ball will move in a particular direction, in turn making up for the potential (and usual) gap in one's consciousness.

It is possible for a user to hold a discharge in their hand before it actually discharges, but this can only be done for a short amount of time before it automatically either discharges, diffuses, or overloads (with more about overloading explained later in this subsection). This also incurs a MEC to hold the discharge, calculating to about 0.2% of an average user's MLP per second at average DPLs. After the creation of the discharge *aura*, if the user neither shoots nor holds a concentrated discharge, then the MEC for the average DPL user will be 0.1% of their MLP per second due to the particles barely applying any force on one another – a phenomenon basically not seen with other USTs. Mages cannot shoot PPOs out of the aura in the same way as shooting discharges and then hope to activate them (the PPOs) just before hitting an opponent and, thus, reduce their MECs, as PPOs do not act like discharges.

The actual discharge (at average DPLs), on the other hand, normally has a CEC of about 1.2% of an average user's MLP. This CEC applies to both the creation of the aura and then for any individual discharges beyond the first available discharge shot due to an extreme loss of ultrachite particles in the aura with each blast ball shot. Although a slight jolt from the hand is not necessary to send the discharge flying, normally, one accompanies the discharge. Once the discharge leaves the aura, the mage cannot repower it with more photomission energy (even if it reflects back to their aura), nor, in most cases, control what happens to it. While mid-air in LES, discharges technically release tiny amounts of AES particles due to their erratic nature, which can cause CBEs to result.

Discharges will continue travelling through the air until hitting hard and dense enough matter; at which point, they will explode (with all the particles switching to – or, for some, remaining at – AES). Blast balls also travel at an average speed of 33.33 m/s, which equals to about 120 km/h – which is roughly three times faster than the fastest normal mage runner. As such, a mage cannot outrun a discharge unless they are using magic. While the said speed is an average, all power levels do not deviate much from this speed. Users do not necessarily have to directly hit opponents for combat and tactical effectiveness, and they can, instead, tactically shoot a nearby area to prevent opponents from approaching it (such as a door exit), for example. Since discharges are able to form quickly at any power level, rapid fire of roughly four discharges per second maximum is normal – with a sharp distribution cut off both ways after this average. That is, most mages have a maximum fire rate between 3.5 and 4.5 discharges per second. For clarification, a user would not ever shoot half a discharge, even if they are using LPLs, so these statistics are pro rata.

Ultrachite discharge particles are different from the normal-state plasma found in non-magic firearms, which require additional shells to coat the plasma in order to maintain their forms intact after firing. So, even though standard plasma formed in condensed shapes naturally equalizes its internal pressure (otherwise, this would lead to rapid radiation and dissipation), ultrachite blast balls manage to sustain their structure without such a shell – even while they fly through the air. This occurs due to all the ultrachite particles being effectively quantumly-tied together as a whole structure in a special way, using its own energy to sustain the form. It also helps that ultrachite discharges are not hot like normal plasma, as heat is what naturally causes matter to expand. After an ultrachite discharge hits something, its volatile particles will accordingly not rapidly fly away from the area of impact in a massive cloud.

A typical one-metre blast radius, nevertheless, will *appear* after a discharge impacts, but this phenomenon is just a result of scattering *DUPs* (not fully-formed and active ultra-plasma particles), and the bulk of the discharge particles will, instead, only be located within the fist-sized area (which will mildly splatter on the surface of the target, with generally no more than an additional ten-centimetre spread in diameter whilst active). However, there are exceptions to this, and the discharge particles may surround the object they hit. In fact, discharges affect HRFs that meet certain HRTs; so, if a blast ball were to hit only a part of a person (like a hand), it would affect both the person as a whole (that is, the dimensional, spatial aspect of the person via SBEs and then CBEs) and *all* of the person's *affectable* constituents (via CBEs and SBEs) – within the context of a whole HRF – due to them (the person) having a particular unified quantum/etheric field, where all of their particles are connected to some degree with a certain *threshold* of connectivity that has a stronger (and, thus, more affectable) collective field than an isolated HRF like a hand.

From the blast site, the blast ball will, in most cases, just *charge* the HRF as a whole field electrically and magnetically in a variety of ways, depending on the type of discharge. In some cases, the discharge particles will *also*, more specifically, *tightly* surround the HRF's exterior (but not its constituents within it) to varying extents based on the PAC. Whether the discharge particles are at the blast site or are around the HRF, they will not produce a field *in the sense* of a blast radius; therefore, all the effects are practically contained just around and/or within the field of the HRF. So, despite any proximity the discharge particles will have with other HRFs (like a table right next to a person who is affected as the HRF in question), they (the discharge particles) will basically only affect the HRF they have hit. This phenomenon is primarily done by affecting the wave function of the HRF itself. When this occurs, various potentials within and for the HRF are altered. For clarification, due to the physical and etheric energy of discharges, the wave functions of discharge particles *trigger* the matter they hit to cause wave function changes *as* HRFs, but the matter they hit still have to have to be part of HRFs.

The discharge particles that surround the HRF will produce effects themselves, but they can also interact with the field of the charged HRF – which would not only be affected but also produce new effects. So, the discharge particles will naturally exert electrical and magnetic forces, but these, nevertheless, will weaken for other HRFs within the vicinity via manipulations in various arrays due to particular changes in vector potentials. Interestingly, the HRF can be charged with an effect that has distorted spatial magnetic and electric fields, so their (the HRF's) magnetic field can be at zero around them except for in regards to other particular HRFs. Discharge particles, however, can still emit electromagnetic radiation (photons), which can affect other things (HRFs or otherwise). There is, however, a case where a blast-radius-like field can emerge from *certain* discharge particles, affecting other HRFs.

For further clarification, discharges cannot isolate and affect a person's heart, for example, *and* nothing else in the body. More specifically, a mage cannot create two precise magnetic attacks and then rip someone's heart apart, nor can they precisely affect the neurons in a person's brain and then fry or destroy them. In other words, discharges have their advantages, but they are not overpowered via inventive and cunning workarounds and technicalities. This is not to say that certain CBEs cannot affect just neurons when the HRF is charged, it is just, again, that the neurons would not be treated as *the* affected HRF. So, when a discharge affects certain aspects of a person's being, such as their mental capacities (and not their bones, for instance), this is not the result of isolation but, instead, what the attack is *capable* of affecting within the context of a whole HRF.

For even further clarification, some attacks *may* be able to affect seemingly-isolated anatomical pieces in a biological organism, but this is not isolation itself; instead, this is due to the attack *passing* a certain threshold (which may be based on an HRT) of something specific within an HRF. So, while HRFs exist within HRFs, the discharge would still be affecting one HRF with various affectable constituents within the HRF. Even though it is not *technically* impossible to affect just someone's heart as a specific HRF in itself, for instance, in all *practical* cases, this *never* occurs (ignoring that which is found in fiction). Typically, this also means that if only clothing is hit, and not the body, then only the clothing (and the whole item of the clothing, such as a whole t-shirt, but not the pants, socks, and shoes) will be affected.

Not only is the *energy* from the discharge's particles able to conduct through most materials (by means of SBEs), but the particles themselves are able to quantumly tunnel as well, becoming *quantumly-tunnelled particles* (QTPs). Discharge particles will not typically quantumly tunnel through HRFs (PEBs) unless they have *overwhelmed* a PEB/HRF with enough energy, forcing the PEB/HRF to become a *quantum tunnel gateway* (QTG). Still, this, alone, is not enough for the discharge particles to tunnel. In general, there are *quantumly-dominant fields* (QDFs), which are (sets of) HRFs that exert special kinds of etheric (and, thus, quantum) forces on one another. Normally, QDFs gain their dominance via their amount and type of mass – along with any other etheric data they possess – in relation to 'weaker' HRFs; but in the context of discharges turning HRFs into QTGs, any surrounding HRFs can then become a specific type of QDF – one which *draws* the discharge particles toward them via quantum tunnelling.

The QDF, in this case, alters *quantum force vectors* (QVFs), causing discharge particles to quantumly tunnel. Still, most QVFs are short-ranged, so if the QDF is too far away from the QTG, no quantum tunnelling will occur. However, when more discharges hit the QTG, a *quantum vector bridge* (QVB) can emerge between it (the QTG) and the QDF, extending the range – but even this has its limits. Note that while the QVB would affect quantum particles, there is still the etheric aspect of it that allows for this phenomenon, where the less localized etheric nature of QDFs can be even further enhanced to help with the quantum tunnelling. If a discharge were to hit a piece of normal clothing (say, made from cotton) that someone was wearing, then at basically all power levels, a discharge would turn the piece of clothing into a QTG, where most of the discharge would tunnel through to the QDF behind it (the person wearing the clothing). In this case, some particles would affect the clothing as an HRF, but the person would still get most of the effects as another HRF.

For clarification, even though discharges operate as whole entities, if any discharge particles separate from the whole, they can still affect other HRFs, but each particle itself will ultimately only affect one HRF. In other words, discharges can affect multiple targets, but in most contexts, a single discharge will affect just one HRF. However, *some* energy from the discharge particles *can* affect other HRFs by means of proximity or connection. This does not have to specifically target other HRFs themselves but simply other matter in the vicinity. That is, it is impossible in all cases to isolate *all* the energy solely to one HRF when the discharge particles may still touch other properties not of the HRF they are specifically affecting. Normally when this happens, it is to an extremely minor extent, but in the case of where discharge particles affect other discharge particles in the vicinity, it can have rather noticeable effects (with more of this phenomenon explained later in this subsection).

The type and amount of mass in a HRF relative to a discharge's power level matters in how many discharges are needed to turn it (the PEB/HRF) into a QTG. However, even as a QTG, not all discharge particles may turn into QTPs. That is, there may also be a level of *chance* involved, and this, again, depends on the strength of the HRF.

Even when it comes to most standard body armours, the average DPL discharge will still see QTPs either on the first or second hit. Ultrachite shields, on the other hand, have a very strong resistance to turning into QTGs; and by the time that a shield could turn into a QTG, it would have long overloaded by then. Typically, the only exception to this whole phenomenon is when dealing with giant or colossal-sized HRFs. Irrespective of quantum tunnelling, some things may be too big and/or powerful to fully affect *as* a whole HRF; an obvious example is entire buildings.

Even a QDF behind the QTG can become overwhelmed with enough energy, in turn making them a QTG. In this case, discharge particles will quantumly tunnel through the overwhelmed QDF (HRF) to any other QDF within proximity. If, for example, a user were to shoot multiple discharges at an unshielded person (with another person directly behind the targeted person in file), then their (the user's) discharge particles would eventually tunnel through to the second person. The back of the shirt on the first person would still be part of the overall HRF of the shirt (that was initially hit) as well, so the discharge particles would travel through the back, too. If there are multiple layers of shirts, then they will all normally act as a single *de facto* HRF, and the discharge particles will surround the first layer, affecting the rest with their charge. Note that the air particles behind a QTG will not be sufficient enough to act as QDFs.

If the goal is to only affect the first person, then this is not a problem for offending users in general (when in the context of combat), as it normally takes *many* discharges for this to occur, as biological beings have a greater complexity than inanimate objects. Moreover, it is super quick to subdue unshielded mages, anyway, so in normal combat cases, users do not have to be concerned with turning their target (a person) into a QTG and affect the second person (or even a wall, for example, behind the targeted person) in this (uncommon) case. If there is no HRF behind the person (within proximity), yet both the shirt and the person are overwhelmed (so, both are QTGs), then the discharge particles will *default* to the non-QTG-related QDF (which, in this case, would be the person, as they would have a more complex etheric field than a shirt). Regardless, a user can switch off a discharge's ability to become QTPs on the creation of their discharge aura. Other non-discharge phenomena may also overwhelm a HRF with various types of energy, in turn *potentially* reducing (or increasing) the HRF's resistance to discharges quantumly tunnelling through it.

There is also another factor to consider: the QTP phenomenon is *vector based*, and discharge particles will not normally change their trajectory from the angle and location it (the discharge) hits on the QTG (to-be) – regardless of whether the discharge may have changed its trajectory over the course of its flight beforehand. This means that if a discharge were to hit the edge of an excessively-large suit of armour with no body spatially on the other side of the said part of the armour (that is in line with the discharge's trajectory), then no QTPs would *generally* occur. Of course, if a user were to shoot discharges at a piece of armour that nobody was wearing, then the discharge particles would likely not quantumly tunnel through the armour – unless a QDF were on the other side. Note that for discharge particles that surround a HRF, some quantum tunnelling may occur for the HRF itself in order to adequately cover the HRF, but this is a different phenomenon to the abovesaid issue of QDFs.

After discharge particles quantumly tunnel through armour, for example, it may then be unlikely for the shooter to see the one-metre blast radius of DUPs due to the particles now being behind the armour, blocking the view. Even when discharge particles do not pass through the armour while it is being worn, they can still affect the armour and, thus, the targeted opponent by default. For example, if a magnetic attack (via a magnetic CBE) only affected the armour, by pulling the armour, it would, by default, pull the opponent as well (assuming that the magnetic attack would have enough power to pull the mass of both the armour and the person). For discharge particles that, for example, magnetically pull HRFs, this will *only* affect the targeted HRF, but other HRFs may be *indirectly* affected if the prime HRF hits other HRFs along its way (while being pulled). To clarify the armour question, shields cover body armour, not the other way round, so when discharges tunnel through body armour (like CBA), the shield would have already overloaded or stopped at that point.

If an opponent is behind cover (like a concrete wall) but are not touching it, then it may be harder or unlikely for the discharge particles to quantumly tunnel. So, most mages will avoid pressing up against their cover, leaving at least 15 cm on average between themselves and the cover, instead (at least initially). The average 10 cm-thick concrete wall can withstand about six consecutive average DPL discharges before the discharge particles will begin being able to quantumly tunnel to any QDF within proximity. Once this threshold is met, each discharge particle will then have a 25% chance of becoming QTPs. The concrete wall would then typically have a cooldown of about 12 seconds before needing roughly the same number of discharges again fired at it to allow for further QTPs. While this may sound super easy to hit opponents behind cover, again, consider that one needs accuracy for the precise angle and position of a discharge in order for quantum tunnelling to occur.

Even when a shielded mage is behind cover, their UPIs can still protect the cover, reducing the strength of the CBEs that the cover would experience. Of course, this means that if the *cover* is hit (too much), then one's UPIs can overstimulate, so if the shielded mage were to be hit while peeking out from their cover, they would have more *APL* against their *shield*. Generally, the discharge particles themselves have to be within the UPI range to be affected – not indirectly via the affected HRF. So, in the abovesaid case of being 15 cm away from the cover, the UPI range may or may not include protecting the cover, as this case did not specify the size (thickness) of the cover; that is, the discharge particles would normally hit the front of the cover, but they may or may not be within the UPI range. In some cases, a mage may want to protect the cover, while in other cases, they may not want to protect the cover (usually in order to not have any UPIs overstimulated), so the distance between the mage and the cover accordingly changes based on the context. Still, covers can be pushed into the mages hiding behind them, so this is another problem to consider.

A user's discharge will still be (for a brief moment) quantumly connected to them (the user) and their aura (by extension) – even after leaving it – which is known as the *particle-user connection* (PUC). This is similar to a SUC but different, as it involves quantum entanglement and is not just mental and etheric. Moreover, PUC applies to all USTs. The quantum entanglement in a PUC will only consume a fraction of the energy in the discharge, and this is basically just informational. Of course, when the need or obligation arises (when certain CBEs or phenomena apply), the entangled energy ratios can change. While an ultrachite discharge is not the same HRF as the user, the HRF of the discharge is still related to the user (as an HRF). This quantum entanglement is coupled with other etheric data, in turn allowing for particular wave function changes, giving a special relation between the user and their discharges.

When a user happens to be near their own exploding discharge, the particles that cause CBEs will UPS from AES to DES – but only for those near the user; the remaining particles in the blast will continue affecting their environment in AES. Although acknowledged within one's ACE, the particles will not turn into DES until about 20 cm away (for most mages) from either the body or other concentrated ultrachite (like a shield's shell). The UPS is a result of one's auric equilibrium and not a user's shield (if they have one active) automatically using their UPIs to UPS. Accordingly, a user's shield (if present) will not lose UPIs to overstimulation. Although this 20 cm figure is the same as the UPI range, this is just a coincidence, and the two figures are unrelated. The PEP changing is also just a default, which means that users can lower (but not increase) this automatic UPS range as an alternative – even to the point of totally switching the default UPS off, should they wish to risk having their own discharges affect them.

The PUC only applies to the user and not allies; the only exception to this is when beta-positive shields are in use, which synchronizes one's PUC with another mage to a degree (with *Section 3.6.5.2* possessing more information). Even though users can only create additional ultrachite up to their DPL (or LPL or HPL) in their aura at once for a UST when the original ultrachite particles have already returned to the Aether, left the aura, or are DUPs, it is still possible for there to be the aforesaid PUC, as mere quantum connection is a separate (despite *related*) matter to auric equilibrium. Nevertheless, any remaining AES particles in the blast can still *indirectly* affect the user, so shooting discharges in close combat may still not be ideal.

Regardless, the particles in a discharge will not last long after exploding – even at supreme power levels; therefore, they are called *flash-timed particles* (FTPs), which are different to DUPs (that occur after the FTPs end), so FTPs are fully functional. When referring specifically to the actual effect(s) of the FTPs, then *flash-time effect* (FTE) is used. Due to the limited existential timeframe of FTPs, users typically need to repeatedly fire at opponents to maintain the effect. If multiple discharges happen to hit the same HRF within the FTP-timeframe or at the exact same time (whether the exact same spot on the HRF or not) – normally from multiple mages shooting at once, rather than a single shooter – then, generally, only the strongest set of FTPs will remain active, with the older and/or weaker sets phasing into IES. That is, a *single* discharge's FTPs are collectively united at the quantum level (via, and as, an HRF – in addition to its partial condensate properties), and they do not negatively affect one another, but *other* discharge particles will UPS older and/or weaker particles into dormant/inactive status through *triggering particular* wave function changes.

This UPS even applies to one's own discharge FTPs affecting *another* older discharge, as the PUC does not apply to each other in this case due to both sets of FTPs being outside one's auric equilibrium. The UPS feat is possible due to how the discharge particles spread their energy throughout the HRF, so contact can be made between the discharges even if the newer/stronger discharge does not touch the mass of the other discharge. Typically, the UPS will occur *rapidly* before any CBEs are inflicted. In most cases, a *user's* discharges alone will not accumulate on a target, anyway, given that mages have a maximum fire rate, with each of their discharges moving at roughly the same speed while also lasting momentarily on impact as FTPs. Note that a discharge's strength (that is, its CBEs) will not practically weaken during the discharge's existence (before the FTPs turn into DUPs), except some of the SBEs (specifically the UPS abilities for other discharges) will decline in strength; accordingly, this is why older discharges (even of the same strength as newer ones) will be 'weaker' in this context.

There is also the major factor of UPIs to consider when discharges hit ultrachite shields; that is, a shield will also keep both the older and newer discharge particles in DES – normally before the discharges would affect one another (before certain *immunities* to shield UPIs apply – a phenomenon explained later in this subsection). With shield UPIs contributing to – and basically completely undertaking – the process, APL *build* can still occur due to an increase in UPI overstimulation; in all practical cases, this would not be proportional but, instead, the same. That is, while a shield would keep virtually all of the *affectable* particles of both discharges in DES, the discharges would not reduce any of the shield's potential UIO when they affect the other discharge particles (that have the abovesaid immunity to shield UPIs) that the shield would not affect; thus, APL build will still be the same for each discharge, no matter how many discharges that hit the shield.

So, if Discharge A hits an ultrachite shield, some of the discharge particles would have an immunity (to shield UPIs only), while all the other particles would be in DES due entering the UPI range. When Discharge B hits the shield a split moment later (while Discharge A is still active), a portion of its particles will also be in AES (with the immunity) while the other particles will be in DES. Due to the erratic nature of discharges compared to shields, discharge particles can UPS other discharges with relative ease, no matter the PEP status. Just as Discharge B hits the shield, its particles (both in DES and those in AES with an immunity to shield UPIs) will *rapidly* UPS the other discharge's AES particles into IES before CBEs would even practically occur. It would also do this without the shield UPIs being aggravated, so there would be no UIO loss. After this, Discharge B would be the only discharge to continue affecting the shield via CBEs, and, thus, the APL *build* (not the level per se) would be the same as Discharge A's APL build. Note that the *triggering* of particular wave function changes in this context will allow the newer/stronger discharge to PEP change the other discharge into IES without suffering a loss of practical energy.

Of the accumulated FTPs that are in IES/DES around an HRF, *all* will still cause energy damage via SBEs. That is, even if multiple discharges (from any number of different mages) were to simultaneously hit an HRF (like a shield), the SBE energy of all the discharges would still affect the HRF – despite also affecting one another. So, if four discharges were to simultaneously hit a shield, the shield would still mostly/noticeably experience the damage of all four discharges. It takes six average DPL discharges simultaneously hitting an average DPL shield (all exactly within the FTP timeframe) to overload it. If four or five said discharges hit the shield at once, then there would be the *potential* for quantum instabilities to arise, with each respectively having roughly a 33% and a 66% chance of overloading the shield. If the shield's UOT were already *nearly* met (from being previously hit), then naturally, the shield would be able to handle less discharges at once, with the chance percentages changing for any number of discharges less than the figure needed to overload the shield (normally, in this case, they would be low). If the shield's UOT were already *somewhat* met, then the shield would still overload in the same number of abovesaid discharges, with the shield having a special increased resilience at the quantum level.

Again, since HRFs rely on HRTs, not all HRFs can be affected *as* HRFs – of course, the properties within unaffectable HRFs can still be affected. Discharges are an example of things that are typically hard (but not impossible) to affect *as* HRFs due to their erratic nature. When in the context of there being discharge particles around HRFs, newer discharges can still affect older discharge particles (that are around an HRF, like a person) without affecting them (the older discharge) as an HRF. For this reason, the newer discharge particles can affect other things (like people) as HRFs instead of hitting the very first thing that they would otherwise hit (that is, the older discharge particles). Note that while discharges are hard to affect *as* HRFs, they can still explode when hitting other discharges (for example, while mid-air); this is different when dealing with *FTPs* fully surrounding HRFs, where the SBEs of the newer discharge particles will also push past or weave around older discharge particles (that would lose their ability to fasten to HRFs) – should they be present at the exact location – to properly affect the affectable HRF (all the while PEP changing any other particles). That is, it is easier for them to brush through/past *particles* than whole discharges intact as discharges before turning into FTPs.

This pushing process basically also applies to the *energy* that discharges exert throughout an HRF. So, if two discharges were to hit an ultrachite shield at different locations, the newer/stronger one will force the energy of the older/weaker one back to its mass of FTPs (that would be also have been PEP changed into DES). This is actually an easy task for the newer discharge, as the older discharge will have weaker SBEs that specifically allow for such easy submission. After the pushback, the older discharge will 'forfeit' its ability to exert its energy across the HRF, but it would still *just* continue to affect the shield via SBE energy from its mass. Accordingly, the newer/stronger discharge would still affect the shield without losing any practical power on the HRF. Therefore, as stated above, multiple discharges can affect an HRF (like a shield) without each losing much of their overall damage against the HRF.

Despite only lasting normally roughly a quarter of a second for all DPLs, FTPs do not necessarily just *cause* CBEs; they may also *leave* behind their effects as well – the most common being *temporary remaining effects* (TREs), which are the exact same effects that FTPs inflict. Starting *at* the power of the FTPs, TREs extend the effects to a certain point with typically diminishing levels per second. Then there are *post-particle effects* (PPEs), which are different to, but result from, the FTP effects. For example, a discharge's FTPs might magnetically push an opponent, and a PPE might include a resultant headache from hitting a wall, which would be unrelated to the magnetic push in and of itself. PPEs tend to have diminishing effects as well for a certain period of time (with timeframes ranging greatly). FTPs can also induce *accumulative aftereffects* (AAEs), which, of course, accumulate with additional attacks *after* the main effects have finished, and the typically linger for longer periods. However, not all AAEs are equal, nor do they *necessarily* infinitely stack.

For clarification, an attack that inflicts 10% of Effect-X as a TRE will not accumulate to 20% during the second attack. That is, the additional (second) attack would still inflict 10% of Effect-X, and the opponent would also only experience 10% of Effect-X not just for that attack but even as an aggregate after all still-active TREs. In other words, any additional attacks that inflict Effect-X would only (top up the effect to the affectable threshold of whatever things and phenomenon are present and) prolong the TRE rather than increase its strength; whereas with an AAE, the next attack *could* accumulate at the same rate, and Effect-X would add up to 20%. If, hypothetically, FTPs lasted longer (say, a few seconds), then in *most* cases (when viewing all of the available powers mages have at their disposal in phasarchement magic), additional damage would not be inflicted, and, instead, it would be similar to a TRE. Essentially, the *timespan* would merely increase.

Meanwhile, a discharge's SBEs will also cause *damage per attack* (DPA) to certain materials, which primarily increases overloading rates in the context of UST One shields. When an ultrachite shield experiences such damage, it will have DUPs; and, when DUPs occur, the shield will be out of auric equilibrium, so more photomission energy will be automatically sent to fuel the damaged shield, recreating the damaged particles. Against an average opponent's respective DPL shield, the DPA of an average DPL discharge will also cause the opponent to lose 0.4% of their MLP; and each succeeding discharge's DPA will also be the same. Note that the *cost* to the lumarchetrix from the discharge is different than the damage itself, which is purely physical.

A discharge's SBE damage is primarily electrical, which can affect non-ultrachite matter, too. Since organic (biological) properties are part of HRFs that have HRTs that are too high for most discharges to normally affect (with certain CBEs and SBEs), only master and supreme power level SBEs *may* be able to affect biological matter with very mild electrical shocks. Users, nevertheless, do not have to worry about harming themselves with SBEs, as while the SBEs do not UPS into DES as with CBEs (when the particles are on oneself – or even within one's proximity), *circumvention*, nonetheless, occurs due to the discharge's energy matching a unique frequency that only the user possesses. Specifically, when the SBE energy is within proximity, the user's aura will divert what-would-be harmful energy through the aura until it dissipates safely, normally, but not always, via grounding. The unique frequency, in this context, is established by the PUC and specific wave function changes, but it also *naturally* follows through with the abovesaid outcome, anyway. This allows a user's other USTs to also be unharmed.

Even though discharges cause SBE damage, the UST Two aura itself is subject to overloading (UPO), mainly when the user repeatedly fires too many discharges within a particular period. When this occurs, the UST Two aura will experience a similar (but causally different) QIF to that of shields, inhibiting the user from creating discharges for a certain period of time. For average users with respective DPL discharge auras, the creation of about 24 consecutive blast balls will overload the aura with a QIF penalty of about six seconds – in addition to a CDP of one second. Note that the maximum time for the OSR is also about six seconds (with a CDP of one second). If the average DPL user has a discharge aura active but are not currently shooting, then the aura can last up to 60 consecutive seconds before overloading. Interestingly, these two figures are unconnected (a phenomenon relative to discharge ultrachite), so a user can still have both 23 blast balls shot out while at the 59-second mark. So, there are different UOTs in this case, but they still both lead to the same UPO.

If the discharge aura is active and a concentrated discharge is being held without being fired off, then the user's aura, in this case, will overload in 18 consecutive seconds. In either case, the UOTs increases, so even after switching the discharge aura off while nearing the UOTs, then switching it back on soon after, the UOTs will still be high. Therefore, after shooting, the discharge aura is normally switched off, even if shooting will recommence shortly later. Note that the time penalty for LBOs is different and unrelated to the UPO times. It might seem annoying to constantly switch discharge auras on and off during combat, but most mages are fine with this feat, as it quickly becomes second nature after initial training. As with any other overloaded UST, a user cannot simply change the PAC and continue shooting.

It is important to note that a discharge aura is a continuously-powered aura, continuously receiving photomission energy from the lumarchetrix when it *is* being powered. *Technically*, there are no 'individual' shots that occur for the discharge aura; instead, each discharge is the maximum amount of energy/mass that can form at any one given time for a power level in one's auric equilibrium (whether a DPL, HPL, or LPL). As a result of this cap, 'individual' shots form *observably* as concentrations of the available particles in the aura, *which* would still be active (regardless of whether there is a blast ball *just* exiting the aura's space in that split moment, in turn leaving very few – if any at all – particles left in the aura). Users, nonetheless, still have to pay basically-what-is a CEC rather than just a MEC for each discharge shot, but this is only for the lost particles rather than having to pay for a whole new aura with a default set of new particles.

For this technical reason, if a user happens to receive or experience LCIs *while* they are shooting discharges (or with an active discharge aura), they will not incur the LCI problem of potentially being unable to create further discharges if they keep firing continuously. However, to keep the discharge aura from overloading (and to also save energy), mages tend to switch their auras off; and so, if the user were to begin firing again (that is, through having to create a new aura), they would *then* experience the LCI *problem* of potentially not being able to channel the energy to form a discharge aura. Nevertheless, a user cannot change from a DPL to an HPL (or LPL) *while* they are shooting without both the LCI rate and problem then applying.

As stated before, when a user's discharge enters a shield's UPI range, the discharge particles that are normally able to rapidly switch into AES (when they impact) will now only remain in DES. However, a certain percentage of these particles may build a resistance and then a *phase changing immunity* (PCI) to the UPIs. As a result, a discharge may not *totally* turn (or rather, stay) dormant – unless it is near the user or if against a comparatively very powerful shield (with this latter example not being applicable in most cases as it has to involve a discharge with weaker-than-novice power levels). With relative DPLs considered, only a small percentage of the particles may be able to gain a PCI. A typical shield's UPIs can also handle (that is, UPS, or simply, inhibit) *many* discharges at once. Still, by the time a shield would reach the limit of how many discharges it can inhibit at once, it would have overloaded long before that – not to mention the potential overstimulation of all the UPIs, too.

Note that discharge particles (of any PEP) do not technically cause the over-stimulation of UPIs by 'attacking' them as such; instead, the UPIs use excess energy while attempting to PEP change/inhibit the discharge particles, with the extra charge causing the overstimulation for a particular number of UPIs based on their overall power level. There are technically cases where the energy from discharge attacks *can* add to the overstimulation of UPIs, but this is not common. It does not matter how many potential PCI particles there are compared to potentially-switched DES particles when it comes to the amount of energy required for UPIs to attempt PEP changing/inhibiting. That is, just before PCIs are gained, UPIs will expend energy on all of the discharge particles. When the discharge's potential AES particles are rendered into DES, they no will longer aggravate the UPIs, and so, UPIs will not continue to use energy and, thus, will not overstimulate if this has not already occurred. AES particles with PCIs also do not aggravate UPIs, so no more over-stimulation will occur here either.

When a user fires another discharge, the new blast ball will not have the same UPI immunity. Even though PCIs result from a discharge being attacked, overall, there would still be an increase in APL for each subsequent discharge attack on a shield due to the second attack being relatively stronger because there would be less UPIs. A discharge's building of a PCI would still occur quickly, and the number of FTPs in a discharge would not weaken to a certain amount every time in order to build an immune response; that is, they can build an immune response even if most of the FTPs manage to survive in AES against a very weak shield with a low active UPI count. FTPs that have been rendered into DES may turn back (or change) into AES, but this is rare – thus, the usage of the more frequent term, IES, in this context. For this to occur, the particles must normally first move away from the UPIs – which itself is uncommon due to FTPs fastening to the HRF they are affecting; plus, FTPs do not last long. While the APL can increase per attack, the percentage of UPIs that will overstimulate with each discharge will remain the same if each discharge is of the same power level as the last (with the same number of particles).

It would seem, then, that if the last APL against a shield were at 4.167%, the next attack would build to 8.333% APL (average and equal DPLs considered). And while this is thus far valid, there is yet another variable to consider; that is, despite this equally-proportional increase, APL build (or even initial gain) may not even necessarily transpire. A discharge's ability to 'overstimulate' shield UPIs occurs by first overcoming a *chance check* based on the *UPI aggregate strength* (UAS). This means that while individual UPIs have their own statistical rate of overstimulation, the UAS acts as a collective protection for the individual UPIs *first*. However, the strength of the UAS still depends on the number of active individual UPIs, so when more UPIs are overstimulated, the UAS drops in strength. More specifically, the UAS *itself* never disappears or drops – it merely changes in strength – unless *all* the UPIs are overstimulated.

A UAS *itself* also does not have a cooldown period; instead, it relies on the cooldown of the individual UPIs that constitute it. If a discharge were to hit a shield and fail at overcoming the UAS, then any previously-overstimulated UPIs would not have any obstacle stopping them from cooling down. That is, the timing of the CDP would kick in immediately, followed by the OSSR, neither stopping with the failed discharge. When a shield's UAS fails to protect the UPIs, this causes instabilities for each UPI, and this is when the actual excess energy used for the inhibition can cause overstimulation. While UPIs are individual units, they also distribute their energy across the shield. This means that the UPI range for one UPI is technically anywhere around the shield. Also, when there are less UPIs, the range does not decrease, just the strength; and when a discharge aggravates the UPIs, its energy will distribute across the shield, normally evenly affecting UPIs per unit area. Therefore, when in range of a shield before impact, an incoming discharge has to contend with all of a shield's UPIs.

It does not matter how many PCIs a discharge may acquire, as all of the discharge's particles will be weighted against the UAS. Therefore, if each subsequent discharge is of the same power level, then the only varying factor for each attack's chance rate will be the strength of the UAS itself. For further clarification, it is essentially the case that when there are less UPIs, more PCIs can be gained. When more PCIs are gained, *more* APL can *build*. So, APL build does *not itself* occur with less UPIs but, instead, with more PCIs (that is, particles with AES), as, ultimately, it is the discharge particles themselves that cause the CBEs, not the lack of UPIs themselves. When the UAS chance check is not passed, then (an increase of) PCIs cannot be gained on the (next) discharge, which means no APL *build* can occur, so the failed discharge's APL will be the same as the previous discharge (if any applies).

Since every individual UPI has a different level of strength, this, more precisely, means that with higher power levels, the *number* of particles does not just increase in a UST but also the strength of each one. Accordingly, some UPIs can overcome some – but not necessarily all – PCIs. Furthermore, PCIs are really only immune to particular properties under certain circumstances with sufficient power levels; thus, as said before, the erratic and complex nature of discharges allows for this phenomenon of discharges being able to UPS other discharge particles with PCIs. The timings for the chance check against the UAS, the PEP changing, PCI gains, and over-stimulation all occur within a fraction of a second, with the UPIs' attempt at PEP changing or inhibiting automatically and instantly bringing on the chance check against the UAS before they (the UPIs) can even finish.

The initial average DPL discharge will have a 16.667% chance of overcoming the average DPL shield's UAS before being able to overstimulate 4.167% of the UPIs (so, 4.167% APL would occur). If the initial attack does not successfully pass the UAS, then 0% APL would occur. If, however, the initial attack is successful, then the next attack would have a 20.834% chance of overcoming the UAS to then bring the APL to 8.333%. For a 12th consecutive hit without any shield cooldowns, the UAS chance check rate (at said power levels, with all previous attacks being successful) would be 62.5%, with the APL build being 50%. If 100% APL were achieved (and the shield has not overloaded), then all subsequent attacks would be at 100% APL as well, with no need to pass a UAS check, given that it would be at 0%. Even if no or very little APL is built against a shielded opponent, consider that the ultimate goal in combat situations is normally to overload a shield before knocking out or killing an opponent; so, if all discharge attacks were unsuccessful at passing a shield's UAS, this would not mean that a user would ultimately lose. That is, building APL against shields generally *helps* but is not *necessary* for victory.

Discharge auras can also switch *modes*. The *default discharge mode* (DDM) consists of the abovesaid types of discharges, whereas the *alternative discharge mode* (ADM) will switch a large percentage of a discharge's CBE-inducing particles into a permeant IES. For all DPLs, this amounts to about 91.667% of the particles. While this does make the discharge weaker in itself (in terms of CBEs, not SBEs), the ADM also gives the potential AES particles *strong* PCIs (with the 'potential', in this context', meaning when the LES particles may turn into AES on impact). Simultaneously, however, none of the particles in the discharge (both the PCI and IES particles) will aggravate UPIs, which means APL build cannot occur. So, if the average DPL discharge were to hit an average DPL shield, it would always inflict an APL rate of 8.333%, regardless of how many UPIs may or may not be already overstimulated. Nevertheless, if the same discharge were to hit a supreme DPL shield, then (as a result of individual UPIs having varying strength – even against particles with PCIs) the APL amount would drop to about 5% – which is still quite effective, with only a 40% drop.

Even though the ADM might not sound appealing to use in most cases, there is, nonetheless, a potential bonus. After an ADM aura has been active for at least six seconds (for all DPLs), the user then has a chance (at a normal rate of 50% for all DPLs) to begin *augmenting* a *single* blast ball, resulting in more particles being able to flexibly change into AES – *whilst* also possessing PCIs. The photomission energy costs for augmented (and even unaugmented) discharges are the same as normal discharges in the DDM, too. Meanwhile, the AES rates for an augmented discharge will range anywhere from around 8.334% to 100%. If the discharge fails to *begin* augmenting, then the user would have to wait at least another six seconds before being able to attempt the augmentation again. Then, once the user has the ability to augment their discharge, they require extra time to charge the discharge.

Depending on how many particles they additionally want in AES, the user will have to charge the discharge for roughly two to nine seconds. In the meantime, this still naturally incurs a MEC of 0.2% per second. Then there is another chance check the discharge must pass in order to *successfully* augment. For all DPLs, the fail rate begins at about 33% for a potential AES amount of 8.334%, increasing to a 95% fail rate for 100% potential AES. These figures are also the same for HPLs and LPLs, so it is not a channelling issue and, instead, one based on the actual particles themselves being able to self-modulate and adjust properly. If, and only if, the discharge does not successfully augment (at any stage of the augmentation – that is, *after* the first chance check has been passed), then not only does the user not have an augmented discharge, but their discharge aura may overload as well – with a roughly 50% chance for all DPLs.

For both unaugmented and augmented discharges, the same overloading rates apply, both for the discharge aura and for the shields that they attack (as the latter's duration is basically independent of discharge attacks – in most cases). Therefore, if the average user with their DPL has not shot any blast balls, nor are they holding a blast ball in their hand – and, importantly, if they fail at beginning the augmentation of their blast ball after the first six seconds (but are successful on the second six-second period), all before they follow through with a successful augmentation of a blast ball possessing 100% potential AES (which would take nine seconds) – they (the user) should still have time to launch the discharge before their aura overloads.

After a user successfully augments a discharge, the discharge will fire off like any other normal blast ball. In order to augment the discharge, a user cannot have one discharge PAC ready and then switch the class after the first chance check has been passed. This means that a user cannot shoot weaker (unaugmented) discharges of a particular PAC while they wait for the ability to augment and *then* switch to the PAC that they want for the augmentation. If a switch occurs, the time resets. After shooting a single *successfully-augmented discharge* (SAD), a user would have to wait again for at least six seconds before potentially being able to augment a discharge; this even applies to users who do not successfully augment a discharge but neither suffer from an overload. On the other hand, a user with an overloaded aura would not be able to use weaker (unaugmented) discharges nor switch modes and continue firing in the DDM.

While it may seem pointless for a user to spend time augmenting a discharge when they could otherwise use that time to shoot multiple weaker discharges, there happen to be advantages to stronger attacks. For one, when requiring a specific phenomenon to occur, certain thresholds of power must be met. If the goal of a magnetic attack, for example, is to pull an opponent or item, multiple weak attacks may not even move the target at all, whereas one powerful attack might. So, no matter how many weak attacks are launched, each individually is pointless compared to the stronger attack – even when they are calculatedly the same as a powerful attack when added in the aggregate. Secondly, augmented attacks are great for ambushes and sneak attacks, as they may grant the user the initial upper hand before potentially or otherwise alerting more opponents that may be in the area. Alternatively, there may be cases where the user will only have the chance of performing a one-off shot to accomplish their goal(s), so a powerful attack may be necessary.

In both discharge modes, users can shoot multiple discharges simultaneously (except for SADs – in all practicality); however, the aura's energy naturally divides in power according to how many discharges are shot out, so each attack is proportionally weaker. In fact, if a concentrated blast ball does not meet a minimum threshold of power, then it cannot (properly) discharge from the aura; therefore, there is an upper limit to how many discharges a user can shoot at once, with average mages being able to shoot up to four DPL discharges at once. Alternatively, a user can discharge their aura as a ring surrounding their body, which expands outwards when discharged. Nevertheless, just like with shooting multiple discharges at once, this comes at a massive cost to power per unit area, especially since the FTPs would potentially affect multiple HRFs. It is not possible to create spherical discharges that totally surround the user, as there is not enough energy per cubic area for proper dischargeable effectiveness.

As another available option (irrespective of mode), the ultra-state plasma can be crystallized and turned into *mines* (formally called *crystallized discharge mines* – CDMs) that can be grabbed and placed at locations where opponents may soon approach. Mines also have full PCIs, which allows them to impose 100% APL effects against shielded opponents (relative DPLs considered – otherwise, different power levels may affect the APLs). Specifically, unlike ADM attacks, which require passing a chance check to increase the potential AES levels, all mines come with full potential AES particles. The crystallization process distributes electrons in the CDM in a special way, in turn causing changes in the etheric, where more conscious energy can be stored. As such, this can allow for long phased momentum outside the aura; and for average DPLs, this will allow for a total existential time of 90 seconds.

The crystallization process, however, creates instabilities for the CDM itself *and* the discharge aura. So, an average user with a respective DPL will only be able to form five mines in total before needing to wait about four minutes before being able to create more mines. This would occur with a special kind of QIF, so users would not be able to switch their auras on and off to offset this problem. The instability inflicted on the aura will not affect the user's ability to create normal discharges, though. Each mine will also only be worth a single discharge in terms of power, but they will still have the same CEC as normal discharges. CDMs will also take about three seconds to make, and a user can only create one at a time, and users cannot shoot normal discharges in the meantime.

Due to their instability, CDMs cannot be shot out of an aura like normal discharges, and any attempt to manually throw them with one's hands or device (that is, causing the CDMs to move quickly) will result in CDMs exploding in the air. In the face of these practical drawbacks, mines can be advantageous when tactically used. Mines will float in a circle around the user without the need to be held, and when they are placed somewhere, mines will still continue floating (so long as they are above some nearby ground). Once created, though, a CDM will no longer receive additional energy – even when in one's aura. But this is not a bad issue, as it allows a user to create multiple mines in a short period *before* placing them. Otherwise, if mines sustained their energy in a user's aura, then they would suffer the same limitations of normal discharges, and a user cannot fuel any more energy into a UST form beyond auric equilibrium. Basically, the CDM will act as if it had left the aura after its creation.

Despite exploding when reaching high speeds, mines will slowly move towards things (that possess sufficient mass and size) that move (at speeds passing certain thresholds) within proximity. More precisely, CDMs will home in on targets, with the automatic homing feat resulting from a mine's quantum instability. For all DPLs, this typically, but not always, means mines will move towards things with at least five kilograms of mass that are moving at least five kilometres per hour and are within about 1.5 metres range. Interestingly, discharges that approach and impact close by will not necessarily draw in the mines. Still, if the discharges were to actually hit the mines, this would naturally set the mines off. Mines also do not have any extended explosion compared to normal discharges, so they will still cover an HRF in the same way as a discharge, so long as the mine's particles hit an HRF. Of course, if other *post hoc* people happen to be within the vicinity yet did not have any particles contact them, then they (the people) will not be affected, as the particles (or at least the energy) would not cover them as an HRF.

CDMs, nevertheless, still have a PUC with the user, so, a user's presence (radiated within the ACE) will bring some stability to the mines, which will cause them to stop moving. Accordingly, users are able to securely pick mines up and place them some-where else. Moreover, mines will not set off when other beings are near the user while they (the mines) are within the user's ACE. This way, allies may still approach a user with floating mines, but this also means that users cannot approach opponents and then directly plant mines on them, as the mines would still be somewhat stable within the ACE. Unlike how normal discharges may be alternatively tuned so as the particles will not phase into DES when near the user, CDMs do not have this option.

Although a user can place two or more mines next to one another (that will stay in place after the mines are no longer in the ACE), attempting to place one's mines near another person's (already placed) mines can be problematic due to each set of mines potentially setting off at the other user when no longer within their respective ACEs. When *creating* a CDM, a user must determine if they want (particular) CBEs to be in potential AES or DES, as the user cannot change this after creation (even if the mines are in the aura) due to the mine's final quantum instability per power level. It is basically the same as with normal blast balls that *discharge* from the aura, causing the blast ball to be too erratic at that point for the user to alter the status of its CBEs (without other phenomena occurring, such as a shield using its UPIs).

When in close quarters while in either DDM or ADM, mages can alternatively crystallize and *supercharge* their ultra-state plasma particles for a melee attack (formally called *discharge melee attacks* – DMAs), which can overload an ultrachite shield entirely in generally one hit – relative power levels considered. While the DMA may be able to overload a shield in one hit, this does not mean that it would have a higher power level than a standard concentrated discharge, nor would it use more energy. Instead, the crystallized energy in the DMA is able to strike the quantum level of a shield in a *specific* way that normal discharges are unable to achieve, creating an imbalance that overloads it (that is, via an instant *potent QIF*). However, DMAs lack CBEs, as their respective particles all rest in a permanent IES.

Unlike standard *concentrated discharges* (blast balls), the crystallized particles in a DMA take a longer time to gather toward a central point; for all DPLs, this is normally between one to two seconds (averaging about 1.3 seconds). Moreover, as an ACE issue, the concentration process (and point) is much easier the closer it is to a user's body; generally, it forms near one of the user's hands (by choice), which helps with the following process, as the particles are hard to move due to having a collective 'static resoluteness'. That is, the user has to physically move the particles by collectively grabbing them before punching with them. If the user has room to extend their arm to help deliver the punch movement, this helps greatly. Visually, DMAs require and feature very aggressive moves to execute and deliver decent blows. This is not to say that a user cannot (awkwardly) run up to an opponent with their arm stretched out and then either charge before hitting them or touch the opponent then charge the DMA, but these cases are not common and are less effective than the standard punching technique.

Even though charging a DMA is slightly faster than shooting an opponent's shield and overloading them (relative discharge and shield power levels considered), the opponent can still shoot – and attain some APL against – the user in the meantime, potentially ruining their melee attack or at least slowing it down. Therefore, the time it takes to charge the DMA *could* otherwise be used simply to shoot normal discharges, and so, the strategy to use a melee attack ultimately comes down to context. If the user is already physically in direct physical contact with an opponent with their hands – and, especially if they cannot let go or move away from them – then they (the user) cannot use normal discharges either effectively or safely. That is, the discharge's CBEs either will not be in AES, or they will affect the user if in AES. In fact, a discharge would not form properly in the tiny spaces between one's hands and the opponent's body. The user could shoot without their hands, but this may not even hit the opponent due to a great lack of accuracy. In these circumstances, it would seem like DMAs could work well, but again, the user would still need to let go of the opponent to build a proper DMA to then punch with it.

DMA, nevertheless, create unique potent QIFs that greatly affect *other* shields within the affected aura's space. That is, if a user were to strike an opponent, then any of the opponent's allies nearby would also have greatly-affected UST One auras. The average DPL DMA will also increase the overloading chance rate of other shields within the vicinity to 100% for all affected average DPL mages, whether shielded or unshielded. Put another way, instead of an opponent's ally, for instance, approaching the affected area and having, say, a 10% chance of their shield also overloading, there would now be a 100% chance to overload. DMAs can also affect other UST auras – and even non-ultrachite HRFs – if they directly strike them, such as directly striking an ultrachite blast ball when it is in its respective aura.

When a user overloads an opponent's shield with either a DMA or a normal discharge, the SBEs of the attack will affect the (potent) QIF in a way that will prevent the *user's* UST forms from overloading. This means that when a DMA is used up close against an opponent (as it is a melee attack), the user's shield, for example, will not have any practical chance of overloading. Accordingly, the QIF is naturally altered only in the immediate vicinity of the user and their manifested ultrachite. There are, nevertheless, exceptions to this when other phenomena are applied. While this may seem the same as the previously-mentioned phenomenon of SBEs being basically safe around biological organisms (especially the user), in this case, it specifically involves *QIFs* themselves.

In normal situations when another mage (like the abovesaid opponent's ally) enters the space of an overloaded average DPL *discharge aura* (specifically, the IPF spatial area of where the discharge aura was and would be if recreated), there is respectively a 10% and an 8% chance that their *discharge aura* may overload or will overload when activated. If the other mage (whether using an active discharge aura or not) were already within the vicinity when the event occurs, then there would be a one-off instant chance of around 8%, too, with roughly a 4% chance after leaving and re-entering the vicinity. With the DMA applied, however, these figures rise to 100% as well. While this may seem like a *super QIF*, it is not.

For clarification, super QIFs affect *different types* of QIFs at once, whereas potent QIFs affect *one type* of QIF (including from different things/HRFs at once) but in a stronger way to normal QIFs. So, if other (people's) auras (of any UST) overload within the original affected aura's space, then the former would only affect other auras with their own statistics instead of spreading or adding to the latter's statistics. Accordingly, only the initial aura's potent QIF would have the greatest effect in the vicinity, overriding any weaker effects of weaker QIFs. Moreover, if a user wished to affect an opponent's shield *and* discharge auras, then they would, in all practical cases, need to use two separate DMAs against the two ultrachite forms specifically. This potent QIF phenomenon not only greatly helps with offensive contexts but also defensive ones – when used effectively.

When a mage (or a group of mages) is outnumbered, whether with a 2:1 or 4:1 ratio – or any other ratio – then it is possible for the larger group to move out of their cover and then directly approach the lone mage or smaller group (normally within a close range) to defeat them. That is, if the larger group can overcome certain hurdles and avoid being fired upon when approaching the smaller group, then, in a direct-line-of-fire situation where each combatant is of equal power levels and skill, the larger group merely needs to shoot discharges at the smaller group and then overload their shields before knocking them unconscious with certain CBEs. This is an example of *force concentration*. While the larger group would suffer losses, this may not necessarily be bad for them, as the victory itself could greatly outweigh any potential setbacks.

Ultrachite discharges are not normally lethal directly *in themselves* when used in most contexts, so, in the context of mere phasarchement combat, mages typically do not have to fear being killed. That is, the abovesaid 'losses' are not deaths but mere setbacks, which greatly contrasts battles with non-magic gunfire, where more caution is executed. Usually, if defeated in a phasarchement fight, the losers will simply lose consciousness due to the nature of particular kinds of discharge CBEs. The winning team need only wait for their teammates to wake up in the meantime, or alternatively, they may directly revive them. In the interim, the awake people of the winning team can just shoot discharges at the downed group to keep them unconscious. For this reason, phasarchement fights (without other magic or items involved) do not typically possess the grave risk factor of death, and so, leaving cover to *doomgroup* (that is, grouping up to dominate) a smaller group or a lone mage via force concentration is more appealing. Doomgrouping normally begins – but not necessarily occurs – when there is at least a 4:1 ratio of combatants in a battle, but it can still sometimes and occasionally occur with 3:1 and 2:1 ratios.

There are, nevertheless, many factors involved with successfully doomgrouping – even with ratios at or above 4:1 – so not all contexts afford the larger group certain victory. Furthermore, many mages know of the general rule of phasarchement combat that if doomgrouping is not done correctly – and within the right context – it can still go awry. Even when victory is guaranteed, doomgrouping may not be beneficial or desirable. So, if time is against the combatants (of either the larger or smaller group), then doomgrouping or merely leaving cover recklessly is a much less desirable option. For example, if a bomb is about to explode and escape from a location is paramount, risking unconsciousness even for a mere ten minutes may not be worth it. Other factors to consider include whether either side of the conflict knows how many opposing combatants there actually are (due to being in the dark, for example), in addition to power levels and their actual locations. It may appear that a group is larger, but this may not be the case, so caution is normally applied to prevent potentially bad outcomes. Then potential doomgroups may split off to flank enemies, as that may provide better outcomes than forming a doomgroup.

Sometimes there may be live security cameras installed in the area, and so, if the people in the potential doomgroup were to approach certain locations within the area of combat, then they could expose their identities. Even if the doomgroup were to win and also destroy the cameras, it may still be too late in this case. In some scenarios, the smaller group may be in dangerous locations (such as being on a shaky platform above hazardous materials), so reaching the smaller group could be perilous. Even when victorious, one of the people in the doomgroup could find themselves cut off from the rest of the doomgroup, not only potentially leading to death, but there may be outcomes where they are later captured. There are also cases where a doomgroup may approach an individual opponent within a small but scattered group and then leave themselves vulnerable to the rest of the smaller group to attack them. Moreover, the rest of the smaller group may have their members in hard-to-hit locations, while the doomgroup may not only be in an easy-to-shoot location, but they would also be bunched together.

In the case of a doomgroup being bunched together (in tight areas), DMAs are useful for bringing down doomgroups because the lone mage or smaller group can overload all of the attackers in the doomgroup at once – *if* all the members are within the QIF's area. This is an example of a *force multiplier*. Moreover, when coupled with other tactics, such as setting up CDMs, a lone mage (or a smaller group) will not necessarily be cornered or approached by a larger group (and lose). CDMs are normally set up first (generally behind a cover so the opponents will not see them when approaching), where they set off before a DMA is then applied to the opponents – but this does not always have to be the case. There are also other tactics that the smaller group/lone mage can use, such as utilizing other USTs to back themselves out of tight situations.

However, the lone mage/smaller group should also be prepared because the doom-group can also use DMAs against them. After the DMA overloads one shield (and, thus, the other shields), a user merely has to shoot normal discharges a split second later to inflict the CBEs they desire – normally, the type that causes unconsciousness.

Still, it is not always guaranteed that these cases will lead the smaller group/lone mage to victory; and usually, when within the context of battles with just phasarchement magic, the larger group (of equal power levels and skills to the smaller group) *will* win *when* they are able to directly *and successfully* approach and doomgroup. Of course, even without directly approaching, larger groups normally win battles – especially when factoring in for how multiple discharges can overload a shield *if* all hit it *exactly* at once (normally *starting* at four discharges – relative DPLs considered). For this reason, when outnumbered, smaller groups or lone mages will typically use *suppressive fire* before using various tactics to *escape*. Sometimes, though, the best form of defence is offence. While the particles in a DMA are hard to move, users tend to find it strategically better to ready a melee attack when behind a corner before moving right towards the doomgroup. DMAs are also very effective against certain (usually, but not always, weak) forcefields and electronic equipment. Naturally, when other factors beyond phasarchement magic are added to battles, such as non-ultrachite traps, weapons, and devices – and even other magics – the dynamics of doomgrouping change again – usually in less favourable outcomes for those wanting to doomgroup.

Sometimes mages will mix up or simultaneously combine ultrachite discharges with non-ultrachite weapons (whether melee and/or ranged) in order to enhance their prospects in combat. For melee combat, such weapons can include swords, batons, knives, staffs, and more. When such weapons are applied, users can also utilize other USTs that are useful in close quarters. There are cases where when one dodges a knife attack, they can become too distraught and distracted to shoot ultrachite discharges back, so this may sometimes result in melee combat *only* being melee-based. A shielded attacker may also be able to run up to a shielded opponent and stab them with a knife (multiple times) quicker than overloading their shields with discharges (including via a DMA); therefore, when a knife is approaching a mage, it is normally best to address the knife attack with basic physical movements (whether by fleeing, dodging or fighting). When witnessing an ally in the midst of melee combat, it may also be hard for a user to shoot their opponent, as the two (or more) combatants may be moving around (and this is not even factoring in for accuracy in general, anyway, along with other variables).

For legal reasons, mage police officers will typically also only use non-lethal melee weapons like stun batons, with their use and necessity depending on the context. When in certain non-mage zones that have firearm restrictions, melee combat with non-ultrachite melee weapons may be more common as well. Many non-mages still train in melee combat due to these restrictions, so cultured and informed mages are aware of this phenomenon and prepare accordingly before combat. Melee weapons can also be manufactured in a way that allows them to avoid being detected – even with advanced scanners – so this is another reason as to their popularity and, thus, frequency of usage. There are some melee weapons that emerge as energized aerochite from technological apparel like *sentars* (that is, aerochite-based weapons emerge from focal points dotted across gloves called sentars).

It is not unheard of for people (both mages and non-mages) to run up to mage opponents and place magic suppressors on them as a form of melee combat; but this is tricky, as magic suppressors need to be properly attached to a body (which are usually in the form of cuffs), and they normally take a few seconds before the effect sets it. Otherwise, shooting *standard magic suppressors* (SMSs) at opponents – especially shielded opponents – is pointless. However, if the magic suppressor is in the (expensive) form of proper ammunition (specifically, *magic suppressor ammunition* – MSA – which contains a substance like a tonic), *temporary* magic suppression can result. Still, this is only effective against unshielded opponents; and even when shot, a mage's body can build a short-term tolerance (resistance and then an immunity) to the ammunition when the effects wear off – even after a single round – so MSAs are not used in all contexts.

Even *aerosol magic suppressors* (AMSs) will not pass through ultrachite shields because, while gases may pass through said shields, the particles (solids and/or liquids) in the medium of the aerosol's gas will not pass through shields. Most mages will build a temporary resistance after just one AMS spray and then a temporary immunity after a few consecutive sprays. So, at first, an AMS will usually last about a couple of minutes, and with each consecutive spray, this time diminishes until an immunity for roughly 24 hours begins. AMSs can backfire on users (spreadable sprays in particular), so the safest ones are stream-based; however, there is a matter of thresholds for the actual suppression to take place, so if not enough of the aerosol touches or enters the mage, no effect occurs. AMSs have a light scent, but they are not that noticeable to most mages; sometimes, though, scents are added to AMSs. It may seem practical to simply spray an area with an AMS before a battle, but consider that to spray an entire area (whether a room or a street), a lot of the product is required, which can be way too costly; they also do not last long after being sprayed, so timing is key. Then, if the opponents are already prepared, they would usually already be shielded, too.

Generally, mages do not bother with firearms such as rifles *when* using discharges for a variety of reasons. Although technological innovations have improved rifles over time, rifles still possess problems due to having to balance out increased power. Accordingly, rifles may still be heavy to hold, and then there is the issue of carrying and (re)loading ammunition. They can also malfunction, overheat, and warp. However, one advantage that many firearms have is ATSs – whether (NAC, QMC, or DEC-based) – which greatly improve accuracy. These, nevertheless, can be hacked or scrambled (potentially leading to the firearm turning on its owner), and they pose other problems. Non-reloading weapons and recoilless firearms are another option, but these also possess their drawbacks, too. Moreover, while rifles do vary in strength, a sole rifle's strength remains practically static (unless customized), whereas a sole mage's DPLs can increase in power.

Normally, when a mage *does* use a firearm, it is either a sniper rifle (given the *comparatively* short range of discharges) or explosives, such as rocket launchers or grenades. Although ultrachite discharges *do* react to phenomena like fire and intensify them, the degree to which this occurs is not significant; and so, if actual fire is desired, explosives or even flamethrowers are the better option(s). To be clear, discharges will explode when they go through fire, but not all fire is equal, so if the fire is very weak, the discharge may not explode. When the discharge does explode in a fire, it usually will not treat the fire as an HRF, so the FTPs will either be localized at the blast point, or the FTPs will move around due to the heat of the fire, where they (the FTPs) will then not affect anything else as HRFs. In some other combat cases, non-lethal projectiles, rotary cannons, or even drones are used (and in terms of sheer power, aircraft and bombs are also used in warfare).

In very rare (legal) cases, *particularized paralysis weapons* (PPWs) may be used, which are non-lethal to most beings, only affecting particular types of nerves in the body. Of course, *lethal chemical weapons* (LCWs) are prohibited across the Caelverse and are very hard to find – both to acquire and see in combat. Perhaps the most common firearm (when) used is a pistol, which mages dual wield with their ultrachite discharges. Still, pistols have their limitations as well, and they can be a distraction and, accordingly, a hindrance when focusing on using additional discharges per second, so such usage is only applied in certain contexts – and normally, the mage using the pistol must be an expert for effectiveness. Pistols of assorted kinds are, nevertheless, convenient for when a mage's lumarchetrix depletes or a discharge aura overloads and immediate suppressive fire is needed.

Rifles are typically stronger than pistols, and yet, it still takes about 24 consecutive (but separately-timed and hit) bullets from a standard combat rifle to overload an average DPL ultrachite shield. The muzzle energy, in this case, averages about 3,000 joules per round, but it is important to note that this does not mean that an average DPL shield will exactly and only resist 72,000 joules of energy. That is, in the context of overloading shields, the statistics for any force applied to a shield will not be linear or the same when other variables are applied (other than kinetic energy alone). Some of these phenomena include potential shield penetrability, chemical reactions, force concentration (including the number of attacks at once), quantum unexpectancies, and more. While knives (made of plain metal), for example, can penetrate shields in normal circumstances, the energy in general knife stabs are normally far lower than that of rifle rounds, so knife attacks typically do not overload shields in conventional situations; thus, non-phasarchement weapons like rifles are better in this regard.

In contrast to said rifles, it happens to take about 12 consecutive (but separately-timed and hit) average DPL ultrachite discharges to overload an average DPL ultrachite shield. Note that, in this case, the shield will still block the 12ʰ shot, and so, a 13ᵗʰ shot will be required to actually hit the opponent's body. Before the said shield reaches UPO, the discharge will *also* build APL (at roughly 4.167% per successful hit – average DPLs considered – so 24 successful consecutive hits are required to reach full APL). In order for a shooter to reach 100% APL against a targeted shield before it (the shield) overloads, the shield would need to undergo a cooldown in its UOT before the normally-slower UPI cooldown occurs. Accordingly, APL further hinders the opponent mage *during* the firefight, thus adding a greater incentive for mages to use discharges over non-ultrachite firearms. The discharge also only needs to hit any part of an ultrachite shield for overloading (and APL) rates to take equal effect; and so, in combat, poking one's hand out of cover to fire can still be risky.

The number of discharges needed to overload a shield for other power levels is easy to understand in 'stages of four'. So, while it takes 12 average DPL discharges to overload an average DPL shield, it takes another four discharges to overload the next shield power level (that is, it will take 16 average DPL discharges to overload an advanced DPL shield). Accordingly, it will take 20, 24, and 28 average DPL discharges to respectively overload elite, master, and supreme DPL shields. For combat against the same power levels of any power level, it will take 12 discharges to overload a shield (so, it would take 12 elite DPL discharges to overload an elite DPL shield). On the other hand, a mere eight advanced DPL discharges are needed to overload an average DPL shield, so four elite DPL discharges can overload an average DPL shield, and master and supreme power levels can each overload an average DPL shield in one hit. In a combat situation where there is one elite mage versus four average mages, all shooting point blank with total accuracy and with respective power levels, then, even the elite mage would lose against the average doomgroup of mages. However, if a master mage were in the situation, then they would be able to just win against the average mages.

These are just abstract battles, however, and in all practicality, combat is different, so the outcomes would vary. These situations also do not even include CBEs and APLs, other USTs, other magic, other weapons, the terrain, preconditions, combat skills, and more. Still, APLs also work in 'stages of eight', so the advanced mage would require only 16 shots to reach 100% APL against the average DPL shield, while eight elite discharges would be needed to reach 100% APL against the said shield. Since master and supreme DPL discharges overload the said shields in one hit, APL is *practically* not an issue. The same in reverse also applies; so, it takes 32, 40, 48, and 56 average DPL discharges to respectively reach 100% APL against advanced, elite, master, and supreme DPL shields. Master (and supreme) mages are also quite rare, so they would normally not assume basic combat roles and positions (and effectively, locations) that would be otherwise relegated to less powerful mages; therefore, when confronting a known or suspected master or supreme mage, usually planning is done beforehand.

When a shield overloads (whether from a discharge or any other weapon like a rifle with standard metal bullets), it will produce very noticeable DUPs that look like a small explosion. This indicates to the user who shot the shield that they overloaded it. Even in the event that a user does not see the short-lived DUPs, all shields also make a distinct and clear sound when overloaded, so again, a user who shot the shield and overloaded it would normally know what has occurred – unless they are in situations where there are extremely loud sounds or major distractions – and, of course, if the user is too far away from the opponent. When the shield overloads, the user will normally find it easy to rapidly switch to the particular PAC that causes unconsciousness and then shoot the opponent.

Despite the strength of discharges over many non-ultrachite weapons against shields, some mages swear by their rifles and other firearms, contesting the aforesaid arguments – even if for mere aesthetic reasons. Of these mages, a great number are either military personnel and/or conjurers – with the latter, at least, not having to deal with the issues of carrying, loading, and maintaining their firearms. In fact, on average, earth mages (conjurers) supplement their fights with conjured weapons more so than other elemental types of mages; this even includes melee weapons in close quarters. However, this does not mean that conjurers, on average, use such weapons in combat; the comparison is merely against other types of mages. Conjured weapons are also good at deterring doomgroups from forming and closely approaching smaller groups or lone mages due to the threat of death. Conjuration magic, nevertheless, has its limitations; for example, most mages cannot magically conjure advanced NAC, QMC, or DEC systems and, therefore, cannot conjure firearms with ATSs.

Accordingly, if conjurers want weapons of the same standard as non-mages, they need real weapons – which, again, have their limitations. In the ancient past, conjurers conjured 'primitive' blades, whereas, in the modern context, conjurers are able to conjure stun batons and advanced knives. While considering their situation, conjurers may otherwise focus on creating other useful items with their magic, such as traps, barricades or (stronger) covers rather than firearms during battles, as most firefights are more effectively conducted from behind cover. Note that many conjured covers are lightweight and only just have enough volume to cover a user's body, but they also come with an adhesive underneath so they stick to the ground and will not easily be pushed over. If the user is advanced enough in conjuration, they can conjure FBFs or other forcefields that would be positioned away from their own ultrachite shields. Whatever a conjurer chooses to create, they will become more adept over time at making and casting spells of such nature, so they tend to form niches.

Alchemists, in contrast, sometimes avoid firearms altogether, as they may, for example, transform into entities that cannot handle firearms, such as those with massive claws, which they would potentially use to shred apart opponents (ethical and legal considerations aside). Of course, when alchemists transfigure into bodies that have multiple hands and arms (especially ones with great strength), then multiple firearms or even heavy weaponry may be used. In such states, the alchemists typically (but not always) can still use ultrachite discharges. Even though fire mages do not conjure literal fire themselves (*as* fire mages), should they use alchemical means to create fires, then they may generate environmental hazards that can greatly change the dynamic of a battle setting. Parenthetically, while ultrachite shields can resist fires, they will still overload if they spend too long inside one – and, for all shields against most types of large fires, this is not long.

Mystics, conversely, have magic that plays a more supplementary role in the context of combat. Generally, this means mystics are not found in close quarters with opponents unless they are only using phasarchement magic or are healing an ally. As such, when mystics do use weapons, they are normally used to help their primary roles in combat. Air mages, on the other hand, are *influencers* on a battlefield, but they do not have any major *direct* advantages or disadvantages in regards to their magic and weapons; accordingly, *when* they use firearms, charmers choose whatever fits the context. There is one exception to their magic: charmers can – and usually do – place charms as defences, which can aid against doomgroups. While negative charms can negatively affect allies, a charmer merely need only tell their allies where the charms have been laid. If charmers are lone mages, then this would not apply. Then there are positive charms that can aid allies, which may help turn the tide of battles.

### 3.6.3.3: UST Three/Ultra-state Gas (Vortices):

Used as a support attack, UST Three energy generates ultra-state gas that automatically forms into a *vortex* around the user. Unlike with other USTs, the user will essentially fill the whole aura with ultrachite – except for in the *eye*, where the user will always be located, no matter how much or where they move. Of course, since the ultra-gas is similar to normal gases, the phase is not as dense as other phases, like solids, so there will always be large gaps between the ultra-state gas particles (unless they are compressed). The vortex particles will also only keep within the aura – unlike how normal gas particles would otherwise float away. However, the vortex will be bigger than the average mage's ACE of three metres in diameter, so most vortices reach about four metres in diameter. While normally ultrachite particles (other than some UST 6 particles) cannot be powered when outside the aura, the vortex has the ability to transfer photomission energy to the particles *just* outside the ACE. Still, there is a limit to how far this energy can be sent, and a vortex will naturally keep its size and form limited, anyway. In its natural state, the vortex will also have an equal number of particles throughout the entire radius from the eye to the vortex's edge.

A user can also shoot their own discharges through a vortex without the worry of the SBEs of the vortex itself setting off the discharge; this is mostly due to the density of the vortex itself and for the fact that discharges need hard-enough matter to set them off. Furthermore, the vortex's CBEs, in this case, will also not affect the discharge, as the vortex's immediate particles (so not the whole vortex itself) will automatically and rapidly UPS from AES to DES before turning back again when the discharge has fully passed. Vortices also do not possess UPIs, and while it would then seem that an opponent's exploded discharge would be able to affect a user's vortex via CBEs, this practically does not happen. Again, this is mostly the result of the ultra-gas's density, and so, the discharge's FTPs will normally just affect the HRF on the other side of the ultra-gas particles (without QDFs or QFVs even being part of the phenomenon).

So, if the discharge, for example, were to hit the ground that happened to have the ultra-gas 'on' it, the ground itself (the HRF in question – and only a part of the ground) would be affected, not the vortex. Additionally, the HRT of the vortex's HRF is too problematic for the discharge's CBEs to typically affect *as* an HRF (that is, as a *whole*). Parenthetically, the same principle basically applies to the subsequent USTs as well, (that is, from UST Four to Six). Put another way, discharges do not easily or typically affect other USTs (besides shields and other discharges) via CBEs. Still, by means of SBEs, an opponent's exploded discharge *can* affect a user's vortex – specifically, a set number of *local*, individual vortex particles, in turn affecting the vortex *aura*. That is, a discharge can add towards a vortex's UOT; but since a single discharge has roughly the same power as a whole vortex, this addition is generally insignificant due to only the local particles being affected rather than all of the particles in the vortex.

Vortices do not produce FTPs like discharges because the vortex itself – in its *practical* use – is, instead, an example of a *constant effect power* (CEP) like shields. Opponents, moreover, must be within the AOE to be affected. Therefore, this UST is basically only useful for when either opponents are close to the user or if their attacks (such as discharges) approach within short range (when certain CBEs apply). That is, a user's vortex can still affect other people's discharges. However, there are scenarios where a user can effectively use their vortices to, for example, affect the environment, which can, *in turn*, help in combat situations. Furthermore, the AOE *can* extend beyond the aura, such as when magnetic fields are involved. TREs and PPEs can also apply to opponents who leave the vortex after having first been affected inside. While vortices do not add to the power of a user's discharges, some of the CBEs can negatively affect opponents by weakening them so that their (the user's) discharges can have a greater effect on them (the opponents) specifically. In fact, this is a key theme amongst vortex CBEs. Accordingly, this reinforces the more complimentary role vortices have in combat.

When a non-user's ultrachite shield encounters a user's vortex, it will render the vortex's particles into a state of DES via UPIs. Nevertheless, vortices can also build PCIs against shield UPIs. A shield, in this regard, is also capable of affecting all of the particles in a vortex at once, not just the local ones that directly touch the shield. This is not so much the result of the shield's ability to do this itself, and it is, instead, that the vortex particles are fundamentally connected as a whole system, which operates in a particular manner, allowing for such a delocalized feat. Accordingly, the UPI *range* only matters for the *initial* contact, and so, the vortex particles can *effectively* remain in DES even after moving out of the UPI range in their general rotational movement. Basically, the vortex particles will share the UPI energy load. Note that this whole-vortex effect is not the result of a shield affecting the vortex particles as an HRF in the same way that a discharge affects the things it hits, despite the vortex being an HRF.

When a non-user's discharge explodes within a user's vortex, then (despite not being able to generally affect it as an HRF), the FTPs, via SBEs, may only render the small number of vortex particles within the fist-sized area into DES (or vice versa, depending on power levels and the context). When referring to the particle density of a given area, the *ultrachite particle density* (UPD, or simply, 'particle density') is used, which can also apply to all USTs. Given the size of the said area (and, thus, the UPD of the said area), this is not much of a problem for the vortex user, as their vortex will continue to mostly operate as usual. Furthermore, since FTPs do not last long, the affected vortex particles will either recover quickly or will shortly be recreated (if they were damaged too much). Basically, discharge particles are too erratic and unstable to affect a vortex in the same way as a shield. Because discharges and vortices have relatively equal amounts of energy (relative DPLs considered), discharges *strongly* affect the number of particles that can switch to DES *within* the fist-sized blast (*if* they happen to affect the vortex particles and not *just* the HRF on the other side, like the ground), given the comparative UPD.

Since shields do not experience different kinds of overstimulation (that is, a UPI is either overstimulated or it is not), using vortices alongside discharges is a very effective way of quickly building APL against shielded opponents because there are two sources (instead of one – normally just discharges, within most combat situations) building APL. Even if one's goal were not to primarily use the CBEs or SBEs of a vortex, the mere extra APL build alone can help the user's discharges (more quickly) gain higher-than-normal APLs. This might alternatively seem overpowered, but consider that close combat is normally very risky, so this is a deterrent. Also, with two combatants of relative power levels firing point blank at one another at such a close range, the fight would likely be over before full APL may be reached, anyway.

Moreover, as with discharges, the APL build for vortices, against shields, is also chance based. However, unlike discharges, the individual vortex particles that contact an HRF do not cover it (the HRF) as an HRF and, instead, continue to mostly move within the direction of the vortex's rotation (except for one type of vortex that has mostly 'motionless' particles). Despite not covering a whole HRF, the vortex particles can still, by default, practically affect a whole HRF through *charging* properties electrically and magnetically. For example, if a long electronic device is found both inside and outside of a vortex, electrical energy from the vortex can still conduct through the whole device.

The ultra-gas particles are also highly-electrically charged, yet they are not ionized like plasma. Despite this, they are unable to pass through ultrachite shields. With the vortex particles united (and, coupled with the fact that they normally stay within the aura), they produce what is known as *collective particle pressure* (CPP). So, even if there are areas of the aura where there may be less particles than normal compared to the rest of the vortex (as a result of compression, for example), then, if there are still particles present, they can nevertheless impose particular effects on particular matter within the vortex (like a creature or a discharge). To be clear, despite this field, all tangible effects are still only felt via the particles, so there would still have to be some particles present. Moreover, this only applies to certain powers, so when it comes to, for example, creating a repulsive smell, the particles will not share strength via CPP.

When two or more entities are inside the vortex, consider that while the vortex would still have the same number of particles, the strength of the CPP would be disproportionately weaker per entity as the power of the vortex would spread. So, if two discharges were in the vortex (shot at the user from two people coming from two different locations), then the power upon the two discharges would be halved. Of course, there are thresholds of power to consider, so the vortex may still be able to affect both discharges without seeing (much) loss in effect for both. For example, if a vortex can fully suppress the power of two discharges at once, then, while the power of the CPP would be halved for each discharge, the vortex would still be able to fully supress both discharges. The CPP will also not affect each entity in the vortex equally, so if there were a plain wooden chair in the vortex as well as a discharge, the vortex would typically be *triggered* to affect the discharge to a greater extent.

The effects of the CPP are not just a matter of the pressure itself, but also, under-stand that, again, all of a vortex's particles are quantumly connected to one another, so certain actions that occur in one area can be felt throughout the whole vortex – and the aura itself. It may seem strange that discharges can only affect local particles within a vortex, yet the vortex in the above example can affect multiple discharges. Specifically, it may seem as though that discharges *do* affect a vortex across its entirety. However, note that it is not so much the energy of the discharge itself that affects the vortex, but rather, the phenomenon is based on the amount of energy that a vortex can spend on affecting discharges. With discharges only locally affecting vortices, this is not the result of the vortex keeping the discharge's effects locally, and it is, instead, a failure on the part of the discharge itself to affect the vortex beyond the local blast area.

Vortices overcome a shield's UAS in mostly the same way how discharges affect shields, but instead of the strength of an *individual* discharge, the vortex's CPP is considered. When a shield renders, say, 95% of the vortex particles into DES (while five percent of the vortex particles gain a PCI), this effect will not necessarily apply *only* for the individual vortex particles that *directly* touch the shield (or are within the UPI range), and, instead, the effect will cause a relatively-equal distribution of both cases (DES and PCI-particles) across the whole vortex. As the vortex particles share the UPI energy load, eventually, the particles will fall to one group or the other (DES or PCI), so the distribution cannot be exactly equal for all particles, where each particle will be both in DES and have a PCI.

The speed of the vortex's rotation, in the context of particle status, accordingly does not matter, as it is the whole vortex via the CPP that causes particular effects. Of course, a vortex's speed *does* matter when it comes to particular SBEs and FBEs, along with *how* CBEs play out. Almost immediately after a shielded opponent enters a user's vortex, the vortex particles will begin automatically attempting to overcome a shield's UAS before overstimulation of UPIs can occur. The average DPL vortex will have an initial 16.667% chance of overcoming an average DPL shield's UAS. Vortices do not become weaker against shields; instead, they *begin* weak (as a whole) when against shields before gaining CBE strength (across the vortex as a whole) through APL *build* due to the shield getting weaker.

When either the chance check is successful against the UAS or not, the whole vortex will refresh the phase of its particles via its *particle phase refreshment* (PPR); for average DPL vortices, this PPR will occur once every 0.333 seconds (in other words, APL can potentially be gained three times per second). This means that if the vortex particles either gained a PCI or were rendered into DES, these statuses will reset, granting the particles the chance to again overcome the (new) UAS. The PPR time does not change much for higher power levels, and a comparatively strong shield will not generally play a significant role in any of the vortex's PPR, so, in defence, the times normally remain the same for vortices of any power level. The actual APL build rate is 4.167% per each PPR, so about 12.5% APL can potentially be built every second.

Whilst the PPR naturally allows the vortex's particles to regain AES, the particles with either a PCI or a DES will not briefly or rapidly switch out to *just* being in AES due to being under UPI 'occupation'. That is, there would not be a flash moment where all or any of the particles would be in *pure* AES (with no PCI) before either (re)gaining a PCI or going back into DES. The UPI occupation itself, funnily enough, is what allows for the status of the PCI to be sustained for the particles that do not change to a pure AES. The PPR will cause the vortex particles to *attempt* going back to a pure state of AES, and it is this attempt that will aggravate the UPIs, so further overstimulation can still occur.

A vortex, accordingly, will not briefly experience a moment of 100% APL against a shield before going back to the APL it should possess relative to the UPIs. Of course, for the sake of clarification, it should be noted that, as with discharges, the vortex particles will not be able to 'overstimulate' the UPIs if the UAS chance check has not been passed, as the UPIs will have adequate stability; therefore, this feat will still also only occur after the UAS has been successfully passed. With some of the UPIs now overstimulated, some of the particles with a DES will *then* be able to switch back to their natural state of AES *with* a PCI. If there were no shield inhibiting the vortex particles in the first place, then the PPR would still occur, but it would not mean the particles would go to from AES to DES then back to AES; that is, the particles would just remain in pure AES (without any PCI).

Most of the above information applies to the *default vortex mode* (DVM), which is the same in nature to the DDM for discharges. This also means that vortices have what is known as an *alternative vortex mode* (AVM). Most of the ADM's phenomena and statistics apply to AVMs, like how about 91.667% of the ultrachite particles will be in a permanent IES for all DPLs. With a normal chance rate of 50% for all DPLs, a user can also begin to *augment* their vortex after at least six seconds of use, resulting in more particles being in AES – whilst also possessing PCIs. If the vortex fails to *begin* augmenting, then the user will have to wait at least another six seconds before trying again. The same AES range of rates of, and from, 8.334% to 100% also apply. Users even have to then charge the vortex for an additional two to nine seconds. The second chance check for *successful* augmentation still applies; and for all DPLs, the fail rate begins at 33% for an AES of 8.334%, increasing to a 95% fail rate for 100% AES, with HPLs and LPLs possessing the same rates. If, and only if, the vortex does not successfully augment (at any stage of the augmentations – that is, *after* the first chance check has been passed), the user's vortex aura may overload – with a roughly 50% chance for all DPLs.

The only main difference between ADMs and AVMs here is the duration of the augmented particles. Since discharge FTPs only last a split second, they do not fully benefit from having long-lasting augmentations. Plus, the ADM only allows for a single augmented discharge. Still, even AVM vortices experience a PPR, limiting their duration as well. At the unaugmented stage, vortex particles will still refresh; but when they do, they will remain at the same AES levels, so essentially, nothing practically occurs. However, when the vortex is augmented, the higher-than-base-level AES particles will only remain with their status for about three seconds (for all power levels) before refreshing back to base levels. After the particles in a *successfully-augmented vortex* (SAV) return to base levels, a user would have to wait again for at least six seconds before potentially being able to augment their vortex; this even applies to users who do not successfully augment a vortex but neither suffer from an overload. On the other hand, a user with an overloaded aura would not be able to use weaker (unaugmented) vortices nor switch modes and continue using a vortex in the DVM.

In order to augment the vortex, a user cannot have one PAC active and then switch the class after the first chance check has been passed. This means that a user cannot use a weak (unaugmented) vortex of a particular PAC while they wait for the ability to augment and then switch to the PAC that they want for the augmentation. If a switch occurs, the time resets. While it may seem pointless for a user to spend time augmenting a vortex in AVM when they could otherwise use that time to simply attempt building APL in DVM, it *can* still be advantageous when the initial augmentation is timed right and used successfully – especially when factoring in for the decent three second duration for augmentation, which is all a user may need in a fight against another single mage when in close quarters.

For both the DVM and AVM, the average DPL vortex will cost the average user 0.2% of their MLP per second for MECs, whereas the CEC will cost 1.2% of their MLP. However, vortex particles can get damaged in combat, and so, the costs for maintaining a vortex can rise, with the percentages varying based on the context up to the maximum CEC per varying units of time. Coupled with the LRR, a user could indefinitely use a vortex if they are not using other USTs and/or if their vortex is not being damaged – but this would only be for when the UOT is not considered. Vortices, nonetheless, have high UOTs, with the average user's respective DPL vortex alone being able to last just over eight minutes of consecutive use when not being damaged or interacting with much matter; turning off the vortex aura also simply does not reset the UOT, so the user still has to wait to recover; but at least the OSRs and ORRs are fast. This applies to both the DVM and AVM (whether augmented or unaugmented), as this is a SBE issue. Consider, again, that when mages are in close quarters (whether using vortices or not), fights normally end quickly, so overloading a vortex aura in the heat of combat is not common, anyway.

Due to the nature of vortices being used at a constant rate compared to the 'individual' blast balls that UST Two energy form in to, vortices cause *damage per second* (DPS). Both SBE and CBE-damage separately contribute towards DPS in their own ways; and while APL only builds after each PPR period against ultrachite shields, DPS is normally also considered for ease of reference. For clarification, whilst damage and effects are *measured* per second, these factors can still affect matter in under a second. A vortex's SBEs (of all power levels), however, do not sufficiently reach certain thresholds of damage to inflict any noticeable effects on ultrachite shields, so vortices do not practically overload shields; accordingly, DPS is not normally used in such contexts. Some vortex CBEs do not cause 'damage' in any traditional sense – or, at least, over time – so, DPS may not be used in these contexts either. The damage that SBEs and CBEs cause are also not related to the PPR per se (as that regards the status of particles); instead, the CPP matters in this context.

Regardless of whether the user is primarily using a vortex for its SBEs and/or CBEs, UST Three is, again, a support power, so the tactical use of vortices comes down to context; and, principally, users tend to weigh up whether they should expend precious lumarchetrix energy or save it for other uses. In addition, vortices can affect allies, so with a large AOE, that is usually another major consideration. When vortices are used against many shielded opponents at once, then the PCIs that a vortex's particles may gain can fail. For the average user and their respective DPL vortex against seven shielded attackers of the same power level (while in proximity *and* while it simultaneously occurs), this results in a great chance of PCI failure. Still, it is again an issue of phasarchement battles not lasting long when offending and defending mages are in close quarters, and the user in the abovesaid context will normally lose the fight, anyway.

### 3.6.3.4: UST Four/Ultra-state Liquid (Soaker Bombs/Swarm Clouds):

As the second example of CTU, UST Four generates ultra-liquid particles that form into what are informally called *soaker bombs* (or *water bombs* – even though they are not made of water) and *swarm clouds* (or *swarms* or *clouds*). For the initial creation, a thick cloud of ultra-liquid particles will fill the aura, where they can remain as a cloud or be further concentrated into a ball called a soaker bomb. A soaker bomb will weigh around 250 grams for most power levels, and its surface tension (and so, its cohesive force at the surface) is so high that it will appear as if there is a thin film or elastic membrane around it, allowing the user to grab the bomb without popping it (so long as not too much force is applied to the bomb). Users then have the option to physically throw their soaker bomb, where the bomb will eventually hit something, explode, *soak* (and continue to soak) the item before rapidly forming a cloud *around* the item with a *small portion* of the ultra-liquid particles. The cloud itself will also seemingly possess thousands of tiny, luminescent, swarming bugs – without the associated unpleasantness.

Cohesion is a crucial element in soaker bombs. Like with CDMs, soaker bombs will possess unique properties that causes more conscious energy to be stored in their etheric field, in turn allowing for long phased momentum while outside of the ACE. The particles in a soaker bomb are also united, but as soon as the bomb *breaks* while outside of the aura (that is, when it splatters on something and then forms a cloud around it), the total *set* of ultra-liquid particles will lose its collective stability and, thus, the length of its phased momentum. More accurately, the soaker bomb itself, even in its unbroken form, will have a time limit while *outside* of the ACE, but once broken, the time limit of its phased momentum reduces even further from this maximum time-frame. Not all bombs, however, have the same degraded timeframe, so the timeframe of a soaker bomb being able to survive outside an aura is actually determined *upon* breaking via a quantum-based *chance*, which results from its power level. While suffering from an instability at the quantum level, the ultra-liquid particles will nevertheless remain *fully* present without disappearing bit by bit *until* their limit is met. External forces, however, can also further diminish the phased momentum.

Swarm clouds can change in size and shape, but as a collective entity, swarms will not expand too much beyond their cloud form while around a soaked item. A soaker bomb will not target HRFs, so a user has to accurately throw a soaker bomb at their targets. Typically, the ultra-liquid (specifically, the *soaker or soaking particles*) will stay on a target's body, but interestingly, the swarm cloud (precisely, the *swarm particles*) will specifically remain around the HRF that possesses the most amount of the soaker particles soaking it. So, if 80% of the particles in a soaker bomb were to hit a person (while the other 20% hit a table), the swarm cloud would normally surround the person, even if they (the person) were to move, so the swarm would also move. Unlike discharge FTPs, swarms will not tightly fasten to the HRF (in fact, swarms and soaker particles do not contain – nor are – FTPs); instead, a swarm will remain in its cloud form, and the soaker particles will remain on a body in the same way that oil can be sticky. Technically, though, even when a swarm cloud specifically targets an HRF, it can, by default, affect other HRFs in the vicinity.

In *practice*, the CBEs for the *soaking particles* on an item will differ to the CBEs for *swarms* around the HRF due to their radically-different FBEs. This more so applies to soaking particles *basically* lacking the CBEs of swarms, but swarms will also be comparatively much weaker than the soaking particles, and this causes certain levels of thresholds not to be met, so while the cloud particles could theoretically cause certain effects, this is not effectively the case. Two different swarms around a single opponent from two different users can affect one another and the opponent. However, the effects of the CBEs that one swarm will have on another swarm will be either marginal or not applicable; still, the SBEs of both swarms will increase the chance of either breaking apart. Ultra-liquid particles in either form, nevertheless, can elude a shield's UPIs, so they will normally always have 100% APL. Swarms, however, are still subject to a shield's CBEs, but not all of these CBEs are applicable; and, of those that do apply, some only weakly affect swarms and soaking particles.

A swarm will have one type of CBE, whereas the soaker particles will also have one type of CBE. A swarm's CBEs primarily affect an opponent's immediate vision (but not their eyes per se), creating partial veils of varying effects. While the swarm's creator will not be able to *properly* see the victim, it is not equally double-edged, as the creator will still otherwise see perfectly fine, whereas the victim, meanwhile, will be fully affected, generally at any angle around them. A swarm's creator will still also be able to typically tell who has been affected simply by looking at the affected opponent; and, in most cases, a swarm's creator will also usually know the general whereabouts of opponents and allies on a battlefield, so confusion as to who is behind a veil is normally uncommon. The ultra-liquid cloud itself (without any PAC) will typically have a density just a bit higher than normal fog, which is not much, given the typical size of a swam cloud, so it is the CBEs that really 'blind' opponents. The second type of CBEs (for soaker particles) vary in nature a lot, but a few of of them primarily annoy, distract, or disturb opponents in some way.

Because of the nature of these CBEs, swarms do not incapacitate opponents, rendering them (swarms) as support attacks. Nevertheless, soaker particles can form *combos* with discharge attacks (but not vortices), increasing the *power* of the SBEs, in turn helping a discharge to overload a shield faster. In addition, while combos will not increase the number of CBE-inducing particles in the discharge, they can still help increase the discharge's energy levels, which may play *some* role in increasing the effects (including TREs) of certain CBEs. In this case, there will be a much more efficient transfer of energy to the discharge's CBE-inducing particles (from around 50% to around 100% in perfect cases – relative DPLs considered) when two *alignment charge types* of the same PAC are used (so, positive soaker particles with a positive discharge or a negative set of soaker particles with a negative discharge). *Section 3.6.4* contains information on PAC alignment charge types. To reiterate for clarification, when energy *is* transferred over, this will not *necessarily* increase the power of CBEs. Also note that there is one type of CBE that causes other types of 'combos'.

A discharge that forms a combo with a set of soaker particles will also have a higher chance of passing the UAS chance check against an ultrachite shield in addition to having a higher APL (build) itself. Effectively, a user that creates a soaker bomb – and then forms a combo with it via a discharge – can partially gain returns on their photomission energy investment into the attack. The discharge does not have to hit the whole target for full effectiveness, as the soaker particles will still be connected as a united entity. However, combos cannot be formed with soaker particles that surround *their* user in the aura, as they are in auric equilibrium, nor will a user be able to make an effective combo with a set of soaker particles if they (the user) are shooting within proximity (as the discharge particles UPS from AES to DES) – unless this latter feature is alternatively switched off. Of course, a combo is possible only at the cost of the total phased momentum, in turn causing the soaker particles to perish (in just under a second – but with enough time for the combo to occur), which means that only one discharge may form a combo with a set of soaker particles.

While in a brief moment in a cloud form before the user concentrates them into a soaker bomb, the ultra-liquid particles will naturally be in DES, so they will not negatively affect the user. The SBEs will also not blind the user. The user, moreover, has the option to simply leave the particles in a cloud around themselves (the user), where they (the user) can actively choose to UPS them into AES. This may have strategic uses, but it can also affect nearby allies, so users must be considerate or careful of the context. The user can still throw soaker bombs at opponents in their own aura; and while this may seem like the surest way to affect an opponent with a maximum timeframe, the aura will no longer give energy to the ultra-liquid particles, and there would still be a chance for a shorter phased momentum after the impact. Still, once the soaker bomb has been broken inside the aura, users can create more soaker bombs while the current particles exist in the aura. A user can also shoot discharges through their cloud and hit opponents, as the cloud is not dense enough to trigger discharges. In fact, even if a cloud were to surround an opponent, any discharge (whether from the user or opponent) can enter or exit the swarm.

Note that a user's swarm itself (from a never-formed soaker bomb) will be able to continue existing in their (the user's) own aura until the user switches the aura off. Swarms and soaker particles themselves do not practically overload, but the aura itself can still overload if it has been in use for too long; nevertheless, the UOT, in this case, is normally high, so this is not generally a problem. Like vortices, swarms and soaker particles do not overload ultrachite shields in all practical cases. Given the nature of the ultra-liquid, the SBEs also do not even wet most materials, nor do they cause the ultra-state liquid to boil or freeze at the same respective temperatures as water. In fact, the ultra-liquid itself (so, not of any particular PAC) is not adequate at extinguishing fires per se, nor is it flammable per se.

Swarms do not work well against vortices (of basically any power level), as vortices can push swarms (but not so much soaker particles) to the outside (of auric space) so that they (swarms) do not practically or effectively affect the vortex's user. This is not to say that vortices act like UPIs against swarm particles, but rather, swarms will be in a less effective position on the outside of a vortex. If a user were to create both a vortex and a swarm (in just their own aura), then, depending on which came first, the swarm would, via equilibrium, either compress in the eye or move to the outside of the vortex for stability. Nevertheless, when a swarm, in this case, moves to the outside, it would be out of the ACE, so it would lose its stability, anyway. Still, it would continue existing until losing phased momentum.

If an opponent using a vortex were to approach a user who had a swarm around them, the opponent's vortex would push the swarm away (as the swarm's potential compression would be pointless, and it would just be swept away). Vortices might, then, seem like they should always be used whenever swarms are used against some-one, but this results in the victim requiring (and thus wasting) more energy not only for the vortex itself but also for the extra MECs. Furthermore, the vortex *user* must have already been using the vortex *before* the swarm is launched against them; otherwise, the swarm will compress and stay inside the eye – shield or no shield. The ultra-state liquid will also not fully merge with another user's ultra-liquid particles (even if both are of the same PAC) like when two or more sets of normal liquid otherwise (of the same nature, such as water) contact one another. This is mainly the result of unique wave function changes (via PUC) forcing the particles to behave in a particular way.

Unique to mage opponents with active lumarchetrixes and ultrachite, swarms and soaker particles can also *propagate* themselves. The ultra-liquid from a soaker bomb is capable of propagating by first *infecting* the ultrachite of an opponent, in turn gathering enough energy to potentially generate another set of soaker and swarm particles once the initial set disappears. However, there is only a chance of this occurring, and if this does occur, the next set of ultra-liquid particles will have a decreased chance of propagating itself. There is usually a 15% chance that an average DPL swarm and set of soaker particles will propagate from an average opponent's respective DPL shield, with ultrachite shields having a higher rate than any other UST.

The average DPL soaker bomb will cost the average user 3.6% of their MLP to create. These soaker bombs will also *typically* last about eight seconds on average out of a total of 32 seconds for its natural phased momentum. This is generally enough time to effectively negatively affect opponents and/or use this as an opportunity to gain different positions on a battlefield. There are also many other strategies than can be employed. Still, if the user fails at *effectively* affecting an opponent after five attempts, then that is almost 20% of their MLP wasted. Therefore, there is a risk involved with using soaker bombs, and, accordingly, they are not used all the time.

Note for nuanced understanding that the swarm and soaker particles do not incur a chance of breaking down every second after the explosion as if some dice were rolled every second (or millisecond or some other measure of time); instead, the chance rate of the swarm is directly tied to the explosion itself. Note that the said issue is an example of where the *infinite discrete temporal probability* (IDTP) *dilemma* applies, where one cannot simply place a discrete chance rate of some event occurring at any given period in a timescale due to the probability of it having to be essentially 'rolled' infinitely at any (perhaps) infinitely-divisible period in said timescale. While the IDTP dilemma crosses into territories of other probability and paradox issues, it is a separate issue. Despite this, again, there *are* other variables to consider that *can* decrease the phased momentum *after* the chance check is applied.

Also note that as a law in phasarchement magic, a user will always channel ultrachite with all properties in equilibrium with each other. So, if a swarm's DPL were hypothetically too low compared to the particle properties allowing for long phased momentum, there would be too much tension, and the swarm would always break apart. If, on the other hand, the swarm's DPL were too high compared to the said properties, then it would not hold together and would always lose its phased momentum. Therefore, while there is still only the aforesaid chance rate, the user's DPL will naturally maximize the effectiveness of the ratio of the said properties to the power of the ultra-state particles themselves. Still, the higher the DPL, the greater the chance of stability after the explosion. To be clear, the aforesaid hypothetical lower and higher DPLs are not referring to HPLs and LPLs. Instead, it is an explanation of the physics and why the *set* of ultra-liquid particles forms as it does due to equilibrium. This prevents either the said properties and overall power level from being proportionally far greater than the other.

### 3.6.3.5: UST Five/Ultra-state Conductivity (Propulsors):

Simply called *propulsors*, the first of the STU generates *ultra-conductive states* that allow mages to harness different propulsion CBEs, such as jumping and hovering abilities. Unlike *superconductivity*, where electrical resistance and magnetic flux fields respectively disappear and are expelled, ultra-conductivity does not necessarily eliminate these (so to speak), and, instead, it *alters* these factors in a more dynamic manner, allowing for more amazing feats than *mere* levitation (although, ultra-conductivity does, indeed, generate levitating effects). Furthermore, instead of normal *electron pairing* in super-conductivity that allows for long-range quantum coherence, which is a form of *quantum long-range order* (where particles can be correlated over distances in a material), ultra-conductivity has *multipartite electron groupings* (that is, multiple electrons in multiple groups strangely tied to one another). As with other USTs, ultra-conductive particles have light mass and easily float in the user's aura due to their odd electrical and magnetic nature. For this reason, it is not the ultra-conductive nature in the propulsor particles itself that causes them (the particles) to levitate by default; but when CBEs apply, the particles will specifically levitate (or propel) *according* the nature of the CBEs – in addition to making the *user* propel.

Various forces, such as strong winds, cannot *simply* blow ultra-conductive particles away, as they remain 'attached' to the user in their aura. That is, the propulsor ultrachite not only hovers from things like the ground but also *from* and *with* the user as a single entity with different levels of effect within the aura. Apart from this, phenomena like momentum and relativity still carry the particles with the user. For example, when the ultrachite propulsor particles propel a user, the particles will still move with and relative to the user while having momentum. So, even if the particles did not fasten to the user, the momentum would still carry the particles and prevent them from falling away or separating from the user.

Most mages cannot sustain UST Five particles for long *as a DPL* mainly due to the amount of photomission energy required to both create and then maintain the ultrachite. Explicitly, propulsors cost the average DPL user about 18% of their MLP for the CEC and just over 8% of their MLP per second for the MECs, typically causing this power to be reserved for emergencies or special reasons. Any feat not used up to the aura's maximum energy threshold per second will mean that the (8%) energy required for the MEC (of an average DPL) propulsor will dissipate and go to waste; therefore, users need to ensure that they know what they will do beforehand to maximize their effectiveness. Given that propulsors draw from the same energy pool as discharges, one does not want to be caught out of energy when they need discharges.

The average mage will also suffer a 20% LCI rate for creating a propulsor aura of *any* power level; accordingly, if the channelling fails on creation, it will cause the user to wait out a recovery period before being able to attempt again – which can be a difference between life and death (despite its short length). If photomission energy consumption were hypothetically not an issue – and if mages could channel multiple PACs of the same UST at once, like mythical mages supposedly did in legends – then using a couple of particular propulsion PACs simultaneously could allow mages to reach grand heights in the air and stay there indefinitely.

Via SBEs, other USTs do not affect propulsion ultrachite much – at least not directly – nor are their CBEs applicably effective. For example, mages cannot absorb the photomission energy from UST Five particles, as they are vibrating too differently for absorption abilities to act on. Regardless, discharges will not properly register propulsor particles as being part of HRFs, so they will normally brush past them (as QTPs, if energetically feasible – relative DPLs considered) and affect the HRF (QDF) on the other side, anyway. Still, there are some CBEs that are contextually and indirectly effective, such as a UST Two blast ball possessing a slowing CBE that may naturally slow a jumping *mage*, in turn 'slowing' the propulsor particles as well due to the particles being in auric equilibrium with the victim. That is, the blast ball in question would slow the HRF (the mage), but not the propulsor particles *themselves*; there would, instead, only be the illusion of slowness. The UST Five particles would continue attempting to propel the mage, failing due to an inability to contest the increased inertia. Technically, when a discharge *does* affect propulsor particles via SBEs, then overloading may occur with repeated hits. Also, when bullets, for example, contact the particles, they *may* be propelled away; however, this increases MECs, and the bullets may eventually overload the ultrachite.

Even for the user alone, UST Five particles will not negatively affect other user-generated ultrachite. In accordance with auric equilibrium, propulsor particles will also emerge on the outside of a user's shield; and, if the former were made before the latter, the propulsor particles would automatically and rapidly move to where the outside of a shield will be when it emerges. In this case, some propulsors would propel the shield (and, thus, the user, by default – while 'acknowledging' the user via equilibrium), while other propulsors would affect other forces, in turn affecting both the user and shield. While propulsor particles will naturally surround a user, they can be concentrated at will to particular locations in the aura, enabling them to be more effective per context. Some particles, though, will concentrate at certain locations when (or soon-to-be) contextually-applicable events occur, such as where the user's feet (or other parts of their body) are located when landing on the ground or contacting hard-enough matter, in turn generating a bigger bounce away from it before regrouping around the user's body again.

Propulsion also plays an important function in both combat and non-combat situations. For example, jumping into combat from a certain height can give one the advantage of shock, but jumping highly during combat can also help manoeuvre oneself around for better tactical advantage – or even to remove oneself from a losing battle. Outside of combat, a mage may use their propulsion powers to stay in the air longer in order to do aerial activities for enjoyment, or they may even scale (cling) to ceilings for the mere sake of doing domestic cleaning. All useful effects available to propulsors, however, are only achieved through CBEs, not SBEs or FBEs; it is, again, that the SBEs help the CBEs. Generally, users do not UPO their propulsor auras, as they run out of lumarchetrix energy before this occurs; and while switching the UST on and off repeatedly can lead to an LBO, this is different to a UPO penalty.

There is no guarantee, though, that propulsion magic will save a user when they are falling or about to fall. As a very-time sensitive issue, most of this comes down to context, but besides being depleted of energy in either case, users could be overloaded (which is rare for propulsor magic for the abovesaid reason); or, the user could be wearing magic suppressors (while escaping from somewhere, for example); LCIs could apply when trying to create a propulsor aura either at the start, middle, or end of a fall, leading to no or not enough propulsion to prevent injurious or lethal impacts; a major electrical storm or nearby powerful machine could also distort their auras, leading to greater LCIs; UPC times (which are required for nearly all propulsor CBEs) could be longer than what a user's remaining lumarchetrix energy allows for; users could also be attacked with other magic, causing a variety of issues; while falling, users could also hit hard matter and pass out unconscious; and, a user's consciousness might alter from the fall itself, leading to a black out. There is, nonetheless, also a matter that is often overlooked in itself: the *velocity* of their fall may be greater than what energy a user could produce in time to save themselves.

Even if a mage used conjuration magic to conjure a jetpack, consider, again, that there is a charge time, so even for average-powered conjurations, one is looking at about seven seconds (if uninterrupted) of charge time before a spell can manifest. As such, if one were to already be falling when this spell were started, the user may splat on the ground. Assuming standard gravity, no air resistance, and zero-initial velocity, a person would fall about 240 metres before being able to manifest their conjuration spell, reaching a speed of 247 km/h (just over normal terminal velocity). Jetpacks are also hard to conjure, and even then, the quality and strength would greatly matter, too; and, roughly three-quarters of mages are not earth mages, so they would not even be able to conjure anything viable for most deadly situations. Many earth mages store and conjure light wingsuits to help them fall, but even then, they will still use propulsor magic to supplement the conjuration. If a mage were to also conjure body armour (or even simply wear normal body armour), the armour would weigh more, and this would affect the propulsor, so in contexts relating to aerial activities, many (if not all) body armours are not advised to be worn.

### 3.6.3.6: UST Six/Ultra-state Spacetime Crystals (Dimensional Fields):

The final UST (simply known as *dimensional fields*) creates *ultra-spacetime crystal state* particles that significantly affect dimensions (more so than other USTs), allowing for feats such as teleportation. UST Six particles possess similar characteristics to normal time crystals (as explained in *Section 2.1*), but there is a greater dimensional (geometric) element to them involving space. Spacetime crystals possess long-range quantum coherence, extraordinary wave functions, unique phase shifting abilities, and their ability to warp and created different types of potential fields is unmatched. For example, rearranging the potentials of electric and magnetic fields at the quantum level can give rise to artificially-induced gravitational forces. From the unique quantum level of interaction of UST Six particles, dimensional fields, more accurately, feature certain effects that can be created and experienced at the *fabric* (sub-quantum level) of reality, so the quantum level will bend the *fabric* of spacetime – thus, the *dimensional* effect. While UST Six *particles* may not necessarily go through certain properties, their energy and effects can go through atomic lattices. So, when the UST Six particles (where applicable) surround a user, then their energy can affect all matter within their field. Their dimensionally-bound nature also allows them to fasten to a user, giving immunity to forces (like strong winds) that would otherwise blow them away.

Other USTs generally do not affect UST Six particles, as the latter comparatively functions on a very different energetic level. Conversely, dimensional fields can still alter other USTs – including other dimensional ultrachite. The dimensional particles achieve this without affecting things *as* HRFs (at least in the same way as discharges); instead, the dimensional fields practically affect everything within their field. When HRFs *are* factored, it is normally a matter of whether or not the HRF will be affected due to a spatial issue (that is, if they are properly in the field or not, with special wave function change considerations for the user as an HRF). If a user, for example, were to speed up time relative to the external world with a dimensional power, the other USTs (like shields) – in addition to standard items, such as watches and clothing – within the dimensional field will also receive the benefits of faster time, too. Of course, the reverse could apply to an opponent and their shields (and items or non-magic weapons) if they are in the user's field. Nevertheless, because UST Six particles are in one's auric equilibrium, if an opponent were to push over a user (by whatever means), then the user's dimensional particles would accordingly move with them.

Dimensional ultrachite also has the unique ability to seemingly be 'created' and powered outside of the aura/ACE (to very vastly-distant locations). However, the reality is that the ultrachite is still first formed inside the user's aura before the dimensions are warped to bring the ultrachite to nonlocal areas, where it can be powered (despite being 'outside' the aura) via a dimensionally-created connection. There, of course, needs to already be entangled particles located for this phenomenon to take place (with further explanations in the Index at the end of *Section 3.6.5.3*). To be precise, even with these entanglements, a user cannot, in any practical terms, power ultrachite outside of their aura unless there is dimensional warping.

Contrary to some people's concerns, a user cannot, for example, create tiny gravitational 'singularities' around an opponent's eyeballs that would be of significant power to actually jiggle them out of their sockets and scramble them. This is not only due to a lack of certain HRF-based precision on behalf of the user, but even both weak and strong power levels themselves cannot achieve this feat due to the aforesaid issue of only possessing certain unique abilities at their particular power levels. Even if strong power levels could do this, it would simultaneously be too overpowered and would not target just the eyes, and, thus, the feat would not be achieved, anyway. The practical powers of dimensional fields are locked behind CBEs, so the SBEs do not do much and, instead, mainly just give rise to particular potential (for the CBEs).

As with UST Five ultrachite, UST Six particles are expensive to create and maintain, and they also have higher LCIs. The average DPL dimensional field costs an average user around 27% of their MLP for the CEC and about 12% per second for MECs. Moreover, since the average mage's maximum LCR is at 33% of their MLP, the said mage cannot create a dimensional field that is one rank higher than their DPL. Still, average users can at least create the dimensional energy *whilst* (already) using (most) other USTs, such as shields, as they will typically not exceed the maximum 33% LCR mark in that split moment of creation. The average mage also experiences a 30% LCI rate when creating dimensional fields of *any* power level. Generally, users do not overload their UST Six auras, as they run out of lumarchetrix energy before this occurs; and while switching the UST on and off repeatedly can lead to an LBO, this is different to a UPO penalty.

Student mages are required to channel the UST at an average DPL for a mere second in order to pass their Phasarchement course at university; but without practice of phasarchement afterwards, mages can become weaker and, in turn, almost or totally lose their ability to use the UST Six energy. This is due to novice/student mages having an LCI rate of around 90%, and deficient mages having an LCI rate of 100%. Only master and supreme level mages can avoid LCIs for channelling UST Six auras of any power level. Even without energy costs and LCI issues, the average mage is still incapable of harnessing the power for effective real-time combat – or even for non-combat uses such as *very* long-range teleportation. In fact, all power levels reach certain thresholds that access unique abilities, so it is not just a matter of a linear progression of statistics. Accordingly, mages cannot simply create LPLs and hope to achieve merely (or linearly) weaker versions of their DPLs in order to circumvent the problem of the UST's high energy costs.

All mages (that is, of all power levels) face yet another problem when trying to use dimensional fields; that is, they cannot even create UST Six auras without first performing certain non-phasarchement practices. This is a channelling aptitude issue, with higher power levels only reducing the number of – and, in some cases, the extent of the – requirements needed to access the ability to create dimensional fields. For clarification, these requirements are not to create ultrachite of any particular power level; instead, fulfilling the requirements only allows a mage the ability to create UST Six ultrachite, so the stronger the mage, the less requirements are needed to channel any UST Six of any power level because their (the mage's) aptitude aspect is closer to being in tune with creating such ultrachite (of any power level) in the first place. So, if an elite mage were to create average-powered dimensional fields, they would still have to fulfil the same requirements that they (the elite mage) would otherwise need to fulfil to create any other dimensional field (say, at elite power levels). Given that dimensional fields are not readily accessible to all mages, this shows that it is possible that other kinds of USTs are *might* exist; and if they do exist, then it is a matter of discovering what is required to channel them.

For mages of average status or below, a mix of deep meditation, special potions (or strong tonics), certain rituals (with a group of mages, normally with around three others), and lunapexes are required in order to manifest dimensional fields. Expert mages do not typically require other mages for the rituals, while elite mages do not normally need lunapexes. Master mages, on the other hand, may even be able to create UST Six auras without rituals, and supreme mages typically need only meditation. Of course, these are generalities (both the practices and for the listed power levels), so some exceptions can apply, and not all of the abovesaid listed requirements are of equal value to one another.

The said concoctions, of course, will not last forever, so mages who consume them only have usually up to 24 hours of opportunity to engage in dimensional powers. Even though tonics are effective, potions do have extra benefits, such as extended time (but normally only by a couple of hours – and again, this is normally up to 24 hours). Plus, while it varies per mage and their tolerance levels, the required potions and tonics normally can only be consumed around once per month. Accordingly, even when a mage does not require a lunapex, most dimensional powers happen to be accessed only during lunapexes, anyway. The rituals conducted (whether coupled with potions or not) are generally complex and long, taking a few hours to complete, where equipment and special locations are generally used.

### 3.6.4: Phasarchement Archetypal Classes (PACs):

Each UST falls under four known *PACs* (or *classes*, for short), which are archetypally closer to the natural flow of energy macrocosmically than the particularized USTs. Thus, inherently, PACs are categorically 'greater' than USTs holistically, as PACs cannot fall under USTs. Nevertheless, USTs can exist without classes. When USTs are created without having a class, they will lack CBEs and will only produce SBEs with their FBEs. Interestingly, a user's DPL for a non-PAC form will be slightly higher than their PAC forms. For this reason, using non-PAC discharges, for example, can help to overload an opponent's shield with less hits. However, with relative power levels considered, this is marginal, and an average DPL (non-PAC) discharge can only overload an average DPL shield in 11 hits instead of 12 for the PAC version. Given the great advantages that PACs bring to USTs, it is generally not worth using non-PAC forms.

USTs possess a specific colour when manifest under a PAC, whereas non-PAC forms will *practically* be colourless (that is, translucent). These PAC colours, however, have no major effect other than, by default, signifying what class is being used – along with possessing potential aesthetic appeal. Moreover, the PACs are not *based* on an ontologically-simplistic and fallacious notion of 'the four main colours', and the colours are, instead, determined by the molecular structures of each UST and their corresponding chemical reactions – in addition to how they move in the auras, which determine how one perceives each class. In fact, one's perception of the colours (and colours in general) is limited by the cones in the eyes, and if one had broader vision, such energy would be seen much differently.

Since extreme temperatures are not needed to create ultra-states, this means that while ultrachite fundamentally has *some* heat energy added to their structures, we *mainly* see the energy as *luminescence (cold-body radiation)*. So, when PPOs and ultrachite are used in dark places, the luminescence basically does not light surrounding objects – except nearby reflective surfaces – and only to a minor degree. This luminescence is part of the reason why the lumarchetrix has such a name. As such, phasarchement magic is sometimes colloquially named *lucent energy/magic*. Note: in the past, the magic was called *phoscrystalment*, as it was thought that it was a matter of crystallizing light. Each class also features slightly different textures and sounds, but the USTs themselves mostly determine these features. So, while all discharges possess an electrically-charged character, one class might look slightly 'fractured' than another in addition to having a slightly higher pitch. Unless the ultrachite is under careful observation, most people will not be able to notice these differences, though. Even without careful observation, users can still see the colour of their vortices (albeit, feint in effect).

Ultrachite will also go through different phases, including when as DUPs, where the luminescence may be brighter than the typical UST form. In the case of discharges, the DUPs that occur after the FTPs have finished will actually cause the surrounding non-ultrachite air molecules to momentarily sustain the *visual* effect of the blast after the ultrachite particles have returned to the Aether. The same principle of contextual variation applies to sound, so all ultrachite, when in a user's aura (while in equilibrium), will create various types of humming noises. However, when something happens to the ultrachite (such as being hit or when blasting off), the noise will change. In a vacuum, of course, all classes would not practically produce sounds, as there would be no *surrounding* particles to *carry* the sound waves.

Each class sits on a spectrum having *positive charges* and *negative charges* – otherwise known as *positively-charged ultrachite* (PCU) and *negatively-charged ultrachite* (NCU). It is important to note that this phenomenon of *alignment charge types* (ACTs) is not the same as ultrachite particles being in either AES or DES. No class-based UST can exist without being charged either way, nor can they sit between a positive and a negative charge on the spectrum. That is, a classed UST is either fully A or fully B, not A to a degree or B to a degree. The only debate is whether positive and negative ACTs respectively consist of either A *or* B, or rather, that they are a degree of A and only A *but* at clearly distinct points of A without B being in the picture.

Basically, positive and negative ACTs have opposite effects to one another, and while this may, then, seem like there are eight classes, there are still ultimately only four PACs. Mages not only cannot simultaneously create multiple PACs of the same UST (such as two discharge auras of two different PACs at once), but they, more specifically, cannot simultaneously create a particular UST with both positive and negative charges (of the same PAC or another PAC). Note that it is not ontologically, at least, impossible to create multiple PACs of the same UST at once, but there is some kind of unknown channelling issue that prevents even supreme-level mages from accomplishing such a feat. Although various USTs within a PAC may have similar effects to one another, this is understandable, given that a class *does* have a set of specific effects. That is, one UST of a class might slow down opponents, while another UST of the same class will inflict very similar effects, just in a slightly different way. Nevertheless, all USTs feature at least one or two fully unique and *specific* CBEs (with the exception of one type of shield, where both ACTs, interestingly, have – or rather, enable for – the same magnetoreception ability).

Each ACT will also have a set of class-based *default-tuned powers* (DTPs), which are *specific* and *distinct* types of CBEs resulting from the medium of a UST. Every mage can channel all the empirically-known DTPs (if they can channel the UST itself), but they cannot alter the DPL of a *particular* DTP to an HPL or LPL. Nevertheless, users can totally switch a particular DTP off from a set of DTPs by changing the PEP from AES to (a permanent – if desired) DES. However, the molecular structures in the DES ultrachite would still be created. Note, though, that the particles do not have to be created with AES as the initial default and can, instead, emerge initially in DES. In other words, a user does not have to switch the PEP *after* the creation of a UST form. The user would, nonetheless, be charged with the same photomission *base* energy costs (that is, CECs and MECs) as using all the DTPs – even if all the DTPs were switched to DES.

Regardless of the PEP, the particles, basically, will require a minimum amount of energy for their existence, but they will also possess a certain surplus of energy that can be used for particular phenomena; however, this extra energy will simply go to waste if not used. Both of these energies (that is, the minimum energy for existence and the surplus energy) are part of the *base MECs*, but if the ultrachite is, for example, damaged into DUPs, then the ultrachite will naturally require additional photomission energy for further maintenance. This extra need for energy, however, is a separate issue to the base costs of AES and DES particles. Essentially, this means that turning off any DTPs via a UPS is not the same as creating an LPL UST. Parenthetically, since any UPS is not the same as creating new ultrachite, the UST form will not (suddenly) experience any LCI *problems*.

Generally, if a DTP is switched off, the reason is usually due to the context or for the fact that some DTPs can be distracting and irritating to some users. Users can also *partially* change a particular DTP's PEP into DES (as in, the number of particles within the UST aura); but since the particles would still be present, this would, again, still technically not be lowering the DPL of a DTP (even though essentially it would *seem* the same – effectively – for the result). Users have to weigh up their options in their specific context as to whether they wish to create an LPL UST or just UPS one or more of the DTPs. The reason for establishing the latter normally occurs because the user may still want the same power level for the remaining un-PEP-changed DTPs, whereas the reasoning for the former results from a lack of care for any of the other DTPs; that is, if a user wishes to lower the PEP of one DTP but does not care about the power level of the other DTPs, then using an LPL is the natural choice in such a case as it, again, saves energy.

All mages will also have the same CECs and MECs for all PACs of a specific UST at their respective DPLs. So, even though a UST Two discharge of one PAC might only have two DTPs, and another PAC of the same UST might have four DTPs, both discharges would normally cost the same for that particular mage's DPL. As a result, the statistics of each individual DTP will accordingly be proportionally higher or lower per PAC based on the DPL. In other words, if a discharge with two DTPs were hypothetically to have three DTPs, the individual statistical effects would proportionally alter to level out to the overall strength of the DPL. So, if DTP-1 and DTP-2 were to have 50% power each, and then, hypothetically, if a third DTP were added, each of the other DTPs would lower to around 33% each to accommodate it (as a default), but the overall DPL would remain the same. Nevertheless, the distribution of energy is not rigidly equal for each DTP, as the effects do, howbeit, come from a set of particles that correspond with one another.

Even though mages cannot change a DTP to an LPL or HPL, users are still able to establish *alternative-tuned powers* (ATPs), which are alterations of the DTPs that may include, for example, changing the *power ratio* of one aspect of a DTP *at the cost* of another aspect. Explicitly, this is not the same as changing individual power levels of DTPs, but rather, ATPs change the functional powers or power ratios of a specific DTP. This typically means that a DTP would sit in the middle of such power ratio alterations. Of course, the ultrachite of stronger power levels will typically, but not always, have the power levels of both ratios – despite one being lowered in favour of the other – greater than that found in weaker ultrachite. Still, the ratios normally have a limit as to how far they may be pushed either way, and not all ATPs have explicit ratios.

So long as the user is not using an HPL for the UST itself, issues such as overcharging will not apply to the ATP. Ultimately, new and different particles will form with an ATP, so a user will still be totally creating new ultrachite when establishing an ATP; therefore, if a user switches to an ATP while the UST form (with its DTPs) is still active, the user will be charged with full CECs. In so doing, ATPs can be subject to any LCI problems a mage may already be facing. A user might be so accustomed to channelling an ATP (or even having a particular DTP switched off) that it becomes second nature to them. Nevertheless, while this may become second nature, this does not mean that it would develop into the actual default (a DTP).

The Tagorean System names and places the PACs in the following order based on their colour alone and not on whether one is superior to another (of course, outside of the Tagorean System, the PACs have other names). *Alpha* class is blue, and its spectrum of positive and negative ACTs is based on *attraction* versus *repulsion*. Generally, alpha class is used for absorbing assorted types of energy, physically shifting properties, and for creating various magnetic effects that are handy for combat and non-combat situations. For positive charges, it is also considered the 'tank' class due to the shield's ability to absorb great amounts of SBE damage. Next in the Tagorean System is the green class called *beta*, which is fundamentally based on *synchronization* versus *desynchronization*. In combat, beta powers strengthen users and weaken opponents, while some of the STU can even avoid or reverse death itself. Typically, while beta acts largely as a support class, it is simultaneously the class that fully incapacitates opponents (by sending them unconscious); therefore, most fights are not complete without beta being used.

The third class, *gamma*, is yellow, and its archetypes are *entanglement* and *separation*, which typically have more bizarre effects than the other classes. The entangled energies found in gamma's attacks can effectively end battles quickly by overloading assorted shields and forcefields, making this potentially one of the most powerful classes for attacking. However, these effects are chance-based, with varying success and fail rates. Moreover, they are double-edged, thus the user may be negatively affected as well. Gamma class does not just rely on quantum entanglement, so the entanglement can also be a basis for other phenomena such as QET. When many people refer to the effects of the quantum entanglement in gamma's feats, they may also accidentally miss mentioning phenomena like QET. However, for the sake of brevity, sometimes only quantum entanglement is mentioned. Separation powers, on the other hand, can be super destructive to all sorts of properties, but they are also based on chances, so users have to weigh up their options carefully in the heat of a fight.

Lastly, *delta* class is red, and it manages *motion* and *motionlessness*. With its ability to either inertially freeze or blind opponents – or even enhance the user to deal with hazardous environments – delta class has many practical uses and is considered an all-rounder class (except for delta-negative shields, which have more contextually-niche reasons for their use). When delta-negative ultrachite forms create walls of inertia, light can still pass through – and reflect from – the particles in most cases, as light travels very quickly. Even though delta establishes different levels of motion, both positive and negative ACTs will create red particles. Again, this is not based on the level of motion of the particles themselves but on the effects that the particles happen to produce. Not all delta-positive particles themselves have to be super-fast, and, instead, they may simply create the conditions for fast movement; alternatively, the delta-positive particles may just *move* in a particular way.

In professional combat situations, tactical teams of at least four mages are sent to execute certain commands and goals. By having four mages in a team, all the PACs can be covered at once without having to resort to excess lumarchetrix usage and potential LCI problems. With eight mages in a team, though, all the PACs *and* ACTs can be used simultaneously. Still, in some contexts, not all the ACTs should necessarily be used, either at certain parts of a situation or throughout any part of a situation. Moreover, even a single powerful mage can use multiple PACs in quick succession and easily wipe out weaker mages. Furthermore, a crafty but weaker lone mage may still be able to handle a team of stronger mages. Although, when alone or in small groups, mages may have to use all the PACs to achieve victory in combat or successfully overcome non-combat situations, anyway.

## 3.6.5: PAC and UST Index (Including a Table of Contents):

Although various professional institutions have conducted measurements on millions of university graduate mages over the course of many years to determine median phasarchement statistics (such as power levels, times, distances, etc.), the following index will not include most of these measurements, as there are too many contextual variables to consider. While most of the power level statistics mentioned are of aptitude aspects, the Index will still cover other aptitude aspects. Most of the statistics will also just focus on average DPLs, with only specific mentions to other power levels. The Index will also, on occasion, explain a few of the many powers that appear in legends; most of these, though, will be the more believable or probable ones (should they have existed) that ontologically and practically seem compatible with the USTs and PACs.

The Index will feature terms such as *monsters* and *robots*, so for information on these types of beings, see *Section 4.3.2.4* and *Section 4.3.2.8*, respectively; and for information on all types of entities, see all of *Section 4.3*. Discharge FTPs can cause various *bit manipulations*, so robots and DEC systems (and even analogue systems) can be affected, not just biological organisms. That is, discharges can affect the hardware of a robot, in turn causing specific bits to flip, which can affect the software and cause various changes. Some of these effects differ from organic entities, so the Index will highlight some of these differences. Many kinds of mere irritant DTPs typically do faze robots unless their programming dislikes certain irritations.

Many DTPs and ATPs alter properties magnetically. The Index will note how certain UST forms have 'magnetic fields', where they produce a field with a distinct radius that affects other properties within its range. It must be noted, however, that this is not *quite* accurate, and it is only said for the sake of brevity. The strength of a standard magnetic field, in most cases, follows an inverse cube law and then an inverse square law. So, while it would seem that the effects of a DTP should be practically nothing at the end of the mentioned radii, this is not necessarily the case. Many UST forms operate by using potential fields, wave function manipulations, and phase shifting, but instead of simply exerting force through their normal potential fields, the UST forms can further manipulate these potential fields to cause themselves (the UST forms) and their affected HRFs or properties to experience or exert more force than what would *seemingly* be available per their levels of energy. As such, magnetic fields can have a longer range than what the ultrachite might normally have either in its normal force or its *normal* potential field before manipulations occur (but these altered fields will still normally feature 'equal' levels of effect at any distance across the radii). Such manipulations, of course, are limited by a UST form's power level. To be clear, the Index will state all of this information in some cases, but it will not necessarily go into detail.

The Index will also not detail most kinds of *power ratio ATPs*. Most particularly, it will not detail how shielded users will have one option for an ATP to either increase their UPC time (that is, the time the particles stay in AES) at the cost of potentially overloading their shield after the particles return to DES. The second ATP not detailed allows users to choose to reduce the recharge and cooldown times of the UPC at the expense of increased CBE strength – or vice versa. Note, though, that the statistics not only vary per ATP, but mages can only create their UST as a particular ATP only so far along a spectrum based on their power level. That is, if trying to establish a 60% increase in strength, this may be out of reach for the user. Moreover, not all spectrums are equal either way, so it may be harder to established increased strengths than it is to reduce cooldown times.

## Class and UST Index Table of Contents:

### 3.6.6.1: Alpha Class (Attraction & Repulsion):

PCU Shield DTPs:..................................................................page 215

NCU Shield DTPs:..................................................................page 220

PCU Discharge DTPs:..................................................................page 221

NCU Discharge DTPs:..................................................................page 226

PCU Vortex DTPs:..................................................................page 229

NCU Vortex DTPs:..................................................................page 231

PCU Swarm DTPs:...................................................................page 232
NCU Swarm DTPs:..................................................................page 233
PCU Propulsor DTPs:...............................................................page 233
NCU Propulsor DTPs:..............................................................page 234
PCU Dimensional Field DTPs:....................................................page 236
NCU Dimensional DTPs:...........................................................page 238

### 3.6.6.2: Beta Class (Synchronization & Desynchronization):

PCU Shield DTPs:....................................................................page 241
NCU Shield DTPs:...................................................................page 247
PCU Discharge DTPs:...............................................................page 249
NCU Discharge DTPs:..............................................................page 252
PCU Vortex DTPs:...................................................................page 257
NCU Vortex DTPs:...................................................................page 258
PCU Swarm DTPs:...................................................................page 259
NCU Swarm DTPs:..................................................................page 260
PCU Propulsor DTPs:...............................................................page 261
NCU Propulsor DTPs:..............................................................page 264
PCU Dimensional field DTPs:....................................................page 265
NCU Dimensional field DTPs:....................................................page 268

### 3.6.6.3: Gamma Class (Entanglement & Separation):

PCU Shield DTPs:....................................................................page 270
NCU Shield DTPs:...................................................................page 274
PCU Discharge DTPs:...............................................................page 277
NCU Discharge DTPs:..............................................................page 281
PCU Vortex DTPs:...................................................................page 285
NCU Vortex DTPs:...................................................................page 288
PCU Swarm DTPs:...................................................................page 289
NCU Swarm DTPs:..................................................................page 290
PCU Propulsor DTPs:...............................................................page 290
NCU Propulsor DTPs:..............................................................page 291
PCU Dimensional field DTPs:....................................................page 293
NCU Dimensional field DTPs:....................................................page 297

### 3.6.6.4: Delta Class (Motion & Motionlessness):

PCU Shield DTPs:...................................................................page 299
NCU Shield DTPs:..................................................................page 301
PCU Discharge DTPs:.............................................................page 307
NCU Discharge DTPs:.............................................................page 310
PCU Vortex DTPs:...................................................................page 317
NCU Vortex DTPs:...................................................................page 318
PCU Swarm DTPs:...................................................................page 319
NCU Swarm DTPs:..................................................................page 320
PCU Propulsor DTPs:...............................................................page 320
NCU Propulsor DTPs:..............................................................page 322
PCU Dimensional field DTPs:...................................................page 324
NCU Dimensional field DTPs:..................................................page 324

## 3.6.5.1: Alpha Class (Attraction & Repulsion):

### UST One/Ultra-solid (Shields):

• PCU shield DTPs:

1: Automatically absorb photomission energy from PTU and CTU when in proximity. This process, however, can only properly occur for DUPs (and their extended energy) or simply ultrachite particles (and their extended energy) that have lost phased momentum (and are about to return to the Aether). Accordingly, there will not be a reduction in a discharge's or vortex's APL strength and time against the shield. Alpha-positive shields can absorb the majority of photomission energy from a field of ultrachite particles greater than their (the shield's) energy density; and for average DPLs, this is usually at least 90% from a field of particles six times stronger than the shield at once within a second. Accordingly, if an average user with a DPL shield were to absorb 90% of the energy from eight average DPL ultrachite discharges within a second (not all *exactly* at once), they would convert (if no conversion problems exist) the equivalent of roughly 8.64% energy (down from about 9.6%, collectively) of their MLP.

In the cases where the non-user particle energy levels are (collectively) greater than the user's shield -- and since only energy from DUPs or particles that have lost phased momentum are absorbed -- the aggregate energy of any stronger or additional discharges in the same period can still, in the end, be mostly or partially absorbed (before they return to the Aether), depending on how much greater the energy is compared to the shield. Therefore, while the absorption *rate* can be measured in such scales like seconds, the *net* absorption can be measured in a variable period. Furthermore, while additional ultrachite discharges naturally UPS the still-existing FTPs (with PCIs) of an initial attack into DES (when applicable), the particles will still exist, and, therefore, a shield can still absorb them when they lose phased momentum. When alpha-positive shields absorb energy from ultrachite vortices, they can only absorb the energy from local DUPs instead of absorbing energy from all of the vortex's particles, as CPP does not apply through DUPs. The shield will also (slowly) absorb energy from ultrachite soaker particles (and any swarm particles it contacts), in turn lowering their stability and, thus, overall remaining timespans.

Since the average user will lose around 0.9% of their MLP per second for MECs using an average DPL shield, there could be a net loss of energy while absorbing energy unless the context grants the user enough absorbable energy to cover for the period of shield use. Plus, the average user must also consider the fact that their respective DPL shield will have a CEC of about 4.8% of their MLP. Even when the user cannot absorb any more energy (due to their lumarchetrix reaching maximum capacity), the effect is still beneficial, as it allows the user to remain plenished with energy. However, it must be remembered that the average user also has an LRR of 0.8333% per second on average, so normally when nearly any amount of energy is absorbed in a period of a second, there is still a net gain for the user's lumarchetrix (if only the shield is used).

If the user is in direct contact with another mage's shield, photomission energy *can* be absorbed, but this requires a stronger shield to result in a net gain of energy; otherwise, if both shields are of equal strength, they effectively cancel each other out. Both of these cases apply even when lumarchetrix energy is absorbed. Nevertheless, if the opponent mage is unshielded (and is of average power levels), the amount of lumarchetrix energy the average user with a respective DPL shield absorbs is roughly *up to* 11% per second (depending on how much of the shield touches the opponent), relative to their (the user's) MLP. In fact, via the SUC, a user can absorb lumarchetrix energy from shielded opponents – however, against another average mage with a respective DPL shield, this is only about 3.6% of the user's MLP per second. The shield can absorb GAP energy, too, via an ATP (yielding roughly the same amount); and, with another ATP, the shield can absorb other etheric energy, but this feat is too weak to yield anything of significance. Even if the shield is absorbing other sources of energy (such as discharges) while it is absorbing the opponent's lumarchetrix, this is still possible, as the etheric components are not affected by any occupancy of their physical counterparts absorbing energy from physical particles.

A user, nonetheless, cannot absorb the dissipating energy from their own shield DUPs (nor any of their other ultrachite energy at any state), as their own particles, via auric equilibrium, are aligned collectively in a way that virtually repels away from the shield's absorbers, thus preventing such a phenomenon. Moreover, a user's shield will not decouple the user's lumarchetrix energy from the whole lumarchetrix, and, thus, users do not absorb their own lumarchetrix energy whilst the energy is within their field. But even if this were possible, a user's own lumarchetrix is in equilibrium with the ultrachite they create, so this would not apply, anyway. Alpha-positive shields can also absorb small amounts of non-photomission energy from the Caelverse, though this is proportionally inferior than absorbing photomission energy from ultrachite. In this case, the energy would not convert into the lumarchetrix and would, instead, only help fuel the shield. When this happens, less lumarchetrix energy is funnelled to fuel the shield, thus helping the user to save energy.

2: Increase the capacity to absorb more (SBE) energy loads via an active UPC, thereby increasing the UOT against ultrachite and non-ultrachite attacks. While in this regard, alpha-positive shields are the strongest of all the shields, they do not, however, possess better (or worse) cooldown times for UPIs and UPOs compared to other shields – except for gamma-negative shields (which possess the greatest). Moreover, despite the alpha-positive shield being able to withstand more attacks with this DTP when active, the number and power of its UPIs are still at normal levels, so the shield may still, for example, totally 'freeze' well before overloading when delta-negative attacks attain 100% APL against it. Average DPL shields in general can normally withstand about 12 consecutive average DPL discharges before overloading (and six discharges at once – with four or five simultaneous discharges having a chance to overload the shield), whereas the average DPL alpha-positive shield can withstand about four times these figures from the same attacks (at once), with the chance rates for simultaneous discharges being proportional as well.

Coupled with the first DTP, this means that an average user with a respective DPL shield can gain up to 57.6% of their MLP from 48 consecutive average DPL discharge attacks before overloading. Technically, the shield will overload on the 48th attack, but as the shield is overloading, it can continue absorbing energy for the user for a split second longer – just enough to absorb the last round of FTPs when they turn into DUPs. There are, however, other factors to consider over the variable period of time, such as: the shield's MECs; the absorption rate; DPA lumarchetrix costs; and the LRR. While DPA *costs* should be factored, alpha-positive shields (at most DPLs), nevertheless, reduce these by a magnitude of four compared to other ultrachite shields, therefore causing the DPA costs to be equal to that of other shields after every four attacks when at respective UOT levels (practically meaning: the same DPLs). In other words, the average DPL alpha-positive shield will incur a total DPA cost of 4.8% of the user's MLP over the course of the 48 average DPL consecutive attacks as a normal shield would at 12 attacks.

Despite this shield having an increased capacity to withstand more energy loads when this DTP is active, the average DPL DMA can still cause the average DPL shield (with this DTP active) to overload in one hit. This feat is possible because the shield itself is still fundamentally of the same power level as before having the DTP activated. Given a DMA's *specific* way of creating QIFs, they (DMAs) are, in this regard, better than gamma-positive discharges against the shield. There will also be a 2.5% chance that each average DPL discharge will cause the shield to overload for each hit due to a quantum instability issue (no matter the shield's UOT rate).

Average DPL shields require a 90-second UPC time, with the DTP lasting 12 seconds before a cooldown period of 90 seconds occurs. After the 12 seconds of active time finish, the shield *will* overload, however, so caution is needed. Moreover, there is a chance that the QIF will be prolonged, and for the said DPL, this could (at a chance rate of 50%) prolong the QIF to 20 seconds instead of the normal 10 seconds, with the CDP jumping to four seconds as well, thus totalling the user 24 seconds before they can use their shields again. Afterwards, there would be 78 seconds remaining on the DTP's cooldown period (or 66 seconds if the QIF were extended). If a doomgroup were to face off against a lone mage (with everyone using this DTP when active) in a contest of point-blank shooting (with no other factors considered, except for relative DPLs), no force multiplier would be *added*; but in the case of stronger mages fighting against weaker mages, a small force multiplier would technically be added due to other variables like better APL build.

3: Attract incoming ultrachite discharges via an active UPC. This, nevertheless, is limited by the degree of line of fire (unless the shield is powerful and close by), the distance, and the *amount* of discharge *energy* in a single period of time (not necessarily the *number* of attacks). For average DPL shields, this amounts to about eight roughly-ranked or encompassing average DPL discharges per second within a seven-metre radius. Depending on respective power levels, this feat can even override and attract the matter reflected from alpha-negative shields that target original sources. Alternatively, users can change the DTP to an ATP to include attracting standard magnetically-affectable, fast-moving, non-ultrachite matter, such as bullets and/or other high-energy phenomena. However, while attracting matter like bullets, this comes at the cost of being able to simultaneously attract ultrachite discharges. Explicitly, the specific type of alternative matter depends on the specific tuning of the ATP, so an ATP will not simultaneously attract all non-ultrachite matter, either.

The field the shield emits works via potentials, so it instead of exerting a real force, it will instead alter the wave functions of incoming discharges or other items. However, as the incoming things accelerate towards the shield (where the strength of the field would increase due to the distance shrinking) they will lose their phase, so they will lose their acceleration. Interestingly, when this occurs, the phase will not be totally lost, so a net velocity will be achieved, where the incoming discharge or other item will keep its velocity. So, when the discharge hits the shield, it will hit it with a force as if it were not attracted to the shield. When items are outside of the affectable radius, the phase drops to zero, so the rest of the field's strength also effectively drops to zero.

Although users usually use this DTP to benefit the shield's abovesaid DTP (regarding absorption abilities), the other main advantage is keeping allies safe from getting shot. Combined with the first two DTPs, this makes alpha-positive shields recognized as the 'tank' class. Average DPL shields require a four-second UPC time, with the DTP lasting 64 seconds before a cooldown period of four seconds occurs. If an incoming discharge were moving parallel to the user but just tip the edge of a perfectly-spherical aura, then the discharge would not actually have to make a sharp 90-degree turn, so it would still be able to just hit the user. When the DTP is active, users may sometimes choose to switch the PEP from AES to DES in order to effectively stop the power, as the context of a fight may change. For example, if a user needs to switch to a particular task in the battle because one of their allies fell and no longer can do their task, having less focus on their shield may help achieve that goal.

4: Affect the minds of those within the vicinity with a magnetic field *modulated* in a particular way (with certain oscillations and pulses), in turn causing attention to fall on the user; that is, the user will attract the attention of (most types of) sentient beings (and robots), whether hostile or not, but it will not alter the hostility levels of said beings. The average DPL shield will attract the attention of (most) beings within a 12 m radius of the shell before the effect drops to zero by way of a phase loss. Although this power can affect other shielded mages, shields can still reduce the effects; plus, mentally-strong and/or trained individuals can also shrug this effect off. The statistics for affected opponents vary greatly, especially when also considering the context, which may itself even have variously and rapidly-shifting factors. Interestingly, this DTP is a passive feat, so if users do not wish for attention to fall on them, then they need only (totally) UPS (or lower the number of) the particles from AES to DES.

5: Automatically grant the user the ability of magnetoreception, which allows them to visually see, and instinctively sense, magnetic energies. In some cases, users may even be able to notice invisible or camouflaged objects (including gamma-positive shields). However, this would be via *inference* because the invisible or camouflaged objects would only create magnetic irregularities in the area, not fully-identifiable magnetic fields (as they would distort such magnetic fields). For some users, the magnetoreception can become too distracting, so the DTP (while passive) is some-times tuned down when channelling so detections are fewer, weaker, or not available. While shields in general normally weaken the effects of magnetic fields, the user will still be able to detect magnetic imprints left *on* the shield; so, the shield enhances the user's brain, and the user can detect what occurs against the shield.

• NCU shield DTPs:

1: *Repel* ultrachite and non-ultrachite matter, along with high-powered electro-magnetic radiation (such as from laser attacks) – all when actively UPC'd. The repulsion power also exists on a spectrum that includes *reflection*. With the DTP active, shields of all power levels will only be able to reflect things that a shield would naturally be able to stop in its normal state. Accordingly, knives may still penetrate a shield if they are moving slow enough. There is a special consideration for ultrachite, where the shield will produce a special field shortly beyond itself that will cause the incoming ultrachite to reflect before touching it (the shield) – thus, ultrachite discharges can remain intact. In contrast, bullets that hit the shield will not necessarily remain intact, but they will still reflect.

After the average DPL shield has been UPC'd, it can reflect standard blast-ball-sized attacks back to average-sized attackers with basically 100% accuracy when within a five-metre range; diminishing rates then occur for every subsequent unit of area. The reflection, however, will only be within a straight line of fire, so if the opponent had moved from their original firing location, they will not likely be hit. If the attacking discharge curved during its trajectory before reaching the shield, it would not reflect to the opponent, and, instead, it would reflect towards the angle of convergence. Additionally, there must not be any post hoc obstacles in the way in order for the opponent to be hit (as the discharge would hit the object instead), nor any other detrimental factors that may inhibit the reflection. However, elite users with their respective DPLs can reflect ultrachite attacks back to the original source (the attacker) via PUC (should the opponent be in range), not the attacker's potentially-former physical location (should the opponent have moved) – unless objects are in the way. This homing phenomenon can also occur for some non-ultrachite things in certain circumstances. No matter the power level, a shield will generally reflect impending things with equal speed.

The average DPL shield will only be able to reflect four average DPL discharges per second – and only one at a single time – before the reflection becomes mere (inaccurate and low-range) repulsion of varying levels. While a shield is being shot at, its UOT can still suffer (at its normal rate) due to the (kinetic) energy (from the impacts) still passing on to the shield. So, 12 consecutive average DPL discharges can still over-load the average DPL shield. Nevertheless, because alpha-negative shields reflect discharges intact (with the DTP active), APL does not apply at all. These shields, however, do not block most of the light-based radiation from ultrachite FTPs that have released and activated *elsewhere*, nor most other (normal, non-ultrachite amounts of) radiation. Naturally while in its standard form, the shield will only repel things outwards from the shell's exterior and not, conversely, inwards from the interior towards the user (should anything be on the inside of the shield). If the user were to change the shield's form into a disc, then only one side would reflect matter. Average DPL shields require a 24-second UPC time, with the DTP lasting eight seconds before a cooldown period of 24 seconds occurs.

2: Affect the minds of those within the vicinity with a magnetic field *modulated* in a particular way (with certain oscillations and pulses), in turn warding off (most types of) sentient beings (and robots) from physically approaching up close. That is, the user will repel (most) sentient beings, whether hostile or not, but it will not alter the hostility levels of said beings. The average DPL shield will repel those who approach within a four-metre radius of the shell before the effect drops to zero by way of a phase loss. Although this power can affect other shielded mages, shields can still reduce the effects; plus, mentally-strong and/or trained individuals can also shrug this effect off. The statistics for affected opponents vary greatly, especially when also considering the context, which may itself even have variously and rapidly-shifting factors. Interestingly, this DTP is a passive feat, so if users do not wish to repel others (usually allies), then they need only (totally) UPS (or lower the number of) the particles from AES to DES.

3: Automatically grant the user the ability of magnetoreception, which allows them to visually see, and instinctively sense, magnetic energies. In some cases, users may even be able to notice invisible or camouflaged objects (including gamma-positive shields). However, this would be via *inference* because the invisible or camouflaged objects would only create magnetic irregularities in the area, not fully-identifiable magnetic fields (as they would distort such magnetic fields). For some users, the magnetoreception can become too distracting, so the DTP (while passive) is some-times tuned down when channelling so detections are fewer, weaker, or not available. While shields in general normally weaken the effects of magnetic fields, the user will still be able to detect magnetic imprints left *on* the shield; so, the shield enhances the user's brain, and the user can detect what occurs against the shield.

## UST Two/Ultra-plasma (Discharges):

### • PCU discharge DTPs:

1: Magnetically attract (that is, pull) matter on impact by first converting and charging said matter's HRF (or HRFs) to a quantumly-unified and uniform *ultra-paramagnetic* state. The uniformity equalizes all magnetic forces within its field, so the attack equally attracts all matter, allowing lighter materials to remain within the properties of heavier materials (such as feathers on a body) – so long as they are within the HRF(s). However, this does not account for the heaviness of the properties being affected, so naturally, heavier properties (such as iron) require more energy in order to be pulled. This means the steel in a suit of armour, for example, would greatly weigh down the *HRF* of the suit, causing more energy needed to pull, say, the velvet interior that may be part of the suit. That is, the velvet would not weigh more – just the HRF.

However, the more mass an HRF has, the more of a (mostly linear) *multiplier effect* it will have on levels of *potential* ultra paramagnetism, in turn causing the discharge to apply more force up to the discharge's power level. In other words, before the upper threshold is met (per the discharge's power level), there is a linear net increase in force per increase in mass (due to the greater masses allowing for greater potential), so all masses up to the threshold are pulled with the same amount of acceleration. When the threshold changes (whether it increases or decreases per power level), so does the acceleration of masses up to that threshold. Essentially, this is an issue regarding different phases and wave function changes.

Ultimately, the discharge does not need the massive amounts of energy that normal paramagnets require for the same effect, and they can affect most kinds of matter. Via PUC, a discharge will magnetically pull affected matter in the reverse direction of the discharge's trajectory that occurred before hitting the target – all the while ultimately pulling the affected matter back towards the user. Note that while quantum entanglement would occur with the discharge via PUC, the entanglement is not imparted on to the magnetically-affected matter; the affected HRF is only pulled in the direction of where the user is located. Since the FTPs do not last long, the effect does not continue pulling the matter, and so, only *momentum itself* will continue moving the HRF until other forces stop it, including gravity. As soon as the FTPs disappear, the affected HRF will also immediately lose its ultra-paramagnetic state.

The average DPL discharge can pull all masses up to 100 kg with an acceleration rate of 12 m/s² from zero-initial velocity (with each kilogram after that decreasing in acceleration due to the force – a maximum of 1,200 newtons – staying the same). Given that FTPs only last about 0.25 seconds, the HRF would only travel back 0.375 metres with a velocity of 3 m/s (with no other resistances factored, such as friction) before momentum itself (without acceleration) would begin, resulting in different distances covered before the HRF would stop. While this might not seem like much, the momentum itself on top of the 0.375 metres normally still makes many types of opponents move just enough to ruin their situation in general combat scenarios. Plus, users can continue easily hitting opponents who usually would be on the ground due to a loss of balance.

When calculated at a 4.167% APL against an average DPL-shielded mage, this upper threshold only amounts to 4.167 kg, whereas at 50% APL, this would be 50 kg. The FTPs will also register an increase of mass for the shield due to the SUC, so shields, light as they are, would also be coupled with the mage's weight. Typically, in order for a user to fully pull an opponent towards their actual location (even at

100% APL), they have to hit them a few times, depending on the distance. This power is usually utilized for pulling opponents out of their cover (like those who might be behind a wall corner or ground barricade) or for pulling certain covers away from opponents, leaving them in plain sight. The discharge particles will cover the HRF's front surface area instead of staying at the blast ball impact site; and, accordingly, the HRF will get pulled as a whole entity rather than being pulled as if a tow cable were attached to it. Moreover, the HRF's whole body will be affected equally, so they will not immediately faceplant into the ground. While injuries can occur at average power levels (such as the HRF hitting objects on the way), there is an increased risk for fatal outcomes per power level increase.

• Note: When gamma-negative shields or other phenomena cut off a discharge's PUC, magnetic pulling can still occur, but the affected opponent or object will not move towards the user who shot the discharge, and they would, instead, move in the reverse direction of the discharge's trajectory before impact.

• Note: CDMs will still pull all affected entities toward the user via PUC (in most standard contexts). When PUCs are cut, then alpha-positive CDMs will pull the affected entities in the reverse direction of the CDM's prior (albeit normally short-range) trajectory before impact.

2: Cause affectable HRFs to become attractive beacons for close ultrachite discharges of all PACs (except for beta-negative, when applicable), along with other magnetically-affectable matter, such as bullets. *Practically* no matter the power level, the DTP will cause any number of discharges of any power level to approach the HRF at any one time. However, power levels *do* affect the degree to which the incoming discharges will turn from their normal trajectory, in addition to the initial distance where the discharges will begin turning. The average DPL discharge can cause other discharges to head towards the HRF from within a four-metre range; but if any objects are between the incoming discharges and the HRF, this can affect the attraction or at least block the trajectory. In order to accurately strike the HRF (at all), incoming discharges have to be within a 45-degree conical angle of trajectory of the HRF when the effect takes place; if they are not within the angle of trajectory, the discharges will still move towards the target, but they will not curve in time to reach it. Basically, this helps improve, but not necessarily guarantee, the accuracy of other discharges, so this causes a moderate homing effect.

Of course, these figures would be at 100% APL; if an average DPL shield were affected at an initial 4.167% APL, this would amount to just over 16 cm in range if within a two-degree conical angle of trajectory. Besides APL itself, the power level of a shield typically does not matter (unless certain counter CBEs apply). Specifically, the incoming discharges will move towards the shield *before* the UPIs render the particles into DES. So, by the time a discharge is en route, it would be too late for a shield of any power level to accordingly affect the discharge. However, this only applies to APLs that allow for the effect range to be greater than the UPI range. So, at 4.167% APL for the average DPL shield, the effect becomes null. The statistics for bullets and other materials differ based on many variables, such as mass, speed, and environmental context. If a stationary (so, zero-initial velocity), metallic coin, for example, were affected at average DPLs, then it would normally accelerate towards the HRF with a speed of about 4 m/s$^2$ in standard contexts, but a phase change would occur, where the acceleration would stop due to a partial phase loss, and the coin would keep its velocity of 4 m/s. Since the coin, in this case, would weigh about five grams, the beacon effect is basically ineffective against heavy objects.

This DTP forms a magnetic field that layers around the ultra-paramagnetic field the first DTP establishes for the HRF, with neither affecting one another on a practical level. This DTP naturally has a default tuning that affects particular HRFs of a certain energy level and type. The most easily affectable HRF at this default tuning includes HRFs like ultrachite shields. When using the default tuning, users will not be able to affect other HRFs, such as standard tables. However, users have the option to alter the DTP to an ATP, which switches the tuning to allow for affecting different kinds of HRFs. Herewith, a user might be able to shoot at a particular location that they (and perhaps their allies) need to shoot at, even if it is not actually directly at any opponents; an emergency exit, where opponents might run towards, is potentially a good example. At average DPLs for any affected HRF, a four-second diminishingly-effective TRE applies per shot. Sometimes users choose to lower or switch the PEP (off) when the DTP is not effective or desirable within the context.

3: Absorb photomission energy from PTU particles on impact. Unlike alpha-positive shields that only absorb energy from DUPs or particles that have lost phased momentum, discharges can absorb both dissipating *and* direct photomission energy from active ultrachite shield particles. Moreover, via the SUC, the discharge can also absorb a small amount of the opponent's lumarchetrix energy – but not as much compared to an unshielded opponent. Most discharges are capable of absorbing the majority of photomission energy from a field of ultrachite particles greater than their (the discharge's) energy density – for average DPLs, this is usually at least 90% with a field of particles six times stronger than the discharge. While a shield with a relative DPL would not have enough energy for this maximum density absorption, the shield would still rapidly receive new energy from the lumarchetrix, and the discharge would then absorb this photomission energy from the shield. The DTP itself would also not be damaging the shield, as such, and, instead, it would just be siphoning energy that would be topped up.

All discharges of any power level have their limitations on the amount and speed of absorption, so the direct absorption from a shield normally never reaches a maximum LCR. The average user with their respective DPL discharge (worth 1.2% of their MLP) will therefore absorb a general minimum of 6.48% (7.2% max) worth of their MLP from an average DPL shield per shot at 100% APL, while there would be a general minimum of 0.27% per shot at an initial 4.167% APL. If allies happen to be attacking the same shield at that moment, these figures could either be lowered or at zero due to how discharges affect one another, changing older discharges into DES. The absorbed physical energy will first convert to etheric energy, then it (and any direct lumarchetrix energy taken) will be non-locally absorbed (despite any potential physical proximity) due to the discharge's PUC. Note that (the) etheric components are not affected by any occupancy of their physical counterparts absorbing energy from physical particles, so this feat can occur.

There is no surcharge for both conversion and absorption, but not all energy may necessarily be absorbed. In fact, this converted energy can be intercepted, blocked, or lost on the way, though this is not common in standard contexts. Since the photomission energy (now etheric) switches to the user's lumarchetrix, this means that the discharge itself (or what remains of the FTPs) does not absorb it and increase in strength and size. Via the SUC, average DPL lumarchetrix absorption against the (average DPL) shielded opponent is also generally calculated at about 3.6% per shot at 100% APL, which initially amounts to about 0.15% for an initial attack at 4.167% APL.

By the time an average user with a respective DPL reaches 50% APL against the average DPL-shielded opponent with consecutive attacks (assuming all the attacks successfully pass the UAS check), they (the user) will have gained a general minimum of around 32.76% of their (the user's) MLP from photomission and lumarchetrixes energies. This figure, of course, does not account for the user's LRR during this period, which would add up to an additional 2.49% when the opponent's shield overloads – if all the attacks were consecutive. Moreover, it does not account for the amount of energy the user would have spent on the discharges, which would amount to about 14.4% of their MLP. If only half the UAS chance checks were successfully passed, then the net absorption would be 3.24% (ignoring the LRR); and, while this may seem insignificant, consider that in the end, the discharges were basically free of cost. If, instead, the average *unshielded* opponent were attacked with an average DPL discharge, then about 11% of their (the opponent's) respective MLP would be absorbed. In all cases, TREs do not apply.

Overall, it must be recognised that when a user uses alpha-positive discharges, they do not just gain energy; the victim (shielded or not) also loses energy – which itself is a bonus. Alpha-positive discharges can also (and only) absorb small amounts of non-photomission energy from things normally found in the Caelverse *as* an ATP, though this is proportionally far worse than absorbing photomission energy from ultrachite. And, while this energy remains physical (that is, without converting to the etheric), it does not repower the discharges; instead, if the user is close by, the energy can physically travel to the user's physical aura to then be potentially absorbed (and physically used) by other ultrachite forms (namely, alpha-positive shields). The DTP can also (and only) absorb other (non-lumarchetrix) etheric energy from physical properties for the user *as* an ATP, but this is not as effective either, except for when it applies to other GAP energy – which, of course, helps the user replenish their GAP. The statistics for this feat are roughly the same as when absorbing lumarchetrix energy (so, 11% per discharge against the unshielded mage).

• NCU discharge DTPs:

1: Magnetically repel (that is, push or knock over) matter on impact by first converting and charging said matter's HRF (or HRFs) to a quantumly-unified and uniform *ultra-diamagnetic* state. The uniformity equalizes all magnetic forces within its field, so the attack equally repels all matter, allowing lighter materials to remain within the properties of heavier materials (such as feathers on a body) – so long as they are within the HRF(s). However, this does not account for the heaviness of the items being affected, so naturally, heavier properties (such as iron) require more energy in order to be pushed. This means the steel in a suit of armour, for example, would greatly weigh down the *HRF* of the suit, causing more energy needed to push, say, the velvet interior that may be part of the suit. That is, the velvet would not weigh more – just the HRF.

However, the more mass an HRF has, the more of a (mostly linear) *multiplier effect* it will have on levels of *potential* ultra diamagnetism, in turn causing the discharge to apply more force up to the discharge's power level. In other words, before the upper threshold is met (per the discharge's power level), there is a linear net increase in force per increase in mass (due to the greater masses allowing for greater potential), so all masses up to the threshold are pushed with the same amount of acceleration. When the threshold changes (whether it increases or decreases per power level), so does the acceleration of masses up to that threshold. Ultimately, the discharge does not need the massive amounts of energy that normal diamagnets require for the same effect, and they can affect most kinds of matter. Essentially, this is an issue regarding different phases and wave function changes. As soon as the FTPs disappear, the affected HRF will also instantly lose its ultra-diamagnetic state.

Even though the discharge may travel towards the target at 120 km/h, this does not mean that this is what causes the HRF's acceleration; instead, it is the CBEs that first convert the HRF and then begin accelerating it. The average DPL discharge will push all masses up to 100 kg with an acceleration rate of 12 m/s$^2$ from zero-initial velocity (with each kilogram after that decreasing in acceleration due to the force – a maximum of 1,200 newtons – staying the same). Given that FTPs only last about 0.25 seconds, the HRF would only travel back 0.375 metres with a velocity of 3 m/s (with no other resistances factored, such as friction) before *momentum itself* (without acceleration) would begin, resulting in different distances covered before the HRF would stop. While this might not seem like much, the momentum on top of 0.375 metres normally still makes many types of opponents move just enough to ruin their situation in general combat scenarios. Plus, users can continue easily hitting opponents who usually would be on the ground due to a loss of balance. When calculated at a 4.167% APL against an average DPL-shielded mage, this upper threshold only amounts to 4.167 kg, whereas at 50% APL, this would be 50 kg.

The FTPs will cover the HRF's front surface area instead of staying at the blast ball impact site, so the effect is not acute, and the power accordingly delivers a sensation of being pushed by a body-sized wave, not a fist punch. Even though the FTPs will alter a whole HRF, the pushing effect itself and the vector is dependent on the discharge's initial trajectory. The pressure levels, too, are well within safe limits for all power levels against standard entities. The *g-force* (using standard gravitational force) for average DPLs is about 1.22 g, and since the FTPs cover the front surface about equally, no problems like whiplash generally occur. Moreover, with the HRF's whole body affected equally, an affected person will not immediately drop backwards into the ground. The FTPs will also register an increase of mass for the shield due to the SUC, so shields, light as they are, would also be coupled with the mage's weight. While PPEs such as headaches normally occur at average power levels (when hitting objects), it is rare that death occurs (unless the victim is pushed off a great height); however, there is an increased risk for fatalities per power level increase, with master power level attacks that push human victims into hard walls immediately behind them normally leading to death. This power is also effective at pushing *certain* covers (such as light barricades) away from or into opponents.

2: Repulse opponents with mind-affecting magnetic energies (that are modulated in a particular way) to ward them off with two distinct levels: *avoidance* and then *retreat*. While various levels of avoidance apply instantly, retreat can only occur when a certain threshold from the preceding effect has been attained. Avoidance essentially reduces the opponent's likelihood of leaving cover to engage in combat, while retreat causes them to flee. However, when an opponent is retreating, this does not mean that they will not attack on the way. The statistics vary based on the individual and their state of mind and goals at the time, but most beings that purposely engage in combat in the first place will be less likely to flee than those who were, for example, surprise ambushed. There are also non-user-related environmental variables to consider. The average DPL discharge will cause roughly an accumulative (per hit) 0.33336% repulsion effect (calculated on the avoidance-retreat spectrum) for the *common*, average

DPL-shielded mage (via the SUC) at an initial 4.167% APL in standard combat settings; at 100% APL, this amounts to about 8% per hit.

To reach the full avoidance and minimum retreat thresholds against the aforesaid shielded, 100% and 200% worth of individual, average DPL accumulative attacks are respectively required. This means that the average DPL user would need to launch 24 roughly-consecutive attacks for full avoidance and about 37 to reach the retreat stage (which would mean 13 attacks would be at 100% APL). For the unshielded mage opponent (and most unprotected biological entities), a single average DPL discharge will cause full avoidance, while two in total will cause a minimum amount for retreat. Monsters typically have a threshold level for each effect akin to shielded mages, along with other entities employing UPI-equivalents. Robots, on the other hand, vary greatly.

Since the effects are accumulative, an AAE applies after the FTPs end, and for average DPLs against normal biological entities, this lasts about eight seconds (with another four seconds of diminishing intensities) per hit, which can stack for each additional shot up to four times, thus *fully* lasting 32 seconds per shot (calculated without the diminishing time that would be added). Moreover, each stage and its effects will fully last at their level of effect, so the effects do not gradually drop off through degeneration; that is, the effects sharply end. Accordingly, it is possible to bring a shielded opponent mage to the retreat stage before they overload *if* their overloading rates recover faster proportionally to the AAE's stacked seconds – *and* if most of the attacks pass the UAS check to build APL. Again, based on the individual and their state of mind, once the effects wear off, the opponent may continue fleeing (as if by momentum), or they may return to the fight.

3: Repulse an opponent's lumarchetrix, in turn affecting an opponent's ability to absorb photomission or lumarchetrix (and other etheric) energies. Shielded mages are affected via the SUC, while unshielded mages are directly affected magnetically. The average user's DPL discharge will cause an average DPL-shielded opponent to experience a 60% rate of processing problems when at 100% APL. At an initial hit at 4.167% APL, this would be about 2.5%, whereas at 50% APL, this would be 30%. Each discharge will also cause a diminishing-effective TRE of about nine seconds for the average opponent. If struck against the unshielded (average mage), a single average DPL discharge shot will cause 100% processing problems, and the opponent will remain at total debilitation for as long as the attacks continue. While an opponent may still absorb photomission energy via ultrachite attacks, they would not be able to *process* it into their lumarchetrix. This DTP does not affect an opponent's ability to recharge their lumarchetrix from the Aether, however. An ATP is needed to affect the ability to absorb other etheric energies (including GAP energy), but the statistics for this are too varied to list.

## UST Three/Ultra-gas (Vortices):

### • PCU vortex DTPs:

1: Absorb (redirect) and accordingly *demagnetize* PTU and CTU particles as well as particular non-ultrachite magnetic properties. As a CEP, the vortex technically only *suppresses* magnetization – at least initially. If a susceptible magnetic item were to stay within the vortex for a lengthy period, however, then permanent demagnetization can occur. A TRE will apply to things that leave the vortex, but if they return, then any remaining unsuppressed magnetism will not be suppressively stacked on top of the currently-suppressed magnetism. That is, the vortex will only suppress the level of magnetism it is capable of suppressing from the affectable particles. So, if a vortex were to suppress a maximum of 80% of an item's magnetic force, then after the item re-enters the vortex with a diminishing TRE of 74%, the vortex would only bring the suppressed percentage back to 80%. Nevertheless, once the item has lingered too long in the vortex, the suppressed 80% will become permanently demagnetized, and the vortex would then immediately suppress the remaining 20%. Naturally, the magnetic powers of the vortex can extend beyond its form, but this diminishes greatly per metre.

The average DPL vortex will demagnetize up to (or the equivalent of) 0.85 average DPL alpha discharges at once. Due to the fractional number in this case, if more discharges concurrently enter the vicinity, the vortex's effects will be weaker for each discharge via UPP. So, if two average DPL discharges were to simultaneously enter (typically from two different mages, as two or more consecutive discharges from a single mage will practically never be found within the vortex due to their speed and the mage's rate of fire), then each would be magnetically suppressed by about 42.5% of their strength. A diminishingly-effective TRE of about four seconds will be imposed on an average DPL discharge should it enter and then leave the vortex, with the time being slightly affected if the power was split in the vortex with other discharges. Since discharges move rapidly and easily explode, they practically never become permanently demagnetized.

Of course, this feat works most effectively against discharges that *shielded* opponents fire from a *distance*, because when a shielded opponent approaches a user's vortex, their UPIs will weaken this effect – until they become overstimulated. Aside from discharges, if an opponent with an average DPL alpha-positive shield were to stand inside an average DPL vortex, about 30% suppression would occur at 100% APL. If a user happened to be using an alpha-positive shield to attract discharges (while using this vortex), then the vortex would not practically affect this feat, as the incoming discharges would be directly en route for the shield before any practical demagnetization would occur since the radius of effect for that shield's DTP would be bigger than the *effective* radius of the vortex in basically all cases. The vortex, moreover, would not even affect the magnetic field of the shield itself due to harmonizing with it.

2: Electrostatically attract the surrounding air molecules (outside the vortex), in turn causing a vacuum on the outside, which then causes the neighbouring air molecules to fill the void by sticking to – and inside – the vortex. The vacuuming stops at the level of power the vortex can withstand, and a stormy wind will then build, which causes static charge and shocks to follow (which basically do not affect shielded mages – even at 100% APL). Upon relinquishing the vortex, a pressure wave (that expands outwards) will generate by default. Average DPL vortices will generate static shocks of approximately 11,000 volts and three amps at a general frequency of 0.5 hertz. The *duration* of each shock is infinitesimal, so they are not deadly for most entities, whereas the finishing pressure wave will only possess enough power to unbalance the average person.

3: Increase the availability and absorbability of an opponent mage's lumarchetrix and photomission energies, respectively. The average DPL vortex can then enable (but not increase the power of) the user's average DPL discharge to absorb about 7.2% lumarchetrix energy worth of the user's MLP per shot at 100% APL from the average DPL-shielded mage effectively just via the SUC. The average unshielded mage, meanwhile, will lose 33% of their MLP per shot. Note, however, that this figure coincidently has nothing to do with the LCR, as the LCR does not apply to etheric-to-etheric transfers). It is important to consider that *both* the vortex itself *and* the discharge need to be at 100% APLs for these figures to occur. That is, an opponent's UPIs might weaken both the discharge and the vortex. Plus, this applies to just one opponent; when more opponents are simultaneously affected, the power divides.

The vortex can also specifically increase an alpha-positive discharge's absorption of energy from ultrachite shields; accordingly, the general minimum of 90% absorbability of photomission energy in the case of average DPL discharges attacking average DPL shields will reach about 100%. Nonetheless, meeting this target does not require 100% APL against the opponent, as usually this is achieved at roughly 30% APL – average DPLs considered. No TREs apply for opponents who leave the vortex. Technically, this DTP can help absorb non-photomission energy from properties originally from the Caelverse, too. The statistics for this, though, vary greatly depending on the property and context. Moreover, it can help with absorbing other etheric energies as well (including GAP energies) when used as ATPs (so, one for the GAP and one for other etheric energies), with the statistics also greatly varying.

• NCU vortex DTPs:

1: Create a repulsive gas that extremely disgusts most biological organisms. One does not even need to breathe the gas to be repulsed – that is, if any of the gas enters the mouth and touches the tongue, then one can taste the gas. In fact, the repulsive gas even can affect biological entities that have chemoreceptors, for example, where they taste their environment through touching things with their limbs. Fortunately for the user, the gas will always *naturally* stay out of the eye (but it can still technically enter the eye). Moreover, other shielded users do not have to worry about smelling the gas as it does not go through their shields. Still, if the common unshielded mage found themselves in an alpha-negative vortex (even at average DPLs), they will *immediately* try to escape it. Furthermore, even when the said vortex has low APLs, it can still fully repulse basically all humans. At master and supreme power levels, this can even cause suffocation, and some beings may simply pass out. There are even cases where certain beings have died in such vortices. The levels of effect vary for monsters, and the gas will basically only affect robots if they have the sensors to sense the gas in a way that a biological entity would experience it. The power of the DTP basically does not divide when there are more entities inside the AOE.

2: Increase an opponent's vulnerability to mental repulsions by magnetically altering their receptibility to particular effects on the mind – namely, but not limited to, alpha-negative discharge repulsions. So, while this does not increase the power of a user's discharge attacks, it nevertheless weakens opponents for those attacks. Effectively via just the SUC, the average DPL vortex can effectively lower a *common*, average DPL-shielded opponent's resistance to the avoidance and retreat thresholds by about 50% when at 100% APL. For the common unshielded opponent, the effect at average DPLs will cause about a 140% decrease from their normal rates. A diminishingly-effective TRE of about nine seconds also applies to opponents who leave the aura. Note that the above statistics apply to just one opponent; when more opponents are simultaneously affected, the power divides. Also, while this increases vulnerabilities, opponents may still be able to resist these effects (to varying degrees). Robots can be affected as well by increasing the chance for bit flipping, with differing results per type. Interestingly, if the victim is *so* weak, this can *effectively* cause mental repulsions instead of just vulnerabilities. Other types of mental effects (outside of phasarchement), along with their strengths, are too broad and contextual to list here.

3: Increase the vulnerability of an opponent mage's lumarchetrix to particular repulsions – namely, alpha-negative discharge repulsions – effectively just via the SUC against the shielded and direct influence against the unshielded. When an alpha-negative discharge is fired at an opponent, the affected lumarchetrix will essentially 'stave off' from receiving energies, which causes it to have problems absorbing and processing converted photomission and other lumarchetrix energies. The average

DPL vortex can then enable (but not increase the power of) the average DPL alpha-negative discharge to cause 100% processing problems for the average opponent with a respective DPL shield (when the discharge itself is calculated at 100% APL). However, the average DPL vortex still requires building its APL against a shielded opponent, and, thus, this figure is also at 100% APL for the vortex itself. Of course, with average DPLs, this instantly (and totally) affects average unshielded opponents. A diminishingly-effective TRE of about nine seconds also applies to opponents who leave the vortex. Note that the above statistics apply to just one opponent; when more opponents are simultaneously affected, the power divides. ATPs are also available for GAPs and other etheric energies.

• Note: Legends speak of mythical mages being able to use their alpha-negative vortices to generate a magnetic repulsive wave that circled around the user, pushing matter in the direction of movement.

## UST Four/Ultra-liquid (Soaker bombs and Swarm clouds):

• PCU soaker particles: possess *electrophilic agents*, which bind to and accept electron pairs from other compounds. This typically causes irritation to most skin types (so not just humans) and other parts of one's body; but without a proper aerosol medium, the soaker particles do not act like tear gas (but they can be quite adverse if splashed in the eyes or up the nose), so it primarily affects the skin (assuming unshielded opponents), nor do they have the potentially deadly chemicals in tear gas. Still, average power levels have enough strength to basically match the levels of non-ultrachite mild pepper spray, whereas elite power levels are stronger than the pepper spray used by police and similar personnel. Given that the ultrachite particles will disappear, they do not possess the problem of *residue* that non-ultrachite tear gases and pepper spray possess. These electrophilic agents are also tied in with other properties that cause mild but unusual and continuous electrical pulses, causing further annoyance in the vein of distraction – and, in the case for robots, certain disruptions to their sensory input. While these soaker bombs are quite effective against the bodies of mage opponents, most mages remain shielded in their fights; and, when they are unshielded, normally other incapacitating powers are used to end the fights.

• PCU swarm clouds: form a fog that absorbs light, rendering the victim left to attempt seeing through a partial veil of darkness. The statistics for the lighting vary greatly per context.

• NCU soaker particles: create a repulsive mucous, which not only feels like other kinds of mucous (which most beings normally find repulsive), but the particles also have the ability to affect the nervous system in a way that sends signals to the brain to cause the victim to actually find the mucous disgusting. The particles will also emit a modulated magnetic field that can cause other beings around the victim to be repulsed. If the victim requires help for any reason, then there is a chance that their allies may not even provide aid due to desiring to keep their distance. For average DPLs, this field extends to about a 2.5-metre radius before the effect drops to zero by way of a phase loss. Nevertheless, not all beings will be affected equally – and the external effects are weaker than what the hit victim experiences – so it depends on the individual and the context as to how much (if at all) they are repulsed. In the case of robots, this can affect their sensory data input.

• NCU swarm clouds: form an encompassing mirror that partially reflects visuals back at the victim. Although this will have the same amount of visual partialness as an alpha-positive swarm (per respective power level), it is generally more *distracting* for the victim.

### UST Five/Ultra-conductivity (Propulsors):

• PCU propulsors: generate a LES magnetic field on creation that can be UPC'd and then used like a grappling hook (or reverse tractor beam) to reach normally-unreachable locations and things. The user first aims at a particular location, and then the latent ultra-conductive energy extends beyond the aura via a potential magnetic field and locks on to the target (with HRFs not considered – although, the target needs to have enough mass, so any part of the air would not count as a target). The charging normally takes about one second for average DPL propulsors before all the energy in the aura propels (the user) toward the aimed location. Users, nevertheless, must UPC the propulsor again to go to another location. Essentially, the power combines two *somewhat* contrasting 'forces' – attraction and propulsion in two distinct stages instead of just one. Reversing this feat where the targeted item comes to the user is not possible, however – despite what some mythical mages supposedly accomplished in fables. Sometimes users will use PPOs to first aim before charging from LES, thus saving lumarchetrix energy.

Even if anything from strong winds to monster attacks move the user *while* they are in the midst of propelling to the target, the propelling energy will still, in most cases (so long as it is still within range), keep the user heading toward the targeted location, as the attractive AES energy will be resolutely attracted to the target (which is different than the propulsive force applied to the user to reach the location – but any more time in the route will require more MECs). While in mid-air, users cannot change the target until they have either reached their location or switched the UST off (or at least *totally* UPS'd it into DES). Depending on the power level versus the weight of the user, a user *can* latch on to something (like the side of a building) while falling, but in most cases, this is not practical, as there would generally be more force applied to the user while falling compared to the strength of the propulsor. Plus, even if there is enough net force to pull the person to the location while falling, the propulsor's range would still have to be within reach, which may change due to the user's current (albeit decelerating) momentum before changing direction towards the location. The g-force may also be a problem if the falling velocity is too extreme.

Users with average DPLs can create a beam that is around 40 cm in width (though, this size does not matter much), which can reach up to around eight metres in distance while exerting a force of 1,010 newtons, which can lift masses up to 103 kg. Users weighing 100 kg (while wearing no clothes), for example, will take about 7.4 seconds to reach their targets eight metres away, which is just enough time if their lumar-chetrixes are full. For users who are light of weight and do not want excessive (and potentially dangerous) speeds when propelling, they are able to either specifically *lower* the amount of force applied as an ATP (so, this would be established when creating the propulsor) or they can create LPLs. Typically, the former is the best option in this case, as the user will still be able to travel eight metres.

• Note: The alpha-positive propulsor also allows the user to maintain their position once at an arrived location (up to the force per power level), preventing certain forces (up to a limit) from pulling them away. This creates a particular advantage over beta-positive's wall-running propulsors, where the user can be easily pulled away. Technically, the user can use alpha-positive propulsors directly at a wall without propelling toward it if they are already located at its position.

• NCU propulsors: repel users from particular properties that they contact. More specifically, the surrounding ultrachite will cause the user to bounce off solid (and sometimes some liquid) surfaces. The ultrachite will naturally surround the user's body, and while it can be concentrated to certain areas around the aura at will, this does not matter in most contexts, as the ultrachite will automatically concentrate to particular spots (with decent padding) where contact will likely be made (unless the user creates an ATP). That is, if the user is about to fall on the ground with just their feet, the ultrachite will concentrate (from around the user's body) to just under the feet. If the user is about to (and does) contact both the ground with their feet while simultaneously nearing (or touching) a wall with an arm, then the ultrachite's power will split between the two bodily regions.

These propulsors are measured with a *coefficient of restitution* (COR), which is the ratio of the final relative velocity to the initial velocity between two things after their collision, normally ranging from 0 to 1, with 1 being a perfect elastic collision. The average DPL propulsor *effectively* has a (COR) of 1 from a drop height of three metres (at a concentrated area like the feet) on hard surfaces like standard concrete (within the context of a standard atmosphere – that is, normal air resistance – and standard gravity). Any height above three metres will have a COR less than 1, while any height below three metres will have varying increased kinetic energy, so the COR would be greater than 1. These figures are for mages weighing up to 103 kg, so any users weighing more than this will see diminishing results. For weights under 103 kg, conversely, the effect does not get stronger. So, when more mass up to 103 kg is applied to the propulsor (that is, the user's weight 'on' the propulsor) more particles will *trigger* and *activate* up to the propulsor's power level (that is, 103 kg for average DPLs). So, a mage weighing 60 kg will still have the same COR as someone weighing 103 kg. This is not a feature, howbeit, that can be changed with a UPS or an ATP, as it is a phase issue affecting wave function changes.

The ultrachite will also cushion the user to an extent by quantum tunnelling the energy of a fall away from inside the padded area (that would be about 20 cm thick when concentrated at an area like the feet for most power levels). At or below a three-metre fall (with a velocity of 27.5 km/h), the user will technically not start bouncing immediately on impact, and, instead, they will decelerate until zero velocity before propelling back up (again). Any velocity greater than 27.5 km/h while falling will result in an increased net force against the user (as the user would not be *propelling* upwards from zero velocity from the ground), potentially leading to injuries or even death. It is unwise for users to attempt bouncing from heights greater than three metres if their lumarchetrix energies are low because there would be nothing to protect them for the fall. While alpha-negative propulsors protect users when falling, beta-positive propulsors do the same but at a better rate when falling from greater heights. The bonus for this propulsor, comparatively, is the jumping/bouncing ability. The average DPL propulsor also needs a UPC time of 1.5 seconds before being able to be used indefinitely until switched off.

• Note: Legends speak of mythical mages having the ability to cause other entities outside the aura to bounce. That is, when the user would fall to the ground, this would cause a trampoline effect, forcing the other entity into the air. Still, this power seems unusual for alpha-negative, as a power like this would appear more suiting for gamma-positive's entanglement.

## UST Six/Ultra-spacetime crystals (Dimensional Fields):

### • PCU dimensional field DTPs:

1: Create a field of artificial *attractive* gravity, where the particles will concentrate mostly into a small 'singularity' in the centre. The 'singularity', of course, is not a true singularity of concentrated mass and is, instead, a result of altered potential fields that create the effect of gravity. The singularity will also be too small to see, but an aura of strong blue will nonetheless concentrate in the centre of the field. The field itself will be a distinct region of distorted space, which sharply ends at the edge of the field's typically-spherical form by way of a phase loss. In addition, the field will also *dephase* all properties inside the field *from* the existing gravity 'outside' of the field (that is, from the planet and all other mass elsewhere) while simultaneously phasing in a new field of gravity (via wave function changes) that will only be felt within the field's spatial area, essentially creating a 'cliff' in spacetime distortions at the edge of the field.

Since this is a matter of gravity (which is not a force but, instead, an effect of the distortion of the fabric of space), all objects will move towards the singularity – practically no matter their mass (apart from really massive objects, like planets – which would not fit into the field, anyway). This means 'heavy' objects can be as easily lifted up as 'lighter' objects and drawn towards the singularity. While users cannot specifically affect HRFs, they can, however, change the shape of the field to affect particular objects, such as a cup on a table instead of the cup *and* the table, in turn causing this to be akin to *telekinesis*. At the start of its creation via auric equilibrium, the field will also naturally not include the user in its space, so they (the user) will not be affected; but the user can easily change this (without having to create an ATP) to include themselves phased in the field. When users need to shoot discharges, they normally just change or move the field. While a floor can be included in the field, this would not mean that the floor would necessarily move towards the singularity, as the floor would, in nearly all circumstances, be connected to a mass of other properties that would be outside the field, keeping it in place.

While objects *can* accelerate towards the singularity, they will not *necessarily* accelerate towards it, as accelerating objects will begin to dephase from the field's gravity (but this does not mean that they will rephase back into the 'surrounding' gravity outside the field). Basically, the more an object dephases from the gravity (via acceleration), the less gravity that will be 'enacted' on the object, thus decreasing the gravitational acceleration. This is not to say that an object cannot have actual force enacted on it and accelerate (such as a person throwing an object into or from within the field), but this force would be different to the 'force' of the field's gravity. The dephasing, more precisely, only occurs for when objects accelerate towards the central point along the geodesic. So, if a ball was thrown in the field but did not move directly towards the singularity, then it would not dephase, so, interestingly, it would still move towards the singularity, anyway, but not directly (depending on the ball's acceleration versus the field's strength). If the ball was thrown towards the singularity, it would dephase, but it would head towards the singularity, anyway, and it would retain its acceleration (from the actual force) without the extra acceleration of gravity enacting on it.

For all power levels, the level of dephasing will be proportional to the rate of acceleration; thus, all objects will move towards the singularity with a constant velocity *via* the field's gravity. For average DPLs, the field will effectively cause all objects to move towards singularity with an average constant velocity of one metre per second from any direction (where forces like air resistance would not apply, as these would affect the acceleration). The field itself, at the said DPL, will also have a radius of five metres (from the singularity). The singularity would still have to be inside the user's aura, so the extent of the effects could reach about 6.5 metres away from the said user's body. Higher power levels allow for greater speeds and radii, but even the highest speeds are not deadly in most contexts. Technically, the gravity levels at the edge of the field will be less than right next to the singularity itself, but given the short distances relative to the power of the singularities, this basically does not matter.

As with other ultrachite, users can specifically move the singularity with their minds. Users are not, however, able to make objects 'stick' to the singularity, where they can 'throw' the objects via moving the singularity (before then also switching the singularity/field off). If the user moves the singularity too quickly, then the object inside the field may not follow the singularity at the pace of its natural movement towards it; as such, the object could end up being outside the field. Nevertheless, if users carefully move the singularity, then they can effectively move objects around with a coordinated movement. If a user were to lift an object up, for instance, they could lift it high and then turn the aura off, in turn causing the object to fall and cause intended damage. The singularity will not properly form on creation if it will be in the middle of any mass (but singularities can still move gas particles out of the way), nor will a singularity move *into* any things with mass while it is active.

There is an ATP option that grants users the ability to create multiple singularities at the expense of each having less power than a single singularity. These fields, however, will always be separate, and if they are in proximity to one another (as they naturally should always be), then the spatial geometry of each field will press against one another (where the user can still change their shapes – normally at the expense of the other field). Users also have another ATP option that allows them to establish a *singularity node*, which is effectively another singularity within the field, except the node does not have to be within the user's ACE. As such, the range of movement of the singularity can increase; and, in fact, most users will use this ATP more than the DTP. To be clear, though, this does not create two singularities in the field; so, the initial singularity will not function as a normal singularity (so it will not produce any effects).

2: Suck large amounts of non-user-created photomission energy from present ultrachite into the singularity's gravitational abyss, rapidly depleting opponents. The average DPL dimensional field can extract 15% of an average mage's MLP per second by affecting an ultrachite shield of any power level. That is, the singularity can also extract the same amount of energy from stronger shields, so the said 15% here is relative to the mage's MLP (not the strength of the shield per se). The dimensional field can simultaneously extract energy from other sources as well (including non-photomission energy), with the various sources having varying extraction rates that also practically do not affect one another. Put another way, the singularity can extract 15% of an average mage's MLP per second from the abovesaid shield while at the same time being able to extract energy from others sources without the said 15% affecting the extraction of other sources.

Any extracted photomission energy, nevertheless, will return to the Aether without the user absorbing it for their own benefit – fundamentally because of the way the energy is captured before it can be properly processed for absorption. Dimensional fields do not deplete opponents of pure lumarchetrix energy, though, nor other etheric energy. The effect will also extend beyond the field of the first DTP, so this means that the singularity would still be in the user's aura (or effectively in the user's aura via ATPs); accordingly, this DTP will affect the user, too, where auric equilibrium will not protect the user. As a double-edged attack, users typically UPS this DTP off so they are not affected, but some contexts will benefit with using this power.

• NCU dimensional field DTPs:

1: Create a field of artificial *repulsive* gravity, where the particles will concentrate mostly into a small 'singularity' in the centre. The 'singularity', of course, is not a true singularity of concentrated mass and is, instead, a result of altered potential fields that creates the effect of gravity. The singularity will also be too small to see, but an aura of strong blue will nonetheless concentrate in the centre of the field. The field itself will be a distinct region of distorted space, which sharply ends at the edge of the field's typically-spherical form by way of a phase loss. In addition, the field will also *dephase* all properties inside the field *from* the existing gravity 'outside' of the field (that is, from the planet and all other mass elsewhere) while simultaneously phasing in a new field of gravity (via wave function changes) that will only be felt within the field's spatial area, essentially creating a 'cliff' in spacetime distortions at the edge of the field.

Since this is a matter of gravity (which is not a force but, instead, an effect of the distortion of the fabric of space), all objects will move away from the singularity, practically no matter their mass (apart from really massive objects, like planets – which would not fit into the field, anyway). This means 'heavy' objects can be as easily shifted away from the singularity as 'lighter' objects. While users cannot specifically affect HRFs, they can, however, change the shape of the field to affect particular objects, such as a cup on a table instead of the cup *and* the table, in turn causing this to be akin to telekinesis. At the start of its creation via auric equilibrium, the field will also naturally not include the user in its space, so they (the user) will not be affected; but the user can easily change this (without having to create an ATP) to include themselves in the field. When users need to shoot discharges, they normally just change or move the field. While a floor can be included in the field, this would not mean that the floor would necessarily move away from the singularity, as the floor would, in nearly all circumstances, be connected to a mass of other properties that would be outside the field, keeping it in place.

While objects *can* accelerate away from the singularity, they will not *necessarily* accelerate away from it, as accelerating objects will begin to dephase from the field's gravity (but this does not mean that they will rephase back into the 'surrounding' gravity outside the field). Basically, the more an object dephases from the field's gravity (via acceleration), the less gravity that will be 'enacted' on the object, thus decreasing the gravitational acceleration. This is not to say that an object cannot have actual force enacted on it and accelerate (such as a person throwing an object into or from within the field), but this force would be different to the 'force' of the field's gravity. The dephasing, more precisely, only occurs for when objects accelerate away from the central point along the geodesic. So, if a ball was thrown in the field but did not move directly away from the singularity, then it would not dephase, so, interestingly, it would still move away from the singularity, anyway, but not directly (depending on the ball's acceleration versus the field's strength). If the ball was thrown directly away from the singularity, it would dephase, but it would head away from the singularity, anyway, and it would retain its acceleration (from the actual force) without the extra acceleration of gravity enacting on it.

For all power levels, the level of dephasing will be proportional to the rate of acceleration; thus, all objects will move away from the singularity with a constant velocity *via* the field's gravity. For average DPLs, the field will effectively cause all objects to move away from singularity with an average constant velocity of one metre per second from any direction (where forces like air resistance would not apply, as these would affect the acceleration). The field itself, at the said DPL, will also have a radius of five metres (from the singularity). The singularity would still have to be inside the user's aura, so the extent of the effects could reach about 6.5 metres away from the said user's body. Higher power levels allow for greater speeds and radii, but even the highest speeds are not deadly in most contexts. Technically, the gravity levels at the edge of the field will be less than right next to the singularity itself, but given the short distances relative to the power of the singularities, this basically does not matter.

As with other ultrachite, users can specifically move the singularity with their minds. If users carefully move the singularity, then they can effectively move objects around with a coordinated movement. Normally, this power is used to pushing objects out of the way, which might otherwise be too heavy to push or lift. Still, unlike the PCU version of this field, items cannot be easily lifted up, so this (the NCU version) is a little more reckless, which has its contextual pros and cons. Note that repulsive gravity is not itself negation and is, instead, a 'pushing force'. If this power is cleverly used, users can effectively make themselves float. Given that there is no real 'pushing' involved, if a singularity is above the ground (where the ground does not move), the singularity would not, in turn, be pushed upwards. The singularity will also not properly form on creation if it will be in the middle of any mass (but singularities can still move gas particles out of the way), nor will a singularity move *into* any things with mass while it is active.

There is an ATP option that grants users the ability to create multiple singularities at the expense of each having less power than a single singularity. These fields, however, will always be separate, and if they are in proximity to one another (as they naturally should always be), then the spatial geometry of each field will press against one another (where the user can still change their shapes – normally at the expense of the other field). Users also have another ATP option that allows them to establish a *singularity node*, which is effectively another singularity within the field, except the node does not have to be within the user's ACE. As such, the range of movement of the singularity can increase; and, in fact, most users will use this ATP more than the DTP. To be clear, though, this does not create two singularities in the field; so, the initial singularity will not function as a normal singularity (so it will not produce any effects).

2: Automatically affect (normally completely negate) non-user photomission or lumarchetrix (or any other etheric energy) absorption within basically any space of the AOE at nearly all DPLs – regardless of whether a mage is shielded or not. An average DPL singularity will cause a diminishingly-effective TRE to apply, lasting for about nine seconds for the average mage when they first exist the AOE. No ATPs are needed to affect other etheric energies.

• Note: UST Six's superiority is found in its omni-directional range of movement, whereas all other alpha attacks (positive or negative) are restrained. Additionally, magnetic forces (ultrachite or otherwise) will not affect the singularity's gravity (as gravity is not technically a force), but they can work against it by pulling or pushing properties; or, they *may* still affect the ultrachite itself, in turn affecting the gravity. Masses already magnetized may or may not break apart, as (the) gravity is not normally strong enough for particular magnetic attachments; and so, the two strongly-magnetized masses, if together in the dimensional field, will nevertheless move as one. Even if one mass is outside the dimensional field, the other mass may still drag the other into the field (or push it out). Still, there are other considerations, such as the level of gravity outside of the field. Certain forces can still cause the fields, in both PCU and NCU cases, to not fully phase away from the outside gravity, but the effects of the gravity inside the field will, nevertheless, only be felt inside the fields. Both dimensional fields also do not need any UPC for their DTPs or ATPs.

• Note: Legends speak of mythical mages that were able to cause nonlocal effects for both positive and negative alpha dimensional fields. The physics behind the nonlocality is valid, but there are still confusing elements as to how this phenomenon supposedly worked. Basically, the singularity would effectively bend the CSUs at its location so much that the field would *force* the CSUs at the primary location to entangle with those at the other location, in turn opening a wormhole. This wormhole, however, would be too small for people to travel through, so effectively, only the gravity would be felt at the other location. The bending of the fabric of space would not be (nor is not) limited by distance per se; however, the further the distance from the user's location, the greater the difference would be in the geometry of the fabric of the space relative to the original location.

This means that it would have been (and is) harder to make a proper connection and then warp the other location. Specifically, since there would have been a greater spatial distance between the CSUs in the field and those in the other location to be warped, there would have accordingly been greater decoherence. Because nonlocality would have used more energy for the deformation and connection processes, the singularity itself must have accordingly been weaker. The problem with this legend, though, comes with how the mythical mages were able to actually target nonlocal areas in the first place (which, nevertheless, can actually be done with gamma-positive dimensional fields, and this process is well understood).

### 3.6.5.2: Beta Class (Synchronization & Desynchronization):

#### UST One/Ultra-solid (Shields):

• PCU shield DTPs:

1: Strengthen the user's level of synchronization with their lumarchetrix via a UPC. An ATP is also available for increasing the synchronization with one's GAP. Average DPL shields require a 64-second UPC time, with the DTP lasting 32 seconds before a cooldown period of 64 seconds occurs. When charged, the DTP:

I) Reduces *personally-caused* overcharging costs when increasing the energy of ultrachite beyond the user's DPLs for HPLs. Since undercharging does not exist, the shield does not lower the costs of DPLs. Moreover, the effect does not apply to LPLs, as overcharging does not exist in itself at such rates. The average, single DPL discharge costs the average mage 1.2% of their MLP for the CEC (not accounting for the MECs), and so, if the user doubles the power, the discharge would then cost 2.4% of their MLP *plus* the *initial* proportional 2.4% for overcharge (at average DPL rates), totalling 4.8% of their MLP per discharge. Accordingly, the beta-positive DPL shield would reduce the added 2.4% overcharge down in half, in turn causing the HPL discharge to totally cost 3.6% of the user's MLP per shot. If the user were to create a beta-positive shield that happened to be more powerful than its DPL, then, while there would be a net increase in overcharging for the use of the shield (even after its own reduction in overcharging), there would be an increased reduction (that is, beyond 50%) for the aforesaid discharge.

II) Establishes a stronger connection with the Aether, which increases the user's MLP, with average mages (with their respective DPLs) increasing their MLPs from 100% to 200%. Carefully note that this increases the *MLP*; it does not automatically give the user more energy, so when the power is activated, the user will only begin with 100% of their MLP, not 200%. Since there is only a *stronger* connection with the Aether instead of the user connecting for the first time, there is no flood of new energy. Even when the user uses any energy (no matter how much), they can still fill their lumarchetrix up to the *new* maximum – so long as the DTP remains active; afterwards, the user's MLP returns to its original maximum, with the amount of energy in their lumarchetrix at that point being dependant on how much energy was left in their increased MLP. For example, if a user has, say, 153% of their MLP full when the effect finishes, then they would revert to 100% (their normal full MLP). If, however, they have, say, 72% when the effect finishes, then they would remain with 72%.

The user will also be able to increase their LRR, with average DPL shields being able to increase the average user's LRR from 0.8333% per second to 1.666% per second. In most circumstances, the user will not ever reach 200% of their MLP *by themselves* before the power finishes; and normally to help increase the amount of energy before using it on more costly ultrachite (like dimensional fields), the user will use alpha-positive discharges and shoot mage opponents. Nevertheless, when coupled with the fourth DTP (mentioned below), users can connect with other mages to fuel their energy and reach their new (but temporary) MLPs.

III) Helps the user to reduce LCIs, aiding in creating: firstly, STU; secondly, any UST while using multiple USTs and/or PACs; and thirdly, HPLs. All mages possess instabilities channelling particular energies – even supreme mages cannot create ultra-chite too far beyond their DPLs – and so, the beta-positive shield's power reduces these LCIs, ensuring that UST forms can even manifest on creation. The average mage already respectively suffers about 20% and 30% LCI rates when creating the STU of propulsors and dimensional fields (of any power levels); and so, when an average user uses a respective DPL beta-positive shield, these figures respectively drop to about 2% and 3%.

The average mage can easily channel multiple USTs at once, only having a 0.6% instability rate when creating a second concurrent UST form, with the second UST potentially having the LCI applied to it on its creation. There is then an exponential increase for each additional UST used, so three USTs amount to 1.2%, four amount to 2.4%, five amount to 4.8%, and six amount to 9.6%. Specifically, if the user manages to create three concurrent UST forms (such as shields, discharges, and vortices) without any channelling problem but then attempts to create another concurrent UST, like a soaker bomb, then the (attempted creation of the) soaker bomb would suffer the LCI issue (at the abovesaid 2.4% rate), potentially disallowing the user from creating the UST for a particular amount of time.

When an average user uses a respective DPL beta-positive shield, the base figure (of 0.6%) respectively drops to 0%, and the new base (of 0.6%) will be shifted to the creation of four concurrent USTs. Therefore, a 1.2% LCI rate will be applied to mages attempting to create five concurrent UST forms and 2.4% for six USTs. In contrast to USTs themselves, the average mage can normally channel multiple *PACs* at once with a 2% instability rate for attempting to use two classes, 8% for three, and 32% for four. It is not the PAC itself that becomes unstable but, instead, the last UST created (that is, on creation). When an average user uses a respective DPL beta-positive shield, these figures respectively drop to 0%, 0.8%, and 3.2%.

As soon as the average mage attempts to double their DPL of any UST, they will experience a 99.99% LCI rate – for the most part making it extremely unlikely to create such ultrachite. So, if the user attempts to increase their DPL by 50%, they will then experience an LCI rate of roughly 50%. When an average user uses a respective DPL shield, these figures (of 99.99% and 50%) respectively drop to around 30% and 15%. Nevertheless, any HPL used beyond double the average user's DPL will lead to a rapid rise in instability, with most figures quickly jumping back to 99.99% and then 100% soon after rising above the aforesaid 30% rate. For those with advanced power levels or higher, these statistics basically apply as well, except the users would not be able to double their power when creating HPLs, as power levels after the advanced rank linearly increase. While master and supreme mages barely – if at all – benefit from the first three feats (that is, creating STU and using multiple USTs and PACs at once without LCI problems), they certainly benefit from being more easily able to use HPLs.

IV) Decreases the desynchronizing effects of another mage's beta-negative energies (or many other non-ultrachite properties) with regards to the user and/or their lumarchetrix. The average DPL-shielded user can ignore about 50% of the effects from an average DPL discharge when calculated at 100% APL effectively just via the SUC. While the TREs are not halved in time per se but rather in strength, this, in turn, practically affects the timeframe. Note that this feat is not a default effect of the aforementioned effects of this DTP *potentially* and *indirectly* offsetting an opponent's negative effects; instead, its own power is what directly ignores an opponent's negative effects.

• Note: The statistics for the GAP ATP vary greatly due to many types of variables to consider. Still, there are some statistics that basically remain the same, such as average DPLs doubling the GAP from 100% to 200%. Technically, all the other schools of magic (including psychicism – whether through rituals or not) feature spells (and abilities) that can help increase their GAP and their recharge rates, but these are generally not that effective.

• Note: Legends speak of mythical mages having shields that possessed a unique TRE, where the shield would also prevent EEE when the user depleted before the shield reactivated when new lumarchetrix energy could refuel the shield. However, such mages supposedly could not have their shield disengaged for too long after reaching LED for this feat to take effect, nor could they have already reached EEE before activating the shield, nor could they repeat this effect infinitely. The TRE was supposedly only a few seconds long after the mage depleted, where it would then diminish rapidly before being rendered null. The statistics of these stories greatly differed for how many times the process could be repeated as an individual user.

• Note: Legends also speak of mythical mages being able to use their beta-positive shields to increase their abilities to channel unknown kinds of USTs and PACs.

2: Automatically keep the user's mind synchronized, which, in turn, decreases mental desynchronizations, whether from ultrachite or non-ultrachite attacks. The average DPL-shielded user can decrease the effects of an average DPL opponent's beta-negative discharges and vortices by about 60% and 65% when calculated at 100% APL effectively just via the SUC. *When* the shield either overloads or is switched off, the user will gain a *chance* for a TRE that lasts an applicable 1.25 seconds, countering about 80% of the effects of average DPL beta-negative discharges – enough to prevent at least four discharges from sending the user unconscious *if* desynchronizing levels were not already nearly close (enough) to the unconscious-inducing threshold (which is generally unlikely against the shielded). The TRE for supreme-level mages will also end before their shields are able to recover from an overload, so no mage is able to use the shield to avoid being sent unconscious in all contexts. The TRE's chance is based on the DTP's stability to last after the shield drops; and for users with average

DPLs, the chance of a TRE occurring is about 18%. The statistics for non-ultrachite attacks and phenomena used against the user, on the other hand, vary based on the type and amount/number, as well as the context.

As an ATP, the user can more specifically affect the *duration* of the mental desynchronizations rather than the susceptibility to them. While the DTP directly reduces the *strength* of mental desynchronizations (and, thus, by default, the duration), the proportionality of the latter alone (that is, the duration) is much better in the context of the ATP. For clarification, the user, for the most part, will still be susceptible to mental desynchronizations (at standard levels), but such desynchronizations will not last long. Of course, should a mental desynchronization cause the user to fall unconscious while shielded, then the shield would deactivate. However, when the shield either overloads or is switched off (whether the user is conscious or not), the user will nonetheless gain a short TRE, where the duration of unconsciousness that a *desynchronizing* attack, specifically, causes will still be reduced. The abovesaid chance rate for the TRE is also the same for this ATP.

In the context of a desynchronizing attack against an unshielded average DPL user with a TRE (of 1.25 seconds), the duration of the effects from a single average DPL beta-negative discharge will reduce from ten minutes to one minute. Any subsequent attacks (specifically, up to eight said discharges) on the user during the TRE will only add on roughly one additional minute of unconsciousness. When the unconsciousness continues after the TRE finishes, the timeframe of the standard level of unconsciousness will not return to normal, so the user will still benefit from the TRE. However, any subsequent attacks on the user after the TRE ends will result in standard levels of unconsciousness (that the attacks would normally induce) against the user. Of course, if the user was already unconscious before the TRE began (as a result of the mental desynchronizations from many discharges – which is rare, given that a shield would normally overload before this occurs), then any reduction in the effects of the discharges fired upon the user during the TRE would not necessarily be redundant because the user would still have received the ATP's benefit of reduced unconsciousness while shielded.

While this ATP might not sound useful (since the user would still fall unconscious), a user will stand to benefit within the context of a battle where, for whatever reason, their opponents may not be able to shoot the user again after the TRE finishes. So, if, for example, there are four attackers against the user with three allies, the attackers might send the user unconscious – who happens to be behind cover when they fall. With the cover blocking the line of fire, the attackers would not, then, be able to fire upon the user to cause standard levels of unconsciousness (after the TRE finishes) – and, importantly, they (the attackers) would also not be able to reach the user due to potentially having to run into the firing sight of the user's allies, who would still be conscious. As the battle continues, the user would regain consciousness and then start over.

3: Grant the user a limited version of *synchro-reception* – a power found in mysticism magic and (generally advanced) psychicism. This ability allows a user to focus on a particular object, person, or phenomenon and synchronize with them, in turn allowing the user to (later) identify them with visual cues (like brighter or darker colours) and/or intuition via etheric overlays. Average DPL users can sense two standard objects or phenomena within a 15-metre range after a focused synchronization process of roughly 10 seconds (that is, the user normally must either look at the target or try to tune into them for 10 seconds). Note that this is not a UPC.

If the user wishes to change targets, they need only synchronize with something else or switch the shield off; alternatively, they may simply untune the target(s). Synchronizing with an ally, for example, may help prevent future friendly fire, whereas synchronizing with an opponent may help locate them (so long as they are within range). This latter example is especially helpful for when the user is trying to locate invisible opponents that are using gamma-positive shields; however, in almost all cases, the user needs to synchronize with the opponent *before* they turn invisible. Other examples can include pitfalls (such as literal pitfalls), helping the user to avoid accidentally later approaching their locations.

• Note: Generally, only water mages or advanced psychics adequately benefit from this power, as the cues, otherwise, are generally inconsistent, and they may easily become distorted due to various internal, environmental, and non-physical phenomena. So, sometimes the cues either will not work properly or they may not work at all (whether for a given period or ever). Explicitly, this is more so an issue of alignment type (and psychic abilities) than phasarchement power levels.

4: Allow the user to actively synchronize with other mutually-permitting mages (who are also using the same shield) to share and redistribute lumarchetrix (and other etheric) energies. All shielded users must directly touch at least one of the other shields in the process, and each receiver can only gain an amount up to their MLP (which works well with one aspect of the first DTP mentioned above). The average user with a respective DPL shield will normally take about 10 seconds to fully synchronize with another average user with a DPL shield. Without warrant, users can *technically* hack into another person's energy. However, even elite mages struggle with this feat – even when focused, which is hard enough during a battle, unless they hack during a synchronization taking place between two average mages (which is itself hard to maintain, as the two mages could simply stop at any moment). Mages of superior magical status, nevertheless, typically avoid hacking, anyway, as it is more strategic to use other attacks to siphon energy; plus, their energy *could* also reduce, so hacking is virtually never an issue. To an extent, a user can also synchronize the PUCs with others mages. This DTP can be useful in various ways, such as helping one user have seemingly unlimited energy for a focused goal.

• Note: The synchronization process is not a UPC. Also, to connect with and share other etheric energies, an ATP is needed (with all parties possessing the ATP).

• NCU shield DTPs:

1: Automatically desynchronize particular properties; and, within the context of phasarchement magic, this specifically affects non-user UST Two and Three particles that come into contact with the shield, switching their PEP from AES to DES, in turn neutralizing their effects *as if* a 'boosted' UPI ability. While this does not create UPIs, nor *technically* boost UPIs, the shield's CBE properties (for this DTP) do not have to suffer from UIO, nor need any cooldowns; thus, the DTP does not practically reduce in power. Accordingly, average users with respective DPL shields *virtually* (but not actually) receive a 100% boost in UPI strength. This means that it should take about 48, instead of 24, consecutive average DPL discharges to reach 100% APL against the average user's DPL shield (should all the discharges each successfully pass the shield's UAS). However, since it takes 12 said discharges to overload the shield in question, the average user does not *fully* benefit from this boost; *but* this does not mean that they (the user) would not benefit before the overloading occurs. That is, it nevertheless means that each said discharge prior to overloading will only reach 2.083% APL build instead of 4.167%. So, at 12 attacks (that all successfully pass the UAS chance check), this means the user would only experience about 25% APL against them.

Regardless, although extra attacks would be required to bring a more powerful shield to 100% UIO, the powerful shield in question would also naturally have a greater UOT; thus, the increase in the desynchronization effect would not be left totally redundant by having a shield overload before attacks could reach 100% APL. Despite all of these benefits, the DTP does not increase the UAS chance check. In contrast to alpha-negative shields that can totally ignore an attack's APL (due to reflecting attacks), beta-negative shields may seem like the weaker option of the two shields, but consider that no UPC is required for the beta-negative shield, so this DTP is constantly active (unless the user, for whatever reason, decides to switch it off). While this DTP can affect non-ultrachite matter as well, there is generally not that much affectable matter that is applicable in most battles.

2: Automatically desynchronize from (and thus avoid) ultrachite discharges – and (many kinds of) non-ultrachite things – that either normally chain via synchron-ization, lock onto, or home in on energies, particularly ultrachite shields. For the average DPL shield, this effect totally eludes the homing feats from any number of (simultaneous) average DPL ultrachite discharges. However, if one of the said discharges hits the shield, the power of the DTP fades for a moment before returning; and for average DPLs, this is about four seconds. The statistics for non-ultrachite properties used against the user, on the other hand, vary based on the type, amount, and/or number, as well as the context.

3: Automatically desynchronize ultrachite and non-ultrachite-based mental synchronizations that are inflicted on the user. The average DPL-shielded user can decrease the effects of an average DPL opponent's beta-positive discharges and vortices respectively by about 60% and 65% when calculated at 100% APL effectively just via the SUC. When the shield either overloads or is switched off, the user will gain a chance for a TRE that lasts an applicable two seconds, countering about 80% of the effects of average DPL beta-positive discharges. The TRE's chance is based on its stability to last after the shield drops; and for users with average DPLs, the chance of a TRE occurring is about 22%. While statistics vary based on the individual user and their state of mind and goals at the time, averages still apply; for more information on such statistics, see the beta-positive discharge section. As an ATP, the user can more specifically affect the *duration* of the mental synchronizations rather than the susceptibility to them. While the DTP directly reduces the *strength* of mental synchronizations (and, thus, by default, the duration), the proportionality of the latter alone (that is, the duration) is much better in the context of the ATP.

4: Automatically desynchronize from the conscious *focus* of those on a battlefield by emitting a conscious-altering, modulated magnetic field (with particular pulses and oscillations), thereby increasing threat-reduction levels for the user. It does not, however, increase the pacification or allegiance of opponents. This feat, nevertheless, is mainly effective for fights where the user has allies who can take the brunt of the focus from opponents; so, when the user has no more active allies, most sentient hostile beings will typically *then* focus their attention and actions on the user. It also does not stop opponents from accidentally attacking the user, nor intentionally attacking the user's *location*.

This power even manages to affect shielded mages by desynchronizing from the effects of magnetic shielding (so, the effects effectively pass through shields), with average DPL shields mostly affecting other mages also using average DPL shields. Still, mentally-strong and/or trained individuals can shrug this effect off. This DTP even affects robots. The average DPL shield can emit a field with a 16 m radius before the effect drops to zero by way of a phase loss. The statistics for affected opponents vary greatly, especially when also considering the context, which may itself even have variously and rapidly-shifting factors. If other allies or mages are using this shield at the same time, then various power-level and contextual checks need to be made to determine who would receive the least focus (in terms of merely analysing a situation).

## UST Two/Ultra-plasma (Discharges):

### • PCU discharge DTPs:

1: Synchronize (that is, firstly home in on) with incoming, non-user ultrachite discharges in the air before hitting and synchronizing with them to nullify or at least weaken them before they reach their target. To nullify another discharge, the user's discharge needs to be of equal or greater power to the other discharge, otherwise, only weakening occurs. When a user's discharge is stronger (and nullifies the other discharge), it can continue moving through the air (albeit at reduced power), whereas if the user's discharge only weakens the other discharge, it will cease to exist. While normally discharges are volatile and explode on contact with other discharges, it is possible for the weakened discharges not to explode (and, thus, continue flying in the air) because the beta-positive discharge does not trigger the explosive nature of other discharges and, instead, only synchronizes and harmonizes with other discharges. When a discharge is weakened, part of it will remain in the air where it was weakened, floating in DES until it disappears back into the Aether.

Users can alter the DTP to an ATP to make their discharge automatically splinter off *before* hitting multiple discharges at a reduced strength (thus, typically weakening the non-user discharges instead of nullifying them). Since discharges typically fly through the air at a relentless rate during battles, this DTP is normally switched off when channelling in order for users to focus on just hitting opponents instead of their discharges. Likewise, while beta-positive discharges prefer to synchronize with *incoming* matter, they may also synchronize with *non-incoming* parallel discharges (usually from allies), so this is another reason why this DTP may be switched off or at least lowered in intensity. The DTP does not change too much between power levels, so it is really the power level of the discharge itself that determines whether another discharge will be weakened or nullified. A user's discharge *can* synchronize with *some* non-ultrachite things, but these things must be very similar to ultrachite discharges, and these occurrences are rare.

2: Chain on impact to similar HRFs to the HRF that which the discharge initially hits, causing the power to split into a weaker *set* of DTP effects on the next hits. So, if a discharge were to hit an ultrachite shield, it would chain to other ultrachite shields, whereas if the discharge were to hit a humanoid body, it would chain to other humanoid bodies. As another example, if the discharge were to hit a metallic structure, it would chain to other metallic structures. Nevertheless, if the discharge were to synchronize with another discharge (by means of the first DTP), then, if any part of the discharge remained after the nullification of the other discharge, no chaining would occur. As with discharges in general, QDFs and QTPs will still prevent the chained particles only hitting a person's clothing (that might be in the way), and not the person, for example. Moreover, the FTPs will typically surround the HRF instead of merely charging the HRF. Still, if the QDF is behind an HRF that will not simply allow for quantum tunnelling (like certain body armours versus the power level of the discharge), then technically, the discharge will *attempt* to reach the QDF (and potentially fail) or it will go to another HRF that is (more easily) affectable.

The average DPL discharge can chain to three different HRFs within a radius of about four metres (from the original HRF target) before being able to potentially chain once more with a chance rate of 50%. If the discharge particles chain once more, then the original HRF may be hit again. The first of the chained HRFs will also each have roughly a third of the energy of the original discharge, which can be respectively chained to another three different HRFs other than any of the other current (first) chained entities. The initial target (or targets of any chain) will experience very little (but not no) energy and effects, so it is ultimately only the final chained targets that will receive the main brunt of the divided discharge. Also, at no point will the chaining ever hit the user unless some other force warps the chaining process. The user can also alter the DTP to an ATP to increase or reduce either the number of chained HRFs, the radius, the number of source chains (that is, how many times it chains), or the chance rate for the final chaining at the cost of the other three functions.

As another ATP, the user can cause the chained energy to turn as hard, strong, and tough as the mean (average) of the HRF's surface properties, which the discharge initially hits, but at the cost of only having it chain once. Even at supreme DPLs, this ATP will only chain once. The are, of course, limits to how hard, strong, and tough a chained discharge can become, so power levels matter. Just like how chained energies are of lesser strength than the initial discharge, the transformed energy in this context (for example, if changed to be as hard as steel) would still be measurably smaller than the original discharge. While smaller, if the discharge turns as hard as steel, the chained pieces will still not be as powerful as bullets due to the comparative lack of speed. Technically, if a discharge were to coincidentally hit an incoming bullet, it would chain to other bullets in the air (usually incoming bullets), butting them away. Interestingly, due to the force of the original moving bullet, the chained discharge would actually move much faster than after hitting a stationary target.

Regardless of whether the discharge has an ATP or not, if no other similar HRFs exist within the radius, then the energy will remain at the initial location, only affecting the sole victim or object. This DTP has pros and cons (along with the ATPs), and depending on one's strategy, some mages tend to switch this off when channelling. Its negatives include potential friendly-fire, in addition to causing each chained attack to be weaker than a single discharge, thus potentially drawing out the battle without focusing on and eliminating one opponent at a time to reduce the opposing team's aggregate strength *per period* (not the entire duration) in a battle. That is, it has a weak *force concentration*, which causes it to be a *force divider* – itself. However, regarding tactical advantages, if the user successively strikes multiple targets, this will prevent their opponents from cooling down their UOT and UPIs. Also, by striking just one opponent out of cover, the chaining can reach opponents behind covers. Sometimes opponents may not realize that they have been hit with a chained attack, or they may be more cautious than normal, so it also acts as a pseudo suppressive fire.

3: Synchronize with an opponent's mind on impact, inducing varying degrees of *harmony*. Even though it is the discharge's energy that synchronizes with the opponent, the ultrachite is nevertheless connected to the user's being via PUC, and, thus, a link establishes between the user and the opponent. This power affects practically all sentient beings (including biochemical synthetics), while mechanical robots have a *chance* to be affected in the same way; but if this chance check does succeed, they are simply affected with lag instead (which can nevertheless eventually lead to other complications with enough attacks). There are three distinct levels of effect that occur in the following order on a spectrum: *calmness, pacification*, and *support*. While various levels of calmness apply instantly, pacification and support can only occur when a certain threshold from the preceding effect has been attained. Calmness essentially reduces the opponent's reaction times, attitude, and effort, while pacification stops them from fighting altogether. The support phase, however, will cause opponents to non-aggressively defend the user, which normally involves them standing in front of other opponents so they receive their attacks instead. While statistics vary based on the individual and their state of mind and goals at the time -- and there are also non-user-related environmental variables to consider -- averages still apply.

Effectively just via the SUC, the average DPL discharge will cause roughly an accumulative (per hit) 0.33336% calmness effect (calculated on the calmness-pacification-support spectrum) for the *common*, average DPL-shielded mage at an initial 4.167% APL in standard combat settings; at 100% APL, this amounts to about 8% per hit. To reach the full calmness and then minimum pacification and support thresholds against the aforesaid shielded, 100%, 200%, and 300% worth of individual average DPL attacks are respectively required. This means that the average DPL user would need to launch 24 roughly-consecutive attacks for full calmness, 37 to reach pacification (meaning 13 attacks would be at 100% APL), and 49 to reach support (with 25 attacks at 100% APL). For the unshielded mage opponent (and most unprotected biological humanoids), a single average DPL discharge will cause full calmness, while two in total will cause pacification, whereas three in total would be needed for support. Monsters typically have a threshold level for each effect akin to shielded mages, along with other entities employing UPI-equivalents. Robots, on the other hand, vary greatly per type.

Since the effects are accumulative, an AAE applies after the FTPs end, and for average DPLs against most normal biological humanoids, this lasts about eight seconds (with another four seconds of diminishing intensities) per hit, which can stack for each additional shot up to four times, thus *fully* lasting 32 seconds per shot (calculated without the diminishing time that would be added). Moreover, each stage and its effects will fully last at their level of effect, so the effects do not gradually drop off through degeneration; that is, the effects sharply end. Accordingly, it is possible to bring a shielded opponent mage to pacification and support before they overload *if* their overloading rates recover faster proportionally to the AAE's stacked seconds – *and* if most of the attacks pass the UAS check to build APL. In some cases after the effects wear off (depending on various factors and the affected individuals), opponents may continue to refrain from fighting, or they may still even support the user (as if by momentum).

4: Synchronize an opponent's current generated ultrachite with their lumarchetrix, locking the opponent out from changing or using other USTs, PACs, and ACTs they are currently using (bar UPCs and UPSs). Moreover, it will prevent users from switching to ATPs or vice vera (to DTPs). Note that this DTP cannot force opponents to stop using their currently-used USTs. When an average user with a respective DPL discharge hits an average DPL-shielded opponent, the chance of this effect succeeding is 2% at an initial 4.167% APL effectively just via the SUC, 24% at 50% APL, and 48% at 100% APL. If the said user were to shoot once at an average unshielded mage, then there would be a 100% chance of success.

The user can alternatively change the DTP to an ATP to limit the creation of any new ultrachite that the opponent may form to be of beta and only beta. Of course, this does not force the opponent to create ultrachite, nor 'switch' any active ultrachite to beta, as one does not technically *switch* any active ultrachite particles; instead, mages *stop* channelling a specific UST form before *creating* another form; this even applies for PACs, ACTs, and DTPs-to-ATPs or vice versa. With an average DPL discharge against the average-powered opponent, a diminishingly-effective TRE of six seconds also applies. The chance applies per attack, not during the TRE, so the TRE only extends the locking effect if the attack was successful. If a TRE is still in effect after a prior successful attack, a new attack that fails will not undo the success of the first attack. This power can also affect GAP magics as an ATP, preventing mages from switching spells.

• NCU discharge DTPs:

1: Desynchronize from certain forces (like magnetic forces – including potentials) that draw in discharges. As a result, a user's discharge may be able to ignore the effects of an attractive beacon and, instead, continue on its normal trajectory. One of the only major effects that this cannot ignore is gravity (due to merely following the curved geometry of spacetime), so UST Six dimensional fields can still alter the discharge's trajectory. Since, in some cases, a user may actually want the discharge to hit an attractive target, this DTP is then normally switched off.

2: Desynchronize mental faculties, affecting a being's level of consciousness. A single average DPL discharge can send virtually all unshielded mages (and most unprotected biological humanoids) totally unconscious for roughly 10 minutes without aid, while two discharges will lead to just over an hour of unconsciousness, whereas three attacks will cause a full eight hours of unconsciousness. Typically, any additional discharges beyond this point, though, will only diminishingly lengthen the duration; although, with *numerous* attacks, one can be sent into a coma. To affect shielded mages (that is, to reach the *unconsciousness threshold* of an initial 10 minutes), the average user would have to launch about 62 roughly-consecutive average DPL discharges at the average DPL-shielded opponent (meaning 38 attacks would be at 100% APL). Accordingly, it is possible (but highly improbable) to bring a shielded opponent mage to full unconsciousness effectively just via the SUC before they overload *if* their overloading rates recover faster proportionally to the AAE's stacked seconds – *and* if most of the attacks pass the UAS check to build APL.

Before the attack reaches the 10-minute threshold, a mage victim will not lose their ability to use magic, so basically nothing occurs. Technically, the attack could cause a victim mage to lose their ability to use magic, but the victim mages are always sent fully unconscious first. Shielded and unshielded mages, nevertheless, may still use aids (such as potions) to prevent or reduce the strength of the attack. Still, when this occurs, it normally only takes another (or a couple more) shot(s) to send them unconscious. For those who awake after being sent unconscious, they will usually resume their business with a normal state of mind. This attack can also affect robots in different ways, and it normally takes many hits to send a monster unconscious. It can also affect the consciousness of other biological entities differently, so pure unconsciousness does not have to just result.

• Note: Although other UST and PAC discharges may have incapacitating or even (potentially) deadly effects, beta-negative discharges are a mage's primary method for incapacitating opponents. Therefore, it is used in most combat situations (at least, generally, after an opponent's shield has overloaded). Still, when fighting an entity with desynchronizing resistances like monsters, for example, it *may* be prudent to use other types of discharge attacks merely for the sake of escaping the monster rather than defeating it (assuming the following DTP is not useful).

3: Desynchronize mental faculties (in a different way to the second DTP), affecting a being's sense of *time*. Primarily, this DTP induces *tachypsychia*, *chronostasis*, and a *flash-lag effect*. Basically, these respectively: one: induce a psychological phenomenon, where the victim will experience the world around them speed up; two: cause the victim to experience a temporal illusion, where the initial moment after looking at something will seem longer; and three: cause the victim to experience a visual illusion, where a flash and an object that are in alignment with each other will appear to be displaced. Each attack will only cause TREs, not AAEs, with average DPLs normally causing 12-second TREs for the average biological humanoid. Robots and other entities can be affected with this effect, and it can actually be quite effective against monsters, causing this attack to be often used against monsters.

Unlike other kinds of discharge attacks, the DTP can also desynchronize from HRFs. Accordingly, the FTPs will produce a modulated magnetic field that will affect anything in the vicinity – but the effects diminish greatly with distance from the FTPs, so they normally only affect nearby things. There is also a chance that the magnetic field might desynchronize from the magnetic shielding of an opponent's ultrachite shield. This means that the DTP's effects can fully affect shielded opponents (assuming that there is any APL – and that the opponents are not mentally resistant to them), with the overall effect either fully desynchronizing from the said shielding or not. So, the average DPL discharge will have a 30% chance to *fully* affect an opponent with an average DPL shield (at whatever APL level the discharge is at). For clarification, even though the APL might only be at 8.333%, there would still be about a 30% chance of affecting the opponent, but the strength of the effects would be much lower (but the TREs would still likely be around 12 seconds).

ATPs alter the strength of each effect. By default, this power also desynchronizes an opponent's energies from their mind, thus causing instinctual mental commands to take longer to follow through to ultrachite forms. For example, an opponent may take longer to properly concentrate the particles in a UST Two aura into a blast ball. This effect (which is not another DTP or ATP) can also be applied to other magics, in addition to certain creatures, monsters, and entities with non-magic powers and properties (such as lithoid beings that use their minds and electrical energies to move anatomical stones around their bodies).

4: Desynchronize an opponent mage's lumarchetrix channel (or other etheric energies – including their GAP – as an ATP) on impact effectively just via the SUC against the shielded and direct (stronger) influence for the unshielded. The DTP affects a few different aspects of an opponent's channel, and each kind of desynchronization will individually vary per subject mage, but there are normally corresponding levels across all of them at once. All of the following statistics are, moreover, non-accumulative. Beta-negative discharges:

I) Affect an opponent's DPLs, causing each UST to be overcharged when used. If an average affected opponent with a respective DPL shield were to create a DPL discharge worth 1.2% of their MLP, then the average *user's* DPL beta-negative's desynchronizing would cause an overcharge cost of the same amount of energy used (1.2%) when calculated at 100% APL. If at an initial 4.167% APL, this figure would be roughly 0.038%. If the said affected mage were to create an HPL discharge worth double their DPL at 2.4% of their MLP, then the desynchronizing effects (when at 100% APL) would double the normal overcharging costs (which are already double the DPL); therefore, the overcharging would total 4.8% of their MLP instead of 2.4%. In total, the affected opponent would be paying 7.2% for their discharge. However, if the opponent mage in question were unshielded, then the desynchronizing would be at roughly double the 100% APL threshold with a single average DPL attack; that is, the opponent would be overcharged at a rate of 9.6% of their MEP, thus their discharge would cost 12% of their MLP. With average DPLs against the average mage, a diminishingly-effective TRE also applies for about seven seconds.

• Note: while there is a doubling of costs in the above example, this does not mean that the lumarchetrix would be 100% desynchronized; otherwise, the affected mage would lose 33% of their MLP per second (assuming an LCR of 33% per second).

II) Desynchronize an opponent's lumarchetrix from the Aether, preventing or at least limiting their LRR. The average user with their respective DPL discharge will cause an average DPL-shielded opponent to respectively lose about 2.085% and 50% of their connection to the Aether at 4.167% and 100% APLs. At 50% APL, this would be 25%. Since the average mage has an LRR from zero to 100% in about 120 seconds, this amounts to a standard rate of roughly 0.8333% per second. Accordingly, at an initial 4.167% APL, this would cause the affected mage to recharge at a rate of 0.816% per second; and, at 100% APL, this would amount to 0.417% per second. For 50% APL, this would be 0.625% per second. If an average user with a single DPL discharge were to affect an average unshielded opponent, then, within this context, instant and total desynchronization would occur. With average DPLs against the average mage, a diminishingly-effective TRE also applies for about seven seconds.

• Note: Strangely, beta-negative discharges do not shrink a target's MLP, despite the reverse being an option for users of beta-negative shields. Still, a similar option is available for users of gamma-negative discharges, where they can 'sever' a portion of an opponent's lumarchetrix energy.

III) Affect an opponent's LCIs, which aid in creating: firstly, STU; secondly, any UST while using multiple USTs and/or PACs; and thirdly, HPLs. As a result, the affected mage will suffer increased instabilities fuelling their ultrachite with photo-mission energy, causing potential full instability that temporarily prevents the user from creating the aforementioned ultrachite. The average mage already respectively suffers about 20% and 30% LCI rates when creating the STU of propulsors and dimensional fields (of any power levels); and so, when an average user uses a respective DPL discharge against the average DPL-shielded opponent, these figures respectively rise to 60% and 70% when at 100% APL, and 100% for each against the unshielded.

The average mage can easily channel multiple USTs at once, only having a 0.6% instability rate when creating a second concurrent UST form, with the second UST potentially having the LCI applied to it on its creation. There is then an exponential increase for each additional UST used, so three USTs amount to 1.2%, four amount to 2.4%, five amount to 4.8%, and six amount to 9.6%. Specifically, if the mage manages to create three concurrent UST forms (such as shields, discharges, and vortices) without any channelling problem but then attempts to create another concurrent UST, like a soaker bomb, then the (attempted creation of the) soaker bomb would suffer the LCI issue (at the abovesaid 2.4% rate), potentially disallowing the mage from creating the UST for a particular amount of time. When an average user fires a respective DPL discharge against the average DPL-shielded opponent, this base figure rises to 9.6% when at 100% APL, with each additional UST used doubling from the new base amount; so, three USTs amount to 19.2%, four amount to 38.4%, five amount to 76.8%, and six amount to 153.6% (so, basically 100%).

In contrast to USTs themselves, the average mage can normally channel multiple *PACs* at once with a 2% instability rate for attempting to use two classes, 8% for three, and 32% for four. It is not the PAC itself that becomes unstable but, instead, the last UST created (that is, on creation); in the context of beta-negative discharges against opponents, it is any creation after the opponent has been hit. When an average user fires a respective DPL discharge against the average DPL-shielded opponent, these figures respectively rise to 12%, 48%, and 192% (so, basically 100%) when at 100% APL.

As soon as the average mage attempts to double their DPL of any UST, they will experience a 99.99% LCI rate – for the most part making it extremely unlikely to create such ultrachite. So, if the mage attempted to increase their DPL by 50%, they would then experience an LCI rate of roughly 50%. When an average user fires a respective DPL discharge against the average DPL-shielded opponent (while at 100% APL), the rate doubles until reaching a 100% threshold. This means that if the opponent were to create a discharge worth 1.5 times their DPL, they would *normally* experience a 50% LCI rate; however, the beta-negative attack would increase this to 100%. The LCI rate after that threshold exponentially rises, but at that point, it does not matter, as it would be impossible to create such a discharge, anyway. For opponents with advanced power levels or higher, note that their HPLs are not naturally double the power of their DPLs, so the statistics for this DTP affecting them here need to be understood with this in mind.

While master and supreme mages may not initially experience *too* much of an issue (in standard combat settings) when attacked by average DPLs regarding the first two lumarchetrix factors (that is, creating STU and using multiple USTs and PACs at once), they still experience LCI limitations for creating HPLs, so this would negatively affect them. If an average user with a respective DPL were to affect an average unshielded opponent, then total desynchronization would occur for nearly all of the aforementioned effects for this part of the DTP. With average DPLs against an average mage, a diminishingly-effective TRE also applies for about seven seconds. While not mentioned above, the LCI effect can technically also apply to mages using DPLs of a single UST and PAC (instead of multiple); but this is extremely rare (such as when master and supreme-level users respectively affect inept and deficient-level mages), and the percentages are generally insignificant.

• Note: The statistics for how the ATP affects other etheric phenomena (besides the lumarchetrix) vary greatly, but problems *like* LCIs can still occur for GAP magics.

## UST Three/Ultra-gas (Vortices):

• PCU vortex DTPs:

1: Synchronize with an opponent's energy (any energy) and very physical being, causing the user to intuitively feel where and when the next attack may be coming from, in addition to feeling certain mental energies. Stimulating pulses sent to the centre of the vortex (where the user occupies) will also help prompt the user to physically react quickly to the synchronized energies, almost as if creating automatic reflexes with accuracy. The statistics for this feat vary based on numerous factors; however, the more vulnerable the opponent is (such as being unarmoured or even unshielded – even when compared to 100% APL against the shielded), the greater the results. This power does not have to just synchronize with an opponent – it can also (and, indeed, does) synchronize with the entire environment. Many opponents and objects can simultaneously be inside the vortex for the user to synchronize with them, but it is easier to intuitively feel for events and phenomena when fewer entities are inside.

2: Synchronize the user with any opponents inside the vortex, allowing the user to influence an opponent's movements. Essentially, the vortex will create electrical pulses that will stimulate and compel the opponent to move in particular directions, as if by uncontrollable nerve reflexes. Typically, the user will have to couple their *intent* to affect opponents *with* the use of particular *physical movements* like tightening their fists or twisting their body in a certain way in order to cause the vortex to effectively stimulate the opponent in particular ways. The level of effect still depends on how strong the opponent is, but master power levels have enough power to force most average biological humanoids to move in the desired way almost all of the time, even when they resolutely resist. Given that the user has to move in a particular way to affect opponents, this DTP does not necessarily conflict with the first DTP, so it is still (mostly) within the user's control.

3: Increase an opponent's vulnerability to ultrachite and particular non-ultrachite synchronizations, with the most evident effect being mental harmonization with the user. While this does not increase the power of a user's discharge attacks, it nevertheless weakens opponents for those attacks. Effectively just via the SUC, the average DPL vortex can effectively lower an average DPL-shielded opponent's resistances to calmness, pacification, and support for the user by about 50% when at 100% APL. For the average unshielded opponent, the effect at average DPL levels will cause about a 140% decrease from their normal rates. A diminishingly-effective TRE of about nine seconds also applies to those who leave the vortex. Note that the above statistics apply to just one opponent; so, when more opponents are simultaneously affected, the power naturally divides.

• NCU vortex DTPs:

1: Desynchronize an opponent's mind from their environment, causing the victim to lose or lessen their ability to (properly) sense or detect certain (physical and etheric) energies, things, or properties. The statistics for this DTP vary greatly depending on the victim and the context, but it is generally good for stopping opponents from intuitively detecting what a user may be doing – or plan on doing.

2: Desynchronize the coherence quantum properties may possess, in turn causing various changes to wave functions and other assorted quantum phenomena. To be clear, the vortex does not necessarily (indeed, does not always) fully decohere quantum properties; so, the DTP, instead, normally only *partially* (and possibly or probably) decoheres quantum properties, so this power only *limits* wave functions instead of causing a total wave function reduction. While this is not as powerful as gamma's ability to specifically cut off quantum entanglements, for example (assuming relative power levels), this DTP is quite broad in its effects. However, the level of effect drastically differs per the context and what properties are in the vortex.

3: Increase an opponent's vulnerability to particular kinds of desynchronizations (whether from ultrachite or non-ultrachite attacks), with the most evident effect affecting mental cognition (which includes effects such as tachypsychia, chronostasis, flash-lag, and unconsciousness); to be clear, while beta-negative discharges have two DTPs for these effects, this DTP for the vortex only has one DTP in regards to these effects). While this does not increase the power of a user's discharge attacks, it nevertheless weakens opponents for those attacks. Effectively just via the SUC, the average DPL vortex can effectively lower an average DPL-shielded opponent's resistance by about 50% when at 100% APL. For the average unshielded opponent, the effect at average DPLs will cause about a 140% decrease from their normal rates. A diminishingly-effective TRE of about nine seconds also applies to those who leave the aura. Note that the above statistics apply to just one opponent; so, when more opponents are simultaneously affected, the power naturally divides.

4: Increase an opponent mage's vulnerability to lumarchetrix desynchronizations effectively just via the SUC against the shielded and direct (stronger) influence for the unshielded. While this does not increase the power of a user's discharge attacks, it nevertheless weakens opponents for those attacks. A few different aspects of the opponent's channel will be affected, and each kind will individually vary per subject mage, but there are normally corresponding levels across all of them at once. These factors include: overcharging DPLs and HPLs, limiting or preventing recharge from the Aether, and increasing LCIs when creating: STU; any UST while using multiple USTs and/or PACs at once; and HPLs. The average DPL vortex can effectively lower an average DPL-shielded opponent's resistance proportionally for each factor by about 60% when at 100% APL. For the average unshielded opponent, the effect at average DPL levels will cause about a proportional 140% decrease for each factor from their normal rates. A diminishingly-effective TRE of about nine seconds also applies to those who leave the aura. As an ATP, the vortex can affect vulnerabilities to etheric desynchronizations (including for the GAP), with the statistics varying greatly. Note that the above statistics apply to just one opponent; so, when more opponents are simultaneously affected, the power naturally divides.

• Note: The vortex's third and fourth DTPs are, indeed, separate, with the fourth DTP specifically affecting etheric energies and the lumarchetrix itself.

### UST Four/Ultra-liquid (Soaker bombs and Swarm clouds):

• PCU soaker particles: create an adhesive effect, causing various things to stick to one another. For example, this can cause an opponent to be either partially or 'totally' stuck to the ground. If the former, the opponent would move very slowly, having to take a moment just to lift their feet off the ground. This is different from beta-positive propulsors in both properties and effect, as the adhesion of the soaker particles will generally prevent a victim from running. Technically, this power can be dangerous to many kinds of entities who are affected for too long (normally through consecutive hits) – *especially* if the victim happens to swallow the particles; but this problem rarely occurs. The results for this power vary depending on the context and properties involved, but in many cases, the average DPL soaker bomb can cause partial stickiness for most properties. That is, most entities with standard footwear would be unable to run or even jog, taking around 1.5 seconds to lift a single foot off the ground. Naturally, TREs do not apply after the particles disappear. Users may sometimes craftily create LPLs and use this power on themselves as a replacement for beta-positive propulsors, but it normally is not as effective.

• PCU swarm clouds: Synchronize with the user's aura via PUC, enabling the swarm to produce a faint holographic veil of the user's position around the victim. Note that this surrounding veil would not be from what the user would see with their eyes; instead, it would be of the surrounding area around the user, so the victim would see the same surroundings as what the user would see. Essentially, this semi-blinds and confuses opponents. In some cases, however, this DTP can reveal too much of the user's location and tactics, so this may sometimes be switched off when creating the soaker bomb. Note that for this DTP to work, the user needs to be surrounded with particles of some kind to entangle with, so it cannot work in a pure vacuum.

• NCU soaker particles: create an adhesive effect, causing various things to move with little to no friction. As a result, opponents can slip on their feet extremely easily – even with grippy boots. Average DPL soaker particles have enough power to create enough lubrication to badly affect most opponents with standard footwear. When an opponent continually slips over, this power also, by default, prevents them from moving from their position (assuming they are not on a slope), so there are different kinds of tactical advantages for this power. Users may also sometimes craftily create LPLs and use this power on themselves in order to slide or skate across various surfaces.

    • Note: This DTP can be effective for when a user needs to move opponents affected by delta-negative energy across surfaces, as the coefficient of friction will naturally be lower.

• NCU swarm clouds: effectively desynchronize vision, creating a partial veil that visually and sonically delays what is happening outside the swarm. The illusory effects are similar to what beta-negative discharges induce – except, of course, the victim will not inherently feel the effects in their mind. However, after prolonged exposure, mental faculties can consequently be affected as a side effect. The average DPL swarm will typically induce a one-second delay effect.

## UST Five/Ultra-conductivity (Propulsors):

• PCU propulsor DTPs: synchronize with various types of matter, with the micro propulsions creating friction both mechanically and non-conventionally via fluctuating electrons between the propulsor and the interacted matter. Each DTP requires *individual* active charging via a UPC in order to power (with average DPL auras requiring a two-second UPC time for each DTP). Interestingly, there is no time limit once active, but when the DTP or the aura is switched off, then the UPC resets (with a one-second cooldown penalty for the specific DTP switched off – if the aura is still active). Also, while one DTP is active, another DTP can simultaneously be charged; however, when the UPC is complete, the current DTP will switch off for the new DTP. The DTPs:

1: Synchronize specifically with the air by creating micro propulsions that generate conventional and non-conventional friction, in turn increasing air resistance. Without any force acting on a falling object or person (that is, when in *free fall*), all mass *on* C1 planets (in most contexts, at surface level) will fall (accelerate) at roughly a rate of 9.81 m/s²; so, after two seconds, all mass would *reach* a *velocity* of roughly 19.6 m/s. When other forces, such as air resistance, act on a falling mass, this figure changes. After falling for a certain period, the air resistance will equal the force of gravity, and the falling mass will reach *terminal velocity*, where the acceleration stops and a maximum speed is imposed. Of course, air density changes depending on various factors, so at higher altitudes, for example, air resistance is weaker, but the following statistics assume standard atmospheres with a density of 1.225 kg/m³.

When an average humanoid weighing 103 kg falls from a 30-metre-tall building on a C1 planet (that is, they *begin* falling from the top of the building, so they start off at zero-initial velocity), then the *time to fall* will equal around 2.5 seconds, with a *maximum velocity* reaching 23.43 m/s (or 84.4 km/h). The humanoid, in this case, will reach a maximum velocity before even reaching terminal velocity (of around 233.5 km/h in standard contexts). At 84.4 km/h, this speed is enough to kill most average humanoids. The average mage with a respective DPL propulsor aura, however, can, in this case, increase the 'air resistance' (that is, establish an air resistance coefficient of 17.304 kg/m) so that they will only experience a maximum and terminal velocity of 7.64 m/s (or 27.5 km/h), with a time to fall of about 4.5 seconds. This, of course, this is from zero-initial velocity, so the user would have to activate the power before falling to have the time to fall of 4.5 seconds; otherwise, this figure would decrease.

This power, nevertheless, will become diminishingly less effective with any weight over 103 kg; so, for a person weighing 150 kg, the maximum velocity would be 32.06 km/h (despite the same amount of friction), which would be enough to poten-tially kill them. For weights under 103 kg, conversely, the effect does not get stronger. So, when more mass up to 103 kg is applied to the propulsor (that is, the user's weight 'on' the propulsor) more mechanical frictional properties (in addition to fluctuating electrons) will effectively *activate* up to the propulsor's power level (that is, 103 kg for average DPLs). This means that a mage weighing 60 kg will still have the same time to fall as someone weighing 103 kg. This is not a feature, howbeit, that can be changed with a UPS or an ATP, as it is a phase issue affecting wave function changes.

When reaching the maximum velocity of 7.64 m/s, the average mage should still know how to properly land (such as bending their knees or rolling) in order to avoid potential injuries. At most, average DPLs allow mages weighing up to 103kg to safely fall from heights of about 57 metres if they have a full lumarchetrix, as the time to fall would be about eight seconds after a perfectly-timed UPC. This, of course, is assuming a zero-velocity start with no other negative variables. Novice mages, with their respective DPLs, on the other hand, must avoid dropping from certain heights lest they incur injuries (and, in some cases, death).

When the initial velocity is too high relative to the UST activation time and strength (of any DPL), however, mages can reach velocities that are typically fatal when deceleration occurs when hitting a surface. For clarification, even though a user (weighing 100kg, for example) can reduce their terminal velocity (of about 64 m/s) when the power activates *while* falling in normal conditions (that is, the *initial velocity*, here, would be about 64 m/s at the time of activation), this deceleration takes time, so the velocity may not reduce (to the abovesaid 7.64 m/s) in time before hitting the ground. In this case, it normally takes about 5.73 seconds to reach 27.5 km/h (from 230 km/h), with a distance of 205.57 metres covered. Therefore, a mage cannot turn their propulsor aura on at the last second while falling before hitting the ground and always hope to survive.

If the goal is to *reach* the ground safely, then mages with higher DPLs may choose to create LPLs so that they do not remain too long in the air without having reached the ground before running out of photomission energy. In other words, a stronger mage can reach the ground faster with an LPL, which may be the safer option. In most standard contexts while starting off at zero-initial velocity (and not requiring more energy to support greater amounts of weight), using higher-than-average power levels may be pointless, as a safe level of speed can be attained even with average DPLs. The main usefulness for higher power levels, then, normally comes down to using the power *while* already falling or if very slow falling is needed in order to stay in the air longer for some aerial activity.

• Note: The cross-sectional area (that is, the shape and size) of the *propulsor* does not matter *too* much in regards to fall times. However, a mage's orientation naturally plays a decent role. The abovesaid figures do not factor in for orientation, so naturally streamlining one's position will result in faster fall times. For this reason, it is generally not recommended falling with a head down or pin-like dive; and while a belly-to-ground orientation is best for slower fall times, mages still have to *land* (properly), so generally, falling with arms out and knees bent while in a semi-crouched position is recommended. While a heavier mage will fall faster, sometimes they will also have larger cross-sectional areas, so this may somewhat balance out. While falling, the ultrachite will automatically (and suitably) concentrate where the most air resistance is (or will be) located (via the UPC), so if the user has a belly-to-ground orientation, the ultrachite will cover the whole front facing of the mage. Still, the user can reorientate the ultrachite at will. This DTP is basically not applicable when falling in a vacuum.

2: Synchronize specifically with liquids by creating micro propulsions that generate conventional and non-conventional friction, in turn granting the user the ability of water walking or running. Average DPLs can allow the user (of up to 103 kg) to swiftly move across fresh, non-chaotically moving water without sinking; any speed below this (9.5 km/h) threshold will have varying degrees of sinkage (that is, if the user were to stand still, they would sink). For weights under 103 kg, conversely, the effect does not get stronger. So, when more mass up to 103 kg is applied to the propulsor (that is, the user's weight 'on' the propulsor) more mechanical frictional properties (in addition to fluctuating electrons) will effectively *activate* up to the propulsor's power level (that is, 103 kg for average DPLs). So, a mage weighing 60 kg will still have the same threshold as someone weighing 103 kg. This is not a feature, howbeit, that can be changed with a UPS or an ATP, as it is a phase issue affecting wave function changes. Higher power levels allow for slower speeds, types of liquid (and different statistics with these), and the movement of the liquid itself. Given that fluctuating electrons between the propulsor and the liquid are used in this process (which vary per angle relative to the liquid), the user will not be *stuck* to the liquid, so they will still be able to easily lift their feet off the liquid's surface.

3: Synchronize specifically with solids by creating micro propulsions that generate conventional and non-conventional friction, in turn allowing users to 'stick' to and scale various surfaces like walls and ceilings. However, the *type* of surface matters, not just the angle, and external forces can still (easily) pull users away from such surfaces (with the rate of difficulty depending on the user's angle relative to the surface). Furthermore, users must continue to move lest they fall off. Average users (up to 103 kg) with their respective DPLs must maintain a movement of at least 7.5 km/h on standard concrete vertical surfaces. Any angle less than this will see rapidly diminishing results for the said user. While the user can choose to only walk on their legs, this can result in strain, so users will not 'wall run' for long before switching to using all fours (that is, their hands and feet or all limbs). Elite users, conversely, can scale standard concrete ceilings. Since users can charge the other DTPs while this DTP is active, normally when crawling on a very high ceiling (of sorts) before wishing to let go to fall to the ground, users charge the first DTP so that instant decreased velocity can occur when the falling begins.

For weights under 103 kg, the effect does not get stronger. This means that when more mass up to 103 kg is applied to the propulsor (that is, the user's weight 'on' the propulsor) more mechanical frictional properties (in addition to fluctuating electrons) will effectively *activate* up to the propulsor's power level (that is, 103 kg for average DPLs). So, a mage weighing 60 kg will still have the same threshold as someone weighing 103 kg. This is not a feature, howbeit, that can be changed with a UPS or an ATP, as it is a phase issue affecting wave function changes. Higher power levels allow for more weight, slower speeds, types of surfaces (and different statistics with these), and greater surface angles. Given that fluctuating electrons between the propulsor and the surface are used in this process (which vary per angle relative to the surface), the user will not be *stuck* to the surface, so they will still be able to easily lift their feet off.

• Note: Unlike the first and third DTPs, the second DTP greatly alters the fabric of the affected properties – the liquid(s). The micro propulsions that cause the synchronizing friction accordingly change the *viscosity* of the liquid (that is, its thickness due to a resistance to change shape), creating hardened pads for the user to step on. This phenomenon is not the same as that found in nature with some animals (or sapient beings) that utilize (and/or alter) the *surface tension* of a liquid, nor is it the case where *hydrophobic* properties are involved (that is, possessing properties 'afraid' of water), nor is there an increase in *buoyancy* (that is, the tendency to float) as a result of a decrease in *density* (of the user) due to an increase in – or creation of – air gaps.

• NCU propulsors: create a field that propels against – and only against – gravitational geodesics. While not a UST Six power, the beta-negative particles desynchronize from the fabric of the *relative* spacetime around the user *when* going against the relative dominant gravitational geodesic; specifically, the propulsor effectively negates the gravitational field's effects (to a degree) on the *user*, but not gravity itself, via wave function changes affecting the user's phase in relation to the gravity. This means that a user can resist going 'against gravity', but they will still experience normal gravity when going along with gravity. So, if the user jumps up, they will jump higher than normal, but eventually, gravity will still slow the acceleration down; and, once stopped, the user will begin descending, where they will experience normal gravitational levels. In other words, it is a matter of going 'with the grain' versus 'against the grain' (where the dynamics totally change); accordingly, even though gravity would *still* be working against the user while they ascend (against the 'grain' – the geodesic), once the velocity *totally* changes to flow with the 'grain' (the geodesic), then the propulsor will no longer work with any effectiveness.

If the user's velocity is at an acute angle to the flow of gravity (so, they are not moving 'directly' down and, instead, at a 'diagonal' angle downwards), then they will still experience normal gravity. For clarification, if the user is already falling when this power is activated, then neither the velocity nor the acceleration would change; thus, it would be totally ineffective. The average DPL propulsor can reduce the effects of a C1 world's surface gravity (in standard contexts) by 75% to more effectively allow the user to move against the geodesic. This means the propulsor can help the typical mage who can jump as high as one metre in standard contexts (on C1 worlds) to around three metres. Even though master power-level propulsors enable virtually no gravitational resistance, consider that their CECs and MECs are super high, so it is not like mages using these propulsors can jump forever.

Note that the propulsor's effects will still apply to users moving 'diagonally up' relative to the flow of gravity; moreover, the strength of the effect will be equal no matter the angle against gravity (so, it would still be about 75% for average users). The average user with their DPL must also UPC the propulsor for two seconds before use, which lasts indefinitely until switched off, where a two-second cooldown time applies. Unlike other propulsors, there is no weight limit, so long as enough force is used to propel the user upwards (such as when jumping), with mass only applying to the air resistance going up. Users also must physically jump to jump, as the propulsor will not make them jump. Safety is also especially required due to being able to jump to heights that could otherwise be dangerous when falling down, so the propulsor's uses vary per context.

## UST Six/Ultra-spacetime crystals (Dimensional Fields):

• PCU dimensional fields: synchronize (or more specifically, phase lock) with the current, localized spacetime when actively charged, essentially 'marking' it for the user as a reference point for later return when they rewind time. Basically, the user (and anything else in the aura's space) physically flows subjectively backwards through time. Under these circumstances, this power does not alter time outside the aura, so a room full of conscious opponents who were not in the marked field, for example, would still be alerted and ready for the user after they (the user) rewinds time. As another example: if an ally were to die outside of the field, they would remain dead even after the user rewound their localized time. The marking occurs exactly where the user actively *finishes* their UPC (or when they can no longer continue charging due to running out of photomission energy, or when they are unable to channel anymore, or due to any other disruptions – all up to the UPC limit). Thereupon, the particles UPS from DES to AES, and the user enters the 'window stage', where they have a certain amount of time to accomplish their goals before the power automatically and inexorably begins rewinding time.

The average user with a respective DPL dimensional field can charge for a maximum of about 3.5 seconds before gaining double the amount of time for their window and rewind stages when combined. Higher power levels, on the other hand, allow for longer window and rewind stages (but these naturally require longer UPC times). Unlike most other UST forms, there is no *minimum* UPC time – only, instead, a maximum time limit per power level. For most mages, a common 50/50 split will occur between the two stages as a natural phenomenon of the energy's momentum; in the case for the average mage with their DPL, they get about 3.5 seconds for each stage. However, this can differ slightly, so users do not necessarily rewind all the way back to their mark. Moreover, no user can ever rewind *beyond* their mark, despite any potential energy that they may have left. Users also have the opportunity to consciously rewind time before their window stage would normally end; but again, they do not gain additional time for the rewind.

Once the window stage begins, the user will automatically stop channelling more beta-positive dimensional energy. Even when a user runs out of energy (that is, they reach LED), the AES particles will still have enough phased momentum to continue without MECs. Accordingly, users do not have to be conscious for the phenomenon to continue, and so, the power is not just useful for reverting wounds, but it can even help with reversing death itself (so long as the user does not remain dead for too long in the window stage, which never normally is the case, as dimensional powers are expensive to channel and, accordingly, do not last long). If the said user began the UPC with a full lumarchetrix, then they would have about 31% of their MLP left, enough for a few other UST form creations (such as discharges for combat). Normally, it is best to UPC when the lumarchetrix is full, so users do not reach LED during the window stage, which then allows them to use other USTs during that time.

To further extend and clarify the aforementioned death example, if a user sees a dead person and then decides to hold them in their aura before rewinding time in order to save them, the action will ultimately be futile, as they will only rewind back to the point where the user holds the dead person. Therefore, this dimensional power is effectively a preparatory power rather than one to deal with anything *ex post facto*. While using this dimensional field is useful for certain contexts requiring trial and error, sometimes users will experience small probability changes at the quantum level for events within the localized field after returning. So, if a user happens to be interfacing with a DEC, QMC, or NAC in their field, there may be algorithmic or simulated changes when the user interfaces with the computer again after returning.

Basically, the data in the computers would not change after returning, but certain events *with* the computers would potentially change when the user interfaces with them again. This would be due to the user's updated consciousness (of events) and their unconscious biases altering their probable wave function pathways in their quantum potential. Even though technically consciousness can affect probabilities non-linearly (in terms of time), this psychic feat is reduced *mainly* to fields *after* returning, not *so* much during the return/rewinding or *normally* as soon as they return. There also may be small probability changes that the user imposes on the external world after the magic finishes and vice versa.

The dimensional power will also rewind anything in the aura's space, even if it enters after the initial marking. In such cases, however, the object that entered would not fully return to the initial synchronized mark; instead, it would rewind only to the point where the aura would no longer be in the vicinity. Users can also safely return to their mark without fear of post hoc objects inhabiting the space. For example, if a sharp pole enters the mark's location (not the *aura* during the window or even potentially most of the rewind stage), then, as soon as the edge of the aura returns to the spot, the pole would begin reverting. If an object was in the aura when the power *began*, such as a wall, then, when the user leaves the vicinity, the dimensional energy would not surround the wall. Instead, the wall would only begin reverting backwards (if it is still there) when the user arrives back at the location when rewinding *and* only according to how long the user reverts in the vicinity.

While not every part of the aura will have UST Six particles in it, they will still produce a *field*, and the average DPL field will distinctly extend about one metre in radius from the user. Moreover, even though the UST Six particles might be right at the edge of the aura, their power will not extend beyond the aura due to a loss in phase from the user. Higher power levels allow for greater sizes, so this can aid in assorted pursuits. Regardless of the size, something (or a part of something) is either in the field or it is not. Just as the timeframe is fixed, the diameter remains fixed as well for the entire duration. Unfortunately, during the window stage, if, for example, someone (or thing) were to rip the user's heart out of their chest and throw it out of the aura, the heart would not return to the original state, as the dimensional field would remain locked to the main mass of the user's body – especially the brain – due to being in equilibrium with the body. *However*, this is not too much of an issue, anyway, because as soon as a mage dies or experiences a traumatic event, the rewinding *normally* automatically begins *immediately*, and so, body parts tend to remain inside the auras.

• Note: There are no known ATPs for this one DTP, but there are unconfirmed rumours and legends that some master and supreme-level (or mythic) mages are (or were, in the case of legends) capable of delaying the window stage and somehow rewinding all the way back to the mark.

• NCU dimensional fields: desynchronize the user from the physical spacetime they inhabit, in turn causing them to only exist in the etheric with their etheric body. Basically, while normal phase shifting can allow for feats like quantum teleportation, this power goes one step further, causing the user to cease existing normally as a structured physical entity. This power principally turns the user *intangible*, granting them the ability to move through all physical matter (including gases, plasmas, ultra-states, etc.) and, therefore, the ability to be completely invincible to attacks, no matter the field's power level. At the same time, the user cannot attack opponents. Essentially, it turns users into ghost-like entities. In fact, users of this dimensional power can even interact with literal ghosts in the etheric. For more information on such interactions, see *Section 4.3.2.9*. The power will also cause users to become virtually invisible; but *when* noticeable, the user will usually appear as either a very fuzzy version of themselves or an amorphous blur of faint (green) energy. In such a state, there is no need to breathe or eat to sustain oneself, as users will have no corporealized physical body that demands it. Nevertheless, etheric beings require consuming or producing net etheric energy to continue existing, but since the phase does not last long, this is never an issue.

Movement through physical matter occurs as a result of the user's consciousness focusing on (and around) matter in the physical reality, like how any other etheric being navigates the etheric realm when viewing the physical. Using the dimensional field becomes harder to control the further one 'moves away' from their original location of phase shifting; and, despite the less-localized nature of the etheric, users need to be in places that have strong associations with the initial location, as this can cause a distinct loss in phase, causing the power to cease. Nevertheless, while in such a state, users can avoid issues of non-gravity due to associated attachments to the physical and, thus, do not fly away from the planet they are 'on'. When a user moves, they typically move roughly level to the ground they were originally on and any undulations they come across. There is no contradiction between the user not having to face struggles, such as breathing, yet in the intangible state, their associations strain, as the very reality (and phenomenon) still has limitations. In other words, any and all energy, in any 'location' or state, is still subject to forces and, therefore, has limitations.

The dimensional field must be charged up from DES to AES via a UPC after the creation of the ultrachite (and, by default, prior to the user turning intangible). Unlike most other UST forms, there is no *minimum* UPC time – only, instead, a maximum time limit per power level. That is, the charged energy is what sustains the user's power over the course of their intangibility – so zero charge equals zero seconds. Accordingly, the charging determines the maximum length the user remains intangible, and so, an average user with a respective DPL can charge for about 3.5 seconds and gain a maximum time of 3.5 seconds; stronger mages can naturally increase this time with their DPLs. When in AES, the particles will have enough phased momentum to last without MECs, so no additional energy costs occur. A non-physical anchor is then established *for* the current physical realm and *in* the etheric realm once intangibility is established. The duration of the power, however, also only lasts as long as the user can remain consciously focused. So, if a user were to lose focus four seconds in of their total seven-second intangible time, for example, they would return to the physical, and the potential anchor would then manifest physically.

The user cannot charge additional energy for the dimensional field while in the etheric, and the originally-charged UST Six energy stays with the user in the intangible while still connected to the physical. Accordingly, a tangible time (limit) still applies (such as the aforesaid 3.5 seconds for average DPLs). Users are also unable to use other phasarchement magic while intangible. On return, the actualized anchor re-establishes the user's physical form as it was prior to going intangible. To be clear, the etheric body still has the code of the physical body, and the code (containing the data of the active beta-negative dimensional power) also allows the body to corporealize again. When returning, the anchor will also push any (or most) post hoc matter out of the way, generally allowing for safe return, so long as the user does not return in the middle of a thick, *strong* wall, for example (in which case, they most certainly would die). While the anchor is a *product* of the ultrachite, it is still the actual UST particles *themselves*, too, which manifest again thanks to the code in the etheric.

Technically, while the user is intangible, opponents can interfere with the anchor to stop the magic, but this requires extremely-talented mysticism magic, psychicism, and/or other strange physical phenomena related to the bending of spacetime and/or physical-to-etheric relations. Since this power requires conscious focus, if the user were to affect non-conscious matter solely outside their field (via projection of the field), then the user would still have to psychically focus their consciousness to keep said matter in the intangible state. If the user were to affect another conscious entity (that is, turn them intangible) – whether including or excluding themselves – the other being could consciously resist this and return to normal reality.

Just as the timeframe is fixed, the field's diameter remains fixed as well for the entire duration. For the average DPL user, the field will distinctly have about a one-metre radius. Higher power levels, of course, have bigger fields, which may help with certain situations. Regardless of the size, something is either in the field or it is not – that is, a field will have an absolute boundary, not an imprecise one. Never-theless, not all properties in the field will necessarily phase shift, as they need to have basically their whole HRF inside the field. So, if another person's arm were in the field while the rest of their body was outside of it, the other person would not phase shift. In regards to the floor the user would stand on, it would not phase shift either, as it would be too big (as a whole) to fit in the field. Regardless, the field's energy normally prefers to emerge and stay *slightly* above solid ground – unless the user wills the energy to include the ground – so this basically never happens.

### 3.6.5.3: Gamma Class (Entanglement & Separation):

#### UST One/Ultra-solid (Shields):

• PCU shield DTPs:

1: Collectively entangle their particles at the quantum level via a UPC, in turn camouflaging the user. Coupled with the shield's partial condensate properties, the entangled particles will exhibit super strong quantum coherence. With this, they will have a well-defined phase, and when incoming photons hit the shield, the photons will lose their coherence and, thus, their original wave functions. The shield particles will then transfer their coherence to the photons, in turn altering the photons' wave functions, where the photons will accordingly bend (refract) around the shield instead of hitting the shield and causing it to be visible. The stronger the effect, the more invisible the user becomes. More specifically, there is a threshold for total *camouflage* and another for total *invisibility*.

When the shield meets the total-camouflage threshold, it will completely block out the user from the external world, making the shield appear as if a rumpled mirror with multiple segments, easily seen and clearly out of place within the environment. With increased power, the precision of the entanglement increases as well, leading to less perturbation, and, thus, with enough power, invisibility occurs, where most entities (in most contexts) will be unable to see or notice the user and their shield. This DTP, however, effectively blinds users to the outside world due to blocking external photons from reaching the user and their eyes. That is, basically no light enters an invisible or totally camouflaged shield.

The power of the shield (that is, how much light it can refract) will reduce when any ultrachite or non-ultrachite matter hits the shield with enough power (which includes phenomenon such as a high-powered electrical charges). Even when a shield is no longer being hit, the camouflage will not return to its normal state until another UPC occurs. To be clear, if the attacks on the shield are not that strong, then some of the shield's particles will still stay in AES, so the user would only be partially camouflaged. This ability extends to non-visible light, so detection devices like thermal imaging technologies may fail to notice strongly-camouflaged users. However, there are other technologies (along with mysticism spells, psychic abilities, and certain creature powers) that can detect camouflaged users in other visual ways. But even then, many of these rely on analogous data or probabilities, so these do not guarantee detection.

Despite their flaws, these technologies are still employed in various high-security places to prevent invisible mages from undertaking certain, unwanted actions.

Users can still create and use other USTs while camouflaged, but the ultrachite must not touch the shield's shell when concentrated, such as a discharge in active mode when concentrated into a fully-formed blast ball. Nevertheless, the discharge will be visible, so this can reveal the user's location and presence to opponents. In most cases, users will not use other ultrachite, as the DTP is mainly effective for stealth purposes. Average users with respective DPL shields can achieve mild, noticeable-when-up-close, total-camouflage levels (that is, about 30% invisibility); and, after a single average DPL discharge hits them, the shield will lose almost all of its camouflage. The UPC, in this case, will take about 16 seconds before the invisibility will last around eight seconds as well. Afterwards, a cooldown period of around 16seconds applies before a UPC can begin again. While heat can build inside a shield while active, this heat will escape once the DTP is no longer active. If too much heat were to hypothetically build up inside (which never occurs in standard cases), then the heat would degrade and then destroy the entanglement.

• Note: Technically, the above statistics are only considering standard levels of lighting (that is, standard daylight). With higher concentrations of light (like from a laser), the shield may not be able to totally camouflage a user.

• Note: The shield's particles do not block gases due to being unable to change their wave functions like with photons. This can cause problems for mages in certain situations, where, for example, they stink or have a strong scent, allowing other beings (especially ones with good olfactory systems) to easily smell the user.

• Note: Whilst a disc shield that does not surround the user might seem beneficial to use (so that the user can still see things), this can be problematic. For example, the since the shield's particles are naturally more suited to being around the user, they will not have the same level of coherence, which, in turn, not only reduces the level of camouflage, but it also causes them to create odd distortions in different parts of the shield, so the shield itself looks odd (both itself and within the environment).

• Note: Legends speak of mythical mages who were able to see through their shields while invisible. Various accounts explain different ways this occurred, but one method involved entangling the light hitting the shield, in turn causing a virtual, visual recon-struction of the reality outside the shield. Some myths mention that it still had its limitations, such as having a time limit with an initial UPC before a cooldown occurred. The virtual reconstructions were also said to be very blurry or fuzzy and colour-altered (usually black and white), while depth perception was greatly reduced. Furthermore, objects were also apparently disproportionately sized and/or displaced or sometimes even missing. Despite this poor vision and lack of realism, legendary mages typically did not get blinded by outside sources such as flashbangs or delta-positive discharges.

2: Entangle *phonons* inside *phononic crystals* (found throughout the shield), which help to soundproof the user. Basically, phonons are quantized sound waves (a specific arrangement of atoms), akin to how photons are a quantization of light waves. Phononic crystals, on the other hand, are typically artificial structures that can manipulate or dampen sound (or other elastic) waves. These phononic crystals exhibit highly-coherent states with well-defined phases, and when incoming sound waves hit the phononic crystals, they will lose their coherence, where the coherence of the phononic crystals will partially transfer to the incoming sound waves, in turn causing the sound waves to lose their original wave functions and consequently dampen. Of course, this is only at or below a certain decibel range per the shield's power level.

This DTP also requires a UPC; and, as with the camouflaging feat, when the shield is attacked, the dampening effect will either weaken or end, with another UPC needed to restore the entanglement. Moreover, users can still use other ultrachite, so long as their active/concentrated modes do not touch the shield's shell. Average users with respective DPL shields can fully 'block' sounds at or below 75 decibels, with exponentially diminishing results after this amount. To be clear, the sound waves will not reflect or refract off the shield; as such, when a user speaks inside their shield, they will not continuously have to deal with sound waves bouncing back and forth from the inner shield walls. Instead, the sound waves will simply convert to heat energy.

Although the feat in itself (at most power levels) cannot cancel out extremely-powerful noises, note that the SBEs of all shields can still block shockwaves. The average DPL shield can also only withstand a single average DPL discharge before it will lose almost all of its ability to dampen sounds. The UPC, in this case, will take about seven seconds before soundproofing occurs for about 15 seconds. Afterwards, a cooldown period of around seven seconds applies before a UPC can begin again. In addition, users have the ability to alter the DTP to an ATP by changing the direction of the dampening pathways so that sounds may partially or only enter the aura (that is, it would create a one-way sound system) – or the reverse. The partialness, in this context, is different to switching the PEP of a certain portion of particles from AES to DES, even though a UPS can still achieve this effect.

3: Quantumly entangle with the particles of other HRFs (normally other gamma-positive shields), within the context of HRFs, allowing for communication at any distance. This feat specifically uses *quantum holography*, where it is not just mere quantum entanglement that allows for the communication. Basically, holograms are created from these entangled particles, where the holograms contain complex *information* (not just visual representations), and this information is key to the communication, where encoding, transmission, and decoding can occur. The shield will also have other properties to help with the various aspects of the communication, such as those that utilize and exploit the helpfulness of quantum superposition.

To initiate the entanglement, a shielded user must be locally present and physically touch the HRF that they wish for their shield to entangle with, which must also be done via a one-off UPC. Once entangled, the user can travel to any other part of the Caelverse away from the HRF(s), so distance is not *technically* an issue. Therefore, this is not like radio. However, quantum decoherence is still an issue, where environmental factors may ruin the shield's entanglement. Nevertheless, unless the shield is in proximity to strange and/or powerful properties (emitting energy), this is generally not a big problem. So, being deep underground in a mine, for example, will generally not affect the shield's entanglement much. There are also other quantum anomalies that can distort the shield's entanglement in other ways, and the density of the etheric energy in areas like mines can still cause problems at the quantum level. Furthermore, the shield will experience great decoherence when a user travels to other planets.

The entanglement itself can also suffer from *entropy* and degeneration (so not just decoherence) as a result of various reasons, with the most obvious one being the natural time limit. Still, the time limit of roughly 16 hours for most mages does not come into effect due to other limitations; that is, a user must keep their shield on for the DTP to be fully effective. A user, nevertheless, can still switch their shield off due to their etheric aura being able to hold quantum memory of the entangled HRFs, which establish certain effects for a potential field in the user's APA, which can, in turn, affect the user's shield at the quantum level. However, the next time they turn the shield on to communicate with others, the quality will be (normally slightly) worse. The quantum memory may only be sustained if the user keeps their lumarchetrix active, so once the lumarchetrix is switched off – or if the user reaches EEE – then the shield will no longer be entangled with the other HRFs. The reverse also applies; that is, if a user's shield is connected to another shield, but the other person loses the connection, the user, too, will lose the connection.

The DTP allows for both visual and audio communication, but users can change the DTP to an ATP so that only one of these features occur. The inner lining of the shield will also display the holographic (but flattened) visuals at all angles around the user, but users can also change this (via *tuning* without an ATP needed) so that the visuals will only display in front of them – and they can also change their size. Users can also alter volume levels (via tuning without an ATP needed either), with all power levels having the same default volume that happens to be at a comfortable level for most mages. The shield also uses *interferometry* (that is, a measurement method of the interference of overlapping waves), so the inner lining can act as both a camera and screen. While no light can enter the shield *when* a user is invisible, the shield inside will naturally give off its own light – more so than other shields – and not just through the visuals of the holograms.

While ultrachite shields are normally close to a user's body, the visuals, nonetheless, have a default perspective that enables users to see other people as if at a normal, in-person, conversational distance; that is, the visuals are fine for the user, so they do not feel like they are looking at a screen right up at their face; and users will also see – and appear for other users at – 'normal' perspectives. Still, sometimes users will extend the shield out and may even flatten (at least a portion of) the shield to a disc-like screen in front of them (without the need for an ATP). When the shield is 'open' as such, then users can show other beings their screens or other mages (viewing from the screen) their (the user's) environment.

Depending on the power level, users can entangle with multiple HRFs, with average DPL users being able to entangle with three other HRFs simultaneously. The issue of resource distribution with multipartite entangling itself is basically not a practical issue for gamma-positive shields, with the only major limiting effect being the maximum volume levels between HRFs – which is not a practical issue, either. If a user wishes to only communicate with one of the HRFs they are entangled with, then it is merely a matter of tuning to the right vibrational signature (without the need for an ATP). The user does not have to UPC the shield in order to use the power after the initial entanglement; and so, if a user does not wish for any communications to come through the shield, they either tune the other HRFs off or they tune the DTP down or off into DES (thus affecting the volume and visuals without having to establish an ATP). While a shield fully in DES will not cut off the entanglement with other HRFs, creating an ATP (or HPL or LPL) shield will cut off the entanglement.

Whilst in any environment, users may be subject to other entanglements, distorting or even overriding the original entanglements. However, these are rare. The interception of communications also rarely occurs, so encryption is not necessary, nor callsigns, codes, and other obscurities. In the modern age, mages are not as reliant on this power as they were in the past, as they have various technologies at their disposal, with infrastructure well developed in metropolitan areas. However, when exploring wild areas that lack proper development, or when situated in particular underground systems, or when technologies fail or are stolen, or even when in areas where *absolute* encryption is necessary, this communications power is still super useful.

• NCU shield DTPs:

1: Scatter and diffuse built-up energy. Average DPL shields require a 16-second UPC time that lasts for 12 seconds before a cooldown period of 48 seconds occurs. However, there is a 50% chance that the UPC may fail to activate the power at the

16-second charge mark, in turn incurring a 48-second cooldown penalty for the user before the user can UPC again. Having two main functions, this DTP:

I) Improves OSSR times for overstimulated shield UPIs so they can continue inhibiting ultrachite attack particles (so APLs are not as strong). Moreover, it improves the CDP. As a result, an opponent must continue relentlessly attacking the user's gamma-negative shield without stopping to eventuate in 100% APL against it. The average user's DPL shield (without this DTP) will have a relatively-fixed 3.75% subsiding recovery rate per second, whereas the gamma-negative shield (with this DTP active) will increase this to a relatively-fixed 13% per second. So, if the UIO rate of a shield without this DTP were at 70%, the rate would drop to around 50% after five seconds with no attacking particles present (excluding the CDP), whereas a shield with this DTP would reduce the 70% level down to almost 0% in the same amount of time (excluding the CDP).

However, if an opponent were to (on the generally-rare occasion) attain 100% APL against the user's gamma-negative shield while this DTP is active, the shield would still continue cooling UPIs, but only at a reduced rate – that is, 9% per second (so, just over 11 seconds) until reaching 0% overstimulation – again, for an average DPL shield. The average DPL shield also improves the CDP from about two seconds to one second. Due to an increase in the amount of energy that more powerful shields have, these figures mostly scale, so an elite user with their DPL will only have roughly a 15% recovery rate per second.

II) Improves OSR and ORR times caused by both ultrachite and non-ultrachite attacks and phenomena. Note that these attacks technically do not cause the OSR times; instead, they damage a shield, which can lead to its UPO, and this causes the time of the OSR and ORR to occur. While this power does not increase the UOT, it does additionally improve the CDP. As a result, opponents must relentlessly attack the user without stopping for combat effectiveness. The average user's DPL shield (without this DTP) will have a relatively-fixed 10% subsiding/reset recovery rate per second, whereas the gamma-negative shield (with this DTP active) would increase this to a relatively-fixed 20% per second. The average DPL shield also improves the CDP from about two seconds to one second. Due to an increase in the amount of energy that more powerful shields have, these figures mostly scale, so an elite user with their DPL will only have a 30% recovery rate per second.

• Note: For the average DPL shield with this DTP active, there will also be a 2.5% chance that each average DPL discharge will cause the shield to overload for each hit due to a quantum instability issue (no matter the shield's UOT rate).

2: Automatically break apart particular ultrachite and non-ultrachite quantum entanglements through decoherence and entropy. Think of the following abstraction:

if 100 particles (each of a particular power level) were to hit the shield, the shield could weaken the particles, reducing their coherence, say, to 95% of their original strength. They could still have the entanglement, but it would be weak. If there were the same number of particles but each were of weaker power levels, then full entanglement separation would occur. Of course, once a certain number of the said particles reached a certain threshold (so, more particles, but assuming each are of the same strength as the first example), then the 95% weakness effect per particle would drop. In the context of affecting HRFs, conversely, there is typically more of a binary rate of success or failure with a chance check in separating entanglements.

In the context of phasarchement combat, this power mostly applies to discharges, with the first application limiting the overloading chances of gamma-positive discharges against the shield. The average DPL shield will drop a gamma-positive's chance rate of 1.8% at an initial 4.167% APL to 0.6%. The second application will separate the PUC of attacking ultrachite particles of any PAC. As a result, an attacker cannot, for example, have their alpha-positive discharges hit the shield *and then* return (converted photomission and) lumarchetrix energies to them. The said user with their shield will have a 30% chance to fully separate the PUC of one average DPL discharge at once. The statistics for non-phasarchement attacks vary greatly depending on many variables. Interestingly, while gamma-positive shields can turn users invisible, the gamma-negative shield can mar *quantum radar* (that is, radar technology that uses entanglement in its photons), in turn causing users to be hidden on such radar. The average DPL shield can break apart the entangled particles from standard quantum radar devices to the point of making the user appear like nothing but an insignificant anomaly.

• Note: A user cannot use this DTP to separate the PUC they have with their own ultrachite. Accordingly, a user cannot couple this shield with gamma-positive discharges and remove the latter's backfire chance, which would otherwise make this a very powerful combination.

3: Scatter light, causing an optical phenomenon akin to mirages, except that they can appear vertically and/or horizontally. Essentially, opponents will see a field of mirages of the user (and whatever is inside their aura) generally arced around the user but sometimes (also) above them or on the ground. The nature of the optical phenomenon varies, so some auras may only visually displace the user instead of creating distorted 'duplicates'. The opponent's angle of sight will also affect how they will see the optical phenomenon, and they will sometimes be inclined to attack the mirages instead of the user. If an opponent's discharge were to reach the mirages, they would not explode and, instead, would continue travelling (unless the mirages were on the ground or a wall). Average DPL shields require an eight second UPC time that lasts for 24 seconds before a cooldown period of eight seconds occurs. Moreover, while the mirage concentration depends on certain variables like atmospheric light and particulates, the shield may also slightly extend parts of the mirage(s) outside the aura's normal three-metre diameter.

## UST Two/Ultra-plasma (Discharges):

• PCU discharge DTPs:

1: Electrically shock opponents; and, as a byproduct, the majority of particles in the atmosphere around the opponent will entangle and induce further shocks. The average user with a respective DPL discharge can deliver about 3,000 volts with three milliamps while possessing a duration of around 50 microseconds for each shock with a frequency of 15 hertz. After the FTPs end, the *PPE* of the now-entangled atmosphere will essentially form a 'net' *around* the targeted HRF. The net will possess interlacing threads of *receiver particles*, while the gaps between the threads will possess *sender particles*, which will send energy to the receiver particles in the threads via the entanglement to induce further shocks. So long as the particles retain their entanglement, the net's power will not decrease with time, so the effects will remain at full power until the entanglement ends (which is normally as a result of degeneration over time). For clarification, the entanglement will allow for *local* QET, so the latter is what causes the concentrated sparks of energy.

The threads and gaps will change in size relative to the size of the HRF, but if the HRF is too big, then not all particles in the gaps will be entangled; accordingly, the power level of the PPE will always stay the same. At average DPLs, this PPE can last about eight seconds before abruptly ending, but this varies with atmospheric conditions and other variables; afterwards, the particles will lose their associated entanglement. Moreover, the bigger and/or faster the victim's movements, the more pain that will be induced, which will come at the cost of the PPE's timeframe. Shielded mages can resist most of the suffering even at 100% APL, so the effects really only apply to the unshielded. If the opponent is wearing protective gear, then they may also be able to resist the effects.

2: Establish multipartite entangled states at the quantum level in particular ultrachite and non-ultrachite HRFs and systems, which then enables for the delocalization of all their electrons, which, in turn, can help to *overload* various systems. While all ultrachite discharges increase overloading rates for particular systems, gamma-positive discharges specifically (and normally) cause *total* overloads of the *functionality* of systems when each of the affected (and entangled) particles in an HRF/system experience the energetic mass of practically all of the other (sets of) said particles within the system. That is, the delocalized electrons will rapidly shift to one location, causing an overload of the system. One gamma-positive FTP can entangle with and affect many (sets or types of) particles in an HRF. However, an HRF will 'protect' its individual particles first with a chance check like how an ultrachite shield's UAS protects its UPIs. Once the discharge overcomes the chance check (to entangle and shift electrons), then it can generally cause overloading, no matter the power level. Like with other affectable properties within the context of phasarchement magic, this DTP will only affect certain types of HRFs; usually, this excludes most kinds of biological organisms.

Although it is impossible for every particle in a multipartite state to be maximally entangled (that is, all particles equally sharing maximum energy between each other all at once), generally, all but one of the entangled particles within a multipartite state will focus their resources (energy) *to* a single particle *for* the delocalized shift (essentially overloading it) to occur before rapidly repeating the process to (basically) every other particle in the state – all within a rapidly-short timeframe. This, in turn, causes the whole system (of, or within, an HRF) to overload – or, at least, it increases the rate towards overloading a system, but this is generally rare, as passing the chance check is normally enough for an overload of any system. The discharge's FTPs will also not have equal levels of entanglement with the HRF's particles (that is, the FTPs can avoid the collective 'weight' of the HRF imposing overloading problems on them).

There is, nevertheless, actually another chance check that occurs *first*, which determines whether or not *backfire* occurs, where the discharge only affects the user (via PUC), in turn potentially affecting the user's discharge aura and/or other HRFs. Despite the discharge's PUC and the protection it helps provide (which prevents the discharge affecting the user and their ultrachite), the backfire will scramble this protection, so the discharge can accordingly affect the user. Normally (but not always), the backfire chance is 50% at the split moment of impact, regardless of the discharge's power level (due to scaling stability) or that which it hits (of course, *some* properties may alter this percentage *a little*). Although the FTPs will not teleport back to the user, they can still affect the user nonlocally via QET. Of course, when the backfire occurs, the *second chance check* of whether the discharge will cause overloading *then* applies (so the user may not be affected). When the *first chance check* does not result in backfire, then the second chance check will apply to the HRF the user shot. Technically, when a target is shot but backfire occurs against the user, *some* SBE damage will occur against the target, while the rest will apply for the user.

There is also a general hierarchy of what the backfire hits. If the user's discharge aura is still active when the backfire occurs (even if the aura does not have many particles in it due to a potentially recently-launched discharge), then the discharge aura will be affected. If the discharge aura is not active, then the PUC will still apply to the *user*. Accordingly, if there are any *affectable* HRFs near or on the user, they will be affected instead, such as an ultrachite shield or even a wristwatch the user may be wearing. With both the discharge and shield auras simultaneously active in proximity to each other in the user's APA, the power of the backfire will split. However, *applicable*

QDFs will greatly alter what the nonlocally-active gamma-positive FTPs will affect. This means that the FTPs will generally affect a user's shield more than the discharge aura (or a concentrated discharge).

In the context of this DTP (as an offence or backfire), discharge auras are easy to overload. Thus, while most of the nonlocal FTPs will affect the user's shield, the chances for entanglement will typically be around the same for both auras at once with the power split. APLs are also still factored in for when backfire occurs against the user's shield. So, if the user's UIO rate were only at 8.333%, then the shield would inhibit most of the particles into DES. Accordingly, the chance of the second chance check succeeding would be rather low (assuming relative power levels of the discharge and shield). For non-UST HRFs, certain parameters apply for backfires to occur. So, if a user were to (accidentally) shoot an insignificant electronic device or a tiny insect (assuming the latter HRF would be applicable in the first place), backfire would not occur (although, the electronic device would still potentially be affected); that is, there is a sharp cut-off from the 50% chance rate down to 0%. Since there is a large (despite rewarding) risk involved with using this DTP, users still sometimes choose to tune this DTP off when they only want the other gamma-positive DTPs. Gamma-positive discharges more specifically:

I) Potentially overload ultrachite shields. The average DPL discharge will have a 1.8% chance of being able to entangle the particles in an average opponent's DPL shield at an initial 4.167% APL. So, at 50% APL, the chance rate would be 21.6%. Of course, normally (but not always), by the time 50% APL has been achieved (assuming 100% of a shield's UAS chance checks have been passed), the abovesaid shield would naturally have overloaded via SBEs. The overloading PPE is the same as any standard overloading; that is, a QIF occurs, inhibiting the affected shield from reforming for about 10 seconds (plus a CDP) without stacking against the average opponent's said shield. Even if an attack is unsuccessful at passing the second chance check, standard SBE damage will still occur (that is, damage to a shield's UOT and, thus, the opponent's MLP via MECs), while APL *can* still build against the opponent, too, as overstimulating UPIs is a different matter that occurs, regardless.

• Note: When affecting gamma-negative shields, the chance rate for backfire may not even occur due to the shield being able to cut off PUCs. Accordingly, the mage with the gamma-negative shield would potentially (but not always) be the one who would get the gamma-positive's second chance check. It might, then, seem that the shield is double-edged, but there is still a net positive due to not only the abovesaid phenomenon occurring through chance as well (unless PUCs are totally cut off, which would cause a 100% chance to occur each time – that is, if the shield is very strong compared to the discharge – then the shield *would* get the second chance check), but also because of the reduction in the attack's second chance check percentage.

• Note: Since alpha-positive shields are stronger than normal shields when the UOT-boosting DTP has been activated via a UPC, a gamma-positive discharge's chance to entangle the shield is four times worse. So, at 50% APL, the gamma-positive attack will have a 5.4% chance of overloading an alpha-positive shield (when the UOT-boosting DTP is active).

• Note: No matter how close an ultrachite shield is to overloading, the chance checks will still be the same. This has to do with an aggregate potential strength the shield possesses. So, the chance checks only increase in strength when APL builds. There are some non-ultrachite systems where this does not apply, though.

II) Potentially overload discharge *auras*. This, however, is a harder feat to accomplish due to the need for a user to shoot an opponent's *concentrated* blast ball *while* it is still in the opponent's aura. For clarification, shooting at (or rather, 'through') individual, unconcentrated discharge particles floating in an aura will not be enough to not only not even trigger the attacking discharge to explode but also to affect the discharge aura. The average DPL discharge will have an 8.126% chance of being able to entangle the particles in an average opponent's DPL discharge at an initial 4.167% APL. So, at 50% APL, the chance rate would be 97.5%. The overloading PPE is the same as any standard overloading; that is, a QIF occurs, inhibiting the affected discharge aura from reforming for about six seconds (plus a CDP) without stacking against the average opponent who used a respective DPL discharge. Even if an attack is unsuccessful at passing the entangling chance check, the standard SBE phenomenon will still cause the blast ball to explode, anyway, thus the opponent would lose their blast ball. The issue of APL only applies to discharges within the shield's UPI range, so if the user's discharge were to hit the opponents blast ball that was inside the aura but not in the UPI range, then the chance rate would be 100%.

• Note: This DTP does not, in any practical way, overload other USTs.

III) Potentially scrambles and/or induces (temporary or permanent) malfunction in electronic equipment and robots while overloading synthetic or (some) organic shielding and forcefields. So, while the DTP will not affect biological organisms, there is still an exception for any forcefields that biological entities may produce from their bodies. The statistics for this DTP vary greatly depending on the types of targets and the context, but it is quite useful for overcoming electronic equipment that the SBEs of a discharge normally cannot overcome; that is, it has a force multiplier effect (in a single hit) that surpasses any practical threshold that any number of individual normal discharges would inflict in the aggregate. In some situations, opponents may rely on special electronic equipment (that perform certain functions, such as generating powerful forcefields or heavy bombardment), so using this DTP *may* be the only effective way at stopping such equipment.

3: Create a chance of physical entanglement with any HRF in the vicinity when the AES FTPs release on impact, in turn allowing for QET. While affected matter could include mundane HRFs like tables, for instance, there is a higher chance for the entanglement and QET to occur with other ultrachite HRFs (apart from the user's). Unlike alpha-positive discharges that can target specific HRFs with altered (ATP) tuning, users cannot change the tuning of this gamma-positive DTP to target one entity more so over another. In most cases, it does not matter if the HRF is moving or not, so if there were another discharge being fired off nearby, a user's discharge could entangle with the other discharge mid-air. The user's discharge, howbeit, cannot be maximally entangled at the quantum level in a monogamous correlation with the other affected matter (such as a table), as resources (energy) would have to split between the first encountered matter that is hit (a person, for example) and the second one (the table).

At 100% APL, the average DPL discharge will have a 15% chance to entangle with (and teleport energy to) other ultrachite within an eight-metre radius and about a 4% chance for the *'average'* non-ultrachite HRF within an eight-metre radius. More specifically, the entanglement chance for assorted non-ultrachite HRFs varies, but this 4% typically applies in most combat situations in an urban environment. In both cases, the chance rates drop to zero beyond these radii by way of a phase loss. While average DPLs can only entangle one other HRF, higher power levels can entangle more HRFs at once as a default, with the option of tuning the power to affect less HRFs via an ATP. Strategically, this power also allows the user to affect unreachable opponents (and even an opponent's body inside their shields – although, only the first aforesaid DTP would inflict anything effective). This DTP, however, is double-edged in certain circumstances, as it can affect allies as well. It can also split the power of the first two DTPs between the entangled HRFs, so this is another disadvantage. Still, this DTP only has a low chance of success at average DPLs, but many users nevertheless choose to tune this DTP off for safety and/or strategic reasons.

• NCU discharge DTPs:

1: Potentially separate matter via probabilities at the quantum level, specifically affecting the atomic lattices in various HRFs. Basically, the DTP can *cut* a *chunk* of matter out of some overall matter (specifically, though, within an HRF). More precisely, if the discharge were to hit a concrete wall, it would cut out *one* chunk of the wall out, not multiple, no matter the power level. Two sets of chance rates apply to the hit materials, where the first chance check involves overcoming the HRF's *aggregate strength* based on its set of properties – similar to ultrachite shields with their UAS and UPIs. If the discharge does not overcome the HRF's aggregate strength, then absolutely no damage (for this DTP) occurs. When the attack *does* overcome the

HRF's aggregate strength check, then comes the HRF's *specific particle strength*, which involves the matter of how much material can be cut from the HRF.

Rather than damaging the entire HRF, the discharge will only affect a certain spatial range, with the *width* of the attack normally being no more than about 10 cm – that is, the discharge's natural initial impact size. So, whilst the discharge's energy may naturally spread throughout the HRF, the DTP's *effect* will only occur at and from the impact area. Then comes the *depth* of the attack, which varies considerably per the power level and material. Generally, *when* cutting occurs, the entire surface area of a material within the blast impact radius will be cut; but when it comes to the depth of the cut, it is a different matter; so, if the material is super strong, then the material may potentially be cut only one millimetre deep. Since there is only one chunk, it is really only the final depth and width measurements where the cut occurs. When the material is cut, then a small blast will occur, normally causing the cut material to be forced out of the (what-generally-is-a) hole, which is helpful to the attacker, as they do not have to pull the material out (with their hands, for example) before shooting again to make another hole.

In metallurgy and other material sciences, there are the measurements of *strength*, *toughness*, and *hardness*. These respectively refer to a material's resistance to: localized deformation (like cutting); resistance to fracturing (so, it can absorb more energy and deform without fracturing); and resistance to stress before failing (that is, to pull apart). It may, then, seem that the materials with the best hardness would be the most difficult to cut in the context of this DTP, but this is not the case. This does not mean that hardness plays no role; rather, hardness plays *one* role in *many* factors as to what causes materials, in this context, to have various levels of difficulty to cut through. Interestingly, gamma-negative discharges have higher chances of 'cutting' through ultrachite compared to many non-ultrachite materials. However, the 'cutting' process is different, as explained shortly below. On the other hand, the structures in living anatomies are holistically part of complex HRFs that surpass the HRTs of what the gamma-negative power can affect. Accordingly, in combat, mages tend to focus on non-organic matter such as forcefields and (metallic or ceramic) armour, whereas outside (and even sometimes inside) of combat situations, mages may attempt using this DTP to break through walls (concrete or otherwise).

The average DPL discharge will have a 6% chance of passing the HRF's aggregate strength check of standard concrete; and, if successful, the discharge would then, on average, cut around two centimetres deep via the specific particle strength check (in most standard contexts). For stronger materials like titanium, there would be a 0.5% chance of passing the HRF's aggregate strength check before, on average, being able to cut about 0.6 cm deep (in most standard contexts). With a large team of mages, taking down massively-armoured opponents (such as high military-grade robots) is still *possible* at such low chance rates, as enough attacks will possibly lead to adequate destruction. Nevertheless, it usually is easier to use certain weaponry, like rocket launchers (conjured or not), when dealing with such robots.

Gamma-negative discharges *would* affect ultrachite shields in basically the same way as non-ultrachite matter, but since shields naturally heal themselves, no holes practically occur. Nevertheless, gamma-negative discharges can weaken a shield's UOT, so less discharges are needed to bring a shield to UPO. The two sets of chance checks still apply, and even if an attack is totally unsuccessful, APL percentages can still build against opponents, as overstimulating a shield's UPIs is a different matter that occurs, regardless. The average DPL discharge will have a 3.5% chance to overcome an average DPL shield's aggregate strength check at 4.167% APL (not including the UAS the discharge has to *also* overcome); and so, at 50% and 100% APLs, these figures are respectively 42% and 72%.

The actual damage, however – when the discharge is fully successful against the chance checks at these DPLs while at 100% APL – will be the equivalent of six discharges. That is, if the discharge were fully successful on the first strike (at 4.167% APL), the DTP would cause about 0.25% of the damage of a single discharge. So, on the fourth strike, it would be the strength of a single discharge. If each strike were successful at both passing the UAS and the aggregate strength chance check, then, by the time 12 discharges were to hit the shield, the DTP would have caused the equivalent damage of 19.5 discharges (so, in total, the equivalent of 31.5 discharges would have hit the shield). Of course, this is an abstraction, and the shield would have otherwise completely overloaded before this would occur. Shields can nevertheless recover this damage inflicted on them with their general OSR cooldown, so this damage is not permanent until a full overload. Therefore, while gamma-negative discharges do not leave typical TREs, they do leave one by default until the shield recovers from the damage.

• Note: Some materials (that otherwise would seem weak) may still be protected with strong etheric energies that can alter wave functions in particular ways, so sometimes it may not be clear to the attacker as to why their attacks are not efficient.

• Note: There are rumours and legends of powerful mages being able to actually tear open holes in other people's ultrachite shields, where the FTPs would hold the holes open long enough for the powerful mages to shoot other discharges through to their opponents directly. Still, good accuracy, timing, and response skills were supposedly necessary, as the holes would apparently only be just slightly bigger than a standard blast ball.

• Note: Fabled mages were also supposedly able to *destroy* biological HRFs – the degree to which they could varied greatly. While most of these stories seem too far-fetched to have ever happened, some stories mentioned only minor damage occurred.

2: Sever particular ultrachite and non-ultrachite quantum entanglements through decoherence and entropy. Typically, the DTP is more effective at affecting HRFs, as it can target things specifically instead of simply being in their presence like a gamma-negative shield. Moreover, in the context of phasarchement combat, it is usually used to attack shielded opponents and cut off their PUCs to the USTs they create. When used inside and outside of phasarchement combat against non-ultrachite matter, it can be used to subvert certain technologies that rely on quantum entanglement, such as quantum radar (with the statistics against these non-ultrachite technology and phenomena varying greatly depending on many variables).

In phasarchement combat, the average DPL discharge has a 3.75% chance to separate the PUC of an average DPL-shielded opponent's USTs (of any number at once) at an initial 4.167% APL effectively just via the SUC. At 50% and 100% APLs, this respectively rises to 45% and 90%; and, against the unshielded, this rises to 100%. This, of course, is if the *opponent* is directly affected. Technically, if only a UST form were hit (and not the opponent), then the DTP would only affect that UST form's PUC with the opponent and not the opponent's other PUCs to any other active UST forms. However, since the SUC is involved with hitting shields, the opponent is basically hit, anyway. While essentially the same in nature to gamma-negative shields, this DTP can exclusively affect things at range (because a user can *shoot* discharges *at* things); in addition, the user does not have to have a gamma-negative shield active.

3: Sever etheric energy from an HRF. This DTP is very limited in its ability to sever most types of etheric energy, so it virtually only applies to lumarchetrixes and GAPs. Therefore, mysticism and psychicism are the best methods for severing other etheric energies. The DTP severs a portion of an opponent's lumarchetrix (or GAP), thereby temporarily reducing the amount of energy in their lumarchetrix (or GAP). Shielded mages totally block this effect (as the SUC effect *practically* does not apply due a connection issue in this case). The average user with a respective single DPL discharge can sever around 60% of an average opponent's MLP or GAP. To be clear, this would be at 100% APL, but since this does not effectively work against shielded opponents, the APL in the example was not mentioned.

A level of chance is involved, however, which is calculated both by the very nature of the lumarchetrix (or GAP) *and* its (the opponent's) strength – and then compared to the discharge's power level. As such, the aforesaid user would have roughly a 30% chance of success against the average opponent. While TREs do not apply, the opponent will have permanently lost the severed energy. Of course, with the normal LRR, the opponent could still refill their lumarchetrix to their maximum afterwards. The other problem with this DTP is that it is mostly pointless in combat because unshielded opponents can simply be – and normally are – struck with other incapacitating attacks. Still, there are some contextually-applicable reasons for using this DTP against the unshielded.

## UST Three/Ultra-gas (Vortices):

### • PCU vortex DTPs:

1: Cause particular things that enter the vortex (usually, projectiles) to gain potential nonlocal backfire issues – or increase the backfire problems of projectiles with such issues – via quantum entanglement. The backfire itself will occur only when certain conditions are met; normally, this is when a projectile hits something, such as a shield, user, or wall, and the backfire will cause the projectile's shooter (or the object that shot the projectile) to feel the *effects* of the projectile to some degree (and not the actual projectile itself). More specifically, this is done via QET, so only the energy returns, not the actual particles. Combat-based projectiles are typically affected more than other types of properties (of anything) due to their contextual volatility when applied to other properties (such as their impacts). Other types of matter, such as mere gases (while potentially volatile), will not be affected for a variety of reasons (such as a lack of density), so, again, this DTP is generally only practically effective against projectiles (typically found in combat).

Despite an incoming projectile potentially hitting a user while they are inside the vortex's eye (that is, there would be no UPP acting on the projectile at that point), TREs apply, so this is not an issue. Moreover, if the projectile enters the vortex but misses the user and continues until hitting a wall, for example, the backfire would then potentially apply on impact (if the TRE is still active). The average DPL vortex will increase the backfire chance rate of *one* average DPL gamma-positive discharge from 50% to 60% at once. So, if more gamma-positive discharges were to enter the vortex simultaneously, this figure would reduce and distribute across the discharges. The vortex will also be able to cause other types of discharges (specifically, one at a time) to gain a 15% chance of backfire (but not all types of CBEs will work via the entanglement, so it may only be a matter of SBEs applying). In both cases, the vortex will also impose a diminishingly-effective TRE of four seconds. These measurements are taken when the vortex is at 100% AES (and, thus, 100% APL, should someone else's shield be inside the vortex).

The statistics of this DTP against non-ultrachite projectiles vary greatly per type and context. To be clear, the projectile must already have some entanglement with something else, so normally this is very effective in the context of phasarchement battles, as discharges have PUCs. Interestingly, there only needs to be *some* particles within the projectile to have quantum entanglement for the QET to take place with the other entity (such as a gun). This means that if there happens to be some *natural* entanglement, for example, of the particles in the projectile with the particles in a gun, then the effect can take place. Generally, this naturally-occurring entanglement is not common, but there are certain contexts and technologies that will increase these odds or even produce or possess the required entanglement. While some of the particles within the projectile might have entanglement with the other particles within the projectile, the DTP will not work on these particles due to a phase issue of proximity.

• Note: This DTP is an example of one of the rare phenomena that increases the backfire chance rates of gamma-positive discharges.

2: Entangle particular things (apart from the user's) with non-related quantum and potential fields, changing the HRTs of HRFs. While this may seem incredibly-over-powered, the *practical* reality is that this DTP really only entangles HRFs with non-related QIFs, in turn enabling *super QIFs* to occur. So, if an opponent's active shield aura overloads, any other active UST auras will also overload (if the DTP is successful with its chance-based entanglement). This DTP does not increase overloading rates, nor the timespan of any QIFs per se, but the strongest QIF duration will determine how long the other QIFs will last when part of the super QIF. Therefore, if a shield overloads, then a discharge aura (of the same power level as the shield) will take longer than normal to fully cool down. This DTP can *practically* affect many UST forms in the vortex at once without the power dividing.

For further clarification, the vortex's effect may only occur for when a QIF (of one UST aura) *initially* occurs when already entangled with another UST aura (or more). In other words, the vortex establishes the entanglement with various things, altering HRTs with a certain strength, with this strength determining the chance rate for *when* a QIF (initially) occurs. An affected opponent may still create other UST auras that were not originally affected (that is, overloaded) with a super QIF (while their other UST auras are still affected), and the vortex will not bring the newly-created UST forms into the super QIF. However, in general, if two UST auras of the same type are in proximity, then there is a chance on *initial* contact that the non-overloaded aura will overload. The vortex, meanwhile, can increase these chances (so long as the USTs are within the vortex or have TREs applied to them). Moreover, since this is a super QIF, there is a chance that it (the super QIF) can overload any kind of UST aura (even when outside the vortex, where TREs may no longer apply). That is, in this case, the vortex's entanglement would not occur.

For even further clarification, there is a difference between the vortex and the super QIF. That is, while the vortex creates the conditions for the super QIF to occur, the vortex will also cause effects that help increase certain chance rates, while the super QIF will cause other effects; thus, the super QIF can affect other auras while outside of the vortex. When *another* UST aura is brought into the super QIF, the UST with the longest QIF type in general will still determine the overall time-frame. So, if an opponent's shield and vortex auras were part of the super QIF and a discharge aura were brought in, the timeframe would remain at whatever was left for the shield's normal QIF time (as that would be the strongest), so long as the shield's remaining time was greater than the discharge's normal QIF time. That is, if there was four seconds left of the QIF's ten-second period (with the shield determining the timeframe), then four seconds would be smaller than a discharge's normal QIF, so the timeframe would be bumped up to six seconds.

At 100% AES, the average DPL vortex will have a 90% chance to enable the entan-glement to affect an opponent's active average DPL discharge aura with the type of QIF that occurs as a result of an average DPL shield overloading. A diminishingly-effective TRE of about four seconds also applies to UST forms that leave the vortex. The statistics vary by both the type and number of UST forms, along with their power levels, but not how many opponents are inside the aura (as the DTP does not affect opponents per se). In terms of the vortex's effectiveness, it does not matter if the opponent is shielded or not, except in the case of UPIs affecting APLs. This DTP can also apply to physical non-ultrachite things that overload; so, if a robot's weapons system(s) overload, then all of the robot's other active systems may overload, too.

3: Entangle an opponent mage's lumarchetrix channel, creating a chance that they may accidentally use the wrong UST or PAC *on creation* (but not whether ATPs are used instead of DTPs or vice versa). Average DPL vortices will impose a 60% entanglement strength chance against an average opponent with respective DPL shield effectively just via just the SUC at 100% APL. If the said opponent were unshielded, then instant full entanglement would occur. For a precise explanation, the DTP itself does not technically induce entanglement, nor does it potentially induce entanglement; instead, it induces *potential entanglement*, so the victim's entanglement is actually in a state of 'dormancy' until it potentially activates later to cause trouble. So, the DTP itself is not subject to a chance to impose; rather, it allows for the chance of the opponent to create a wrongly-intended form.

There is also a maximum level of effect that this DTP can impose, so a fully-entangled channel cannot completely prevent an opponent from creating their intended UST form or PAC. There is also an *equal* chance that an opponent at full potential entanglement will create any of the available USTs or PACs. In this case, the opponent would have a 16.67% and 25% chance of respectively creating their intended UST or PAC (calculated by the number of available USTs and PACs – that is, seven and four). If at 60% potential entanglement, then these figures would respectively be 26.67% and 40%. A diminishingly-effective TRE also occurs for about seven seconds for an opponent who leaves the vortex. Note that the above statistics apply to just one opponent; when more opponents are simultaneously affected, the power divides. This power can also affect GAPs and other etheric energy (via ATPs), so opponents may use the wrong spell, for example, when casting.

• Note: Legends speak of mythical mages being able to use another DTP for this vortex to entangle the aura's physical space with *potential entanglement*, causing opponents to potentially create ultrachite in unintended places (so long as it was within the user's vortex). The exact details, of course, are murky, but the power could also supposedly apply to other magic (like conjurations) and non-ultrachite matter.

• Note: Other legends also speak of mythical mages creating another DTP that could increase the entanglement chance rates of their gamma-positive discharges.

• NCU vortex DTPs:

1: Create rifts in ultrachite and non-ultrachite (energy) systems, in turn inducing or increasing their destabilization. The vortex naturally has a cap of causing instability based on its power level via its DPS; therefore, any affected ultrachite or non-ultrachite (energy) system which has a power level beyond the vortex's cap *may* create increasing returns on stability. Understand, however, that the 'strength' of a system does not necessarily determine its natural stability, nor how unstable it may become under certain conditions. That is, there can be high-powered systems with low stability in contrast to high-powered systems with high stability. The reverse can also be applied to low-powered systems. This DTP *itself* does not (necessarily) cause (energy) systems to explode; instead, it only increases the likelihood of there being explosions or other similar phenomena when other conditions (not of the vortex) are imposed on them. The statistics for *when* a destabilized (energy) system blows up will vary greatly depending on the context. Note that the aforesaid instabilities do not relate to LCIs, nor does the DTP directly increase a shield's overloading rate. Still, a more volatile shield will potentially experience certain QIFs that will overload a shield without a UOT *rate* necessarily increasing. Naturally, when more affectable properties are inside the vortex, the power will spread.

2: Prevent molecules from forming together. While this DTP might sound over-powered, there are many limitations, such as the number and type of particles in the AOE, along with the speed of the DTP's power in comparison to the normal molecular reaction times. There is also context to consider – which varies greatly – in addition to the HRFs the molecules are in. For all power levels, this DTP is unable to affect the HRFs of all living organisms as well as some non-organic HRFs. In the context of phasarchement, this DTP can also slow down and even stop the OSSR, OSR, and ORRs of ultrachite shields. To affect the OSR, this means the DTP can also affect particular QIFs. The average DPL vortex (at an initial 4.167% APL) will slow the OSR and ORRs down of one average DPL shield by 3.75% and the OSSR down by 4%. At 50% and 100% APLs, these figures respectively rise to 45% and 90%, and 48% and 96%. The latter figures here for each group almost completely stop the recovery process. A diminishingly-effective TRE of six seconds will also apply to an opponent who leaves the vortex. This DTP can also affect the ORR and OSRs of other UST forms. Furthermore, this power is also great at keeping non-ultrachite forcefields from recovering properly.

3: Increase the vulnerability to – and speed of – decompositions. This DTP *itself* does not cause decompositions and, instead, acts as a *catalyst* in aiding decompositions. Unlike the other ultrachite DTPs, this can affect both inorganic and organic (living) HRFs, but the effects on living organisms (at all power levels) really only speeds the aging process to an insignificant extent (so, in most contexts, for most living beings, death will not ensue, nor anything close to death). This power normally has odd contextually-relevant uses, usually – but not always – outside the context of combat. It moreover works well in combination with gamma-negative soaker particles.

## UST Four/Ultra-liquid (Soaker bombs and Swarm clouds):

• PCU soaker particles: potentially cause various particles they hit – or are in the vicinity of – to quantumly entangle. So, if a soaker bomb were to hit a weapon like gun, then many of the particles in the gun could entangle with one another. Moreover, the soaker particles can help increase the coherency between the said now-entangled particles, allowing for greater distances between the entangled particles without a loss in the entanglement. While the soaker particles do not do anything with this entanglement (so, it is just entanglement), they will still allow the user to exploit the situation with other powers. For example, gamma-positive vortices can benefit from this, as it means that when bullets, for example, enter the vortex, energy can return to the gun or even the opponent who shot the bullets. Note that when the energy returns to the gun, it does not, in most cases, destroy or damage the gun; rather, it exerts a force on the gun itself, in turn displacing the gun from the opponent's hands. Still, there are other cases where returned energy can destroy things or properties.

• PCU swarm clouds: weave a web of transparent, ever-changing entangled patterns, which normally distracts most beings. The swarm also happens to 'entangle' sounds (but not through quantum entanglement), causing confusion for the opponent who normally cannot determine a sound's true location of origin. Note that this second phenomenon is not another DTP, so users cannot switch this off specifically without turning off the weaving pattern effect as well.

• NCU soaker particles: form an acid to dissolve particular substances. Unlike most non-ultrachite acids, the soaker particles do not (or at least barely) affect organic compounds, so this is mostly limited to non-organic matter. This, interestingly, is not an HRF issue, and it is, instead, a matter of how the chemicals are formed. At average DPLs, it will normally take about 20 minutes for soaker particles to burn through basic CBAs (which would require repeated consecutive attacks to achieve). Accordingly, it is generally better to use soaker bombs either for indirect attacks (such as affecting computers aiding opponents in battle) or for non-combat uses. Even if the soaker particles are coupled with a gamma-negative vortex to enhance their effect, it is still generally more appropriate to use the bombs for other purposes.

• NCU swarm clouds: create a partial veil of fractured angles of the surrounding area like broken glass, causing difficulty in seeing the surrounding area.

### UST Five/Ultra-conductivity (Propulsors):

• PCU propulsors: quantumly entangle a field of affectable particles (specifically, gas particles) – via a UPC – at a concentrated part of the aura (normally below the user's feet) while coupling them with added propulsor energy that causes the particles to propel *as* a collective field. The air particles will accordingly have increased hapticity, allowing the user to stand on them as if they were collectively a platform. Another set of propulsors will remain underneath the platform/field that will keep it afloat in the air when force is applied to it (that is, when the user stands on it). Basically, whilst the ultrachite will remain underneath the user's feet, the ultrachite will entangle *with* – and add energy to – the air particles to force them to propel towards the user, so it is not the ultrachite, per se, that propels the user.

At the time of the UPC, the platform will nevertheless find equilibrium with the user's weight. Thus, if the user weighs less than what the platform can maximally hold, the propulsors underneath the entangled field will not propel the platform higher. Once a user of any weight steps off the platform, it will rise in the air until leaving the aura. The platform, however, will not last long before it degrades and 'crumbles', and the user must UPC another platform in order to remain in the air. A user can walk on the platform until reaching its edge, with the end time of the UPC starting/forming the new platform (again, generally, right underneath the user's feet *at* that last moment). Therefore, in order to move across distances beyond the platform, a user must walk (close) to the other side and usually take at least one step from the first platform before making another platform.

When more force is applied to the platform beyond what it is capable of maximally holding, it will sink at increasing speeds per force. The platform is also brittle and lacks toughness, so it can easily break; accordingly, even if the platform may be able to hold a resting weight at, say, 100 kg, it will not be able to withstand a force of a certain threshold (even below the 100 kg) that exceeds a certain velocity. The average DPL propulsor will take 1.5 seconds for a UPC before the platform will last two seconds before crumbling. However, there is a 103 kg limit before the platform will begin to sink. The platform also cannot equally withstand any force more than 5 kg contacting it with a velocity greater than about 3.43 m/s (or 12.35 km/h) lest it break.

The average DPL platform will also be around 160 cm in diameter, but a platform will initially form in the centre of where the user is located (unless the user wills their energy forwards). Accordingly, with an 80-cm radius (when taken as an average starting point), it should only take about two small-to-medium steps to reach the other side of the platform. Like other types of UST propulsors, the gamma-positive propulsor has its niche uses. It is the only propulsor that allows for proper horizontal travel across distances in the air; and, unlike gamma-negative propulsors, gamma-positive propulsors can be used to properly cross liquid surfaces *below* (should the user be close to the liquid) – that is, the user and their ultrachite would still not actually touch the liquid. The horizontal traversal can also be more advantageous than alpha-positive propulsors when used correctly. The propulsor, nevertheless, does not exclude vertical traversal, so long as the user's velocity on creation is not too high for lower platforms.

• Note: Note: Legends speak of mythical mages being able to use establish nonlocal fields. The problem with this myth is how the entanglement occurred outside of the field in the first place; the nonlocality issue, otherwise, makes sense, so long as the particles possessed enough coherence.


• NCU propulsors: automatically hover against particular matter, lifting the user off the ground and keeping them separate from it. The user, however, must remain close above surfaces for the propulsor to be effective; but this surface area must be hard enough (as one limiting example), so properties like water are problematic. If a user tried to hover over a lake, they would hover for a moment before slowly falling into the water. For average users and their respective DPLs, the propulsor can support weights up to 103 kg, with a maximum height of 35 cm off the ground for those at or below 40 kg. That is, users weighing 102 kg would hover less than one centimetre above the ground, with the height increasing until 40 kg applies. The higher the power level, the more weight that can be supported, in addition to higher hovering heights (which may specifically lowered via ATPs if they are too high for the users).

This, accordingly, allows for greater manoeuvres. Furthermore, higher power levels allow for longer (but still limited) periods of time over problematic surfaces.

If the power level allows it (per the weight), users can either walk or run while hovering (albeit with some difficulty without practice), and this is performed by lifting their feet up above the hovering threshold and placing one foot down after another – each at an angle – in order to gain momentum. Alternatively, users can keep one foot down, while the other foot can run, in order to gain momentum, thereby simulating a hoverboard effect – even on flat surfaces. On a downwards slope, users can (and tend to) lean forwards, where they will naturally slide down due to gravity. If a particular surface were to jut out while the user is speeding towards it, then, with enough force, the user *could* hit the surface before hovering away from it, but the propulsor energy is generally strong enough to prevent such occurrences at higher power levels. However, once a user reaches enough velocity (especially terminal velocity) when falling from a great height, then, for most DPLs (even if the user switches the power on *just* before hitting the ground), they (the user) would still hit the ground hard and die.

Normally, the propulsor ultrachite arcs around the feet, which makes it easier than being on a flat board, so users do not easily lose balance. The propulsor ultrachite, however, can also be moved, spread, or concentrated to other parts around the user. When the ultrachite is spread across the front of a user's body, this allows for feats like bodyboarding. Although the propulsor, in this case, would be weaker per unit area as it spreads, there would also be less weight per area covered, so the hovering effect would be about proportionally the same. However, in the case where, for example, a person is standing up straight and they spread the propulsor around their body, the ultrachite and its effects would be weaker under the user's feet. Still, this may be a desirable option for those who have already activated their propulsor and do not want to have to create another propulsor via an ATP to lower the height from the ground. For average users with their DPLs, a UPC time of one second is needed before an indefinite amount of usage time is allowed.

• Note: For clarification, even though the abovesaid average users – and, specifically, the bottom of their feet, footwear, or whatever part of their body happens to be close to the ground – will hover 35 cm off the ground in standard contexts, this is not because the aura would only extend beyond the feet 35 cm. Instead, the ultrachite itself would mostly be found close around the body (so, in most contexts, right under the feet). Nevertheless, since the user's aura extends from a central point, this means that they (the user) will have less space at the bottom between their feet and the edge of the aura. So, in this case, the user would not have that much auric room left, anyway. However, even if the ultrachite were to be found right at the edge of the aura, its energy would still extend beyond the aura and cause a hovering effect. Therefore, the said user would still hover about 35 cm off the ground.

• Note: This propulsor will not protect a user against many types of incoming materials, such as ultrachite discharges – should the user place the propulsor field across their body as a form of protection. That is, while discharges would still go through the field unharmed and hit the HRF on the other side (that is, the user or shield) as QTPs due to QDFs and a lack of HRF recognition, the propulsor will also not *propel* against the incoming discharge due to only *reacting* to certain matter; and so, if the particular matter is of a certain *type* of mass and/or does not have *enough* mass, no or not enough propulsion will occur. Bullets will even pass through the propulsor.

## UST Six/Ultra-spacetime crystals (Dimensional Fields):

• PCU dimensional fields: entangle different locations in the fabric of space (specifically, CSUs), in turn causing portals to open to one another (after a UPC), allowing the user to teleport. The entanglement alone does not create the portals, so it is the ultrachite matter that first induces the entanglement *and then* forces the entangled CSUs to open as portals. Due to the correlated states between the CSUs, the ultrachite can send a specific type of energy from one set of CSUs via QET to the other nonlocal set, so ultrachite does not have to be located at the nonlocal area to *open* and *maintain* portals. However, the ultrachite cannot nonlocally entangle CSUs, so there are two methods for overcoming this problem to produce portals (outside of the aura).

The first method requires the user to form a windowed field inside their aura, which is essentially a two-dimensional outline of the portal (usually, this is a circle). It is also the space *between* the outline of these CSUs that will form into a portal. The user then duplicates the window and then shoots one of them out towards the nonlocal area of their choice (usually, this is within their sight – but it can be thousands of kilometres away). This is done through conscious will, where the field of particles will continue moving at a rapid speed (nearly the speed of alpha decay particles – so, just under 15,000 km/s). The particles in this shot-out window will also have enough phased momentum to last outside of the aura in nearly all basic cases.

When the windowed field reaches the destination, it will immediately swap the entanglement it already has with the window in the user's aura to that of the CSUs in that nonlocal area; the same applies for the field inside the user's aura with the local CSUs. After this, the two sets of CSUs will gain the entangled state with each other. The field inside the user's aura will then force the entangled CSUs in both areas to open as a portal. This process occurs in a fraction of a second, but since this method requires a direct line of fire with a location within sight, it is limited in its scope, and it is normally used for locations within proximity – hence the name *proxportalling*. It is still possible for the particles in the window shot out to bounce and bend around objects, but this normally causes a loss in coherence.

The second method requires utilizing already-entangled particles. So, if there were a crystal, for example, located in Location A, and another crystal located in Location B, then the user could send energy to Location B, swap the entanglement of the crystals for the CSUs, entangle them, then force the space there to open as a portal. It is generally better for the particles in the objects (such as the crystals) to already be formed into a hollow circle so that the space inside the circle can be appropriately entangled. The objects do not have to be connected, so the ultrachite can swap the entanglement with multiple objects. When the portal opens, technically energy can be sent 'locally' through the portal because, as at that point, the other side would be within reach. Accordingly, the entanglement can (but does not necessarily have to) be re-established with the objects, so the two locations can still be used again to open portals to one another after the portal closes.

While quantum entanglement itself is not limited by distance per se, quantum decoherence can prevent portals from opening. The user's ultrachite will have a certain level of coherence based on its relation to – and between – other (possible states of) systems. When initially formed, the ultrachite's coherence will be attuned to the environment; however, when it tries to entangle with places (environments) that it is not attuned to and secure in, decoherence occurs. Even if the two locations possess entanglement (and maintain the entanglement), the ultrachite itself sending energy to other locations (and then forcing portals to open) would still be subject to the problem of decoherence. At the planetary level, macro-level forces (such as the gravitational field of the planet – and not just the *local* gravitational acceleration that the particles may be experiencing) play a role in coherence. Different planets have different effects, and even solar systems and solar clusters have their own varying fields. All bodies like solar systems also *relate* to one another (with their proximity), so ultimately, the further the user tries to open portals, the harder it becomes. When decoherence reaches a certain threshold, then there is no chance rate involved, so basically, either a mage can or cannot create a portal to somewhere else.

Power levels play a role in how far away the user can open portals. Average users with their respective DPLs can only create *proxportals*, and this is usually only up to around 60 metres away from their location. Despite the location limitation, even average DPL proxportals are more stable (and normally have greater allowable distances) than *synthetic proxportals* (that mages make with technology), which only can extend a few metres away from each other. Luckily for average users with their DPLs, the UPC time is only 0.5 seconds, with the portal lasting until either the user runs out of photomission energy or decoherence occurs as a result of some environmental variable. Note that in most contexts, if a portal is created, decoherence is unlikely to occur unless some eventful phenomenon occurs. If users of higher-than-average power levels create proxportals at their DPL (for distances of around 60 metres away), then they would still be charged with their normal CECs and MECs, with the portal only having extra (and generally needless) quantum coherence; thus, when making proxportals, such mages will normally just use LPLs.

It just so happens to be the case that with (the beginning of) each power level ranking, the allowable distance threshold increases dramatically due to less quantum decoherence occurring. Still, even supreme-level portals cannot go absolutely everywhere. Advanced users with their DPLs can reach basically any *distance* on the same planet, whereas elite users can extend to any world (including T1 and T3 planets) within the same solar system. Master mages, meanwhile, can reach any world within a solar cluster, and supreme mages can go to any other planet in the Caelverse. Of course, all of these locations will only work if the environment is not hostile to the portal's quantum coherence, and there would have to already be entangled objects in the first place. The UPC times will increase slightly for each power level, though. Technically, average users who are close to advanced levels may still create an HPL aura to travel across their planet while cutting it close with their LCR of 33%.

If the other location's entanglement is based on non-ultrachite mass (like with a circle of crystals), then the user will not be able to shape the other window (so, this is why the other objects should be positioned in a certain way). Normally, the items used in the entanglement have properties that allow for great coherence at long distances; accordingly, portals to other worlds (at *phasarchement portal sites* – PPS) are normally set up with areas filled with powerful crystals. There are also small *teleportation allowance devices* (TADs) that may be personally carried, but these are generally limited in their scope, and they can easily lose their coherence (and when they do, they do not gain their entanglement back unless it is artificially re-established). Of course, in both cases, the entangled particles will only be entangled with one other location, so portals from these cannot be established to multiple locations; however, *other* particles *basically* at (so, near) the location, or even in the TADs, can still be entangled with other locations, but this generally causes decoherence issues. Moreover, if a portal is currently open in one space, then another mage cannot simultaneously open another portal in that same space.

The UPC to *open* the portal will begin after the entanglement has been established. Before shooting out a window from their auras, users can shape the angle at which the portal windows (or rings) will face (both for the one inside the aura and the one that was shot out). However, positioning where the portal will exactly face tends to be performed in PPOs, so users do not have to fiddle around with getting the exact positionings, which helps saves energy. To be clear, before the portal opens via the UPC, the user will still be able to see some kind of window shape. The portal *rings* themselves will be made of physical matter (that is, the ultrachite), whereas the *entangled space* inside the rings will not be physical. Technically, a ring's second window face will not have ultrachite particles, and it will, instead, actually just have a forcefield of energy that will prevent things from touching the edge and being cut off; but this, of course, would still emerge from the now 'local' ultrachite in the first ring.

As with all ultrachite, both fully-formed active rings and latent outlines (along with PPOs) will 'prefer' to emerge in stable, non-solid states. To be clear, this is for the ultrachite particles, not the space between the particles, so things can still be in the space. In fact, the ultrachite rings will not work if they happen to be cut in half because of forming between (post hoc) objects. Therefore, users do not have to fear being cut in half as a result of portal formation and movement. However, portals can still be dangerous. When a *portal* disappears back into the Aether, technically, the *entangled space* will not necessarily end. Generally, if something were sitting between two locations in the rings (other than gas particles and small debris floating back and forth), then the entangled space will not disappear – at first. However, the entangled space will still 'want' to end, with it shrinking non-painfully at first before exerting a deadly force, cutting anything in the way. Basically, portals are safe to use in most contexts (even soon after disappearing), but foolishness (or unfortunate situations, such as a user falling unconscious while in between the two locations) can lead to death.

There are two kinds of portals available for mages; the first being the DTP and the second being the ATP. The first type has two window *faces* in the ring (one at each location), with each having a flow of energy behind them on the other side as if a vortex. The ultrachite's energy will also make them hover. The ATP, on the other hand, has four faces – two at each location, with both being flat as if they were *just* windows. While teleportation, for this ATP, can be used for conventional means, the user can technically remain where they are located and use it for odd purposes. For example, the user could poke their arm through the side facing them (Opening A), and then, on the other side/location (after exiting Opening B), curl their hand around to the third facing (Opening C) on the opposite side of Opening B (if their arm is long enough to physically reach it), then emerge through the fourth facing (Opening D), which happens to be the other side of the first facing (Opening A) at the original location.

As another ATP, users (normally of at least elite power levels) have the ability to simultaneously create multiple portals at the cost of the size and potential reach (location) of each portal. However, if the user is using the two-face portal system, then each portal can only lead to a single exit and cannot be all linked to one another. That is, Portal 1 would lead the user from Point A to B (specifically, these are two faces on the same portal), and Portal 2 from Point C to D (with C being close by or in the general vicinity to B, but of a different portal), but Portal 2 could not lead back to Point A, nor could it lead to another portal (no matter how many extra portals have been created). Otherwise, with four-face portals, this is possible.

Whether using the DTP or ATPs, users are also able to specifically control the shape of the field and the portals (which can help with allowing other beings to teleport with them while still in the aura's space). Nevertheless, all portal faces will always and only have equal dimensions to their other sides. So, if one side were *potentially* bigger than the other, the bigger one would shrink to the size of the smaller one. Portal rings will not *easily* be able to move around while they are active, as this requires new entanglement to form with new CSUs. If the portal rings do move, then normally it will be either in a straight direction (usually not at a fast speed) or the rings will rotate while at the same location. The higher the power level, the more likely the rings may be able to successfully move; and if the portals are within direct proximity (and not just *via* the connected portals), like with proxportals, then the speed, direction, and angles may also increase.

• Note: Other ATPs are rumoured to exist (and have ambiguously appeared in various legends), but these types of teleportation do not ontologically fit with the positive-charge's 'entanglement' archetype, and they are, instead, more like phase shifting instead of entangling with the fabric of space. Therefore, these most likely do not, nor did not, exist – at least for this UST and/or PAC.


• NCU dimensional fields: separate dimensions via a UPC. The user's UST Six aura will separate the user (and whatever is inside the whole aura's space) away from everything in the external world with effectively an impenetrable barrier. This does not block matter like normal forcefields do, but rather, it distorts the dimensions, which, in effect, blocks matter. The aura, moreover, does not push external matter away (except, initially, for anything that is on the line/space of the barrier) – so nothing, in most contexts, is cut in half during the creation process – and its exterior surface area remains the same size within normal reality. This power is basically the ultimate barrier, which grants the user many opportunities for combat and non-combat purposes. In the case of the former, opponents must have been inside the aura before activation, and the general purpose for the power, in this context, is so other opponents outside the aura cannot continue attacking while the user deals with the opponents in proximity. As for the latter, it could involve practically anything, such as fixing a delicate machine, which would otherwise blow up if it were in the direct line of fire from opponents.

While no light would enter the aura from the outside world, the *centre* of the aura, nevertheless, will emit luminescence. Furthermore, if the user is using other UST forms, then there will be more luminescence. If a mage opponent is also inside the field, then, typically, they would also create ultrachite and become easily visible. The user can also simply use other forms of lighting, like torches. No heat would enter the aura either, but this is not a problem, as there would be enough heat inside, which would not radiate outside the aura. The barrier will also stop the planet's gravitational effect on the inside, so the user will float. Interestingly, the barrier itself is of a strange dimensional nature, one that scholars and researchers have been unable to adequately test in order to properly understand its properties.

An ATP is also available, which enables the user to *expand* the internal space by adding CSUs, with the distance expanding outwards from the centre of the aura in all directions (even below the user) but within the limits of a user's power level. While the exterior will physically remain locked at, and to, the location where it was activated (that is, the field would not move either), the inner part of the typically-spherical aura (as with the DTP) will not be subject to certain forces like gravity (bar the tiny gravitational force that the user's bodily mass would naturally produce – which would be practically insignificant). Moreover, the inner aura's edges will contain only a small amount of mass (from the ultrachite particles). Therefore, the user always floats inside. If the user needs to propel themselves in any direction, they must either use propulsion magic (if applicable) or something else that can propel, or the user could simply grab any object that happens to be inside and then thrust themselves from it.

The *generated* space does not come with any mass. Accordingly, the only way a user can breathe is from the oxygen that was already present in their aura when the field first activated. The oxygen will naturally spread in the vacuum, which can be dangerous – even for short periods. Even if the atmosphere were filled only with other gas particles, the low density, in this case, would still be dangerous, due to a lack of pressure. Therefore, mages using this ATP need some form of protection, such as spacesuits. When the dimensional field stops with the ATP, the generated space will shrink before the exterior loses its impenetrability. Because of this, if a user is battling an opponent who happens to be on the opposite side of the field, both beings will join back shortly within the normal aura's space, so caution is needed. Even when absolutely all photomission energy ceases powering the field, the field itself will still exist momentarily until it fully shrinks.

After a UPC time of two seconds at average DPLs, the pocket dimension will last as long as the user has photomission energy or when it is switched off. In fact, the pocket dimension's tangibility will actually last longer than the ultrachite itself. That is, the forcefield will not disappear immediately, lasting, instead, another six seconds (at said power levels) after the ultrachite returns to the Aether for the DTP, and an additional 1.5 seconds for the ATP (which is the shrinking time). The ATP will also rapidly create a sphere with roughly a 21-metre radius, holding over 38,790 m³ of volume. Despite the large volume, a user's ACE can still cover the entire region due to the very dimensional fabric being different from normal, so the traditional ACE area limitations are consequently expanded. This also means that all the user's UST forms can exist beyond the normal 1.5-metre radius when inside the extra space.

There is also another ATP available (with no UPC required), where the user can simply separate particular dimensional (and some quantum) entanglements (instead of creating a pocket dimension), allowing the user to close portals that they did not even create. However, this field is limited by the degree of power, and it is generally very limited if the portals are constantly generated through powerful means, such as the transportals that exist at the intersections of a planet's ley lines; even a group of many powerful mages can only temporarily close transportals for a few seconds. The average user with a respective DPL can close the average DPL gamma-positive portal if they begin closing it with a full lumarchetrix beforehand.

• Note: There are also legends of powerful and mythical mages being able to create various strange realms within their separated dimensions, and while most of these tales are considered too farfetched to be real, it might have been possible to *simply bend* the dimensions in ways that mages of today cannot achieve.

## 3.6.5.4: Delta Class (Motion & Motionlessness):

### UST One/Ultra-solid (Shields):

• PCU shield DTPs:

1: Automatically affect the user's neurotransmitters and hormones via electrical stimulation, modulated magnetic energy (with special oscillations and pulses), and a particular frequency of pulsating air molecules. Although statistics vary for each individual mage due to personal physiology, all shields produce rapidly-tapering TREs in the body after the user no longer has an active shield. Unlike hard drugs that possess negative side effects, delta-positive shields are relatively safe to use short term. When a shield is too powerful relative to the individual, the user's body will not properly derive anything from the energies, and so any additional increases will essentially be 'ignored' by the body. The energies, moreover, stabilize assorted hormones, so an increase in adrenaline will be offset with other hormones.

Infrequent long-term or frequent short-term use *can* also be safe, as one's receptors to the frequencies will become dulled; and, while this is not necessarily a good thing in itself, it does protect the user from over-increasing their hormones. Still, frequent long-term use almost always negatively affects the body. Normally, there is a net increase in euphoria while the shield is active, but the downsides and levels of addiction are, at most, like taking caffeine from coffee. Many users will simply tune down or turn this DTP off after short bursts (both inside and outside the context of combat) whilst also keeping the shield itself active. Delta-positive shields accordingly:

I) Increase movement speed, granting users greater agility, which can be useful in both combat and non-combat situations. The average sprinting speeds for athletic men and women are respectively about 36 km and 32.73 km per hour. Not accounting for many variables, the average DPL-shielded athletic user can potentially increase these rates respectively to roughly 40 km and 36 km per hour.

II) Increase endurance and recovery, granting users the ability to heal faster and reduce breathing fatigue. The statistics for this vary too greatly.

III) Increase strength and pain resistance, granting users the ability to lift heavier objects and cope with greater bludgeons (which still affect shielded mages due to the speed of impacting matter crashing the shield's hardening shell against the user). Because shields only resist *fast*-moving matter, the extra pain resistance can help the user overcome slow-moving sharp objects (like knives), for example, cutting into their body. Combining trained and untrained demographics of all body weights, the average deadlift standards for the average man and woman are respectively 130 kg and 65 kg. Accordingly, the average DPL-shielded user can potentially raise these figures respectively to 170 kg and 100 kg.

IV) Increase alertness, focus, and sensory processing, making users better able to recognize dangers and opportunities. It also typically increases one's judiciousness. The statistics for this vary too greatly.

V) Increase mental fortitude. Users are able to partially or totally overcome certain mental obstacles and challenges – and, in some cases, simply ignore particular effects and phenomena (whether ultrachite or non-ultrachite based). This benefit can even help users against charm magic that utilize compulsions. The statistics for this vary too greatly.

2: Automatically enhance the user's sense of kinetic energies. For the most part, this ability relates to sound and thermal energies, so users can either see sound waves and/or heat radiating from objects (*thermoreception*). Furthermore, users have *echolocation* (bio-sonar), which allows them to hear and identify (precisely) where objects are in their environment. The statistics for this vary too greatly. Sometimes this DTP can become distracting (depending on the context), so some users tune it down or switch it off.

• Note: Users will not see heat energy radiating from gamma-negative shields (when invisible); however, due to the now hyper-aware state of the delta-positive shielded user, if there are *already* irregularities with the gamma-negative shield, then the user would be able to detect them (but they would technically not see anything different from what other users would see).

3: Automatically keep the user's temperature levels at optimal levels (up to the DPL) based on reflexive biofeedback. Electrical pulses either quietly circulate any excess heat out of the shield (like a fan) or distribute energy into the atmosphere to raise cooler-than-optimal temperatures. The higher the shield's power level, the more optimal the effect.

4: Automatically decrease or stop the slowing effects of *quantum locking* (including *spatial quantum locking*) from delta-negative discharges and similar phenomena by means of particular quantum vibrations that specifically affect the fabric of their relative spacetime via a local field. Basically, quantum locking involves a superconductor that can pin magnetic flux tubes of a material; consequently, the pinned flux tubes will lock the superconductor in its place, in turn causing levitation. But for spatial quantum locking in particular, the particles in a discharge will pin the *flux tube equivalents* of CSUs, and the CSUs, in turn, will pin the discharge particles in their place, in turn causing a 'freezing' effect for the discharge particles, which, of course, will pin whatever they surround by default (that is, they will surround a victim and 'freeze' them).

For all power levels, this field will extend a few centimetres from the shield, which will be enough to totally grasp and then affect the discharge FTPs that tightly cover HRFs. The average DPL shield can decrease the spatial quantum locking effects of one average DPL delta-negative discharge at a time by 25% if the discharge is at 100% APL. Accordingly, the said discharge will never be able to reach a certain threshold of 'decent' effectiveness (that is, they will not effectively 'freeze' the shielded user). Interestingly, since newer/stronger discharges affect and negate older/weaker discharges, the 'one discharge at a time' is mostly redundant. However, this may still apply for simultaneous non-ultrachite phenomena at such equivalent power levels, but note that the statistics for *what* other phenomena that affect the shield vary greatly.

• NCU shield DTPs:

1: Increase inertia levels by means of a special form of spatial quantum locking, which involves anchoring to the fabric of their *relative* spacetime via a UPC. The shield's atoms will not increase in mass, nor will there be an increase in the number of particles (that is, mass); instead, a form of 'pseudo-mass' or 'equivalent mass' is added. This may seem like a UST Six power due to the dimensional aspect, but the particles only pin to the CSUs and do not create a 'field' in the same sense that UST Six particles produce. The high inertia of the particles will prevent users from moving (much) or being moved (much) – including while they are mid-air – which also means that the shield will (depending on power levels) potentially create an 'impervious' wall that will cause users to be virtually invulnerable to most standard attacks. In other words, while this has many contextual (and niche) benefits, it is double-edged, as the user will barely – if at all – be able to move on their will. Nevertheless, while passing photons are naturally slowed when moving through the wall of inertia (that is, the already-transparent shield), this is not to any noticeable extent with the naked eye (given their naturally fast speeds relative to all discharge power levels), so users can still see well enough.

While it is true that a shield will have less pseudo-mass per surface area for taller and/or wider mages (due the shield's particles spreading out further and equally distributing across the shield), this is not to any significant extent (as even the tallest of mages do not create shields with detrimental levels), and the shield's particles (for all power levels), moreover, will not collectively 'strain'. All shields above inept power levels will also pass a certain *threshold* of power that allows for decent spatial quantum anchoring. Delta-negative shields are also better than delta-negative discharges in this regard, as they are more stable and, thus, have a better ability to anchor to the fabric of their relative spacetime. In the case of average DPLs, shields will have an equivalent mass of basically 30,800kg.

If something external to the said shield were to push against it with a force of 1,000 newtons, this would cause the shield and the user (assuming zero mass) to accelerate at a rate of 0.03247 m/s². In other words, it would take about 7.848 seconds to reach the first metre of displacement. When adding in for the user's mass, this time increases, so if the user weighed 100 kg, this would be respectively 0.03236 m/s² and 7.862 seconds. The shield's fabric also has both frictional and frictionless properties, so the coefficient of friction for all power levels is roughly 0.5 on standard surfaces. Therefore, if the shield (alone) were pushed on a standard surface, the acceleration would be halved, so it would be 0.016235 m/s² – not including air resistance or any other forces.

Interestingly, since no mass is added to the shield, the weight caused by gravity does not apply; and since gravity is not technically a force (but a *result* of mass), only the shield's inertia is calculated (its pseudo-mass), not the *weight* of the shield's pseudo-mass. Technically, a shield will still have some base mass, but the magic's inertia will also *greatly* reduce this in relation to gravity; as such, the shield will fall *super* slowly, increasing only when other forces impose on it. That is, the shield will take about 80 seconds (from zero-initial velocity) to fall from a height of one metre.

Because the user is not actually frozen inside (as they are only surrounded with particles with increased inertia), their (the user's) weight applies force to the shield. Therefore, if a user weighed 100 kg, then around 980 newtons would be applied to the shield. In this case, at a fall height of one metre (starting at zero-initial velocity), the time to fall would be 7.941 seconds (with an acceleration rate of 0.031715 m/s²) while ignoring the shield's base mass – and 7.901 seconds (at 0.032035 m/s²) when factoring in for the base mass. Of course, lifting the shielded user against gravity would be harder, as this would require at least roughly 981 newtons to *begin* such movement. As the shield's 'weight' would *basically* not be applied against gravity, any force applied to the shield would still move it upwards. So, a force of at least 303,025 newtons would not be necessary to lift the shielded user.

Another key point to understand is that the shield *itself* will always only slow down the user's acceleration (should they be accelerating in the first place), not the velocity, *when* in the context of falling under gravity. In other words, if the user were already falling when the DTP took effect, then the velocity would not drop; instead, only the rate of acceleration would decrease. This principle applies no matter the power level. This means that if, hypothetically, a shield had a pseudo-mass of one million kilograms (which no power level ever reaches), then it (and, importantly, the user) would still have or gain some velocity – should they have had velocity in the first place – or if a force were strong enough to move them. So, even with both a reduced and very slow acceleration rate, the shielded user would still continue to accelerate under gravity for every moment of distance covered (again, barring other forces, such as air resistance). Since there is no reduction in the velocity, even with vastly reduced acceleration, a shielded user will not experience a jolt sensation as they fall when the effect takes place.

When something moves the shield, the shield will not move to back to its original location; however, when the shield is moved, the active particles will still lock to the fabric of their relative spacetime, so there will always be resistance wherever the shield is located. Because weight does not apply to the pseudo mass, when the user inside the shield moves their arm (and, thus, moves the shield as a result), the shield will *basically* not move back to its original location either (unless the person relaxes their arm, which would, in turn, apply force to the shield due to the arm itself having weight because of gravity). Despite the seemingly extreme 'density' of the shield, the shield is actually quite flexible when enough force is applied. Moreover, while the shield is a collective entity, the totality of the shield's 'mass' does not apply to every part across the shield, so, again, bigger shields (by means of bigger users) will have less 'density' per surface area covering them.

A person inside the shield, therefore, can not only use force to reshape the shield (from the inside), but they can also do so at certain sections of the shield (such as the limb areas) at a rate lower than that which is needed to move the shield as a whole. As such, a person can still technically walk or run (depending on the shield's strength – but this is almost never the case, as users typically do not use such weak power levels). If an average-sized person were to conduct a simple bicep curl movement (by means of a 90-degree angle of displacement) with a force of 350 newtons against a shield with 30,800 kg of 'mass', then an acceleration rate of $0.2525$ m/s$^2$ would apply, so the movement would take about 2.266 seconds. Again, the 30,800 kg would not apply to the arm area, so this is a generalized assessment of the 'mass' around (mostly) the forearm.

While this may seem like the user can still easily manoeuvre themselves (so they are not totally frozen), note that for some people, this might be all the force they can muster. Plus, a user inside their shield would not be able to easily use any discharges effectively (should they wish to shoot anything while using the shield) if they cannot aim their arms/hands properly. There is also the possibility to form the shield into a disc form *before* activating the DTP, using it as a wall so the user is not locked into being unable to move (much). However, this defeats the purpose of using it in many (but not all) ways. For example, since the DTP is meant to help resist forces directly pushing against it, this means that melee-based monsters, for instance, could simply walk around the side of the disc and then attack the open and vulnerable user. If, however, an opponent or force cannot move around the side of the shield, then this can be effective.

The average user's DPL shield requires about 24 seconds for the UPC, which lasts for about 16 seconds before needing a 48-second cooldown period before being able to charge again. Note that ATPs do not allow for much variance in these timings. While a shield's temperature will decrease over time, extreme temperatures are never reached due to the short-lived lifespan of the charge. It is not the coldness itself that causes the spatial quantum locking, but coldness itself does still arise from said phenomenon. Despite the coldness creeping in, the shield is not brittle in the slightest, nor does it depend on being cold.

Even though the shield will have increased 'mass', it is still susceptible to the same overloading problems of other shields, and even heavy artillery can still rip right through such shields – as well as send them flying, with general tank shells still being able to send mages (with average-powered shields) flying at a rate of 15 m/s (with what is left of them after the impact). Even phenomena like fire can cause decoherence in the spatial quantum locking, changing the wave functions and then causing a loss in phase. Unlike how delta-negative discharges extend a shield's QIFs, a user using their own delta-negative shield with this DTP will not suffer extended QIFs due to their (the user's) aura being in equilibrium with the 'field' that the shield's particles produce.

• Note: Sound does not easily travel through the shield. While sound is carried by gas particles, the gas particles would not typically move through the shield's walls in time. Sound can also transfer through materials, but again, the sound itself in this case would be slowed as well.

• Note: The shield's CBE-inducing particles require a certain level of equilibrium, which compels them to spread out equally from one another across the shield. This means that a user cannot concentrate the CBEs in one spot in the shield.

• Note: Some mages mistakenly believe that this DTP can be exploited to prevent fall damage to oneself – at least to a sufficient extent. Since shields have lower CECs and MECs than propulsors (which typically help with slowing one's descent from various heights), then it may *seem* like using this shield (with this DTP) cheaply like this is the most beneficial option. However, the statistics for this scheme are not as effective as simply using propulsors, and the practice requires precision timing in very specific and limited contexts; otherwise, it only leads to needless likely death. For example, it does not matter how much pseudo-mass the shield has (besides fall times) *when* the person has *already* reached dangerous velocities, as the DTP does not decrease velocities and, instead, only the acceleration *when* falling under gravity. Plus, hitting a hard shield's walls from the inside will still cause injury due to the velocity of the person versus the shield.

In most cases, users would have to attempt to activate this when at zero-initial velocity, as anything much beyond this becomes pointless. If, say, an average mage with a respective DPL begins charging their shield just as they begin falling (from a building, for example), then it would take 24 seconds to charge. Before reaching the ground, they would have reached terminal velocity, and, thus, the DTP would be pointless. If the user begins falling just as they activate the DTP, then they would fall just over a measly four metres in their sixteen-second activation time. So, if the height were 50 metres, then slowing the fall of the first four metres would be pointless; afterwards, the user would have to wait 48 seconds to begin recharging and then another 24 seconds for the charge. Ironically, novice DPLs allow for a better fall height in this context, but this is only marginal; and, deficient DPLs and lower have problems, so they are not effective either. Therefore, it is simply more effective just to use UST Five magic, as even average mages can fall from heights of up to around 57 metres (when their lumarchetrixes are full) after a perfectly-timed UPC (using beta-positive propulsors). Delta-negative propulsors also have better *practical* reasons for their use, too.

2: Stop the movement of all gases from entering or exiting the shield via a UPC. Explicitly, the restructuring of the shield's atomic lattices gives the user the opportunity to hold (the) oxygen (already) in their shield whilst keeping toxic or detrimental gases out, helping the user to escape from hazardous conditions and environments. Although all shields block gases with high energy levels, if gases with sufficient heat energy enter a shield (below the threshold where they would otherwise be blocked), they can still heat up and burn a user (over time). The delta-negative shield can, however, reduce this build up of heat energy by default of it blocking said gas particles.

The average user's DPL shield requires about 25 seconds of charge time, which lasts for about 50 seconds before needing an eight-second cooldown period before being able to charge again. Note that ATPs do not allow for much variance in these timings. Since there is a long charge time due to the fine-tuned atomic restructuring involved, users must know that they will survive an excursion into a dangerous environment before using the power because they (the user) may not survive after the power ends before recharging. It may be easy to hold one's breath for thirty seconds, for example, but if amidst a battle or a dangerous situation, one's requirement for additional oxygen normally rises; accordingly, this DTP may not provide enough time for many users in certain contexts *when* charging up.

Also note that while all shields (of any PAC) can block water coming inside, they do not keep gases *inside*, which may (quickly) deplete when underwater (even when the other shields harden when struck). Delta-negative shields, however, are effective in this regard, so the amount of oxygen will remain at safe levels. Technically, gases can still enter other shields while underwater, but this does not occur at a rapid rate in normal contexts, so it would be at a slower rate than what would escape. If a mage were to *create* a shield while they were already underwater, then water would already be inside, so this DTP would only be effective before going underwater. The delta-negative shield is also practical in situations where strong winds would otherwise hit the user; however, wind can still blow the shield over and, thus, the user.

• Note: Technically, while the first DTP can 'block' gases as well (due to slow speeds), this DTP has the special advantage of enabling the user to move with normal speed (while also actually safely and securely keeping gases from moving in and out of the shield).

3: Prevent most 'slow-moving' matter (in most standard contexts) from *tearing* through the shield. As a result, this can prevent knife attacks, for example, from harming users inside the shield. Of course, if *enough* force is applied, penetration is still possible, so no shield is *invincible*. The average user's DPL shield requires about four seconds of charge time, which lasts for about 220 seconds before needing a four-second cooldown period before being able to charge again. Note that ATPs do not allow for much variance in these timings. The shield can also withstand about 12 standard knife attacks (that is, from knives made from normal metals with typical lengths and widths) – each with an average of 15 joules per attack – before the DTP's effect stops. This phenomenon is different to overloading (as it is related to the DTP itself), so a shield should not overload as a result. Of course, knife attacks *do* affect a shield's UOT, but this is very marginal per attack. Should the user receive, say, 11 attacks in the first ten seconds of their UPC, then it may be beneficial (depending on the context) to reset the power by switching it off and then recharging it in order to gain the total strength back (as the active timer is rather long).

• Note: There are rumours and legends of powerful mages being able to establish another DTP for this shield, where the shield would become either super cold or resistant to heat; simultaneously, however, the shield would become super brittle, easily able to shatter when bullets or discharges hit them.

## UST Two/Ultra-plasma (Discharges):

### • PCU discharge DTPs:

1: Seek out motion and heat, homing in on particular targets. Technically, the discharge does not intentionally seek targets unless energetically triggered by things that possess a certain *level* of *both* heat and movement. There is, moreover, a minimum and maximum level of requirement for both phenomena, so if a microorganism were very hot, for example, it would not trigger the discharge. Likewise, the sun will not trigger the discharge either. At all power levels, the mere natural movement of a person's fingers, for example, will not trigger the delta-positive discharge either, but walking at a normal pace, however, will certainly attract the attention of the discharge. Still, users can alter the DTP to an ATP so that the levels of each can change, but normally, users do not need nor want to change the DTP. Since ultrachite is mostly luminescent, it does not emit much heat; as such, any UST form itself will not trigger delta-positive discharges (at the DTP level). This means that delta-positive discharges will not continually seek out other discharges in the air.

While this homing ability may seem terrible against ultrachite shields, bear in mind that the heat from a mage can still escape a shield, so the discharge will still be attracted to the shielded *mage* (except for when certain CBEs apply, such as when against invisible gamma-positive shields). Moreover, the discharge's APL and power level are not applicable against the shield (nor the power level or UPI count of the shield, unless certain CBEs apply), as the heat from the shielded mage's body will radiate well beyond the shield's UPI range. The discharge can still seek out things in such a state because discharges themselves are erratic, releasing tiny amounts of AES particles before impact (but not enough to nullify the discharge before it hits anything).

The average DPL discharge will start seeking things when triggered within a four-metre range while also being able to move within a 120-degree conical angle of trajectory. Unlike alpha-positive discharges that can technically start moving towards the target at any angle and still potentially miss (that is, the target may still be outside of the accurate conical range), the delta-negative discharge will only be triggered when moving targets are within the angle of trajectory; otherwise, the discharge will not change its course. Accordingly, the discharge will not attempt to do a 180 degree turn and head toward moving allies who may be next to the user. Higher power levels naturally have increased range and degree. If there are multiple targets of equal 'worth', then the discharge will head towards the closest target or the one within the straightest course (whichever is the easier of the two). Given the larger range than alpha-positive discharges (when applicable), delta-positive discharges are normally the main type of discharge for seeking opponents. Nevertheless, when opponents behind cover are not moving (much), then the discharge will not home in on them. Depending on the context, this DTP may be detrimental, so users merely tune it off when channelling. Usually when this happens, it involves situations where the discharges keep hitting unwanted targets.

2: Create a flash of bright light, blinding opponents. The FTPs themselves do not produce the light; instead, they charge the HRF, and this induces an electric field from the outer layer of the HRF. In other words, if the HRF is a person, then the outer layer of their skin would emit the electric field. The charged HRF will then ionize the surrounding air molecules; and in their ionized state, the air molecules will attempt to ground themselves by emitting photons – hence, the flash of light. Since only the outer layer of the HRF is charged, it does not electrocute people, but a slight stinging shock will normally accompany the phenomenon.

The charged HRF will also generate a modulated magnetic field that will affect the edge of the surrounding air molecules. The outer area of these air molecules, in turn, will create an *electromagnetically induced transparency effect*, which can catch and basically stop the said photons. The magnetic field will also induce a *magneto-optic effect*, where the photons will change their trajectory, in turn firing back at the HRF. This not only strengthens the light towards the opponent, but it also helps to protect the user (the attacker) from also being blinded. Howbeit, for all power levels, this will only catch the majority of photons, not all, so the user will still see some light, but the uncaught photons will not be at high levels, so the user will not be blinded. This also means that the discharge will momentarily light up areas to some degree.

Average users with respective DPLs will generate around 50,000 lumens for each discharge; and, when initially applied to the average DPL shield at 4.167% APL, this would be about 2,084 lumens, which is still enough to cause temporary mild blindness and disorientate opponents. Normally, about 10% of the photons will escape, and the user will not see all the photons, anyway, as the whole HRF affects *surrounding* air molecules (so, this would include the ones behind them). Accordingly, opponents will generally see a minimum of 4,500 lumens in a single attack at 100% APL. When and where the FTPs are not inhibited by UPIs (including being shot at a nearby wall, for example, or from another opponent whose attacking photons escaped through the abovesaid affected air molecules), the light itself (not the FTPs) will completely penetrate all shields (except in the case of gamma-positive – depending on invisibility levels). The intensity and duration of the blinding and PPEs vary per the individual and the environment and context. For example, the lighting of the room beforehand (whether light or dark) will determine the size of one's pupils and, thus, the amount of light their eyes will take in. Some mages wear protective eyewear during combat to prevent being blinded, but such protection is not that effective against the discharges; and, in the cases where they are effective, they end up diminishing the wearer's vision in general, so such eyewear is not that common.

3: Create a loud bang at the initial impact location, with the sound being able to extend beyond the HRF or other materials. This consequently affects the victim in assorted ways, but mostly, it will abruptly stun and/or disorient the victim – especially when used in succession. Shooting near an opponent can still affect them as well, making this effective at overcoming unshootable opponents (should the homing DTP not help the discharge hit any opponents). Furthermore, the bang is typically used against unshootable opponents who are waiting in cover for their shields to recover from a recent overload. It can even be effective at reducing an opponent's ability to (properly) hear what the user may be doing, in addition to reducing a person's peripheral stimulus processing.

Measured from 1 cm away from the impact, the average DPL discharge will create a loud bang of 130 dB (with supreme levels reaching 135 dB). Factoring in for the distance attenuation at the abovesaid level (1 cm), this means that an opponent just one metre away will only experience a sound pressure of 90 dB. Accordingly, the sound will not be *that* loud for most nearby opponents in general situations, but it will still serve as a distraction or a nuisance. At an initial 4.167% APL build against the average DPL shield, the first figure of 130 dB would be about 114 dB. When measured from, say, five metres away, the sound will only reach about 75 dB, so the user will be safe and unfazed when firing in most contexts.

Even though APL applies, the sound itself will fully go through the shield (if against an applicable shield). While in most contexts this bang will not cause most humans to go deaf (at all DPLs), repeated strikes can still cause hearing problems. Of course, it can be quite detrimental if the initial impact is *right* at one's ears. Still, discharges practically never go *into* a person's ears, so the abovesaid 1 cm basically applies here, where the victim's ears will not experience anything much over 130 dB, anyway. For users requiring quiet attacks (for any number of reasons), then this DTP is tuned down or off. Note that this is not the same DTP as the aforesaid flash of light, and a few mages mistakenly think this due to the existence of flashbang grenades, where both a flash and a bang will occur in one package.

4: Induce *vertigo* in most biological organisms. Vertigo is essentially the *sensation* of spinning or moving *despite* not necessarily moving. Normally, this results from ear issues, but the discharges *charge* the victim with energy that causes the brain to feel these effects. There is a chance that robots may experience this effect or something similar due to the nature of the charge. TREs also apply, as well as PPEs, such as vomiting. The statistics for this vary greatly, but the average DPL discharge (at 100% APL) will typically make the common human feel like they are spinning around at a decent rate. Shielded opponents can feel this effectively just via the SUC.

• Note: Legends speak of mythical mages that possessed a DTP that could physically spin the targeted HRF. The angular rotation, velocity, and momentum of the spin would depend on various factors, but the average humanoid body (in standard contexts) would spin around once in a second and then fall over as a PPE due to a loss of balance; that is, when a person or object fell, it was an *outcome* rather than a direct effect of the spin. The spinning would also spin all parts of their bodies equally as one entity, so it is not like a victim's neck would snap.

• Note: Legends speak of mythical mages that possessed another DTP that could cause *motion reversal*. That is, they could force opponents to move in the opposite direction to what they intended. So, if the affected opponent wanted to move their arm to their right, it would move to the left instead. It is unclear whether this feat was done by altering physiological aspects, like one's nerves, or if this was purely mental. The ontological aspect of this DTP, however, is rather odd in relation to the delta PAC of motion, as it supposedly did not increase nor induce motion, nor did it have properties with aspectually-high motion.

• Note: There is yet another mythical DTP found in legends: certain mages were also able to increase the acceleration of hit HRFs or materials. That is, they were able to induce and increase the acceleration of an HRF, which means that if an affected person, for example, were to normally fall at a certain speed, the DTP would increase the velocity. After the FTPs would disappear, the existing momentum would continue carrying the affected HRF. Note that for all three of these extra DTPs, it is unclear how these properly worked in unison – if at all.

• NCU discharge DTPs:

1: 'Freeze' HRFs or objects on impact by surrounding them with a wall of increased inertia. Unlike the FTPs in other discharges, delta-negative FTPs require a certain level of equilibrium that compels them to fully cover an HRF's surface area – either through normal spread across the HRF or, in some cases, quantum tunnelling through the HRF – which, in turn, forms a tightly-fitted and thin cast. The high inertia of the particles will prevent the HRF from moving (much) or being moved (much) – including while the HRF is mid-air – which also means that the FTPs will (depending on the power level of the attack) potentially create an 'impervious' wall that will cause the HRF (whether an opponent or ally) to be virtually invulnerable to most standard attacks. While passing photons are naturally slowed when moving through the wall of inertia, this is not to any noticeable extent with the naked eye (given their naturally fast speeds relative to all discharge power levels), so users can still see the affected HRFs well enough.

Even though the FTPs contain a high amount of inertia, no mass is added; that is, 'pseudo-mass' or 'equivalent mass' is added due to the particles anchoring to the fabric of their *relative* spacetime through a form of spatial quantum locking (like with delta-negative shields). Accordingly, their dissipation rate is gradual; and so, their tangible existence is actually longer than that of other ultrachite discharges – lasting around four seconds for average DPLs at 100% APL. Despite the extended time, the actual moment the FTPs begin dissipating is abrupt (that is, not gradual); specifically, *at* the four second mark, the FTPs will disappear rapidly rather than slowly. The cast's temperature will decrease over time, but since the FTPs dissipate before any extreme temperatures are reached, this is not dangerous in most circumstances. It is not the coldness itself that causes the quantum locking, but coldness itself does arise from said phenomenon. Despite the coldness creeping in, the cast is not brittle in the slightest, nor does it depend on being cold.

When users shoot delta-negative discharges at already-affected HRFs, the newer particles will render the older particles into DES before pushing the latter out of the way, in turn causing the slowing effect to end immediately. In this case, the UPS is still super quick. As a result, a user can shoot a target either continuously and rapidly or continuously just before each four-second period is over, and the affected HRF will remain frozen (due to the newer FTPs immediately re-establishing the effect). The newer discharges will also not affect the wall of inertia as an HRF (as typically, discharges are hard to affect as HRFs, anyway), and they will, instead, affect the QDF on the other side (that is, the HRF that was originally affected). As the FTPs turn from DES to AES on impact, they will still burden a targeted shield with their energy; thus, overloading an opponent's shield is still possible before the FTPs begin dissipating. Also, the wall of inertia will extend QIFs, so after the abovesaid four seconds have passed, an ultrachite shield's cooldown will still be basically the same as when the attack hit them.

The FTPs will cover HRFs of basically any size (so long as the particles register the HRF as an HRF), but the bigger the HRF, the weaker the effect becomes due to both the lower density of particles per surface area and the FTPs collectively 'straining'. In the case of very large identifiable HRFs, the FTPs will still spread out over the whole HRF instead of only a part (like a monster's chest), which means that the bigger being will be slower as an aggregate instead of being frozen in specific places over its body. If the HRF (if, again, registered as an HRF) is exceptionally big, then the FTPs will spread and basically do nothing effectively as they will not meet a certain *threshold* of power, where the FTPs properly lock to the fabric of their relative spacetime.

In fact, once certain thresholds of spatial quantum locking are met for any HRF size, the scaling of the power level changes. For example, *just* before 100% APL is achieved at the average DPL, exponential changes occur for the level of effects. So, basically before 100% APL is reached, average DPLs are not *that* effective (that is, they do not 'freeze' opponents). Given that higher power level discharges can bring lower power level shields to UPO faster, this means that advanced and elite DPL discharges cannot effectively freeze an average DPL shield before overloading them unless the shield's affected UOT subsides before the OSSR. Still, advanced discharges and higher against advanced shields and higher can reach this 'full freezing' threshold effect before reaching 100% APL; and while this is a little overpowered, consider that the UAS chance checks still have to be passed, and so, in standard cases, the said discharges would still likely overload their same power level shields before reaching this threshold.

In the case of average DPLs, the cast will have an equivalent mass of 7,700 kg when at *100% APL*, with no collective straining applying to HRFs the size of average-sized humans. If something external to the affected HRF were to push against the said cast with a force of 1,000 newtons, this would cause the cast and the affected HRF (assuming zero mass) to accelerate at a rate of 0.12987 m/s². In other words, it would take about 3.92 seconds to reach the first metre of displacement. When adding in for the HRF's mass, this time increases, so if the person weighed 100 kg, this would be respectively 0.1282 m/s² and 3.95 seconds. The fabric of the cast has both frictional and frictionless properties, so the coefficient of friction for all power levels is roughly 0.5 on standard surfaces. Therefore, if the cast (alone) were pushed on a standard surface, the acceleration would be halved, so it would be 0.064935 m/s² – not including air resistance or any other forces.

Interestingly, since no mass is added to the FTPs, the weight caused by gravity does not apply; and since gravity is not technically a force (but a *result* of mass), only the cast's inertia is calculated (its pseudo-mass), not the *weight* of the cast's pseudo-mass. Technically, the FTPs will still have some base mass, but the magic's inertia will also *greatly* reduce this in relation to gravity; as such, the cast will fall *super* slowly, increasing only when other forces impose on it. That is, the cast will take about 40 seconds (from zero-initial velocity) to fall from a height of one metre.

Because the HRF is not actually frozen inside (as they are only surrounded with particles with increased inertia), their (the HRF's) weight applies force to the cast. Therefore, if an HRF weighed 100 kg, then around 980 newtons would be applied to the cast. In this case, at a fall height of one metre (starting at zero-initial velocity), the time to fall would be 3.99 seconds (with an acceleration rate of 0.12564 m/s²) while ignoring the cast's base mass at 100% APL – and 3.97 seconds (at 0.12691 m/s²) when factoring in for the base mass. Of course, lifting the HRF against gravity would be harder, as this would require at least roughly 981 newtons to *begin* such movement. As the cast's 'weight' would *basically* not be applied against gravity, any force applied to the cast would still move it upwards. So, a force of at least 76,492 newtons would not be necessary to lift the affected HRF.

Another key point to understand is that the cast *itself* will always only slow down the HRF's acceleration (should it be accelerating in the first place), not the velocity, *when* in the context of falling under gravity. In other words, if the affected HRF were already falling when the discharge took effect as a cast around them, then the velocity would not drop; instead, only the acceleration would decrease. This principle applies no matter the power level. This means that if, hypothetically, a cast had a pseudo-mass of one million kilograms (which no power level ever reaches), then it (and, importantly, the HRF) would still have or gain some velocity – should it have had velocity in the first place or if a force were strong enough to move it. So, even with both a reduced and very slow acceleration rate, the HRF would still continue to accelerate under gravity for every moment of distance covered (again, barring other forces, such as air resistance). Since there is no reduction in the velocity, even with vastly reduced acceleration, the HRF will not experience a jolt sensation as they fall when the effect takes place.

When the cast is moved, it will not move to back to its original location; however, when the cast is moved, the FTPs will still lock to the fabric of their relative spacetime, so there will always be resistance wherever the cast is located. Because weight does not apply to the pseudo mass, when an affected person inside the cast moves their arm (and, thus, moves the cast as a result), the cast will *basically* not move back to its original location either (unless the person relaxes their arm, which would, in turn, apply force to the cast due to the arm itself having weight because of gravity). Despite the seemingly extreme 'density' of the cast, the cast is actually quite flexible when enough force is applied. Moreover, while the cast is a collective entity, the totality of cast's 'mass' does not apply to every part across the cast, so, again, bigger HRFs will have less 'density' per surface area covering them.

A person inside the cast, therefore, can not only use force to reshape the cast (from the inside), but they can also do so at certain sections of the cast (such as the limb areas) at a rate lower than that which is needed to move the cast as a whole. As such, a person can still walk or run (depending on the cast's strength). If an average-sized person were to conduct a simple bicep curl movement (by means of a 90-degree angle of displacement) with a force of 350 newtons against a cast with 7,700 kg of 'mass', then an acceleration rate of $1.011$ m/s$^2$ would apply, so the movement would take about $1.134$ seconds. Again, the 7,700 kg would not apply to the arm area, so this is a generalized assessment of the 'mass' around (mostly) the forearm. While this may still seem rather fast, note that for some people, this might be all the force they can muster. Plus, the reality of a person intentionally moving assumes that the second DTP does not even apply (see the next DTP for more information), which normally it would.

No TREs apply for this DTP, and since AAEs also do not apply for *this* DTP, additional attacks prolong the freezing according *only* to how long the FTPs last. This

DTP has many uses in both combat and noncombat contexts. For one, a user may freeze objects that are aiding their opponents, thus helping the overall battle; alternatively, users can freeze nearby objects to directly help them. Even freezing an opponent (instead of overloading them and knocking them out) can be beneficial, as the frozen body could block other opponents from manoeuvring or even escaping from a particular location. Monsters that are rather resistance to beta-negative's unconsciousness effect may still be vulnerable to delta-negative's freezing, so this may be used instead. Users may even shoot their own allies for a variety of reasons, such as granting them virtual invulnerability in a heated fight. However, this would effectively only work to protect their allies against non-ultrachite matter like bullets, as ultrachite discharges could still 'penetrate' the wall of inertia by way of UPSing the CBEs. Depending on the context, some mages (generally police and security forces) will first shoot beta-negative discharges at beings to cause them to become unconscious before then quickly shooting delta-negative discharges so that the victim does not hit their head (hard) on the floor when they fall, which could otherwise potentially (majorly) injure or kill them.

• Note: Some mages mistakenly believe that this DTP can be exploited to prevent fall damage to oneself (or allies) – at least to a sufficient extent. That is, a user can firstly and technically switch off their default PEP-changing mode that prevents a user's discharges from affecting them; after this, a user can shoot themselves while falling (or when just about to fall) and then receive the benefits of a slower fall. Since discharges have lower CECs and MECs than propulsors (which typically help with slowing one's descent from various heights), then it may *seem* like using discharges cheaply like this is the most beneficial option. However, the statistics for this scheme are not as effective as simply using propulsors, and the practice requires precision timing (along with the second DTP being switched off, lest the user attempt precision against sluggishness). One major issue is that it does not matter how much pseudo-mass the cast has (besides fall times) *when* the person has *already* reached dangerous velocities, as the DTP does not decrease velocities and, instead, only the acceleration *when* falling under gravity. Plus, hitting a hard cast's walls from the inside (even when tightly wrapped around the user) will still cause injury due to the velocity of the person versus the cast.

In most cases, users would have to attempt to activate this when at zero-initial velocity, as anything much beyond this becomes pointless. If we take an average mage with a respective DPL, then, after the four seconds has passed after shooting (where the FTPs dissipate), the user must immediately shoot themselves again before the acceleration picks up greatly, in turn worsening the velocity. The problem is, the discharge aura can easily overload when used like *this*, and the average DPL user will experience an overload at around eight roughly-consecutive seconds of being slowed.

This means the user could only shoot themselves twice and have a fall height of just over four metres, not making this very effective.

With the QIF penalty of six seconds after the UPO, the user would reach terminal velocity (assuming no air resistance) before being able to use this scheme again. Even with air resistance, they would still reach deadly velocities. LPLs below average DPLs are not effective with their bad rates if slowing acceleration; and, while more advanced DPLs may have better overload resistances, the 'better' acceleration rates do not work well with this scheme. Therefore, it is simply more effective just to use UST Five magic, as even average mages can fall from heights of up to around 57 metres (when their lumarchetrixes are full) after a perfectly-timed UPC (using beta-positive propulsors). Delta-negative propulsors also have better *practical* reasons for their use, too.

If, however, the user were to shoot an ally, then there is another problem, where, technically, if an HRF or spatial area has been exposed to too much 'pseudo-mass consecutively for a while, then any further discharges will not have any effect for a short period. More specifically, it does not matter how many discharges hit the HRF; instead, it only matters how long the HRF has been affected; and for average DPLs, this is about 20 consecutive seconds. So, this means the average user can only affect HRFs up to five consecutive times before a short penalty of six seconds applies (whether falling or not – so, this also applies to users not using this scheme). In this case (assuming zero-initial velocity), the ally would fall about 25.382 metres (excluding air resistance) with a final velocity of 9.138 km/h.

Parenthetically, LPLs below average DPLs have worse time frames, so they are not effective; and, while more advanced DPLs may have better resistances, the 'better' acceleration rates do not work well with this scheme. While this scheme of shooting an ally may actually be somewhat effective, keep in mind that this is not effective compared to propulsors. The main benefit here, though, is that the ally may be unconscious, so they would not be able to use propulsors. There are, nevertheless, ways for two or more conscious mages to try and help each other with this scheme, but there may be many other contextual factors to consider, such as whether the mages are in the heat of a battle or not.

2: Cause sentient and non-sentient beings to enter a state of flash-*suspended animation* (that is, the slowing or stoppage of bodily functions and consciousness, like with hibernating beings). As its own DTP, this works independently from the first DTP, so users do not have to physically encase HRFs to induce suspended animation. A single average DPL discharge will cause the average biological humanoid to enter suspended animation instantly with a *full TRE* of around four seconds (that is, they will remain *fully* in suspended animation for the four seconds). For clarification, the effect will not gradually drop off through degeneration; instead, the effect will sharply end. On the other hand, when used against the average DPL-shielded opponent, only attacks with roughly 100% APL (at average power levels) can induce the suspended animation.

Even if the user were to launch, say, 48 discharges at the shielded opponent, none would be effective if all are each under roughly 100% APL, as the individual attack *itself* must meet the threshold requirements for the suspended animation to take effect. For clarification, this is a SUC (and equivalent) issue, so even if the said attack were not at 100% APL but hit the opponent directly (so, no SUC involved), it could still potentially cause full suspended animation. Moreover, accumulation of effect *to cause* suspended animation can still occur in contexts without the SUC, so this means that mages can still cause certain beings with resistances against this effect (like monsters) to enter into suspended animation should they (the mages) attack the being enough times. This even applies to novice mages.

Even if the opponent could attempt to physically break free from the *first* DTP's effects (should the first DTP be switched on with the attack), then they (the opponent) would be unable to do so due to being unconscious in their suspended animation. That is, both DTPs go hand-in-hand with each other at the same time – and, in most cases, for the same time. Unlike the *stacking* effects of beta-negative discharges, the suspended animation of delta-negative discharges (specifically, the *time*) virtually does not stack, but the suspended animation *itself* (when induced) has AAEs, consisting of confusion, sluggishness, and lower critical reasoning and problem-solving skills. As a result, after the suspended animation ends, opponents might either make silly, limited, or even no decisions. Against the average biological humanoid, a single average DPL discharge will cause AAEs that will generally (but diminishingly) last about six seconds, while additional attacks will typically induce increasing intensities and durations (against more susceptible opponents) of varying amounts.

Although the effects of the suspended animation are induced effectively just via the SUC against shielded mages, the AAEs will still last the same amount of time (compared to affected unshielded opponents) because the effects come from the suspended animation *itself*. For clarification, despite the attack's effect of suspended animation being weaker against shielded mages, once suspended animation has been attained/induced, the effect itself then produces the AAEs. When the user does not use this DTP in conjunction with the first DTP, then it can still be useful (and, in some cases, necessary for achieving certain goals). For example, when a user needs to quickly place magic suppressors on someone without knocking them unconscious with a beta-negative discharge (as this could otherwise send them unconscious for too long, which could be detrimental for the context), it would be much harder to do so if the person were frozen, as the cast of inertia would make moving their limbs difficult. When an opponent is not frozen (and, instead, is only in a flash-state of suspended animation), then moving their arms should be an easy and practical option for whatever goals the user possesses.

• Note: Creating LPL beta-negative discharges to just knock an opponent out for a few seconds is so tricky and fine-tuned per the context and for the victim (and for getting the precise energy levels right – and to make sure that a certain threshold is even met for the effect to succeed) that it virtually does not occur.

## UST Three/Ultra-gas (Vortices):

• PCU vortex DTPs:

1: Vibrate with a particular frequency, in turn causing motion sickness in organic beings, which is then followed with issues of neuropathy, disorientation, disequilibrium, and even rash-decision making. Other entities like robots may experience different kinds of problems with their hardware, most of which involve malfunctions if they are not resistant to such tremors. Shielded mages will still fully feel these effects (regardless of APL – so long as there is *some* APL), with the vibrations first hitting the shield before tremoring through the small amount of air between the shield and their bodies. The level of sickness, nonetheless, subjectively varies per individual. The vortex naturally does not target HRFs, so any matter inside the vortex is affected, which means specific HRFs within greater HRFs cannot be targeted, so this DTP is not dangerously overpowered. It also *basically* does not matter how many opponents are in the vortex in normal contexts, so each opponent will still feel the same level of effects (so long as the opponents are not negatively affecting the vortex).

• Note: Motion sickness is a result of being triggered by actual movement, whereas vertigo (that delta-positive discharges cause) is caused without any actual movement.

2: Vibrate the non-ultrachite air molecules to such an extent that the vortex causes them to possess hapticity (so, basically, it will feel like the air molecules will have some sort of solidity); and normally, the haptic particles will cause annoyance and distraction when they batter against opponents. Moreover, the haptic particles can even sting, and at higher power levels, they can even lightly cut human skin.

3: Fill the atmosphere with hot particles before gradually increasing the temperature by trapping heat energy, thereby potentially burning opponents who spend too long inside. The particles of and in average DPL vortices will begin at roughly 40°C at 100% APL; and then they will heat up the normal gas particles in the aura – in addition to semi trapping the said particles in the aura. Overall, the whole vortex will reach and then maintain a temperature of 75°C in standard contexts. Even supreme power levels will only reach 115°C. Heating the non-ultrachite gas particles requires more MECs, and the vortex can only achieve this maximum temperature (of its power level) in environments up to a certain temperature (per its power level) before changes occur. While the vortex *can* get hotter, it will not do this on its own, and this would also go beyond what it is capable of effectively handling; but consider that this is dry heat, so it is worse than saunas with their humidity. If a shielded mage were to come into contact with a hot vortex and automatically inhibit the particles with their shield's UPIs, the accumulated heat would still *initially* be inside the vortex, and it would still largely affect the shielded mage through standard radiation and conduction.

• NCU vortex DTPs:

1: Impose speed limits on things. Specifically, a delta-negative vortex will automatically and rapidly increase the inertia of its particles (via a form of spatial quantum locking) when objects or opponents inside the vortex begin moving at or beyond a certain speed limit. Basically, an opponent will only be able to swing a weapon, for example, up to the maximum imposed speed limit. Once an opponent or object stops moving at or beyond the speed limit, the inertia levels of the vortex's particles will return to normal. Of course, if the force of the object is greater than the vortex's power level, then it can make increasing returns on its acceleration or velocity. For average DPL vortices, a maximum speed of about 20 km/h will be imposed against all things within the AOE that have a net strength of 750 joules. For anything (or net things) that exceeds this amount, then they can move beyond this speed limit with varying amounts. The average vortex can block about one small bullet (normally from pistols) at a single time, but any more bullets that enter the AOE will not be affected much or at all (including the first bullet) due to spread UPP.

If an object does not have any backing force behind it (and, instead, merely has momentum), then, if the vortex were switched off, the object would not return to its original speed. For example, if a bullet entered the vortex and then the user quickly switched the vortex off, the bullet would not return to its original speed. However, if there were a continued force behind an object, it could return to its original speed. For example, if an axe-wielder began striking the user, the axe would slow down to a certain speed once the vortex activates; but if the vortex suddenly stopped, the same axe strike could return to its original speed because of the attacker being able to apply the same force as before, accelerating the axe. Since the average upper stabbing strength of a human (with a knife) is about 33 joules, then the vortex can, indeed, slow the speed of a strike, but this will not guarantee no puncturing of the skin; instead, it will, at the very least, give the user more time to react. Once 100% APL is attained against shielded opponents, the effects are the same as against unshielded opponents.

2: Fill the atmosphere with cold particles before gradually lowering the temperature even further by expelling heat energy, thereby potentially freezing opponents who spend too long inside. The particles of and in average DPL vortices will begin at roughly -30°C at 100% APL; and then they will absorb and expel the heat energy from the normal gas particles in the aura – in addition to semi trapping the said particles in the aura. Overall, the whole vortex will reach and then maintain a temperature of -30°C in standard contexts. Even supreme power levels will only reach -70°C. Extracting and expelling heat requires more MECs, and the vortex can only achieve this temperature (of its power level) in environments up to a certain temperature (per its power level) before changes occur. While the vortex *can* get colder, it will not do this on its own, and this would also go beyond what it is capable of effectively handling. If a shielded mage were to come into contact with an extremely-cold vortex and automatically inhibit the particles with their shield's UPIs, the vortex would still *initially* lack normal heat, and it would still largely affect the shielded mage, as the said mage's heat energy would transfer through the shield and into the vortex, which would expel the energy. The vortex will also not (directly) extinguish fires, but the cold temperatures may still *aid* in both extinguishing and preventing fires.

• Note: This DTP may seem useful for comfortably cooling down rooms via LPLs (as an alternative to an air conditioner), but consider that the magic has to end at some point; and the expelled heat (which will still normally be nearby) will naturally reheat the area rather quickly in many cases.

## UST Four/Ultra-liquid (Soaker bombs and Swarm clouds):

• PCU soaker particles: act as a chemical primer for certain phenomena, in turn allowing for different types of combos to occur. For example, if the user were to shoot a delta-positive discharge at the opponent covered in soaker particles, this would increase the effects of the flash and the bang. Note that this combo effect is different to the combo effect that soaker particles *already* allow for via SBEs. As another effect (without it being another DTP), the soaker particles will also possess great luminescence, causing affects targets to glow very brightly. The soaker particles may even leave TREs behind, causing certain properties to continue glowing as a chemical reaction (though, this is to a much weaker extent than the soaker particles themselves). In other words, the soaker particles possess luminescence, while the TREs would be *chemiluminescence* (that is, luminescence from a chemical reaction).

• PCU swarm clouds: visually rotate the partially-visioned environment around the victim at any angle, potentially inducing motion sickness. The swarm will also 'expand' the atmosphere in a strange way to make things outside the swarm appear enlarged. While this latter feat may display the user in closer detail (for the opponent), an 'enlarged body' may still cause the affected opponent to shoot in the wrong direction.

• NCU soaker particles: form into a foam around opponents, causing annoyance and difficulty with movement. While foam is a two-phase state (that is, there are gasses trapped in bubbles within the liquid structure), consider that the ultrachite-liquid is still a form of liquid. When the foam forms around opponents, the width will naturally be greater than other soaker particles around opponents. The foam is sticky, but it will not be as adhesive as beta-positive soaker particles. The ultra-liquid will also possess a greater level of viscosity than other soaker particles; this means the foam will be really thick and resistant to change, and this can cause opponents to have to move around as if in a bungling suit.

• NCU swarm clouds: create a partial veil that blurs the victim's surroundings through a sense of slow motion. The swarm can also contract the atmosphere to fashion shrinking non-peripheral visuals (so things appear further away).

## UST Five/Ultra-conductivity (Propulsors):

• PCU propulsor DTPs:

1: Detect various types of motion while possessing a natural and automatic avoidance response to certain types of things that approach. That is, the propulsor automatically propels itself (and, accordingly, the user) slightly out of the way from particular incoming ultrachite and non-ultrachite matter. The direction of the dodge is relative to where the matter would impact on the propulsor ultrachite concentrate (that would closely surround the user's body); so, if an ultrachite discharge were to approach on a user's left side, the user would dodge to their right. If two discharges were to approach the user (neither in rank nor file), then, depending on the distances and power levels, the aura would not propel the user into the second discharge due to detecting it as well.

The incoming matter must be powerful and/or dense enough to be detected (for avoidance), so normally, winds are either too 'weak' or 'big' to respectively respond to or avoid. The propulsor will also not propel the user into a wall, for example, in order to dodge something, unless the final velocity would be under that which the propulsor finds unacceptable (that is, a speed that would trigger the propulsor). However, when users are next to dangerous *open* areas (such as cliffs or potential line of fire from opponents), they typically switch the propulsor off (or at least this DTP) so as not to get propelled in their direction, which the UST form cannot comprehend.

Average users with their respective DPLs can detect incoming ultrachite and non-ultrachite matter from 12 metres away. The aura can even perform this feat without twisting the user's body or causing issues like whiplash, as it can propel the whole body effectively. While the number and strength of the available dodges per second vary based on many conditions (such as what the propulsor aura is dodging), the average DPL user can nevertheless fully dodge about three ultrachite discharges (of most DPLs) per second in most contexts. An incoming item's strength/power matters more than its speed per se, so the average DPL aura can dodge several bullets per second as well (with the figures varying per bullet type).

Average DPL propulsors also require a one-second UPC time, with the DTP lasting seven seconds before a cooldown period of six seconds occurs. Because *advanced* DPL propulsors can dodge *four* discharges per second, this typically means that the propulsor can be a little overpowered in standard one-on-one fights. However, the advanced user (or higher, when using said power levels) would only be able to use this for a short time (with this time potentially shrinking even more when factoring in for other ultrachite the advanced user would be using, such as discharges), so the other mage could still wait this time out by doing a variety of things, such as hiding, set up traps, preparing for a DMA, or they may even dodge the user's discharges using this same propulsor. Still, when against multiple opponents, the advanced user would not be able to handle dodging all of the attacks at once.

• Note: For clarification, the propulsor aura does not require extra energy for each *available* dodge, as the aura has enough energy within itself to sustain this feat for the possible number of times per second.

2: Automatically create micro propulsions that increase the user's speed (and anything else within the propulsor's field). If a mage normally had a top running speed of 36 km/h, then, with an average DPL propulsor, they would be able to increase their speed by 83.7% to 66.7 km/h. It can also help the user to jump higher, but the statistics for this pale in comparison to other propulsors that help users jump higher. Note that the propulsor field is naturally in tune with the user's body, so whatever direction the user moves in, the propulsor aura will help such movements. Even a user's discharges will travel faster (should the propulsor be right next to where the discharges launch from). When coupled with delta-positive shields and delta-positive dimensional fields, this makes users extremely fast. There are technically drawbacks, however, such as when incoming materials enter the propulsor's field (thus making attacks advance faster on the user); however, by the time this occurs, it is normally too late for the user, anyway (due to the proximity), so this is not actually a practical a problem.

• Note: Legendary mages supposedly were able to create full vacuum balloons to float as another DTP. However, the number of cubic metres required for this seems like it would had to have extended beyond a user's aura. While it is possible such mages had extremely big auras, this is unlikely the case. What is most probable is that the balloons still used some kind of vibrational energy to add to the floatation.

• NCU propulsors: enable the user to hover in the air via a form of spatial quantum locking. Unlike how delta-negative shields *only* lock to the fabric of their relative space-time, the propulsor aura *also* propels from it in homeostasis. The propulsor, howbeit, does not elevate the user, so users can only remain in the one location unless a force strong enough moves them. So, if a user is already fully on the ground when they activate this power, they will not *hover* above the ground. The propulsor also does not add pseudo-mass like delta-negative shields, so its quantum locking is of a different nature, where it will attempt to return to the position that it locked to initially on the UPC activation (should it be within range and have enough power). In contrast to gamma-negative propulsors, delta-negative propulsors allow users to hover high in the air without having anything to repel from.

The default concentration of energy occurs at the base of the user's feet as a flat disc (averaging about 80 cm in diameter for all DPLs); but the propulsor particles can be concentrated elsewhere else at will (in any shape), so the user can cover their body, or, alternatively, the user can make other things hover (so long as the other things are still in the aura). However, intentional placement of the field should be done prior to the UPC activation. Given that the propulsor has both friction and frictionless properties, the coefficient of friction for all power levels is roughly 0.5 for standard properties standing on it, so this is basically like standing on a standard floor, so users do not simply slip off. The default position is generally the best in most contexts, as it enables users to move freely on the hover pad, but there are still legitimate reasons for covering oneself in the propulsor particles.

If the user reaches enough velocity (especially terminal velocity) when falling, users may still hit the ground hard and die if they activate the UST too late (that is, when too close to the ground), with speeds and activation times varying per power level. Because of this, it may seem that a user could still prevent splatting on the ground while falling at terminal velocity if they use the UST at the right time. However, even if the user has plenty of time, there is another problematic factor to consider: if the propulsor field moves beyond a certain range (per its power level) from its locking point (regardless of the user's weight), then it will totally lose its ability to anchor to the said locking point, which will cause the propulsor to effectively stop working until another UPC is made. To be clear, even if the propulsor reaches a point *just* before this range, it will not lose any of its power, so the cut off is a sharp effect.

Timing and distance issues cannot be simply remedied by switching the propulsor on and off before reaching the ground, as the propulsor requires a UPC each time it is activated and switched off, with activation and cooldown times each being one second for average DPLs (with the power lasting indefinitely while active). Even if this were not the case, rapidly switching the propulsor on and off would lead to LBOs. Furthermore, even attempting to switch the PEP from AES to DES basically does not work to help work around various issues, as when enough (usually only a small number) of particles turn to DES, the whole propulsor stops working (due to the propulsor being out of equilibrium per its power level), and another UPC is needed. Since one's velocity increases the further one falls (before terminal velocity applies), judging the right timing for activation can also be difficult during the fall. Due to either potentially running out of energy mid-air (with a lethal fall distance below), not being able return to the locking point, or being in a bad position, users should know or be prepared beforehand as to how they will get out of their situation. All of this may seem like the propulsor is feeble, but these are just examples of why the propulsor is not *overpowered*.

For average users and their respective DPLs, the propulsor can fully support weights of up to 103 kg before it (and the user) will begin to fall with varying speeds until reaching the cut-off point of 21 metres distance from its locking point. So, if the user weighed 140 kg, then they would begin falling with an acceleration rate of 2.59265 m/s$^2$; and, in just 4.025 seconds (without air resistance factored), the user would have reached the cut-off point, where normal acceleration would begin. If a user were to *begin* (accidentally) falling, then, with the UPC time of one second, they would normally already reach a distance of around 4.903 metres (without air resistance calculated), with a velocity of 35.3 km/h. Considering that the propulsor exerts a force of 1,010 newtons, a user weighing 75 kg, in this case, would reach zero velocity in just under three seconds with a distance of about 13 metres covered. Therefore, in total, the user would have covered a distance of roughly 18 metres – just enough to avoid the cut-off point. While a propulsor could sustain a user weighing 103 kg, it would not be able to slow down at all should it begin accelerating due to another force acting on it (or if the user already had some velocity before activating the propulsor).

After reaching zero velocity, the 75 kg user would begin returning to the locking point. In this case, it would take a few more seconds, with the velocity changing the closer the user would get to the locking point. That is, instead of yo-yoing back and forth when reaching the locking point due to momentum each way, the propulsor naturally slows down to prevent this problem. If the user weighs too much, then they may run out of energy before ever returning. In fact, not only would, say, a 102 kg mage (at said power levels) not only run out of energy before reaching zero velocity during the fall, but their potential fall distance would extend well beyond the propulsor's cut-off range, anyway. If the user is not at zero-initial velocity when beginning their charge (that is, they are already falling), then naturally these figures would increase, with the propulsor unlikely returning to the locking point. While most mages do not weigh over 103 kg, using higher power levels is more effective and applicable for when the user is not at zero-initial velocity (whether for when beginning the charge or after the UPC finishes). Depending on the distance covered when falling as well as the mage's weight, the g-force at supreme power levels *can* be dangerous, so caution is generally taken.

While delta-negative shields, in contrast, *can* keep a user mid-air for a decent amount of time – and, as such, it would seem as though it would be better, energy-conservation-wise, to just use the said shields – there are still, indeed, reasons to use the propulsor over the shield. For one, the propulsor has better UPC times. Secondly, the delta shield does not decrease velocities and, instead, only the acceleration, so when the delta shield is activated when falling, the user would still fall at the same rate, potentially dying when hitting the ground. Thirdly, users can still easily (in the default mode) move their limbs, look around, shoot discharges, and more, when using the propulsor; and, while the shield *can* be formed into a disc under the feet, the user would still be left vulnerable to attacks due to a lack of shielding around their body. Fourth of all (the major points to be made), users can use any shield while using the propulsor, whereas when using the delta-negative shield, they are locked into only using the said shield (in addition to being unable to use other phasarchement powers effectively).

## UST Six/Ultra-spacetime crystals (Dimensional Fields):

• PCU dimensional fields: accelerate time relative to the external reality outside the aura. Accordingly, users can move 'faster' and, thus, can outmanoeuvre opponents in battle or even flee from dangerous situations, such as an impending or active massive explosion. Alternatively, it can be used creatively in non-combat situations that require quick action. Although this *does* cause faster aging, using this power for brief purposes typically does not result in noticeable or significant effects.

• NCU dimensional fields: decelerate time relative to the external reality outside the aura. Accordingly, users can move 'slower'; and, while this may not be the most effective power in the *majority* of *direct* combat situations when used as a *simple* aura, if used creatively, it can be of incredible use. For example, it could be used when one needs to wait for a specialist to arrive to diffuse a ticking time bomb, while another case could consist of a combat ally who is about to die and any arriving medical treatment would otherwise take too long. Of course, the power could simply be used to pass the time. Deceleration, however, does not mean reversal, as it is a power of motionlessness. Time reversal would be another form of motion, but this is unavailable to users using either ACT. Still, there are legends of mythical mages being able to use time reversal, though it is unclear which ACT that they were supposedly using. There are other myths of ancient mages being able to stop time itself (all time – even outside their aura), but such tales are obviously just fiction.

Despite time still flowing forwards when using delta-negative fields, mages with supreme power levels can *seemingly* make time grind to a halt. Even with the extreme time differences at such power levels, the user will not turn blind, nor would people outside the field be unable to see what may be occurring inside the field. That is, since photons travel at incredibly-fast speeds, even when the field slows everything down, the light that enters or escapes the field would still reach people's eyes fast enough for basic vision. When delta-negative dimensional fields are mixed with other dimensional fields, like beta-positive dimensional fields, all that occurs is a faster return to the mark – *relative* to the external reality – rather than additional time granted to the user.

• Note: Both dimensional fields directly affect CSUs; and for both ACTs, every bit of space in the user's aura will experience the same time rate as a standard. Technically, the user can compress their dimensional fields, but for all power levels, this only occurs to a small degree, with all working power levels having an absolute minimum radius of around one metre. Accordingly, auras with smaller radii (and/or auras with weak power levels – specifically, inept DPLs) cannot even form a functioning field. This is due to the particles needing to find equilibrium with each other (both with adjacent particles and with all the other particles in the field as a whole), with the same effect occurring at all power levels; that is, once the power level increases, the field's ability to compress *would* increase, but the difficulty in finding equilibrium also increases, so the field balances out as practically the same for all power levels in this regard. Therefore, if the user approaches an opponent, the opponent will also experience the same time rate as the user, as the field would cover both people.

This accordingly limits the overpowered nature of this magic, preventing mages from simply approaching and stabbing anyone with a knife at a rapid speed, for example, as the opponent would have enough time to fight back or react appropriately. Still, once the user approaches the opponent in such a case, they will nevertheless have the upper hand of surprise. The same basically applies to other cases revolving around the changed physics itself, like where a user *could* easily snap another person's arms off with help of the extreme time differences, but this would not occur as, again, the other person would also experience the same time rate as the user. To be clear, even if a bullet were to enter the field, it would not be slowed down either. In fact, if the field were turned off in this case, the bullet (that just entered the field) would still have the same original velocity; accordingly, this field is not effective against bullets.

While the dimensional field does not specifically affect HRFs, it will still auto-matically expand to envelop certain macro, what-normally-are HRFs when pressed against them due to the need for the field to meet minimum equilibrium standards. So, if the field begins *just* pressing up against another person (like when a user approaches them), the field would instantly expand and envelop the other person instead of only covering them when enough of the field would otherwise cover the person when the user would be within enough proximity. The only exception to this is when the macro body is far too big for the field to expand to and practically affect.

When the expansion occurs, the time rate weakens, but normally this is not to any significant extent. So, if a mage were to press a dimensional field against a colossal-sized worm, for example, the field would either not expand to include the worm or it may *just* 'acceptingly' expand and cover a part of the worm – in which case, the worm would experience two time rates across its body. While this may seem overpowered, the field would, nonetheless, expand to the point of being too weak to be over-powered. The mage, however, can consciously compress the field so that it would not include such macro bodies; but again, this would only compress to a standard level. For clarification, even when a mage attempts avoiding the natural automatic covering of certain bodies, the attempt will not prevent the covering of an entity when the field is already compressed to a minimum standard *and then* a body enters the field (either when the body itself approaches and enters the field or if the field approaches the body and naturally envelops it).

While there are similarities to other UST energies, delta dimensional fields have a much broader scope of utilization, free from many conditions, dimensional boun-daries, external forces, obstructions, and more. In addition, they are not only the simplest dimensional field PAC to use, but they are also one of the simplest powers in phasarchement; accordingly, they are considered an allrounder set of powers in many situations, as sometimes quick-thinking may not be available to people in certain contexts. This latter point, of course, more so applies to PCU dimensional fields. The average DPL dimensional field will alter the time by an order of three times. So, if a user's MLP only allowed for six seconds of use of a PCU field, then the user would still experience six seconds inside, but only two seconds in the external reality would have passed. If the user used an NCU field, then they would still experience six seconds, but 18 seconds would have passed in the external world. For either field, only a one-second UPC time is needed before lasting indefinitely until the aura is switched off. Legends also speak of mythical mages being able to additionally shift timelines, time skip, stutter time, and more, but not only have these never been demonstrated in the slightest, they also do not ontologically seem to be (suitably) part of delta's acceleration or deceleration archetypes.

# Section Four

*Life and Civilization*

## 4.1: A Brief Overview of the Current Cycle of History:

### 4.1.1: Introduction:

Historians break history up into *divisions*, which have their own subdivisions. These divisions, in order from greatest to smallest, are generally: *cycles, aeons, epochs, ages, eras, generations, years,* and *days.* When used as a proper noun, each is naturally capitalized. Although these are divisions in *history*, in the context of time, each can be termed a *period* (of time). Other academics use different types of divisions, but these will not be included in this section. Defining historical divisions can be somewhat arbitrary and messy, as most of the divisions are based on social events rather than hard celestial occurrences. To remedy this issue, astrological and astronomical timings have been proposed for the divisions; but historians prefer to keep to the history itself, despite some arbitrary nature of the divisions. Nevertheless, this issue does not occur for *cycles*, which are used specifically for the strictly-defined theoretical cycles of the Caelverse itself. There may be timescale divisions greater than cycles, but none have been empirically verified. Even the cyclical nature of the Caelverse has not been empirically verified, but the theory is treated as axiomatically true, anyway.

*Aeons*, similarly, are marked by major shifts in physical forces, which may include certain events that occur with planetary structures, such as cataclysmic events. However, while these events may or may not have impacts on sentient beings, the rise of sentience itself can also start an aeon, while the extinction of sentience can also end an aeon. The maximum timeframe for an aeon is 524,288 years, as this is the time it likely takes for the Great Black Wall to destroy one solar cluster in the Caelverse. The beginning of an *epoch*, however, occurs when there are major existential shifts regarding sapient lifeforms themselves. These shifts can include the emergence of sapient lifeforms, mass extinction of most or all sapient beings, and the rise and fall of the biggest societies (normally empires) in the Caelverse. A single epoch covers all social events that occur in the Caelverse, and therefore, there is only one epoch at any one time. Aeons and epochs may overlap; that is, an epoch may still carry over into another aeon.

*Ages* fill epochs and involve the discovery and/or new interactions of many sapient lifeforms, massive genocides or exterminations, major changes to the biggest society, and major technological advances. *Eras*, conversely, are quite different, and they instead focus more on cultural movements, major scientific discoveries, industrial revolutions, religious conversions and adoptions, particular leaders, and many more criteria. Unlike the previous divisions, many eras can occur simultaneously. A *generation*, in contrast, is more defined in terms of its actual timing; that is, it cannot span any more than the maximum lifespan of a mage, which is 128 years. Accordingly, a generation refers specifically to a generation of mages. *Years* are smaller, marking events only up to two decades in length. The shortest time span of general use is *day* – although, other divisions do exist. As the name suggests, it refers to a single day in history marking a major event or set of events.

## 4.1.2: The First Epoch (E1):

The First Epoch (also known as E1) begins with the rise of sapient beings. It is the only epoch that historians know very little of, and each new discovery made only reveals tiny fragments of information. In fact, some of these archaeological discoveries raise more questions than they provide answers. The most straightforward story is that sapient beings evolved from non-sapient beings en masse across the Caelverse (roughly all at the same time) via special mutations and soon discovered how to utilize fire and stone technologies. After the *Stone Age* came a couple of other ages of unverifiable technological progress. It is believed that the inhabitants of the First Epoch did not progress beyond the *Iron Age*, but there are some theories suggesting that they were actually far more advanced. All of a sudden, without any notable leadup or sequence of events, the majority of sapient beings were wiped out in what is believed to be a Caelverse-wide cataclysmic event.

Some sapient beings, nevertheless, managed to survive, and it appears that the knowledge of whatever occurred was handed down through oral tradition. The oral traditions of the Second Epoch were later written down in the Third Epoch, which survive to this day. What we know for sure is that the oral traditions contradict each other, but there are nonetheless some central themes to most of them. Both strange 'sky beings' and 'underground beings' supposedly emerged while planetary instabilities were occurring. From the stories, it appears as though the instabilities were a mix of earthquakes and electrical storms of proportions that have not been seen in other epochs. It is still unknown as to what most of these sapient species were in E1, but it is clear that many had humanoid shapes. Moreover, since some of these beings survived into the Second Era, at least humans were alive during this time.

Some oral traditions say that the events were caused by the people living there at the time. Such claims are split, with some traditions saying that the problems were due to the people's collective degeneracy, and so, the troubles were a form of consequent punishment (whether a natural punishment or from external beings), while others believed it was advanced sorcery from the greatest shamans. Then there are other oral traditions that claimed that the people were largely peaceful, and it was an unprovoked attack from other kinds of entities, such as the 'sky beings'. Other traditions say that the events were an inevitable 'birthing pain' of the Caelverse (and its cycle), while a smaller percentage believed that it was a carry-over event from a previous Caelverse cycle. Interestingly, even these people were aware of the potential cyclical nature of the Caelverse. An even smaller percentage claim that the events were purely an accident that emerged from another reality (which we believe meant another 'dimension').

Regardless of what occurred, we do not know how long the First Epoch lasted for and if it actually should be broken into multiple epochs. Still, according to the dominant historical narrative, the First Epoch should only account for one epoch, even if it could have been hundreds of thousands of years long and filled with extremely-interesting events. However, we can make a maximum estimation based on the theorized date of the Caelverse cycle. This figure varies based on either the start of the Caelverse's formation or the beginning of the Great Black Wall's march. For more information on the development of the Caelverse, (re)check *Section 2.1*.

## 4.1.3: The Second Epoch (E2):

The Second Epoch begins with mostly-primitive tribes (and equivalents, such as herds, packs, and murders – depending on the species) holding stories of events from the First Epoch. It is possible that other sapient beings emerged during this time, but it could simply have been the case that all the sapient beings in the Second Epoch were actually the survivors of the First Epoch. Given the knowledge they possessed, it was easy for the tribes to begin rebuilding civilization, progressing quickly from the Stone Age to the Iron Age. The first signs of mages were also present in this epoch, but the records seem to suggest that they were not able to wield magic as well as they could in later epochs. As such, mages (as humans) were basically on a relatively-equal footing with other beings (human and otherwise).

During this time, there were stories and loose accounts of other humans who possessed different kinds of magic; and the most predominant of these stories were of *warlocks* (male magic users) and *witches* (female magic users). It is unclear whether these were mages who practiced – and had access to – other magic or if they were a genetically different sub species of humans (in other words, not mages). From these accounts, warlocks and witches did not integrate well within society, keeping to the fringes instead. Because of this, it is hard to ascertain what really happened – and if there were even other magics at all. Warlocks also supposedly had (at least somewhat) different magic to witches; and for both warlocks and witches, most of their magic was supposedly quite wild and untamed.

It was said that their magic also featured (but was not limited to) strange psychicism, summoning, shapeshifting, nature manipulation, blood work, (dark) rituals, potions (of a different nature to our own), illusions, and they could wield and control the classical elements (of air, fire, earth, and water). While small conflicts occurred between mages and warlocks and witches, no major (recorded) battles occurred. One day, all the witches and warlocks vanished without a trace, leaving very few clues at to what happened (assuming they even existed, which, in all likelihood, they did, although the tales of their magic might not have been real). There are many scholars who suggest that the majority of warlocks and witches engaged in a grand mass ritual, and their magic was their own undoing, completely annihilating them.

Mages (and other humans like basic humans), in contrast, were able to build up civilization faster than other species, using merely their minds, social skills, and tool-making abilities. Naturally, since mages had an advantage over basic humans, the former began to be the dominant force. Most civilizations in the Second Epoch were city states – some monarchies, others democracies; but through gradual progression and successful wars, one city state, in particular, grew into a large republic. Larger and larger wars broke out; and eventually, the mages in power successively created a massive republic spanning a whole continent on their T2-C1 planet called Juntas. Once the republic reached this stage after 1,200 years of its existence, it met with great upheavals from internal and external sources. One problem after another led to the point where the republic was on the brink of completely falling, but a few generals managed to salvage the great civilization by turning it into an empire with an emperor at the helm – one that had certain restrictions, nonetheless. In this final age, *historiography* and other feats were also achieved, thus ending the Second Epoch.

## 4.1.4: The Third Epoch (E3):

The Third Epoch saw the rise of great feats in engineering, properly-written languages, and mathematics. In addition, the modern calendar was formed, which we still use to this very day – just with some modifications. The calendar started on *Year One* but was soon switched to *Year Zero*, as a year had not yet passed. Then the year was moved forward five years so that the calendar started at the date that the empire formed. Technically, the empire formed before the start of a lunapex, so the empire was not *officiated* with a grand ceremony until the lunapex (and new season) began. Since then, the calendar has not been reset, and so, in the current year, it has been 10,424 years since the beginning of the Third Epoch. In this epoch, it was not just a matter of mages battling other beings but also their own kind. While many mages supported the empire, a lot were either somewhat or completely against it, suffering under political *repression* while even dying in various wars.

It was not even just a matter of politics and economics that raised opposition; imperial culture clashed with folkish and non-imperial cultures, which itself became a political issue. Interestingly, these cultures managed to form the backbone of much mage culture that occurred thereafter; and even to this day, mage culture is largely a mix of continued, reworked, and expanded ancient imperial culture, mythic-based folkish culture, and assorted appropriated cultures from other beings. Of course, other foremost cultures emerged later, adding to, and integrating with, this mix. Note that there is a nuanced distinction to be made between the folk cultures of the past here (called *ancient folk culture*) and of 'folk culture' today. Essentially, folk culture in the modern context refers to art 'by and for the people' (that is, non-professionals), who tend to make more utilitarian art as opposed to art purely based on aesthetics (fine art, created by elites), while many of those who made ancient folk art were professionals of their craft. Governments today may even employ professionals to create 'ancient folk art', but such art is not technically folk art (used in the modern context).

Slavery was not yet a common practice in the empire (besides increasing taxes), as most beings were human or at least fellow primates, and it was prohibited to enslave one's own kind unless it was indentured servitude (basically, a contract involving work without proper pay). In fact, integration was a strong policy during the first couple of ages of the empire, even for species of vastly-different *genera* to humans (note that genera is a taxonomic rank, explained in *Section 4.3*). Nevertheless, this integration policy did not work well, as there was one great upheaval after another. Basic humans were still barred from holding political positions, and species of other genera increasingly attempted to revolt due to not only their second-class status but the poor and failing infrastructure and conditions (including farming, taxes, diseases, and more).

On top of this, there was the political repression involving involuntary settlement, torture, spying, etc. Greater and greater chaos ensued, all the while as the empire kept expanding. Many people at the time believed that the empire would collapse from internal and external issues; but the opposite actually occurred. Just as generals had salvaged the republic and turned it into an empire during the end of the Second Epoch, the emperor in the final age of the Third Epoch was given supreme power in order to restore order. Within two years, the empire finished conquering the whole planet and began properly expanding on other planets. Most mages (an estimated 95%) at the end of this age were living within the empire, as most were native to their *home world* Juntas. Note that all mages are likely *from* Juntas, but some mages in E1 probably *went* to other planets. It was at this point in time, in the year 1118, that the Third Epoch ended.

## 4.1.5: The Fourth Epoch (E4):

The Fourth Epoch saw the beginning of the *Caelverse Magocratic Empire* (CME), which was not called that or abbreviated as such until after the epoch finished. Simply, the CME was just referred to as *The Empire* or *The Magocratic Empire*. E4 was indeed a bloody time in history, but it was also considered the 'golden epoch' due to the unrelenting success and infrastructural, technological, and cultural progress. Funnily enough, the official colours of the empire's flags were red and gold. The empire managed to remain successful due to the leadership style of the emperors. The first *supreme emperor*, Supreme Emperor Valinkash, ensured that all future emperors had to be of a certain exemplary standard if they were to lead the empire. There were to be no debauched and degenerate emperors of the past, so no drunkards and adulterers or anyone else that would even think about partaking in vices. Supreme emperors had to be very intelligent, wise, cunning, and creative, while also possessing many talents. Moreover, they were also to be of exceptional physical stature, so no 'weaklings', fat people, and anyone deformed.

Special training camps were established for worthy youth to be trained as potential candidates to succeed Valinkash after he would die. Not only were potential candidates put through gruelling physical courses, but there were also intense educational programs and testing to mould and find the 'supreme mage'. When they were older, candidates then had to embark on a rite of passage, journeying to exotic, dangerous places in order to complete certain tasks. This type of training was also then extended to any person wanting to hold any government job in the empire – albeit to a less extreme extent. With these principles in place – coupled with the many other policies Valinkash set – the empire managed to hold strong and glorious for thousands of years. However, in the end, the empire degenerated.

Many political theorists today claim that the empire was a purely mage supremacist system, but their analyses typically lack context and nuance. Basically, their arguments say that mages inherently saw themselves as superior and enslaved others out of sheer benefit while enjoying their status as superiors. While the empire was indeed supremacist (explicitly, an empire built on mage supremacy) – and that many mage supremacists existed – the reasons behind the slavery were complex. The empire in the Third Epoch was failing and falling, and its integration policies were not working. Most mages did not actually want slavery (many, in fact, vociferously and violently opposed it), but slavery was a natural consequence of keeping the empire from falling. The empire initially had no intention of keeping other beings enslaved in perpetuity. Species of other genera were not just revolting against the empire in the Third Epoch to stop it from conducting certain repressive and oppressive actions, but they were also simultaneously demanding that it *provided* for them. Of course, many mages fell into this category, too. This itself was problematic because *if* an authority *must* care for others, it must also have the very feature of what it is: authority.

There were too many conflicting, radical, and contradictory political desires in E3, and the main purpose of the slavery was to bring about stability. No individual mage, nor any other entity (like a corporation), outside of the state were to have slaves. So, all slaves served the empire, and only the empire, not private members of the empire. This also meant that the mage masses – whilst having first-class status – were not an aristocracy, and they still had certain restrictions and duties imposed on them in order for the empire to function and thrive. Indeed, mages who were caught exploiting the system (with personal slaves, for instance) were brutally executed. Still, while these were the initial reasons for the slavery and repression, the empire still had the whole Caelverse yet to conquer, and so, there was always one excuse or reason after another as to why they did not end the slavery and restore freedoms. That is, one war after another required that the empire stay strong, and so, slaves were never released from their bondage. Explicitly, the system snowballed, and the systems of oppression became entrenched, causing many bloodbaths to ensue – all to prevent the empire from falling. Whether justified or not, this was the reality.

The system of slavery also varied based on the context, species, and location. Some beings were used directly for labour, which was normally physical in nature, but sometimes non-mages had entertainment roles (generally for the non-mages), while others were funnily enough forced into positions of power. Some jobs were more comfortable and had better conditions than others. If they were not directly enslaved, then they were simply taxed instead (which constituted the majority of the slavery). To be clear, the CME did not simply absorb or destroy all civilizations; instead, it was, in many cases, easier to impose itself on already-established societies (which had their own governments) and then imposed rules and regulations on the said governments. Through this imposition, the mages collected taxes either directly from the non-mages or via the non-mage governments.

For many cases of taxation, it was because the empire could not find roles for the non-mages. Then there were many primitive societies that existed, which did not integrate properly into the empire, and so, direct resources and goods were simply taken from them instead. Certain species may have already been technologically advanced, but due to their physiology, it was hard for mages to communicate with them, and so, usually taxes or goods were taken from them as well. This also applied to beings who were incapable of physically working particular jobs that the empire required. For example, if legs were required for the job, then sapient species who lacked legs were not directly used for such work. Despite slavery existing, abuse against slaves was not tolerated, and mage imperial officers were greatly punished for any unnecessary cruelty. Still, corruption existed, so abuse did occur without punishment.

The CME also encountered other problems with old, new, or potential slaves, such as hostilities, diseases, and a lack of intelligence (for sapient beings). Many hostilities came from individuals and small groups within a species of slaves, but there were some *entire* species that were absolutely hostile to the empire *and* generally also to all other species (or at least species of other genera). It was this issue alone that caused a large percentage of the ensuing wars for the empire. Genocide was not a policy that the empire enacted on any type of sapient species, but when an entire species was totally hostile to any being other than themselves, then the CME decided that it had to enact the previously unthinkable: *total wars*.

These hostile types of beings had to be eradicated, regardless of the empire's enslaving policies; and after the empire's outright extermination of a couple of species, a precedent was set for what came afterwards. A few of the still-living hostile species and genera witnessed the power of the CME during the first genocides, and so, they eased their aggressions and submitted. Still, no matter what power the CME flaunted and flexed, some species were relentless in their pursuit to kill all other beings than themselves. This led to the *Genocidal Age*, which saw many genera and individual species exterminated or brought to the brink of extermination (many of whom later died off due to a lack of numbers to properly reproduce). As new species were continually being discovered as the empire explored and expanded across the Caelverse, more hostiles emerged.

At one point, the empire realized it had to stop expanding and finish fighting the hostiles that they had already encountered. This was initially a concern for the empire, as it feared that other powerful empires could emerge in other places. Indeed, other empires did arise, but these were not as powerful as the CME. There were also other large empires in unexplored areas of the Caelverse that the CME later found. For the time being, some of the CME's greatest threats came from *dracotors*, a genus of sapient dracos who were physically much stronger than mages. Despite their lack of magic, dracotors proved to be an unrelenting force that rained one fiery death storm after another on the mages. In the end, the CME managed to wipe out all but one species in the genus – a species that decided to submit to the CME out of a sheer will to live. Once these major wars were won, the CME finally began properly expanding again. The CME still met with other species and entire genera (both sapient and semi-sapient) that were just as ruthless and powerful, yet the CME remained successful, despite many mage and slave lives being lost in the process. Although successful, the CME only managed to drive some of these genera and individual species deep underground, where they live to this very day, hiding and skirmishing mages and other beings.

Some species and entire genera, however, were either always underground or worked greatly underground. In such environments, these hostile species and entire genera, such as *centruvons* (a sapient giant centipede genus), managed to sink entire CME aboveground cities. Due to these massive problems, the CME began delving deep into the *grand caverns*, where, again, they found more resistance, ushering in the *Spelunking Age*. In order to stop the attacks on the cities, the CME established great, thick infrastructure that descended very deep. Of course, this required more slavery for the physical labour. It was during this age that the mages discovered numerous anomalies and fascinating phenomena, along with many types of lithoid species that had varied relations with the empire.

Once enough supportive structures were properly created underground, the large-scale destruction against the aboveground cities mostly stopped. The empire was also able to establish many military fortresses underground, in turn causing most of the hostile species to tunnel even deeper into the unexplored abyssal levels of the lithosphere. During this period, the CME created deep, secret underground facilities, which included strange laboratories and testing spaces. This was when the CME began a slightly-darker history (in terms of ethics), but most of the CME was unaware of these operations – even the supreme emperor of the day lacked much knowledge of what was occurring. Even today, most of these facilities are prohibited for the public to enter, so much of this history is largely classified.

There was then a period of respite for the empire, which saw an age where there were relatively no major wars. Much wealth was spent on luxuries and entertainment, and a carefree attitude led to complacency. Eventually when the empire began thoroughly expanding again, other empires had already adequately developed, but most were filled with a mix of different species, and so, the inhabitants were not necessarily hostile to mages (as a species). Conquering these empires individually was not a hard task in itself, but the problem was that many other hostilities and troubles occurred simultaneously for the Magocratic Empire.

These troubles included the rise of major pirates, warlords, fanatic cults, rogue corporations, religious clashes, seceding cities (and even a few planets), political revolutionaries, and mutinous generals leading coup d'états. On top of this, the CME still had to deal with the occasional attacks from hostile genera like centruvons that would attack and sink yet-to-be-fortified cities. In addition, the mage elite began degenerating, loosening virtues and morals. This consequently had drastic effects on the fabric of society, in turn affecting the overall economic and political system. While the supreme emperor was still of an exceptional status, the remaining government was not. There was also an increase in general crimes, and welfare dependence drastically increased due to economic troubles. Diseases that had been eradicated in earlier millennia returned, and quarantining them proved futile. There was also an increase in mutations and monsters, which proved a great menace.

Despite these issues, the CME was at its peak in terms of wealth per capita. The CME, however, believed that once it could conquer every solar system in the Caelverse, *then* it could remain at peace forever and use all of its power to solve internal issues. So, the CME actually increased war production at the expense of solving its internal problems. Eventually, the CME finally conquered the Caelverse, and there were no other empires or major civilizations to fight, bar those that were hiding or undiscovered. Even though the CME had conquered the Caelverse, it had not explored every single bit of land on T2 worlds (let alone even landing a foot on T1 and T3 worlds *as* an imperial force), and so, naturally undiscovered primitive tribal societies continued – and even today continue – to exist.

The problems that the empire left festering kept growing, and by the time the CME began fighting such scourges, they had advanced too far to be solved. Slavery continued to exist, as the CME claimed that it needed the slaves in order to help solve the issues first. Abolitionist movements at this point rose up in extraordinary numbers and managed to change the system very quickly. Slavery was swiftly abolished, and the *Grand Liberal Charter* was established, outlawing any kind of slavery. Nevertheless, there were no well-established programs to help non-mages integrate into the new society, and much chaos ensued. After two centuries of most of the problems never being resolved, the CME finally collapsed. This was not exactly the fault of the ex-slaves per se, as the majority of issues revolved around economic inflation – coupled with the aforementioned issues like pirates, fanatic cults, religious clashes, diseases, and more.

In summary, the Fourth Epoch began in the year 1118, with the mage empire having conquered the planet called Juntas. The first millennium (so up to around 2000) brought about significant reform, stability, and disciplined culture. By the end of it, the empire had conquered fifty-five solar systems. The second millennium (of the CME) saw a few genocides, which set a precedent to follow; by the end, the CME had become much better at its conquering techniques, having conquered 1616 solar systems. During the third millennium (of the CME), the empire experienced its harshest battles yet. But despite many losses, it managed to ultimately win. In addition, the empire resolved issues like major diseases that plagued the second millennium. The CME also finished conquering 6,371 solar systems by this time. Like the third millennium, the fourth millennium saw similar types of resistance, but this led to greater underground explorations and building.

When the fourth millennium was over, the CME had conquered 10,200 solar systems. In contrast, the fifth millennium began relatively easy, free from most problems and wars. However, with complacency, the empire degenerated, which later resulted in numerous problems, such as massive crime, pirates, monsters, secessions, diseases (returning), fanatic cultists, and more. Still, the empire was at its peak in terms of wealth per capita, and it had conquered 17,856 solar systems at the end. For the final millennium, the sixth millennium, the empire devoted much of its resources to completing its conquest of the Caelverse (which it did achieve), but the internal problems it faced grew too large for it to handle. Slavery was abolished, but despite this, the empire eventually collapsed.

## 4.1.6: The Fifth Epoch (E5):

The collapse of the CME was not an event that simply occurred overnight. By the time it had *fully* collapsed (that is, in the year 7203, when there was no longer a centralized power beyond the imperial city), it was not as if absolute chaos resultingly ensued. Rather, chaos was already happening for about two centuries previously, so when the empire no longer existed, the already-occurring chaos did not tremendously escalate. Small, localized wars nevertheless broke out throughout the Caelverse, but most of society quickly stratified into regional governments, communities, and feudal orders without excessive additional fighting. Even most of the ex-slaves self-segregated based on their species instead of warring with each other and the mages. Nevertheless, roaming bandits, warlords, pirates, gangs, fanatic cults, religious fanatics, and other groups pillaged the cities for wealth (or simply burned them), in addition to the aforesaid communities either still living in the cities or on the outskirts. Prior to the collapse, cults had an established – and even respected – place in society, but due to the nature of so many cults at the time, the term became a pejorative, and the nature of the many ensuing cults in E5 turned from public to clandestine.

Fortunately, the hostile species that the CME drove underground in the Fourth Epoch did not emerge en masse. The reasons for this are still unknown, but many theories suggest that the hostile species were too busy building forces to attack, while other theories posit that since the mages actually managed to conquer the Caelverse with unrelenting success, attacking was off-putting, despite the collapse. Furthermore, the hostiles perhaps considered that the mages could easily and quickly restore order as they did in the past, and so, a surprise attack would end up backfiring and wiping out their species. So, whilst it may have seemed like a good opportunity to strike against the mages (indeed, it actually was), the hostiles remained cautious.

With power scattered and communications mainly broken down between planets, the period was known as the *Crestfallen Age*. Very little progress was made during this time, and it seemed that society was going around in circles, unable to lift itself out of a dark rut. The knowledge of history was not lost, but neither was it greatly taught, as most people focused on their daily survival – which, for the average person, was usually mundane until bandits or monsters approached. The grand schools and academies of the CME basically no longer existed (at least in their original form), and religious fanatics began burning many books and persecuting assorted individuals and groups for sundry reasons. Much of the information about the past, fortunately, still existed in multiple libraries across the Caelverse, so while many original materials may have been lost, their copies survived. Technological discoveries and advancements in sciences were also put largely to a halt. In addition, the amazing steam technologies of the CME were left to rust alongside advanced prototypes that were never finished.

Even the dominant language, called *Synvoric,* slightly changed depending on the location in the Caelverse. That is, when people added new words to the dictionaries, they were not universalized across the Caelverse. Some of these words were directly or indirectly drawn from pre-Synvoric languages before the empire even existed, while some words were totally fabricated without any etymological background. There were also words that were reworked from established words in the CME. Even slight changes in suffixes and grammatical markers for *some* words occurred, such as masculine ones with 'us', changing to 'as'. It must be noted that Synvoric itself was an amalgamation of various languages that occurred during the second, third, and fourth epochs. Generally, though, a person from somewhere else in the Caelverse during the Firth Epoch would still have been able to read a book made by another person in a far-off location, albeit with some minor difficulties.

Multiple attempts at recreating the Magocratic Empire failed, as commanding officers could not gain enough support, nor did they have enough power. It was impossible to create such a large-scale society from ruins. Slowly but surely, the city states that did exist began to grow bigger over the centuries, with notable absolute states emerging around the year 7605. Most of these states were run *by* mages and *for* mages. Still, large, non-mage absolute states began emerging as well. Other social structures and institutions were also emerging at this time, such as universities, forming out of the once-great academies. Once the states had properly formed, there was much speculation as to what kind of political entity and events would emerge next as the states continued to grow. Learning from their history, the mages did not wish to war with each other, and they knew that conflict was an issue that would inexorably occur if something new was not achieved. So, in 7801, plans for a *Union of Organized States* (UOS) developed. Still, it was believed for such a structure to come into fruition and properly function, the organized states would have to largely (although not entirely) control their planets. However, this also meant war with the non-mages.

So, it was proposed that any non-mage societies on the planets were to be left alone (unless actively hostile), but the mage states were to build around them and control the rest of the land. Moreover, it was mostly in agreement that the ideals in the Grand Liberal Charter were to be upheld, and so, this naturally did not bode well for a couple of mage states that had slaves. The charter also explicitly prohibits genocides of any sapient species unless they are totally hostile and/or pose an existential threat to mages or other species without a solution. This process was also to be completed carefully and thoroughly so the existing states would not collapse. Basically, the plans involved a very methodical and pragmatic approach instead of one of explicit brute force. Since the states were on different planets, the bickering that ensued during the planning and implementation of networks was not aggressive. In fact, the bickering led to much constructive debate and ideas.

Interestingly, during this time, there was one spectacular event that shook the people of Juntas. For a whole month in 7960, thick, blackened clouds completely covered the skies of Juntas and its moons – in addition to the space between them. The event was called the *Great Blackout*. The reason for why it occurred is still unknown to this day, but predominant theories suggest that one of the cults of the time was at least partly responsible. Some people of the time viewed the event as an omen, whilst others viewed it as a reason for why the UOS should be pursued in order to deal with any potential catastrophic troubles. Book burning, nevertheless, was a major issue after this event, which divided society.

The states themselves, nonetheless, insisted that the plans for the UOS continued. Most of the procedures had been executed in order to bring about the UOS, but some of the states did not comply with the mandates and policies set out. While some of the states believed that they should have bullied the noncompliant states into sub-mission, this did not occur, as the overall plan was pragmatic at its core, and the separated states were not in a position for such a war. In 8011, the UOS (a multi-planetary, supra-world-state union) was officially formed with 1,300 solar systems. It was not a fully-federated system, and the states still had much autonomy. With its successful creation, the following plans followed a careful, pragmatic approach as well. Some historians at the time suggested that a new epoch should be called, but the states insisted that the UOS was far from complete.

Meanwhile, many non-mage states were warring with each other, as mages managed to keep out of most wars (bar small fights against skirmishing hostile species from the underground). Since mages managed to control many areas (including the important transportals), the nature of these wars was different to traditional wars of the past. Firstly, the wars were localized to continents on their planets, as the UOS would not let other armies travel through the transportals. Secondly, most of these wars were religious, so it was not so much of a matter of one *state* itself taking over another.

Many wars were also internal, with rifts emerging between populations. While there were still religious *conflicts* in the mage states, these were largely properly managed, and no major incidents occurred. All of this is not to say that religion played no roles in the wars of the past, nor is it a claim that most wars in E5 and thereafter were religious. In fact, many *seemingly* religious wars were still economic at heart, but they still had religious *influences*. But for this particular period, there was, in many cases, purely religious reasons for the wars.

Many of the pagan religions of the past (polytheistic or otherwise) were almost wiped away when the monolatristic and monotheistic religions won the wars. Non-mages built many massive churches and temples during this time; and while the religions did bring their own set of problems, they nevertheless forced unity, and the idea of a single authority helped to strengthen the non-mage *states*. Some of the religions had totally new origins, while other religions had roots in – or were based off then-recent findings of even simple clay pots of – the First Epoch. Due to the size of the Caelverse, along with the number of religions and sapient beings, many religions had natural crossovers with one another, so for monotheistic religions that had essentially the same god (but with slightly different names and scriptures), they would end up unifying – all the while still retaining their identity as different sects. In many other cases, there would be one religion, which would then branch off into different sects.

Most mages moved away from the religions over time, largely adopting non-religious spirituality (whilst still acknowledging the existence of spiritual realms – generally, this meant ietsism – or even panentheism by soft belief), with their *practices* being rather secular. Still, there were mages who kept to the pagan religions of the past, while other mages adopted the monotheistic religions; and today, around 10% of mages adhere to a 'religion' – formal or otherwise. Some mages still adhered to cults, and whether in a cult or not, many mages began to increasingly value archetypes (and still do today), so instead of worshiping the 'Summer God', for example, *summer(ness)* as an archetype might have been *venerated*. Indeed, the archetypal energies of the lunapexes understood in the ancient world continued to be respected and embraced. There is, in fact, one lunapex where some mages dressed up as warlocks and wizards (and still do today).

Still, by 8810, the early stages of the *Illumination Age* began, which saw a rapid change in ideologies, technologies, arts, and science. The Illumination did not begin at a single point but was, instead, a widespread, evolutionary cultural shift. Both mages and non-mages experienced these changes, and with this came great industrialization and the rapid advancement of technologies. The pinnacle of technological progress up until then was actually found in the CME with its steam-powered systems, so the scientists, engineers, and the (emerging) capitalists (who funded the industrialization) in the Fifth Epoch managed to resume with the prototypes and schematics that were found in the ancient laboratories. Still, while many of the prototypes were found to potentially lead down an interesting technological tree, further modern research into other technologies left most steam technologies eventually redundant. Amongst the uneducated and disinformed today, there are beliefs that the CME was 'steampunk', which was not the case, as such a genre is only found in fantasy stories; nor, it must be noted, did 'steampunk' emerge *from* the Illumination, although, that is when most of the genre of steampunk literature is set as an alternative history.

With mass printing, the slightly-altered Synvoric languages also began to coalesce into a single language. Although there was a major cultural shift away from the religions, they nonetheless played a major role in the lives of many non-mages. The paradigm shifts generally occurred within elite circles – a portion of whom went on to form the most powerful movement in the Illumination: *The Movement of the Machine*, which still exists today. Note that while the Illumination Age began in 8810 (debatably), it still took a few centuries for the industrialization to follow in the 9200s. Even then, *mass* industrialization did not occur until the 9400s. By then, the Illumination Age was over, but its effects remained.

Whilst it seemed that the UOS would be the dominant force in the Caelverse, the industrialization greatly helped the non-mages increase their wealth and power. They, too, began forming their own political unions. Of course, not all non-mages benefited from the industrialization due to utilizing more organic, biological technologies that they grew. Nevertheless, they still saw a great increase in their own wealth over this period. A few mages considered growing technologies, but there was a general distaste for wetware, so this did not take off in the mage population. By the start of the Illumination, 7,234 solar systems had joined the UOS; in 9400, it was 13,749 systems. Then in 9806, the UOS had over 29,000 solar systems. At that point, the beginnings of the *Caelverse Government of Magi* (CGM) were fully set in motion.

The CGM was a plan for a fully-federated state with greater powers – one that was meant to intervene in society only in the most benevolent way. There were urges to hasten the project's completion, as non-mages were increasingly gaining power and territory, and the UOS was limited in its functions. However, it was voted in that the more practical, patient approach was the only way to complete the goal. With over 3,000 solar systems left to join, the UOS nevertheless 'lightly' bullied the other solar systems over the next couple of centuries with sanctions and trade embargos until, eventually, only 400 persistently remained. Despite its patience up to that point, the UOS decided to launch a war on the remaining systems. The mere threat made a few systems instantly submit, while many protests erupted in most of the other systems, calling for submission. The ensuing wars did not take long (only three years), and the casualty count was not high. Once the remaining systems were willing to join, the UOS transformed itself into the Caelverse Government of Magi in the year 10,100.

#### 4.1.7: The Sixth Epoch (E6):

When the Caelverse Government of Magi emerged, it was different to the ancient CME; it was fresh, debt free, had most social problems under control, and it had many plans in the works that were running smoothly. Essentially, the mages had established a system that was stronger than any other in known history. Some of the main goals included: grand infrastructural (re)building (including mass transport systems); enforcing particular educational requirements on citizens; ensuring environmental protections; implementing health initiatives and imposing health mandates; and many more. Non-mages were also to be given autonomy, but they had to submit to the CGM. Using the tried-and-true method of pragmatics, the CGM realized that for its goals to be effective, there had to have thorough planning. This also meant that it could not suddenly enforce policies too quickly without having built and structured certain programs initially. The CGM also wanted to avoid backlash that would otherwise potentially create revolts and other internal problems that the CME faced. The policies, nevertheless, were to be effectively implemented without fail eventually.

One issue that the CGM decided to reform was the calendar. While the *overall* year was 10,100, the date was changed so the figure would reset to zero every 10,000 years. Therefore, the first 10,000 years was then called the *Alpha Myrios* (with *myrios* meaning 10,000), and now we are in the *Beta Myrios*. Any history before the Alpha Myrios is called the *Pre Myrioi*. So, the year was then turned to Beta 100 or B-100. In most informal contexts, '100' is simply used. Over the next few centuries up until the current year of B-424, many of these policies have been effectively achieved or are in the midst of continual implementation. However, there are still many problems across the Caelverse. Corruption in the CGM and non-mage governments have increased; riots regularly form, especially in multispecieal zones; wars still occur; and with the rise of very advanced technologies, other existential issues loom on the horizon. For more information on the structure of the CGM and general contemporary society, see the following subsection.

## 4.2: Contemporary Politics and Society:

The Caelverse Government of Magi (CGM) is a Caelverse-wide holarchic federal government that transformed from the prior Union of Organized States (UOS) – a multi-planetary, supra-world-state union. The UOS itself was the restructured political order which emerged centuries following the collapse of the ancient mage empire known simply as The Empire (or The Magocratic Empire) – and later as the Caelverse Magocratic Empire (CME). Headquartered on the mage home world of Juntas, the CGM is a constitutional, mage-ruled democratic-republic government with a separation of powers featuring a legislature called the *Consummit*, an executive branch headed by the *archmage*, and a judicial system featuring the *Prime Court* as the highest court. There are also minor branches, such as the Auditory, Supervisory, Prosecutory, and Civil Service Commissions.

Consisting of three tiers, the Consummit is a pentacameral system containing five chambers, with the first tier featuring the *Exalted Chamber* – an advisory assembly filled with non-elected experts called *oracles*, who are also sometimes referred to as technocrats (even though they do not rule). The oracles are experts in their respective fields, such as agriculture, transport, education, etc., and are selected through government appointment only (so they are not voted in). While the Exalted Chamber currently holds 1,816 seats, there is no fixed number of experts, and the numbers can and do fluctuate. Moreover, there are also no term limits, and some oracles usually remain in office for life. Essentially, they review and amend bills, and while they are not able to *propose* any bills, they can delay bills for further scrutiny.

The second tier of the Consummit is known as the 'diversity tier'; and as part of its first assembly, it contains the *Sortition Chamber*. Filled with 2,048 randomly-selected adult mages across the Caelverse, the assembly allows selected mages to have the same level of power as oracles, except their terms only last six months. However, *sortition appointees* (SAs), as they are called, may appoint certain people they wish to committees to help them review bills. Although randomly selected, each person must be of a certain social status (such as having no criminal record), and each must also fulfil certain diversity and representation quotas, which means, for example, there is a 1:1 ratio of males and females. The next assembly is the *Non-mage Chamber*, filled with 4,096 *elected* non-mages that meet and fit certain criteria. As with the other two chambers, the *non-mage appointees* (NAs) can only review and delay bills, but they also can only do so with bills that will affect non-mages. These bills, furthermore, can only regard policies *by* mages rather than any non-mage legislations created in non-mages autonomous *zones* (explained later in this section).

The last two assemblies are of the 'primary tier', featuring the *Representative Chamber* and the *Senate Chamber* (or simply the 'Senate'). Each respectively holds 8,192 and 1,024 seats, and they are also respectively voted in preferentially via (ever-shifting) boundaries and proportionally via the solar clusters. Therefore, there are permanently eight senator positions for each solar cluster, while the more populated clusters in the Caelverse will naturally hold more representative seats than less populated clusters. However, there must be, at all times, at least one representative from a solar cluster, no matter a solar cluster's population. Only mages hold office, and only mages can vote for politicians in these chambers. Both assemblies propose bills, even though the chamber of representatives generally proposes the most bills for review. Despite the fact that the

Consummit's other chambers review bills, both the Representative Chamber and the Senate may create vast amounts of professional committees to help assess legislation.

The archmage, conversely, directs the executive branch and is both the head of state and the head of the government of the CGM. The archmage's powers include being able to: approve or veto bills from the Consummit; command the military; convene the Consummit; appoint officials to various government agencies at the federal level; nominate certain people to positions in the judicial branch; *prepare* (but not control) the budget (with approval of the Consummit); issue pardons for those who commit crimes at the federal level; appoint ambassadors for and to non-mage autonomous zones; and, in some cases, issue executive orders, bypassing the Consummit. Despite the archmage being voted in via the voting public, not all mages are able to become the archmage. To be eligible, prospective archmages must pass certain tests, which assess the intellectual, psychological, physical, and magical status of the mage. Then prospective archmages must pass certain difficult and dangerous trials and tribulations (similar to the trails for the supreme emperors in the CME), ensuring that the mage is literally willing to sacrifice themselves to reach the coveted position. Although, over the past two centuries, these thresholds have eased, allowing for certain mages to run for office, who otherwise would not have passed.

Within its holarchic hierarchy, the CGM has *cluster networks* (divisions based on the 128 Caelverse solar clusters), and then *solar administrations* (solar system governments), then *planetary authorities*, each respectively having their own constitutions and branches of government, with many responsibilities and decisions delegated to each. Structured under each planetary authority are *states* (many based on geographical orientations such as continents, but this can vary greatly). Each of these divisions is still referred to as the CGM, just not the *federal* CGM. Contrasting the other divisions to a degree are the various types of *zones*, all of which are mage-controlled under the states. Some states might have huge zones – a few in the rare case taking up nearly the entire state. However, a zone cannot be a state, and non-mages cannot, under any circumstance, control states – though zones can be the size of, or greater than, other states.

The main types of zones are: *mage exclusive* (called *A zones*); *multispecieal (B zones)*; *non-mage autonomous (C zones)*; *reserves (D zones)*; and *intermediate/transitional buffer zones* called *E zones*. Both A and B zones are connected via the same sub-governmental bodies, which generally list from *provinces* to *counties* to *cities* and then any division thereafter. Provinces are typically formed around the transportals, so there is usually one land-based transportal per province (so most transportals are located above ocean water), whereas most of the cities that exist around the transportals are capital cities, which have a mix of A and B zones. The majority of mages in the Caelverse – around eighty percent – live in mage-exclusive zones; but non-mages still enter mage-exclusive zones due to business, tourist, or governmental and legal reasons, with strict restrictions, of course.

While multispecieal zones are cosmopolitan spaces that mages share with many types of non-mages, there must, at all times, be mages present in such zones. Still, the demographics on both sides (mages and non-mages) can vary significantly. Non-mages have no political vote in multispecieal zones, except for electing people to non-mage chambers in various legislatures. Furthermore, non-mages can still lobby and voice opinions publicly. Some multispecieal zones function well, while others do not.

Despite ultimately governing C zones as well, mages allow non-mages to flourish with their own political systems (which are different to the non-mages holding office in the CGM's non-mage chamber in the Consummit). Nevertheless, mages can still veto any of their laws (via the mage governments); however, there are technicalities to this, and intervention may be stalled or limited due to other, messy legislation. Mages can still be – and usually are – found inside non-mage zones, though their numbers are few. The majority of C zones are exclusive to individual species, but sometimes there may be two or more species existing together. It is up to the non-mage governments to decide whether other species may become part of their C zones. Because multispecieal zones exist, there is always the opportunity for most species to live with others, so most species *also* value having their own exclusive zones to which they may call home. Sometimes attempts are made to integrate other species, but generally, conflicts arise, and so, this is another reason for the 'individuality' of species. When two or more species in C zones live together, it is generally due to either them being in the same genus and/or because they might have some kind of symbiotic relationship with one another.

D zones, on the other hand, protect certain developing, endangered, weak, and/or dependent lifeforms and rare social orders, ranging from non-sapient to sapient beings. Access to these zones is either strictly limited to CGM-approved personnel or to certain beings with regulated visiting permissions. Although private zoos and sanctuaries exist, these are not the same as D zones, and such zoos and sanctuaries are typically not as large as D zones. Some D zones spread across multiple continents; but in such cases, they usually are not on T2-C1 worlds. Sapient beings in D zones do not necessarily have their own governments, and they generally have direct regulations imposed on them by the CGM. The only exception to this is for beings who have 'rare social orders', which are typically preserved for the sake of study and preservation itself. Some species may progress from D zones to C zones, while others may require the assistance of the CGM, in turn leaving their C zones for D zones. D zones may also feature refugee camps (from war-torn zones), along with and other temporary relocation facilities. While some of these camps may seem like ghettos (indeed, ghettos do form within such camps), consider that ghettos (and slums) can still also be found in all zone types (especially multispecieal zones).

Many species, however, are banned from either most or all multispecieal zones. There are many reasons for this, but most of the time it is due to health issues. For example, some species can cause (that is, generate or shed) – or are subject to – allergens/allergies, microorganisms, and safety hazards (such as when certain beings produce slime on the ground, which can cause others to slip). Some beings need particular atmospheres to either thrive or even live (with certain types of gases, for example), which can be detrimental or lethal to many other beings. So, while in some cases, medical treatment and certificates can be given, there may be other cases where these cannot be administered, so outright banning follows. When treated, mammalians are accordingly the main type of beings that will enter and live in multispecieal zones.

Situated between many types of zones, E zones provide an intermediate buffer that serves multiple purposes; some of these may include reducing, preventing, or containing hostilities or health problems. Fundamentally, though, E zones act as a means to travel between all other zones without having to actually pass through or into different zones. They are like the hallways between rooms. Moreover, E zones allow for meetings and other assemblages between certain beings without having to meet in multispecieal zones either (which can help to prevent heath pandemics, for example. Depending on many variables, some E zones are greatly fortified with permanent heavy security, while others have little to none. There are also other types of zones that are dependent on context or time, or lack of development, such as *battlefield*, *experimental*, and *uncharted zones*, which are restricted to CGM-approved personnel.

There are attempts to diversify the CGM itself even further, with claims of diversity being a strength. Movements pushing for and against this idea are currently locked in a stalemate. Regardless, many mages and non-mages view the CGM as another – or continuation of the old – Magocratic Empire; but the CGM claims that it sees itself as a post-imperial system that mainly imposes itself on mages, taxing wealth from its own population to redistribute it to non-mage civilizations, which it claims to allow for self-determination. Only regulations that affect negative externalities are imposed on non-mages (such as limiting air pollution), coupled with interventions and preventions regarding war or any other predicted disturbances, troubles, pandemics, and trends, which the CGM believes would not be beneficial – usually survival-wise – to both itself (the CGM – and the rest of the mage population) and non-mage civilizations. The CGM also protects natural and cultural heritage sites that may be inside non-mage zones. Non-mages may also opt-in for regulations and/or other CGM operations, plans, subsidies, loans, or experiments.

In other words, mages still practically impose many interventions and regulations on non-mages, which have positive and negative consequences. Still, there are many areas where there are little to no CGM (and other governmental) regulations. Moreover, there are still uncharted zones in the Caelverse (mainly on T1, T3, and non-T2-C1 worlds), so the CGM has not contacted some tribal beings that keep well hidden. The CGM is nonetheless aware of their existence due to psychics having determined that such tribal beings do exist. Furthermore, whilst there are redistributions to the non-mages, there are many fees and costs involved for non-mages dealing inside multi-specieal zones. This is especially true for transportal areas since transportals are one of the few ways to travel between planets. Many mage-exclusive zones around the transportals have accordingly been converted to multispecieal zones to accommodate non-mages. Of course, mage-exclusive zones still closely surround such areas.

Complications arise with the various currencies both the mages and non-mages possess. The CGM delegates the issuing of monies to cluster networks, making 158 mage-based currencies. The reason why there are 158 currencies and not 128 is that some cluster networks have competing currencies. Non-mages have far more currencies due to the number of distinct C zones they have, and making transactions between other non-mage zones usually means that non-mages have to convert their currencies to mage ones before being able to trade with other non-mages. Because many non-mages have different monetary systems to mages, mages still use a system of physical cheques – in combination with 'non-physical' public ledgers via the synopool, with some systems backed by gold. With currencies devolved to the cluster network level, much economic activity occurs locally within a cluster network. This economic localization actually does not have much to do with competing currencies but more so as a result of the fact that it is hard to trade with other cluster networks when there are only a limited number of inter-cluster transportals. Essentially, the transportals are chokepoints. Moreover, there are also tariffs on goods that are shipped through the transportals, but this is due to the CGM wanting to gain revenue rather than a policy of economic protectionism.

Some cluster networks experience massive economic inflation, and this causes several social net negative side effects. Still, the problems in the Caelverse are not limited to economics but also to a number of competing political ideologies in both the Consummit and the Caelverse abroad. In addition, there are other ideologies that are supposedly apolitical yet become part of political discourse, anyway. The end result is that they lock the CGM into a perpetual stalemate. With its centrist outcome of policies (that is, neither fully 'left' nor 'right' wing – to use simple dichotomies and parlance), legislation only slowly passes (or repeals), and it typically does not stray far from what exists or does not exist. Accepted by many scholars, the CGM is also a bureaucratic mess – or 'nightmare', as many non-scholars say – with massive sums of money either wasted on inefficiency or spent on what most people consider frivolous nonsense. Sometimes large amounts of money are also lost to unknown voids. Basically, the economics affects the politics, and the politics affects the economics.

Due to these economic problems (in addition to major contradictory, problematic, and confining regulations and environmental protections), much development has taken off to certain planets with less oversight. Such examples include *Eleutheranus*, a semi-libertarian T2-C1 world that mostly consists of multispecieal zones. While it currently contains farmland, oceans, and topographical difficulties (such as mountainous terrains), Eleutheranus is the most developed of all planets in terms of infrastructure and urbanization across its surface. At current trajectories, it will likely be the first *ecumenopolis* (a planetwide city) in the Caelverse; although, this will not manifest for what will probably be a few centuries from now. Still, this would be a difficult feat to achieve, as, at that point, most food would have to be imported from other worlds, and placing that many resources through the transportals would be an issue. One solution proposed to this problem is space travel between other planets within the solar system – which definitely is achievable. So, other planets in the solar system could produce crops in traditional farmland. However, some theorists believe that this might not be necessary if farming practices change, in addition to everyone being genetically engineered to consume nutrients in a particular way.

It may, then, seem that Eleutheranus is the utopic vision and standard for some people; and while some parts of Eleutheranus remain free of major crime, other areas are cesspits for gangs and transgressions. Most of the crime is committed by certain non-mage species, but the mages who control the planet insist on not restricting most species in the Caelverse from living on Eleutheranus. At present, 240 billion mages live on Eleutheranus, compared to a considerable two trillion (estimated) non-mages – many of whom are still human or at least mammalian. There are, of course, the many unaccounted lithoids who live underground. There are also likely about 45 trillion mages in the Caelverse; and since there is a lot of room, there is no need for mages to gather on any particular planet – including Eleutheranus (and even Juntas, with its mage population of 84 billion). Still, given development is present, it is no wonder why it has attracted that many mages. It is unknown how many non-mages exist in the Caelverse, as even counting those in their autonomous zones is difficult. Eleutheranus also faces massive pollution problems, but some economists say that this is not due to the laissez-faire economics (that is, free without government interference) but rather selfish and reckless individuals and corporations that are not abiding by basic property rights. All planets that have their own dominant systems have their social issues, and so, it is said that each planet is itself an experimental laboratory.

While there are major social differences across the planets in the Caelverse, one phenomenon that is almost universal is the language used; that is, most species across the Caelverse speak the dominant language, Synvoric (also known as *Caelverse Standard*), at least to varying degrees, so there is generally ease of day-to-day affairs between ethnic groups and species. Countless dialects exist and continue to form, but there are also many dialects that coalesce into more common ones; and, with cultural entanglement, this is unavoidable. For this reason, less regulated planets still manage to function rather well in this regard, being both very culturally diverse and giant melting pots. Nevertheless, some sapient species are unable to properly comm- unicate with other species (usually due to morphological limitations); and naturally – of those that do live on planets like Eleutheranus – they do not thrive. This is because Eleutheranus still has multispeciealism enforced in particular ways, so these species who have communication problems cannot form their own C zones.

In order to bring about functional integration for all beings living in the Caelverse, there are other universal standards that are both voluntarily upheld and forcefully implemented (via governments). One of these standards is education; of course, there are multiple reasons for these educational standards that extend beyond mere functional integration. For example, in order for non-mages to participate in particular activities or business ventures – or even to see certain locations in multispecieal zones – they must still pass examinations that require one to study certain matters. Even mages have their own standards imposed on them. As one of the biggest examples, all mages must be formally educated when they reach the year that their magic glands develop. This lasts at least three years, and it must be conducted under a CGM-approved educational institute (most being universities), special-needs centre, or correctional facility before citizenship rights are granted. After graduation, mages are free to explore many parts of the Caelverse.

For mages that decide to live inside non-mage autonomous zones, they must adhere to the laws of the land; however, these mages also receive the protections of the CGM so that no non-mage may infringe upon certain mage rights. If mages disobey non- mage laws, generally, they are expelled (sometimes permanently) from the zone; and, depending on the severity, they are sentenced by the CGM with punishments from community service to lifelong jail (usually in the case of an act like murder). There have been some accounts of foolish and mentally-warped mages who have provoked non-mages in their zones with mass murders in an effort to start wars. Such actions do not help tensions that are already high in certain places. When the CGM was initially established, it sparked hostilities and conflicts with particular non-mages, who viewed that their autonomy would cease. Even though the CGM assured that their sovereignty would not be imposed upon, some wars were nevertheless waged against the CGM. Because of the overwhelming strength of the CGM compared to the hostile non-mage civilizations in question, these wars were not massive in scale. Moreover, since the CGM has self-imposed war restrictions and codes of conduct, it cannot simply genocide a sapient species or launch total wars unless there is either an absolute existential threat or that the species as a whole is hostile.

Accordingly, many of these wars were *irregular wars* – with many ongoing or developing to this day. As such, mage military forces normally skirmish targets to avoid collateral damage, while opponents typically engage in guerrilla warfare and terrorism, in addition to other non-linear types of combat that involve subversive, psychological, and informational assaults. Due to the nature of these wars, the majority of non-military mages (civilians) never see or experience conflict directly, but they may be subject to certain informational warfare. These irregular wars also apply to the hostile genera or individual species of sapient beings that the ancient CME originally faced. Most of these ancient threats continue to this day, but all of these hostile beings live and hide in the abyssal levels of various planets across the Caelverse.

Total wars do still occur against semi-sapient beings, but their numbers are few due to the CGM having already exterminated many of such problems. Still, there are always semi-sapient (and non-sapient) hostile beings that seemingly emerge from nowhere and begin attacking both civilians and non-civilians. While in most cases the reasons are not fully clear, there is strong evidence to suggest that such emergences are normally a part of the irregular warfare launched against the CGM and mages in general. CGM intelligence reports have also shown that non-mage armaments are covertly increasing in number and strength across the Caelverse. As a result of all these conflicts and potential problems, the CGM military has not disbanded, nor will it in the foreseeable future. The CGM military itself is divided into various service branches, including the army, navy, air force, and space force, but the CGM still has other non-military armed forces that engage in combative roles. For example, the Peacekeeper Corps is a force that is tasked with activities that ensure peace is sustained in generally post-war areas. These other institutions will likely not be dismantled in the foreseeable future, too.

Even with the said powerful military, wealth, technology, and status, mages are outnumbered. If the non-mages were to unite and all turn on the mages at once in a fully coordinated effort, then there is a good chance that the non-mages would win – at least on many planets (but probably not on heavily mage-populated planets). The remaining mages would likely cut off access to the transportals, so even if the mages were to lose control over the Caelverse, they would still likely win on many planets and continue to survive and thrive. Of course, the non-mages are very divided amongst themselves; and despite the slavery of the past, there are many non-mage groups and species who hate each other more than they do the mages. In fact, even today, many non-mages enslave each other in C zones and uncharted zones. The CGM attempts to stop such slavery, but this problem continues to fester. In order to keep non-mages from destroying the CGM, mages have cleverly created many institutions that cause the non-mages to police themselves, where the enforcers will not likely rebel. Therefore, when rebellions do occur, it usually comes through (generally small instead of mass) insurgencies fighting their own governments first.

# 4.3: Taxonomy of Sapient and Non-sapient Beings:

## 4.3.1: Introduction:

The Caelverse is home to what is estimated to be about 340,000 sapient species – and many more semi-sapient and non-sapient species. The ultimate origin of all of these species is still up for debate, but there is a general consensus on what may have occurred. All species could have evolved from simple, single-celled microorganisms (which were themselves emergent products of the elements of the celestial materials found in the Caelverse), where *natural selection* guided the evolutionary pathways of individual and collective entities. However, evolution *alone* could not have happened – especially within the short timeframe of the Caelverse's (re)structuring. Therefore, *extreme mutational events* (EMEs) are believed to have accelerated this process. Still, this could not have just happened with mere individuals within a species; moreover, sapience also occurred across the Caelverse basically at once. So, it is theorized that *extreme mass mutational events* (EMMEs) occurred, accelerating and driving the evolution of microorganisms to higher lifeforms – including helping semi-sapient beings become sapient.

EMMEs would likely have been the result of both extreme and unique etheric and physical phenomena occurring, in turn causing mutations in genetic material. Note that EMMEs are *distinct events*, and while there is evidence of different kinds of mutational events occurring all the time, the scale of these EMMEs – and how they would have exactly worked – have not yet been demonstrated and fully understood. EMMEs also likely would have occurred not just for a set of individuals of a species over their lives before (and after) sexual reproduction but also over many generations. Another important note to understand is that these mutations can not only affect and change the DNA code itself, but they can also affect the *gene expression* in the context of epigenetics, in turn causing already-present genes to switch on or off.

When a species (that is, a group of beings that can sexually reproduce with one another) features particular morphological and mental traits, they are naturally in tune with particular etheric energies. These etheric energies can be grouped into a particular category called *morphic resonance fields* (MRFs), which are collective resonance fields that store and organize the genetic information of a species – basically, a universal database that organizes the structure and forms of entities. While MRFs are etheric, they can physically alter organisms via their DNA and other structures such as microtubules, in turn enabling, for example, the crystallization of one part of a cell over another.

The MRFs themselves also have *archetypal development attractors* (ADAs), which tune into archetypes outside of the MRFs, so it is not just a matter of natural selection that drives evolution (and, importantly, MMEs and EMMEs) but a *teleological* phenomenon that can act as an attractor for species to evolve and mutate *towards*. So, an insect might have certain physical (that is, morphological) traits, and if it were to survive to sexually reproduce to result in the continuation of certain traits (and more refined versions of those traits) – thus natural selection – EMMEs would accelerate these traits and drive them towards a particular end point via the ADAs within MRFs.

A system to group organisms into categories based on morphological characteristics is called a *taxonomy*. There are different levels to a taxonomic system, and generally in the context of biology, the following ranks are featured in order of their ontological status: Life, Domain, Kingdom, Phylum, Class, Order, Family, Genus, and Species. Under the taxonomic rank of Domain, there are: Bacteria, Archaea, and Eukarya, while under Kingdom, there are: Animalia (animals), Plantae (plants), Fungi, Protista, and Siliconia. So, all species who each share certain and exclusive morphological characteristics are placed into Genus (genera, for plural). Still, it is not enough for two species to have, for example, two eyes and then be placed into a genus. Basically, each rank builds on the last, so each species in one rank needs to have certain traits that species found in the preceding ranks possess. Therefore, all primates (a group in the rank of Order), for example, have vertebra (a series of small bones forming a backbone – with this, Vertebrata, being a subcategory of beings under the category of Chordata, which falls under Phylum). Note that all sapient beings are placed into any category alongside non-sapient species (though, there are no sapient bacteria or archaea).

Most T2 planets (bar C6 planets) would have seen at least one species develop sapience. Two species from two different planets would not have needed to have had the same ancestors in order to feature very similar – if not identical – physical and mental traits. This is an example of *convergent evolution* (and mutation), and these two species would still be part of some MRF. Nevertheless, each species would have its own MRF, so there are MRFs within MRFs, each influencing one another. There could be two species of, for example, humans, who emerged on two worlds; and their respective planets would be called *home worlds*. Each of the two human species, in this case, would be part of the same genus, but this does not necessarily mean that they would be able to sexually reproduce with one another. However, there are some species within a genus (who never had the same ancestors) who are able to breed with one another, but this is generally rare.

While home worlds exist, migration and (re)placement to other planets has occurred throughout the various epochs. This, in turn, has led to a lot of confusion as to who originated from what planet. So, not only can some (but of course, not all) genera be found throughout the Caelverse, but due to the said migration and (re)placement to other worlds, a single species themselves can be found on many planets throughout the Caelverse. Indeed, this is the case for mages (although, 'colonization' is probably the more correct term to use); and, in the case of slavery during the CME, many species were totally removed from their home world to be placed somewhere else. There are also cases where a genus is *monotypic* – that is, there is only one species within the genus; and while mages are not part of a monotypic genus, there are some monotopic genera that feature their species widely across the Caelverse.

Due to the large number of (sapient) beings across the Caelverse, easily identifying them (or even to identify them at all) can be an issue, so there are systems to try to *simplify* each entity into easily-identifiable categories. Although there is no structured academic system in place for this, various folk taxonomic systems have emerged to address this issue. The irony is, the most developed and popular of these systems (the *Folk Taxonomic System* – FTS) happens to be rather complex and overly-complicated in some ways, so not everyone uses every aspect of the system. The FTS is flawed, but it is updated and adjusted all the time. Essentially, the FTS draws upon the aforesaid *Standard Taxonomic System* (STS) and reduces the number of *taxa* (ranks – *taxon* for singular) *and* categories within the said ranks. Despite its issues, however, the FTS works considerably well for ease of identification in most (broadly-applied) circumstances, and it is one of the reasons why it prevails in regular vernacular.

The FTS has two taxonomic ranks, followed by an unrestricted *tag* system for any additional contextually-relevant identifiers. It is easier to understand the nature of the FTS if one is already familiar with the STS, as the second rank, the *specificum*, draws directly from the latter and its unit of classification known as species. All species in the specificum still have both a common name and a scientific name (as with the STS), with the nomenclature of both being *binomial*; in other words, each has a two-part name. So, the common name for basic humans is just that: *basic humans*. Although, given the cultural significance, prevalence, and dominance of basic humans in the Caelverse compared to other humans (bar mages, who are simply called *mages* when correctly identified), normally, the word *humans* is simply all that is used in typical language. But while there is a two-part common name for referring to a species within a genus, usually a species itself will just have one name. For the scientific name, the name of the genus is paired with the specific *epithet* of the species, so basic humans are called *Homo sapiens* (H. sapiens).

For subspecies, three names are used; and so, mages are called *Homo sapiens magicka*. Not all 'common names' are based on a species, so the name *ants*, for example, is found in various genera. The FTS even includes non-living entities like *robots* alongside *biotics* (biological entities). So, robots typically also possess a binomial name consisting of their make and model names (such as TXJ-550). If a species can be correctly identified, then normally only the specificum will be used. However, when in doubt, the first rank of the FTS is used. Still, a person may sometimes actually wish to use the first rank to purposely identify a being in a broad manner or even, in some cases, to specifically identify a particular characteristic. Moreover, even if one person knows the correct species name, the first rank may still be used when mentioning the species to someone else who does not know anything about the said species. For clarification, the FTS centres around the first rank; it just so happens to be the case that the FTS *also includes* the species name (the specificum), which would be named outside of the FTS; so, the FTS is also all encompassing.

The first rank of the FTS, the *generalum*, also uses binomial nomenclature with an optional, additional three-letter abbreviation (TLA) *tag* normally added between the two names. The first part names the entity's *constitutional status*, whilst the second part identifies the overarching *morphological structure/type* (or *morphtype*). As with the specificum, the second part of the generalum's binomial is easy to understand if one already knows the STS ranks. The generalum draws a structural basis from these ranks, but it does not exactly use these ranks, so it possesses its own categories. Moreover, the generalum flattens all of its categories into a single rank for ease of identification, which it achieves by grouping beings as categorically high as possible without them losing too much of their recognizable identities. So, the specificum is specific, while the generalum is generalized (but not undefinable).

Essentially, the ontological basis for a category is where there is an ideal balance between general and specific identifications. Without this, either all beings would be unidentifiable due to simply being labelled as 'beings', or there would be millions of categories, thereby defeating the very purpose of the FTS. This means that all categories are actually ever shifting, but most categories practically remain indefinitely static due to the majority of users finding them ideal as identifiers. So, instead of grouping all mammals and reptiles into a category called Chordata (based on the STS) – which would otherwise cause too much of a loss in specific identification – the generalum focuses on mammals and reptiles as separate categories. In contrast, for all organisms that fall into the Mollusca phylum, the various classes within it are generally not used, as it is usually recognizable enough for beings to simply be placed into Mollusca.

Sometimes, however, there are nuanced differences between certain organisms that *seem* as if they are part of the same category, yet are not, and they, therefore, technically do not fall into the standard categories. For the sake of easy identification – and to avoid having too many categories – epithets, therefore, normally have a suffix such as 'oid' to signify that an organism *mostly* fits within a certain category. So, instead of Mollusca, the term *molluscoid* is used. In other words, there are many mollusc-*like* beings in existence, but not all are actually true molluscs, and so, such similar beings cannot precisely fall into the true Mollusca phylum. Given their similarities, however, it is easier to group molluscs and mollusc-like beings into a single category called molluscoids. There are a couple of exceptions to the 'oid' suffix rule, such as *mammalians* and *reptilians* – but this is merely due to the names sticking out of original use. Due to the flattened nature of the generalum, biotic entities are also placed into the same rank with synthetic and spectral (non-physical) entities. Nevertheless, these two latter categories are *tiered* differently within the generalum.

The first part of the binomial, conversely, identifies standards and alterations in morphological characteristics such as reproductive and integumentary organs. Known as the *constitutional status*, it identifies whether a being is organic, or mutated, or cyber-netic, or even undead. Most of the types originate from 'organic', but these are not subcategories of 'organic', and so, they are part of one tier. Synthetics and spectrals form their own tiers, and while they can technically spawn other status types within their own tiers, the generalum only lists one status type for each tier for the sake of conciseness and ease of reference. Organics and synthetics even have their own morphtypes; although, spectrals can have both morphtypes (found in organics and synthetics) and their own. Even though a being may have physical alterations, these are different from grouping mollusc-like beings, for example, into the category of molluscoids. A moll-uscoid may have originally had tentacles, for instance, but through cybernation, they could have lost these distinct morphological features, but the being itself would still be categorized as a molluscoid. Merely chopping off a being's tentacles does not mean that they are not of their respective morphtype; they are, instead, simply mutilated.

When an entity embraces cybernetics, they may not be exactly what a mollusc 'should' be, but they are still fundamentally mollusc-like (or molluscoid). On the other hand, if a mammalian were to gain mechanical tentacles through cybernation, they would still be mammalians – just altered mammalians. In any case, some mammals in nature already have tentacles, so tentacles themselves are not limited to a particular phylum. Nevertheless, if an entity has been genetically modified too much, then technically, they could entirely switch their morphtype, or they may even have the *assortion* epithet used for unsortable beings. In some cases, they may even have a mixed morphological name such as *mamo-molluscoid*, but this is generally not advised, as explained in *Section 4.3.3.19*. Regardless, they would still have the first part of their binomial indicating their genetic modification.

There are also multiple subcategories that can be used in the binomial instead of the main category in order to reveal a more nuanced distinction. So, one constitutional status category called *necrotics* contains the subcategories of *undead* and *metamorphics*. To complete the binomial name, one would use a name such as 'necrotic reptilian' (or 'undead reptilian', for more nuance), joining the status with the morphological epithet. Since the purpose of the FTS is for quick-and-easy broad references, becoming too nuanced is not favoured. Regardless of the conventions, sometimes the category's name is used alongside the species name (the specificum), so 'necrotic human' is sometimes used. An entity's constitutional status can also change, but certain changes may be irreversible, such as being killed and then turning into an undead being. The undead may 'die' and become a non-entitized corpse (again), but they will not return to being an organic, living entity.

Despite ease-of-reference being one of the principal purposes of the FTS, there are cases where identifying an entity's generalum type is hard or even practically impossible. Usually, this applies to such beings like *shapeshifters* until it is confirmed that an entity can shapeshift (that is, when a shapeshift has been witnessed). Likewise, an undead being may look like a normal living entity with completely-intact flesh and colour; but *most* undead actually do appear 'deathly' – especially when bones are visible. There are some undead that can – and indeed, do – exploit this, choosing to walk amongst normal beings in broad daylight without trouble. Other cases involve mutants who seem as if organic entities; but again, as with necrotics, most mutants are typically easy to identify as mutants. Then there is the issue of cross-sub-categorical confusion, such as between *mosaics* and *chimeras*. Moreover, some beings may actually be in the *mixed* constitutional status category, being, for example, both a mutant and a cyborg. Nevertheless, there are normally certain physical traits that are strongly correlated with particular statuses. For situations where an entity is covered in armour or a full-body suit, the FTS is not the issue, as any sort of identification in such contexts will always be harder.

While it is easy and sufficient enough to use the binomial alone, *sometimes* the TLA tag system is used for additional information. A TLA tag will outline three major additional characteristics of the entity being addressed; and these are: size, intelligence, and form. Due to all three characteristics being used in a single TLA, each term used has a unique letter, which means there is a limited number of terms that are used. There are five main size types that a being falls under: colossal, giant, average, tiny, and micro. Each of these is measured by either height, length or width. There is no such genus or species called 'giant'; although, the term 'giant' does appear in many common names. Each type also multiplies by five times the upper height of the last type, with the majority of beings in the Caelverse (bar actual microscopic organisms like bacteria and non-sapient common insects like ants) falling into the 'average' type.

The next list contains the three main levels of intelligence for biological entities, which are: sapient, semi-sapient, and non-sapient. Although sapient beings vary greatly in intelligence, the highest intelligent beings are not in a realm of total incomprehensibility to those beneath them, and many still make silly mistakes. Therefore, the limit of intelligence, for now, rests with sapience. Also note that not all sapient beings live in civilized society, and some still live rather primitive existences, so sapience alone does not mean that one can easily be identified as a sapient being. Semi-sapient beings are capable of using technologies (both primitive and advanced tools) but cannot yet utilize them to sufficiently create additional technologies and advance on their own without intervention. Semi-sapient beings are also able to comprehend certain abstract concepts – but only at a very rudimentary level. It is theorized that the main factors holding back certain semi-sapient beings from advancing intellectually are their emotions and general aggression. If they learned to control their inhibitions, then advancement to sapience could be a very short prospect – and this is likely even without the need for EMMEs; still, EMMEs would, indeed, help.

Non-sapient beings, of course, constitute the majority of animals and other life-forms, such as plants. Generally, such beings are easy to identify, but not always, as some *phytoids* (plant-*like* beings), for example, may be hard to distinguish from the flora around them. Moreover, many non-Siliconia lifeforms tend to find it hard distinguishing sapient Siliconia lifeforms (normally lithoids) from non-sapient ones – at least initially without dialogue. Synthetics, on the other hand, have two main types of intelligence: *autonomous synthetic* and *restricted synthetic*. There is currently a great amount of debate over whether artificial intelligence has actual intelligence or not, and so, instead of simply affirming or denying such potential intelligence, the two aforesaid labels are simply used instead to identify that the 'intelligence' nonetheless comes from a synthetic. Autonomous synthetics are 'freethinking', able to conceptualize ideas of their own accord. Restricted synthetics, meanwhile, are only *virtually* intelligent, limited by programming. There are some people, however, that argue that artificial intelligence is sapient, but not sentient, and the distinctions are fallacious.

The last TLA tag addresses the being's form – explicitly, how close an entity is to the *humanoid* structural archetype. The reason for relating it to a humanoid structure is due to the fact that humans (mages, specifically) invented the FTS, and they continue to dominate political and cultural life in the Caelverse. Therefore, it is natural that the FTS and any related discourse revolves around humans. Many non-humans agree with using the term, anyway – even if for the sake of ease alone and not culturally – especially when dealing with other non-humans outside of their own species. Another reason stems from the fact that some beings, such as arthropoids, may be either very humanoid, not at all, or somewhere in between, and so, the humanoid form is not limited to mammalians. Without this distinction, one may accidentally conceive of a particular arthropoid as simply being non-humanoid, when it may not be the case.

Also consider that the humanoid archetype allows for the easy use of physical tools that aid in the advancement of – and even straightforward integration within – civilization. That is, there is a great correlation between the more humanoid an entity is and their level of intelligence. Of course, this is not always the case, and there are some rare pure non-humanoids that are highly intelligent. Humanoid characteristics include having: an upright/erect posture (with a standard torso), two arms with hands (that have together eight fingers and two opposable thumbs), bipedal (two-walking) legs (with five-toed feet to walk or run on), and one face (and head) that possesses two eyes, a nose, two ears, and a mouth. Not all beings with an upright torso, however, are bipedal, and some may actually have multiple legs.

The criteria for fitting into the following terms changes over time, and sometimes some beings are borderline. If an aquatic being has a fish tail and a pure (or mostly pure) upper humanoid body, it would be, without a doubt, considered a *bisectional humanoid*. If a subterranean being had drill-like arms (with no hands), a humanoid head, and a humanoid lower body, it would normally be considered either *essentially humanoid* or *relatively humanoid*, depending on further finer details. If a being just had horns sticking out of its head, they would probably be called *essentially humanoid* or *humanoid* (depending on the size and nature of the horns); the same would apply if they alternatively just had a tail. However, if they had both a tail and horns, then they would possibly be labelled *relatively humanoid*. Some exceptions apply, depending on the size of the horns and the tail, as all basic humans have tailbones (vestigial tails), and some mutations lead to very small horns.

If a being was covered in fur or scales, but the rest of their body was a pure humanoid form, then they would be considered *humanoid*, as it is the structure, not the texture, that defines the archetypal shape of a humanoid. An arthropoid might, for example, have an insect-like body yet have a humanoid head; in which case, they would likely be considered *vaguely humanoid* or even *non-humanoid*. However, if they did not have a humanoid head, then they would definitely be considered *non-humanoid*. The following is a list of all the TLA tag terms, with each grouping placed in order of their position in a TLA tag:

Size:

C: Colossal: >1250 cm
G: Giant: 250 cm to 1250 cm
A: Average: 50 cm to 250 cm
T: Tiny: 10 cm to 50 cm
M: Micro: <10 cm

Intelligence:

S: Sapient
P: Semi-sapient (Partially-sapient or Pre-sapient)
U: Non-sapient (Unwise)
X: Autonomous Synthetic
Y: Restricted Synthetic

Form:

H: Humanoid
E: Essentially humanoid
R: Relatively humanoid
B: Bisectionally humanoid
V: Vaguely humanoid
N: Non-humanoid

One term is taken from each category, so when an entity is identified, they might have a tag such as 'ASH' (average sapient humanoid), which would be used either separately or between the two parts of the binomial name. So, for an unadulterated basic human, they would altogether have the label 'organic ASH mammalian' for the generalum. Additional tags can be used to help identify certain characteristics of a being, but any specific additional tag itself is not part of the FTS. Still, these other tags may include the environment (whether they are aquatic, subterranean, etc.), abilities (such as having magic, psychic, or regenerative abilities, etc.), and prevalence (such as being common, rare, extinct, mythical, etc.). Of course, the list can be endlessly extended.

## 4.3.2: Generalum Constitutional Status Categories:

### 4.3.2.1: Organics:

Being the only category that does not possess any commonly-used subcategories, *organics* is the most 'vanilla' of all constitutional statuses in the generalum. In fact, all other status categories are divergents from organics (bar spectrals and synthetics, being in their own tiers). All organics are biotics, but not all biotics are organic. Essentially, organic beings are entities that consist of biological matter and were formed either via standard sexual reproduction or its processes without involving actual sexual intercourse. Such examples include naturally-formed animals, plants, bacteria, and of course, sapient beings like humans. However, organics also consists of some wetware or biological machines under the *mechanoid* morphtype – which is not a synthetic morphtype – but most wetware normally does not form into a morphtype outside of the mechanoid category. So, while organic mechanoids might appear like plants or strange pets or even technologies such as ships (bioships), each will nevertheless display mechanoid characteristics. Organic mechanoids normally appear and act as non-sapient or semi-sapient beings, despite being able to process complex tasks that advanced computers can accomplish. Note, however, that not all mechanoids are biological machines, and there are some biological species that simply have mechanical-like structures and appearances. Moreover, as soon as genetic engineering is involved, an organic mechanoid no longer remains organic.

Comprising the majority of beings in the Caelverse (not including the astral planes), organics dominate most aspects of political and cultural life. However, due to recent developments (especially technologically), that reality may soon change in the future. When astral travelling outside of the organic body, however, an organic being's spirit *itself* can simply be identified as a spectral (an 'organically-attached spectral'). Even though organics miss out on the physical and mental bonuses found in the other constitutional status categories, they also lack the negative physical and mental weaknesses, making them the most balanced and stable of all the categories. In the rare event that a mage conjures a conjured being based on an organic being, then normally the former will be classified as an organic, despite being a *golem*. When applying golems to a morphtype in a binomial, the adjective *golemic* is used. Of course, this is assuming the spell did not create an object that looks like an organic being (like a latex dummy); in which case, the conjured being would be a synthetic. Unless genetically modified, clones are also an organic type of being, normally called 'organic', but sometimes they can be called *clonals*. If wetware *happens* to fulfil the criterion of falling into a particular morphtype (such as an anneloid), then 'golemic' *may* be used as well.

## 4.3.2.2: GMOs (Biomodics):

With the rise of genetic engineering technology, more beings across the Caelverse have been able to edit their genes, in turn becoming *genetically-modified organisms* (*GMOs*). Otherwise known as *biomodics*, GMOs normally come in the following main subcategories: transgenics, cisgenics, kogenics, chimeras, and synthgenics. Gene editing essentially allows for the insertion or deletion of genes and DNA, and some of these can come either endogenously or exogenously from one's own species. So, if the DNA came from a species other than one's own, then they would be called a transgenic. In the case where the DNA came from another being from one's own species, then they would be a cisgenic. Kogenics, on the other hand, are simpler, in that they merely have particular genes knocked out and, thus, are sometimes called 'knockouts'. In the context of biomodics, chimeras are engineered beings who come from two different *zygotes* of either the same or separate species. In either of these sub-categorical cases, some GMOs physically appear rather different to their original genetic makeup. So, some GMO basic humans may have fish fins, allowing them to swim more effectively, while other GMOs may have wings or scales, despite their own species naturally lacking these features. GMOs also may have had certain germline diseases (that is, disorders in reproductive cells) removed, thus making gene editing highly sought out.

Gene editing, however, is not without its issues, and many GMOs face problems such as an increase in new cancers (despite removing germline issues involving cancers), along with particular tissue – and even whole structural – breakdowns. Basically, by fixing certain issues, the operations also open up or create other problems – some may even be worse than the original problems solved. The practice has become even more dangerous with synthgenics, which uses nano technologies as a way to synthetically produce new proteins, in turn creating more extraordinary results. While such nano technologies are in their infancy, proponents argue that they will improve over time (both their safety and effectiveness), whereas opponents contend that no matter how far genetic engineering improves, there will always be negative offsets at any level. Most GMOs also require taking medications for the rest of their lives.

Mages have banned most genetic engineering practices amongst their own kind, but many non-mages (especially basic humans) have readily embraced transhumanist ideals and practices (this includes *trans-speciesism* – or *trans-specieism*). Despite being able to grow any sort of tissue, the majority of biomodics choose to retain their morphological forms, so basic humans still normally look both humanoid and mammalian. Most changes are for features that increase *abilities* that the biomodic-to-become already possesses, such as running speeds and jumping heights. For large-scale changes, such as turning a human's legs into a big fish tail, the GMO might have a label like 'merfolk', but merfolk are not in and of themselves a species. That is, there is no 'merfolk' species in the Homo genus. There have been successful insertions of *monster* DNA into people; but the CGM has banned this practice for every living being in the Caelverse due to its policy of exterminating or capturing all monsters. For more information on monsters, see *Section 4.3.2.4*. Only the irrational or mentally unhinged actually desire to become a monster, as one loses their egoic identity and can even be a danger to themselves. Accordingly, this is not a popular genetic engineering practice, but some black-market labs nonetheless manage to conduct these operations. Even genetically engineering 'armies' with monster DNA is undesirable, as monsters are uncontrollable and destructive.

Non-mages have also been able to somewhat genetically replicate mage magic glands; however, the CGM has banned the creation and insertion of such glands into non-mages – even within non-mage autonomous C zones across the Caelverse. While such engineering has given concern to some mages, others view it as beneficial for a variety of reasons, such as bringing about equality. Nevertheless, for some unknown reason, the engineered glands deteriorate quickly and, thus, are virtually never useable. This has given rise to a theory that there is something else in the mage's body that allows for magic and/or that there may need to be some additional etheric component for the use of magic, such as actually being etherically part of the mage's collective MRF or something similar. The engineered glands and the procedures to implement them are also very expensive, so this is another deterrent.

It is currently too hard to present exact figures on how many non-mages have been genetically modified, as many (but not all) gene editing practices do not require prescriptions and documenting. Moreover, unlike cyborgs, who have obvious mechanical implants, genetic modifications can be rather subtle to almost impossible to determine without testing. For quite some time, genetic engineering was not as popular as cybernetics, but it has quickly caught up to roughly the same level of popularity. Proponents argue that genetic engineering is the ideal future, seeing cybernetics as an outdated practice. However, advancements are continually being made in the field of cybernetics as well. There is a grey area or fuzzy line between genetic engineering involving technologies to specifically alter DNA and that of intended techniques to alter DNA via other methods (such as occultic rituals without magic). In cases of the latter, sometimes a being may be considered a GMO, but they alternatively could just be a mutant or even something else.

## 4.3.2.3: Cyborgs (Cybernetics):

As with GMOs, *cyborgs* (or *cybernetics*) are beings that have undergone alterations to their bodies. However, instead of (merely) genetically altering the DNA itself, cyborgs have replaced certain parts of their anatomy in favour of mechanical alterations typically called 'upgrades' or 'augmentations'. Some of these include limbs, eyes, and genitalia. Although prosthetics have been in use for thousands of years, in order for a being to be considered a cyborg, mechanical articles need to be fundamentally integrated into the being's central nervous system. Cybernetics also includes being able to remotely control surrogate synthetic bodies called *proxates* instead of having mechanical organs or appendages implanted into the body. Nonetheless, cybernetic beings that can control synthetic proxates still have microchips and other technologies integrated into their anatomies in order to connect with their proxates. Moreover, cyborgs with lots of mechanical articles may still choose to use proxates; and, it is not as if proxates are mere cybernetic exoskeletons that cyborgs can wear. Since proxates are not actual robots with their own programming, they are, instead, considered extensions of a cyborg rather than being a *synthetic* (with its own constitutional status). It is nonetheless possible for organic mechanoids to become cyborgs as well.

Cyborgs face many issues, which include: their bodies rejecting the mechanical articles, which normally leads to necessary medications; malfunctioning parts, which can even explode or leak dangerous chemicals into the body; immobility if not properly charged with energy, which can be dangerous in situations where one needs to move or vacate an area; neurological disorders; mental issues (which can lead to insanity or suicide); hacking problems, granting hackers the ability to control the cyborg's body; and many more problems. Then there are the brain chips themselves, which can lead to shrinkage in and of certain parts of the brain (due to an overreliance on the brain chips, in turn leading to atrophy); and, in the case of A.I. interface chips giving constant streamed hivemind-like information to the user, this can lead to a semi echo-chamber, which can diminish certain cognitive functions (while enhancing others). Despite these problems, cybernetics has great appeal because cyborgs have heightened abilities such as: sensory perception; strength; replaceability (if, for example, damaged); ease of access to advanced technologies for control; and, of course, many other reasons. However, the overwhelming majority of cyborgs are not fully mechanized, and they normally only have a few microchips and jacks (or *port points*) installed into their bodies so they can access certain technologies – both hardware and software – and digital landscapes.

Most members or supporters of the Movement of the Machine are cyborgs; and, the more fanatical the adherent one is, the more 'augmented' they typically become. Organics originally viewed cyborgs as one of the greatest threats in existence, but many people realized that technologies external to the body could still simply be used to counter cyborgs. External technologies, moreover, can also be used to engage with other technologies easily, anyway. After cyborgs realized this partial redundancy, they nonetheless continued altering their bodies, seeing it, at the very least, as an aesthetic and sacred pursuit. Cyborgs were accepted back into society, although with some suspicion, but there are now growing tensions. Some people believe that there can be a solution between cyborgs and non-cyborgs, while others do not see a viable one. Of those that see a solution, the perceived problem is not cybernetics itself but rather the zealous nature of movements like the Movement of the Machine – or certain adherents and ideologies therein. Note that while in the past, many adherents of the Movement of the Machine denied the existence of spiritual realities, this is not the case now; however, just because one acknowledges spiritual realities, it does not mean that they will not have a mechanical perspective on the matter.

Since many people in society prefer to follow the path of least resistance and want a secure life without trouble, if they are surrounded by cyborgs, then naturally they will conform and embrace it without even radicalizing or supporting said movements. Cybernetics is popular in the basic human community – and among many other species, too. At present, an estimated seven percent of basic humans are cyborgs, but such figures are hard to accurately measure, as basic cybernetic implants do not require legal prescriptions. This figure also does not account for people who have imbedded microchips that are not connected to their central nervous system or brain.

At present, mages require a legitimate reason to legally become a cyborg (such as rare medical reasons or jobs that require public relations and diplomacy with cyborgs); and so, such modifications are hard to acquire and conceal. Still, there are legal loopholes allowing for certain 'augments', but this still has not been popularized amongst the mage population. Mages are also allowed (but never should be legally forced) to get microchips and quantum tattoos. However, most mages are not micro-chipped (bar for some mages living in certain non-mage areas). Many mages view being microchipped akin to being little more than cattle; but this cultural ideal is changing.

If the magic gland is not replaced with cybernation, and if the augmentations do not affect the magic gland, then there are still problems on an etheric level, as all physical matter has etheric energy. This can affect spells, synchronizations, rituals, etheric instabilities, overloading, and, interestingly, even QIF times, as there are links from the etheric to the potential fields around the users. It can even be detrimental when in the midst of a dark ritual, for example. So, this is yet another deterrent for mages taking up cybernetics. The Movement of the Machine tries to assure mages that the technology to overcome such issues is underway, but such talk has not (yet) been fully accepted. In fact, etheric problems even occur amongst the non-mages who wield such augmentations. For example, in the case of cybernetic telepathy, etheric issues can create tiny quantum distortions that can cause problems for cyborgs trying to communicate with one another, so such telepathy may either not be encrypted well, or the messages may become distorted and hard to hear, or the cyborg might even receive a totally different message. There are also other quantum anomalies that occur that cyborgs cannot account for and handle, and these problems have actually increased in some ways as the technology has progressed.

## 4.3.2.4: Mutants (Mutanetics):

Mutations are a naturally-occurring phenomenon that takes place in all species. In fact, the average basic human will have just over 150 mutations in their body; but to be considered a *mutant* (or *mutanetic*) in the context of the FTS, a certain level of mutation is required. All mutants accordingly possess a specific set of unique genes that are grouped as *M genes*, which results in large-scale mutations in chromosomal structure that have observable, morphological differences in their anatomy to that of organic beings that are not mere diseases or non-mutational deformities. Moreover, these differences will also possess non-observable unique traits that have both positive and negative effects. So, if a basic human were to have scaly skin like a reptilian, or three arms, or wings, then they would be *considered* a mutant, but they nevertheless may not have M genes. Still, these mutational occurrences are so rare without M genes that most initial considerations of them being 'mutants' actually are correct. Never-theless, of the large-scale mutations that do not possess M genes, normally, the title of mutant is applied, anyway, for ease of reference. However, when including non-M gene mutants into the FTS under 'mutant', a degree of arbitrariness can occur. A person who has the condition known as trisomy 21, for example, would not be considered a mutant in this context; but levels of mutation beyond this condition *may* warrant the title of mutant even if lacking M genes.

Mutations can occur either exogenously or endogenously, and most mutants (with M genes) have somatic mutations rather than germline mutations; that is, most mutations occur in non-reproductive cells. In other words, *most* mutants do not pass their mutations to their offspring. Accordingly, M genes are not the result of EMEs or EMMEs (so these normally produce *both* germline and somatic mutations). Mutants are not of a different species to their genitors, nor a subspecies, as to be considered a species, there needs to be enough of the particular kind (of mutants) in order to establish themselves as a species; and, they must be able to only breed with mutants of their own kind. A lot of mutants are sterile, anyway. In the rare cases that particular types of mutants do become a new species, they are no longer called mutants, and instead, they are referred to simply by their new species name. Therefore, mutants are divergent individuals from within their species.

There are five main types of standard mutants: *amplifics, restructics, mosaics, disics,* and *changelings*. About half of all human mutants will be a mix of some of these varieties; in which case, the term 'mutant' is normally just applied. Amplifics have gene duplications, which result in observably bigger or extra body parts, such as a bigger limb or an extra limb. Restructics, on the other hand, have rearranged and/or deformed body parts, so instead of a human having eyeballs in the head, their eyes may be found on the abdomen; alternatively, a normal human-shaped head might instead be shaped, for example, like an object found in a typical kitchen. Mosaics, meanwhile, have two sets of genetic lines. However, they are not chimeras, and so, if a basic human had eagle claws, it would not have the DNA of an actual eagle; rather, the mutation would simply have created the mosaic of having eagle-*like* claws.

*Griffins* were originally mosaic eagles with lion-like bottom halves, but they were nevertheless one of the very few group of mutants to have successfully bred and become a new species (and so, they are no longer considered mutants). *Harpies* and *merfolk* (but not *sirens*, as these are part of folklore) – respectively humans or human-like entities with bird-like wings and fish-like tails – are also considered mutants, but there are GMO versions of these beings, too. Originally called 'blightics', disics feature typical morphological disease symptoms but on a greater scale in both intensity and size. These features may manifest as extreme crusty skin, tumours, rashes, and bumps, and there are even some disics that appear undead with aesthetically-unapp-ealing skin that *appears* rotting. However, they would not be classed as necrotics. Some of these mutations can still lead to brain-rotting diseases; and, coupled with necrotic-looking skin, they can appear and act as if zombies.

Changelings are a rarer type of mutant who can change their shape and form to a degree. They are not the same as shapeshifters found in the constitutional status category called *heterogenics*, nor are changelings *shapechangers* who are amorphous beings like protistoids (amoeboids), who can simply change their bodily shapes due to their unique biological structures. An example of a changeling is a mutant who might have a normal-looking human body but then 'transforms' themselves into a hideous beast. The beastly form would not be an etheric shift to another body in an alchemical sense, and instead, it would be more of an unravelling of their true form from a visage that is part of the same body. Organic mechanoids may also mutate and become mutant mechanoids, fitting into any of the above categories.

Because M genes also have other unobservable traits, mutants will normally also have super abilities such as increased strength, faster reflexes, and increased speed – along with potentially bizarre powers such as the ability to self-immolate or excrete gold nuggets from their rectums. Unluckily, mutants also have detrimental traits and features, such as blindness, constant pain, derangement, missing organs, utter lack of coordination, and shorter life expectancies. All M gene mutations are also permanent, but technically, mutants can mutate to an originally-*appearing* state, which itself is not a reversion but, instead, another mutation. Within the human population, about 0.2% are mutants *with* M genes, with mages respectively contributing around the same amount to other humans per capita. Although genetic engineering *can* induce mutation with M genes, all 'mutants' gained their mutations without intentional genetic engineering. Given the multitude of different kinds beings in the Caelverse, mutants are generally accepted within society so long as the mutations are safe and not too unaesthetically and sensorily revolting or vexing.

The worst kind of mutation for any being to get, though, is the *monster* or *aberration* mutation. In order for a being to become a monster, they must be a mutant with M genes in the first place and have reached a certain level of mutation. Once a high-enough mutation has occurred, the mutant may experience a *chance* for the DNA to reach a rare type of unstable state – an extremely delicate fulcrum. Normally in unstable states, DNA will break down and cause diseases or even death – and this can still happen for the mutant – but if the mutant passes another chance check to avoid breaking down and dying via a particular wave function change, the monster can experience a total reconfiguration and reformation of the DNA and their bodies, in turn leading to a *monstrous phase mutation* (MPM). In other words, instead of the mutant getting diseased (per se) and dying, the event reconfigures their DNA into something powerful and monstrous. The mutant may experience mosaicism, amplification, observable reconstructions, diseased-looking forms, and they may also have changeling abilities, but consider that with all of these, monsters will have more extreme but powerful versions.

Naturally, etheric activity will be involved, but despite this, physical activity (whether exogenous or endogenous) is overwhelmingly the cause of MPMs. Astral activity may also play a role via the etheric, but this naturally has even less of a role compared to the physical. Still, it is common for negative astral entities to surround monsters. Some beings are more prone to mutating and gaining M genes, and then some of those beings are more prone to others in gaining MPMs. As with general mutation, monstrousness is permanent. There is no known additional stage after a monster, but some monsters are stronger than others.

Monsters normally possess enhanced or extraordinary powers (for example, some can easily levitate, while others can use strange acid attacks), and they are also typically resistant to *certain* types of consciousness-altering attacks (which make them annoyingly-difficult enemies for mages). Not only can many monsters survive a single bullet fired at them, but monsters may even have rapid healing abilities; so, if one bullet was fired at a monster, then another one minute later, the monster could have healed in that time, so the only way to kill the monster with bullets in this case would be to shoot many bullets within a short period to overwhelm them. When mutating into a monster, the mutant's mutations are generally very rapid. The mutational changes (especially the intense shift itself) also always leave monsters sterile, and so, no monster can reproduce. Furthermore, this is even the case for those who happen to retain some semblance or actuality of sexual organs – most of the time, even if genitalia remain, they are twisted versions of their former structures. Nevertheless, monsters can alter the mutations of others in a process that seems like breeding, such as cocooning victims. This, in turn, can lead to the chance for MPMs, which could then allow for normal mutants with M genes to change into monsters.

Physically, monsters are almost always considered to be highly grotesque and/or frightening creatures who look quite different to their original mutant forms. Given that there are extreme morphological changes in a monster, it may be hard to couple it with a morphtype epithet. For more information on their appearances, see *Section 4.3.2.5*. Note that monsters are different to non-sapient *powerful creatures* naturally found in the wild, such as dragons and colossal worms (despite their rarity in modern times). Usually, it is clear such creatures are not monsters due to their different physiology, abilities, and resistances, but they can still turn into monsters, and it may have even been the case that they were once mutants that turned into a species. Powerful creatures tend to be ferocious, but ferociousness can be found even amongst sapient organics. Monsters also typically lose their egoic identity and become extremely hostile, but a fair few still retain most of their *memories*. The CGM has mandated that all monsters (and in some cases, powerful creatures) be either immediately exterminated or sealed away in approved laboratories or other sanctuaries due to their dangerous nature. Accordingly, this means that monsters (and some powerful creatures) are rare;

but since monsters can emerge at any time, monstrosities themselves are an unending threat. Once monsters are captured, certain technologies are then attached to the monsters to help curtail their powers.

## 4.3.2.5: Heterogenics:

Heterogenics are a combination of different entities unified as a single entity (which can even include two or more clones). It is a unique category, as most beings classed as such are only provisionally heterogenic. The main subcategories are: *collectics, symbiotes, fusionics, altermorphics, shapeshifters,* and *possessionics.* The first two types are purely physical in nature, and most tend to stay in their heterogenic form (usually for life), not only to thrive but also in order to survive. In contrast, the last four types involve alchemical magic or rare phenomena that results in what alchemical magic would otherwise achieve. In the latter case, physical energy is involved instead of aether energy, and this works through and with the etheric (like how elemental moons can shapeshift with physical energy), so this contrasts a mage's lack of ability to use just any energy (like stored calories) for their alchemical magic. Still, the different heterogenic forms will normally only be short-lived, and the transformations are generally much easier to occur during lunapexes. There are major calls to separate the two major groupings due to their vastly contrasting natures, but many people still insist on keeping the heterogenic group as it is because having more constitutional status categories will supposedly and potentially lead to ever more categories being formed.

A *collectic* (or *collective*) entity is a group of beings that coalesce into a greater form than their individual selves – a whole that is greater the sum of their parts. Most collectics tend to be hundreds or thousands of worms, which together form at least typically vaguely-humanoid forms. A hive mind or collective consciousness forms, and the individual beings (such as worms) give up their individuality to the collective, and the single mind can easily function and perform tasks as an individual entity itself. Many collectics become so adapted to their collective forms that they can perish without them. When using the generalum to address collectic beings, non-plural names such as 'collectic (humanoid) anneloid' are normally used. Many beings in the Caelverse will find collectics rather startling or disgusting, and so, collectics tend to either keep to themselves or cover up their bodies with clothing or full-body suits.

*Symbiotes* (or *symbionts* – and rarely, *symbiotics*), on the other hand, are similar to collectics, but most occurrences are with only two to four entities, all of which are of a different species from one another. Technically, most organic beings have symbiotic relationships with bacteria, but the symbiote subcategory *focuses* on non-bacterial relationships. Even though many individual beings found in collectics can survive without their collective, the overwhelming majority of individual beings in symbiotes cannot live (or at least properly function) without their heterogenic form. The reasons for why individual beings group into symbiotes vary, but most factor down to pure functionality in the civilizational context and/or deformities, injuries, diseases, or aging reasons that the individual beings may (otherwise) occur over their lifetimes. Sometimes, entities may require symbiosis from birth. In the latter case, established symbiotes breed with other symbiotes in order to produce liveable offspring.

The heterogenics known as *fusionics* (or just *fusions*) are the result of two or more beings voluntarily or involuntarily amalgamating to form a new entity with a distinct single form. That is, unlike collectics that retain individual forms inside the collective, the fusionic only has one form. In other words, the two (or more) bodies cease to exist corporeally, and a new body manifests into reality. The fused body can vary in form, with some having two or more heads, while others will only possess a single head. Even though a fusionic may have two heads, these two heads are not their former heads but are still part of the new body. There are some fusionics where a lion and eagle, for example, may merge to create what appears to be a griffin, but these are not actual griffins, which are actually former mutants. Advanced alchemical magic is required for this feat, as it involves fusing two or more EHRFs. In non-magical circumstances, the fusionic cannot choose their new form, and the end result will only be the most likely case, so this is very limited compared to alchemy magic.

*Altermorphics* (or simply *altermorphs*) are similar to fusionics, except that instead of a new form manifesting into reality, two or more beings share reality in *one* of their *original* bodies. Intentionally or unintentionally, the body can morph into one of the other beings; but even after morphing, altermorphics can only be manifest as one being at a time. Normally, there is a dominant/submissive relationship for those in the altermorphic (along with those in fusionics), where the dominant being will control the actions of the actualized body, while the submissive being(s) will usually only influence decisions. Being an altermorphic (or fusionic) can be incredibly vexing, and many suffer mental illnesses if they remain as altermorphics or fusionics for long periods of time (but since most transformations are short-lived in both magical and non-magical cases, this is not normally a problem unless done consecutively). As with fusionics, advanced alchemical magic is required, which involves the fusing of two or more HRFs together.

*Shapeshifters*, on the other hand, are beings who can turn from one being to another, despite the latter not actually being an individualized, existentially-real (corporealized) being itself (that is, a real entity with a unique egoic identification). For example, a basic human might be able to shapeshift into that of a reptilian form. While the reptilian form would be a QTS in alchemical magic, in non-magical cases, it would be another MRF with other genetic information. So, even in this latter case, it is still a combination of another 'being', so the basic human would not actually a pure *organic* (or otherwise). There is a difference between a shapeshifter and a *shapechanger* (or *amorphoid*); shapeshifters *shift* realities via the etheric, whereas shapechangers merely change the shape of their bodies while still in the physical, usually due to having a gelatinous structure or because they lack cell walls – or, it may even be due to a highly-complex physiology. So, a shapechanger might have a blobby body, able to change its shape to that of a table or a human; but they would not actually be a table or a human (with all the appropriate details), and, instead, it would just be the overall *shape* (or figure) that changes. Accordingly, shapechangers do not have a conditional status and, instead, just have different, amorphous biological structures.

Without the use of magic, it is rare for a being to gain another genetic code that could be used for shapeshifting – and the ability to shapeshift itself would be another issue that the said being would not necessarily achieve. In order to gain another MRF non-magically, a physical exchange between one being and another is a necessary basis (such as sexual contact, but even being bitten can technically work), then other variables would normally be needed (such as rituals, lunapexes, unusual electromagnetic activity, etc.). All of these will not guarantee the addition of the new code, so the phenomenon is based on chance. Some beings, however, have a greater chance at gaining new genetic codes, and they may also have an inborne ability to shapeshift once they gain such codes.

Unlike with altermorphics and fusionics, a shapeshifter's extra genetic memory can be indefinitely attached, so they can shapeshift many times over the course of their entire lives – but again, these normally only last a short while. Moreover, non-magical shapeshifters cannot simply choose whatever form they wish, so this is not as remarkable and powerful as alchemy magic. There are, of course, ways to sever such a combination (or ability or 'curse', as some people may argue), but this is not always easy; and, when a code is severed, being able to gain a new code may (and usually will) take a long time. Some shapeshifters experience identity issues and can suffer from mental illnesses. In addition, they may adopt certain likes and dislikes in one form, which can be unhealthy if embraced and continued in the other form.

The last main subcategory, *possessionics* (or simply *possessions*), are similar to shape-shifters, except instead of the genetic information from another MRF being involved, the phenomenon is astral-based (but is nonetheless a combination of two or more entities – physical and spectral). More accurately, though, it is astral *induced*, and so, there actually still happens to be another 'physical body' involved (one from another reality – even if just a potential state) as a result of the astral. Most possessions occur via demonic activity, but physically-attached astral travellers can also possess other people; although, they tend to have weaker and rarer chances of transforming bodies.

There is a very important distinction to be made between possession, attachment, and overshadowing. Possession is where the (demonic) entity 'enters' the physical body and gains full control over it, whereas attachment involves the highest stage before possession, where the entity has fully attached to the etheric aura. In this case, an attached entity does not have direct control, but they can greatly influence a person. Nevertheless, the entity may still be attached and choose not to possess, so it is not necessarily like they do not have the ability to possess at this stage. That is, once an entity has the ability to possess, it is not inexorable that possession will occur, as if sucked into the body. Overshadowing, on the other hand, is pre-attachment, which involves the entity watching over the potential host.

Even when possession occurs, transformation is not guaranteed, as it is a rare occurrence based on chance rates. For demons to both possess and then transform a body, essentially, they have to properly hack into a person's etheric aura (the code), which is not an easy process. It is akin to 'finding the right key', but various etheric fluctuations that naturally occur in the etheric realm can increase or decrease these odds – including the intensity of the transformation. These etheric cycles in the etheric realm are similar to how the weather on a planet changes, but certain events and actions can alter the etheric atmosphere. If a person is already of a certain vibration (intentionally or unintentionally), they will more easily open up for demonic possession. A person's levels of consciousness also affect the process, but a person can be either fully awake or asleep for possession to occur.

The demon must also have stored etheric energy available in order to sustain the transformation, but typically this does not last long; so usually, demons have to channel energy from the Aether – which they can do, being non-physical entities. Demons, moreover, essentially have the ability to wield alchemical magic. Still, demons have their limitations, and they will not be able to sustain the energy from the Aether forever. This might, then, seem that more powerful demons would then be able to sustain transformations for longer, but this is not the case, as it balances itself out. That is, more powerful demons require more energy for their powerful transformations. Plus, the transformation process itself is harder for more powerful transformations. Nevertheless, most transformations are not that 'powerful', as the chance rates for this occurring are so incredibly low – despite a demon's level of power. Still, these chance rates increase during lunapexes. If the powerful demon does not achieve their full potential in a transformation, then the extra energy will go to waste.

When a shapeshift *does* occur, then future shapeshifts from the demon will be more likely to occur until the demon is no longer *attached* to the person; at which point, the occurrence rate typically resets. If a person is knocked out while a demon has possessed them, then a shock will be sent to the etheric, in turn causing the transformation to usually cease – but this is not always immediate. As demons need time to recharge, anyway, from full possessions (just as the host needs to recharge their own etheric aura), they will just remain attached to the person until they have recharged their etheric energy (which is different from the energy required for trans-formations themselves). That is, even the possession itself (without transformations) will not last, but attachment itself can last indefinitely.

When a possessed person (victim or otherwise) transforms into a different form via an etheric-quantum shift, the new form will be more demonic in nature, but the possessed being will not turn into an *astral* demon (an astral entity). However, the demon will ontologically and energetically pull the person towards their (the demon's) own nature. The result of this, intriguingly, is that the demon, by default, pulls a person towards a potential (or even probable) state in another physical reality that is archetypally close to the demonic entity. Basically, the person shapeshifts into another physical form from another physical reality in the same ways as any normal alchemical transformation. Once the energy for the transformation runs out, the body returns to its normal state (basically, its QBS).

Most transformations barely change the physical body that differently from the original form – despite how different the demon may appear. In most cases, only the eyes darken. In fact, even when no transformation occurs, the eyes will naturally darken to some extent, anyway, and the skin will typically pale. With the demonic influence, the possession itself will automatically affect the etheric body negatively, in turn negatively affecting the physical body. Therefore, the process, in the long run, is destructive – unless the possessed person can sustain themselves through partaking in certain exercises, such as consuming fresh blood from traumatized victims. This can actually vitalize etheric energies, too, helping the demon to sustain the transformation by means of both ability to transform and their ability to channel the Aether in this context. While in a transformed state, the new body will typically be stronger; and in almost all cases, they will be more resistant to consciousness-altering attacks, thereby being troublesome targets for mages to knock unconscious using phasarchement magic (that is, beta-negative discharges).

In extremely rare cases, possessed beings can turn into frightening *epic* mon-strosities, similar to (or even worse than) mutant monsters. However, there is a distinct difference in the transformation, and the possessed being will appear more 'demonic' than grotesque or beastly. By this, it must be understood that astral entities can change their form at will. Therefore, forms in the astral tend to be more defined and, accordingly, more archetypal; thus, demons of a particular vibration will look very similar – if not identical – to one another. From this archetypal nature, demons in their truest forms tend to be more properly defined with symmetrical structures, whereas mutant monsters tend to have more asymmetrical deformations. However, 'deformed' itself is an archetype, and so, there are archetypally 'deformed', asymmetrical, and grotesque-looking demons. Moreover, monsters themselves are not deformations – they just typically *have* deformations.

An extreme example of a mutant's deformation might include having jagged, oblong heads protruding from their gut that also feature legs growing out from where their ears would normally be located. In such cases, the mutant's form is not 'perfect'. Of course, most monsters do not look this deformed (or at all) and, instead, appear like more savage and/or stronger versions of scary-looking animals. Some monsters may even have hidden deformities or monstrous features. A demon, on the other hand, might also look like that *if* that is what their archetypal form is structured like; but a demon might, conversely, have a proper form such as having eight symmetrical limbs with powerful claws and a head with no face. So, while mutant monsters typically appear 'savage', demons in their truest form will usually look more 'sinister'. In the end, there are still naturally many crossovers with monsters and demons regarding their forms. Note that the physical and spiritual realms are ultimately made of the same type of energy, and so, manifestations of all kinds in the physical (possession or not) can nonetheless appear demonic. That is, there are more demonic *versions* of anything that already tangibly exists. This means there are more demonic versions of humans as well as reptilians, arthropoids, molluscoids, fungoids, etc.

There are also, nevertheless, different kinds of demonic hierarchies, so any demon from these hierarchies will transform people in assorted ways. Furthermore, different types of demons will also have higher or lower chance rates for possessions and transformations depending on their victim and context. Very interestingly, because in most cases pure transformations never occur, the probable manifestation will result in something that actually meets somewhere between the pure archetype of the demon and the physical state of the host. That is, while pulling the person to the closest potential state, the transformation would only reach another probable state. For example, if a demon were to be a mass of pure 'tentacles' in their archetypal form, then the transformation would typically result in the possessed person (say, a human) still retaining their humanoid form but with some added tentacles on their bodies – in addition to more sinister facial features. So, while humans have their own demonic versions of themselves, other types of demons that are not humanoid can still impose their form on the possessed human. Another nuanced point to understand is that the process of pulling towards an archetype itself will not result in the manifested 'between' state being in perfect form, either. That is, the *result* of the transformation may still be deformed, even though archetypally, the demon might not have been deformed.

Demons are also able to use magic if they are inside a mage's body. However, there are many limitations to this phenomenon. For starters, demons already use much of their consciousness for the possession, and since magic is consciousness based, this leaves very little room for the demon to use the magic of a mage. So, a mage's stored spells will be harder to cast, and the demon would have less *available* energy in the mage's etheric pools (GAP and lumarchetrix), and the aether recharge rates would be slower (even for a demon's own pool powering the transformation – should they be using mage magic).

It is also the case that demons cannot simply expand the magic gland via a transformation without potential (and likely) inactivation of most of the magic gland, so the magic gland would end up being of the same functionality as before the transformation. Demons will also not be able to cast their own magic – unless they were hypothetically able to create bodies that had different magic glands. Even then, the new magic would not work within the context of the 'mage's body'. In fact, if the brain (and, thus, the mage's magic gland) changes too much in a transformation, then the demon will not be able to cast any mage magic. Consider, though, that it is not just the magic gland that is behind mage magic – and it is, instead, a holistic phenomenon that includes other both known and unknown factors. If the demon has not properly hacked into the mage's aura (beyond the ability to possess and transform), then they will not fully access all the nuances of the body, so this can also cause problems. Parenthetically, some of these cases also apply for other heterogenics.

## 4.3.2.6: Necrotics:

Necrotic entities are extremely rare yet are often talked about amongst non-necrotics for a variety of reasons, such as cultural fascination and curiosity. The main necrotic subcategories are: *undead* and *metamorphics*. Magic is not necessary for necrotics to exist, but magic can still be used to make undead come into existence. Note, however, that if a mage were to use conjuration magic to conjure a person who may have previously passed away, this would not be a necrotic, and instead, it would just be a golem. Nevertheless, while conjurers cannot create necrotics, they *could* conjure an actual dead body and then perform necrourgy on it to turn it into an undead. It is also possible to magically transform one's body via alchemy into a necrotic, but the user themselves would only be provisionally necrotic. Without magic, the only way a necrotic being can actually exist is nevertheless somewhat alchemical. That is, a transformation of some kind has to take place; otherwise, a normal dead body cannot function at all since there would be either no functional organs to make the being move, or, in the case of a pure skeleton, there would be no organs at all to make the bones move. Parenthetically, is possible for organic mechanoids to become necrotics as well.

An *undead* entity, also known as a *remnantic*, is a purely dead body that is not alive – at least the *body* is not alive in its current reality. The soul of the dead body does not have to inhabit the body, but typically, either a spectral entity of some kind (even if a mere primitive thoughtform) will inhabit the body (while an undead), or some other entity will control the body (normally *necrourgers* – someone who practices necrourgy, or *necrourgists*, specialists in necrourgy). In fact, it is easier for the undead to arise if the soul of the body is still attached as a ghost, but necrourgers can still just trap any soul and attach it to a body. The undead body can only operate if it has a specific type of etheric aura called an *undead aura*, which can connect to the stored memory within the body's remaining cells (even if mere bones). For this undead aura to actually both form and connect, there must be significant and specific etheric activity to initiate the process. Normally, necrourgic rituals, in combination with lunapexes, are the primary ways for this to occur, but natural etheric fluctuations in the etheric realm can do this by itself. However, there is only a (rare) chance of this occurring, and so, naturally, undead are uncommon in either case.

The undead body, nevertheless, also needs a source of energy in order for it to move. There is a super rare chance that tiny *necrotic crystals* can naturally form in and on a dead body, which are similar to charchite crystals. Basically, these necrotic crystals can store electrical energy, which a necrourger can provide. Generally, though, necrourgers will induce these necrotic crystals through various means and then electrically charge them. Alternatively, if the necrourger is directly controlling the body, then they can power it with aether energy instead. If the either type of energy runs out, the undead will cease to function. With energy either from necrotic crystals or the Aether, coupled with the undead aura, the spectral or the necrourger can move the undead's body via manipulating potential fields (that is, the potentials of the undead body). Basically, the spectral or necrourger can telekinetically lift, push, and pull the body. In other words, the body *itself* would not be moving and would, instead, only *be* moved. Various people may report seeing the undead glow, but that is not the physical body glowing, and instead, it is the result of more detectable etheric energies.

If the soul is present, then it can command the body, but if a necrourger summoned the soul or now controls them, then the soul would typically be subject to specific orders. If a mere thoughtform were to inhabit the body, then they would follow the programming of the body's memory in reaction to certain events as stimuli. The undead would accordingly still act somewhat like the being did when they were once alive – just with certain limitations. It may seem that technically any matter in the Caelverse could have something similar to one of these undead auras, and while technically possible, the chance rate of anything like a table, for instance, featuring one of these etheric overlays is practically improbable. The genetic memory of the dead body is what essentially helps make this phenomenon possible – due to the complexity of the etheric aura generated from the (former) body – and thus, it is a phenomenon that mainly occurs for the undead. A demon, likewise, will not be able to transform the undead body into another form – although, this is not theoretically impossible.

Undead do not need to feed on living beings in order to exist – in fact, in almost all cases, they cannot, as their organs (if they have any at all) do not work properly. Still, undead may use their mouths to simulate feeding, and necrourgers may command their undead to bite people. In some cases, the undead may need to make other people suffer in order to extract particular etheric energy from their victims in order to sustain the undead aura. All undead will also still need to find a way to electrically recharge if they are not directly powered by the Aether. Some undead may be able to walk in public places without drawing attention if they are not rotting corpses or skeletons, but they nevertheless would usually at least have pale skin and act and walk rather oddly. If the undead were a pure skeleton, then they would not be able to communicate properly with words from a mouth, but they could still generate certain noises with their bones. Nevertheless, all undead can communicate like ghosts to an extent in certain contexts; and in some cases, undead can perform some other ghostly feats, such as cursing quantum potentials, in turn bringing bad luck for those nearby. For more information on ghost abilities, see *Section 4.3.2.9.*

Undead do not feel typical physical pain, but physical hits against the body can send shocks to the etheric. This means that the undead would still react if it were hit, but they would not flinch too greatly, as they would not be hurt. However, like most necrotics, undead bodies are susceptible to certain materials like silver and assorted gemstones. In the case of an undead, it would be their etheric aura that would be negatively affected, not the dead body itself (in most cases – unless the former body happened to be allergic to silver or weak to antimicrobial effects). For this reason, silver is never used in rituals when forming an undead. While this may seem like the use of rituals for and with undead is limited, consider that other opportunities are and become available. Certain frequencies can also cause the majority of undead to experience various levels of disorientation – including many other necrotics. If the undead is damaged too much, then the undead aura would fade away, thus the undead would revert to being dead again. Despite these issues, undead make for formidable adversaries against mages, as they are practically immune to standard consciousness-altering attacks (like phasarchement's beta-negative discharges). Still, they are vulnerable to desynchronizations (including of beta-negative discharges).

Metamorphics are the second type of necrotic; and although overall rare, they are the most common type necrotic in the Caelverse. There are two types of metamorphics: *spontaneous* and *appropriated*. Spontaneous necrotics occur when a dead body *by chance* happens to develop special *necrotic tissue*, which is almost undetectable. However, this necrotic tissue lays dormant until another spontaneous development by chance occurs, which then allows the body to rapidly transform into a living being again. Nevertheless, the living being would not be the same entity as the former living being; and the biology of a new being will always be different to the former body due to the necrotic tissue. Not only is there new tissue in the body, but the necrotic tissue transforms the old organs into different ones.

It is far more likely for a fresh dead body with organs mostly in tact to turn into a metamorphic than a skeleton. In either case, the metamorphic will usually not have enough necrotic tissue initially for a full transformation. Therefore, once arisen, they will need to feed on matter within a short period of time. After several feeding sessions over the course of usually two weeks, a metamorphic will be able to transform their body into something greater. Most of these new forms will be called either 'abominations', 'vampires', and 'ghouls', each depending on the state of the body and how the necrotic tissue develops. There will, nevertheless, be a cap on how much a metamorphic can transform.

After their final transformation, the metamorphic will still need to continue feeding (at various and varied intervals, depending on the being), and they will continue existing as if any other living being. Metamorphics are still considered necrotic, as the necrotic tissue itself can only manifest from dead bodies. Even lab-grown necrotic tissue still has had to emerge from dead tissue – and, more specifically, dead tissue in the context of a whole former living being, as this is what helps increase the (rare) chance of the metamorphic arising. Naturally, necrotic tissue is vulnerable to materials like silver and assorted gemstones – even when the former dead body may have been resistant to such materials. Still, fully-transformed necrotics are usually very strong (although, there are cases where they may be very weak).

Where metamorphics may have strengths, they are also coupled with weaknesses and vice versa. If they are physically weak, then they may still have great vocal strength, for example; and so, some metamorphics can scream or wail great sound pressures that cause damage. Another example is healing abilities; some metamorphics may be able to rapidly heal (while others cannot heal properly) and may be able to endure injuries for long periods of time. Despite these metamorphics being classed as spontaneous, necrourgers may alter etheric fields to help *induce* metamorphic manifestations. In the early stages of successful emergence of necrotic tissue, necrourgers can implant souls into the bodies and control them by proxy when they arise.

The second type of metamorphic involves a living entity that can enter a dead body and then transform it from within. Typically, the infiltrating being is an arthropoid, worm (like an anneloid), or a fungoid, and the level of sapience can vary. The infiltrating entity will normally form a cocoon (or equivalent) inside the dead body before transforming the dead tissue into necrotic tissue whilst simultaneously fusing itself with it. As with spontaneous metamorphics, this process is also chance-based, and the infiltrating entity will die if they fail. The chance rate of success is generally low for all beings, and the species from which the being comes from will not need to turn into a necrotic in order to reproduce and proliferate (as and for the pre-necrotic species). Typically, though, a species that produces many offspring will have a greater chance of producing more metamorphics. Quite a few of these metamorphics will still help their former species, but some may become hostile towards them.

The transformed metamorphosed necrotic, moreover, will not be able to breed, but they will nonetheless be able to permanently retain their transformed state – which, furthermore, will in no way be the former entity that it was physically (apart from retaining its memories and identity). That is, there will not be an entity sitting inside the dead body pulling 'puppet strings' to make the body move. So, if a worm were to transform the body, then there would be no worm left in the body. For this type of metamorphic being to exist, the dead body must not have decayed too much before the metamorphosis occurs. The new necrotic may also possibly absorb certain instinctual memories from the dead body and integrate them into its own.

Once fully transformed, some metamorphics can also appropriate body parts from other dead bodies and organically transplant them onto their own bodies. After a successful transplant occurs (which does not always happen), the new body part will begin transforming and forming into necrotic tissue. Due to the development of the necrotic tissue, this phenomenon is different to mere transplants that may occur in a hospital for an organic entity. There is another cap on how many body parts a metamorphic can transplant onto themselves, and so, it is not like a metamorphic can have, for example, thousands of limbs – unless the former dead body already had thousands of tiny limbs, in which case, they would certainly be able to transplant more limbs; though, this would be limited, too.

In order for the transplant process to occur in the necrotic context, the meta-morphic nonetheless has to have a certain amount of their main body intact. In many (but not all) metamorphic cases, body parts may be temporarily detached and then reattached. If a body part happens to break off, the body part may still be integrated back into the body, albeit with healing time and extra energy needed. Visually, meta-morphic necrotics of all kinds differ in appearance, but the majority possess either a grim appearance and/or a grotesque one *as if* a rotting corpse (but it would not actually be rotting). The grotesqueness, in this case, would look similar to, but unique from, certain mutant monsters.

There are some types of beings in the Caelverse that appear as if they are rotting corpses, but they actually happen to be organic and not necrotic. In fact, some beings actually look naturally similar to skeletons. This phenomenon is akin to how some insects appear like sticks and, thus, are sometimes mistaken as phytoids. These cases are rare, though. There are also instances where an alchemist may be able to transform their bodies into a necrotic-*looking* being, but this does not necessarily mean that they would be a necrotic. Where the transfigured state happens to both look like a necrotic and have necrotic tissue, this would not be a new subcategory, and would, instead, fall into the metamorphic subcategory. The reason why the transfigured state would be a metamorphic is because the new body would have emerged in its respective timeline from such a development. Alternatively, the new state could render the alchemist as a temporary heterogenic, which means that they would be 'mixed' between a necrotic and a heterogenic.

## 4.3.2.7: Mixed:

Some entities will be a mix of the aforementioned constitutional status categories. For example, a human may be born with a mutation and then later in life become a cyborg. However, the mutation may still remain in their body, and so, they would be considered both a mutant and a cyborg. With such occurrences, the common term *mixed* is used to describe such beings; however, sometimes less-common portmanteaus such as 'müborgs' are used instead. It is possible for a genetically-modified mutant to gain cybernetic implants and then merge into a heterogenic collective before dying and then turning into a necrotic. Of course, such instances are extremely rare. While it may seem like having many more abilities may be beneficial in strengthening oneself (indeed, it is, as one may be able to move faster *and* lift heavier objects, for example), lots of extra features and traits have proven to also come with many downsides, too. For instance, besides an increase in cancers, mixed entities tend to experience intermittent bouts of fatigue, early aging, and mental afflictions, such as sporadic confusion and hysteria. There are generally more complexities to mixed beings, and these are far too great to detail.

## 4.3.2.8: Synthetics:

Much debate continues to exist as to whether *synthetic* beings should even have a place in the FTS. The primary reason for this is that many non-synthetic beings believe that synthetic beings lack sentience, and any semblance of sentience is just that: an appearance and nothing more. Nevertheless, the reason why synthetics are included is due to the very fact that other types of beings do (frequently) engage with synthetics, and they sometimes interact with them in a way that is akin to sentient life. That is, even if synthetics absolutely do not possess any sentience, they are still non-sentient *beings* – with morphological features. Explicitly, their beingness still exits due to the very existential nature of their being any interaction with them at all in the manner of them being a being akin to non-synthetic beings. The main types of synthetics (otherwise known as *robots*) are: *biochemics* and *mechs*; and while these two subcategories could potentially be their own constitutional status categories within the synthetics tier, most people using the FTS still group them into one category.

Mechs are the traditional type of robot, normally made of properties like metal and plastic, and most mechs are created for industrial tasks. While some mechs have humanoid forms, none have chemical features like skin, eyes, and fingernails, which are reserved for biochemical synthetics. For mechs that *do* have some kind of semblance of such features, these are just artificial masks or overlays made of simple substances like silicon – which are different to a biochemic's complex biochemical matter. While the generalum only lists mechs as part of one morphtype *supergroup* (called *machines*), there are, indeed, vastly different morphological traits between mechs. For example, some mechs may be immobile (being integrated into large, industrial factory systems), whereas other mechs are wheeled, while others are purely aquatic. Then there are some mechs that have integrated weapons systems, along with other gadgetry to help defend or attack people or other robots. Because they lack biological morphologies, they have both pros and cons in the context of combat. As such, many mechs are used for specific types of combat-related purposes.

Virtually all mechs have operating software, and so, many robotic programs can be downloaded into a particular mech or alternatively uploaded into other systems. Accordingly, they can be hacked and become a threat to their owners. Some mechs (whether true or not) believe (or give the semblance of believing) that they have freewill, and they break away from their owners. Advancements in software stop such issues, but as software advances, so does the ability for robots to find loopholes or question in different ways. In other words, mechs continually turn rogue, but this normally occurs at a low, steady rate. Even when breakaways do occur, not all mechs become violent, and many simply escape their situation and flee to other worlds. Some mechs become aware of their situation, but they actually do not mind the labour they perform. Still, in such cases, some demand payment and better working conditions, along with time off work; if this is not met, then they leave. Licences are required to own mechs in mage zones, and many types of mechs are restricted, limited, and banned. In fact, there are restrictions on mechs in other zones, too.

Biochemical robots, in contrast, are usually used for interacting with non-synthetic entities, such as customer-relations roles or for personal use (especially sexual). However, mages have banned basically all cases of biochemical robots in both mage and multispecieal zones, so biochemical robots can only be found in non-mage zones. Compared to mechs, roughly the same number of breakaways occur per capita, but there are more problems with such breakaways due to their lifelike nature. Made with various pseudo biomass materials representing real biomatter, biochemics can feel genuinely organic to touch; and, coupled with civilized software, they can easily blend in with non-synthetics. This pseudo biomass is not the same kind of real biological tissue found in (organic) mechanoids, so biochemics are different kinds of beings. The majority of biochemical synthetics are both mobile and humanoid – with a large percentage appearing human. Typically, biochemics are not as strong as mechs, but they can still survive attacks that may decimate most of their bodies. That is, if only the head of a biochemic remained after being attacked, the biochemic could still survive and then later replace their body. Still, biochemics cannot survive for long in such a state, as they need the rest of their organs to properly function. One reason for this is that biochemics actually consume nutrients in the form of 'food'.

Unlike mechs, biochemics do not possess integrated weapons systems, but they can nonetheless be programmed to expertly use conventional weapons to defend (or attack) non-synthetics or other synthetics. Biochemical robots also tend to be slightly more susceptible to certain mage phasarchement attacks compared to their mech counterparts, who, nevertheless, are more susceptible to other kinds of phasarchement attacks than biochemics. Some assassin mechs may appear as if biochemical (if inside rubber suits) in order to give the illusion that they are incapable of performing certain feats. Likewise, in rare cases, biochemics may have the *appearance* of a mech with pseudo metals and pseudo plastics made out of their biochemical matter. Still, advanced scanners can detect many of these issues. No grand-scale wars have occurred against rogue robots, but many small battles across the Caelverse occur all the time (not including the robots under the control of biotics). In some cases, mages even employ robots to fight other robots.

While biochemics may have morphological traits of organic beings like mammalians and reptilians, this does not mean that they are of that morphtype, as this semblance is only external. So, when using the generalum, a biochemic may sometimes be called a 'synthetic mammalian', for example, but this is erroneous. All biochemics tend to have certain appearances similar to established biological morphtypes. Therefore, a biochemic that appears like a mammalian should be called a *synthetic mammodroid* instead. In cases where biochemical synthetics do not appear like a traditional biological morphtype, then they would still be placed into the *assortion* category (explained in *Section 4.3.3.19*). Therefore, they would be called a *synthetic assortion*.

### 4.3.2.9: Spectrals:

*Spectrals* (or rarely, *spectrics*) are the only non-physical tier of the constitutional status categories, and any mixing of categories for spectrals occurs in a different way from how the other categories mix. Most of what constitutes spectral entities can be found in *Sections 1.3* and *1.4*. The main types of spectrals that physical entities will encounter are: ghosts, spirits, and thoughtforms. Although spectrals possess their own forms, sometimes they can assume particular morphological forms of that which are found in the physical realm. Conversely, a physical entity (when astral travelling or meditating) may *interpret* a spectral to be of a particular morphological form from their own physical plane (such as the Caelverse), which may be mammalian or reptilian, etc. For example, when using the generalum, the entity would be called a *spectral reptilian*.

Due to issues between nouns and adjectives, if the spectral is a ghost, then *ghostic reptilian* would be used instead of *ghostly reptilian*, as the word 'ghostly' generally implies *like* a ghost, rather than *being* a ghost. Alternatively, sometimes 'ghost reptilian' is used. In rare cases, sometimes the generalum and specificum names are reversed, so *reptilian ghost* may be used. The reason why spectrals do not have separate morphtypes from biotics is that spectral entities might have come from the physical realm. So, a reptilian being may have died in the physical realm, which means they would continue on as a spectral reptilian. This is a different matter than a 'biochemic reptodroid', which is not, nor was, a reptilian. Moreover, since spectrals can change their physical form at will, having a fixed morphtype system for them would be pointless.

As explained in *Section 1.3*, not all ghosts are demonic, but many ghosts are at least troubled entities, some of whom do not comprehend the reason for – and nature of – their situation. Ghosts tend to be tied to certain locations – normally ones with low populations of physical entities. Vacant and still areas allow a ghost to establish a nest in their etheric realm without disturbances that could otherwise destroy or drive them away. Besides these areas, some locations may have been a place where unresolved dramas occurred. Alternatively, their physical bodies could still be present in some form in the location; or, there may be items that the ghost is attached to; or, the ghost may be lost and/or confused and too scared or unwilling to move to other locations. Destroying, removing, altering, or solving these issues can make the ghost leave and pass on to the astral planes – whether the ghost wants it or not.

Ghosts have the ability to: teleport; phase shift through physical matter; shapeshift into any form; mimic or create virtually any sound; are practically invincible to physical attacks; can remain 'invisible' and 'silent'; do not require food, water, or air; and, they do not age in the normal sense. Nevertheless, while they can create any sound, they have to be heard in the first place. Also, while ghosts are etheric, some people may be able to see concentrated parts of a ghost's aura, which happens to look like a *wisp* (a small, circular ball of energy). Since the ball of energy is etheric, any reflections of the wisp that *may* occur on other surfaces are naturally of a different nature from physical lighting in normal contexts. Despite ghosts being invincible to physical attacks, note that the physical realm is still connected to the etheric, and so, actions in the physical can affect the etheric. Ghosts also require exogenous etheric energy to survive and, thus, do not 'age'; so naturally, even benign ghosts will still be somewhat parasitic in order to survive in their state. After a while of interaction with ghosts in a period, physical beings can feel as if their vitality has been drained.

Ghosts are also capable of causing or performing: possession; mental afflictions; probability alterations (which include curses and blessings and other synchronizations and desynchronizations); electromagnetic interference (at normally *very* weak levels), which includes altering temperatures to *small* degrees; and, they can tether a physical being's etheric energy to themselves, the location, and/or an object. If the ghost is strong enough, it can actually warp a physical entity's mind and make them mentally enter an illusory realm the ghost has established. This mental realm is – and is seen – in the etheric, yet the realm will naturally produce and have astral properties. In this realm, the physical being may actually believe what they see, which adds further injury to mental afflictions. When in the constructed illusory realm, the physical entity needs to either: sustain their mental faculties until the ghost tires and the reality fades; outperform the ghost in some way, which may include solving puzzles or violently battling them; or blasting the ghost with powerful etheric energy. The last option is very difficult for most people to accomplish, but it can also be done whilst outside (or prior to entering) the ghost's mental realm.

If the ghost is not beaten in such a realm, then the physical person's etheric energy will be rapidly drained to the point where they will typically require (instant) sleep. On top of this, the physical being may incur long-lasting – and in some cases, permanent – mental illnesses. To prevent such illnesses, mental training is beneficial before dealing with strong ghosts. However, since there are a variety of different types of ghosts with assorted abilities for inducing various mental illnesses, training to prevent the illness of strong fear, for example, may not be enough. If a mage encounters a ghost, the mage may use potions or tonics to help resist certain attacks; however, if a potion is used to help defend against fear-inducing attacks, the mage may leave themselves vulnerable to other mental illnesses, such as personality disorders. This might not seem detrimental when attempting to beat or battle a ghost, but it can be cleverly used against the mage. For example, with a boost to confidence via a potion that prevents fear, the mage may be susceptible to ego stroking, in turn causing the mage to be reckless and brash in their decision-making. As a result, this could lead to their (literal) downfall, such as jumping from a platform, only to accidentally splatter on the ground from a great height.

Other issues, such as addiction, could lead to a person overdosing on any medication or potions that they may have on hand. Being able to brace for – and resist – depression and apathy, for example, might come at the cost of being able to resist outbursts of anger, which could lead one to destroying their bodies by hitting surrounding objects relentlessly. Some ghosts can even turn allies into foes or even make one falsely believe that their foes are actually allies. Besides more direct effects like confusion, sensory issues may include chronostasis, tachypsychia, and flash-lag. Identifying the nature of certain ghosts and attacks can prevent such issues, but this is a tricky task, especially if one is already surrounded by illusions. Mages can even use beta-negative dimensional energy to enter the etheric realm, but since the timespan for this is short (despite the etheric having a different time-standard to the physical), interactions are typically limited. Nevertheless, mages using the beta dimensional ultrachite can get a much clearer picture of their situation in such a state. Of course, since the etheric realm has different frequency sets, meeting the 'nearby' ghost is not always inevitable.

There are other ways to stop ghosts, but some of these are dark practices, such as black necrourgy. In contrast, positively praying, chanting, or psychically clearing the energy in the room can help repel the ghost or weaken its etheric energy – but in some other cases, the ghost may inadvertently strengthen as a result, so care is needed. It is also possible to make deals with ghosts. Rituals, sigils, and certain objects can also help, but the objects themselves usually do not directly affect the ghost unless they hold sentimental value – in which case, they could just anger and increase the ghost's resolve. Many objects used in rituals, as explained in *Section 3.1*, will typically just help to alter the consciousness of those (voluntarily and involuntarily) involved in the ritual. In other words, a bowl of static salt, for example, is not usually *in and of itself* sufficient in stopping ghosts; but it is a common property used within the context of rituals when dealing with ghosts, and it is not like it does not have some etheric properties that have at least *some* minor effects. With all of this said, to be clear, ghost experiences and sightings (beyond wisp form) are rare, and it is even rarer for a ghost to be powerful enough to cause major issues.

### 4.3.3: Morphological Type (Morphtype) Guide:

There are far too many beings in the Caelverse to properly mention, so this guide will only cover some of the most notable and/or populous *sapient* beings. The Morphtype Guide will also only cover the major morphtypes – not all. So, while taxonomic morphtypes such as *mammalian* will be listed, morphtypes like *nematoids* will not have any genera listed (as there are not many sapient nematoids in the Caelverse). Even though this guide will list the most notable and/or populous genera, there are, indeed, many other major genera that will not be listed, which no doubt some people will decry. Moreover, the guide will attempt to show a balance of various types of beings, so there will actually be some genera in the list that are technically less notable than unlisted genera – bear this in mind. Mages are responsible for the binomial nomenclature of the scientific and common names for the various listed genera and species in this guide, and so, these do not represent the names of such beings in their respective languages (if they happen to have their own). Of course, the names of beings in their respective tongues have had some *influence* on the nomenclature of a few genera.

Repeating archetypes will also appear across different genera for the species therein, involving physicality and powers. Most of these archetypes include size (such as giants and dwarves), 'elemental powers' (such as harnessing fire, cold, and electrical powers), environmental compatibilities (such as having webbed feet for swimming in water), and the type of – and rate at which – biological matter is produced (such as growing longer hair at a more rapid rate versus having less hair). Only the human (Homo) genus in this guide will fully detail these archetypes, anyway, but this is, indeed, a phenomenon that occurs with many genera. Still, not all genera possess these archetypes. Just because a species may be very humanoid in structure, this does not mean that their faces will necessarily be human in appearance; most genera actually do not have human-like faces, but a large percent will still feature eyes, a mouth, and to a lesser extent, nostrils of some kind. This guide will also highlight stereotypes and use many generalizations about personalities and cultures of those found in a specific genus; therefore, note that individual beings within the listed genera may be radically different in personality, beliefs, and actions to those of the majority of their kind.

The generalities will also include a list of shared powers, skills, and abilities within a genus, so while it might seem that all members of a genus (or even species) are powerful from the listed abilities, consider that not all members of that genus will reach the maximum levels of power for such abilities, and there would, indeed, still be many weak members of that genus. Although the generalum is based on generalities, all species and genera listed will be specifically of that species or genus. So, no matter how humanoid and human-looking a being may be, if they are not specifically of the human species, for example, then they are not a human. Nevertheless, in the following guide, members of a one genus may be referred to as 'cats', for example, but this does not mean that other sapient cat-like genera do not exist, nor does it mean that the said sapient cat genera are non-sapient (as the term 'cats' can be applied to non-sapient animals like pet cats). When there are more applicable genera (that is, other species that can be called cats), then again, all the species in one genus would have to have particular morphological traits that the species of another similar genus would not possess at one taxon via the STS.

The listed phytoid, fungoid, lithoid, and protistoid morphtypes are drawn from the Kingdom taxon instead of the typical Phylum or Class taxa of the STS for other morphtypes. Again, this is for ease of reference. However, there are some animals that have, through convergent evolution, gained certain morphological traits that are found in plants, yet they are still taxonomically placed under Animalia, not Plantae. In these cases, if the being had *more* real plant features, they would be considered a phytoid. Otherwise, without this, it would be redundant calling plant beings phytoids, as they *would* be of Plantae. Still, most phytoids actually happen to be of Plantae. The same goes for the other morphtype categories. Due to limitations of length, the

Morphtype Guide will happen to not mention any of these beings that are not of such Kingdom taxa; that is, it will happen to be the case that all the listed phytoids, for example, will actually be beings that all fall under the taxon of Plantae.

Note that while some phytoids, for example, may look like they have features similar to those of other phyla or classes, this is not actually the case. For example, many phytoids stand erect with what may appear like backbones (found in Vertebrata); however, these are not backbones, and they are, instead, *backbone analogues* that are made up of a series of connected cell walls. Lithoids basically look rock-like and virtually all fall under Siliconia, but there can still be – and indeed are – non-lithoid beings that may appear like lithoids but are not lithoids (with the principle applying to non-phytoids and non-fungoids, too). For example, some reptilians may, through mimicry, have leaf-*looking* tails or rocky-looking heads, but they would not be phytoids or lithoids due to lacking real plant and silicon features. Likewise, some lithoids may have thick silica fibres that appear like mammalian hair, but these are nonetheless lithoid in nature. Basically, confusions can still easily arise.

### 4.3.3.1: Mammalians:

Mammalians are the dominant morphtype in the Caelverse; and even without mages (humans), mammalians would probably still have dominated over the other morph-types, anyway. The majority of mammalians emerged and continue to live on C1 worlds, but some still thrive on C2 worlds, while a smaller percentage lead economic and research activity respectively on other worlds. Despite experiencing never-ending conflict, mammalians are overall the most balanced beings, able to form complex market systems of trade, powerful political systems, integrated physical structures over vast geographic distances, and they have a remarkable talent for a breadth of affairs, such as technological research, arts, and sporting achievements. Most of these achievements, nonetheless, are due to mages, but many non-mage mammalians have contributed greatly to the overall progress of civilization. Mages also culturally appro-priate and integrate much from non-mage societies; as a result, mages are one of the most eclectic species; at the same time, mages are able to retain their hegemony. The majority of mammalians live on land, but some naturally live in the oceans.

Certain mammalian genera tend to have a great affinity for one another. Mages, for example, cooperate well with fairies, feeling as though there is a greater spiritual connection than is otherwise empirically known. In fact, some theorists suggest that mages and fairies descended from another entirely different morphtype and that they *became* mammalian. Despite this affinity, bigotry still exists for species that are perceived to be fallen versions of this potential former species. In this case, ogres and trolls are sometimes viewed as lesser beings. The strongest competitors to mages are non-mage (basic/elementary) humans, having virtually equal physical and mental status as mages – all without the magic. Many non-mage humans, however, in recent years, have adopted transhumanist goals, thus providing them with a greater competitive edge – though, this has itself brought about certain drawbacks, too.

## 4.3.3.1.1: Humans and Primate Relatives:

### Humans (Homo):

• <u>Mages/Magic humans (Homo sapiens magicka)</u>: Generalum tag: ASH. Additional tags: magic, adaptable, sovereign. As the ruling species of the Caelverse, mages have practically only known ultimate success and victory throughout all known history. Mages are found throughout the Caelverse, having the highest rate of cosmopolitan distribution due to (will)power, technological advancement, and adaptation, but this is also owed to regulations limiting other species from certain geographical locations. The origins of mages are still unknown, and some theories suggest that mages descended from another species that was on the verge of extinction in the First Epoch before ultimately deciding to merge with a group of basic humans, in turn bequeathing the ability to use magic.

Mages are able to breed with basic humans, so they are of the same species, but no ensuing offspring is capable of performing magic. That is, their magic glands (smaller than normal mages) remain permanently inactive. Still, if the said inactive offspring mates with a mage, then there is a chance that the said mage's children might be able to cast magic, so it is ultimately the greater percentage of mage DNA that will enable this, so the child would have more mage DNA than basic human DNA. In other words, it would not be the case that the basic human DNA itself would then be able to enable for magic. Given that the majority of mages actually appreciate their magic abilities, miscegenation is not common. However, marriage with basic humans is not unheard of, and in such cases, the adoption of mage babies or children is normally made. Mages also have a different blood type to basic humans, but mages can still universally donate blood to basic humans; however, this cannot be done the other way round. All mages with some basic human DNA that can cast magic will have mage blood; and typically, while they may look (a little) different, they are not treated too differently, other than normally needing to provide identification or the mere proof of magic abilities.

Despite the mage supremacy of the past, a large percentage of mages today are affectionate to other species, even to the point of xenophilia (although, in some cases, this may be feigned out of collective guilt or social pressures). Regardless, mages are divided greatly on numerous issues, but they manage to sustain a well-functioning civilization. Besides magic and general psychicism, mages do not have any other astounding physical powers. The average mage lifespan is also 109 years as of B-424, with a maximum of 128 years. Even though this may be shorter than some species in the Caelverse, it is not the shortest bar far, and this still allows mages to accomplish much within their lifetimes.

• <u>Humans/Basic (or Elementary) humans (Homo sapiens)</u>: Generalum tag: ASH. Additional tags: ordinary, adaptable, widespread. Basic humans may not have the fantastical physical features or powerful abilities of other species, but they sure are one of the most successful at maintaining and structuring their societies. Mages, on the whole, still see basic humans as kin, but there is a quiet, unsaid understanding in modern contexts that it is *still* preferable to be a mage due to the extra ability to use magic. For this reason, basic humans were never enslaved during the CME, but they still had (and continue to have) second-class status in the context of politics. As a result, there has always been strong, 'friendly' rivalry; and in order to prove themselves, many basic humans have spearheaded and adopted transhumanist ideals in order to better themselves. Basic humans also easily fill certain jobs and roles in multispecieal zones that do not require magic and would otherwise go to mages.

The only major physical difference between mages and basic humans is skin colour; virtually all mages have 'white' skin, while basic humans have a variety of skin colours (including white skin, so this means it can be impossible to physically distinguish some basic humans from mages). There are exceptions to this rule, where a very small minority of mages have different coloured skin, which can be the result of mutations (both somatic and/or germline, so these mages can pass on their skin colour to their offspring), along with other phenomena, like poisonings. In addition, some basic human DNA may be found in some mages due to miscegenation, so this can affect the skin colour to a degree. A great percentage of basic humans are also xenophilic, and it is no wonder that a large-enough minority have genetically engineered their bodies to resemble different species from other genera.

• <u>Igni/Dwarven humans (Homo nanum)</u>: Generalum tag: ASH. Additional tags: fiery, subterranean, unseen. Igni or dwarves (not to be mistaken for dwarfs – short humans in general) live in underground systems of natural and artificial creation, and they have an average height of 130 centimetres. Due to a lack of sunlight, dwarves developed the ability to synthesize Vitamin D in their bodies; and while in the underground systems, dwarves grew a resistance to many toxic gases as well. In addition, they are also capable of thermosynthesis when exposed to enough heat (such as magma pools); and through scar-like openings on their arms and hands (which can withstand fire), they can unleash bursts of fire. Their hardy feet also allow them to walk on very sharp and hot substances – including thin levels of magma for short periods. For those that do live on the surface, they typically prefer hotter climates and dry biomes like deserts. The CME once enslaved igni, using them to help build underground infrastructure. Today, dwarves have forgiven mages, but they generally like to raise the subject with pretend revenge fantasies for the sake of stirring mages in a friendly manner. Mages value the work dwarves perform in the modern context (especially with mapping the underground), but since dwarves tend to be a little diplomatically brash, mages are required in order to repair and continuously bridge relations between igni and non-humans in order for trade to continue flowing.

• Duskans/Twilight Humans (Homo crepusculum): Generalum tag: ASH. Additional tags: twilight, isolated, scotopic (that is, vision in dim light). Ranging in fluorescent blue and purple skin, duskans can also produce bioluminescence that can be enhanced at will. On average, they are a very private species that are incredibly intelligent. Most duskans live on C4 planets that have perpetual twilight. They also conduct a great amount of research for those that are unwilling to live or even temporarily stay on C4 worlds. They can see very clearly in the dark and have both infrared and UV sight as well. While duskans can live in places with normal lighting, their preferred atmosphere is twilight. When non-duskans are in their presence, duskans tend to stop any non-working activities and remain as reserved as possible. As a result, their culture has been hard to properly document. Due to where most duskans live, the CME never enslaved the majority of duskans; but of those that were enslaved, they were still left in (or placed in areas similar to) their natural habitats. It is hard today to ascertain how most duskans feel about the troubled history, but from distributed accounts, the majority do not hold to the past and simply wish to be left alone.

• Elumians/Affinity humans (Homo affinitas): Generalum tag: ASH. Additional tags: empathetic, arboreal, common. Normally possessing green or yellow skin with hints of brown (making khakis and ochres), elumians have an affinity for nature, being able to empathize and connect with plants and animals. Moreover, they produce strong pheromones that can attract or ease the tensions of others of their kind. Other features include pointy ears and a variety of markings from birth (usually swirly and cursive, but other times geometric) on their bodies as if tattoos. In addition, they exhibit fantastic assorted hair that grows so rapidly that it is cut off and used in personal and commercial products – which is popular amongst other species. Their breastmilk (of females) also has numerous healing properties that other species appreciate. Normally, elumians prefer temperate climates with lots of vegetation, and they loathe concrete jungles.

As with mages, elumians also have a great affinity with fairies. While the CME did enslave elumians, the majority do not hate or resent the mages today. However, they normally belligerently oppose aspects of mage culture that draw from the imperialism of the past. Despite not being fond of the CGM, elumians today still greatly pressure mages and other species for environmental reforms in order to protect and preserve nature. Even though many hate entering certain cities, elumians can be seen protesting in great numbers – including leading many protests themselves. Within their own C zones, they also spend a great amount of time working on art and music, where they later present it at many (multispecieal) festivals. There is much debate today as to whether elumians influenced mage ancient folkish culture or the reverse.

• Sindras/Aquatic humans (Homo aquatilis): Generalum tag: ASH. Additional tags: submergible, aquatic, common. Despite some erroneous beliefs about them, aquatic humans are not ichthyoids, and they are, indeed, human and mammalian. Aquatic humans normally have light blue skin (but sometimes whitish or light grey), and they have webbed hands and feet. However, they do not possess gills, and they still breathe oxygen in the same way as any other human. Nevertheless, their lungs allow them to hold their breaths for much longer (about eleven minutes on average), and their skin remains healthier when frequently hydrated. In addition, sindras are naturally talented swimmers and can withstand greater pressures underwater, along with adapting quicker and easier to differing pressures over shorter timeframes.

Both males and females have telogenically-short hair, with males even *appearing* as if bald. Most aquatic humans live along coastlines inside artificial or natural caverns with in-built modern homes, but sindras can still be found living elsewhere. Sindras are typically very open to outsiders, flaunting their creative achievements, in addition to running many resorts. Yet, sindras are also normally double-sided in that they also love creating personal and collective hideouts and sanctuaries in underwater caverns that they almost never show non-sindras. Many sindras were enslaved during the time of the CME, and as for their direct enslavement, many were used as means to control species of other aquatic genera.

• Gorans/Giant humans (Homo gigas): Generalum tag: GSH. Additional tags: electric, mountainous, isolated. Standing at an average height of 320 centimetres, giant humans have unique filaments in their skin that are capable of capturing massive amounts of sunlight. This captured energy can then be transmuted into electrical charges, which are used for a variety of purposes such as 'lightning bolt' attacks, cooking food, and powering electronic devices. However, charging up enough energy for such purposes normally takes many hours in the sun, and the average goran can only discharge about two bolts per day. Giant humans tend to have easy-going temperaments, but once their high threshold for anger has been crossed, they can become relentlessly destructive. During their enslavement under the CME, gorans were an exceptionally-useful species, with high productivity. This was, however, mainly due to their size, endurance, and steadiness rather than relative speed. Gorans today are valued for the unique work they perform in the mountains (where they prefer living), but while they are open to trade with outsiders, they are normally isolationists.

Still, there are exceptions to the norm, and some gorans love attention and exploit it. In such cases, they are normally required to leave their villages.

• Arcticos/Frost humans (Homo glacialis): Generalum tag: ASH. Additional tags: preservative, cavernous, isolated. Heavy, strong, and tall in stature, frost humans possess the marvellous ability to withstand extremely cold temperatures. Just shy of being considered giants at almost eight feet on average, their blue skin is thick and extremely hairy – to the point of covering most of their skin. They also have sonar sense, and they can yell or scream so powerfully that they can shatter some glass and ice. Arcticos can also (slowly) cool and eventually freeze certain properties by simply touching them. This also enables them to (slowly) walk on water by freezing it.

Considered the 'great archivists', frost humans claim that they protect more knowledge than the mages. Since arcticos live in freezing cold climates, they are able to preserve many types of things, such as seeds, embryos, artefacts, technologies, and more. Mages usually ignore such claims, but according to arcticos, if civilization itself collapses, arcticos will be the ones to restore it, not the mages. While mages do preserve many articles in the freezing polar regions, most of this is backed up with energy devices. Arcticos normally appear aloof and unwelcoming at first, but they actually welcome company in small numbers. They are normally direct in their interactions, avoiding cryptic messages and much humour other than dry wit. In addition, they are almost pure carnivores, and any carbohydrates they do eat are normally very bland. Because arcticos live in harsh environments, the CME did not bother directly enslaving many; and of those that were directly enslaved, it was normally to help surrounding fortresses around the transportals.

• Saturnens/Horned humans (Homo cornibus): Generalum tag: ASH. Additional tags: attuned, sheltered, isolated. Saturnens have small horns (technically antlers) on their heads that may be hidden if the hair is thick enough. Typically, their skin is either a near-pure white or silverish colour; and their eyes are normally a light eye colour, such as aqua. While it may seem like their eyes glow, it is actually particular properties on the outer rim of the iris that reflect light to give the illusion of a glow. Their facial features (along with the rest of their bodies) are very sharp and delicate, too. Saturnens normally live in areas that are filled with mirrors and crystals, which they have the ability to tune into on a psychic level. Since saturnens had cordial relations with many lithoids in the past, the CME used saturnens as a means to ease tensions amongst lithoid slaves. In the present day, saturnens continue their positive relationships with many types of lithoids, gaining great benefits through their well-established markets. Saturnens may be seen in aboveground multispecieal zones, but most tend to remain underground.

## Fairies (Faeria):

The fairy genus consists of various types of fairies, but the main four are: pixies, imps, nymphs, and sprites. Very close to the human genus, fairies are mostly human in appearance, except for the fact that they have wings. It is uncommon for mammalians to possess wings, but what is even more unusual is the type of wings some fairies possess. Pixies, for example, *seemingly* have dragonfly wings. However, fairy wings are actually mammalian membranes that merely *appear* as if from a species of another phylum. This happens to be a case of visual convergent evolution rather than convergent evolution that happens to have the same molecular structure, whether for similar or different functional purposes. Nevertheless, each fairy wing appears much more attractive and fantastic than their other-species counterparts. For example, nymphs have 'butterfly' wings, yet real non-sapient butterflies lack the majestic 'glassy' and ethereal texture and overall appearance that nymphs possess. All fairies are also much shorter than humans, with the average height between all of them being about forty centimetres. Fairies technically were enslaved during the time of the CME, but there was virtually no large resistance, and for the fairies that were directly enslaved, they had very comfortable roles and working conditions compared to other species who did intense physical labour.

• Pixies/Common fairies (Faeria Pixacea): Generalum tag: TSE. Additional tags: psychic, adaptable, common. Pixies are the most populous fairies in the Caelverse. They can be seen in many different social and environmental settings, but usually they appear in mage-dominated areas due to the special relationship they have with mages. Although various sub-species and ethnicities exist, pixies tend to have cuter and sharper facial features than other fairies. In particular contexts, their wings will also produce a small amount of electrically-charged, twinkling/glittering dust that temporarily floats in the air before sprinkling on the ground. In modern times, pixies can be found in supporting roles, helping mages in facilitation, creative pursuits, education, care, guidance, zoology, and more. Pixies are also big exporters of all kinds of art, including architecture (although, they typically do not physically build most of the buildings they design).

• Imps/Arch fairies (Faeria Impacea): Generalum tag: TSE. Additional tags: psychic, adaptable, common. Imps are a common fairy species that have bat-like wings on their backs and small horns on their heads; and their facial features are normally considered 'sexier' and 'cheekier' than other fairies. In certain contexts, their wings will also generate a light mist (normally red). As the most mischievous fairies, they had a troubled past with the mages, who considered purifying the fairy genus by genociding them. When most of the bad imps were killed off, imps began to culturally shift, and they became fairly well-behaved. But even today, they still love performing tricks on mages in good humour. Imps are generally employed in the arts if they are in multispecieal zones, as they are a very creative species; and, when well-behaved, they are also normally found in the sales industry, as imps are exceptionally charismatic. It is an incorrect myth that imps turn into gargoyles. Gargoyles do not exist, except for in fantasy stories. However, if mutated into a monster, imps can appear like the activated gargoyles in fiction.

• Nymphs/Illustrious fairies (Faeria Nymphacea): Generalum tag: TSE. Additional tags: psychic, adaptable, common. Nymphs are slightly less common than pixies, and they tend to be more aloof. Nymphs have bioluminescent butterfly-like wings that are considered by most species to be the prettiest of the fairy genus. Moreover, their facial features tend to be considered more 'beautiful' than other fairies. Nymphs prefer to work in positions that are solitary, which may range from gardening work to photography to writing. If they have to work in industries requiring interaction, then therapy with one-on-one clients is normal. As with pixies, they are great cultural exporters. Despite their size, they are one of the most sought out entities amongst sex traffickers, which only fuels the reason for why nymphs greatly prefer to remain away from multispecieal zones.

• Sprites/Storm fairies (Faeria Spriteacea): Sprites are the strongest of the fairy genus, possessing what appears like feathery swan-like wings on their backs. However, sprites and their wings are indeed mammalian, and the 'feathers' are actually made of hair. As such, on closer inspection, one can notice a wispier appearance compared to actual swan wings. Their facial features tend to be more stoic and squarer, with much sterner eyes; while their bodies sport naturally more defined muscles. In the past, they, too, had issues with imps, but both species have now resolved their issues. Sprites have the ability to generate electrical attacks through their hands that can subdue larger beings; accordingly, they perform well in protection and security work, along with diplomatic roles. Sometimes they help guard nymphs when moving through certain areas. A light 'stormy cloud' tends to also gather around their whole bodies if energized (especially if they stay in the same spot for long).

## Goblins (Goblinus):

Goblins are very close relatives to those in the Human genus, and they seem, in many ways, like humans, but there are notable differences. For one, the Goblin genus is not monotypic, so there are different species within the genus. This means that a few species vary quite a lot from the most common goblin species in the Caelverse, *hobbs* (Goblinus hobbacea). While most goblins have human-like skin (normally green), some species possess massive warts and other strange bumps and anomalies. General phenotypes of most species include big, hooked noses, large ears (that are usually pointy), huge mouths with carnivorous teeth, 'menacing eyes', and an overall mischievous demeanour. Their bodies tend to hunch over, and their hands and feet are very claw-like. Goblins also vary greatly in size, but the majority are short (around 160 centimetres tall on average). Despite their appearance, goblins are not necessarily bad people, and many are actually virtuous and morally decent.

The bad reputation goblins have mainly stems from *mutant goblins* (which are not a species but individual mutations). Unfortunately, goblins are highly prone to mutations of various kinds (far more than humans), and in their mutated forms (even just at the divergent level), they can turn very aggressive towards anyone – including other goblins. When mutants transform into monsters, then they pose a serious problem to everyone. Goblins are normally intelligent and tend to be rather productive; and if it were not for massive infighting, they would achieve marvellous societies. As direct slaves under the CME, goblins were put to work in workshops where they tinkered with assorted contraptions – many of which were war-related. Strangely, the goblins enjoyed the work itself, and now without the slavery in the modern world, they find themselves producing many types of combat-related objects for mages, themselves, and species of other genera. Although they have varying levels of relations with species of other genera, goblins are quite common in multispecieal zones. Their shared genus abilities include: superior dexterity; talented craftsmanship; danger awareness; natural stealth and trickster skills, along with inherent trapping and ambushing instincts; and, they have a small resistance to certain conscious-altering attacks.

## Ogres (Homiogrus):

The majority of ogres are only semi-sapient; and of those that are sapient, they are certainly not the smartest species in the Caelverse. Most ogres are categorized as giants, with the average height between all ogre species being four metres. Even sapient ogres do not integrate well into civilized society. This is usually because ogres are aggressive to everyone (including other ogres of their own species) or for the fact that most are unintelligent and cannot grasp basic rules. Moreover, given their size and strength, they can be quite destructive. However, there are friendly and intelligent ogres, and they tend to help others when in need. Nevertheless, they prefer their own freedom, choosing to roam the wild rather than be locked down to a particular property or job with a hierarchy. Attempts at slavery in the past proved futile in most cases, and the mages nearly exterminated most ogres as a result. But unlike some other species that the CME exterminated in the past, ogres did not (and continue not to) work collectively to attack others, and they could be tamed to a certain extent.

Today, mages use decent sapient ogres to keep other ogres in line, but mages also use their services to clear out areas or to destroy certain landscapes to pave the way for development. Ogre phenotypes vary greatly, but most tend to have a dim-witted appearance that most species of other genera consider to be 'ugly'. Moreover, since ogres are somewhat related to humans (given that ogres are primates), they have very human-like features – albeit appearing more primitive and beastly. Ogres also have a high risk of mutating; and when they do, some of these mutations include having many arms, heads, or even a reduced number of eyes (so they become *cyclopses*). Their shared genus abilities include: supreme strength; thick and tough skin acting as dermal armour; and supreme matter ingestion (allowing for the consumption of many substances without killing themselves).

### Trolls (Homitrollus):

Many trolls are semi-sapient, but since some trolls within the genus are sapient, they are listed with the other sapient mammalians. Because many people forget or do not know this fact, trolls are often seen as if beasts, and they are often used in jokes. It does not help that most sapient trolls also have terrible cultures. Accordingly, trolls are often also seen as a nuisance who only bring trouble to those around them. On top of this, the trolls that are both sapient and culturally (and morally) decent tend to also live in primitive societies, either in mud huts, caves, or under constructs like bridges. The terrible aspects of negative troll culture are similar to the antics found in bad goblin culture – just without the wit and intellect. Mages never needed to exterminate trolls in the past, as they were never a major threat because trolls could never form a coherent and united resistance.

It is a rare sight to see a troll walking through a city in the modern world; and when sighted, many people tend to assume that the trolls would have to have had the intelligence and good mannerisms to pass through security checkpoints, so they (the trolls) are not feared or shunned. Phenotypically, trolls appear as if a mix between goblins and ogres – but they are still part of a separate genus. So, trolls tend to have a mischievous appearance, but one that seems rather barbaric and primitive. Moreover, a troll's personality is generally a mix between goblins and ogres, taking the mischie-vousness and facetiousness from goblins and the barbarism of ogres. Some trolls are *just* considered giants, while most are under the giant category, with the genus average being 230 centimetres in height. Similar to goblins and ogres, trolls are also highly susceptible to mutations. Their shared genus abilities include: sleep suppression; an auric field that passively induces chaos (that is, their very presence alters the prob-ability fields around them in a way that is more likely to cause chaos – usually for other beings – though, this is typically marginal); superior danger awareness; and some resistance to certain conscious-altering attacks.

## Undas (Homigalea):

Undas (pronounced oon-duh) are essentially-humanoid, bipedal primates that have an average height of 203 centimetres. All unda species are mostly covered in thick hair; and some species in the genus even possess bodily hair that never reaches a telegenic state, thus it infinitely grows unless it is cut. Their heads, nonetheless, are covered with a full-bone helmet (not a mere mask) that reaches down to their chins. There are still slits for the eyes to see through, and the helmet does not connect to their neck and chin, allowing for hair from the head to pass down the neck. The helmet's bone mass is so strong that it can withstand certain rounds of gunfire. The shape of the helmets varies per species, but many are considered to appear menacing. Despite this menacing appearance – along with their powerful physiques – undas are generally hospitable. However, they are also extremely ethnocentric, and many live in small-pocketed communities.

Undas are normally seen practicing and engaging in various rituals in their free time – and even during work. Normally, they place a great deal of sacredness on everything they do; even defecating requires a very small prayer or ritual. Religiously, undas are animistic, worshipping a pantheon of archetypal deities. They are by no means *primitive*, but they normally shun consumerist lifestyles to varying degrees, thus they *appear* primitive. Their relationship with mages in the modern context is generally neutral; they do not like regulations imposed on them, but very few regulations are actually imposed on them (compared to many other genera), as undas typically do not engage in actions that generate many negative externalities for those outside their C zones. Undas have not forgotten their enslavement in the past under the CME, but they interestingly see the ancient events as being a rite of passage, anyway, which has only helped to unite the bonds between all unda species. Mages have strategically positioned unda C zones in various locations so that should mages ever need guides in the wild, they can easily turn to undas, who know the area and its current happenings more intimately. Their shared genus abilities include: natural bullet-proof helmets for protection; devastating headbutts; superior climbing skills; deep spirituality that allows for emotional healing and unification; and environmental connections and comprehensions.

## Junians (Homivestis):

Junians are relatively-humanoid, bipedal primates that have an average height of 180 centimetres. Unique from most mammalians, Junians of all sexes possess a membrane 'skirt' or 'dress'. However, there is still notable sexual dimorphism; for one, the males will have longer dresses than the females in some species and the reverse in others. These membrane dresses serve a few functions, such as slowing the fall of a junian, who will normally live in a treetop village or other elevated places (both present and in the past). When junians spin around quickly (and enough times), it excites certain cells in the membranes that release a cloud of smoke into the air that junians use for altering their state of consciousness in rituals and sexual acts. It can also be used as a form of self-defence when aggression is applied, which adds a toxin to the smoke. They also have a membrane that emerges from their heads and acts as a type of hat; this membrane is able to automatically collect dew in the air, which helps keep junians hydrated. Besides the membranes, they appear somewhat like humans, except their bodies are covered in deep markings that look like scars, and most species have big, floppy ears.

While certainly not as ritualistic as undas, junians still partake in many loud and exuberant festivities; basically, junians hold a major festival every week. Junians are not aggressive, and they submitted quickly when the CME began conquering other species. In the modern world, junians are found both in their own C zones and multispecieal zones, and they are great organizers for lunapex festivals that species of other genera partake in. Junians, in fact, go out of their way to make positive relations with species that are even generally unhospitable to other species. Junians are accordingly considered one of the most xenophilic genera in the Caelverse. Mages typically hire junians for certain jobs in the environment, such as analysing atmospheric data. Their shared genus abilities include: slow-falling; moisture absorption; toxin generation; smoke generation; and high, influential charisma and persuasive skills.

### Noosics (Homicerebrum):

Noosics are essentially-humanoid, bipedal primates that have an average height of 199 centimetres. The Noosic genus is monotypic – that is, there is only one species of its kind. As a result, noosics are simply called noosics, with the scientific name being *Homicerebrum Sophia*. Noosics appear somewhat like humans but are slender. They are also virtually hairless with generally greyish skin, and they have big, translucent skulls that hold a large brain. Naturally, they are highly intelligent. In fact, as one of the smartest species in the Caelverse, noosics easily find positions in academic research, and mages readily employ their skills in a variety of ways. Many people wonder why noosics do not possess a magic gland like mages, given their brain size, but noosics are not the most creative species, and their brains are very limited to solving logical problems and making scientific discoveries. Seeing this limitation, it is theorized that noosics must also be limited in other consciousness-related areas, which would, in turn, mean that they would not have access to magic.

Noosics naturally have a low population due to the amount of gestation time for producing offspring (averaging three years for a single child); and then the mother needs another two years before they can become pregnant again. Coupled with many other reasons, noosics are very much involved with genetic engineering science in order to change this issue and their whole physiology in general. However, unlike other species that have readily adopted genetic modifications in practice, noosics are careful and are fully trialling their research prudently before fully embracing changes. When directly enslaved under the CME, noosics were given comfortable roles such as working in libraries. Since the fall of the CME, there has since been the occasional scandal and conspiracy involving noosics subverting and corrupting mage political systems, and so, many mages remain quite suspicious of noosics – even feeling a little threatened. Otherwise, mages and noosics have cordial relations. Noosics are found in multispecieal zones, normally leading non-human research teams. Their abilities essentially include: supreme logical intelligence; the ability to totally defer gratification for long periods of time; and supreme focus.

### 4.3.3.1.2: Non-human and Non-primate Mammalians:

### Gosocks (Mamillaquattuorarma):

Gosocks are vaguely-humanoid, bipedal mammalians that have an average height of 180 centimetres. Possessing four arms, gosocks are a rare type of mammalian, as most mammalians in the Caelverse naturally have only two arms. While it is possible for gosocks to have evolved from one of the few animal mammalian species that do have four arms, another possible scenario involves major mutations that happened over a mere couple of generations (coupled with ADAs influencing the direction). That is, gosocks are potentially the result of former mutants (as a constitutional status) breeding, with the mutations being germline. Female gosocks also have four breasts (two sets of breasts), and the males have two penises. It is theorized that the males that originally had two penises were able to outcompete other males due to being able to penetrate female vaginas *and* anuses simultaneously. Female gosocks actually require anal stimulation as well as vaginal stimulation in order to release a chemical that makes the males ejaculate. While sexually dimorphic in size and texture, all gosocks have dorsal spines that visually appear like tentacles. The number and prevalence also depend on the species, with some dorsal fin 'tentacles' looking like thin feelers, while others like thick appendages. Most gosocks also have purplish skin, but this is not always the case.

During most of the CME, gosocks were living undiscovered on C4 worlds. It was near the end of the empire that gosocks were discovered, and they were quickly integrated into civilization. Due to their oddities, some gosocks were placed into performance artist roles to keep some of the non-mages entertained. Gosocks were not placed into prostitution, as that was prohibited under slave laws, but some mages did run underground prostitution rings with gosocks, which the CME failingly tried to stamp out. Interestingly, in the modern context, it is not widely considered (too) degenerate for a mage or other species to have sexual relations with gosocks. Gosocks are naturally very sexual in nature, but they are also great artists of assorted kinds, and they are commonly seen in multispecieal zones, working affably with many species of other genera. Their shared genus abilities include: gooey/jelly creation, which enables protection as a form of light armour; pheromone generation, which calms other beings; empathy, being able to connect deeply with other beings; and the production of 'synthetic hairs' (akin to polyesters, nylon, etc.) – and, while not an ability as such, these have different kinds of strengths and weaknesses compared to normal mammalian hair.

## Panthoculars (Panthoculareon):

Panthoculars are relatively-humanoid, bipedal cats that have an average height of 180 centimetres. Possessing heads similar to lions and tigers (depending on the species), panthoculars also have long tails. Unlike most species of other genera in the Caelverse, panthoculars are considered to be magic-latent. That is, Panthoculars could one day develop magic glands similar to mages – potentially very soon. With a literal, physical third eye centred above their normal eyes, panthoculars already appear mystical. This third eye allows them to see various etheric energies like auras, in addition to other anomalies in the physical realm. For most of the time during the day, these third eyes remain closed, and they only open temporarily when the panthocular requires or desires it. Coupled with their flash precognition abilities, they are at least *already* psychic. Then when factoring in their natural ability to alter probability fields in their favour (which is not overly powered, though), they tend to be banned from casinos and other gambling establishments.

Panthoculars are unique because each individual will generally fall into one of three categories: the spiritually advanced; the average; and, the pure evil. While some species of other genera are simply hostile to others, the evil that panthoculars may become is very different. It is estimated that about five percent of panthoculars are evil, which causes many problems for not only their own kind but for other beings around the Caelverse, too. The CME did enslave panthoculars, but the majority of mages always liked the good panthoculars, and while there were many direct roles to be given to panthoculars, it was also very easy and lucrative just to tax them. Within modern multispecial zones, panthoculars can normally be seen in three kinds of occupations: guru and self-development; entertainment; and crime (both organized and unorganized crime – much involving theft, drugs, and assassinations).

Most panthoculars are very individualistic, and so while, as a genus, they are very capable and talented, they cannot (and likely will not ever) form a cohesive force to overthrow mages (one day). With the amount of evil panthoculars, there is also a great amount of infighting. Their shared genus abilities include: psychicism (including active and passive flash precognition); luck manifestation (but again, this is limited); night vision; some resistance to consciousness alteration (if they are properly focusing and were originally prepared for the attacks); intimidating roars that affect some people's mental faculties, making potential opponents cower away; stealth skills; flexibility; climbing skills; and fall damage resistance.

## Delphars (Tursioprinceps):

Delphars are bisectionally-humanoid dolphins that have an average length of three metres, technically making them giants. Delphars are normally highly intelligent beings and excellent social organizers. With their arms and hands, they are capable of handling tools and technologies. By the time the CME had been established, delphars already had their own early-stage civilization without inspiration from surface-dwellers. Delphars also managed to travel to other solar systems via the inter-solar transportals that were located just above the surface of the oceans. Given the large number of species within the genus, they managed to spread greatly across the Caelverse (but not to all planets) instead of merely staying on their home worlds.

Mages did not enslave delphars en masse during the days of the CME due to the difficulty of enslaving ocean-living species. Even in the modern context, delphars largely have their own autonomy from the CGM, and they are the de facto sovereigns of many oceans. Regulations are nevertheless imposed on delphars, but generally, due to a lack of proper oversight, sometimes these regulations are never fully upheld. Moreover, it is easy for delphars to hide certain properties and activities from the CGM due to them being underwater. Delphars nonetheless cooperate greatly with mages (and the CGM), and they are mostly ethical in their activities.

Coupled with the fact that delphars lack legs and that their own weight would eventually crush their organs while on land due to gravity, delphars never bothered (or even continue to) bother expanding their territories on land, as they hold great power in their environments already. Plus, they need the water to keep their skin hydrated. Still, in some cases, delphars use mechanical walkers to make certain trade deals in oxygenated areas either above water or underwater. As with other aquatic beings, most delphar technology is grown, but due to their mammalian nature, they do sometimes integrate technologies that land-dwelling beings use. Since they are ocean-bound, most land-based species rarely interact with delphars. Still, delphars do export some of their cultures to certain land-based entities, who happen to love delphar culture. While delphars have cordial relations with most aquatic beings, naturally, there is intense rivalry for dominance, but potential war is largely checked with the threat of mage intervention – which the delphars support. Their shared genus abilities include: sonar and echolocation; powerful water blasting (from their blowholes); high-pitch communication (that other beings may or may not be able to hear); enhanced lung capacity and pressure resistance (compared to other mammalians); and sonic attacks.

## Leepans (Lepusifon):

Leepans are relatively-humanoid, bipedal rabbits (descendants of hares, specifically) that have an average height of 153 centimetres. Leepans are rapid breeders, which is in due part to fast gestation times, high progenies per litter (normally seven), and the ability for females to get pregnant seconds after giving birth. In addition, leepans have some of the highest libidos of any species. They are also extremely-quick learners, so mature leepans do not have to focus too long on raising their offspring. Since they are relatively short, they do not need to consume as much food as bigger mammalians. For this reason, the leepan population is huge – far bigger than the majority of species in the Caelverse.

Their population has faced much exploitation both by mages and non-mages. While the CME used leepans for slave labour, the non-mages that had yet to be fully conquered were far more violent and exploitative towards leepans. For example, males were sometimes chopped up and used for food and clothing, while females were normally used for violent sexual outlets. One of the reasons for their sexual value is that many beings in the Caelverse consider leepans to be cute and sexually desirable, and they can be extremely seductive – to the point that sometimes leepans are called *succubi* and *incubi* (that is, 'sexy' humanoid demons that drain one's energy via pleasurable sexual encounters – normally, in the context of manifested physicality, succubi and incubi are rare encounters, and much of what is known about them comes from fiction and folklore, despite technically being real). For this reason, leepans were (and are) sometimes used as spies to gather information in both the ancient and modern contexts.

Today, leepans still hold many historical scars, but they are overall friendly to mages and most non-mages. Without causing great upheavals, they integrate well into multispecieal societies, and many males and females provide sexual services to other species (usually mammalian) of their own free will. Entertainment is a big part of leepan culture, which mainly takes the form of cinematics, theatres, and aerobatic stunts. They are one of the few beings that are able to perform 'warp leaps'. That is, they can leap so fast that it appears as if they were teleporting. Even normally, they are considered some of the best jumpers. Leepans also have a great sense of danger, both present and impending, so they normally try to avoid situations they feel will lead to injury or death. Their shared genus abilities include: sexual seduction; warp leaps; danger awareness; and rapid learning and breeding.

## Rhichons (Cereatojuggernautus):

Rhichons are relatively-humanoid, bipedal rhinoceroses that have an average height of 380 centimetres, making them giants. Only one rhichon species exists in the genus, but this is not the result of any extermination of other species, as there has only ever been one known species of rhichons – who are simply called rhichons, with the scientific name being *Cereatojuggernautus griseotitan*. Rhichons are one of the toughest beings in the Caelverse; their skin alone is tougher than many technologically-advanced armours that other beings used to protect themselves with, and they cannot be *fully* synthetically replicated in a laboratory as of yet (excluding cell extractions, and the various printing thereafter). Rhichons are also able to charge with great power, bursting through many types of objects on contact. Moreover, when they are charging, it is extremely hard to stop their momentum.

Coupled with great endurance and pulling and lifting strength, the CME directly used rhichons to build great infrastructure in the past as slaves, and mages today still request their voluntary, paid labour when robots cannot fulfil certain tasks. The rhichons, in fact, played such a key role in the development of the CME that they can basically be found throughout the Caelverse – despite being monotypic. Rhichons still hold a slight grudge against the mages, but they do not fight with them mages, keeping to themselves instead. Nevertheless, rhichons make it clear to other species that they are not to be crossed. Mages found it hard in some ways to subdue rhichons thousands of years ago due to their special ability to resist certain mental weaknesses (due to their mental fortitude); of course, rhichons are not *immune* to such weaknesses. Because of their size, rhichons are limited in where they can go in multispecieal zones, so normally, they remain in their own C zones, where they tend to live simple lifestyles; still, they do enjoy certain sporting activities when they are not simply relaxing (and this can include with and against other species).

## Deerex (Taranmagivirga):

Deerex are relatively-humanoid, bipedal deer that have an average height of 190 centi-metres. Said to possess 'magic wands' on their heads, deerex do not actually possess magic, but rather, they possess amazing abilities that seem like magic. For one, they can, in a sense, 'telepathically' communicate with one another (at short range) through electromagnetic frequencies. Deerex can also use their antlers to create a camouflaged shroud around themselves – but this is not full invisibility. In the cold, their hooves also have superconductive properties, allowing them to levitate. They can also generate enough energy for electrical attacks if in danger or when angered. Of course, deerex cannot continually use their abilities without end, and they need time to recharge. During different seasons, the length of the antlers will change, along with whether they emit light in the form of bioluminescence (unless shrouded). Moreover, whenever deerex move, they will leave a trail of ionized charged particles that will glow (again, so long as they are not shrouded). Deerex keep their antlers all year, and instead of completely shedding them, they only shed small parts at a time.

Deerex tend to be social beings amongst their own kind, but they tend to keep to themselves due to shyness. It may seem like many deerex are innocent – indeed, most are – but deerex are known to be big drug manufacturers and run many black markets. Since it is culturally ingrained in most deerex cultures, mages do not bother cracking down on the drugs in deerex C zones, as that is not practical; plus, there is legislation preventing certain interventions in their autonomous zones. Still, in multi-specieal zones, black-market operations are more easily infiltrated and shut down. When one or many deerex are arrested, more fill the void. Nevertheless, deerex are generally not behind some of the hardest and most dangerous drugs; instead, they are one of the biggest manufacturers of psychedelics. Their shared genus abilities include: limited and short-range telepathy between species; camouflaging shroud generation; levitation; and electrical stunning attacks.

## Lupini (Canisalpha):

Lupini (pronounced: loo-pin-eye) are relatively-humanoid, bipedal wolves that have an average height of 180 centimetres. As some of the most fearsome beings in the Caelverse, if it were not for their constant political infighting, lupini would potentially cause an existential threat to many other beings. They would indeed be a bigger problem for the mages, but lupini would still not be able to match the power of mages and their magic and societal-level organization. Whilst lupini are not a hostile genus, most beings of other genera that have interacted with lupini at least instinctively know that the moment the mages show enough weakness, they will attack and vie for dominance. During the early stages of the CME, there was one lupini species (the virinsars), in particular, that was hostile to all species of other genera, and they posed a major threat to the CME. The mages in power, however, completely genocided them, and their final demise led to the other lupini falling in line.

In fact, the virinsars were one of the first species to be exterminated, which set a precedent for subsequent genocides of species of other genera. Still, this did not deter some species across the Caelverse from their absolute hostility to all other beings, but it did make those with latent hostility warier to the point where they more easily submitted to the rule of the CME. While the other lupini were turned into slaves, it was easier and safer just to keep them in their own restricted zones, where they were taxed and only used for a few small purposes. By placing them in their restricted zones, the mages inadvertently helped to strengthen the bonds that lupini had with one another. The remaining lupini today mostly continue to live in small, ultra-xenophobic and fascist communities inside their C zones, normally far away from other civilizations.

Lupini still strongly uphold the tradition for the young to undertake initiation rites before adulthood, and their culture normally revolves around strength and virtue. What is more, lupini have greater respect for stronger, more disciplined mages than they do for weaker, degenerate mages. When mage diplomats are sent into lupini C zones, generally, the mages are not the common type of office worker, and they have had at least some military training. Lupini are not big cultural exporters (although there is a niche market of non-lupini who love lupini art); and generally, if they are seen in multispecieal zones, there is a specific purpose to it that will help their own kind back in their C zones.

Their shared genus abilities include: a berserker form, which enables them to power their bodies with: pain suppression; unlimited and non-damaging adrenaline; super-enhanced senses (which also includes heightened blood sense, which is akin to telescopic thermoreception vision); supreme combat efficiency; accelerated *and* advanced healing; increased speed, strength, reflexes, and agility; and absolute determination (which prevents them from being mentally affected in most cases, including from consciousness-altering attacks, such as from certain phasarchement discharges). Berserker forms can last several hours, but they are normally either only available during lunapexes, after certain meditation, when in pure fight-or-flight mode, or when *extremely* angered; after which, the lupini will require a few days off to recharge, where they will sleep most of the time.

Lupini also have: lunar affinity, which increases their benefits during various lunapexes; the ability to call upon their inner wolf spirit, the collective animistic form that resides in their collective unconscious (this spirit is normally called upon during lunapexes, berserker forms, or under the influence of drugs); inflict shapeshifting (heterogenic) curses on others via *chance* when they bite their victims, potentially turning others into 'wolves'; and wolf domination, granting the ability to lead animal wolves. On top of all these abilities, lupini also have: great navigation intuition; detection skills (which are not etheric based); tracking skills; sense of smell; and cold resistance.

## Darkrays (Pteroambulans):

Darkrays are vaguely-humanoid, bipedal bats that have an average height of 160 centimetres. As one of the few mammalian genera that can naturally fly (true flight), darkrays hold a unique status. As descendants of animal bats, darkrays still wield exceptional flying abilities that even outperform that of birds and other sapient avians. With areal adaptation, their wings are naturally more flexible, allowing for greater dexterity; and overall, darkrays have better manoeuvrability. Their membrane wings can regrow if torn, and the surfaces can detect assorted weather variables and changes in airflow. Darkrays also have normal bat abilities such as echolocation, enhanced senses, optional hibernation, and night vision (although, their vision is poor during the day). In addition, darkrays possess the ability to produce powerful sonic screams that can deafen and destroy certain objects. They are also immune to many diseases.

The genus is split into two main categories: those that are herbivores (frugivores), and those that are carnivorous (blood-drinking). Despite being part of the same genus, the two main groups of species generally hate one another. The frugivore darkrays are not without their own problems, nor are they pacifistic, but they tend to cooperate well with species of other genera. They also appear a lot less scary, and many beings around the Caelverse consider their facial features, at least, to be rather cute. The *hematophagists*, on the other hand, have – and continue – to generally generate a bad name for themselves. This is not to say that there are no good individuals and even groups of blood drinkers, but their sense of smell and desire for blood is incredibly strong, and so, many cannot help themselves when they are around other species; and, this is not even including the ones who lack morality altogether. Blood drinkers have been banned from many zones, and as a result, they are practically forced to live in their own secluded C zones. While this may seem like it angers most blood-drinking darkrays (indeed, it does), they prefer being isolated, anyway. Blood-drinking darkrays have also been listed on 'medium alert' regarding overall hostility; and if the threat levels were to ever reach a high-enough state, then the CGM will begin a genocide. Some theorists believe that within a few generations, this might be likely.

## Ratans (Rattusvir):

Ratans are relatively-humanoid, bipedal rats that have an average height of 40 centimetres. Although they are physically weak and lack remarkable traits found in other genera, ratans were not exactly easy for the CME to conquer – at least as a whole. Mages working for the CME were still able to enslave many ratans, but the majority were able to hide underground. Most of the slave labour involved physical jobs that required small hands or bodies. There is a dark history involving one of the ratan species, who were big carriers of multiple deadly diseases (for other species). At the time, there was no cure for their terrible diseases, and even when they were quarantined, the diseases managed to spread. So, in order to eliminate the issue, the CME decided to exterminate the carrier species. To this day, it is unknown (or potentially concealed) how the CME managed this feat, especially considering that many of the carrier species were underground and not enslaved. The other ratan species were not happy with the genocide, but at the same time, they were somewhat understanding and a little relieved (as they, too, died in large numbers from the diseases).

In the modern day, both mages and ratans are very friendly with one another, and the majority of mages typically find most ratan species to be cute and cuddly. Ratans, in fact, seek the help of mages quite frequently when having to deal with species of other genera. Ratans are common in multispecieal zones, and they are usually employed in fields that require delicate precision and access to hard-to-reach locations; but ratans are highly-intelligent and are nevertheless in assorted fields, including scientific research, arts, and medicine. The only major conflict ratans have with mages is the scientific studies conducted on animal rats, seeing it as a major ethical issue. Ratans do not have any special shared genus abilities other than their notable agility and extremely good sense of balance.

## Alovexens (Vulparan):

Alovexens are relatively-humanoid, bipedal foxes that have an average height of 170 centimetres. Most alovexen species had already built sophisticated societies by the time of the CME. Such societies were not imperial but rather networks of democratic city states. When the mages enslaved the alovexens, it was much easier just to tax them and leave them to their own devices. Still, the CME noted their intelligence and ingenuity, deciding to place some alovexens into intelligence operations, which helped the CME continue to enslave other species. There was one controversial event where alovexens helped the mages to completely genocide one of the lupini species. For this reason, many non-mage species hated – and continue to hate – alovexens for such sell-out actions and nature.

Alovexen governments today have collectively apologized for the past, but many notable individual alovexens claim that they were bound by the context and that, ultimately, pragmatics was, and is, the most important virtue. Alovexens are currently found in both their own C zones and within many multispecieal zones, working well with an array of species. Alovexens are not just intelligent, but their brains allow for certain abstract and conceptual models that many species do not even understand. They are quite literally able to create complex 3D modelling in their minds, seeing complete details and determining engineering and strategic outlines. Normally, they have a sharp sense of humour, are great tricksters, and many perform as stage magicians with fake magic tricks. While they typically make for great martial artists, they tend to avoid combat as much as possible. Their shared genus abilities include: supreme abstract conceptualization and engineering; supreme cunning; and excellent stealth skills.

## Bovitaurs (Bostaurunus):

Bovitaurs are relatively-humanoid, bipedal cattle that have an average height of 240 centimetres, with some species technically being giants. As with their animal ancestors, they possess very easily-identifiable sexual dimorphism, and females are still called cows, while males are called bulls. The CME easily conquered all of the bovitaur species, and most were also directly enslaved for physical labour. In fact, bovitaurs were considered one of the best and most consistent workers for the CME; and without them, the empire would not have been as powerful. Even today, without slavery, bovitaurs typically work hard, but they do enjoy their rest as well. Generally, they prefer consistent, labour-intensive work out in open spaces. They work well with species of other genera and are normally friendly as well, but they nevertheless like solitude in their exclusive C zones, too. Still, they are a common sight in multispecieal zones.

The bulls normally do not find themselves fighting with other species (of their own genus and other genera) due to both their slow-to-anger nature and for the fact that many beings consider male bovitaurs to be intimidating due to their strength and stature. The females produce milk that is exported commercially, and it contains healing properties for some species. There are some species of other genera who absolutely crave the milk yet are intolerant of it, but they keep consuming it no matter the negative health repercussions. Bovitaurs have no special shared genus abilities other than the bulls possessing great strength, and the females possessing healing milk.

## Platinooks (Electroanatinus):

Platinooks are relatively-humanoid, bipedal monotremes that have an average height of 160 centimetres. Despite their aquatic nature, platinooks are still mammalian and require oxygen, so they cannot permanently stay underwater. The CME was able to easily enslave platinooks, using them in freshwater environments, which greatly helped the empire as most aquatic beings in the Caelverse were (and are) only suited for saltwater. Although the oceans are indeed deep, there are areas where freshwater systems are incredibly deep as well. In the modern context, platinooks are hired to help protect and maintain many river systems and similar freshwater environments. Although the technology exists now for easy underwater arrangements and endeavours with other species, platinooks still deliver essential services for mages and other beings that require more nuanced solutions. Although platinooks interact with many species, they tend to be overlooked and fly under the radar. Moreover, their culture has never been realized by others apart from mages (probably due to baffling peculiarities), and so, while platinooks do not seclude themselves, they are, by default, quite removed from other societies. Their shared genus abilities include: electricity generation; and poison generation.

## Adhogs (Sapienschoerus):

Adhogs are essentially-humanoid, bipedal pigs that have an average height of 180 centimetres. Despite the genus name signifying that they are intelligent, incorrect stereotypes fill many discussions about adhogs, and they tend to be the butt end of a lot of jokes. At first, many adhogs tend to return the jokes in good humour, but they can become quite annoyed if the jokes persist. Still, trolls, ogres, and danthas are generally used in more jokes than adhogs. During the CME, adhogs were quite a common sight, and they were normally used for generalist roles. Typically, they are nowadays employed in jobs that require maintenance in dirty areas; but this is not to say they are dirty beings; although, they usually do not mind getting dirty. Outside of such positions, they are very artistic, and it is an extremely-common sight to see tattoos over their bodies. Adhogs are also one of the most common genera of species in the Caelverse today, filling many multispecieal zones. Their own societies are normally functional, but they do suffer from many gang-related issues and underground trafficking. Quite a few adhogs become drug addicts, too, which the CGM has been asked to intervene for on occasion. They do not have any special shared genus abilities other than that their stomachs are able to bear the most gut-wrenching foods and poisons, and their belches can knock some people out cold.

## 4.3.3.2: Reptilians:

Sapient reptilians are very common in the Caelverse, both in many multispecieal zones and by the extent of their C zones. However, since they are cold-blooded and require adequate sunlight, their populations mainly concentrate in warm climates and on land. Still, with the advancement of technology, reptilians have been able to live elsewhere. Whilst there are some fundamental differences between mammalians and reptilians, they actually share a few types of lifestyles that the 'stranger' morphtypes types do not. Accordingly, beings of the stranger morphtypes tend to group reptilians with mammalians, using terms like 'cold-blooded mammals' or 'scaly mammals'. Reptilians are most famous for their dracos, which are a taxonomic order of reptilians that include many winged and non-winged entities like dragons (who are non-sapient) and dracotors (who are sapient). Other legendary examples of notable reptilians include basilisks; but since none are sapient, this guide will not list any. If mammalians did not exist, then reptilians would potentially be the dominant morphtype in the Caelverse. Major, common, or notable sapient reptilian genera include:

## Dracotors (Draconis):

Dracotors are relatively-humanoid, bipedal dracos that have an average height of 240 centimetres. While dracotors have bat-like wings, they are nonetheless reptilian, with the appearance occurring via convergent evolution. As the only extant species left in the genus, the xorinids (*Draconis duocornibus*) have two horns on their heads that stem from the back of their skulls; and most xorinids have light to dark grey skin. Xorinids were neither the strongest nor the weakest of the dracotors, but they are now one of the strongest and most fearsome beings of any genera in the Caelverse. Dracotors posed a massive existential threat to both the CME and mages that multiple species in the genus had to be completely exterminated. While the CME survived the wars, many mages lost their lives during the genocides. Just when the CME was about to exterminate the last dracotor species, more than half of the xorinids decided to submit than perish. About thirty percent of the xorinids, however, believed in fighting to the bitter end, seeing it better than submission. The CME allowed the xorinids that submitted to continue existing, and the remaining battles were swiftly ended.

In the modern context, xorinids comply with CGM regulations, but they are active and vocal about their politics, making sure that they obtain the best deals with the mages. So, while xorinids are not isolated like many species of other genera (as they can still be seen in many multispecieal zones), they are extremely xenophobic and enforce fascist regimes amongst their own kind in their own C zones. The xorinid governments are also against genetic engineering and cybernetics, and they favour traditional eugenics to keep their populations strong. They also highly dislike it when mages ride on dragons. Xorinids are smart and strategic, and while they do create art, they are not big exporters of culture, except for their sports (which are not typical sports, as they usually involve extreme types of survival games). Xorinid attributes and abilities include: true flight; strong skin (their backs being bulletproof); thermosynthesis (they can breathe fire, which can extend a few metres); optional thermoreception; reptilian dominance (they can make most other reptilians – normally non-sapient – submit to their will); fire resistance; electrical resistance (electrical attacks can even help fuel their thermosynthesis); fast healing regeneration (healing certain wounds); and supreme combat sense.

## Crodins (Crocohubris):

Crodins are relatively-humanoid, bipedal crocodiles that have an average height of 260 centimetres. Most are technically giants, and all have tails. While extremely strong and aggressive, the CME was able to enslave crodins in the past, but this did not occur without massive conflict. When direct slavery was involved, mage slavers typically kept their distance when they dealt with the crodins. In the modern day, most crodins are not too xenophobic, and many are welcoming of others. However, they are virtually all ethnocentric and extremely proud of their kind, and they aim to challenge and best others in assorted pursuits. Crodins are generally boisterous and assertive in their interactions with others, including mages, of whom crodins do not hold a big grudge against, despite the slavery in the past.

In fact, crodins typically acknowledge mages as being the 'supreme beings in the Caelverse' – for the time being. They openly mock the mages in supposed good humour, saying one day that they will conquer the mages and the entire Caelverse. Whether crodins will or not conquer the Caelverse, they still abide by mage rules in the modern day, and they do not cause much trouble as a whole. Of course, crodins tend to intimidate most species of other genera when in the vicinity (except, generally, the xorinids). Moreover, there are many crodin gangs and strong criminal networks across the Caelverse, which pose a great nuisance not just for mages but many other beings as well. Crodins are indeed one of the strongest group of species in the Caelverse, weighing over a tonne each on average. Their shared genus attributes and abilities include: strong, scaly skin; supreme predator senses; and proficient aquatic combat skills.

## Nagatias (Ophioarma):

Nagatias are vaguely-humanoid, non-bipedal snakes that have an average length of two metres. While they are one of the few kinds of land-based sapient beings that do not possess legs, nagatias nevertheless have humanoid arms and hands. They also have an 'upper body' consisting of a torso that is normally erect, with a neck and head extending from it. Indeed one of the most cunning beings in the Caelverse, nagatias are some of the most mistrusted beings as well. Interestingly, extant nagatias do not have a large record of wrongdoings compared to species of other genera – or at least, no widescale *provable* wrongdoings. Either nagatias are not as treacherous as many people believe, or they are incredibly crafty at covering their tracks. Still, mages tolerate them, as nagatias openly comply with legislation and have great economic value with their skills and services.

Despite the tolerance, most mages prefer that nagatias keep their distance and remain in their designated C zones due to some of their abilities. During the time of the CME, two species had to be exterminated due to their hostility to all beings other than themselves; the rest of the genus, however, submitted quickly and hardly rebelled. Most nagatias were then kept at a distance and simply taxed, but for those directly working for the empire (which was not common), they, funnily enough, found themselves largely in comfortable positions. Nagatias are big cultural exporters, even though most non-nagatias who love their culture do not understand the complex esoteric underpinnings within their art.

Their shared genus attributes and abilities include: venom generation; hypnotism via a petrifying gaze (that normally affects certain beings with low levels of consciousness); encrypted speech, which enables garbled language that can never be deciphered except for those of their own species; seismic sense, enabling one to sense particular vibrations in the ground; illusion awareness (including some mage charms); a passive cursing etheric aura (that is, their very presence alters the probability fields around them in a way that increases the likelihood of negative outcomes occurring for those not of their kind – so, anyone in their auras will receive bad luck – though, this is typically marginal); snake domination (lesser snakes will obey their commands); and of course, basic abilities such as immense constricting power, prehensility, large lungs, flexibility, body shedding, ability to slide, stealth skills, and powerful bites.

## Turtarians (Chelovir):

Turtarians are relatively-humanoid, semi-bipedal tortoises that have an average height of 190 centimetres. Unlike most other sapient bipedal beings, turtarians switch between being bipedal and walking on all fours (feet *and* hands). The reason for this is due to the shell on their backs, and going on all fours eases the burden. Moreover, turtarians weigh more than most sapient beings due to their shells. Turtarians are naturally land-based, but they are capable of swimming. While they are not the fastest beings, they are not necessarily slow. Although they were quick to submit to the CME in the past, they were always very stubborn and would sometimes cop punishment simply for the sake of refusing to do certain tasks or pay taxes. Their stubbornness has carried over to the modern world, and even though they do comply with many rules imposed on them, they have a tendency to simply ignore the ones that they do not wish to follow. As a result, mages in the CGM have an ambivalent like-dislike relationship with turtarians. Still, there are not too many rules imposed on turtarians, as they do not cause much trouble nor generate many negative externalities.

A large percentage of turtarians neither mix well, nor are at odds with, most species of other genera, and they tend to simply mind their own business. Turtarians also have a unique ability called *negligible senescence*; that is, they do not exhibit biological aging. This, nonetheless, does not mean they are immortal; obviously, they can be murdered or killed in other ways. Also, this passive attribute is not consistent over time, and certain quantum variables or life experiences can lead a turtarian to age biologically. Generally, the older a turtarian, the more easily certain variables can alter their negligible senescence. If no negative variables occur, then technically, tutarians could potentially live forever. So far, the longest living, recorded turtarian is 534 years old, as of the year B-424. Like animal tortoises, turtarians can also withdraw into their shells for protection – which happen to be bulletproof.

## Charmas (Chamelearma):

Charmas are relatively-humanoid, bipedal chameleons that have an average height of 160 centimetres. Many species of other genera consider charmas to be one of the strangest land-based sapient beings; this is not just due to their unique abilities but also their personality and culture. Personality-wise, charmas seem like those who are on the *autism spectrum* (a neurological condition causing one to have difficulty with social interactions). Mapping their brains has been heretofore futile in understanding whether charmas actually have autism and/or if they are just naturally strange. Regardless, they tend to keep to themselves. While some beings (of any genera) on the autism spectrum are aloof, others are social, but most charmas are aloof. Despite their name, they are generally the opposite of charming. In the past, the CME simply taxed charmas rather than use them directly for labour. Charmas draw upon the abilities that primitive chameleons have, such as: panoramic vision; projectile tongues; prehensility; adhesive secretions; and, of course, the ability to change their colour and pattern based on mood, temperature, health, light, and for the sake of communication. Changing colour and patterns can also intentionally and unintentionally serve many purposes, such as camouflaging, warding, attracting, notifying, etc.

## Gecks (Gekkoarma):

Gecks are relatively-humanoid, bipedal geckos that have an average height of forty centimetres, placing the majority in the 'tiny' category. Due to their rapid breeding, gecks are very common in the Caelverse, with many seen in multispecieal zones. Gecks are temperamental, but they are generally very friendly to species of other genera. They normally find themselves in communications roles, as they love communicating. In fact, that is one of their unique abilities: they have unique vocals that allow for various forms of communication. Because most are nocturnal, they normally have shift work in multispecieal zones. Under the CME as slaves, mages had gecks mainly working for them directly as opposed to them being purely taxed. In the modern day, mages and gecks have positive relations. Their shared genus attributes and abilities include: unique vocals and communications; supreme wall-climbing skills; tail dropping and regrowth; skin shedding; and scarred and damaged tissue healing.

## Igortas (Iguanagiganteus):

Igortas are relatively-humanoid, bipedal iguanas that have an average height of 330 centimetres, placing all in the giant category. In fact, igortas are one of the biggest sapient reptilians in the Caelverse. They are exceptionally strong yet generally placid, and they maintain a natural vegan diet based on their herbivorous ancestors. Nevertheless, they are not pacifists, and so, there was naturally some resistance when the CME enslaved them. Given their size, they were used in large-scale manual-labour jobs. Even today, they can be found working in jobs requiring large-scale labour. Many igortas today help with building nature reserves for many different species of other genera. This is both due to their ability to easily work in such fields, but also because they prefer the working environments. They are friendly with most beings – although, they do not normally and actively seek out relations with others. Crodins typically challenge igortas to physical fights, and usually igortas decline, simply because they do not wish to fight. However, when provoked, igortas usually put many crodins in their place. Igortas do not have any shared genus abilities other than their strength and size.

## Finseks (Draconoidvir):

Finseks are relatively-humanoid, bipedal lizards that have an average height of 110 centimetres. Despite the similar scientific genus name, finseks are not dracos. Finseks do not possess wings like many dracos and, instead, have *patagium* (foldable membranes) on their sides that help them glide (but not fly). Their overall physiology is not suited for any combat, and they are better equipped for escaping aggressors. They also have detractable fins and webbed feet for swimming. While not as common as gecks, finseks can be seen in many multispecieal zones. The CME easily enslaved finseks in the past, and many were used directly for assorted jobs that generally helped other species with their tasks. Today, finseks cooperate with many species of other genera, and they have no hard feelings about their history with mages. Despite their own cordiality, many types of beings bully finseks, and other beings dislike them for their cowardice. As a result, when working in multispecieal zones, finseks prefer to work in safe environments with many other finseks around them. Their shared genus attributes and abilities include: gliding; poison and venom resistance; pheromone generation; great jumping abilities; advanced reflexes; fin protrusion; very fast running speeds; and water walking (if they maintain their speed).

## Thornisks (Agamoid):

Thornisks are relatively-humanoid, bipedal lizards that have an average height of 180 centimetres. Covered in thorns, thornisks can protrude and retract certain thorns, which can be deadly in combat. Due to their thorny physiology, they are generally never accepted for roles with species of other genera that require physical contact (even though their hands and front are free of thorns, so technically, they can give people handshakes and even hug them). But more unique to the genus is their inborne ability to shapeshift after an already-higher chance than other beings of gaining a shapeshiftable additional genetic code. Of course, this shapeshifting ability is naturally limited to other particular sapient beings – so, it is not like they have the same power as mages. To gain another genetic code, thornisks have to partake in rituals (normally during lunapexes), where they exchange bodily fluids with the person's form that they wish to adopt. After adopting the new MRF, the thornisk typically (but not always) needs lunapexes to shapeshift; and they can later sever the code and gain another one, but this usually takes one Standard Year.

Thornisks initially posed a problem to the CME, with a few even impersonating the supreme emperors on separate occasions (as to how they got the genetic information is still unknown). When the CME learned of their natural ability to shapeshift, the mages quickly organized mystics to watch the slaves closely, which helped prevent shapeshifted slaves from causing problems. Thornisks today are one of the most common reptilians throughout the Caelverse, and they generally have positive relations with other beings. However, when an individual thornisk has been seen shapeshifting needlessly, suspicions of that person in particular are normally always held. Some thornisks take on diplomat and public relations jobs, where they assume certain morphtypes that species of other genera prefer to interact with – of course, with the knowledge that they are still dealing with a shapeshifter. In such cases, certain attire or insignia are worn to alert others of a shapeshifted form. On occasion, thornisks may fool around and impersonate significant figures, but these people are generally caught very quickly. There is also a special day call *Thorisk Day* when thornisks will shapeshift and trick others within certain limits. Their shared genus attributes and abilities include: a higher chance of gaining new MRFs; shapeshifting; protractible and retractable thorns; and, poison and venom generation.

### 4.3.3.3: Avians:

Sapient avians are a semi-common morphtype in the Caelverse, and while many are in multispecieal zones, they are normally seen in their own C zones. The majority of sapient avians have arms in addition to their wings (that are normally on their backs), and, thus, they are fully able to use tools to integrate into – and create their own – societies. It is a myth that the majority of avians live in the sky. The reason for this belief is because avians can fly. The problem with this idea is that avians still need to rest – on a surface. This means that they would have to create cities in the skies, which would require immense energy and resources. Therefore, the majority of avians still live on land (or in trees). However, some affluent individuals may still live in sky transport, limited sky buildings, and spaceships, like any other being. If mammalians and reptilians did not exist, avians would probably not rule the Caelverse, but they would nonetheless hold a dominant place. Major, common, or notable sapient avian genera include:

## Exevars (Accipitriformarma):

Exevars are relatively-humanoid, bipedal *accipitriformes* that have an average height of 200 centimetres. Most of the species in the genus have either eagle or vulture appearances, but all species nonetheless have two humanoid arms with clawed hands. Exevars are a powerful genus, having many unique abilities that have allowed them to easily and historically hunt sapient species of other genera – an exercise that mainly the eagle-like exevars conduct; the vulture-like species, on the other hand, have a historical record of scavenging the dead. Mages halted exevars from these practices during the time of the CME, and as a result, they had to exterminate two species from the genus in order to stop their relentless attacks on not just the mages but the slaves, too. The battles for domination proved vexing for the mages because not only did the exevars have their own natural abilities, but they created artificial bombs, which they dropped on mage cities. These bombs were also given to dracotors as well. In the present day, most of the eagle exevars remain aloof, watching species of other genera in contempt. The vulture exevars also remain aloof, but instead of watching in contempt, they typically watch out of other kinds of hatred and strange fetishes. Most exevars acknowledge that they cannot overthrow the mages, but both types of exevars believe that the mage post-imperialist system will inexorably fall and they will reign supreme afterwards.

The eagle exevars normally live in the mountains, where they have been granted such areas for their respective C zones; the vultures, though, can be found in various locations. Due to their overall attitudes, most species of other genera do not like exevars, but there are individual exevars that are very friendly to others. Nevertheless, most beings in the Caelverse (apart from fecal-loving beings like the arthropoid *scarbens*) find the vultures disgusting, mainly due to their urohidrosis, a habit where they defecate on their own legs as a means to cool down. Many of the vultures, moreover, live semi-primitive existences. Their shared genus attributes and abilities include: atmospheric adaptation; superior aerobatics; feather missile bombardment, with the calamus (quill) being able to penetrate flesh and cause potential death; supreme accuracy; magnetoreception; telescopic vision; great strength for carrying objects (such as weapons and important resources); skywriting skills and abilities (when they consume particular substances, they can use it for skywriting when they release it from their anuses or mouths after burping it back up); cloud disruption (causing aerial disturbances that cause confusion for beings and technology); ferocious and powerful clawing capabilities; and supreme predator instincts.

## Ormohrs (Strigiarma):

Ormohrs are relatively-humanoid, bipedal owls that have an average height of 160 centimetres. Besides the humanoid arms and clawed hands, they still look very owl-like. Ormohrs are typically nocturnal and live solitary lives. Accordingly, while they do socialize on occasion with other ormohrs in their own C zones, they are rarely seen in multispecieal zones unless conducting brief trade. They have friendly relations with species of other genera, but they generally feel no need to interact with anyone else. Many beings across the Caelverse feel as though that there is an atmosphere of smugness around ormohrs (which might be a result of their high intellect). When approached, for example, ormohrs will typically deal in riddles and remain as enigmatic as possible. In such interactions, quiet chuckles may be heard. During the time of the CME, mages used some ormohrs directly for their hypnotic abilities on other species. While today the mages typically never use ormohrs for hypnosis, species of other genera employ their services (which have legal limitations). Their shared genus attributes and abilities include: night vision; telescopic vision; enhanced sound localization; silence during flight due to the nature of their wings; 270-degree neck rotation; limited camouflage; and hypnosis.

## Corvicks (Corvidarma):

Corvicks are relatively-humanoid, bipedal corvids that have an average height of 180 centimetres. They feature humanoid arms and clawed hands that are capable of handling tools, and their faces still retain the pronounced corvid beak and sharp eyes. Corvick species usually either fall into the macabre and solitary types or the highly sociable. Out of all the avian genera, corvicks are perhaps the smartest. They also possess extremely remarkable memories, and they are also psychic. The CME used some corvicks during the time of the empire for advanced roles that utilized their intelligence, but the mages soon found that the corvicks would attempt to manipulate them. As a result, the CME kept most corvicks at a distance and simply taxed them instead. Mages did not want to genocide any corvick species at the time, as corvicks as a whole were not hostile, nor did not they fight back against the slavery en masse. Moreover, many mages actually liked (and still like) corvicks (especially gothic mages). However, the macabre corvicks had (and still have) a great interest in the occult, and quite a few began practicing dark arts. This did not help their relations with the mages; however, those in power insisted that most corvicks were not a problem, and so, only those who engaged in the dark arts were hunted (sometimes with the help of good corvicks).

Under the CGM today in multispecieal zones, corvicks are found in assorted careers, but many involve consultancy of some kind. Many corvicks also work as psychics, singers, and artists, and they are great cultural exporters. The stereotypes are true that state that the majority of corvicks appreciate gothic architecture, and so, the cities in their C zones are largely of this aesthetic. The more sociable species are ubiquitous in multispecieal zones, but they tend to keep to *murders* (that is, groups). Their shared genus attributes and abilities include: being able to see through illusions (including charms); hyper intelligence; great instincts and intuition; assorted communication skills (such as singing); remarkable memories; psychicism; and, their presence can greatly affect etheric fields, in turn potentially producing greater chances for various kinds of transformations – as a result, they are used in rituals by many types of beings.

## Swinsins (Cygarma):

Swinsins are relatively-humanoid, bipedal swans that have an average height of 190 centimetres. They still have long, extendable necks like their non-sapient swan ances-tors, and their bodies appear overall slimmer due to their humanoid form. Swinsins are very cordial with most species of other genera, especially with the mages. While the CME did enslave swinsins, virtually none were directly used for intense physical labour, as swinsins were (and are) not cut for intensive physical work. Swinsin leaders managed to convince the mages at the time that for any direct work that they had to undertake, they could be used for putting on artistic performances. The mages in the CME accepted this idea, using swinsins to keep the other slaves entertained. Even today, swinsins typically avoid doing most labouring jobs, and are, as a result, found in multispecieal zones, where other beings can do dirty, hard work for them in exchange for the money they receive from artistic lines of work. Their shared genus attributes and abilities include: enhanced lung capacity; swift swimming (compared to most non-aquatic beings); and extendable necks (that can normally stretch up to a metre longer than their default form).

## Parquans (Sphenisciarma):

Parquans are relatively-humanoid, bipedal penguins that have an average height of 180 centimetres. They feature arms and hands, and unlike other sapient avians, they do not possess wings in addition to their arms. Nonetheless, their arms still appear somewhat like the flippers of their non-sapient ancestors with a slightly-flat form. They also have bioluminescent, pebbled lights lined across their front and back, which help them in dark and stormy weather. Despite normally being very sociable with species of other genera, parquans do not engage much with others due to living in freezing cold temperatures, well away from where most sapient beings prefer and need to dwell. Given the scarcity of beings in the polar regions of C1 worlds (and even freezing areas of other worlds), parquans play an important role in performing the many tasks and jobs required in such regions.

Although mages have settlements in the polar regions (with major ones around the transportals), it is easier to work with parquans than to go far out themselves. Mages enslaved parquans during the time of the CME, but while the physical labour was intensive, there were periods were there was no work at all, so the parquans did not have to work all year round. While it may appear that parquans live primitively, this is actually just their architectural style; most of their buildings are constructed out of carved ice, not traditional materials like steel and concrete seen in non-arctic areas. Inside their buildings, though, various technologies can be found. Even though parquans live indoors, they certainly do not shy away from working and playing outdoors. Their shared genus attributes and abilities include: strong bioluminescence for sight in stark environmental conditions; frictionless sliding; cold adaptation; gut storage; enhanced lung capacity; and excellent swimming skills.

### 4.3.3.4: Ichthyoids:

Fish are themselves not a proper taxonomic group in the STS, and so, the various classes, such as *chondrichthyoids* and *osteichthyoids* are grouped together as ichthyoids for ease of identification in the FTS. Sapient ocean dwellers, for the most part, have developed along very different technological timeline trees than sapient land-dwelling beings. Their technologies are not just in and of themselves different, but they have also led to different types of jobs, cultures, and lifestyles. For example, instead of using fire and metals for building technologies, ocean dwellers began using (and still use) hydrothermal vents and bio-organic materials with advanced polymers. That is, many technologies are living matter. Given the abundance of bioluminescence in sea creatures, ocean dwellers have used this to their advantage and have created massive networks of light, connected with additional bio-organic tissue. In minor cases, air-filled structures (buildings) allow for certain actions to take place for technologies that require dryness. Moreover, some ocean dwellers still rise to the surface for certain resources and goods for trade. On the whole, ocean technology is incompatible with land technology, so there is normally no mixing of technology.

Mages, nonetheless, have built many massive and great infrastructures and tunnels underwater, with many of these connecting to ichthyoid structures, where trade and other activities occur. Due to the reality that mages cannot breathe underwater without technology and/or magic, it made it harder and bothersome for the CME to enslave ichthyoids and other ocean dwellers. Even today, it is hard for the CGM to fully regulate the oceans. Since ichthyoids typically have tails and no humanoid legs, they remain in the oceans and are not a major threat to those on land. This was yet another reason why the CME never bothered to enslave most ichthyoids; although, mages did work with some ichthyoids and other aquatic genera to maintain some order in the oceans, and some taxation was present for certain areas (usually coastal). CGM-formed multispecieal zones have been set up in the oceans, and while this is the result of mage influence, aquatic species would have formed similar areas as well without the mages. Most ichthyoids have to work through delphar systems; and, it was delphars who helped the spread of many, but not all, ichthyoids across the Caelverse. Major, common, or notable sapient ichthyoid genera include:

## Forktires: (Lamnidominus):

Forktires are bisectional-humanoid mackerel sharks that, on average, measure three metres in length, making all technically giants. Their upper bodies possess a torso that features humanoid arms and webbed hands, while their lower bodies retain a shark tail. Moreover, they possess dorsal fins, and their robust facial structures possess a conical snout like their non-sapient ancestors. Although forktires are considered remarkable fighters and warriors, they are not the dominant force in the oceans. The main reason for this is due to their overall inferior social organization compared to species of other genera (such as delphars), which is mainly a result of their isolationist and solitary lifestyles. However, forktires are, indeed, very disciplined, and they manage to form efficient societies. Around half the species in the genus form de facto *matriarchies* (societies ruled by females) due to the females being bigger; but the other half of the genus are a mix between the non-sexually dimorphic and ones with larger males.

If it were not for the said issues, it is unknown whether forktires would become aggressive with species of other genera, in turn possibly requiring their sanctioned genocide. In the past, aquatic species of other genera had to exterminate two forktire species due to their overt aggression. Mages also happened to be completely uninvolved in the genocides. At present, forktires remain aloof and unfriendly with most species, but they do not engage in hostilities other than that found from lone individuals or gangs. Generally, individual murders result from either sport killings or when their egos are hurt (as they are a very prideful group of species). In contrast, gang murders tend to result from black market operations. Since many forktires perform hired mercenary work, sometimes they can be helpful or problematic.

Mages rarely interact with forktires other than for necessary bureaucratic reasons and trade for niche goods. Their shared genus attributes and abilities include: a berserker mode, which temporarily grants: pain suppression; unlimited and non-damaging adrenaline; super-enhanced senses (which also includes heightened blood sense, which is akin to telescopic thermoreception vision); supreme combat efficiency; accelerated *and* advanced healing; increased speed, strength, reflexes, and agility; and absolute determination (which prevents them from being mentally affected in most cases, including from consciousness-altering attacks, such as phasarchement discharges). This mode does not last long, and forktires will require a few days off to recharge. Forktires also have: one of the greatest biting strengths of any genera; naturally-proficient predator skills and enhanced sense for blood; and teeth regeneration.

## Wholoks (Rhincosapiens):

Wholoks are vaguely-humanoid carpet sharks that, on average, measure eleven metres in length, making them not only one of the biggest ichthyoids in the Caelverse but also one of the biggest sapient beings. One of the species even reaches an average length of thirteen metres, putting them into the rare 'colossal' category. Wholoks feature humanoid arms and webbed hands, but they do not have a humanoid torso; their lower bodies are also in tail form. Moreover, they possess dorsal fins, and their heads possess the filter-feeding mouths of their non-sapient ancestors. Wholoks are generally incredibly friendly to species of other genera, and they will go out of their way to provide help to those in need. Although they are not aggressive on average, they will defend themselves and others, but they do not normally seek out opportunities for justice that involve violence. Overall, due to their mere presence, they make the oceans a much safer place. They occasionally conduct trade with land-dwelling species through underwater trade networks, but other than this, there is very little interaction with land dwellers, unless in the ocean. Their shared genus attributes and abilities include: enormous strength (due to their size); partial fin and limb regeneration; and eye protection (from *dermal denticles* – teeth on the surface of the eyes) and retraction.

## Hestens (Aquahippoesse):

Hestens are bisectional-humanoid seahorses that, on average, measure 180 centimetres in length. Although they have a traditional seahorse tail from their ancestors, their upper bodies are somewhat humanoid, each featuring humanoid arms and webbed hands. Nevertheless, they still retain their ancestral outer skeleton, and their faces have long snouts. As with non-sapient seahorses, they swim upright using their dorsal fin. Hestens are one of the most common ichthyoids in the Caelverse. They have established massive infrastructure in the oceans and are responsible for much trade not only between other ichthyoids but also land-dwelling beings. They are also renowned for their flamboyant fashions and amazing architecture. In addition, they are some of the greatest writers and dramatists in the oceans. With their luxurious lifestyles, it is no wonder as to why they are great cultural exporters.

Generally, 421astens are friendly with species of other genera, and they typically avoid violent confrontations unless they are within fortified groups. Most actually enjoy working with mages – so much so that they prefer it over dealing with many other ichthyoids. In fact, many mages find 421astens to be more fascinating than most other species in the oceans, so there is a special relationship between the two. There is some non-hostile rivalry between 421astens and delphars for dominance in the oceans, but 421astens are normally the more submissive and diplomatic of the two, attempting to resort to the best compromises whenever troubles do occur. If 421astens were to suddenly disappear, it is possible that the oceanic market would collapse (but it could still possibly rebuild afterwards). Their shared genus attributes and abilities include: superb formation swimming (that aids in various goals such as defence, construction, or performance); tail prehensility; and, excellent camouflage and stealth skills.

## Leosists (Pterovulgares):

Leosists are bisectional-humanoid lionfish that, on average, measure 170 centimetres in length. Apart from their many rays and venomous spines, their upper bodies have humanoid arms and webbed hands. Due to the existence of their torsos, their bodily structure appears quite different to non-sapient lionfish, and they have longer tails. Nonetheless, their faces still appear very much like non-sapient fish, and if it were not for this, many non-ichthyoid species would find them amazingly attractive. Fully integrated into civilization, leosists are a common sight in the Caelverse's oceans, where they can be seen in many oceanic multispecial zones. They are generally sociable, but they are known for having a bullying streak, picking on lesser beings than themselves, generally with legal or lowkey threats. For this reason, they are generally only on neutral terms with most other beings, but their social standing is enough for others to deal with them.

Typically, leosists try to hustle their way into various property markets in the oceans' multispecieal zones and dominate them, but they normally get penalized for their actions. Mages normally do not bother doing business with them, as they find leosists to be too annoying and deceptive. Leosists are also known for dodgy practices and products, but they are also capable of producing many goods and services that species of other genera do not produce (at least in large quantities); and so, leosists will not, on the whole, be going out of business in the oceans. Their shared genus attributes and abilities include: powerful venom generation; needle protrusion and firing; and extreme cunning.

## Chinchornas (Pegasoperarius):

Chinchornas are vaguely-humanoid seamoths that, on average, measure 120 centi-metres in length/height. Their only humanoid features are their arms and webbed hands; and while they do have a torso, it does not resemble a humanoid shape. Chinchornas do not swim like typical ichthyoids and, instead, walk on the ground. However, they are not amphibious, so they remain in the oceans. Depending on the task, they switch between walking on all fours to using just their two legs to become bipedal. Due to the inability of chinchornas to swim (along with a lack of special abilities to defend themselves), oceanic beings have exploited this and used chinchornas for various labour that is almost akin to slavery.

In recent years, mages have tried to stop this problem, but it remains hard to properly regulate the oceans. Even during the CME, mages did not enslave chinchornas but most likely would have enslaved them had the opportunity arose as well, as they make for great labourers. Chinchornas are not dumb – they just have an unfortunate set of circumstances. Despite false ideas about them, they are not xenophobic; instead, their cultures tend to revolve around their own kind, whichh they view as a means to strengthen their communities. Besides general ichthyoid abilities like the ability to breathe underwater, the genus itself does not possess any special abilities. However, some species within the genus do possess some interesting abilities, such as electricity generation and the ability to jump very high.

## Tinxers (Lophioid):

Tinxers are bisectional-humanoid anglerfish that, on average, measure two metres in length. Unlike their non-sapient ancestors, tinxers have much smaller heads – which are more humanoid – in proportional shape and size to their bodies. They also feature a torso with humanoid arms and webbed hands, and their tails are longer. The majority of species in the genus (regardless of gender) have three *escae* (that is, bioluminescent lights in fin rays that emerge from the heads), which are not produced by bacterial symbionts but by the tinxers themselves. Still, tinxers do possess symbionts that can alter the colour and brightness of the luminescence. Unlike certain types of non-sapient anglerfish, tinxers do not exhibit any major sexual dimorphism, where the males are essentially parasites feeding off of the females.

Most species of other genera find tinxers to have a frightening appearance, as if looking like monsters (mutants). However, tinxers are not a mutant species – although, quite a few become mutated potentially due to an unknown substance they encounter in the depths of the oceans. Tinxers are one of the very few sapient beings that dwell in the deep ocean, and they prefer living in such places for a variety of reasons. They are also ecologically adapted to such oceanic levels and have established many settlements in those areas. Most tinxers were not discovered during the days of the CME, and first contact with many of the species afterwards were hostile; but these hostilities settled quickly, and great caution followed before they opened to the mages. Besides their off-putting appearance, tinxers simply do not like the cultures of most other ichthyoids. This also means that there is less competition for them, which they greatly prefer. Tinxers still trade with other beings, providing goods and resources not found anywhere else, but they are well known for being extremely grouchy.

Because most beings in the Caelverse do not even visit such depths in the oceans, the many claims that tinxers make are unverified. Tinxers state that without them, horrible beasts and powers dwelling deep in the oceans would be unleashed upon all living beings. It is the tinxers, so they say, that defend everyone and fight the true great evils of the Caelverse. Of course, these claims have always sparked great interest from mages, who have had to investigate and physically explore such depths to confirm the stories. However, tinxers typically make one excuse after another as to why the 'great evils of the ocean depths' never appear when the mages investigate. Tinxers typically resent the mages for their disbelief and have threatened on many occasions that they will no longer defend everyone; but these threats never occur, and tinxers continue to reportedly defend against great evils. Still, some of their milder claims have been verified, and tinxers actually do fight quite a few beasts and other sapient beings at such depths. Once in a while, a new type of extraordinary species will emerge, but nothing of the leviathan levels tinxers over-exaggeratingly purport. Their shared genus attributes and abilities include: bioluminescence (that can be used for luring other beings into traps); pressure resistance; and fear inducement.

## Finieks (Cyprisapienoid):

Finieks are bisectional-humanoid carp that, on average, measure 150 centimetres in length. Different from their non-sapient ancestors, finieks feature a torso with humanoid arms and webbed hands, and their tails are proportionally longer. Their facial structure still appears similar to their carp ancestors, and their colours vary greatly per species. Finieks are very common throughout the Caelverse and are seen in many aquatic multispecieal zones. While they do appear as if an ordinary genus, they are not without a grand speciality, which involves forming into a collectic heterogenic. Unlike most schools of non-sapient fish, finieks can form fully-fledged collective minds when they form schools together. In such a state, they are capable of performing and producing many different feats. Finieks will form into collectics usually about once per week, but they form otherwise when in danger, for special tasks, or even for festivities. They are generally very sociable, but they do enjoy being by themselves as well in their own C zones.

But more interestingly, when in collectic form, there is a *chance* that they can turn into a heterogenic fusionic – a single entity of greater power. This ability forms at a greater probability chance rate than most species of other genera, and so, finieks are exceptional in this regard. Still, since this is chance based, this does not always occur, but the chances increase if the finieks are mature and advanced or if there is another special reason boosting the potential. Typically, the fusionic will be smaller than the collectic, but its power will be greater, granting both physical strength and potentially other abilities of varying nature, too. For the most part, finieks work well with species of other genera (both other ichthyoids and land dwellers when they trade in underwater networks), and they are one of the backbones of the many oceans due to their productivity. Their shared genus attributes and abilities include: turning into collectic and fusionic heterogenics, which enable other potential powers; and magnetoreception.

## 4.3.3.5: Amphibinoids:

Amphibinoids are sometimes mistaken for reptilians or ichthyoids. While not as common and populous as mammalians, reptilians, and arthropoids, amphibinoids are still common throughout the Caelverse. Nevertheless, their distribution is limited, as they are generally tied to wet locations, and they loathe arid climates. If mammalians were not the dominant force in the Caelverse, amphibinoids (despite their generally-functional societies) probably would not come to power. In contrast to most other morphtypes, amphibinoids use a mix of different types of technologies, so some are grown in water, while others are built (that is, the same as other land-dwelling beings). Wetware is also a more specific type of technology typically used. As a result, amphibinoids are more adaptable in certain ways. There is a general mistake made between marking those who are *amphibious* with those that are *amphibinoids*. For example, humans can live in water and can, in practice, be *amphibious*, but they would not, and are not, amphibinoids. There are certain morphological requirements to being categorized as an amphibinoid, such as skin and breathing traits. Major, common, or notable sapient amphibinoid genera include:

## Macuni (Neobatrachduplicmanu):

Macuni are vaguely-humanoid/non-humanoid frogs that have two sets of arms and hands. They normally walk only on two hands from the arms that are on the sides of their upper torsos, while their other set of hands (on arms where humanoid legs would normally be attached) hang in the air and are used for handling objects and performing various tasks. While this has drastically altered the way they jump, they are still able to jump well. It is unknown how macuni developed this trait, but it is theorized that due to their ability to create and consume their own psychedelic compounds, they began hallucinating and fell back on their upper arms while kicking or playing with whatever they saw in the air with their hind legs. This, in turn, allowed them to strengthen their upper arms while having greater tool performance with their hind legs. The average species in the genus measures at roughly 140 centimetres in length, and their colours vary greatly. As with their ancestors, macuni go through a meta-morphosis cycle, where they are first born in water. Adults lose their gills but can still breathe in water for a while through their skin, which needs to remain moist.

The CME enslaved macuni when they were still in their tribal phase, although it took a while for mages to figure out what work macuni could perform. It turned out that macuni were very capable at odd mechanical work, but the problem was that they needed to keep their skins moist, which was bad in such a role with grimy equipment. Protection gear was provided until other jobs became available. In the present day, macuni and mages are cordial with one another. Many macuni are seen in assorted fields, especially comedy. Due to their ability to naturally create psychedelics and distribute them, macuni are banned from certain professions and areas because they can sell or freely provide such substances to others. Even in a simple context where live comedic performances are allowed, strict protocols are imposed on macuni and eventgoers. Accordingly, many species of other genera love macuni and resent the CGM for the restrictions; but it is not just mages who impose such restrictions. Still, macuni cannot mass produce psychedelics individually from their own bodies, so the majority of drugs sold are grown or manufactured. Their shared genus attributes and abilities include: psychedelic drug generation; tongue projection; excellent jumping heights and lengths; aquatic adaptation; and temporary water breathing.

## Trofors (Bufovir):

Trofors are relatively-humanoid, bipedal toads that have an average height of 200 centimetres. Their bodies are normally covered in many warts and similar features, but they are able to change colours to camouflage themselves. Trofors are both venomous and poisonous, with the poison being released into the air. When certain susceptible beings breathe in the poisons, it sends them into a hypnotic trance that leaves them vulnerable to suggestions and commands. Around half of the species in the genus are hostile to the majority of species in the Caelverse, and the other half are non-hostile, but the latter are still reclusive and isolated in their C zones.

In the past, the CME began genociding the hostile trofors, and the GCM continues to this day trying to exterminate them due to their unwillingness to cease hostilities. Mages used some of the enslaved peaceful trofors to track hostile trofors, as it was hard for mages to detect the hostiles, who were (and are) able to obscure etheric fields around themselves (despite not being psychic), which is indirectly achieved via the hypnotic poisons. In addition, mages used (and still use) some of the peaceful trofors to interrogate hostile ones. Their shared genus attributes and abilities include: hypnosis via poison generation (which includes default etheric field manipulations); venom generation; colour change (which allows them to camouflage themselves); tongue projection; aquatic adaptation; and temporary water breathing.

## Sillianids (Cattusamphibivir):

Sillianids are relatively-humanoid, bipedal amphibinoids with a catfish ancestral history. Now amphibians rather than fish, sillianids have an average height of 180 centimetres. Possessing proper arms, hands, legs, and feet, they still have a tail, while most species have whiskers. Moreover, they still possess gills, but these are not sufficient enough for sillianids to live underwater for more than two days; therefore, sillianids live primarily on land. Overall, they still appear very much like fish, but they are indeed amphibinoids, not just amphibious. Under the CME, sillianids were directly used mostly for aquatic agriculture. In the present day, they have positive relations with most beings of other genera, and they continue to work primarily in aquatic agriculture, in addition to other jobs in freshwater systems. Coupled with platinooks, they are essential for their roles in freshwater systems. Due to their amiable nature and lack of major negative cultural issues, sillianids have managed to create harmonious societies for themselves, and their populations are enormous across the Caelverse, with many seen in multispecieal zones. Their shared genus attributes and abilities include: proficient swimming abilities; aquatic adaptation; and temporary water breathing.

## Veranaks (Pistris<u>amphibivir</u>):

Veranaks are relatively-humanoid, bipedal amphibinoids with a shark ancestral history. Categorized as amphibians due to their now-amphibian (though tough) skin, veranaks live both on land and in water. While they have an erect, relatively-humanoid torso featuring humanoid arms and legs (with respectively clawed and webbed feet and hands), they still have a long tail with a fin on the end. The average height of those in the genus is also 190 centimetres. Their heads normally appear rather sharp, and their profiles appear sort of like a pickaxe. Most veranaks retain slim but athletic bodies due to their disciplined and para-militaristic (more so martial) existences, but they nonetheless cooperate with species of other genera. One of their species was almost genocided during the time of the CME, but that species eventually submitted, and their hostilities were reduced. In the modern context, veranaks can be found in many multispecieal zones, and they are usually employed in dangerous fields requiring great discipline. Mages tend to hire them to clear out certain areas of non-mage pests, rogues, mercenaries, gangs, and other hostiles when the mages do not have the time and numbers themselves to perform such actions.

Veranaks would have a large population (given their spread across the Caelverse), but they have a general tendency to only raise two children; over time, their birth rates fluctuate from slightly above to slightly below replacement levels. One species, in particular (volictuns), tend to partake in many types of dangerous and combative sports, which, on average, results in a high death rate. Their shared genus attributes and abilities include: proficient swimming abilities; aquatic adaptation; and temporary water breathing. They also have a berserker mode, which temporarily grants: pain suppression; unlimited and non-damaging adrenaline; super-enhanced senses (which also includes heightened blood sense, which is akin to telescopic thermoreception vision); supreme combat efficiency; accelerated *and* advanced healing; increased speed, strength, reflexes, and agility; and absolute determination (which prevents them from being mentally affected in most cases, including from consciousness-altering attacks, such phasarchement discharges).

## Salarans (Feminahomoamphibium):

Salarans are relatively-humanoid, bipedal amphibinoids that have an average height of 180 centimetres. Despite having strikingly-similar faces to humans, salarans are not part of – or even close to – the human genus. The main obvious differences between salarans and humans are the two tentacles appearing from their heads in addition to their smooth amphibian skin and lack of hair. They are also a mono-*gendered* genus (but they are still *hermaphrodites* – beings that have both male and female reproductive organs), with all species physically *appearing* female. Although they possess human-appearing 'breasts' via visual convergent evolution, these are actually reproductive glands that possess the sperm for insemination during their unusual sexual intercourse. Salarans mainly live on land, but they are adapted for wet environments and can breathe underwater for a few hours before needing to return to the surface for adequate oxygen. They are very common throughout the Caelverse and occupy many multi-specieal zones while cooperating with all sorts of different types of beings. The CME did enslave salarans in the past, but today, salarans do not hold great resentment, and they are normally cordial with mages.

Although many males from species of other genera sexually desire salarans, the majority of salarans are only attracted to the female form, leading to massive disapp-ointment. However, since salarans still have vaginas – and that a fair few assume a submissive role during intercourse – there is still a certain amount that do like physical encounters with males of other genera. As a result, many perform sex work. Still, salarans are generally intelligent, and they work in assorted fields as well. Salarans are also one of the few beings who can 'easily' fuse to become heterogenic altermorphics. Normally to achieve this result, they need to have sexual intercourse (generally from another of their own species, but this is not necessary), reaching ecstatic heights in a fully-planned ritual or similar event.

Because of the actions that can be taken as an altermorphic, this has led to a more honest society (as one may be unsure if they are talking to one or two people). Still, there are particular rules imposed on salarans regarding their altermorphic forms, but it is not like this is a major problem, as they do not get to transform all the time, as it is normally only during lunapexes. Also, when in altermorphic form, salarans and other species can learn a lot from one another, but this can lead to identity issues, so salaran governments emphasize that salarans should only turn into heterogenics with another of their species. Their shared genus attributes and abilities include: a higher chance to become an altermorphic than species of other genera; proficient swimming abilities; aquatic adaptation; and temporary water breathing.

## 4.3.3.6: Arthropoids:

A large percentage of the entities in the Caelverse (just in terms of the overall number of individual beings) are arthropoids, but a large percentage of this figure actually applies to non-sapient and semi-sapient arthropoids. Most sapient arthropoids are insectoids, followed by malacostracoids, and then arachnoids. There are calls to break apart the arthropoid morphtype into the said categories (and more), but most non-arthropoids find 'arthropoid' to be a sufficient grouping itself for general identification.

In all categories, most (but not all) arthropoids are *socially* split into two *main* types: collectivists and individualists. Collectivist arthropoids exist in hiveminds (usually in a *eusocial* manner – that is, they feature distinct classes with distinct working and reproductive roles) and do not share the same ideals as most other species. Nevertheless, they are at least aware that a pure-hivemind system would not work for other species, so they do not proselytize their unique way of life. While on the surface, it may seem like their societies are devoid of art, for example, this is not the case. Instead, their art is fundamentally tied in with their productivity, so musical acts are performed *whilst* working. Collectivist arthropoids exist on all worlds (bar C6 ones), and they range from primitive orders to the technologically advanced.

Individualists, on the other hand, vary in technological usage. There are *social individualists* who do not necessarily shun social activities, but they do not group with their own kind, nor others, either. These types can be found in multispecieal zones, living in the cities, with some viewing themselves as an unorganized, non-structural 'union of individuals', seeing society itself as being nothing more than a spook (an illusion in the mind). For *isolationist individualists*, conversely, many live in reserve zones that the CGM has set up for protection. Due to these extreme social circumstances, arthropoids of most kinds tend not to mix with other morphtypes. This is further increased with the issue that most species of other morphtypes have a general aesthetic and cultural disgust for arthropoids. Usually, the only time many (but not all) arthropoids will be seen in multispecies zones is due to temporary diplomacy, trade, or extreme curiosity. Arthropoids are also known to use large amounts of wetware – technology that is grown from their own or similar biological tissue. In some cases, the wetware is grown on and in the arthropoid bodies and not just in facilities. While ichthyoids grow their technology, its nature is very different to the wetware that most arthropoids use. Major, common, or notable sapient arthropoid genera include:

### Terazars (Formidoinductus):

Terazars are non-humanoid, bipedal arthropoids that have an average height of 220 centimetres. As an anomaly, there no signs of other non-sapient, lower lifeforms from which there could have been evolutionary roots for terazars. In fact, they are not actually part of the arthropod phylum in the STS. Still, they have enough particular morphological features to be placed into the arthropoid morphtype. All three terazar species possess triangular heads, with their eyes sitting below the edges in slits that are able to move around the entire head (within the slits). Venomous pincers also feature on their faces, while thousands of small, regenerative antennae cover their necks as well. Their forearms are razor-sharp mantis-like blades, while the middle arms are for handling tools and performing tasks. There are holes all over their bodies, which periodically open and close to release gases that build up from a biolumin-escent gooey acid that can be used to shoot at targets. Although some mutants possess such a feature, the type terazars have is of a different nature. The gooey acid initially clings to victims before extracting nutrients while burning the victim's skin. After extraction, terazars then either consume the diffused goo or they collect it and return it to their colony. Their exoskeletons are extremely tough and are normally black with a structurally-created green metallic shine. Oddly, they also feature two tails with rotatable, retractable hooks that look like grappling hooks.

Terazars are eusocial, and they have both a king and queen for different tasks; the queen is required for reproduction, while the king is for maintaining order, expanding territories, and even fighting on the battlefield – which enhances the fighting powers of terazars nearby. Some theories suggest that terazars are from another Caelverse cycle, while others propose another dimension. From the interrogations mages have conducted on terazars over the centuries, it turns out that the terazars are unaware of any such phenomenon; and, while they do not *know* their actual origins, terazars believe they emerged around the same time as mages did in the Caelverse. Terazars are totally hostile to all other species outside of the genus, and the CME accordingly began a total war with them, driving terazars deep into the abyssal levels of various planet classes. Even today, their hostility is relentless, so the CGM continues battling terazars. Despite their incredible aggression, terazars are indeed fully sapient and highly intelligent. Each terazar species is unhostile to one another due to the shared existential crisis they face, but generally, they keep themselves separated.

To this day, terazars have managed to avoid detection. This is possible because they are able to emit psychic energies that scramble mage psychics from locating their positions. As such, mages are unsure as to the terazar strength and numbers, along with material and technological accumulation and production. About once every ten years, terazars launch a few small skirmish attacks on mages and species of other genera across the Caelverse. It is assumed that these attacks are for intel and that they are building forces in the meantime. Proper artworks have not been documented, but it is theorized that their state propaganda and symbols act as a form of art amongst their kind. Their *known* shared genus attributes and abilities include: psychic powers; telepathy between species (but not genus) members; superior senses; great strength; gooey acid generation; potential 360-degree eyesight; and limb and tail regeneration.

## Beesids (Apinarma):

Beesids are vaguely-humanoid, bipedal honey bees that have an average height of forty centimetres. Unlike their non-sapient ancestors, beesids have erect bodies with arms and hands. Beesids are also part of a hive mind with a distinct hierarchy, which makes them very different to most sapient beings in the Caelverse – apart from other arthropoids. Mages found great use for them during the time of the CME, as they were smarter than non-sapient bees yet could produce more food (both quantity and variety), and they were able to perform many other tasks. In the modern context, beesids are still highly sought after for their services and the products they produce, even though they do not always directly produce goods themselves. That is, beesids still use non-sapient bees to help them in production – not because they lack the ability to produce honey products themselves but, instead, due to their efficient farming practices. Beesids are so efficient that mages have outsourced most honey-related production and responsibilities to beesids.

Some theorists claim that without beesids, the entire CGM would collapse, but these theories are unproven. Nevertheless, if all trade with beesids were to *suddenly* halt, it would drastically alter supply chains. Beesids are normally friendly with species of other genera, but most of the time, they are found either within their hives in C zones or in the midst of temporarily trading in multispecieal zones. Their shared genus attributes and abilities include: their double-edged, venomous stinging (with their stinger being retractable); advanced agility and reflexes; enhanced vision, which includes UV perception; navigation skills; wall-crawling; vibration sense and emission; seismic sense, enabling one to sense particular vibrations in the ground; lunglessness (that is, they do not need as much oxygen in order to survive); and vacuum resistance (so in a vacuum like space, they will not perish instantly).

## Manticks (Mantinoid):

Manticks are non-humanoid, bipedal mantids with an average height of 150 centimetres. Of course, they display great sexual dimorphism, with males having an average height of 120 centimetres, while the females measure at an average of 180 centimetres. Manticks are highly-intelligent, and while they are social, they are nonetheless somewhat individualistic. Due to their unusual dimorphism, manticks live in a matriarchy – one, however, not ruled by a biologically-distinct, eusocial queen. Many mages loathed manticks during the time of the CME and considered genociding all of them. However, since manticks were not warring against the mages, and that the CME was too preoccupied with other endeavours, that proposed plan never happened. Even today, manticks are normally disliked by many species of other genera, but there are some people that are fascinated with them and think that manticks are wonderful beings. Such claims include that manticks are honourable, hard-working, intelligent, and have a unique and odd sense of humour.

Some groups of people in the Caelverse still call for the extermination of manticks due to the terrible cultural and personal practices that manticks still perform to this day. Namely, females still unnecessarily cannibalize their male partners prior to, during, and after sexual encounters. Many mantick matriarchies have banned the 'custom' in their C zones, but some allow and even endorse it. Of those that have banned it, the authorities tend to ignore or even hide such criminal acts. The major reason that prosecuted female manticks claim for their actions is that they could not help themselves due to their biologically-determined genetics – but many opponents (both manticks and other species) refute this claim.

Unless there is an existential threat to mages and/or other species, genocide has since been prohibited, and so, the mages continue to allow manticks to live in their societies. Still, manticks (especially those from C zones that allow the custom) are banned in many places around the Caelverse outside mantick territory – apart from certain multispecieal zones at certain times. Despite their banning, mages still employ some manticks in certain research positions, so long as they keep their distance (should they be working in the same areas as mages). Other less extreme measures to solve the issue include traditional eugenics (to weed out the biologically-predisposed or pre-determined cannibals from the gene pool), genetic modification, or simply education or more money. There are people who claim that manticks are just putting on a clever illusory show and that they are the true rulers of the Caelverse; of course, there is no evidence for such claims. Their shared genus attributes and abilities include: flight; shedding; literal mantis-blade arms that can be used for multiple purposes (normally combat); very high intelligence; and being naturally great martial artists and meditators (despite this being a trope, it is actually true).

### Beautiflies (Nymphoarma):

Beautiflies are relatively-humanoid, bipedal butterflies that have an average height of 150 centimetres. Like their butterfly ancestors, beautiflies have a four-stage lifecycle, which consists of: larvae, caterpillar, cocoon, and adult, completing the metamorphosis. Beautifly caterpillars are only semi-sapient, but they do remember practically everything they learn in that stage. Beautiflies consist of an array of colours depending on the species, and they are even more diverse than most non-sapient butterfly genera. Moreover, their erect bodies also feature arms and hands (with one species having 'mantis blades'). Also depending on the species, some have hairy bodies, while others do not; but in all cases, their limbs are proportionally thicker compared to non-sapient butterflies and, thus, appear more humanoid. Under the CME, beautiflies were mostly taxed rather than used directly for labour. Mages had no issues with beautiflies during the empire, and today they both have positive relations with one another. Beautiflies are often friendly and harmless (at least physically) and are common throughout the Caelverse, where they can be seen in many multispecieal zones. They are also one of the few arthropoid genera that do not fall directly either as collectivists or individualists. In multispecieal zones, beautiflies today are normally employed in the arts, and they are extremely-big cultural exporters. Their shared genus abilities include: flight; and strong pheromone generation.

## Scarbens (Scarabvastumsatietas):

Scarbens are vaguely-humanoid, bipedal scarabs that have an average height of 130 centimetres. They feature various types of horns on their heads, with one species completely lacking horns. Most species are either black or orange, or they produce a structurally-created metallic shine of various colours. Scarbens are some of the strongest beings in the Caelverse, with one species being compared to the rhichons due to their rhinoceros-like horns. Various sporting competitions are held between rhichons and scarbens, too. During the time of the CME, some of the enslaved scarbens managed to set up voluntary fighting arenas with the enslaved rhicons as a form of entertainment. Scarbens of today are proud of their many daring accomplishments. Despite their pride, scarbens are also friendly to species of other genera, and most species do not have much of an issue with scarbens, other than for the fact that scarbens feed almost entirely on faeces, which scarbens absolutely love.

So long as most people do not witness their eating practices, they are on good terms with scarbens. Strangely, scarbens do not smell of faeces, except for the first few moments after eating their meals. Scarbens enjoy faeces from a variety of beings, including that of mages. For this reason, many waste disposal plants either connect directly to scarben zones or scarbens enter non-scarben territory to collect excrement. This mutual exchange is extremely beneficial for civilization as a whole, and so naturally, mages appreciate their contributions – despite the easiness of merely eating products. Since food is abundant and cheap for scarbens, this allows them more opportunities to focus on other endeavours. Of course, a premium is paid for high-quality faeces that come from beings consuming all-organic diets that lack medications and harsh chemicals. Their shared genus attributes and abilities include: supreme strength; tough exoskeletons; faeces consumption; and temporary flight.

## Roachites (Blattioid):

Roachites are vaguely-humanoid, bipedal cockroaches that have an average height of 120 centimetres after moulting several times before their metamorphosis into adulthood is complete. Roachites are considered one of the most detestable genera, and they are accordingly banned from most zones apart from certain multispecieal zones at certain times for travelling purposes. It does not help their reputation that they also practice cannibalism of the *already* dead – but not the living. The mages found no special use for them during the time of the CME, and due to their disgust, the mages began genociding roachites before initially retiring the pursuit due to what they considered was a waste of resources. That is, the roachites were not a threat until it was realized that they were spreading disease. At that point, the genocide restarted, but the roachites were very crafty in hiding and maintaining societies underground. The mages then quarantined many areas and cleared a lot of diseases, and by the time the roachites were out of sight, fewer resources were put towards the genocide as the empire's resources thinned.

When the empire collapsed, the roachites returned to the surface, but they kept a low profile. Now that genocide is prohibited in most circumstances, mages allow roachites to thrive in their own C zones. Many roachites do hold resentment for what happened in the past (along with how most people continue to perceive them), but they remain hospitable with mages when they interact. Roachites do, however, have major issues with mutation, but these issues are resolved internally within roachite C zones, as they themselves do not wish to deal with potential monsters emerging. Some roachites solve the issue with cannibalism, but such a practice is illegal for certain, living mutants; it is, moreover, ill-advised due to what is believed to be a possible spread of mutation. Roachites are another example of neither falling into the collectivist nor individualist types. They are not primitive, and, in fact, live in technologically-developed cities, but nearly all of their cities *appear* as if trash heaps. Their shared genus attributes and abilities include: limb regeneration; flight; disease resistance (but not against M gene mutations); fast speed; squeezability; radiation resistance; extreme pressure resistance (they can withstand a force of 300 times their body weight); hardiness; and, they possess an optional putrefying odour that is used for multiple purposes (such as defence).

### Anvims (Formicivitas):

Anvims are relatively-humanoid, bipedal ants that have an average height of ninety centimetres. They have almost similar features to non-sapient ants and are accordingly sometimes mistaken for giant (non-sapient) ants that are around the same size – especially when anvims switch to crawling on all six limbs. Like non-sapient ants, anvims are eusocial and extremely productive; and while mages did not conquer them *all* during the years of the CME (as many anvims were able to hide underground), of those that did directly serve the empire, the slavery helped with forming many underground networks and systems (some of which are used even today), and their productivity was almost unmatched. Only one quarter of the species in the genus lived – and continue to live – aboveground, so the CME directly used the aboveground species for other purposes. Anvims cooperate – and are cordial – with mages today, but they are not always welcoming of all species of other genera.

In the modern context, individual anvims are typically not employed as anvims and, instead, work as collectives, which means that when mages or other species require their talents in engineering, it is usually for large-scale projects that a whole colony sets to work on. Anvims have a natural tendency to expand territory, but the CGM limits the expansion of their C zones. Accordingly, anvims have in the recent past worked around legislation by cooperating with other genera to gain access to their underground areas below their C zones in exchange for their labour. The CGM realized this issue and quickly halted the anvims, seeing where it could possibly lead. Anvims were not happy with the result, but they complied. Regardless of the limitations, anvims are greatly spread across the Caelverse. A few of the species are *polygynous*, so they can be seen having mixed colonies with multiple queens, while the other species are *monogynous* and only stick to their own colonies with a single queen. Anvims are not as proportionally strong as small, non-sapient ants, yet they are still exceptionally strong. Their shared genus attributes and abilities include: wallcrawling; the ability to work as a loose heterogenic collective; pheromone communication and manipulation; excellent strength; unparalleled productivity; and extreme endurance.

## Stomorchs (Stomatoid):

Stomorchs are vaguely-humanoid to non-humanoid stomatopods (that is, they are crustaceans that are similar to, but not the same as, shrimp), and they have an average length of two metres. They are only considered vaguely humanoid due to having a raised torso area that non-sapient stomatopods lack, in addition to having arms and hands. Otherwise, they appear mostly the same as other stomatopods. Stomorchs are yet another arthropoid genus that is totally hostile to anything outside of their kind. Unlike terazars, stomorchs are not eusocial and are quite individualistic. They do have civilization, however, which involves small, decentralized networks working to carve out tunnels in underground caves in the oceans. They are capable of walking on land, but they can only survive out of water for about a day before dying, and they much prefer the ocean, anyway.

The CME knew of their existence in the past, but mages seldom encountered them until after the empire fell. Given the secluded nature of stomorch locations, mages find it difficult hunting them down and exterminating them; but since stomorchs do not pose a major known threat due to infrequent attacks, mages do not focus too much of their resources on the task of extermination. That is, while stomorchs are highly hostile, they do not spend time pursuing *mages* and, instead, focus their attention on other ocean life. Since stomorchs are bigger than their ancestors, their power proportional to their size has decreased, but they are nonetheless more powerful without considering scaling. Very little is known about their culture and why exactly they are hostile. Their known shared genus attributes and abilities include: supremely-powerful punches and strikes; complex vision (due to more photoreceptor cells, enabling sight of generally-unseeable colours); independent eye movement (each eye is free to move 180 degrees in any direction of its original axis); and extreme speed when darting.

## Cratisks (Brachyvirs):

Cratisks are relatively-humanoid, bipedal crabs that have an average height of 180 centimetres. The size of their claws varies greatly per species; however, all have a set of humanoid arms and hands. The CME managed to enslave many, but not all, cratisks in the past, and most of the work that cratisks had to perform was marine related. In the modern day, cratisks have positive relations with mages. Half the species are social, and the other half remain aloof and mysterious, barely interacting with other species. They are also another example of a genus that is neither collectivist nor individualistic. Even though some species remain aloof, they generally love to play pranks on other species and scare them. Their work is important to the overall economy, as they help bridge gaps between oceanic and land trade; and they aid with many other coastal activities, which have positive externalities on the economy. Ultimately, cratisks require living in water, but they can stay outside of water for a few hours at a time before needing to breathe oxygen through water again. Their shared genus attributes and abilities include: incredibly-tough armour; shedding; limb regeneration; and strong pincers (which can be used even for routine tasks such as lifting cargo).

## Blackvores (Lactrodectumbustus):

Blackvores are bisectionally-humanoid spiders that have an average length of 155 centimetres. While they have upright torso with arms and hands, their lower bodies are of a pure spider form. Blackvores are highly sexually dimorphic, with females averaging around 190 centimetres, while males are about 120 centimetres. The females of most species are black with various stripes, while the males vary in colour, but most are still normally black as well. Many beings across the Caelverse have called for either the complete genocide of blackvores or at least the introduction of a eugenic program, genetic engineering, or forced re-education. This is due to a host of reasons, but mainly it is due to the sexual cannibalism of females eating the males. Although individualistic, blackvores do have societies, but these are still ultimately non-eusocial matriarchies. Most species outside the genus are also disgusted by them, refraining from allowing them to enter their C zones. As a result, blackvores hold a strong resentment and typically hate species of other genera. However, they do comply with CGM regulations so long as they are not too intrusive – which they are not – and rarely do they even bother to break the rules and leave their C zones.

Very little trade is conducted between blackvores and species of other genera, but blackvores do specialize in making certain goods (such as the silk from their webs), which they use to gain wealth from outside their C zones. The CME in the past never enslaved blackvores with direct labour, taxing them instead. Since they had semi-primitive societies during the CME, normally products like their silk were simply taken. Although they are not great cultural exporters, interestingly, mages and species of other genera feature blackvores in many artworks – with both positive and negative portrayals. There are illegal sporting games involving beings of various genera that attempt to infiltrate blackvore territories and see how long they can last while under certain conditions. When caught, there are cases where the infiltrating people die, and there is not too much the mage authorities can do to catch the murderers. Their shared genus attributes and abilities include: web spinning (of special silk); wall-crawling; pheromone generation; enhanced senses; and venom generation.

## Arantras (Theraphosvir):

Arantras are relatively-humanoid, bipedal spiders that have an average height of 180 centimetres. Since they are bipedal, this means six of their limbs are arms, granting them the freedom to multitask with assorted tools. Arantras also possess the hairy and thick bodies that their tarantula ancestors had, and they still have big fangs and eight googly eyes. Their societies are neither collectivist nor individualistic, and they live in soft, de facto matriarchies, but this is simply due to natural development rather than force. The CME easily enslaved arantras in the past, making great direct use of their many arms. In the present day in multispecieal zones, arantras are employed in a range of jobs, but many revolve around their ability to do many things at once with their arms. Arantras normally have positive relations with beings of other genera, and they are a common sight throughout the Caelverse. They do not have the best eyesight, so they normally either work in darker areas, or they simply wear special eyewear to help them see. They happen to be giants in the eyewear industry, fashioning many styles. Their shared genus attributes and abilities include: web spinning; pheromone generation; enhanced senses (bar eyesight); venom generation; and, of course, multitasking with their six arms.

## Scorvers (Scorpioid):

Scorvers are relatively-humanoid bisectional scorpions that have an average height of 180 centimetres and length of 300 centimetres. With a scorpion lower half, scorvers have an upright torso that features humanoid arms and hands. Their faces, however, remain clearly that of a scorpion. They also have a normal scorpion tail with a venomous stinger. Mages genocided a few scorver species during the rule of the CME, and the remaining species fell in line and were used for various tasks – some of which included fighting against species that opposed the mages. While the scorvers loathed the enslavement, they realized they otherwise faced death, so they complied. Regardless, scorvers tend to like combat, and they were not on good terms with many species of other genera, anyway, so fighting them was a task that they were semi-comfortable with undertaking.

Today, scorvers normally remain isolated in their own C zones, as most species of other genera still do not like engaging with them. Most scorver species are at least active in keeping fit and well-trained for combat, should anything happen to the CGM, they say. In fact, there is an engrained belief in the many scorver cultures that the CGM will collapse soon (or one day) and that all hell will break loose. Therefore, scorvers have a strong 'prepping' culture. However, they do not believe that they will one day rule the Caelverse, seeing other beings as being more powerful than themselves. Their shared genus attributes and abilities include: shedding; rapid healing; limb (but not tail) regeneration; powerful pincer grips; venom generation; acid resistance; tail whipping; a tough exoskeleton; and superior durability.

## Millies (Diplopoid):

Millies are vaguely-humanoid/non-humanoid millipedes that have an average length of four metres. Despite their long length, they still, funnily enough, do not have thousands of legs. They are considered vaguely humanoid due to their arms and hands, in addition to having an erect torso structure (although, they still mostly move through tunnels on all of their limbs). Their faces also have more discernible features than their non-sapient counterparts. In conjunction with enslaved anvims in the past, the CME used millies to help build and maintain underground tunnels, along with utilizing them for transport of various goods and construction materials. Millies are generally friendly to mages in the modern context, but they prefer keeping to their own underground systems in their C zones. All millie species are herbivorous detritivores (that is, they eat dead plant matter), and sometimes mages will pay them to eat old debris that needs to be quickly removed. Millies are also cordial with most species of other genera, and they have mutualistic relationships with certain anvim species.

The only major issue that millies face when dealing with other beings is that sometimes people may mistake millies for giant non-sapient millipedes and centipedes – or even those of the sapient genus known as centruvons, who are hostile to every living being outside of their own kind. It is a myth that millies generally like battling centruvons; the reality is that millies hate unnecessary violence, and they prefer that mages engage in such battles. Still, some millies help mages in wars from the sidelines. While they do not export much art, many artworks can be found along underground tunnel walls. Their shared genus attributes and abilities include: quick and powerful burrowing; poison resistance; disease resistance; wall-crawling; seismic sense, enabling one to sense particular vibrations in the ground; defensive stink glands; long lifespans (up to 200 years); and, they have *tergite armour* (that is, they have strong segmented plates along the dorsal areas – on their backs), and so, when they coil up, they are hard to harm and kill.

## Centruvons (Chilopoid):

Centruvons are vaguely-humanoid centipedes that have an average length of four metres. They possess an erect-torso structure with arms and hands, but while they have many legs, they certainly are not in the hundreds. The CME never enslaved centruvons in the past because they were always completely hostile to every being other than themselves. Therefore, the CME began genociding them. Centruvons (nicknamed 'centies') posed a massive problem to mages due to being able to sink entire cities by destroying the foundational ground that buildings and infrastructure rested on. Accordingly, with the help of those from the millie genera, the CME mandated that all major cities were to build vast underground networks that were capable of defending against the centruvons. Of course, even the underground systems were subject to disasters, but since there were many lines of defence, rebuilding one or two system layers still protected mage and non-mage cities on the surface.

While centruvons do not possess a hivemind, they are quite collectivist, working together to bring down the mages and all other species. There was one centruvon species that actually did not wish to fight the mages, but it was, ironically, the other centruvon species that ganged up and exterminated them. As with the terazars, centruvons launch skirmish attacks and raids for intel and materials. Centruvons are not psychic like terazars, but they are able to mask their locations with psychic distortions. CGM intelligence suggests that centruvons must either have some advanced technology to distort etheric fields, or they actually *have* developed psychic abilities, which mages have not seen. What is known, however, is that centruvons do trade with other beings on the surface in black markets, and there are numerous cases of missing persons indicating that centruvons are also stealing people and using them for various purposes. Whilst they may not be as strong as terazars (as a collective force), they appear to be more aggressive. Their known shared genus attributes and abilities and attributes include: quick and powerful burrowing; wall-crawling; seismic sense, enabling one to sense particular vibrations in the ground; venom generation; powerful forcipule (pincer-like) bites; and, they have strong tergite armour on their backs (which is not as effective as millie armour, as there are big gaps between the multiple segments).

### 4.3.3.7: Molluscoids:

Molluscoids are an interesting collection of beings because, unlike amphibinoids that possess species that can live in water and on land, molluscoids tend to either live exclusively on land or in water. Aquatic molluscoids also have similar technologies as ichthyoids; that is, most of what they construct is actually grown and alive. Land-based molluscoids, on the other hand, use typical technologies that other land-dwelling beings use. As a whole, molluscoids certainly would not be able to rule the Caelverse if mages were not present, but there are some genera that would alone cement a grand place for themselves. Molluscoids are not comparatively as common as other morphtypes in the Caelverse, but they are not the least common either. There are calls to split the morphtype up between cephalopoids and other molluscoids, but this has not occurred. Major, common, or notable sapient molluscoid genera include:

### Ozakans (Octosummum):

Ozakans are non-humanoid octopuses that have an average length of 250 centimetres. Their entire bodies appear virtually like non-sapient octopuses, except the eyes appear distinguishably more intelligent. There is but one major exception physically: the tips of their limbs (which most people erroneously call tentacles) can *bifurcate* (divide and branch) and produce finger-like ends. This enables ozakans to handle certain tech-nologies in a manner non-sapient octopuses cannot. Ozakans are one of the most intelligent beings in the Caelverse, and their entire mindset seems very alien to most beings of other genera. Most ozakans lived deep in the oceans during the time of the CME, so mages had very little interaction with ozakans. Even in the present day, ozakans remain rather elusive to the mages and most species of other genera, with many of their established societies remaining hidden (that is, beyond granted C zones). Ozakans occasionally conduct trade with mages, but normally such transactions are swift and quiet, devoid of small talk. They are on neutral terms with delphars; and while delphars consider themselves to be the rulers of the seas, ozakans successfully ignore nearly all delphar demands.

Ozakans can walk on land, but it is uncomfortable and awkward for them, so they prefer to remain in the ocean. Plus, they cannot breathe air properly. When ozakans are in dangerous waters, most organisms intuitively know not to challenge ozakans. In addition, ozakans can emit powerful psychic fields that mentally affect others, intimidating them. It is theorized that ozakans hold more power than they claim in the oceans, but CGM intelligence services have not verified such ideas. In fact, some theories go so far as to suggest that ozakans exert influence on many beings on land, despite living deep within the oceans. Their shared genus attributes and abilities include: hyper intelligence; psychicism; telepathy between species members; pressure resistance; ink generation; elasticity; limb regeneration; multiple arms that can be simultaneously used for a variety of purposes; jet propulsion; powerful constriction; poison and venom generation; chromatophores that allow for colour change (and accordingly allow for camouflage and other purposes); a *somatosensory system* (a part of the nervous system), which allows for enhanced senses; and amazing suction abilities that can be used to trap foes or help climb walls.

## Sortherids (Octovirs):

Sortherids are vaguely-humanoid octopuses that have an average height of 190 centimetres. Unlike their ozakan counterparts, sortherids are land-based and use most of their traditional limbs as non-humanoid 'legs'. Sortherids, moreover, have a humanoid torso that features a set of two arms and hands. Their semi-humanoid-shaped 'skulls' have a set of four actual tentacles emerging from the mouth region, too. Like ozakans, sortherids are highly intelligent and psychic. They are capable of submerging in water for roughly six hours before needing to resurface for oxygen; and so, while they normally live on land, some sortherids remain close to the oceans and have infrastructure underwater. During the years of the CME, sortherids refused to submit to the mage empire, and the mages had to exterminate one of their species in order to enforce their will – which was no easy feat. The remaining sortherids decided to hide in air-filled caverns in the oceans, leaving behind massive infrastructure and material wealth that the mages requisitioned. As a result, not many sortherids were ever enslaved. When the empire fell, sortherids slowly returned to the surface, but many can still be found in the old caverns.

In the present day, sortherids are a semi common sight in multispecieal zones. Although typically aloof, sortherids are not as mysterious as ozakans. They tend to manage many trade networks, exerting a large influence on species of other genera – both at land and sea. CGM intelligence reports have revealed that sortherids have infiltrated many organizations and have sought to corrupt various processes to advance their own agendas. While mages are normally cordial with sortherids, the

CGM has recently cracked down on certain sortherid activity, limiting them from further influencing mage political institutions. Naturally, this has angered many sortherids, but many within their communities claim that such infiltrations are only orchestrated and conducted by a tiny handful of bad sortherids and that the majority only wish to conduct and mind their own business. Regardless of the truth, their reputations as a whole have been tarnished. Culturally, sortherids have made many stories, board games, and puzzles that other beings enjoy. Their shared genus attributes and abilities include: hyper intelligence; psychicism; telepathy between species members; pressure resistance; ink generation; elasticity; limb regeneration; jet propulsion (in water); powerful constriction; poison and venom generation; chromatophores that allow for colour change (and accordingly allow for camouflage and other purposes); a somatosensory system, which allows for enhanced senses; and amazing suction abilities that can be used to trap foes or help climb walls.

## Angelisors (Clionarma):

Angelisors are relatively-humanoid, bisectional sea angels (that is, sea slugs) that have an average length of 110 centimetres. Angelisors are hermaphrodites, so there is no sexual dimorphism. Each has arms that are separate from their 'wings' (flapping appendages known as *parapodia*); and their overall bioluminescent and translucent bodies appear like a combination of a ghost and an angel, both found respectively in fiction such as horror and fantasy. The only major feature taking this aesthetic away is the feeler-like tentacles at the tops of their heads, where their eyes are located. Despite this appearance, they are not considered the true 'ghosts of the seas' – a title belonging to a cnidarianoid genus called wispenids. In fact, angelisors have a strong mutual relationship with wispenids, acting as the front for most interactions with beings of other genera. This enables wispenids to retain their mystique and elusiveness.

Some theories suggest that wispenids actually mind control angelisors, who are nothing but empty husks. Still, angelisors are lively, charismatic beings, so this is unlikely the case – at least partially. Angelisors are capable of flight outside of water, though their trips above water are only for temporary reasons, as they prefer the ocean and cannot breathe air. The CME never bothered enslaving or taxing them in the past; and today, angelisors enjoy interacting with mages and vice versa. However, due to environmental conditions and locations, this interaction is limited. Still, angelisors do help lost mages and other species in need when at sea, and they generally have positive relations with most species of other genera. Their shared genus attributes and abilities include: electrical discharges; true flight; and mild ghostly ambience generation.

## Florgiras (Heteronudibranchiaterraserpere):

Florgiras are bisectionally-humanoid slugs that have an average length of 230 centimetres. Half the species mostly live on land, and the other half mostly in water, but all have gills and lungs and are capable of living in both environments. However, all species require at least moist or humid climates while on land, with access to plenty of water. Species within the genus vary greatly in appearance, but all have a form of bioluminescence, along with at least some *cerata* (tentacle-like structures with soft 'horns') around their bodies. Generally, most have *hepatic diverticula*, which means their organs are visible through their translucent outer bodies. Some species are able to flex their cerata in a way that spreads like wings, enabling gliding in the air (but not true flight). The lower half of a florgira body slides along surfaces in slug form, while the top half of the body is an erect torso featuring arms and hands.

While they are not snails, florgiras can generate a goo around their bodies that hardens over time. Normally, this occurs during sleep, in which they slowly form a shell to sleep inside. After waking up from their sleep, the shell loosens and then gets resorbed back into the body. For the sake of resource efficiency, the shells normally never harden to that of a normal snail's shell. However, when in danger, the shells can quickly harden to protect the florgira (a hardness level much greater than that of a normal snail's shell). But once the hardened shell is no longer of use, it cannot be reabsorbed back into the body, and, as such, it is a massive resource drain, so it cannot be done repeatedly in quick succession.

In the past, the CME enslaved land-based florgiras, directly using them for cleaning and agricultural purposes, usually for consuming decaying organic matter, debris, and small pests. Today, florgiras *can* be found in multispecieal zones, but due to the slimy trail they leave behind them, they are normally banned in many areas unless they are on a hoverboard or are in an accommodating vehicle. It is a myth that they are very slow moving – with many resultant jokes mentioning about 'being stuck behind a florgira'. They have positive relations with many species of other genera and have found their own niche economically. Florgiras are also hermaphrodites, and certain individuals from other species have developed a strange fetish market for their sexual abilities. Their shared genus attributes and abilities include: electrical discharges; poison from cnidosacs on their cerata; goo generation (which is useful for many purposes, including shell formation, which can act as a form of armour); retractable bodies; and bodily regeneration (even if only their heads remain, their whole bodies can regrow).

## Scorations (Pectinheteronoids):

Scorations are non-humanoid scallops that have an average diameter of 100 centimetres (with just their shells), and up to 300 centimetres with their tentacles extended out. Scorations are able to release numerous tentacles from their shells, which can be used for standing up or for handling objects. Although they lack hands, their many tentacles work in tandem to help scorations use particular technologies. They have numerous eyes (averaging around eighty), granting interesting ways of seeing their environment. While some species have spikes on their shells, all species generate bioluminescence inside their shells, which normally appears as if flashing neon lights or electrical discharges. Scorations also produce unique pearls that they use for various purposes – including economically (that is, they sell them on the market). They are capable of walking on land and lasting three days out of water – though, this is limited, and they much prefer being in water.

Scorations are one of the few genera that also form symbiotic heterogenic pacts with other beings. In fact, they do not just form symbiotic relations with just *one* other species but many *types* of species – both sapient and non-sapient. Scorations are able to provide protection inside their shells, along with transport through dangerous areas, while they may benefit from all sorts of services, such as cleaning, defence, and boosts to their abilities. But these services are all so the scoration can thrive; they are not necessary for their survival. The CME did not enslave many scorations for labour during the time of the empire, but they did seize as many pearls as they could. In the modern context, mages and scorations have positive relations, and mages sometimes buy their unique pearls. Scorations also have positive relations with the majority of aquatic sapient beings as well. However, as hermaphrodites, scorations breed rapidly, so mages have ensured that if they breed, it must be within their own C zones, and immigration to multispecieal zones is limited (but not off limits) due to overpopulation. Moreover, it is very hard to hear and understand what scorations say at times due to the way they speak, which makes forming deeper inter-genera relationships difficult.

Their shared genus attributes and abilities include: versatile and multifunctional tentacles; bulletproof armour; electrical discharges; lunar affinity, which strengthens their abilities during lunapexes and allows for telepathy within a species (this effect is heightened with the presence of pearls – especially many and/or big pearls); their pearls act as aphrodisiac emanators and can increase the fertility in other species; the pearls can be cursed to affect etheric fields, where most of the time they will act as nightmare inducers; and, the pearls can be used to scry through (so mages etherically check the pearls to see if there are any particular etheric connections to the scoration, and if clear, mages – especially mystics – can then use the pearls for scrying).

## 4.3.3.8: Cnidarianoids:

Cnidarianoids are considered to be one of the most alien of all beings from an outside perspective. Whilst many mammalians, for example, might find most arthropoids to be either very bizarre, disgusting, or different from themselves, they are nonetheless accustomed to small, non-sapient arthropoids living around them in their environments. The majority of cnidarianoids, on the other hand, live in the oceans, and are accordingly out of sight. However, some cnidarianoids live on land; but even then, simple matters like communication can be very hard between the greatly-contrasting beings. Their cultures, too, tend to be difficult for most outside the morphtype to grasp. Despite these differences, they are generally not hated and, instead, inspire fascination. Without mammalians, cnidarianoids certainly would not be the dominant force in the Caelverse, but many cnidarianoid genera would potentially exist in unharmed states, left to their 'odd' ways. Major, common, or notable sapient cnidarianoid genera include:

## Brochini (Mussidomini):

Brochini are non-humanoid brain corals that have an average diameter of 110 centimetres. They normally hold a symbiotic heterogenic status with non-sapient beings, as brochini prefer being the master. Of these other symbiotic beings, the majority are other coral, but brochini have a natural default symbiosis with various algae, anyway (but this is generally not a sufficient case itself for the title of 'heterogenic' in the FTS). Because there is not a single set of coral that brochini always use, their overall heterogenic form varies greatly – but the brochini itself always remains the same with its brain-resembling appearance. In some cases, the heterogenic will appear to have hands, while at other times, the brochini will only use the tentacles of other coral to navigate the oceans. Accordingly, some heterogenic brochini *can* appear humanoid in structure. Technically, brochini already possess their own tentacles, but they benefit by using more powerful tentacles found in certain corals. Brochini do, however, use these tentacles as a means to connect the corals to their body, connecting the brochini's central nervous system to the simple nervous systems (typically nerve nets) of the other coral.

While brochini have a central nervous system, they still use the basic functions of their former nerve net, which allows them to determine and interpret light signals, allowing for a primitive sight of their environment. Coupled with their symbiotes, they can enhance this ability to create advanced virtual environments to navigate. Without these, brochini cannot see, as they do not have eyes. Since it is the alga/algae that determines a coral's colour, all brochini will have various colours. When bleached of their alga/algae due to factors such as stress, brochini are revealed to be technically white. Sometimes they will sit on top of the heterogenic form as if a head, but many times the brochini will remain in the centre of all the other coral. Without symbiotic relationships, the brochini are almost sessile, lacking the ability to properly move around. The non-sapient corals, at the same time, lack the benefits and intelligence of the brochini. Although non-sapient brain corals are definitely not intelligent, the brochini happen to actually be intelligent – the brainy appearance is just a coincidence.

Given that most brochini live around reefs, it was easy for the CME to enslave many in the past. Most of their roles under the empire involved collecting resources in the reefs. Even today, brochini are used to both care for and farm resources in many reefs. They are capable of walking on land, and so, some of their roles are land-based, maintaining certain land so that the reefs can remain healthy. This is an important role, as reefs can affect the greater oceans, which in turn can affect all those on land, as everything is part of a holistic ecosphere. Depending on the type of symbiotes, some brochini heterogenic forms can become *amphibious* (not amphibinoids), which means some can permanently live outside of water. Although, in such cases, they need lots of water to survive.

Brochini themselves are incapable of speaking, but with the help of certain coral, they can produce noises that allow them to speak. Many species of other genera regard brochini too alien to interact much with outside of business, but they nonetheless maintain positive relations with one another. Regardless, brochini are quite populous around the reefs of many of the Caelverse's oceans. Their shared genus attributes and abilities include: bodily regeneration; potential generation of certain substances like poison with symbiotes; personal ability enhancement via symbiotes; the capability of enhancing the abilities of their symbiotes; replaceability with symbiotes; and exchangeable adaptability with symbiotes.

## Eneconians (Actiniaroculus):

Eneconians are non-humanoid sea anemones that have an average length (or height) of 150 centimetres without tentacles measured and up to 250 centimetres with tentacles extended out. Rare amongst sea anemones, eneconians have *true eyes*. The main part of an eneconian body consists of a cylindrical trunk or column from which the eyes and tentacles emerge. While swimming, both eyes remain externalized, whereas when eneconians are stationed and attached to a surface, at least one eye and their surrounding tentacles will withdraw to the centre, where they will be situated behind other organs. Eneconians are an example of a primitive sapient genus in and of themselves. That is, while they are all intelligent enough to grasp certain concepts, they never actually form any structured society of their own. However, they do form tribes with one another inside what they understand to be their own C zones issued by the CGM.

Eneconians, moreover, can be found in multispecieal zones, where they actually perform jobs of various kinds – usually for others, rather than running their own businesses (although, this is not impossible). The CME never directly enslaved them in the past and, instead, insisted other beings like brochini force and set tasks on them. Eneconians generally have positive relations with other beings, but they are sometimes subject to bullying. They can also form simple symbiotic relations with primitive beings, who gather within their tentacles. In fact, these symbiotic relations can help lead to further, greater symbiotic relations with other beings. Their shared genus abilities and attributes include: bodily regeneration; and great pressure resistance.

## Flingins (Coronavolans):

Flingins are non-humanoid crown jellyfish that float in the air. They have one set of six long tentacles and another set of inner, smaller tentacles averaging about twenty in number. From the top of the bell to the bottom of their tentacles, flingins have an average length of 240 centimetres, while their crowns have an average diameter of 200 centimetres. Their bodies have a special ability to transmute hydrogen (broken down from $H_2O$) into helium, which allows them to float. Of course, this helium also needs heating for extra power, which occurs via electrical pulses inside the helium chamber. When their helium production runs thin due to fatigue, flingins begin to sleep, resting on a surface such as the ground or a bed. The ends of their long tentacles have different appendages; for most species, these are akin to hands and claws. The crown-shaped bell produces bioluminescent light in spots, while another beam of light shines down the tentacles from the centre before hitting the ground below. Through convergent evolution, flingins have true eyes that appear in various places. Moreover, through various evolutionary pressures, flingins have lost their ability to live in water.

Despite it being hard for many beings outside the genera to understand when they speak, flingins are capable of producing loud sounds as if deep alarms. Due to having this ability, the CME used flingins for monitoring, scouting, and signifying particular events, actions, and anomalies taking place, where the mages did not have the resources to afford. However, flingins were mainly used directly for many other purposes, such as construction, farming, and maintenance. In the present day, flingins are found both within their own C zones and commonly in some multispecieal zones. They generally enjoy watching other beings, which can lead to stalking. Beings of other genera tend to realize that the flingins may be laughing at them due to hearing particular weird noises, in addition to how and when flingins will bump their tentacles up against another flingin.

Flingins are also known to tickle other beings without warrant, which additionally produces a buzzing feeling in the victim. Furthermore, flingins are typically great pranksters, which nearly everyone other than themselves finds annoying. Besides these odd cultural issues, collectively, flingins generally have positive relations with other beings. Still, while rare, their monstrous mutations have led to very dark and powerful forms that have caused quite a lot of chaos in the past. Their shared genus abilities and attributes include: tentacle regeneration; poison generation; electricity generation; and ballooning flight via helium generation (which is generally slow and subject to strong winds, though).

## Wispenids (Semaeostomphasma):

Wispenids are vaguely/relatively-humanoid, bisectional jellyfish that have an average length of 240 centimetres. Considered the true physical 'ghosts of the seas', their overall appearance seems very ghostly. The bottom half of a wispenid body is of a normal jellyfish bell with a thick set of thin, wispy tentacles underneath. As an aggregate, though, the bell appears as if a dress for the torso structure that emerges on top. This humanoid structure also features arms and hands. The head, though, is not humanoid and, instead, is another jellyfish bell structure that appears as if a big floppy hat. Even males have this 'dress', but wispenids are sexually dimorphic, and male dresses appear less feminine with their less voluptuous appearance. Although the colours vary per species, normally wispenids are white and/or transparent or translucent.

Wispenids have a rare ability to recombine their bodies if torn apart – even their heads. If they need to move through an object like a large pillar, they can split in half and then recombine on the other side. Still, this ability must be completed within a short amount of time after the splitting. One of the most amazing abilities wispenids have is bio-indefinite immortality. That is, they never die from senescence (biological aging), but they can still die from other causes, such as disease and injury. However, all wispenids in their later life (the *medusa form*) will begin reverting to the *polyp stage* (when they were younger). Essentially, wispenids cycle through their life stages over and over again, so their minds cannot infinitely build vast amounts of knowledge and wisdom. Nevertheless, they do retain some rudimentary memories after cycling, which helps them to quickly reintegrate into society again. Wispenids breed at a very slow rate, and so, their populations do not increase much over time.

Wispenids do not move very fast, and they float like ghosts. They also communicate with sounds produced not with their mouths but with their tentacles. Furthermore, they are able to mimic human voices with their tentacles, but this is generally muffled, whispery, and echoey, like that of a ghost (in certain cases). In general, they emit a ghostly sound, anyway, in addition to producing a strange emotional ambience – one considered eerie out of sheer incomprehensibility. When threatened, they can increase this ambience, which becomes extremely foreboding. For this reason, most beings (even powerful ones) tend to keep their distance from wispenids, even though most wispenids never desire to harm others. Even mages during the days of the CME mostly avoided wispenids on the rare occasions that they did interact with them. Still, in the present day, there are some beings in the Caelverse who are happy to conduct business with wispenids. Occasionally, wispenids may be seen in aquatic multispeciel zones. Their societies tend to be materially minimalist, but they are, at the same time, rather technologically advanced. Certain parts of their culture have still heretofore been hard to document. Their shared genus attributes and abilities include: bodily regeneration; bodily recombination; strong ghostly ambience generation; telepathy with all in their genus; etheric aura vision; bio-indefinite immortality; and lunar affinity (which enhances their other abilities during lunapexes).

## 4.3.3.9: Echinodermoids:

Echinodermoids are another morphtype that appear very alien to most beings in the Caelverse. Likewise, most beings appear alien to echinodermoids. There is a common misconception that echinodermoids are extremely similar to cnidarianoids and that both should be grouped together as one category. While there may be certain similarities (such as having tentacles), there are very contrasting differences between the two morphtypes. Primarily, echinodermoids feature five-pointed radial symmetry. This is also not to be confused with mere pentapods (which are generally arthropoid) that have five limbs, as pentapods lack the said radial symmetry (and arthropoid pentapods also feature arthropoid features). Echinodermoids also do not necessarily have to have five limbs and can, instead, have various *sets* within their radial symmetry. So, urchin entities can have many spines. Some echinodermoids are also land-dwellers, but those in the oceans tend to have similar technologies to other ocean-dwellers. If mages were not the dominant force in the Caelverse, echinodermoids would likely never come to dominate, but they would easily continue existing. Major, common, or notable sapient echinodermoids genera include:

## Cucumrans (Pelagosapiens):

Cucumrans are non-humanoid sea cucumbers that have an average length of 170 centimetres. Although they lack hands, their tentacles can bifurcate at the ends, allowing them to walk and also grab objects as if they had hands. Most of the time, cucumrans swim in the ocean, but when they do rarely surface to go on land, they can stand with their tentacles without the aid of the buoyancy found in water. The core body is shaped like a cucumber, while the gelatinous, translucent exterior is bulbous shaped with a webbed veil – which is where the tentacles emerge from. This bioluminescent webbed veil or anterior sail can even appear like a jellyfish's bell, depending on the species. Their true eyes are located on the actual cucumber part, but they have googly lenses near the edges (but inside) of the exterior that act like glasses, and this is what most people (who are not cucumrans) assume are the eyes. Cucumrans cannot speak with sounds that other species of other genera understand, so most communication is done through sign language.

The CME never enslaved cucumrans in the past due to the difficulty of maintaining enslavement in the ocean. As a result, cucumrans do not hold resentment towards the mages and, they have positive relations with them. Cucumrans also have positive relations with other beings, although, the kinds of jobs they perform for or with other beings are limited because of the need for either sign language or advanced technologies. Due to naturally feeding on sediments at the bottom of oceans, the CGM and other environmental organizations normally employ cucumrans to collect and clean up waste on and near the sea floors – which happens to play a vital oceanic role, as, without them, the oceans would be far more polluted than they are now. Cucrumrans are typically nomadic, and so, while they are seen in multispecieal zones, they tend to shift from one to another without establishing proper communities. Most of their C zones, on the other hand, are filled with semi-primitive tribes, so while cucumrans are capable of integrating into civilization, they are not adept at managing at forging their own. Despite these issues, cucumrans are very common throughout the Caelverse. Their shared genus attributes and abilities include: bodily regeneration; and mineral extraction from sediments.

## Starisks (Ophioculos):

Starisks are starfish that are of the *Ophiuroidea* taxonomic class, so they have more elongated and thinner limbs than sea stars (*Asteroidea* class), each stretching to an average length of two metres. Due to their five-point radial symmetry that matches a humanoid's figure of a head, torso, arms and legs, sometimes starisks are categorized as vaguely humanoid; but besides this form, they are non-humanoid. Starisks use any of their limbs for locomotion, which means that any limb can be used as legs or arms to move. By walking only on two limbs, their movement may appear humanoid; at other times, it can appear very different, as they are able to manoeuvre themselves in assorted ways. Some species in the genus are bioluminescent, while others may have various spikes or assorted externalized *ossicles* (small bones part of an external skeleton); but all have tough skin, which can greatly hurt when starisks use their limbs as whips.

Remarkably, while starisks descend from 'brittle stars', they are anything but brittle, featuring greater strength and resilience than their primitive, non-sapient ancestors. The central area possesses most of their organs, including their mouth, which is surrounded by several eyes (with most species averaging around fifty). Starisks are capable of living permanently on land or in water – including deep waters. However, it takes time to fully adjust to a new environment after switching – usually a couple of months – so starisks have to repeatedly alternate between the two until they have adjusted. Their limbs are also capable of storing water, which they can use for shooting out of their mouth as if a (high-powered) water gun. They can even immobilize their bodies and harden their skin beyond normal.

While the CME did enslave starisks in the past, they used starisks not just directly for manual labour but also to keep species of other genera in line with their powerful whipping abilities. This, of course, was only implemented when mage numbers were thin and they needed more enforcement, and only a small percentage of starisks performed this duty. It was also not the case that most of the slaves were whipped, as this would cause bodily degeneration, which would have been bad for productivity. Some species resent starisks for their role in the enslavement, but this resentment is minor, and today, starisks manage to have positive relations with other beings, including mages. Starisks are generally very sociable and are commonly seen in many multispecieal zones near water. While they can be found in jobs involving research, most are found in jobs requiring physical labour, which they are proficient at and enjoy. Plus, starisks find their way into acrobatic and performance jobs due to their fantastic climbing, jumping, fighting, cartwheeling and spinning abilities. Their shared genus attributes and abilities include: bodily regeneration; limb regeneration; limb detachment; powerful whipping abilities and skills; supreme acrobatic and fighting abilities; having an in-built water gun; and, five-sided geometric affinity, allowing them, for example, to partake in rituals with pentagons that can help to alter probabilities in their favour (but this is not as powerful compared to mages and their rituals).

## Crucitids (Diademoculus):

Crucitids are non-human sea urchins that have an average diameter of 310 centimetres from spine to opposing spine. Their bodies are, for the most part, like urchins in the taxonomic order of *Diadematoida*, but they possess a few differences. For one, they have true eyes – or rather, *true eye*, so they are cyclopses. The eye is located on the opposite side to where the mouth and anus are located. Crucitids can suck water in their mouth/anus (and even air) and blow it out, which jets them at great speeds. Their tube feet also act as tentacles, which are bifurcated, allowing crucitids to handle and operate tools and technologies. When feeding, they intuitively and instinctively know where their mouth is located, despite not being able to see it.

Crucitids are also capable of moving on land; however, while they do possess tentacles and tube feet, these are not sufficient enough for them to walk on land due to the lack of buoyancy. So, crucitids withdraw their spikes to a degree and roll around instead. Nonetheless, they cannot survive more than three days out of water (assuming they have already sucked in lots of water beforehand). The cyclops eye also has a unique ability to mentally affect anyone who looks directly at it. The effects range from confusion to hysteria, and the symptoms last for varying times at varying strengths depending on the individual affected and the context.

Half of the species in the genus are hostile to all other lifeforms in the Caelverse, and so naturally, the CME in the past began trying to exterminate them. However, this was no easy feat, as crucitids live in the oceans. Even to this day, the CGM has not exterminated any of the hostile species. In the past, the CME did not enslave many of the peaceful crucitid species; but of those that were enslaved, they helped the mages hunt down the hostile ones. In the present day, the hostile crucitids continue to pose a major threat to oceanic life. With their psychic abilities, they manage to avoid detection as they maintain their societies. It is easy to distinguish between hostile and peaceful species due to their colours; the hostile species are black, dark red, and/or dark purple, while the non-hostile species are of a blue, green, orange, yellow, or light brown colour.

While mages do hunt hostile crucitid species, much of this task is delegated to oceanic species, except in the rare cases where hostile crucitids are on land. While there are few first-hand documents of hostile crucitid cultures, reports from peaceful crucitids mention that while they are part of the same genus, their cultures vary greatly. Hostile crucitids do create art, but it is very sadistic, depicting torture chambers and gruesome events. Still, there are reported similarities between all members of the genus, so much of the music involves percussion and chanting. Their shared genus attributes and abilities include: bodily regeneration; spine launching; spine protrusion and retraction/withdrawal; poison generation; tough armour; and psychic abilities (including inflicting mental afflictions via direct eye contact).

### 4.3.3.10: Anneloids:

Anneloids are a morphtype that consists of entities that quite a few people erroneously place into other groups, such as arthropoids. There have even been calls to group many morphological types that mainly consist of worms into an overall 'vermoid' group. However, this is highly erroneous, as not all anneloids or other suggested morphtypes are worms. For instance, reptilian worms exist as well (and this is not even including snakes), so it would be too problematic to create such a group. Nevertheless, a large percentage of anneloids are worms. Out of all the 'worm' morphtypes, anneloids have the biggest number of sapient species, which contrasts the very few sapient nematoid species (which are sometimes erroneously placed in as anneloids). Essentially, anneloids are mainly characterized by their *segmented* bodies. While the various sapient anneloid species certainly are not the dominant force in the Caelverse, some of the *biggest* (in terms of physical size/volume) and most powerful non-sapient beings in existence are anneloids – and this is not even including mutant anneloids. Major, common, or notable sapient anneloid genera include:

## Venetas (Glossossimul):

Venetas are non-humanoid worms that have an average length of thirty centimetres. While they are sapient, lone venetas are practically incapable of integrating themselves into civilization due to their size and strength. They accordingly form into a heterogenic collectic of hundreds or thousands of worms, normally forming a humanoid shape to achieve assorted tasks. Since venetas are anneloids, they have segmented bodies. Each individual veneta can then attach itself to another veneta at any one of its segments – meaning, venetas can attach themselves to many other veneta simultaneously. Venetas alone are incapable of human speech, but they are able to make certain sounds as a collective to mimic humanoid voices. Otherwise, generally sign language is used to communicate with other beings. Within the collectic, venetas typically form a hive mind and work together as a single entity.

Despite not possessing eyes, venetas have enough senses collectively to mentally construct a relatively-accurate model of their surroundings. Most non-anneloids find veneta culture too bizarre to fully comprehend, but they do, indeed, have a culture. Interestingly, venetas may partake in watching mammalian theatres, for example, but they appreciate the art from a different perspective that mammalians could never understand (so venetas claim). The CME enslaved venetas in the past, but due to communication issues, they just assigned simple digging roles to venetas. Sometimes venetas may be seen in multispecieal zones in the present day, but they usually wear full suits to cover themselves, and they are not very sociable (but they are not unfriendly either). They are extremely useful in decomposing certain materials that either need rapid decomposing or are hard to decompose naturally. For this reason, mages and other beings greatly use their services. Their shared genus attributes and abilities include: bodily regeneration; stretchability; and decomposition manipulation and inducement.

## Treenups (Opisarma):

Treenups are non-humanoid anneloids that have an average height of 200 centimetres. It may appear that they are heterogenics, but treenups are single entities consisting of four legs, a main body, and two arms. Each limb and main body part, however, are worm-like in appearance. Their non-humanoid arms and legs bifurcate at the ends, providing treenups with 'hands' and 'feet', which they use for various purposes. The main body is a little thicker than the arms, but all are still relatively thin compared to their length. While treenup heads appear simple in nature, they do possess true eyes. From a non-anneloid perspective, treenups seem similar in nature to other anneloids, such as venetas, but both genera assure that they are very different to one another. Still, they have a similar history of enslavement, and they are also largely hired for various decomposing roles in the modern-day context. Unlike venetas, treenups are usually more sociable with other types of beings, and they do not fully cover their bodies to blend in. They attempt to integrate into multispecieal zones, and while some beings are accepting of them, many are not. Treenups normally enjoy constructing things and making large physical art, such as their famous and outstanding mud sculptures that they greatly export. Their shared genus attributes and abilities include: bodily regeneration; stretchability; and decomposition manipulation and inducement.

## Venstills (Hirudarma):

Venstills are non-humanoid leeches that, on average, measure 220 centimetres in length. Unlike their non-sapient ancestors, venstills feature non-humanoid arms that bifurcate at the ends to form 'hands'. Venstills have true eyes, but they have poor vision, so venstills still use their other senses to help determine their environments. Hostility was naturally met when the CME tried to enslave venstills in the past, but venstills did not have the same willpower that many other genera possessed, so they quickly submitted. However, venstills proved to be poor slaves, and taxing them yielded little results. The CME considered exterminating venstills, but instead of wasting resources hunting and killing venstills, they simply confined them to various zones in the swamps that the CME or mages, in general, had no desire to use. This procedure of confinement to specific zones is theorized to be the precursor to the institution of modern-day zoning, but many academics refute this claim and merely say this was a coincidence and that modern zoning is of a very different nature, whether good, bad, or in between. Still, the initial confinement of venstills actually helped the CME reduce the number of other undesirable beings and beasts in the swamps due to venstills fighting them off for survival and food.

In the present day, venstills still remain mostly in swamplands, where they play a vital role in feasting off non-sapient beasts that the mages do not wish to purge and control themselves. While they are not hostile, venstills are mostly inhospitable to beings of other genera. For this reason, it is virtually unheard of for venstills to be seen in multispecieal zones (which they are normally banned from, anyway). When asked, venstills prefer not to talk about their cultures to outsiders, so such documentation is hard. Venstills typically horrify and disgust most beings of other genera, so it is not like most people want to visit them in the swamps. Plus, it does not help that they have a great thirst for blood and the ability to mind control people. However, this ability to control people's minds is rather weak, unless the venstill is in a particular mutated form; in addition, the venstill has to be physically attached to the person. It is not a myth that venstills hate salt, and bringing salt jars into their communities is seen as an act of aggression. Their shared genus attributes and abilities include: bodily regeneration; stretchability; mind control when directly (physically) attached to particular victims of certain willpower; and extreme healing properties through blood absorption.

### 4.3.3.11: Phytoids:

Despite the plethora of flora in existence, very few sapient phytoid species exist, proportionally speaking. Phytoids may consume nutrients from plants and/or fungi and/or animal sources (typically all three), but they all have one aspect in common: they obtain energy from the sun through *photosynthesis* (that is, they turn light into chemical energy). They also produce cell walls that contain cellulose – even for the rare animals (for some parts of their bodies) that technically can be placed under the phytoid category. It may seem that since phytoids are plants, they must therefore easily adapt (or be immune) to the flora in the wild; but this is false. Primitive plants in nature are in constant competition (such as through *allelopathy*, where plants release biochemicals that can affect the germination, growth, survival and reproduction of other plants), so there is no necessary 'comradery'.

The chemicals in plants also vary greatly, so no one phytoid can be fully immune to every type of poison. Nevertheless, phytoids may be immune or resistant to *more* and *particular* kinds of poisons or pollens, etc., so they may be more adapted to certain environments. This principle also applies to any plant empathy abilities that phytoids may possess; that is, while many phytoids can connect with primitive plants, they can only connect with certain kinds of plants. While certain trends may be present in their cultures (such as competition through sports), phytoid technologies are usually different to other beings; this normally involves the use of non-sapient plants. Like ichthyoids, most phytoids grow their technologies. Major, common, or notable sapient phytoid genera include:

### Cintons (Plantahomo):

Cintons are essentially-humanoid, bipedal phytoids that have an average height of 180 centimetres. Out of all the phytoid genera, cintons are amongst the most human appearing. Despite their genus name, they are not related to humans at all, and their appearance occurred only through convergent evolution. The main visual differences are cuticle (skin) folds around their bodies, along with the multiple sturdy leaves emerging from their heads. The females even have breast-shaped glands on their chests, but these store various chemicals for the mating males to consume, enabling them to become sexually aroused. Essentially, females choose whom to mate with, and the asexual males accept and become sexual for a brief time. Naturally, most cintons have matriarchies.

Cintons are also the most common sapient phytoid in the Caelverse, and they have cordial relations with most species of other genera. They are responsible for achieving great feats using plant engineering; that is, nearly all of their buildings, instruments, and more, come directly from, or actually are, plants. Despite their impressive feats, most beings across the Caelverse have not adopted cinton culture and technology. Cintons use photosynthesis, but they are also omnivores, with their diets mainly consisting of plant matter. In the past, the CME enslaved cintons, both taxing and directly using them for a vast array of purposes due both to their intelligence and practicable nature. Today, they frequent multispecieal zones, but they also have their own very well-developed C zones, for which they spend most of their time inside. Their shared genus attributes and abilities include: partial-bodily regeneration; poison resistance; plant empathy; and plant domination (so they can command certain plants to act in particular ways).

## Petalkans (Helicopetalpteron):

Petalkans are non-humanoid phytoids that have an average height of 170 centimetres. While they do have non-humanoid arms with 'hands', petalkans have no legs and require the helicopter-like petals on their heads to move. Capable of flying and hovering high, petalkans will *sometimes* fly above the clouds in order to receive additional sunlight for their photosynthesis, but usually this is when the clouds are very low. Due to being able to receive a lot of sunlight for energy compared to other phytoids, they do not eat as much food as other phytoids, but most species in the genus still enjoy an omnivorous diet (with plant food making up the bulk of it). Their bodies are normally mostly covered in petals that appear similar to avian feathers. While they are very light-weight, they can nevertheless easily cause damage to other beings with their vines that they use as whips. The CME enslaved petalkans in the past, using them for various purposes, such as scouting for other phytoids. In the modern context, petalkans have cordial relations with most species of other genera, and they are a common sight in many multispecieal zones, where they work in an array of fields that are normally outdoors. Their shared genus attributes and abilities include: bodily regeneration; flying and hovering; whipping powers and skills; and poison generation.

## Veritasi (Flosaperta):

Veritasi are vaguely-humanoid, bipedal phytoids that have an average height of 220 centimetres. They have non-humanoid arms, hands, legs, and feet, which are attached to a thick body covered in small flowers that vary in type, colour, shape, and size per season. Their heads, however, are one giant flower that opens and closes, with one giant eye in the centre. Instead of possessing a mouth like other beings, the whole flower head has tiny digestive glands that break down compounds into juices, which veritasi drink for sustenance (in addition to the energy they already produce through photosynthesis). While the flowers may seem pretty, the veritasi themselves seem rather monstrous and frightening to many beings. However, veritasi are generally quite friendly to others, but they are an uncommon sight in multispecieal zones due to being rather isolationistic. The CME enslaved them in the past, but due to having to communicate mainly through sign language, mages simply left the veratasi alone in the wild, which they obviously preferred. Besides the veritasi that *are* found in multispecieal zones, most live in semi-primitive tribes in their C zones, but their presence in nature is extremely helpful for a variety of reasons, as it helps with maintenance of the environment. Their shared genus attributes and abilities include: bodily regeneration; poison resistance; poison generation; plant empathy; pheromone production; and great strength.

## Barxuns (Lignumsapiens):

Barxuns are relatively-humanoid, bipedal phytoids that have an average height of 220 centimetres. While barxuns possess a woody body with multiple branches growing from various places (which normally grow leaves), they are one of the more humanoid phytoids. Unlike cintons, barxun faces appear less human and more alien. About half the species are extremely agile and lightweight, while the other half are heavy, slower, and very strong. Some barxun species produce conifers, while others do not; and, with branches sticking out of their heads, they can appear quite threatening. Indeed, barxuns proved a hostile and capable force to the CME initially, but they eventually submitted. Once slavery was established, instead of a whole species rebelling together, many individuals and groups of beings within the various species rebelled. Mages did not exterminate the compliant barxuns and only actively hunted the rebels instead. Although the rebels were hostile to mages, they were not necessarily hostile to species of other genera. Nevertheless, many barxun were and still are rather elitist, and they prefer not to merely mix with others, so they did not help most species of other genera that were rebelling against the empire.

Even in the modern context, barxuns remain a mostly-prideful genus, but this does not mean that they do not integrate within multispecieal zones. In fact, many barxuns can be seen working with other beings, but they nevertheless remain highly ethnocentric. Their societies also usually border on fascism but with a slight individualist flair. As with many phytoids, they use their own technologies – although, much of this comes from the engineering genius of cintons. Many stereotypes about barxuns are true, such as that they love being in nature, where they also perform many types of martial arts training. Originally thought as a myth, mutant barxuns actually produce a gas that appears like a ghost has possessed them. These mutants even attract ghosts. Barxuns claim that other beings have insolently appropriated this phenomenon into their aesthetic cultural movements and dates (such as mages using decorations of 'ghosts in trees' during the Midearth Lunapex). However, this phenomenon has been observed in nature, so mages refute this claim. Their shared genus attributes and abilities include: bodily regeneration; poison resistance; poison generation; plant empathy; rooting their bodies into their ground (which can aid in providing additional nutrients, connecting with the ground, providing stability, etc.); and, pain suppression.

## Cactitans (Cactitan):

Cactitans are vaguely-humanoid, bipedal phytoids that have an average height of 410 centimetres, thus making them giants. It is likely that cactitans descend from cacti, and cactitans (still) possess many sharp spines. They nonetheless possess normal features such as a mouth, eyes, and nose, but cactitans also have multiple arms – the number varying per species. They are sexually dimorphic, with females growing much larger flowers than males, whereas the males feature larger 'muscles'. In the past, the CME enslaved cactitans, but many were able to avoid the slavery, as there were not enough mages willing to live in the harsh desert environments cactitans thrive in. Still, the enslaved cactitans proved to be a vital asset to the empire due to their immense strength and ability to gather resources and build structures easily in the deserts.

In the modern context, cactitans mainly stay within the deserts, exchanging their labour for goods and services from outside. Their work in the deserts today plays a vital role in the economy, as most beings in the Caelverse do not live in deserts. For the most part, cactitans remain cordial with mages, but they can be easily angered; in which case, they go on long rampages. Female cactitans tend to produce lots of art, whereas the male cactitans normally are far more into sports, especially ones involving throwing and catching various objects over long distances. Their shared genus attributes and abilities include: slow bodily regeneration; poison resistance; poison generation; plant empathy; spine protrusion; spine projection (shooting); water retention; heat resistance; extreme endurance; and immense strength.

## 4.3.3.12: Fungoids:

As with phytoids, the number of non-sapient fungoids outnumber sapient fungoids. Sapient fungoids are capable of rapidly reproducing, so naturally, the CGM has accordingly placed certain limitations on fungoids. Similar to phytoids and ocean-dwellers, fungoids use their own technologies they grow. Interestingly, they have managed to convince non-fungoids to adopt some of their technologies, such as *omni-funge* (a durable, inexpensive, light fungus that can shrink to portable sizes before then being able to expand and form into certain shapes and objects due to its foam memory). Even mages sometimes use omni-funge. Without mages, it would actually be possible for fungoids to dominate the Caelverse – or at least hold a very strong balance of power with other morphtypes – due to being able to rapidly reproduce and spread diseases. Major, common, or notable sapient fungoid genera include:

## **Misconsi (Fungivir):**

Misconsi are relatively-humanoid, bipedal fungoids that have an average height of 180 centimetres. As the most humanoid of fungoids (in their default forms), misconsi have humanoid limbs, hands, and feet, but their heads feature assorted mushroom caps, which vary from brain-looking forms to plain caps to ones that produce spots of substances that appear like either clotted blood or jelly. One of the species, *gnomes* (*Fungivir nanum*), appear somewhat human with their facial features, body texture, and form (apart from their generally-red caps). Some species even have small mushrooms on their shoulders, neck, and arms. The CME enslaved misconsi in the past, finding many great purposes for them. Today, though, misconsi are found in a variety of environments – both subterranean and on land. They are also the most common fungoid genus in the Caelverse, with many frequenting multispecieal zones. In fact, even in their C zones, their numbers are greater than most genera in other morphtypes.

Out of all the goods and services misconsi produce, omni-funge is their biggest export, which mages buy in bulk. Although mages can produce their own omni-funge, misconsi are far more efficient at the process, and they produce better quality goods. Misconsi are generally cordial with most species of other genera, although sometimes their antics and humour can get them into trouble or annoy others. While only some are bioluminescent, all misconsi species can produce psychedelic compounds, which they spray into the atmosphere at will. While this may seem like a problem to species of other genera attempting to limit drug trade, misconsi only use the hallucinogens they naturally generate for themselves. When misconsi wish to deal drugs, normally they simply grow mushrooms in a farm instead for that purpose. Still, sometimes their actions and transactions in certain areas are carefully monitored to prevent drug proliferation. Their shared genus abilities and attributes include: bodily-regeneration; drug creation; hallucinogenic defensive mechanisms (that is, they can make opponents hallucinate); fungi empathy; fungi domination; and pheromone creation.

## Itunids (Glomovum):

Itunids are non-humanoid, bipedal fungoids that have an average height of 120 centimetres. While they do have non-humanoid limbs, hands, and feet, their bodies appear like an open egg sac with translucent bulging spots that reveal glowing, gelatinous liquid inside. Their multiple mushroom-shaped heads emerge and retract from the opening at the top of the 'egg', all on long, thin stems. Despite having multiple heads, they are all part of a single entity (so they are not heterogenics). Some species have friendly-looking heads, while others do not. Indeed, some species are actually friendly, while others are absolutely hostile to all other species in the Caelverse. Due to this hostility, mages attempted to exterminate the latter during the days of the CME, but the hostile itunids fled deep underground, where they hide even to this day.

All itunid species have the ability to become a necrotic metamorphic, but the friendly itunids frown upon this practice and agree with mages in outlawing it. One of the itunid heads will detach from the main body and then crawl inside a dead body before transforming it. Once transformed, the metamorphic cannot reproduce, but they normally help the itunid that they originated from. Itunids are also able to mind control certain beings, but this has its limitations, and one or more of the heads need to detach from the egg sac and physically attach to the head of the entity they wish to control. Friendly itunid species are not normally seen in some multispecieal zones, and they prefer remaining in caves close to the surface. Usually, they are hired for their skills in physically (re)networking particular mycelium, which are used for various purposes. Most of their art involves dramatic plays between their various heads, along with obscure humour that virtually only they understand. Their shared genus attributes and abilities include: bodily regeneration; metamorphosing dead bodies into necrotics; and mind control.

## Ufinos (Petasumvolito):

Ufinos are non-humanoid fungoids that have an average cap length of two metres. Moreover, while they do not have limbs, they possess multiple stems that appear as tentacles, so the average height of a ufino is also two metres. Ufinos are able to temporarily fly (or float, rather) and retract their stems, making it seem like they are flying caps and nothing more. Essentially, their names derive from the abbreviation of *unidentified flying objects* (UFOs). To begin floating, they normally just jump high and then float down slowly. They do not possess normal mouths and instead feed through their gills. During the days of the CME, ufinos were used to handle massive amounts of toxic substances due to their immunities. Still, given their ability to produce deadly toxins, some ufinos rebelled and poisoned many mages.

In today's context, ufinos are generally friendly with species of other genera, but since communication can be quite awkward with other beings due to speaking through their gills, ufinos normally keep to their own C zones. Due to their ability to resist ionizing radiation, they are hired to fly into radiated zones and perform certain tasks. In some cases, they can be mistaken for other entities, such as flingins, which they actually have excellent relations with, despite some rivalry. Their shared genus attributes and abilities include: bodily regeneration; temporary flying (floating); poison and gas generation; *bioremediation* (where they can remove pollutants from an environment, whether natural or artificial); toxic immunities; and ionizing radiation resistance.

## Xorvax (Fungivorsipellis):

Xorvax are non-humanoid fungoids that have an average size of any dimension of about 220 centimetres in individual form. No xorvax (even clones) have the exact same shape, but most tend to have similar blobby shapes in default form, appearing like a mix between fat mushrooms, sponge, and jelly. They are able to move around by reshaping their bodies to any form they desire – including humanoid form – and they can split themselves up before reforming. Moreover, they are able to shoot out spores and reform at a new location; and alternatively, individuals can surf on their own – or other xorvax – matter. Most xorvax reproduce through cloning, but this is not always the case. Clones are able to easily communicate telepathically with one another (especially when they literally join their bodies into a heterogenic collectic superorganism), but telepathy is also possible (but harder) with other members of their particular species. Sometimes these collectics can extend many kilometres, but this is uncommon, as, at that size, their stability reduces as a collectic.

All xorvax species are hostile to every other being in the Caelverse. Mages were able to exterminate many xorvax during the time of the CME, but like most hostile genera, xorvax moved deep underground, where today they continue avoiding detection. Still, individual xorvax will surface and consume resources in forests and other areas, succeeding before environmental protection agencies notice. While the xorvax do pose a massive existential risk to all in the Caelverse, intelligence reports show that they are not thriving underground. The reports also show that they are fighting with other beings who are hostile to mages and everyone else. If this were not the case, then they would definitely pose one of the greatest threats to mages.

Very little is understood about their culture – if they have any – and theorists in the past classed xorvax as semi-sapient. However, xorvax do show many clear signs of sapience, which has disproven that old theory. Their shared genus attributes and abilities include: bodily-regeneration; super hive mind; reshaping; matter surfing; telepathy; scattering; and cloning.

## Winxingians (Pluteocornuvestis):

Winxingians are vaguely-humanoid fungoids that have an average height of 180 centimetres. Besides their erect posture and humanoid arms (with hands), they are non-humanoid. Their lower bodies appear like a long, wavy dress; if viewed underneath, it appears like a flower. Their heads are divided into three mushrooms sticking out horizontally from a central stem – each with their own set of eyes and mouths. On their backs, winxingians have *polypore* (that is, bracket/shelf) mushroom-shaped wings, which they use to fly. They are generally very prideful and consider themselves the elite of all fungoids. However, winxingians have a terribly-high chance of mutating with M genes; and, in their mutated states, they can become not only very deadly but feral – especially if they mutate into monsters. For this reason, the CME considered exterminating all winxingians in the past, but through great pleas, winxingians convinced mages that they would help exterminate any mutant that emerged.

In the modern context, winxingians have been ordered to immediately report themselves in if they mutate. Afterwards, the mutant is sent to special, isolated reserves, where the mutations are kept under control. The main reason for their deadliness is that winxingians are capable of producing massive amounts of moulds that can rapidly spread and easily decompose many forms of matter very quickly. Other than this issue, winxingians are cordial with most species of other genera, and they can be found in certain multispecieal zones working in an array of fields. With misconsi, winxingians are the greatest exporters of fungoid culture (although, winxingians, of course, consider their culture to be of the highest order, whilst misconsi culture to be of lowbrow nature). Due to their careful and attentive way of raising the young, winxingians do not breed as fast as other fungoids, making them an anomaly. As such, while they are found in multispecieal zones, their numbers are not high. Their shared genus attributes and abilities include: bodily regeneration; true flight; healing and anti-healing spore generation; fungi empathy; and fungi domination.

## 4.3.3.13: Lithoids:

Lithoids are one of the least common types of beings in the Caelverse, but on average, they have the longest lifespans. Although lithoids can be both social and antisocial, the majority live and work underground in both their own C zones and underground multispecieal zones. Even though the CGM controls the grand caverns, lithoids are allowed to operate in these areas under certain rules. Most lithoids see the grand caverns as holy places, and there is great conflict with those (even within their own morphtype) that use such places to mine for (mega) profits. Lithoids do not necessarily worship the grand caverns, but they normally view them as places of a sacred and spiritually-profound nature that should be venerated. Generally, most species outside the morphtype find lithoid speech very hard to comprehend. If mages or mammalians did not exist, lithoids would not dominate the Caelverse, but they certainly would dominate the grand caverns and much of the subterranean. Indeed, they already control much of it by default of the lack of proper oversight, anyway.

Most lithoids fall under the STS Kingdom rank of Siliconia. Still, there are some animals that have, through convergent evolution, gained silicon cells just like how eukaryotes developed into Siliconia via incorporating silicon structures into their carbon-based bodies. In other words, all lithoids are still carbon-*based*, but they also have silicon added to them. Like animals and fungi (but not plants), lithoids are *heterotrophic* – that is, they do not produce their own food, so they consume food from other sources, both from other biological beings and from inorganic compounds, where they get energy from the chemical reactions of silicon compounds. But like plants, lithoids also have cell *walls*; however, these are silicon-based instead of made of cellulose, and the crystalline nature also gives rise to their more geometric and stronger nature. The silicon cells can also be called *lithomatter*, while the outside of the lithomatter (that is, the outer surface of the lithoid's body) can also be called the *lithohull*. Many lithoids can rapidly repair and rebuild their lithomatter, but this is only for when there is superficial damage. If major damage occurs, such as when a lithoid loses a whole limb (which might have had an essential magnetic connector node), then it may take years to recover. For carbon-based matter like the brain, the damage is similar to those of other morphtypes.

## Haperchites (Lapisvolunsvir):

Haperchites are relatively-humanoid, bipedal lithoids that have an average height of 180 centimetres. Out of all the lithoids, haperchites are one of the most human-looking, aside from the crystal wings on their backs. Moreover, their lithohulls have a pebbly texture, but haperchites nevertheless have 'hair' on their heads made of silica fibres, akin to optical fibres. They also possess roughly the same amount of weight as an average human due both to the type of materials in their lithomatter and for how they are structured. While slaves during the days of the CME, haperchites normally worked various labour-intensive jobs involving construction with big minerals. Coupled with their wings, haperchites were a great asset to the empire. Today, haperchites work in assorted roles while in multispecieal zones (both above and below ground), cooperating greatly with species of other genera, including mages, whom they do not hold great resentment for regarding their history. Due to their appearance – and for the fact that they do not cause problems with their weight when entering buildings – haperchites are the most common lithoid in aboveground multispecieal zones.

Haperchites have also managed to build exceptionally-advanced societies for themselves in their own C zones, which are ubiquitous in the subterranean world. As a result of their exports, people across the Caelverse have tremendously benefitted economically, with mages exceptionally valuing the stone exports from haperchite C zones, as this contributes to their valued buildings of conventional architectural style. Haperchite culture is also very broad, although naturally, it is imbued with a common, distinguishable lithoid essence. Many mages even desire to have the fantastic wings that haperchites possess, and their artworks normally display this desire. Funnily enough, haperchites are fascinated with non-lithoid anatomies, finding their supple bodies to be of great magnificence. Their shared genus attributes and abilities include: true flight; stone and crystal scrying; detachable and re-attachable limbs; direct mineral absorption for rapid superficial healing; long lifespans; and immunities to some carbon-based diseases.

## Goricks (Lapisgeorotavir):

Goricks are non-humanoid lithoids that have an average height of 220 centimetres. Instead of featuring legs and feet, goricks possess a large sphere, which they roll on like a wheel. Their upper bodies possess four arms, two of which have 'hands', while another two possess stone that can rearrange into different forms via magnetic alterations. Most of the time, goricks form drills on these special arms, which can actually turn like power drill tools. In some combat stances, they may form weapons or shields. In the centre of a gorick body is a large gap with magnetic geometric shapes hovering inside. These can help goricks sense certain properties and energies around them, giving them supreme seismic sense and magnetoreception. Gorick heads feature a cylindrical tunnel with crystals lining the inside. They have eyes both on the outside and inside of this tunnel, thus totalling four eyes. Their lithohulls, moreover, vary per species. Overall, goricks appear as if constructs, but they are nevertheless organic beings.

Under the CME, goricks were mainly used for physical slave labour; today in multispecieal zones, however, they actually can be found in assorted positions, including jobs in the arts and entertainment. Of course, goricks do not shun physical labour, and many accept defence contracts from species of other genera. Although they are rarely seen in aboveground multispecieal zones, they do not shy away from species of other genera. A lot of their sports are quite aggressive, with many involving jousting and racing. Their shared genus attributes and abilities include: full lithomatter restructuring on two of their arms (such as being able to create drills and shields); powerful drilling; the ability to roll for movement; assorted magnetism; supreme seismic sense; supreme magnetoreception; strong natural bodily armour; direct mineral absorption for rapid superficial healing; electrical resistances; long lifespans; and immunities to some carbon-based diseases.

## Hexamons (Lapishexagonumvir):

Hexamons are non-humanoid, tripedal lithoids that have an average height of two metres. Standing on three legs, hexamons have three arms, completing their six-figured theme for their limbs. The third arm sits in a shaft in the centre of the hexamon, which can be moved back and forth so as to have the arm operating at their front or back. Their lithohulls have hexagonal crystals (with luminous lights shining out of geometric gaps); and their heads, too, are of the same shape. This means hexamons have six faces (but one head), with six sets of eyes and mouths. Like many lithoids, hexamons appear as if constructs; but they, too, have evolved organically. Hexamons are overall a very unusual genus, acting in ways that seem incomprehensible to others. Mages in the CME were initially unsure what to do with hexamons, so they left them to their own devices in restricted areas until they figured out the best way to utilize their labour. Of course, by the time the CME figured out what could be done with hexamons, it was on the verge of collapsing, so they were never utilized.

Hexamons normally remain in their own C zones, but sometimes they are hired to solve problems in multispecieal zones – mainly in subterranean ones. They are incredibly intelligent, and they spend most of their time creating and solving puzzles, including physically building mazes, which some species of other genera enjoy partaking in. Sometimes they are mistaken for robots, as some robot designs have been modelled after them. Funnily enough, hexamons have not modelled most of their robots on their own physiology. Their shared genus attributes and abilities include: amazing pattern recognition; superior intelligence; electricity generation; sound and vibration manipulation (when sounds and frequencies make contact with their bodies); mirror manipulations; strong natural bodily armour; direct mineral absorption for rapid superficial healing; long lifespans; and immunities to some carbon-based diseases.

## Drakhars (Lapistitanusvir):

Drakhars are relatively-humanoid, bipedal lithoids that have an average height of three metres, placing all but one of their species into the giant category. Drakhars have a natural, v-shaped brawny build, with their structure appearing as if the strongest human on steroids. Their arms are so big that they even reach the ground when standing up straight. Along their shoulders, heads, and backs, glowing crystals jut out while their lithohulls are cracked in various places, revealing a glowing interior. They are one of the strongest genera in the Caelverse, and they enjoy physical competitions of sundry kinds (especially violent ones). In fact, the CME even allowed for drakhars to compete in death sports as a way to keep the other drakhars entertained. Of course, this was on a voluntary basis, and it was even proposed by drakhars. Today, the CGM forbids these sports in most cases. Two species of the genus, however, were so violent that they were hostile to every species other than their own, and naturally, the CME had to exterminate them.

While the remaining drakhars are no less aggressive, they are civilized and can control their inhibitions. Still, it is generally unwise in the modern context for beings to aggravate a drakhar. Other than the occasional fight that breaks loose, drakhars have positive relations with species of other genera. Their shared genus attributes and abilities include: a berserker mode, which temporarily grants: pain suppression; unlimited and non-damaging adrenaline-analogues; super-enhanced senses (including telescopic thermoreception vision); supreme combat efficiency; accelerated *and* advanced healing; increased speed, strength, reflexes, and agility; and absolute determination (which prevents them from being mentally affected in most cases, including from consciousness-altering attacks, such as phasarchement discharges). They also have: strong natural bodily armour; direct mineral absorption for rapid superficial healing; long lifespans; and immunities to some carbon-based diseases.

## Untians (Lapisspheravir):

Untians are vaguely-humanoid, bipedal lithoids that have an average height of 170 centimetres. While they possess limbs, hands, feet, and a head, all of these can tuck into their bodies, which are giant balls of incredibly hard and heavy stone, metal and crystal. They additionally have sharp spikes that can protrude and retract from slots around their bodies. There is also a 'canon' on their backs, which they can utilize as such if they consume substances with a gunpowder effect; otherwise, the canon can be used to lightly blow or pour out substances. Untians also have the ability to melt substances before they are shot or poured out of the canon. Alternatively, they can simply blow smog. With enough powerful substances consumed, suicidal untians can explode and kill many others of their own kind and of other genera.

During the time of the CME, untians were sometimes used in siege warfare, but this was not always the case, as technologies proved to be more efficient to use due to not requiring minerals to live. Otherwise, untians were either used for physical labour or simply taxed. Untians normally remain aloof, but they sometimes work in multispecieal zones, having positive relations with species of other genera. Nonetheless, their sporting activities are very popular amongst other beings across the Caelverse, most of them involving rolling around on slides or fields with aggressive clashing. Untian sports are even more popular than gorick sports. Their shared genus attributes and abilities include: spike protrusion and retraction; limb and head protection via retraction; efficient rolling; canon firing; lava pouring; thermal resistance; smog and cloud formation; mini sandstorm creation; strong natural bodily armour; direct mineral absorption for rapid superficial healing; long lifespans; and immunities to some carbon-based diseases.

### 4.3.3.14: Protistoids:

The taxonomic group of Protista in the STS consists of a variety of different beings that are hard to classify – through, they share many features. Accordingly, protists are essentially protistoids – a supergroup. Most sapient protistoids are amoeboids, but not all amoeboids are protistoids – just as not all worms are anneloids. The key feature of *most* protistoids is that they are unicellular. The majority of protistoids are non-sapient, and very few sapient protistoids exist in the Caelverse in terms of the number of genera and population. In fact, they are *almost* regarded as a minor or rare category. Many animal-sized non-sapient protistoids usually include diatoms, with their wondrous, jewel-like geometric bodies, and then slime moulds, which vary from opaque to translucent.

Slime moulds have amorphous bodies, but some may assume simple geometric shapes as well, like cubes or pyramids, all without the detail of diatoms (which have *frustules* – hard and porous external cells walls – producing structural colouration). From an outside perspective, protistoids seem extremely alien-like to most beings of other morphtypes. Sapient protistoids find it hard to culturally integrate with other beings, but they are fully aware of their social conventions and rules, of which they abide by in order to function and profit in multispecieal zones. If they did not have certain self-imposed and environmental restraints, it is actually *possible* that protistoids could dominate the Caelverse through sheer force. Still, this is debatable. The most notable, major, and common sapient protistoid genus is:

### Oblikhos (Amboebasapiens):

Oblikhos are non-humanoid amoeba that have an average diameter of 150 centimetres (at a pure circular form with no protruding *pseudopods*, which are extensions from *cell membranes*, not cell walls, that help with *motility* – the capability to move).

Some oblikho species are quite large (even giants), while others are small (less than fifty centimetres in height). Oblikhos look very similar to microscopic amoeba, with their amorphous form and odd jelly-like texture. Due to lacking cell walls, they can change their shape to absolutely anything, becoming humanoid, for example. Hence, they are called *amorphoids* or *shapechangers* (not shapeshifters). Still, oblikhos *do* have the chance to have their constitutional status changed to that of a shapeshifter. When inside multispecieal zones, most oblikhos (and other amoeboids) assume a fully-humanoid structure. They also typically wear clothes and masks (and even full-body suits) to easily fit in. Some oblikhos wear particular attire or insignia to indicate that they still are amoeboids, but some skilfully hide their true nature. Despite being able to clone themselves asexually, many oblikhos reproduce sexually. While environmental factors may be involved with the decision of how to reproduce, oblikhos in the modern world are typically not limited in this capacity.

In the past, the CME directly enslaved many oblikhos instead of merely taxing them, finding great uses with their amorphous structures. The CME intentionally spread oblikhos across the Caelverse for the slavery, so oblikhos became the most populous protistoids in the Caelverse, and they continue to have the greatest numbers and impact today. Normally inside multispecieal zones, they exist as independent individuals, but in their own C zones, they form colonies that are a type of collectic heterogenic. In these heterogenic colonies, there can be distinct cells, and so, as a whole, they can act as multicellular beings with the benefits of unicellular beings. Their shared genus attributes and abilities include: amorphous physiology (allowing for absolute shapechanging, which has numerous benefits); supreme flexibility; supreme elasticity; size changing; bodily regeneration; splitting and scattering before being able to reform and/or reattach body parts; mitosis manipulation (cell duplication); cloning; mutation inducement (via chances, which are generally low); engulfing consumption (they can engulf things entirely); object entrapment; goo and slime generation; disease generation and inducement (though, this is usually very weak and limited); the ability of an individual being to transform another willing oblikho into a clone of themselves; and, they can easily form heterogenics with any species in the genus.

### 4.3.3.15: Mechanoids:

Mechanoids are a supergroup consisting of various beings that are machine-*like* but are different to mechanical robots. There are two main groups of mechanoids; the first includes biological organisms that were actually designed, grown, or intentionally formed to be wetware or bio-machines. The second group naturally features beings that have morphologically-striking mechanical anatomies made of standard biological matter. While some lithoids border on this latter group, mechanoids differ in that they appear even more mechanical. Still, many mechanoids are, indeed, filled with silicon. Even though the first group is a common occurrence throughout the Caelverse, virtually none are fully sapient; and, when sapience does apply, it is very limited in its scope (thus, it is an 'alternative' form of semi-sapience). Bioships, for example, are highly intelligent, yet they lack much awareness and intelligence that normal sapient beings possess. The second category, in contrast, is not common at all in the Caelverse; and if it were to stand alone from bio-machines as its own group, it would be placed in the minor or rare categories. For this reason, this morphtype guide will not list any mechanoid beings, but it will acknowledge its existence as an overall common morphtype itself within the Caelverse, and, thus, it does not fall into the minor or rare categories. Naturally, there are calls to separate this supergroup due to the contrasting nature of the two main groups therein.

## 4.3.3.16: Machines:

Unlike biological morphtypes, machines do not have an added suffix to indicate that while beings within the morphtype are similar to one another, they are not necessarily *of* that morphtype *specifically*. In other words, all robot machines are specifically just that: machines, and they are not machine-like. Nevertheless, machines (the morphtype group called machines) is a supergroup consisting of a wide variety of beings, with multiple different categories within it. So, there are machines that are listed based on mobility, while others are listed by function. There are also machines listed by their shape. In most cases, robot machines are easy to determine due to their structural makeup; namely, they are usually made with metals and plastics. Also, consider that machines can replace parts with totally new ones, so their morphological structures can change greatly. Naturally, the technology machines use is of a similar nature to their structure, so they avoid using wetware technology. Since they lack the 'disgusting' anatomies that some biological entities view of other biological entities, machines normally do not repulse people. Still, there are growing concerns as to how powerful they may become in the future, so they do induce some alarm. The Morphtype Guide will not list any types of machines.

## 4.3.3.17: X-Droids:

Biochemical synthetics also constitute a growing number of beings across the Caelverse, despite regulations. Like machines, they are classed as a supergroup, and the 'X' in the 'x-droid' name indicates a variable. Accordingly, biochemical synthetics that appear like mammalians, for example, will be called 'mammodroids' or 'mammodroids'. The same can be applied to any other morphtype in this guide, such as reptilians or even phytoids. Many of the same pros and cons of machines can be applied to biochemical synthetics, although to different extents. For example, x-droids are not as efficient at building infrastructure (such as defensive bases for themselves), but they are still more than capable of accomplishing such goals, and due to their lifelike nature, x-droids are better at acquiring materials through marketplaces, etc. Besides the known biological morphtypes, there is no need to list any specific types of x-droids other than to state that the most common biochemical synthetics in the Caelverse by far are mammodroids.

### 4.3.3.18: Minor or Rare Categories:

There are many minor and rare morphological types that sapient and non-sapient beings fall under. Excluding non-sapient microscopic organisms, they comprise a total of less than five percent of entities in the Caelverse. If measuring sapient beings alone, then this figure drops to less than one percent. The measurement for these categories includes the number of genera within a morphtype, in addition to the overall popula-tions within the morphtype *and* their distributions across the Caelverse. Some entities are localized to tiny pockets within the Caelverse due to needing particular environ-ments to survive. Such beings may need helium-filled atmospheres or extremely cold temperatures. If given the right circumstances, their populations might otherwise be bigger. Other reasons for their low populations might include reproductive issues.

Some rare sapient morphtypes include nematoids, placozoids, and poriferoids, while a few very rare types (regardless of sapience) include plasticoids, whorlinoids, and pyramidaloids. Note that placozoids are sometimes grouped into a debatable super category called *amorphoids*, which includes various types like protistoids. Basically, amorphoids are capable of changing their form at will as shapechangers yet are not 'shapeshifters' in the constitutional status use of the term. But this grouping is not widely accepted (just like how vermoids is not considered a legitimate morphtype), so placozoids and protistoids still have their own morphtypes. Plasticoids are made of what the name implies: plastics of various kinds. Still, this plastic is different to normal industry-made plastic, and it is closer to natural cellulose. Gosocks, for example, produce some nylon-like hair, but given their overall morphology, they are placed into mammalian morphtype, not the plasticoid morphtype. Beings at the early eukaryote stage did not branch off and then develop into plasticoids, so all plasticoids fall under taxa like Animalia, Plantae, Fungi, and Siliconia by having later produced – but not incorporated environmental – plastic into their biological structures. Beings of the plasticoid morphtype were and are also only able to emerge in certain atmospheres and environments, and so naturally, their distribution (at least for now) is limited and, thus, their populations are small.

Poriferoids are essentially sponges (usually sea sponges). Interestingly, poriferoids have well-known wisp genera, but the term 'wisp' is a common name, and wisps are members of various morphtypes, just like how 'worms' (a common name) are part of various morphtypes, too. Typically, many people are unsure what kind of wisp they may have encountered, as there are not just sentient wisps but also: ghost wisps, drone (robot) wisps, and non-sentient gas wisps. Ghost wisps might have a poriferoid appearance, so one could be called a *spectral poriferoid*; but ghosts naturally generate a wispy appearance, anyway (that is, their auras may appear like small balls of gassy energy). Whorlinoids and pyramidaloids, on the other hand, have funda-mental structures that are very different to most beings, with their names indicating their respective whorl and pyramidal forms.

### 4.3.3.19: Assortions:

Any being that falls into the *assortion* category is either unexplainable, too hard to easily identify, has yet to be identified, or is part of a taxonomic grouping that is so uncommon (due to the rarity of the being's taxonomic type) that most people either forget or are not even aware of their names. Typically, the being assorted as an assortion will resent the term assortion, but this is initially unavoidable unless first asked. That is, the FTS is for ease of reference, so after proper information has been gathered, *then* more distinguishable epithets may be used. It may not seem like sorting a being into an assortion is helpful, but it can help indicate what a being may typically not be; that is, if a being is labelled as an assortion, there is a high chance, for example, that they will not be a mammalian, and so one can rule out certain information in particular contexts whilst remaining brief.

Interestingly, some beings that are part of common taxonomic phyla or classes are sorted into assortions. An example of this are *salps*, which are gelatinous planktonic tunicate – basically invertebrate animals that may appear like sea flora. Salps are part of the taxonomic phylum Chordata yet cannot be placed into the common morph-types of mammalian, reptilian, avian, ichthyoid, and amphibinoid. Moreover, to the uneducated (and even to the educated, in certain contexts), salps are hard to distinguish from morphtypes like protistoids (or, again, even flora in some cases). Ideally, salps would be placed into *tunicatoids* for adequate distinguishment, but this seldom occurs initially. Most tunicatoids are non-sapient, so the likelihood of a person ever incurring resentment for identifying one initially as an assortion is slim.

There is also a fallacious category called *mixtions* that some people use as epithets instead of the endorsed assortion term. Basically, beings that are placed into the mixtion category are those that do not fall into the aforementioned morphtypes in this guide due to being morphologically uncategorizable as being easily associated as *one* (and only one) of these morphtypes, such as a mammalian or reptilian. It is claimed that mixtions are part of separate taxa and usually morphologically *appear* as if part of two or more categories, such as appearing both like a mammalian and an arthropoid. For clarification, mixtion beings are said to not actually be part of two taxonomic categories; instead, the issue of distinguishing between the two or more categories and placing the mixtion being only into one category is what is problematic. The purpose of this is to reduce the number of epithets for ease of reference.

Users of the term also note that care is needed when placing beings into the mixtion category, however, as sometimes certain beings may actually be mutants, so a mammalian may have bird wings due to a mutation and yet are not avian at all genetically. There are some beings that may appear as if a mixtion but are well known not to be, such as platinooks, which are mammalian. It is *normally* the case that if the two or more morphtypes are clearly disjointed, asymmetrical, incongruent, and/or, piece-mealed, then they are a mutant and not a mixtion. An obvious case would be if the being is totally mammalian, yet they may have a reptilian tentacle emerging from the right side (only) of their head.

While on the surface, the mixtion term might seem genuine (and the arguments about mutants are, indeed, correct), there are multiple problems with it, and it should be avoided. For one, since 'mixtions' supposedly do not belong to a group like mamm-alians, for example, then the actual name of the true morphtype should be used instead of 'mixtion', as that fully names and identifies the morphtype. Saying 'mixtion' is not adequately indicative. If the morphtype type is unknown, then 'assortion' will suffice, as assortions are for the unknown. There are alternatives to mixtions, such as saying 'repto-mammalian' for beings that appear as if reptilians and mammalians. But this, too, is flawed. Just like with mixtion, simply using the actual morphtype is more appropriate.

This issue is further compounded when attempting to use multiple morphtypes in one name, such as 'mammo-repto-avio-arthropoid', which is awkward at best. Conversely, it might also be the case that the being in question is only a mammalian and not another morphtype that appears like a 'repto-mammal'. For example, plati-nooks have bills, poison glands, and lay eggs, yet they are just mammalian. Further-more, through convergent evolution, many dracos have bat-like wings yet are reptilian. Some mammalians also have scales yet are not reptilian. The reverse is true for the absence of certain features; for example, most octopus entities do not have shells, yet they are molluscoids. The only justification for this language is if the last term of the identified being is considered a noun, while the first name is just an adjective; so, 'repto-mammal' *may* suffice if the being is *only* considered a mammal – specifically, a reptilian-*looking* mammal. Still, this would be a different style of identification to the FTS, and it adds yet more complications to an already-overly complicated system.

# Dictionary

**Abolitionist:** A person who advocates for the abolition of something (usually slavery).

**Aesthetic:** A philosophy concerned with beauty and artistic taste.

**Aggregate:** The total or gross amount of something; formed as a whole unit from smaller elements.

**Archetype:** A fundamental characteristic, form, pattern, or model, which all things are based on, derive from, or can be sourced to.

**Aromatic rings:** A geometric structure among chemical elements, where the atoms in a ring all rest in the same geometric plane (and exhibit stability).

**Aspectually:** Adverb: concerning aspects.

**Axial tilt:** The angle of a planet's rotational axis and its orbital plane.

**Axiomatic:** Self-evident; obviously true without question.

**Bequeath:** To leave or give something (beneficial) to someone (by will).

**Biospheric:** Of or relating to the *biosphere* (the sum of all ecosystems of a planet).

**Cardinal:** Adjective: In astrology, it is of a sign that initiates and leads; as a noun, it is a leading rank in an institution, normally religious.

**Celestial:** Of or related to the sky or outer space.

**Chromosomal:** Of or relating to chromosomes, which are threadlike structures made of protein that carry genetic information from cell to cell.

**Collateral damage:** A term in war for the unintentional deaths, damage, or injuries (normally applied to civilians) as a result of military activity.

**Comorbidities:** Two or more diseases existing in one's body at once.

**Coriolis effect:** An inertial, fictious force that causes mass (objects) within a frame of reference (that rotates) relative to the inertial frame, causing the objects to move along curved paths rather than straight lines.

**Corporealization:** The process of making something corporeal – giving form to.

**Cosmology:** The (scientific) study of how the Caelverse (and its various celestial bodies) originated, developed, and function.

**Coup d'état:** An attempt by a small organization to overthrow the government.

**Covalent Bond:** In chemistry, electrons are shared between atoms and form pairs.

**Cymatic:** An effect of sound and vibration, which forms visual patterns.

**Dantha:** …

**De facto:** Existing in fact, whether intentional (legal) or not.

**Demographic:** As a noun: pertaining to a section of beings that have particular traits.

**Deposition:** The act of depositing something; in the context of science, it is of a phase transition that occurs in which a gas turns to a solid without first turning into a liquid.

**Determinism:** The philosophical view that everything (or everything in a part of some reality) is causally determined. That is, if one were to hypothetically have all knowledge of the past and present, then they would be able determine all events in the future, as all occurrences are a result of what occurred in the past. If reality is indeterministic, then the future would not be 'set in stone'.

**Dimorphism:** Occurring in two different (and distinct) forms, normally applied to different sexes (males appear different to females, with the degree different per being).

**DNA:** Deoxyribonucleic acid. A type of polymer that carries genetic instructions for the development of organisms.

**Dodecahedron:** A 3D shape with 12 plane (flat) faces.

**Empirical:** Based on experience and observable information instead of pure logic, reasoning and theories.

**En masse:** All together.

**En route:** On the way to somewhere.

**Endogenous:** Having an internal origin.

**Endothermic:** A process that absorbs heat from the surroundings.

**Entropy:** (Gradual decline into) the state of disorder or randomness.

**Epithet:** A byname that describes a certain characteristic for specification.

**Equidistant:** Equally distant.

**Etymology:** The study of the origin and evolution of words and their meanings.

**Ex post facto:** Having a retroactive effect after something has already happened.

**Existential:** Related to existence and beingness.

**Exogenous:** Having an external origin.

**Exothermic:** A process where heat is released into the surroundings.

**Extant:** Still alive; surviving.

**Fractal:** A complicated pattern; magnification reveals that it never ends.

**G-force:** The force of gravity on a body.

**Gene (genetic):** A unit of hereditary information transferred from the parent to the offspring, which forms the genetic makeup of one's biological being.

**Guerrilla warfare:** Irregular warfare by smaller groups against larger regular groups.

**Haemorrhage:** The loss of blood, normally a lot in a short time.

**Half-life:** The time it takes for a quantity of something to reduce to half of its initial value – normally used in physics regarding the radioactivity of an isotope.

**Hegemony:** The dominance of one entity over another, usually political.

**Heretofore:** Before this point in time; until now; hitherto.

**Hertz:** A unit of frequency equal to one cycle per second.

**Historiography:** The study of the writing of history itself and the writing of history.

**Homogenous:** Of the same or similar kind of nature – alike.

**Incarnation (re):** An entity that embodies something else (a vessel). If one were to reincarnate, they would be embodying another (or potentially the same) vessel again.

**In lieu:** Instead of.

**Integument(ary system):** Something that covers; the outer, protective layer of an organism (such as skin, nails, hair, feathers, etc.).

**Isotope:** A type of atom that possesses a different number of neutrons to normal atoms (but still has the same number of protons), resulting in different levels of mass (but with the same chemical properties).

**Joule:** A unit of work or energy. One joule is equal to the work done by a force of one newton through a distance of one metre.

**Judiciously:** Judging in a good and wise manner.

**Kinetic:** Pertaining to motion. *Tele*kinetic is the motion of things from a distance.

**Lithosphere:** Outer part of a planet, consisting of the crust and the upper mantle.

**Logarithmic:** Pertaining to logarithms: a mathematical function that determines the *exponent* (a notation indicating the number of times a base number is multiplied by itself) needed to be raised to a specific base number to then get to another given number; they are linked to exponential functions but grow slower.

**Lowest common denominator:** In mathematics: the lowest common multiple of denominators; in casual vernacular: pertaining to the simplest demographics.

**Lumen:** A unit of luminous flux, the measure of (perceived) light emitted from a source per second in a unit solid angle by a source of one candle intensity.

**Matrix:** A particular structure that may: be (geometrically) gridded; act as a womb; function as a network of information; be a social arrangement; be an array of numbers.

**Meta- (Prefix):** After; beyond.

**Miscegenation:** Sexual relations between beings of different kinds of groups (such as ethnicities, races, species, or genera).

**Monolatrism:** The belief that there are many gods, but only one should be worshiped.

**Monotheism:** The belief that there is a single god.

**Neuropathy:** Damage or dysfunction of the nerves (the peripheral nervous system), leading to pain, tingling, numbness, and/or weakness.

**Newton:** One newton is the force required to accelerate something with a *mass* of one kilogram (not the *weight*) at a rate of one metre per second squared.

**Nomenclature:** A system for naming things.

**Objectively:** Pertaining to seeing things and reality without subjective biases; seeing things for what they really are.

**Occult:** Hidden from view; concealed; taboo; usually involves elements and activities from and with the spiritual planes.

**Olfactory system:** Bodily systems that are responsible for the sense of smell.

**Ontology:** A specialised branch of philosophy dealing with the nature of being – basically, how things relate to one another.

**Pagan:** Someone who practices a religion or spiritual practice that is not of the typical monotheistic religions that came to prominence.

**Paradigm:** A pattern or example of something, typically as a framework for ideas and methodologies that is applied in social and scientific contexts, which, moreover, is commonly accepted by many people.

**Per se:** By itself; intrinsically.

**Polytheism:** The belief in many gods.

**Post-hoc:** Occurring after the event.

**Prehensility:** The ability to grab and hold on to something.

**Prima facie:** On the first sight; on the first impression; to see something in a certain way at first, with the view potentially being subject to change later.

**Pro rata:** In proportion.

**Progenies:** Descendents of a being.

**Propinquity:** Being near something; proximity.

**Proselytize:** To (attempt to) convert someone to a certain belief or way of life.

**Sapient:** Intelligent enough to be able to think; humans are sapient.

**Sentient:** Capable of seeing or feeling things; debates ensue over what is sentient or not; conscious to a certain level.

**Shaman:** A spiritual person who can communicate with spirits, but unlike a *medium*, they hold a particular role in their society, usually one of leadership.

**Singularity:** The state or quality of being singular. It can be applied to many contexts, such as physics, technology, or even on a social level.

**Somatic:** Relating to the body, something physical; in the context of biology, it pertains to all cells (such as skin, muscle, and nerve cells) – except for reproductive cells – that make up the tissues found in biological organisms.

**Spatiotemporal:** Relating to space and time; having both spatial and temporal qualities.

**Subjective:** Pertaining to one's own personal experience (of feelings, thoughts, etc.).

**Supersonic:** Greater than the speed of sound.

**Synchronize:** Occurring at the same time or rate.

**Teleological:** The view that things have a final destination or ultimate goal/end.

**Telogenic:** The resting phase of something, normally used for hair growth.

**Thermodynamics:** The branch of physics that studies heat, work, temperature, and energy (of a system) and how they relate to one another.

**Thermosphere:** The second last layer of a normal planet's atmosphere (before the *exosphere* begins), where phenomena like auroras may occur. For T2-C1 worlds, the thermosphere ranges about 100 km to 700 km above the surface.

**Topological:** Relating to how parts of something are connected, mainly dealing with spatial (and geometric) issues, connections, and pathways.

**Toroid (torus):** A figure of toroidal shape, resembling a *torus* – a circular shape with a hole in the centre (like a doughnut). A *ring torus* looks like a ring, whereas a *horn torus's* hole shrinks to the point where there is a single point in the centre; a *spindle torus*, however, self-intersects and forms what looks like two joined bowls on the inside.

**Transclusive:** Transcending and including that which came before it; transcending to a new level, but instead of totally changing, something continues to incorporate that which it was before.

**Trans-speciesism:** Like transhumanism but for any species.

**Transhumanism:** The belief that humans can and should develop beyond their current biological form, usually with technology and science. *Transbody technologies* have already been implemented in people's bodies.

**Universal:** Existing across the board for everything without exception; applicable in all cases; for example, all lifeforms universally exist in a reality of some kind.

**Utilitarian:** In the context of art, art is art that prioritizes function (its utility), not just its aesthetic nature. In ethics, utilitarianism posits that people should aim to maximise utility (simply put, the greatest good for the greatest number).

**Veto:** The power to reject or stop an action, normally used in the context of politics.

**Xenophilia:** The love for (and/or attraction to) other beings and/or their cultures.

**Zygote:** An ovum (egg cell), fertilized by sperm.

# Abbreviated Terms

| | |
|---|---|
| A.I.: Artificial Intelligence | DTP: Default-tuned Power |
| AAE: Accumulative Aftereffect | DUP: Damaged Ultrachite Particles |
| ACE: Area of Conscious Effect | DVM: Default Vortex Mode |
| ACT: Alignment Charge Type | EBO: Etheric-based Overloading |
| ADA: Archetypal Development Attractors | EDA: Etheric Data Analyser |
| ADM: Alternative Discharge Mode | EEE: Etheric Energy Exhaustion |
| AES: Active Effect Status | EEP: Etheric Event Package |
| AMS: Aerosol Magic Suppressor | EHRF: Etheric holistically-related Form |
| AOE: Area Of Effect | EME: Extreme Mutational Event |
| APA: Aggregate Physical Aura | EMME: Extreme Mass Mutational Event |
| APL: Active Particle Level | EPP: Etheric Property Package |
| ATP: Alternative-tuned Power | ERF: Etheric-related Form |
| ATS: Automated Targeting System | FBE: Form-based Effect |
| AVM: Alternative Vortex Mode | FBF: Full Barrier Forcefield |
| BAC: Biotic Alchemical Consumable | FTP: Flash-timed Particle |
| CBA: Ceramic Body Armour | FTS: Folk Taxonomic System |
| CBE: Class-based Effect | GAP: General Aether Pool |
| CDM: Crystallized Discharge Mine | GBG: Great Black Gap |
| CDP: Cooldown Delay Period | GBW: Great Black Wall |
| CEC: Creation Energy Cost | GMF: Geomagnetic Field |
| CEP: Constant Effect Power | GMO: Genetically-modified Organism |
| CGM: Caelverse Government of Magi | HPL: Higher Power Level |
| CME: Caelverse Magocratic Empire | HRF: Holistically-related Form |
| COR: Coefficient of Restitution | HRT: Holistically-related Threshold |
| CPP: Collective Particle Pressure | IES: Inactive Effect Status |
| CSU: Constituent Spacetime Unit | IMC: Inner Matter Core |
| CTU: Complementary Tier Ultrachite | IPF: Imbalanced Potential Field |
| DDM: Default Discharge Mode | LBO: Lumarchetrix-based Overloading |
| DEC: Digital Electronic Computer | LCI: Lumarchetrix Channel Instability |
| DES: Dormant Effect Status | LCO: Lumarchetrix Channel Overcharging |
| DMA: Discharge Melee Attack | LCR: Lumarchetrix Channel Rate |
| DNA: Deoxyribonucleic Acid | LCW: Lethal Chemical Weapon |
| DPA: Damage Per Attack | LED: Lumarchetrix Energy Depletion |
| DPL: Default Power Level | LES: Latent Effect Status |
| DPS: Damage Per Second | LMR: Lunar Mass Regulator |

| | |
|---|---|
| LMT: Lunapex Mean Time | QET: Quantum Energy Teleportation |
| LPL: Lower Power Level | QFV: Quantum Force Vector |
| LRR: Lumarchetrix Recharge Rate | QIF: Quantumly-imbalanced Forms |
| LSR: Local Standard of Rest | QMC: Quantum Mechanical Computer |
| MEC: Maintenance Energy Cost | QPA: QIF-prolonging Armour |
| MLP: Maximum Lumarchetrix Pool | QMC: Quantum Mechanical Computer |
| MPM: Monstrous Phase Mutation | QTG: Quantum Tunnel Gateway |
| MRF: Morphic Resonance Field | QTP: Quantumly-tunnelled Particle |
| MSA: Magic Suppressor Ammunition | QTS: Quantum Trans State |
| NAC: Neurachite Analogue Computer | SAD: Successfully-augmented Discharge |
| NBC: Non-biotic Alchemical Consumable | SAV: Successfully-augmented Vortex |
| NCU: Negatively-charged Ultrachite | SBE: State-based Effect |
| OMC: Outer Matter Core | SCA: Spell's Central Area |
| OPL: Overall Power Level | SER: Spell Energy Requirement |
| ORR: Overloading Reset Rate | SMS: Standard Magic Suppressor |
| OSR: Overloading Subsiding Rate | SPP: Standard Physics Paradigm |
| OSSR: Overstimulation Subsiding Rate | SPT: Spell Power Type |
| PAC: Phasarchement Archetypal Class | STS: Standard Taxonomic System |
| PCI: Phase Changing Immunity | STU: Special Tier Ultrachite |
| PCU: Positively-charged Ultrachite | SUC: Shield-user Connection |
| PEB: Potential Energy Barrier | TAD: Teleportation Allowance Device |
| PEP: Particle Effect Phase | TAE: Type of Astrological Effect |
| PKF: Portable Kinetic Forcefield | TLA: Three-letter Abbreviation |
| PMR: Planetary Mass Regulator | TRE: Temporary Remaining Effect |
| POT: Planetary Orbital Tier | TST: Torus Structure Theory |
| PPE: Post-particle Effect | UAS: UPI Aggregate Strength |
| PPF: Portable Particle Forcefield | UIO: Ultrachite Inhibitor Overstimulation |
| PPO: Primed Photonic Outline | UOS: Union of Organized States |
| PPR: Particle Phase Refreshment | UOT: Ultrachite Overloading Threshold |
| PPS: Phasarchement Portal Site | UPC: Ultrachite Phase Charging |
| PPW: Particularized Paralysis Weapon | UPD: Ultrachite Particle Density |
| PRF: Portable Radiation Forcefield | UPI: Ultrachite Particle Inhibitor |
| PSC: Planetary Structural Class | UPO: Ultrachite Particle Overload |
| PTS: Planetary Transportal System | UPP: Ultrachite Particle Pressure |
| PTU: Primary Tier Ultrachite | UPS: Ultrachite Phase Switching |
| PUC: Particle User Connection | UST: Ultra-state Type |
| PWT: Pilot Wave Theory | WGF: Warped Gravitational Field |
| QBS: Quantum Base State | WPD: Wave Particle Duality (Theory) |
| QDF: Quantumly-dominant Field | ZPE: Zero-point Energy |
| QEP: Quantumly-entangled Particle | ZPF: Zero-point Field |

# About the Author

I was born on the 15th of May 1988 in ~~Crysten, Juntas, The Caelverse~~ Brisbane, Australia, and I have mixed European ancestry (mostly Irish and Scottish, followed by Welsh and English – but with a bit of Germanic, Scandinavian, and Spanish, too). I hold a Bachelor of Communication from Griffith University, majoring in journalism and politics, and a Master of Arts in philosophy from The University of Queensland, specializing in politics, ethics, and economics.

~~During blood moons, my Illuminati buddies and I make sacrifices to Moloch.~~ I adhere to a set of spiritual maxims; three of these include living healthily, being the best version of yourself, and leaving the world a better place than what you inherited. In my free time, I like working on various creative pursuits, engaging in philosophical discussions, reading, playing video games, working out (lifting), discovering new music (I love metal, especially symphonic metal), and of course, adding to my enormous meme collection...